D1443117

The Possessors and the Possessed

Other books by Samuel A. Schreiner, Jr.

Thine is the Glory
Pleasant Places
Angelica

The
Possessors

**THE SAGA OF THE
VAN ALEN FAMILY
OF NEW YORK**

and the

Possessed

A novel by
Samuel A. Schreiner. Jr.

ARBOR HOUSE
New York

130194

Library of Congress Catalog Card Number: 79-54009

ISBN: 0-87795-229-9

Manufactured in the United States of America
10 9 8 7 6 5 3 2 1

Authors of historical works quite commonly, and rightly, salute the legions of diligent researchers and flights of nimble-fingered secretaries who have made their work possible. Perhaps unfortunately, the author has enjoyed no such private services in creating this work. He did, however, avail himself of a public service that must be mentioned: The Darien Library. While the whole library staff was helpful, special thanks should go to Jean-Jacques Strayer and Ms. Janis Rodman of the reference department, who went out of their way to find and produce obscure and ancient books from all over the country to satisfy the author's demands, and to Ms. Virginia Wellings who, as head of circulation, was patient in forgiving the author for keeping books long past the statutory and reasonable time limits for borrowing.

But the most significant help the author has had, not only on this book, but on all those that have preceded it, has come from his agent, Ms. Phyllis Westberg of Harold Ober Associates, Inc., and from his publisher, Donald I. Fine, president of Arbor House. Phyllis, first, and then Don have repeatedly gambled on the author's ability to turn an idea into a book, a sustaining faith without which it would be impossible to work. In addition, Don's general suggestions and detailed editing on the manuscripts has proved a discipline without which the work might have been futile. In thinking of both Phyllis and Don, the author is reminded of a phrase that he wishes he had the wit to invent, "no man is an island unto himself . . ."

Samuel A. Schreiner, Jr.
Darien, Conn.
February 1, 1980

To my wife, Dorrie, and her mother, Carrie Moon, whose stories about their Van Alen ancestors, including one great lady who attended school in Kinderhook with President Martin Van Buren, inspired and provided a name for this tale about a fictional Van Alen family. I pray that they, and all other Van Alens living or dead, will not feel that I have taken their good name in vain.

Prelude

Sometimes she thought that she'd seen too much, more than the human eye was meant to tolerate. Right here in New York she'd witnessed the birth of a nation, and right here in New York in this year of our Lord eighteen hundred and sixty-three she was watching it writhe in the throes of death. Rioting, looting, shooting, burning. She'd stood in a dreadful dawn, hand-in-hand with her son Peter, and seen the light creep across the smouldering ruins of the house in which her other son Cornelius died. She hadn't been able to cry then, and she probably wouldn't cry now. She knew that she'd get over the burning, as she'd gotten over so many other things. It was a matter of survival, and she was a survivor.

Her father-in-law, old Cornelius, used to complain that it was hell to grow old, and now she was beginning to understand what he meant. *Old* Cornelius? Why did she still think of him that way? He'd died at sixty-seven, and she was unbelievably eighty-three and still surviving. Why that, too? Why she and not all those others so dear and important to her? Her lover Aaron, who'd been often to China, used to say that she was like the bamboo tree which the Orientals held to be stronger than steel because it bent with the wind. If she was, she wondered whether the bamboo felt, as she did, the pain of its bending.

Still here she was—this person who was christened Sarah, who was called Sally, who was first a Schuyler and then a Van Alen. And still she didn't know why she was here. Wisdom was supposed to be the priceless gift of age, but, although a lot of people thought so, wisdom didn't come from just living. She almost had to laugh at the way people treated her as if the number of her years had given her some sort of secret knowledge. Instead, the years had only deepened the mysteries, added to the questions, subtracted from the answers. She'd searched for wisdom in the poets, the prophets, the philosophers, but she hadn't found enough. Like the candles she'd burned before the gas came in, their insights were pinpoints of light that deepened the shadows in all the corners.

If age did not give wisdom as a gift, shouldn't it grant time to acquire it? But days, and even those nights when so often now she couldn't sleep, passed faster than they ever had. She'd thought about this not long ago when she'd persuaded her son Peter to take her on a sentimental journey to the manor near Kinderhook where she'd been born. They were rattling along on the Hudson River Railway, jouncing so that she feared her insides would turn over, and a young man, holding a watch in his hand, shouted triumphantly, "Yippee! A mile a minute!" That was how fast the world was going by her now, by everybody.

She was suffering from a kind of panic. It had come upon her as sharply as the angina spasm in her heart when she'd seen in that dawn the evidence of deaths that made the whole world look mad. Soon she herself would join all those others in the grave, would become part of Mr. Bryant's "innumerable caravan." Had old Cornelius felt this way, and was this what he meant by the hell of growing old?

It would be much easier if she could be sure of heaven like her father Jacobus, like her nephew James, and—yes—like her first-born son Cornelius, or even if she could be certain of hell. She believed in God, but she'd never known, as those others claimed to know, what God was going to do, and she didn't know now. Some would say that she'd already paid over and over again for her own sins, if sins they were, and yet they'd given her in Peter and his children reward beyond measure. It would be much easier, too, if she could accept the polemics of political leaders as assurances of public virtue, but she'd known too many of them as private persons—General Hamilton and Aaron Burr, her brother Peter and her cousin Matty Van Buren, her son Peter and Abraham Lincoln—not to be too acutely aware of their human frailities. It would also be much easier if she could be content with the glowing visions of poets, but she'd seen them consume her friend Mr. Poe and wither with age in her friend Mr. Bryant.

Matters like this kept turning and turning in her mind these days like the flywheel of a steam engine out of gear. Perhaps if she really looked at her life, if she spent these days when she could no longer go out without help from Peter or his wife, Martha, or one of the grandchildren and these nights when she lay awake examining all those things she'd seen that were stored like a stack of daguerreotypes in her memory, some meaning would emerge. If she were lucky, her mind might work like that new stereopticon that Cornelius had bought just before the fire and put a new dimension into what she saw. Life was living, and she had surely done more of that than most, not only in years but in experiences. She could start with that and see where she arrived. It could be a surprise, for, having seen so much, she was at least sure of one thing: you never knew what you might see next. Yes, life was living, and living was full of surprises.

She would see what she would see . . .

Chapter 1

The Rockets' Brave Glare

Although life could present few wonders to surpass the imaginings of the child Sarah Schuyler was, one of them had to be the city of New York on the night of April 30, 1789. Not that it wasn't exciting by day to eyes that had never seen a collection of houses larger than the little village of Kinderhook. Down by the wharves, there were some crooked streets running between lines of familiar Dutch cottages with their stepped roofs like funny peaked hats, but for the most part the buildings were grand in the English manner, tall and square and faced with brick. There must have been a dozen churches sending up spires to finger the sky, and, if you were as lucky as young Sarah to have a fourth-story room, you could look east, west or south and see above the rooftops a fringe of ships' spars as high as the steeples silhouetted against shimmering waters. It was these ships, come from every port in the world, that she found most fascinating. Along the East River where Uncle Cornelius took them to see his sloops, the huge square riggers snuggled up to the bank, rubbing salt-encrusted shoulders and poking long snoutlike bowsprits over the cobbled wharves like pigs at a trough, and, like pigs, they were feeding and feeding off the markets and shops along Front Street and Water

1

Street and Little Dock street. Their crews babbled in strange tongues as they grunted their loads ashore, and auctioneers cried bids for casks of wine, bales of cloth, boxes of tea, cartons of trinkets, beams of iron. She loved the commotion, but it could not compare in magic with that night.

As darkness came on, so did the lights. It seemed that every window in every house and building from river to river was winking and blinking, and the black waters surrounding the town were transformed into a rippling field of stars by the reflection of lanterns hung high in the rigging of ships still at anchor. To her, it seemed the gift of a thousand thousand Christmas trees, as if Nicholaus, that special saint of good Dutch children, had lost track of the seasons.

Sarah was proud that she had contributed her own touch to the magic. It was she who suggested that they cut the bases off half a dozen candles to expose the wick and bind them in the middle into a kind of wheel so that when the points were lighted they resembled stars. One of these was hung in each window of the upper stories of the Van Alen residence on Broadway and another in the fanlight above the front door, adding up of course to thirteen. It was far from being the most splendid of displays. Down by the Bowling Green the French and Spanish ministers were outdoing each other in tribute to the new republican court. M. de Moustier's talented sister, Madame de Brehan, had hastily painted scenes from the young American Republic's history and mounted them in windows ringed with lamps; Don Gardoqui had erected a huge transparency depicting the Graces he called into blessing on the infant nation. Still, no house in town showed a more patriotic front than that of the Van Alens.

In her innocence, Sarah did not know that her thirteen stars provoked sniggering comments from some of the guests who began arriving promptly at seven. One of them, Attorney Aaron Burr, surveyed the scene carefully to make sure that the pattern was not accidental and then said to his fellow lawyer, Colonel Hamilton, arriving at the same time, "Well, it looks like the worm has really turned."

Though at the moment Hamilton had need of Burr politically, he was not amused; his wife, Betsy, at his side must have overheard. "You forget yourself, sir," he said. "We are here to meet Mrs. Hamilton's relatives, and Mr. Van Alen is a good client of mine."

Burr's black eyes seemed to dance with the lights, taking on that look of mischievous amusement that so annoyed Hamilton. "Ah, yes, the law and politics make strange bedfellows, don't they, colonel—or is it Mr. Secretary?" he said.

Hamilton pretended not to hear the remark. Taking his wife by the elbow, he shoved past Burr and went into the house. Burr shrugged and followed, muttering to himself, "Pompous ass . . ."

Inside, the Van Alen house, one of the few to escape the ravages of the great fire during the war, literally smelled of wealth. The odor of the tea in which Sir Robert Wentworth had so successfully traded lingered in the marbled foyer which was surrounded by the rooms where his business and now that of Van Alen & Son Shipping and General Merchandise went forward during the day. The foyer itself was the base of an open stairwell that rose four stories to a skylight in the roof. On the second story, there was a parlor running the length of the house to the left, and a dining room and library, thrown together by opening sliding connecting doors for such occasions as this, to the right. In these rooms, the candles of chandeliers, magnified and reflected by hundreds of crystal drops, created a glittering, shimmering light that bounced off the polished surfaces of furnishings by Chippendale, silver by Bateman, china by Wedgwood. Portraits of Sir Robert and his lady and their daughter Lydia, hanging above the marble mantles, were by the hand of Sir Joshua Reynolds. There was nothing to be seen of American manufacture or even of the Dutch heritage of the present master of the house. It was exactly the sort of establishment that a woman who persisted in calling herself Lady Lydia six years after the last British soldier was withdrawn from the city in which it stood would be expected to maintain.

Still, only a few of the people gathering in little knots of conversation under the shining chandeliers or moving through the reception line to meet the Schuyler family found anything strange in this. Most of their own homes were similarly furnished; for more than a century the wealthy of New York had looked to London, or in some cases Paris, for the latest fashions in household goods and clothes. Indeed, and particularly among the ladies, much of the talk about the great event of that day centered upon the way General Washington had chosen to dress himself to take the oath of office as president. He wore a plain brown suit said to have been ordered from Hartford and a dull, steel-hilted sword. For many of those attending the Van Alen levee that humble touch was a bit disconcerting; they had given

3

liberally of their own funds to remake Federal Hall into a background for what they hoped would be more like a coronation. Notes of bewilderment and derision sounded in the hum of conversation.

"I should think he would have worn his uniform or at least a suitable black like Chancellor Livingston . . ."

"Perhaps Hamilton put him up to it. You know he's always talking about how we should have our own manufacturing."

"What will we call him—your highness, your excellency?"

"He prefers Mr. President . . ."

"Can you imagine? They say he's been seen walking the streets from place to place. You would suppose that Mr. Van Alen or somebody would lend him a coach."

"Well, his own is coming up with Mrs. Washington. Bright canary yellow, I hear, with his Washington coat of arms guarded by cupids painted on the doors. Drawn by six white horses. That should make a splash."

"I do hope so. It's been so drab since Sir Guy left . . ."

"Do you think he'll shut himself away? They tell me he sent regrets to Lady Lydia even though Cornelius was one of the heaviest subscribers to the fund."

"Well, I'm told he doesn't want to favor one citizen over another with his presence. When Mrs. Washington arrives, they plan to hold their own levees . . ."

"They'll be dull affairs, I should imagine. They both retire at nine like country people, and from what Mr. Burr says the general is as solemn as he looks. I've watched him all the week and never seen him smile."

"It's his teeth, my dear, didn't you know? They say he's ordered a new set of seahorse teeth from Mr. Greenwood. I do hope they're ready before the ball. I'd hate to dance with a man so grim."

Fidgeting by her mother's side, Sarah Schuyler heard little of this talk. She was too busy manufacturing smiles for all the strangers who patted her on the head or shook her hand. Her cheeks ached from the effort, and her neck was beginning to hurt from looking up at them. Even at ten, she was aware that most of them were prominent people and that she should be impressed, but she would much rather be out in the streets looking at the lights; her abiding fear was that the reception would go on so long that they'd miss the fireworks. She was also aware that few of the faces smiling back showed a flicker of real interest in her; like herself, they were just being polite. She was, after all, only a child. One comment she had overheard was, "Fancy having all those children at an affair like this. But the Dutch do that, don't they?"

The Dutch. Until she heard that, she'd never thought about being Dutch, or rather that being Dutch might mean being something different. Anyway, she wasn't all Dutch, because her father's mother had been French. That was how they explained to her why, with her black hair and eyes and olive complexion and skinny legs and arms, she didn't look at all like her pink, plump mother or sister or even like her half brothers and sister except perhaps Peter whose eyes were like hers. She was rather proud of not looking like the rest of them because the way her father would smile at her when he said she reminded him of his mother made her feel somehow special. As for being Dutch, her father wouldn't allow Dutch to be spoken in their home and had even started holding services himself at the manor when the dominie in Kinderhook refused to use English in church. "We're all Americans," he'd keep telling them, "and we must put an end to this divisiveness."

What she was was a Schuyler which she knew was the real reason that she had to endure this boring reception. She hadn't thought that being a Schuyler meant being anything different, either, until they reached New York; now she was beginning to realize that it was something to be proud of. Her aunt Lydia—Lady Lydia—had suggested this thought when her parents protested her going to so much fuss to entertain them. Tall, gaunt, wattled and beaked like a turkey, Lady Lydia was possessed of a tongue so sharp that it seemed to scissor her words. "Don't talk nonsense," she said. "You, my dears, are my drawing cards. With you in the house, General Schuyler—he's a senator now, you know—and his daughters, Mrs. Hamilton and Mrs. Church, won't be able to refuse me. Neither will the governor, now that your Janet is engaged to a Clinton. And I'm sure Chancellor Livingston will want to be in the same company with Colonel Hamilton since he's still seeking a position with the administration. Ours should be the first house in the city that night, thanks to you."

Lady Lydia had been right. All those people were here—and more. Mr. and Mrs. John Jay. Vice-President and Mrs. John Adams. Mr. and Mrs. Isaac Roosevelt. The James Madisons. The Waltons. The Van Courtlands. The Van Rensselaers. Mr. Aaron Burr, making excuses for his wife who was ailing. Of them all, only Mr. Burr made Sarah forget for a minute her misery. Though he was a small man, he dropped to one knee when he took her hand so that he could look her full in the face. He had soft features, a mouth meant for smiling and lively eyes blacker than her own.

"Well, it's Sarah, is it? Does anyone ever call you Sally?" he asked. "I just lost a little daughter named Sally a few months ago, and I'm looking for another Sally to take her place. So you won't mind if I call you Sally?"

Nobody had ever called her Sally, but she liked the sound of it. "Oh, no," she said.

"Good. Then that's settled. You shall be my Sally. I often stay over at the Van Buren tavern in Kinderhook, and I could come to see you —that is, if your mother wouldn't mind. Would you like that?"

"Oh, yes." She didn't know what else to say without giving offense; she was both pleased and a little frightened to be singled out for such attention from a man she'd never seen before.

"Well, then, I'll ask your mother," he said, rising and taking Catharina Schuyler's hand. "You have a most beautiful daughter, Madam," he said. "But then, of course, you should."

The pink in her mother's cheeks deepened. "Thank you, Mr . . . . uh . . ."

"Burr. Aaron Burr at your service, Madam. I've been telling your daughter that Mrs. Burr and I sadly lost our little Sally, so she's agreed to take her place so to speak. It would give me great pleasure if I could call upon you when I'm up Kinderhook way."

"As Mr. Schuyler says, our latch string is always out, Mr. Burr."

"Ah, thank you, Madam. I should very much like to watch my new Sally grow into a lovely young woman . . ."

"Mr. Burr, I'm afraid you'll turn the child's head."

"Why not? Why not? I say a woman should be proud of her beauty —and her brains. I hope you've started Sally on her Latin and Greek."

"Well, Mr. Burr, we've never thought . . ."

"I know. I know. You've never thought that a girl has need of a classical education. Most people think me queer that I do. My little Theodosia's only six, and she can already read a little French and decline a dozen Latin verbs. I've mapped out a whole program of education for her, and I'll share it with your Sally as I would have with my own. Would you like that, Sally?"

"Oh, yes," she said again, though she wasn't so sure. She'd seen young Jacobus and Peter struggling over the lessons that their father insisted they master and felt lucky in that respect to be a girl; she didn't think she could sit still long enough to learn all that. But what this strange Mr. Burr seemed to be saying was that there was nothing a girl couldn't, shouldn't, learn, and maybe he was right; maybe it was worth a try. The thing that puzzled her, though, was why he was so interested in her instead of Rebecca, standing on the other side of her mother and looking, as everybody always said about her, "like a little Dutch angel." Just as nobody had ever called her Sally before, nobody had ever suggested that she was beautiful. Yet she knew from the way Mr. Burr had looked at her so steadily with his restless black eyes that he meant what he said. It was her first sense that she might possess within her some kind of mysterious personal power, and if that was what her mother meant by turning her head, Mr. Burr had done it.

She wished that she could think of something more to say to him than yes or no, but he'd been holding up the receiving line long enough, so he moved off with a wink and a promise to see her again. Then a blur of a face took his place, and another, and another. How long would this go on? The fireworks were supposed to start at nine.

Jacobus Schuyler was as conscious of the time as his youngest child. He had not gone to all the expense and trouble of bringing his family down from Kinderhook to be social drawing cards for his wife's in-laws. Indeed, he'd accepted their invitation with misgivings only because he wanted his children to witness the great events that would be transpiring in the city and, what with the crowds pouring in, there was no other place to stay. He had no use for Cornelius Van Alen, even though he was Catharina's only brother, and couldn't abide that woman who called herself Lady Lydia. Hamilton may have convinced a court, but he couldn't convince Jacobus Schuyler that Cornelius Van Alen hadn't been trafficking with the enemy during the war. The circumstantial evidence was too strong to leave much doubt. Though it was argued that Cornelius kept himself to the river, serving the continental forces with his sloops, it was never denied that Lydia and the children had stayed on in the city, right here in this house, where she'd quartered some of the highest ranking British officers. Why then wouldn't Cornelius, as rumors had it, slip his sloop into the city at night and take advantage of the high prices the British were willing to pay for the very food that his own family needed? If more proof were wanted, it was all around them this minute in most tangible form—in those massive chandeliers dangling from the ceiling, in that rich rosewood piano imported from Astor & Broadwood in London rising from the floor, in the black slaves slipping through the crowd with trays of punch, in the shiny satin that draped Lady Lydia's scarecrow figure and the figured silk that rode Cornelius's ample paunch. Nobody got that rich serving the continentals, as Jacobus Schuyler had more reason than most to know.

He'd heard that it was said around Kinderhook that Jacobus Schuyler was jealous of his brother-in-law. Jealousy was the wrong word for the righteous anger a man had a right to feel at going deeper and deeper into debt as the paper promises Congress had issued to pay for the produce he shipped to their armies proved increasingly worthless. He'd had to sell at a discount to speculators who would grow rich if Hamilton could push through his plans to have the new government assume the debts. He had no doubt that Cornelius had his share of that paper, as most of Hamilton's friends did. But jealousy was definitely the wrong word for his feelings. It was absurd to think that a Schuyler could be jealous of a Van Alen, so absurd that it would be laughable under any other circumstances. The Van Alens were freeholders, but just; the few acres on which they tried to subsist weren't much larger than the slave patch on the Schuyler manor. And the circumstances of his marriage to Catharina Van Alen were too plain to be denied. He'd needed someone to look after the children when Jannetje died, and Abraham Van Buren had recommended one of his new wife's relatives. The rest was a matter of propinquity and convenience, though Jacobus would have to admit that it had worked out very well indeed, except for that brother of hers.

Feeling the way he did, he'd had to choke down a very large lump of pride to accept the Van Alen invitation to stay with them in the city during the inaugural festivities. He'd been surprised, in fact, that it had been issued to them since Cornelius had to be aware of his sentiments. He'd been goaded into expressing them often enough over drinks at Van Buren's when some stupid Dutchman would start bragging on the success of Kinderhook's native son. To many of them the fact that Van Alen's money might be tainted with treason simply proved how smart a Dutchman could be. The whole area was full of secret Tory sympathizers, and no wonder with Johannes Ritzema openly preaching loyalty to God's minister on earth, George III, from the pulpit. A good thing that Jacobus had withdrawn his family from the church to get them away from Dutch influence when he did. Well, he'd set those braggers straight whenever he could and had probably established the basis for the talk that he was jealous of Cornelius. In his letter of invitation, Cornelius had gone on so much about binding up the family ties severed by war that he'd reduced Catharina to tears and very nearly convinced Jacobus that there might be some good in the man. In a way it was a relief when Lydia who, unlike her husband, was at least honest let the cat out of the bag: they just wanted to make the most of the Schuyler name. After this evening, Jacobus could go on despising his brother-in-law and feeling that he owed him nothing.

Still, Jacobus was struggling hard against a disillusionment he didn't want to acknowledge. Like many men who've never gone to war—lamed in a fall from a horse and burdened, besides, with the care of the manor by his father's death, he'd elected to stay home—Jacobus had an exaggerated notion of war's glories and capacity to purify by fire. He'd followed avidly the details of every battle in the press, and the images of many of the men he was seeing for the first time this night were as bright in his mind as blades of steel. Hamilton, for example, exposing himself to the blast of cannon as he vaulted the parapets at Yorktown ahead of his men; Burr, slogging through the snows of Quebec and cradling the dying Montgomery in his arms. Yet here was Hamilton, one arm around Cornelius Van Alen's fat waist as they exchanged pleasantries that provoked them to laughter; there was Burr, bowing and kissing Lady Lydia's veined, bejeweled hand. Beyond, warming his stout backside at the fire, was John Adams, a hero with words if not bullets; he seemed charmed by whatever the Van Alen's oldest daughter, Amelia, whose Tory husband de Lancey was killed in a raid on a patriot farm in Westchester, was telling him. How could these men forgive and forget so soon? Was it a largeness of mind that he, Jacobus, did not possess, or a smallness of personal interest? If the presence of Schuylers had been an excuse to open the Van Alen house, it was clearly apparent where the real attraction lay from the perfunctory way in which he and his family were greeted compared to the deference shown the Van Alens. It was money—money, money, money. Jacobus knew from his reading that men sold their souls for it, but he had never watched it happen before.

A loud voice jarred him out of his bitter reflections. "Jacobus Schuyler! It's long since we've met, and how are you keeping?"

Governor George Clinton pressed one of Jacobus' small hands warmly between both of his large ones. When Jacobus looked up into the governor's craggy, open face, he thought he caught a wink. "I never thought to see you in this household, Jacobus."

"Well, I . . ."

"Never mind. We all have to bury the hatchet some time. Look at me, surrounded in these very rooms by the enemies who crammed this Constitution down my throat. But they're good fellows all the same. Anyway, I really came to have a look at that Janet of yours who I understand is marrying into the Clinton clan. I can say now that it is our good fortune."

"Thank you, governor . . ."

"George. It's George to you, Jacobus, particularly now that we're almost related. I don't know young Robert very well, but they tell me he's a tolerable good farmer. Of course, you'd know better than I."

"Yes, he's doing well with his sheep, now that he can send the wool to England again."

"So I understand. I gather he bought one of those merino rams the chancellor's importing to Clermont. Why don't you give it a try, Jacobus, with all that grass you have between you and the river?"

"To be honest, I can't afford to buy one. I was left with a lot of worthless scrip, and . . ."

"Yes, yes. It's the sad story I hear all up and down the river. That's one reason I fought so hard against losing all the power of the state to this federal government. I tell you when Hamilton over there and his people get control of things, the money will all be right here in New York, in his bank or the treasury, instead of out feeding the land where it belongs. But . . . well, you've never concerned yourself much with politics, have you, Jacobus? And you can thank the Lord for it. There isn't a man here in this room who doesn't envy your kind of life. What's money compared to that?"

"Power," Jacobus said.

The governor laughed. "You never did waste words, did you, Jacobus? Well, you're right, I guess. Hamilton certainly understands that, and that's why he's bound to take the handling of money away from the states if he gets his way. I'm afraid Washington will be putty in his hands . . . . Ah, but there's Chancellor Livingston. Excuse me, Jacobus, I must have a word with him. A politician's work is never done, you know."

Jacobus found the governor's talk more upsetting than warming. His attitude about these people who had been, to say the least, half-hearted about the war, about those who had defeated him in the convention to ratify the Constitution, seemed almost a shrug. If the leadership of a great state required such an attitude, it was well that Jacobus had had the good sense to stay out of politics. There were those who called Jacobus Schuyler a brooder, and they were probably right. What else could a man of intelligence do during long days on horseback tending his lands? To make up for his education being cut short by his father's death, he read and thought a great deal. Along the way he had become a man of convictions, and apparently convictions did not mix well with politics. He would have had these Van Alens and their like on the first ship to Nova Scotia with the other turncoats, and, while he did believe in a federal government, he'd see it in the hands of a sound man of property like Livingston instead of an adventurer like Hamilton whose only claim to being a true American was his marriage to a Schuyler, a marriage that, as Jacobus understood it, the girl's father had sensibly opposed, and he counted General Schuyler weak for not having worked his own will with his child.

The governor's hint that Washington might be putty in Hamilton's hands was, therefore, most distressing to Jacobus. For Jacobus the Revolution had been a holy crusade, and George Washington, a lofty Virginia landowner, had been the perfect knight to lead it. Since logic did not always play a predominant part in Jacobus' thinking, perhaps also because of a foreshortened education, he arrived at his feeling about the Revolution largely as an emotional reaction to the way a closed Dutch community had treated his mother. It had been regarded as quixotic, if not sinful, for his father to come back from his one trip abroad with a French bride, and, although most of the Dutch had to doff their caps to *any* Schuyler, Jacobus knew that, behind his parents' backs, his mother was ridiculed for her looks, her language, her Huguenot faith and what were considered her high and mighty ways; he himself was probably looked upon as a half-breed since he had none of the Dutch coloring. So Jacobus saw in the Revolution not only a way of transferring real power from London into the hands of colonial landlords like himself but a way of crushing Dutch exclusive-ness which he thought to be fostered by the British on the divide-and-conquer principle and nurtured by Dutch religious and cultural ties to the Old World. Moreover, his dabbling in history and religion had led him to the conviction that America's Puritan fathers had been truly led by God to a land where they could better worship him, an impossibility until and unless the evil influences of the Old World could no longer prevail. It was to see the birth of this new nation under God and his anointed servant, General George Washington, that caused Jacobus to come here, and, until this evening, he had been able to believe that this was happening.

Perhaps the most convincing evidence was the figure of Washington himself, a man of such impressive dignity, sobriety and size that he personified all of Jacobus' ideals. He could only thank God that Washington had remained aloof from this gathering; he didn't want his children, or himself either, to dwell upon the man's blemishes like those shallow-minded women talking about the teeth he'd probably sacrificed to his country by eating rotten army food. He wanted them to remember him as they first saw him a week ago, standing in the stern of the crimson-draped barge bearing him over from Elizabeth-town Point in New Jersey to the City. He'd have to say this for Cornelius Van Alen's wealth: by being taken aboard one of his sloops, they were brought close enough to see everything clearly. It was a show worth whatever he suffered from that indigestible lump of pride in his belly.

As the barge, rowed by a dozen New York pilots in white uniform, moved sedately across the harbor, it was surrounded by vessels of all description, their yards and rigging fluttering with flags. The largest, the Spanish sloop-of-war, *Galveston,* saluted the general's passing by firing thirteen guns and breaking out the banners of every foreign nation. Washington, tall and stiffly erect, dressed in his continental blue and buff, white-powdered head bared, acknowledged this trib-ute with a majestic bow, as he did again when a band on another barge struck up "Yankee Doodle." Then twenty or so men and women, lining the rails of a sloop that sailed in close to the general's barge, broke into an anthem, ironically set to the tune of "God Save the King." The women's high voices carried the words distinctly to where the Schuylers stood on the high poop of the Van Alen sloop:

Hail thou auspicious day!
Far let America
Thy praise resound:
Joy to our native land!
Let every heart expand,
For Washington's at hand
With glory crowned!

Hearing this, Jacobus felt his eyes grow moist. Sarah, holding his hand, tightened her grip, and when he looked down at her, he saw that her intense black eyes were also flushed with tears. It was a time for even strong men to cry. The shoreline from the Battery around to Murray's Wharf at the foot of Wall Street where carpeted stairs had been laid out for Washington's landing was a moving mass of people, all cheering and waving their hats so that it looked to Jacobus' farmer's eye like a wind stirring a field of grain. Declining the carriage waiting for him, Washington chose to walk through the press of people to the house prepared for him in Cherry Street, and it was reported by those close enough to notice that his eyes, too, were so wet that he had to wipe them several times.

Washington wept again this day when he stooped to kiss the Bible after repeating the oath administered by Chancellor Livingston. This time, and also thanks to the Van Alen connections, the Schuylers were on the roof of a nearby house in Broad Street and able to witness the great man's emotion themselves. Below them, the crowd, larger than the one that had greeted his arrival, made a thick tapestry of heads covering the square before Federal Hall and along Broad and Wall Streets. Some said a count of those heads would add up to more than the city's entire population of 20,000 since people had been coming in all the week from as far away as Boston and Philadelphia. Yet at that moment, there was an eerie hush, as if each individual were joining the general in silent prayer. When Washington lifted his head, Chancellor Livingston stepped forward to the railing of the gallery on which the ceremony was taking place and just managed in a voice already choking from his own tears to cry, "Long live George Washington!" Everybody let go with answering cheers that rose into a steady roar, and the guns in the Battery erupted in a rumbling thunder that shook the house on which they stood, and the bells in every steeple set up a clangor that became an ear-splitting dishar-

13

mony. Jacobus, usually an undemonstrative man, found himself hugging and kissing his wife and children and crying over and over again, "This is the greatest day in history, the greatest man in history. None of our lives will be the same again."

Yes, it was impossible to believe that this Washington could be described as putty in anyone's hands. It was, in fact, a near thing that he hadn't been crowned king, and Jacobus was sure that all of those thousands of people, himself included, would gladly have accepted a crown despite the irony of trading one King George for another. At the services in every church in the city that morning God had been rightfully thanked for blessing America with this man. So, despite what he was sensing and seeing around him in these rooms full of cynical and sophisticated people, Jacobus was determined to go on believing that Washington who had somehow held a slovenly, starving, contentious army together would mold a Godly nation, too. He didn't want to lose this mood which was why he was anxious as his children to get out again into the streets, among the simple people who were celebrating the coming of their country's savior with all of their hearts.

Somewhere near him he could hear a voice with an edge of laughter to it saying, "I'll give this noble experiment fifty years at the most . . ."

The answering rumble was recognizable as Governor Clinton's. "Well, as you know, Mr. Burr, I wasn't for it in the first place. Fortunately, Schuyler's short term runs out in '91, and we'll have need of a candidate to replace him and keep a check on Hamilton. Perhaps you could come to see me at your convenience, Mr. Burr?"

"I'd be delighted, governor, delighted . . ."

Jacobus had had enough. He broke out of the receiving line, took his two small girls by the hand and gestured with his head to the rest of the family. "Come along," he said, "we are going to see the fireworks."

"May I join you, Uncle Jacobus? You'll need a guide through the back streets to get down to the Battery. Just look out the windows there—the Broadway's so crowded you wouldn't be able to move."

It was young George Van Alen. At nineteen, he was tall and reed-thin like his mother but blessed with the glowing cheeks and golden hair of the Van Alens. With curls at his ears, dark-lashed blue eyes and full lips, he had an almost feminine beauty. A dandy as well, he was suited in fireworks; his dark green velvet coat was trimmed along its opening and at the cuffs with bright orange and yellow sunbursts of tropical flowers to match the decoration on his white silk waistcoat. Not a young man to Jacobus' taste, but it would be rude to reject him, and having him along as guide did make some sense.

"Yes, come along, George," Jacobus said.

Sarah was delighted. Immediately, she dropped her father's hand and took George's. Along with the piano, which was the first she'd ever seen in her life, this handsome cousin was one of the unanticipated surprises of the city. He seemed as full of life as she felt herself to be. At dragging dinners, she would often look down the table to find him sweeping those long lashes over one of his dancing blue eyes in an elaborate wink. This would set her to giggling so much that once she was sent away hungry to her room to dwell on her sins; that time, George came up the backstairs with a plate of food for her. He was always teasing her, calling her his "little Miss America," for instance, when she came up with the idea about the candles. She was no wiser about why George paid particular attention to her than about Mr. Burr. Certainly, he didn't call her beautiful; in fact, when he came up with the food that night, his excuse was that "we can't have you getting any skinnier than you already are." She was content with the fact of his attention, and, skipping to keep up with his long strides as they set out for the park, she was supremely happy.

Even the back streets were so full of people that they finally had to form a single file, hand to hand, and work their way through in a kind of snake dance. Here, too, there was an abundance of light; as many lamps and candles as householders could afford had been set out. Women must have been working overtime, for there were banners with the name Washington stitched into them hanging from windowsills or sometimes stretched from house to house clear across the street. Fortunately, horses had been banned from a large area for blocks around the Federal Building and the Battery in the interests of public safety, and the pigs that usually snuffled and rooted in the debris of the streets had been frightened into hiding by all the confusion. But the incredible number of people out braving the chill of the spring night more than made up for the missing animals. They could get no farther than the fringe of the Battery. It was as if some giant hand had lifted the city at the Collect Pond along Division Street and tumbled all of its inhabitants into a crush at the point.

Neither she nor Rebecca could see a thing. George hoisted her up on his shoulders with her legs astride his neck, and her father did the same for Rebecca. There was no way to keep their drawers from showing, but in all the excitement nobody seemed to mind. She was happy that George was so tall, because she could see over all the heads and hats a lot better than Rebecca could. George pinched one of her knees and said, "I'm awfully glad you're so skinny or you'd break my neck. You'd make a good jockey."

She dug her hands into the curly mass of his hair, pulled on it and shouted, "Giddyap!"

"You do that again, you little devil, and I'll dump you in the street. Don't you know horses aren't allowed here?"

They both laughed, and she could feel his bony shoulders shaking under the press of her legs, and she was aware of a strange sensation that would haunt her long after the fireworks faded. But just now, they were starting, and they were all that mattered. Rocket after rocket shot high into the air and exploded with bangs that hurt the ears and shook the ground. Out of the explosions came huge blooms of light with petals of every color in the rainbow. Under their slow fall back to earth, the texture of the walls of the fort, the leaves of the trees in the park, the features on upturned faces in the crowd became as distinct as in the light of day. Each blast was greeted by cheers, claps, gasps from people whose own strong emotions were being expended up there in the sky. Word ran through the crowd that General Washington himself was watching the fireworks from Chancellor Livingston's house on the Bowling Green. It was near where they were standing, so, during one bright shower, Sarah looked and thought she saw the white image of that now familiar face floating in the darkened recess of a balconied window. What must it be like to witness such a thrilling display and know that it was all in your own honor? She simply couldn't imagine. At last one rocket whistled higher than all the rest, emitting as it fell thirteen bangs and thirteen blooms. When its last fire died, the crowd gave off a collective sigh. Whether they articulated the feeling or not, they all knew that the day was finally over, that tomorrow they would shoulder again the crushing work they'd given up for this glorious week, that, as always, the wonder of birth would give way to the drudgery of living.

On the way back, Sarah, still thinking of that face in the window, asked her cousin, "Were you named for Mr. Washington?"

"Oh, no, silly. He'd hardly been heard of when I was born. I was named for King George III like my sister was named for Queen Charlotte. What do you think about that?"

"I think you ought to be glad the president's named George, too."

He laughed. "You're a bright minx, Miss America, but you're right: I am glad. Matter of fact, I think I'll let you go home with your father and run over to Fraunce's to drink a toast to my new namesake. Want to come with me, Jacobus?"

Her oldest brother jumped at the invitation, and their father called after him, "Don't be late. We leave for home early tomorrow."

Dumped as rudely as if he'd actually tossed her off his shoulders, Sarah felt suddenly drained of joy. She was after all just a little girl to whom he was being polite when there was nothing better to do. He probably wouldn't be up in the morning to see them off because she'd already noticed that he often stayed in bed until noon after a night of drinking. They would go, and he wouldn't care, wouldn't care at all. She watched him vanish, arm in arm with young Jacobus, into the jostling crowd without a backward glance, and she wanted to cry. No good saying to herself that it was silly to make so much of a little teasing, or that she really was just a little girl; she couldn't help how she felt.

While they walked back from the park, candles were being snuffed out in houses all around them, and the thousand Christmas trees vanished. When they reached the Van Alen house, the stars there were snuffed out, too; the distinguished company long gone. As she tucked her young daughters into bed, Catharina Schuyler, suspecting that they might be overwrought from all of the excitement of the day, lingered to sing them the little Dutch lullaby by which she herself had been soothed into sleep as a child. It was a secret ritual they shared and kept from Jacobus, and oddly it worked all the better for that reason: the nursery became an escape from the discipline and demands of the lord of the manor.

> "*Trip a trop a tronjes*," she sang,
> *De varken in de boonjes,*
> *De koejes in de klaver,*
> *De paaden in de haver,*
> *De eenjes in de water plas,*
> *De kalver in de lang gras,*
> *So groot myn klein poppetje was.*

17

Pigs in the bean patch. Cows in the clover. Ducks in the water. Home. While her mother sang, Sarah's thoughts for the first time in weeks turned back to the manor. She wondered whether Liberty her pony had grown fat for want of riding, whether Lafayette her dog had missed her, whether the heavy-bellied cows had been delivered of calves, whether the lilacs were in bloom by the cookhouse path, whether the weeping willow down by the river had hung out the green curtain that made a perfect hiding place to read and dream, whether . . . . Oh, there would be so many things to catch up with when she got back, and then that Mr. Burr would be coming and maybe she would learn French, if not Latin, and wouldn't George be surprised if she wrote him a letter in French? Tomorrow didn't seem such a bad day after all, but when she actually closed her eyes to go to sleep, all she could see behind the lids were bursting rockets, falling, falling, falling into dark.

Chapter **II**

The Season of Love

She had lots of hiding places all over the manor; she needed them. When she'd learned to read French and Latin and a little Greek, Mr. Burr started smuggling novels to her—Fanny Burney's *Evelina*, Rousseau's *La Nouvelle Héloïse,* a French translation of Goethe's *Die Leiden des jungen Werthers,* Goldsmith's *Vicar of Wakefield*—as a sort of reward. He'd once run those flashing eyes of his over the jumble of books in her father's library and pronounced it good enough for anyone who wanted to become a dominie or a farmer but wholly inadequate to the needs of a young lady. Jacobus thought novels frivolous, if not dangerous, and he would have only one of them on his shelves—*The Life and Strange Surprising Adventures of Robinson Crusoe,* the reading of which he hoped would teach the boys self-reliance. Since it had been hard enough for her and Mr. Burr combined to convince her father that she should learn anything beyond how to do simple sums and write a tolerable hand in English, she thought it prudent to keep the novels out of his sight and had, therefore, become as cunning as an Indian guide in finding spots where she could read unseen and undisturbed.

Discovered with such innocent intent, these hiding places met a need she never had anticipated in that summer when George Van Alen came to stay with them on the manor. She was almost sixteen, and, stimulated by her reading, more than ready for a romantic adventure. Had he planned it, George's timing could not have been better. A year either way, and she might have seen through him. But the very fact that he arrived under such a dark cloud of dishonor that she was forbidden to speak to him alone made of him a figure more alluring than any in fiction. Where she could safely read, they could safely meet, and the temptation of reaching for forbidden fruit was more than she could resist.

It was six years since that memorable visit to New York, and Sally, as she now liked to think of herself although the family went on calling her Sarah, was in her own opinion quite grown up. She had very nearly forgotten George Van Alen. Or rather he had faded into a kind of blurred memory against which to measure the few young men she met and the many she imagined. Even though she had written to him in her first halting French, he had not responded, and she had assumed that he'd forgotten her, too, until Peter went down to the city to live with Mr. Burr at Richmond Hill and read law. It was a grievous loss since she and Peter shared much more than their black eyes; he'd taught her to swim and skate and sail, and she'd soon found herself able to help him with the studies that he found so irksome. Writing to her alone, he had reported: "Don't tell Poppa or your mother or that little tattletale, Rebecca, but I'm seeing a lot of cousin George. He takes me around with him to the taverns and other places of amusement. Poppa wouldn't understand, but the people I meet through George will be the making of me when I go into practice. He still remembers you and calls you his little Miss America. He's quite the beau of New York, and I'm afraid if you were here you'd lose your heart to him, cousin or no. But he'd surely break it, so, as a brother, I'm glad you are more than a hundred miles away." If Peter had thought that this sort of thing would make her glad, too, he hadn't read her very well, for it had been his letter that made the news of George's coming a matter of exciting anticipation for her.

Her father had been as nearly in a rage as she'd ever seen him the day the letter from Cornelius Van Alen arrived. He'd exploded to his wife right in front of Rebecca and her, something he'd never done before. "I told you, Catharina, that he'd call his loan," he said, "but I never imagined it would happen this way."

Her mother who was stitching as she forever seemed to be doing snipped off a thread with her teeth and said, "You could consider it a compliment, Jacobus; he evidently thinks we can succeed where he's failed."

"Compliment? Having that young man around this house will be like having a rotten apple in a barrel."

"Where else could he go?"

"To hell, as far as I'm concerned . . ."

"Now, Jacobus, Neel has been good to us, and . . ."

"I know it. I know it. Oh, how I know it. I wish that I'd never gone to him."

"Like Neel now, you didn't have much choice then, did you?"

It was a wounding truth. Hamilton's fiscal policies had worked out as predicted: the city was where the money was, and Cornelius, along with friends like Isaac Roosevelt and William Walton, was a director of its only bank, the Bank of New York. Having exhausted the patience of his creditors and the personal resources of his country friends, most of whom were in as bad straits as he, Jacobus had nowhere else to turn. He could perhaps have sued his tenants for arrears as one of the Van Rensselaers was doing, but a suit would have dragged on in the courts and probably produced the same kind of riot on his own peaceful manor. So he went to the city, to Cornelius. It was more galling by far than the last visit which he'd been able to rationalize as a kind of gift to his wife and children. Though that visit had reestablished some casual contact between the families, Jacobus had no more liking for his brother-in-law than before. If anything he felt more aggrieved since Cornelius had profited from the exchange of government paper to the point where he was building a vessel for the China trade. All he would ask for would be an introduction to Mr. Roosevelt at the bank.

But Cornelius would have none of that. He'd sat back like a fat Buddha, blinking and smiling infuriatingly, while Jacobus struggled to produce facts and figures to prove that the loan he was seeking would be good business. Finally, he'd interrupted, "Jacobus, Jacobus, there's no need for all that. I've enough in my own account to advance you, and there won't be any call for interest until you get on your feet. I know what it's like farming, which is why I went on the river . . ."

Farming? Didn't Cornelius realize that he wasn't talking to a grubbing farmer but to the lord of a manor? Jacobus picked up his hat and started to leave. "Never mind. I'll go to Mr. Roosevelt myself . . ."

Cornelius wasn't smiling now; the muscles under his fat cheeks hardened. "It will do you no good, Jacobus; he'll want my endorsement. All you Schuylers are proud, aren't you? Well, I admire that, because I'm a proud man, too—proud of what I've made of myself and not what I inherited. Well, if I want to use what I've made to help my little sister and her younkers, why shouldn't I? What's money for if you can't help your own family? Whether you like it or not, Jacobus, you are family. Now sit down and be reasonable."

Cornelius had made it easier for him to be reasonable by arguing that, since his sister and children would be inheritors, protection of their interest was more than a matter of sentiment with him. In any event—and here he surprised and somewhat disarmed Jacobus with confession—he had a sense of guilt about those who, like the Schuylers, had suffered from the war; this would be a way of easing it. "Oh, I know what you think of me, Jacobus, and maybe you have a right," he said. "But you're forgetting that I didn't have all your advantages and education. I'm nothing but a simple sailor who knows how to pick up a fair wind and ride it. I never did think much about politics, still don't. You know, we Dutch were brought up to mind our own business . . . but . . . well, I know we'll never see eye to eye on this anyway, but the war's long over, and you'd be doing me a favor to let me help you. How much do you really need?"

That need had made Jacobus want to believe that Cornelius was as he pictured himself, a simple and lucky sailor, but he should have known better. Out of a cunning instinct, men like Cornelius always had ulterior motives for anything they did. His, as it now appeared from the appalling letter in Jacobus' hand, had been buying his way back into a family. What was left of Lydia's family had fled to Nova Scotia or England, and the Schuylers were the Van Alen's only immediate relatives. That instinct of his must have told Cornelius that there was no substitute for family in certain crises of life. As now. Cornelius was, of course, not so crude as to mention the loan directly, and he swaddled his words in sentiment, but the meaning beneath the message was clear. If Cornelius had no choice, as Catharina said, neither did they.

Though his face was still red with anger, there was a kind of defeat in his tone when Jacobus said, "You're right, Catharina, you're right.

But I insist that the girls stay away from him. With your permission, I'd like to read this letter since I think they are old enough to understand why I feel this way."

"Whatever you think best, Jacobus," her mother said, but Sally thought that there was considerable doubt in the look she gave her husband when she glanced up from her sewing.

Her father slid the glasses that had slipped down his thin nose back into place, and, pacing to work off his emotions, read aloud:

"My dear Catharina. I—that is, Lady Lydia and I—badly need help from you and Jacobus. Though it may seem strange to you, we have a problem that money cannot solve. It concerns our son George whom I'm sure you will remember from your visit with us. I wish that I didn't have to write these lines, but I must confess that through his foolish behavior he has gotten himself into a situation that endangers his life as well as some of my most important business affairs. A jealous husband has threatened to call him out. Such a meeting must be avoided at all costs, for the man, a veteran of the war, is a notably good shot, but even if George should prevail, injury or death to this man, who is of considerable standing in the financial world here, could bring retribution. We have decided that the only way George can avoid this meeting with honor is to leave the city before it can be arranged and to stay away for a sufficient length of time to let tempers cool. Although it might be possible to send George elsewhere on business, I must confess again that I do not trust him to avoid a similar situation in another city, and it therefore occurred to me that this might be the perfect time to expose him to an experience of country life which he has so far missed and to the association and instruction of people as God-fearing and steady as you and Jacobus. Quite honestly, George does not look forward to such an exile from the idle pleasures of the city to which he has become too addicted, but both his mother and I have made it plain to him that he will be disinherited if he does not submit to our will in this matter. For all his faults, George can be a likeable and amusing fellow, and he is strong enough to be of considerable use in your work, so I doubt that you will find his presence an intolerable trial. I hope that both you and Jacobus will regard it as a tribute to your character and to that of your children that we entrust this matter to you in all confidence and good faith that by living with you George may repent of his ways and return to us a better man. It is a bitter thing to have to admit to

23

failure in the raising of a son, and, although I am no longer a religious man, I have been brought to praying to God for some kind of miracle for which you could be the agents. In trust that you cannot find it within yourselves to refuse this request, we are sending George to you by the company's next sloop to Albany. Your loving brother, Cornelius.''

When their father had finished reading, Rebecca, eighteen and grave beyond her years, reacted with suitable and satisfying expressions of shock. But for Sally the letter had the same effect as Peter's earlier one; it honed her anticipation to a cutting edge. Challenged to a duel for what her books would describe as an illicit love affair— how daring and romantic! She wondered how such an experience must have changed him, and she was surprised to find when he at last arrived that, except for a blond stubble for want of shaving water aboard the boat and a slight bag and crinkle around the eyes, he looked almost exactly as she remembered him: still thin, still almost pretty with his curly hair and high coloring, still . . . well . . . clean. His voice, however, had deepened and taken on a note of what Sally liked to think of as world-weariness. After a reception that was pointedly cool and formal and in which Sally, too, felt obliged to play a properly stiff role, he was blunt, "I don't suppose any of you are any happier in having me than I am in being here."

Jacobus was equally blunt. "For a number of reasons, we feel obliged to your father but not to you. We feel under no obligation whatever to tolerate offensive behavior or feed idle hands."

"Oh, I shall work, Uncle Jacobus. Otherwise I'd go mad . . ."

"And you'll stay out of trouble, too. There's only one tavern near here, over in Kinderhook, and I've already told my good friend, Abraham Van Buren, who runs it to forbid you the house. I want it understood by you, as it is by my daughters, that you're never to be with them except in the presence of the family."

"Really, Uncle Jacobus, I'm not an ogre," George said and broke into a smile that gave his face the look of a boy-angel in need of a shave.

"That remains to be seen, as far as I'm concerned. Now you'll have the chamber above the cookhouse. Dinner is at four."

George sent out the first feeler in search of some human warmth the very next morning which happened to be a Sunday. They were at services, held in the warm seasons in the orangery that Jacobus'

French mother had insisted on having added to the house to give her a place to sit in the light. Though it had the imposing look of a miniature castle from afar, the stone-walled Schuyler manor house was rather gloomy within except when fires were burning against the winter cold. Its builder, Jacobus' grandfather, had made the windows small and high to double as gun ports in the event of Indian attack —an event that in this long-settled valley partook more of myth than reality, though there were several scars in the heavy oak door said to have been made by arrows and left there as reminders of the courage that had been involved in the winning of these acres from savage hands. The orangery, on the other hand, might have been lifted intact from the side of a civilized French chateau; indeed, it almost had been, since it was built to plans for one just like it at the home of Jacobus' mother, with tile for the floor imported from Italy, as specified, glass from France for the tall windows and skylight, friezes in an arbor motif sculptured and shipped in pieces by a Florentine artist. No oranges now grew in its cheerful light, but Jacobus thriftily employed its southern exposure to start vegetables for the kitchen garden. As for conducting services there, Jacobus added a touch of sanctity by installing a pulpit, built by the slave Sylvanus and embossed on its front with a crude cross of his own carving.

It was a curious thing about this pulpit: Sylvanus had constructed it to his own measure instead of that of his master's short, slight frame with the result that Jacobus had to rise on tiptoe to read from the thick family Bible laid out on it or to peer over to look down upon his small congregation. The effect was to give him a kind of Sunday stature that, together with the solemnity of his pronouncements, made it possible to think of him more as a pastor than husband, father or master. The presence of the Negroes at the services—there were only three of them now, Sylvanus and his wife Florence and their daughter Flossie, Sally's own slave—also helped to create a religious atmosphere, for they would mumble "Amens" and "Praise the Lords" to punctuate the reading of the word. Flossie was Sally's one legacy from her grandmother who just before she died decided that the little black-haired, black-eyed baby would grow up to look like her and changed her will to leave her the most personal remembrance she could think of. But for all practical purposes, Jacobus and Catharina, feeling that none of their children should enjoy such special favor, had ignored that clause, and Sally had grown up with no sense of personal possession of Flossie. Several of the tenant farmers and their families, as disturbed as Jacobus by Ritzema's loyalist sentiments, had taken to coming regularly to the manor house for services, so that on this Sunday when Jacobus rose on his toes, opened the Bible, adjusted his glasses and began to read, there were twenty or more souls in front of him, much more than the gathering of two or three that Scripture required to make of any place a church.

But Jacobus seemed to be glancing down only at George Van Alen, as he announced a text from Deuteronomy 22, verses 22 through 28, and began to intone:

"If a man is found lying with the wife of another man, both of them shall die, the man who lay with the woman, and the woman; so you shall purge the evil from Israel. If there is a betrothed virgin, and a man meets her in the city and lies with her, then you shall bring them both out to the gate of that city, and you shall stone them to death with stones . . ."

Sally could hardly believe what she was hearing. How could her father do this? Was he going to shame his nephew before all of the neighbors and the slaves, too? She started to squirm, wanting to get out of there. She risked a glance at George and was totally surprised when, catching it, he very deliberately lowered one of those dark lashes in a wink, just like he'd done at the dinner table so long ago. His nonchalance, his assumption of her sympathy, so shocked and intrigued her that she had to cough and choke into her handkerchief to keep her control. Fortunately, her father appeared not to hear her, reading on:

". . . the young woman because she did not cry for help though she was in the city, and the man because he violated his neighbor's wife; so you shall purge evil from the midst of you. But if in the open country a man meets a young woman who is betrothed, and the man seizes her and lies with her, then only the man who lay with her shall die. But to the young woman there is no offence punishable by death, for this case is like that of a man attacking and murdering his neighbor; because he came upon her in the open country, and though the betrothed young woman cried for help there was no one to rescue her.

"If a man meets a virgin who is not betrothed, and seizes her and lies with her, and they are found, then the man who lay with her shall give to the father of the young woman fifty shekels of silver, and she

26

shall be his wife, because he has violated her; he may not put her away all his days."

At this point, Jacobus closed the book with a thump, cleared his throat, and said, "I suppose you are all wondering why I chose to read such a text, especially in the presence of innocent young ladies. So I owe you an explanation . . ."

Now it was coming. Her father was clear up on his tiptoes, leaning over the pulpit, and . . . smiling! Smiling? He was enjoying this terrible thing he was doing. She wanted to sink right through the floor, and a quick look at George made her realize that he felt the same way. His fair face couldn't hide a blush, and he was wringing his hands and staring at his feet. When he did look back at her, there was no wink left in him.

"Well, my friends," said her father's voice, "it's not that I think any among you could be guilty of such sin . . ."

She only realized that she'd been holding her breath when it came back to her in a quick gulp.

". . . It's that I think that in these modern times when so many of us deem it fashionable to be rational or, as lately in France, to be natural, we ought to be reminded that our God is neither. He is just —consider the woman pardoned because her cries couldn't be heard. But he is not open to reason when it comes to sin, nor does he use nature as an excuse. Sin in this case is giving in to a *natural* desire, yet its wages is death . . ."

On and on he went, but Sally stopped listening. He'd been clever enough in disguising his real intent from those who didn't know, but she and the rest of the family and George, of course, could not doubt that he was using the occasion to assault his unwanted guest. He was saying quite clearly that, to him, George was a sinner, deserving of no less than death. Why did he do this? Did he think it was a way of living up to Uncle Cornelius' expectations and throwing the fear of God into George? Or was he trying to throw the fear of George into them by emphasizing his misdemeanors? Whichever, it only heightened for her the drama George's arrival had created. She felt sorry for George whose head, bowed in embarrassment, was incongruously surrounded by a halo of curls, turned golden by a shaft of sun falling from the skylight. Who was to say that he hadn't loved the woman, as young Werther had loved, and that this kind of talk by her father might not drive him, too, to suicide? It was shivery to think about, and she decided then and there that, come what may, she at least would be nice to George.

It wasn't going to be easy. Not surprisingly, George shut himself away in his room until dinner which was eaten in heavy, embarrassed silence. Once Sally thought she saw her mother's eyes, so like George's, give him a sympathetic appraisal, but she wasn't sure until, having bolted his food, George excused himself. Then her mother said, "I think you were a little hard on him, Jacobus."

"I did nothing but read the law laid down in Scripture. At least I wiped that smirk off his face, and he's got something to think about now. Tomorrow we'll get him out in the fields and put some blisters on those tender hands of his."

"You'll drive the boy away . . ."

"He's no boy, Catharina. He's what—twenty-five, twenty-six? We live here by the word and work, and if he doesn't like it, he's free to go."

"As you say, Jacobus."

That was the way that the threat of contention between them usually ended, for Catharina Van Alen Schuyler believed that keeping peace in the home was a woman's first duty. She might not have held to this, however, if Jacobus had not proved to be in most things a reasonable man. He was fair and kind to the children, hers as much as his own by Jannetje, and completely trusting in giving her a free hand with the household and accounts. Although she lacked the education and therefore the interest to share the intellectual pursuits he followed in his library on long winter nights and bad days, she did feel herself an equal partner in all the practical details of running the manor, including the finances. He often complimented her on her "level head" which she learned to cherish in lieu of other endearments. She was levelheaded enough to know that it was her competence, more than anything else, that had caused Jacobus to propose marriage to her and honest enough to admit that she'd accepted the contract on those terms in order to become a Schuyler, the lady of the manor. On the whole, she had no regrets, for Jacobus had been gentle, if not passionate, in intercourse, both in and out of bed, and, regardless of temporary financial difficulties, the social and economic future of her children, as Schuylers, was far brighter than her own had been.

The only real sorrow in her life, aside from the death of little Ann whom she'd loved as much as her own daughters, was her estrangement from Cornelius. In this, as in his insistence that there be no Dutch in his home, Jacobus was not reasonable in her terms. He could not, of course, have any idea of what Cornelius had been like as a big brother in those good days before the war. Eleven years older than she, just about Jacobus' age, he'd been more father than brother and a tower of strength to her and her mother when her father and two other brothers and sister died within weeks of each other from the fever. Though he'd been rounder, more heavily muscled, he'd looked then a lot like his son George and had been full of some of the same nick. Even tragedy hadn't kept him from bringing a kind of sunshine into the house; he'd taken her and her mother, too, out skating and sleigh racing and sailing to help them forget. Neel Van Alen had turned his high spirits into friendship and friendship into profit when old Captain Polhemus virtually gave him his first sloop. He'd left behind him a lot of broken hearts, and, some said naughtily, maidenheads, too, when he'd sailed away to New York and married Lady Lydia Wentworth, the catch of the city. She and her mother had been proud of Neel, as were most of their neighbors. "Some smart Dutchman," they'd call him. Though he'd dropped by when he was sailing through and kept them alive with gifts of money and promises to bring them down to New York, the war had put an end to all that, and she'd felt obliged to take a position at the Schuyler manor.

Perhaps because she didn't fill her head with reading and political talk in the tavern as Jacobus did, she was more confused than anything else by the war. Her mother died in '77 still feeling herself a loyal subject of King George, and most of the people she knew and trusted around Kinderhook like Pastor Ritzema honestly thought that the Dutch would be better off under the English who'd granted them their lands and let them pursue their own ways undisturbed for more than a century. Nobody knew for sure but what the patriots might confiscate property, as the wealthy de Lanceys feared, or force people to conform to their beliefs, as the pastor feared. A lot of patriotic fervor came out of New England where there was a sorry history of religious persecution, he contended, or out of Virginia where, judging from men like Jefferson, there was no religion at all. "If we have anything like democracy where the majority rules, we'll lose our Dutch ways, the ways of God," he predicted. Statements like that would cause Jacobus to storm, "But that's just the point. It's time we stopped being colonies, being appendages to some state or church in Europe, and became a new people, a free people, one people." Catharina had never felt unhappy being Dutch or felt anything but free, but she had felt unable, and unwilling, to argue with the lord of the manor in matters like this. Still, she'd never been able to think of Cornelius as a traitor, whatever he'd done, since he quite probably was as confused about what was right as she.

With the ending of the war, she had patiently hoped that some cause for reconciliation would arise and had been more delighted than she ever let on to Jacobus when his own patriotism, his desire to witness the inaugural, had made him act reasonably over the Van Alen invitation, however he felt. She'd been happy, too, to discover that in her own way by becoming a Schuyler she had something to offer Cornelius and that proud wife of his. She could see now that the hand of God was behind it all, for she didn't know what they might have done without that loan from Cornelius. She hoped that God would be with them, too, in this business about George. Unlike the God Jacobus talked about this morning, the God she thought about would not wish George dead; he was after all her own flesh and blood and looked so like his father had before he took on the fat of good living.

Reading her own heart, Catharina was a bit apprehensive about the girls, not so much Rebecca who had inherited her own level head along with some of her father's righteousness, but Sarah. Sarah had always been somewhat of a puzzle to her; like Jacobus, she thought that the girl took after her mother-in-law, and she often wished that the old lady had not been so sick and died so soon, leaving her with no real clue as to her nature. As a child, Sarah had been a trial. As high-strung and fidgety as a boy, she was forever tearing her clothes, scraping her skin, breaking a bone in trying to keep up with Peter. There was no stopping her, for she would sulk herself into actual sickness if her freedom were denied. Then along came Mr. Burr who really did turn her head. She'd been reading so much lately that Catharina was afraid that she'd burn her eyes out, and the Lord alone knew what was going on in that mind of hers. Neither Rebecca nor she could understand much of anything Sarah said these days, and even Jacobus would sometimes shake his head as if an educated daughter were a phenomenon beyond his comprehension. Catharina would have to admit, though, that sitting still for a change had put some becoming flesh on Sarah's small body, and the swell of breast above her tight waistband left no doubt that she was a woman. Catharina had not been entirely unaware of the teasing going on between Sarah and George on their visit to New York nor of the excitement Sarah tried to conceal over his coming here. As far as Sarah was concerned, Catharina wasn't at all sure that Jacobus was handling matters right: making George a kind of pariah could make him all the more enticing to such a headstrong girl. Under the circumstances, it was a blessing that George was a cousin, although entanglements between cousins were too common in the Dutch community to put Catharina's mind entirely at rest. Maybe she should try to have a talk with her.

As they were rising from the table, she said, "Sarah, why don't you sit and sew with Rebecca and me instead of reading this afternoon?"

"Oh, I can't, mother, I absolutely can't. Mr. Burr wrote from Philadelphia asking for a translation from a passage in Cicero that he wants to use in a speech in the Senate . . ."

"Couldn't Peter do that? He's right down there with him, isn't he?"

"Pooh. The only Latin Peter ever knew was what I drilled him on —just enough to fool father . . ."

"Sarah . . ."

"Sally. I wish some of you would start calling me Sally, because that's who I am."

"You were christened Sarah . . ."

"But can't people change if they want to, mother? Isn't that what growing's all about—changing? I may have been a Sarah, but I'm a Sally now," she said and, lifting her skirts, ran up the stairs to her room.

Catharina sighed and said to Rebecca, "Sometimes I don't think I understand your sister."

"Neither do I," Rebecca said.

It may have been just as well for the peace of the household. Sally did not pour over Cicero that afternoon. Instead she drew a map of the manor, marking with little x's her hiding places, and writing boldly across the top of it WHERE TO FIND ME. She thought of signing it and specifying dates and times but decided against it; he might find this more intriguing and it would create at the very least an interesting game of hide and seek. When everyone else was asleep that night, she sneaked out to the room over the cookhouse and slipped the map under George's door.

He found her the very next day. He was certainly no woodsman; he hadn't seen the path that she and her horse had made with repeated comings and goings from the main trail, and he came crashing through the underbrush like a wild boar. His curls were darkened and pasted down with sweat, his shirt torn, his breeches burred, but he was smiling. "I was sure it was you, my little Miss America. What fun!"

She was suddenly too nervous to share his exuberance, and she felt a kind of premonition. "Where's your horse?"

"Oh, I left him out on the trail—and thank God for that," he said. He began hobbling around with an exaggerated bow to his legs and rubbing his backside. "Your father's had me in the saddle since dawn, and I'm a city boy, you know—tender in the rear."

"But they'll find him and . . ."

"Don't worry about that," George said. "I left your father way out by the Phillips place. He decided to have dinner in the fields and sent me to fetch it. This was the only x on my way, so I decided to check it out. And . . . well . . . here you are! You don't know what this means to me, little one. I was beginning to think that nobody up here loved me."

She started to breathe a little easier. "I don't know whatever gave you that idea . . ."

They laughed together, and she asked, "How is Peter?"

"Oh, I haven't seen much of him since Burr started dragging him off to Philadelphia. You know you do look a lot like him—but of course you're prettier."

"Well, thank you, kind sir . . ."

"No, I really mean it, Sarah . . ."

"Sally. I'm Sally now."

"Then Sally it shall be . . ."

From the trail came the sound of horses' hooves pounding, her father's voice hallooing his name. Instinctively, George started to answer, but she jumped up and clapped a hand over his mouth. "Don't, for heaven's sake, don't," she said. "If my father finds us here, he'll kill me."

"You don't mean that?"

"Well, no, but he'll have you off this place by sundown."

They kept silent until the sounds died away, and then she said,

"You'd better go now—and come up with a good story."

When she got back to the house, she discovered that her father and George were having dinner with them after all, and her father set out to humble George in front of them. "What happened to you, young man? When your horse came back empty, I was sure from the way you ride that you'd fallen and broken your neck. Why didn't you answer when I called?"

"I was . . . well . . . I had to relieve myself, and . . ."

"Never mind," her father said quickly as if to avert the revelation of further details on such an indelicate subject. "I guess your long walk taught you something: always tether or hobble a horse when you leave it. Anything can spook them, as even the girls here know."

"Yes, sir . . ."

That near miss and the continued uncertainty as to where and when they could take place added spice to their brief and furtive meetings. The fact that they were meeting at all set up a kind of delicious tension when they were with other people and had to avoid revealing themselves. She'd lie awake at night thinking of what to say to him, ask him, and wondered if he did, too. Though it was somewhat of a disappointment to find that he didn't share her interest in literature, he more than made up for it with humorous accounts of his romantic misadventures in real life. A thread of drunken derring-do that ran through the tapestry he wove simply glittered in her innocent eyes. He was a man of the world, and he treated her as a woman of understanding. Perhaps it was because he was a cousin. She knew that a brother would never talk to her that way, and she doubted that a suitor would either.

Once he seemed serious. "You don't think I ought to be stoned to death and sent to hell, do you, Sally?"

"Oh, no. Why?"

"Your father obviously does."

"Well, he takes the Bible too seriously, or at least I think so. Don't you?"

"Obviously. The thing your father doesn't understand from burying himself up here in the country is that I'm in the best of company. Look at Hamilton, an upstanding churchman if there ever was one, and yet he had to admit to adultery down there in Philadelphia to get out of being blackmailed by the husband. And your Mr. Burr . . ."

She was defensive. "What about my Mr. Burr?"

"Well, everybody knows he chases every skirt from Albany to Philadelphia, particularly now that his wife is dead."

"I don't think that's nice. Are you trying to imply that he . . . ?"

"Oh, no. Oh, no. Don't get me wrong. Mr. Burr loves children."

"And so I'm just a child?" She accompanied this with a pout that
turned her rather thin lips into an inviting little bud of flesh.

George didn't miss it. "No more. Sometimes I wish you were, so
I wouldn't feel this way."

"What way?"

"Oh, Sally, don't you know anything about how a man feels in the
company of a beautiful girl?"

"I'm not beautiful."

"You are, and you know it. Stop fishing for compliments. You
ought to be glad I'm your cousin, or I'd . . ."

"You'd what?"

"This," he said, and he clamped his mouth hard against hers.

Then he stood back and grinned. "There! I've been wanting to do
that all these weeks. Did you like it?"

She didn't really know whether she liked it. Pushed back against
her teeth, her lips had hurt; she'd had trouble getting her breath. But
the shock of it, if nothing else, had left her heart pumping a not
unpleasant flush to her skin. Her hesitation and the flush that looked
like a blush made him laugh. "That was your first, wasn't it? You
don't know how to kiss; I could tell. You really ought to learn, and
you couldn't have a better teacher than your cousin George. Think
about it . . . . Well, I've got to go or that old Puritan will miss me."

She did think about it, thought and thought. He'd ruined everything. It was one kind of thrill to share confidences about his distant
conquests in the city, quite another to flirt with the possibility that
she might be his next. He'd tried to be flip and friendly and cousinly,
but, innocent as she was, the urgency she'd felt in that kiss troubled
her. Yet more troublesome were the involuntary and teasing sensations aroused in her own body by his touch as on that long ago night
she'd ridden his shoulders. Fear of what might happen when they met
again was thus added to the fear of being discovered, and she started
hanging around the house, avoiding her hiding places. She tried to
ignore the kind of laughing question that stood in his eyes when they
met at table or sat pretending to read in the parlor of an evening. The
tension that had once been pleasant became a torment. Finally, the

desire to have it out with him, a consuming curiosity as to how the drama might unfold, became more pressing than her fears.

When one morning her father announced that he had to go to Albany, leaving George to his own devices for a few days, Sally went to her favorite place, one that George had not yet seen. If he made the effort to find her, she'd know for sure that he was as fascinated with the game as she and for once they'd have time for more than a few quick, light-hearted exchanges. Too restless to read as she waited, Sally sat on a little grassy knoll with her back against the oak tree that shaded her from the hot August sun and looked out over the river, infested with sloops that looked from here like busy white-winged insects, to the cloud-dappled mountains beyond. It was the kind of scene and atmosphere that a poet would have compared to heaven, and yet it left her unmoved. She was tired, tired of gazing out at this wide and beautiful and empty countryside. It held nothing for her, none of the exciting events and stimulating people with which, as her reading assured her, the earth abounded and with which she yearned to be involved. She wanted to be down there on one of those sloops, going somewhere, getting out of here. What would happen to her if she didn't? What was she waiting for? The coming of some dull and acceptable countryman like Janet's Robert Clinton who would lead her off to a similar place a few miles up or down the river where she'd watch the slow turning of the seasons until death? Yes, that was her probable fate, the abiding hope of her parents, and yet she simply couldn't imagine herself living it out. Something, some-one had to intervene to save her from this fate, like the *deus ex machina* in those old Greek plays. Sitting there awaiting George and wrestling with this vague and vast feeling of expectancy, Sally came close to achieving a wisdom beyond her years: she realized that she was toying with George, not out of any love or understanding of him as a person but out of some hope that he was that *deus ex machina* sent to save her restless soul from an infinity of boredom.

By the time George did arrive, she was almost unbearably keyed up, ready for some unusual happening. It irritated her that he seemed only interested in relaxing. He stretched out on the grass beside her, took a long cigar out of his pocket, lit it and puffed at the sky. "Ah, this is the life," he said. "A pretty girl, gorgeous scenery, the old slave driver off the plantation—and a good smoke. One of my father's. He smokes only the best cigars imported from Spain, says you can always tell a gentleman by the quality of his cigar."

"And not by the way he acts?"

"Ah, now, I suppose you're going to say I'm not a gentleman because I kissed you the other day. It was just an impulse I couldn't resist. I'm sorry if I scared you."

"You didn't scare me."

"Of course I did. Why else have you been avoiding me?"

She was angry with herself that she had no quick, pert answer. Instead, she took a look at him to try to read his expression and noticed that his eyes were resting on the spot where her skirt had pulled up to reveal her ankles. Instinctively, she reached down to cover them, and he laughed, "Don't do that. Your lovely ankle is a more filling sight to these starved eyes than all this scenery . . ."

"Stop that, George," she said, although it was really pleasing to have confirmation of her secret—and, she was sure, sinful—vanity about all of her features. "We have to be serious. I only came here because I think we should have a serious talk . . ."

"And not another kissing lesson? I'm disappointed, devastated," he said, but then he threw away his cigar, rolled over on his stomach, propped his chin on his hands and stared at her without the suggestion of a wink in his clear blue eyes. "You're right, Sally, it is time to be serious. I just wish we weren't cousins—oh, God, how I wish we weren't cousins. I'm in love with you, have been I know now ever since I first looked into those teasing, mischievous black eyes when you were a little girl. I tried to forget you, but your brother Peter will tell you that I never really did. And now that I'm here, every second that I'm in your presence is a torture and every second that I'm alone and near you and yet so far is worse. Well, you wanted to be serious, and I am serious. It's more shocking than a kiss, isn't it?"

"Yes," she agreed, for there was something frightening in the intensity of his voice, the plea in his eyes. Still he was telling her that he loved her; nobody had ever told her such a thing before. But she was puzzled. "Why is it a torture? I . . ."

"Ah, Sally, Sally, you're so innocent, and it may be your innocence I love. I want to kiss you, to hold you in my arms, to . . . but don't you feel that way a little about me?"

"I . . . I don't really know . . ."

"Yes, you do. I know it. Otherwise you wouldn't so cleverly have arranged these meetings. You'd be like Rebecca. And you're right,

36

Sally, right to feel that way. Love is the most wonderful thing in the whole world. It won't hurt you. Let me show you. I'd never hurt you, never . . ."

He jumped up, fell to his knees beside her. Lifting her chin with one hand, he kissed her again, lightly, tenderly this time. He smelled of smoke, of the sweat from his long morning ride, but it was not entirely unpleasant to her; it was somehow the smell a man ought to have. He laughed and said, "That was better, wasn't it? Now that we have time, I can be a better teacher. Try closing your eyes and kissing me back . . ." It was better, and she did, and, as she did, his other arm went around her back and pulled her close to his chest; the hand on her chin made a delicate, tickling tracery down the curve of her neck, under her scarf and along her bare shoulder, down into the fold of her dress until it closed around her breast. Her skin tingled, her nipple stiffened at his touch; it was teasing, terrifying. This was more than kissing, much more, and she had to get away, jump on the horse munching grass not a yard from her ear and flee.

"George, no . . ." she said, putting her hands against his chest and pushing.

But, strong from his summer of work, he held her firmly and said, "Why not? Why not, Sally? You like it; I know you do. I can feel it, can't you? Your little breast is like a bud in bloom . . ."

Somehow he'd unbuttoned the back of her dress and was sliding it down over her shoulder. Then her breast was exposed, lying like a treasure in his hand, and, even as she squirmed to be free, he bent to kiss the stiff bud, tease it with his tongue. Little strings of fire ran through her chest and down into her belly and on down into her loins. It was awful, wonderful, weird. Her body seemed to be slipping its moorings to her mind. Her will to fight free grew feeble, as if instinct told her that they were both in the grip of a force beyond mortal control.

Like a wind on fire, the slack in her will sent him raging. His hands were all over her, up under her skirts, tugging at her stockings, her drawers. His lips ranged her neck, her shoulders, her breasts. He kept murmuring, "Sally, Sally, oh, my Sally, oh, my Sally . . ." He pressed her back onto the grass and kneeled between her legs, spreading them with the power of his own thighs while he tore at his belt and the buttons of his breeches. She closed her eyes against a sight she didn't want to see, and the last image imprinted behind her lids was of sun lighting up the underside of a thousand leaves as if the great oak above her were bursting into flame. But it was she who was on fire. The searing, shocking pain of it made her scream. He clamped a hand over her mouth, and the terrible tearing went on. She sank her teeth into his hand until she could taste blood, but he was evidently beyond feeling pain until at last his whole weight collapsed on her. He kept moaning and saying something like, "Oh, oh, oh, oh," as if in this animal act he'd lost the human power of speech.

Her pain subsided to an ache, but she could feel the warm ooze of what must be blood. She was grievously wounded, but George, stirring now, looked at his hand and actually laughed. "Why, you minx, you bit me . . ."

"You hurt me . . ."

"It's nothing; it always hurts the first time."

"But you said it wouldn't. You promised. You lied to me . . ."

He was sitting up, sucking at the wound on his hand and still chuckling. "You wouldn't have let me otherwise, would you? Every man since Adam has lied about this . . ."

"Oh, I hate you, hate you, hate you. I never want to see you again."

She did what she could to get dressed and headed for her horse. George simply sat there and grinned at her. She hated the horse, too, for munching so steadily away at the grass that she had a hard time getting its head up. How could any creature go on eating while the whole world, her world, was being torn apart? She hated the sky that was still blue and the sun that still shone. But most of all she hated herself. She whipped the horse into a gallop, dangerous on the narrow trail and aggravating to her wound. Maybe dodging low branches and keeping the animal on its feet would keep her from thinking, from feeling. But it didn't.

She rode blindly, instinctively, while her mind reeled the whole experience backward. How could something like this be the longed-for climax of all those romances she'd read? How could she have been blind to the beast lurking behind beauty? How, of all things, could she have let herself go, let him do it? The worst thing she had to face was the remembered sensations of her own body before the pain. She'd been out of control, her very loins working with wanting . . . what? . . . something. But this? Oh, God, no wonder you call it sin. Yes, she'd sinned, and she was paying for it. But what about him? Laughing, grinning, as if they'd been playing a game. It had to be his fault. He'd done it all wrong. He was experienced and should know better. Cousin George, the teacher. She hated him, hated him. It was better, easier, made more sense, to hate him since she didn't know whether she could go on hating herself and go on living.

What would George do now? She didn't think that she could endure having him around winking at her ever more boldly, as she was sure he would. Just the thought of it gave her a scary sense that she might be capable of killing someone. Her father would certainly kill him if he knew, and she thought of telling her father when he got back. Why not? After all, she had screamed and hadn't been heard like the girl in the lesson. But then she wasn't betrothed, so her father might exact from George fifty shekels and a promise to marry, cousin or no. That would be the worst of fates, living with that grin that she now considered evil for the rest of his days, or hers. No, she couldn't tell her father, tell anyone.

But maybe George had really heard the lesson, too. She prayed that he had, and her prayer was answered. That night George vanished from the manor, leaving behind a note thanking his Aunt Catharina and Uncle Jacobus for their hospitality and assuring them that the affair in the city had probably subsided. Still shaking her head over this at breakfast, Catharina was in for another surprise when her daughter Sarah said somewhat shyly, "I think I ought to help you with your sewing today, momma." For the rest of the summer, only the wind haunted the hiding places on the Schuyler manor where once a young girl had dreamed of romance.

Chapter **III**

The Flawed French Gem

Her Uncle Cornelius came to get her himself, as if he feared that, in any other hands, she might do something foolish again, might escape him. He covered what were probably his real motives with a good excuse: he had to bring down a new sloop that had been building in Hudson over the winter, and she might as well come along; a person in her delicate condition could never go overland in the spring, what with the carriages sinking to the hub in mud every other mile so that she might end up walking half the way. In any event, it was most appropriate that he come to claim her, for she was in a very real sense his property. Cancelling her father's debt to him had amounted to a great deal more than fifty shekels, and, if she had any longer the capacity for curiosity, it was to wonder why he'd paid so much for what everybody else considered damaged goods.

During a long, dreary, never-to-be-forgotten autumn, Sally had become gradually aware that there was something wrong with her. When, for the second month in a row, she did not suffer cramps or bleed, it was logical to conclude that it was the result of what she still considered the wound her body had taken. While specific sexual mechanics was not a fit subject for discussion in the Schuyler household, Sally had read too much, observed too much around the farm, to be innocent of the facts of life. She was with child, and she hadn't the slightest idea of what to do about it. As time went on, her whole body began to rebel. She started throwing up, and food became abhorrent. But she had to hide her illness and stuff herself at table to conceal her condition in the vain hope that some miracle would occur before she had to confess. All day and every day and most hours of sleepless nights, panic sat in a lump at the bottom of her throat, wanting to burst into a shattering scream.

It might have been more bearable if she had been able to think of even one person in whom she could confide. The irony of her situation was that, far from feeling that the people around her were mean or misunderstanding, she had always felt that they loved her in a special way. As the youngest in the family, she'd been a kind of pet, the recipient of indulgences that the others had been denied. She was thoroughly aware, too, that this position as family pet was enhanced by her exotic good looks. Despite his shy austerity, her father's pride in her as a reflection of his own lineage came through in many little ways; despite her repeated and rather good-humored expressions of bafflement about her behavior, her mother's sense that this odd daughter of hers might have a peculiar and fascinating destiny was also evident. Her older brothers and sister had played with her like an interesting toy; only Rebecca seemed to find her less than enchanting. Who of all these doting people—with the possible exception of Rebecca—would not be shocked and hurt into unpredictable reaction by the revelation of her sin? Yes, sin. Nothing whatever in her knowledge or experience left her with any doubt that all of them —with the possible exception of Peter who was so far away—subscribed to the explicit moral laws their father laid down every Sunday. If she'd felt unloved, or even unappreciated, she might have seen her condition as a kind of revenge, but she could not grant herself that ease.

Once she almost broke down and talked to Rebecca who caught her in the act of vomiting. "What's wrong with you, Sarah? Do you have the fever? You ought to tell mother so she can send for the doctor."

"Oh, there's nothing wrong. Just something I ate."

"There is, too. You've been looking terrible lately—white as a sheet. If you don't tell momma, I will."

"Oh, no, don't. All the doctor would do is bleed me or give me a dose of salts, and either of them are worse than this. I think it's just the beastly weather. You know how I am when I can't get out and exercise."

Rebecca was riding a horse she wouldn't get off. "But you've never had a sick day in your life. I don't understand . . ."

There was so much that Rebecca, good, sweet and dull, didn't understand, never would, which was why in the end she couldn't bring herself to the truth. Though it was possible that Rebecca wouldn't tell, it was certain that she would take a holier-than-thou attitude and perhaps get an unconscious enjoyment out of Sally's predicament. To be honest, if the shoe were on the other foot, Sally doubted that she would wear it with more grace. But she had an inspiration.

"Listen, Becky . . ."

"Don't call me Becky. You know I don't like it."

"I'm going to call you Becky until you call me Sally. But listen, if you don't tell them about me, I won't tell them why you're always going over to visit brother Jacobus."

It was ammunition she'd been saving for the right battle, and she'd hit the mark. Rebecca's pink cheeks turned fire red. "How did you know?"

Ostensibly to take care of baby James, Rebecca had been spending a great deal of time at the house that their father had built as a wedding present for his older son. Actually, she'd been seen by Flossie, who really was taking care of the baby, sneaking off to meet Jacobus' young brother-in-law, John Livingston, and Flossie had relayed the news to her mistress. Sally had no doubt that the affair was innocent, but the fact that it was so far secret would make the telling an unbearable embarrassment for Rebecca whose stock in trade in the family was her innocence and honesty.

"Never mind how I know, but I know. So is it a pact, Becky?"

"Yes, S . . . Sally."

"That's better, Rebecca," she said and then impulsively hugged her sister. "Oh, I do hope he's nice to you."

"Oh, he is. He says he's in love with me, and I . . . I think I love him . . ."

"I'm glad, Rebecca, glad."

She was only lying a little. Rebecca's goodness deserved reward, and it looked like it was coming to her exactly as promised in all the fables. Not that she, Sally, would want to spend a lifetime with John Livingston from what she'd seen of him. He was far too short and scowly and tongue-tied except when talking about the merino sheep he was helping young Jacobus breed from the stock at Clermont. By marrying into the Livingston clan Jacobus had brought upon the Schuylers a blessing their father couldn't afford, and she had no doubt that another Livingston would be welcomed with open arms. There would be a big wedding at the manor, as there had been for Janet, and the punch would flow, and the orangery would be cleared for dancing, and for a night Rebecca would be a princess with no peers. Yes, Sally was glad for Rebecca but sad for herself since, whatever happened, she was unlikely to see this event and sure never to experience the like herself. She had forfeited forever the right to that kind of happy ending to love, possibly to love itself.

She knew this because of what happened when desperation made her humble herself and reach out for some kind of understanding, if not love, from the one person who ought to share her trouble. George had made no effort to contact her, proving, as she'd suspected, that his protestations of love had been false, a way of opening the gates to lust. Words of gratitude had come through from Uncle Cornelius that George seemed much improved by his stay in the country and was at last settling down to his duties in the firm; if ever they wished to reciprocate by sending their daughters down to the city for a season of social polishing under Lady Lydia's tutelage, they would be more than welcome. This time, however, never wanting to see George again, she had been grateful for her father's mistrust of the Van Alen influence. Otherwise, her parents would certainly have taken advantage of the opportunity, as did most of the other families along the river with eligible daughters. But when her condition left her with nowhere else to turn, she finally wrote a letter to George. It was short, blunt, without sentiment.

"Cousin George—I am carrying your child. What shall I do now? Nobody here knows about it. Please help me. Sally."

She sent the letter, heavily sealed, to her brother Peter for personal delivery so that it couldn't fall into the wrong hands in the Van Alen household. She waited and waited. No reply came from George. At last, though, there was a letter from Peter:

"Dear Sally—I can't imagine what is going on between you and

George, but I hope that it is not serious. I delivered your letter to him, as you asked, and he tore it open in my presence. Whatever you wrote seemed to upset him, for he turned pale and started to shake. I asked if he had an answer, and he said no but he would give me one to send to you later. I waited for weeks. He didn't come to see me or show up at any of the taverns where we usually ran into each other, and so I finally went around to the Van Alen offices to find him. He wasn't there, and Uncle Cornelius told me that he had suddenly volunteered to ship out as purser on the firm's China trader. The old man was proud as punch, saying that George's decision to forgo the gay life of the city for a year or more showed how serious he was at last about the business. He attributed it to the good influence all of you had on him up in the country last summer, but from what I've seen of George lately I thought that there must be another jealous husband on his heels. Then I figured out that the ship sailed not long after he got your letter and put two and two together. I guess your business will have to wait, but if you are in some kind of trouble that can't wait, please let your big brother know.—Peter."

Long and long she thought about taking Peter into her confidence, but every time she sat down to write to him something stayed her hand. The very fact of their special relationship made it a dangerous course. Peter could be hot-headed, and she was sure that, whatever else he did about the situation, he would put his life on the line to call George out as soon as he got back from his voyage. No, she didn't want to add blood on her hands to her other sins. She'd have to solve the problem herself—or let God do it. Though the God she'd been reared to fear seemed the least likely source of help, she began praying, as she'd never prayed in her life, confessing her sin and pleading for a miracle.

But no miracle was wrought. With the thickening of her body, the process seemed to push that sickening lump of panic higher in her throat. Fortunately, her physical sickness subsided, and she began to take on a glow of good health that allayed Rebecca's suspicions. Fortunately, too, her high-waisted dresses could be cinched in above a swelling stomach that didn't yet show under the loose folds of the skirt. But for how long? Weeks, another month? It was January already, and nothing whatever had happened to stay the relentless course of nature. What she wanted but tried not to admit to herself because that, too, might be a sin was to lose the growth inside her.

It happened all the time to women who really wanted a child, why not to her? In fact, women like her were always said to be in a "delicate condition," and she'd often heard her mother say that so-and-so couldn't risk taking the stage for all the jolting or a walk on ice lest she fall. Once free of nausea, she felt anything but delicate, and, as part of her concealment, she went on riding, skating, sleighing as she always had without incident.

As she always had—that was the trouble. Peter had trained her too well, and one of her glories had been that she was very nearly as good as a boy at any of these activities. She couldn't fall off a horse or take a spill on the ice if she tried, or perhaps *unless* she tried. But wouldn't creating a deliberate accident be a greater sin than wanting it to happen? She couldn't bring herself to do this, but she could throw away the caution that is always one of the secrets of the expert in any endeavor. She began galloping her horse without regard to the flint-hard, ice-pocked footing on the paths and, unfortunately, without consideration for the animal. When she brought it in foaming and frothing one cold January day, old Sylvanus screwed up the courage to scold her. "You gonna kill dat horse, missy, gettin' him so heated up this kind of weather," he said. "You don't stop, and I'll have to tell your father. You know, he thinks there's no sin like abusing a horse." She'd always remember the look of surprise on Sylvanus' face when she broke into a crazy laugh, close to the hysterical scream always clogging her throat. No sin greater—oh, if they knew, if they knew.

On the ice, she cut figures, joined the boys in jumping barrels and racing, once clear across the river and back over patches so rough that her teeth rattled. Rebecca scolded her for being unladylike, and she laughed at that, too. Oh, how unladylike; she was better than the boys, and her sharp runners stayed securely under her as if glued to the ice. God was evidently not going to answer her prayers. Instead, he was condemning her to hell. She had never really believed in hell before, but she entered it on the ice on a day in early February.

That morning she was awakened before dawn by a new sensation in her belly. It was a tickling and tapping as if a small fish were flipping around inside her. It could be a gurgling of gas, but she felt no other discomfort. She knew that it had to be the first stirrings of life, and with the coming of this life all hope of saving her own life from the imagined horrors of disgrace and dishonor vanished. She could not kill this new life, did not want to, and go on living herself with sin compounding sin. Oh, God! Oh, God! A vain cry, for this tickling and tapping, she knew, was promise of the only form of miracle she could expect. Her life had been taken out of her hands, and she would have to go this very day and throw herself upon the mercies of her mother and father. The thought of their hurt, their wrath, gripped her with such cramps of fear that the signs of life were overwhelmed, and she had to keep shivering into the cold to use the chamber pot. She felt the strength to do what she knew she had to do literally draining away.

As if in cruel mockery of her own mood, dawn raised one of those rare midwinter days that assert the coming of spring. The sun, riding an empty blue sky, was so warm that by early morning icicles on the eaves began shedding rainbow drops into a gentle breeze. The tiny window in her room brought into focus like a telescope a blazing and cheerful light bouncing off the river's ice and empty fields of snow. At any other time a day like this would have lifted her spirits like those of the birds, chirping and fluttering snow from the boughs with their wings as if to hurry spring. Looking out on such splendor, it was almost impossible not to think of the world as beautiful and good and full of pleasant promise for all of its creatures. It was obvious from the way they were twitting that God did care for sparrows, making more cruel his desertion of her. The very least he could have done this day was to produce gray skies and rain, a kind of universal weeping for one who was lost.

By the time she got down to breakfast, everybody else was as bright as the day, busy with plans to use the reprieve in the weather. Her father wanted to ride into Kinderhook; Rebecca and her mother decided to go along in the sleigh. Would she join them? It was no time to spring her dreadful news, and the idea of spending hours wedged into a sleigh and enduring the cheerful chatter of her mother and sister while her own mind wept was beyond her strength. Oh, no, she'd go skating. Didn't they know how wonderful and free it felt to skate without a muff and scarf and cloak? There mightn't be another chance this year. Well, it was like her, and none of them were surprised at her decision. "Best watch the melt," was all her father said. "Oh, I will, I will," she promised.

Although it had been an excuse to avoid the trip to Kinderhook and although she felt weak from her morning attack, she did go skating.

Wandering around the empty house, rendered gloomier than usual by the contrasting sunlight outside, made her strangely nervous. Every effort to rehearse some appropriate speech of confession, to pick some proper time and place to deliver it, seemed worse than the last. She simply could not imagine the scene in any real terms. She wished, as she'd never wished before, that she could imbibe what her father called "Dutch courage" in a sneering reference to his neighbors' drinking habits. But, beyond an occasional glass of wine at dinner or a cup of punch on festive occasions, she'd had no experience with alcohol; serious drinking was another of those activities reserved for the male of the species, and they were welcome to it from what she'd seen of it. Decanters of brandy and rum stood on the sideboard, but she passed them by and responded, as she'd always responded to emotions she couldn't control, by throwing herself into violent physical activity.

Surprisingly for such a day, the river for miles around was an empty, glowing mirror. The young children who would normally be out there hailing the sun with shrieks and calls as spontaneous and joyful as the song of birds were still shut up in the village school. It was one of the few mercies granted her, for she wanted to be alone to try once more to imagine the terrible scene in store. Without even thinking about it, she found herself skating very carefully, taking little, ladylike bites into the soft ice, and she guessed it was some kind of instinctive response to the awful knowledge of life within her. She was surprised to find a wink of humor in her mind—"If Rebecca could only see me now!" She was not surprised to find that the skating didn't help. Indeed, as she drifted alone through a glittering white world, an overwhelming sense of the darkness in her own mind and spirit seized her.

There had been nothing like this in all of her dreams and expectations of life, never a clue that she might find herself in circumstances beyond her control, never a hint that the special attractions she prized could draw upon her evil as well as good, never a whisper that her will to be different could lead to ruin instead of romance. The pet, the pretty pet, who could do no wrong, had sinned and must suffer for it all of an endless, endless life. She'd long since lost the early consolation of feeling wronged, of loathing him instead of herself. It was her body after all that had betrayed her, that made it now impossible to escape the consequences of the act. Nor was it a

47

consolation to think that others had gone through the same experience and survived. Those others, whoever they were, were not Sally Schuyler. Survival had never been among her concerns, for simply by being who she was survival had been guaranteed. More: by simply being who she was, who she was becoming, some wondrous adventure in life had seemed guaranteed. These guarantees had proved as worthless as the scrip which leached away her father's wealth. The only sure thing remained the revenge of an angry God, and it would be taken today, within hours.

Unconscious of where she'd been going, she was suddenly startled by the sound of cracking under her skates. She was out near the middle of the river, and she could see the crack she'd started, running ahead of her as if an invisible knife were slicing the ice. Frightened out of her thoughts, she instinctively whirled to head back to the surface she'd found safe. Then, again instinctively it seemed, she stopped. What if she skated on and the ice broke and dropped her into the cold, black river? She'd die, of course—and quickly. All of her life she'd been warned against the perils of soft ice and freezing water. A person won't last more than a few minutes under such conditions, the sage river hands would say; in fact, just last winter a boy had given his life to prove their point. She'd also heard that freezing and drowning brought gentle death, though how the living knew for sure puzzled her. They based their assumption on the testimony of those who had nearly died and been revived which wasn't in her mind the same thing as actually dying. Still, they could be right, and there was something appealing in the thought of being overwhelmed by a force of nature, having life snuffed out with one pinch like the flame of a candle, instead of painfully rotting from within. Thinking about it, she felt her whole body begin to react queerly, almost as it had to that other overwhelming force of nature by which she'd been ravished. Tingles ran through her and broke out in gooseflesh on her skin and sweat in her palms and under her arms. As if shoved by a giant hand, she turned again and began skating toward the west, into the sun.

She did something she'd never done before. She looked straight into the sun, letting its light blind her, for she didn't want to see, didn't want to know the exact moment. The crackling in her ears was enough to tell her that it would be soon, soon. Her mind no longer turned in tightening, torturing circles; it ran free as her runnered feet: *This is it! This is it! This is what I've been waiting for and didn't know it. God has been good to me after all; he would not let me do it if it weren't right, if it were going to hurt. He'll take me and hide me under the ice, and they'll never find me and never know. Their sorrow will be sweet, not sour, and their memories of me green. They will set a stone for me beside the one that covers little Ann who died in her innocence and was buried in white and grace it with plantings of petunias in the spring. They will . . ."*

But God was not good after all. One of the many eyes he uses to keep tabs on sparrows and people and other foolish creatures was in the head of the slave girl Flossie who had been sent from the house of young Jacobus to the manor house to borrow some salt. Dawdling along the river bank to prolong a few moments of a kind of freedom and having nothing else to watch, she was looking at the trim, tiny figure of her mistress gliding gracefully along when it simply disappeared, dropped out of sight, leaving a shining wasteland of ice. Flossie screamed louder than the steam siren on the new pumping station, and old Sylvanus, hearing her and fearing for his daughter's life, came running faster than anyone would believe possible. When he heard Flossie's babbled story, he didn't hesitate; he'd fished foolish kids out of crackling ice more times than he liked to think about and even kept some planks by the landing for the purpose. With Flossie to help him and point the way, he lugged the planks out to where they could see a dark hole in the crackles, laid them end to end and crawled across them on his stomach. Though he couldn't see her, Sylvanus plunged his arm into the cold black and seized a fistful of hair floating like dead weed under the surface. He yanked her up onto the planks, dragged her back to safe ice and began kneading her ribs. She gasped, choked, vomited and opened her eyes. Despite the familiar black faces floating above her, she knew she'd gone to hell.

For the next two months, she was virtually a prisoner in her room while her parents alternately raged, wept and debated what to do. The news had come to them in the worst possible way. In the midst of their wild and prayerful elation that her life had been spared, the doctor called in to treat her for shock and chill had come down the stairs after his examination and said quite casually, "You have a double blessing, Jacobus; her baby is still alive, too."

If the heavens had fallen above him or the earth opened beneath him, Jacobus Schuyler could not have been more devastated by shock. He knew at once what must have happened, and his first rage

49

was vented on George Van Alen. Words his wife and Rebecca had never heard before fell from his lips as he tried to describe his despicable nephew. "I told you death was what he deserved, and death he'll get," Jacobus screamed. "I'll go to New York and call him out myself. I'll take the next sloop. And I'll kill his fat father who foisted him on us, too. I'll . . . I'll . . ." To the women, the wrath choking Jacobus was almost as alarming as the news the doctor had brought, and they began to cry. Suddenly Jacobus, his thoughts turning to the girl lying upstairs, joined them, for he was shaken by an unutterable sadness. His little girl, the French gem that so delighted his eye when all else often seemed to be lost, was flawed beyond value. He never wanted to see her again, and he said so, "I don't want to lay eyes on that . . . on her . . . God help me, I don't know what I might do . . ."

Neither did Catharina Van Alen Schuyler, for she'd never imagined her husband capable of such wrath. She needed her level head more than ever before in her life but it went into a spin, a vertigo of conflicting emotion. She felt at once bitterly disappointed in her daughter and unbearably sad about her plight. Knowing her husband's deep convictions, she also felt real fear over what he might go on to do to the Van Alens, to Sarah, to himself, to all of them. What she needed to bring her out of her spin was the facts, all of them, and before her eyes were dry she dragged herself up a flight of steps that had grown steeper and longer within minutes and went in to see her daughter. Still in shock, the girl poured out everything, including the fact that her fall through the ice was no accident, and then she delivered herself into her mother's arms as she hadn't done since she was a baby. Catharina could think of nothing better to do than to cushion the girl, sobbing uncontrollably now, against her soft breasts and rock her back and forth while she let the facts level her mind. The most important of these was that George's flight would make it impossible for Jacobus to add death, perhaps his own, to an already sorry situation before they all had time to think; the next was that George apparently remained unmarried and, while he was deservedly loathed by her daughter and husband—by her now, too—this fact did make possible a common and accepted solution to the problem. It was all she could see to do, and it would take time to bring it about. Meanwhile, she would keep Sarah out of her father's sight, keep her in this room. She needed the rest and deserved the punishment.

Moreover, if she'd tried to kill herself once, she couldn't be trusted; they'd move Rebecca in to watch her at night.

The last was an unnecessary precaution. The minute she knew that she hadn't died, Sally knew, too, that she would go on living through whatever fate she faced. It was God's last trick, and she had no more cards left to play. The shock to both her mind and body left her listless and uninterested in anything. She couldn't focus her mind on reading and would pass the hours of light at her window, watching the gradual greening of a spring that was passing her by. The blind, persistent punches of the life trying to release itself from her were only an annoying reminder that she would have to go through pain, though perhaps she could no longer feel pain. She didn't know. She didn't care. Her opinion was not asked or offered in the bitter debate that went on below, once elemental rage and sorrow subsided. When at last they told her that Uncle Cornelius was coming for her and that she would eventually be George's bride, she knew few of the particulars. All Rebecca told her was that their mother had finally written to her brother, and that Uncle Cornelius had seemed delighted: he would make George marry her and forgive Jacobus' debt besides. When he heard this, their father had, according to Rebecca, started to laugh in a scary way and said, "Good Christians, eh? Must know about the fifty shekels, eh? Well, I guess that's the way the Good Book said it should be, and so it shall be, and so it shall be . . ." Then he'd ridden furiously off to Kinderhook, probably to Van Buren's, and come home roaring drunk for the first time in anybody's memory. It was a measure of her despair that she couldn't bring herself to care about what she'd evidently done to her father, too.

The sloop that rounded up at the manor's landing on an April morning seemed more an elegant barge to convey a princess in triumph to her new realm than the means of rescue for a fallen woman. Called the *Lady Lydia*, she had been built as a packet to capture a share of the anticipated increase in passenger trade now that Albany had replaced New York as capital of the state. She was seventy-five feet long and carried a mast to match with a boom close to ninety feet. She was painted bright red with royal blue stripes; a gilt figurehead under her bowsprit and a gilt carved taffrail trimming her high poop glittered like real gold in the sun. Below, she had a

51

main cabin large enough to hold a ball in the waist and separate sleeping cabins aft for men and women, each with twenty-five bunks. Against the dark mahogany paneling, more gilt glittered in the frames of mirrors mounted above the bunks and the partition between the main cabin and sleeping quarters. Forward, she had a compartment for four in crew and a galley with a brick fireplace larger than the one in the manor's cookhouse.

Welcoming her aboard, his round face as sunny as the day, Uncle Cornelius took in his sloop with a gesture and asked, "Isn't she lovely? Best that money can buy. I always say get the best that money can buy."

Sally struggled not to respond with a bitter laugh. Was *she* the best that his money could buy? Suspicious of his motives and put off by his cheeriness, she said nothing at all, hoping he'd see that she wanted only to go below and be alone. She did know that, because this was *Lady Lydia's* maiden voyage and there was need for testing the strength of her stays and the tightness of her planking, Cornelius and she would be the only passengers, and she was grateful for that. Now she could only hope that he would be spending most of his time on deck, as he should.

He did seem to have some sensitivity to her silence. "Well," he said. "Well, well. Make yourself at home; we have to get underway."

Cornelius headed for the poop, and she started for the companionway. Just then there was a commotion on the pier. Sylvanus appeared, half dragging Flossie who was crying and complaining. With tears in his own eyes, he lifted her and tumbled her over the rail, saying, "Now you go along with your mistress . . ."

"We don't need any more niggers down there," Cornelius shouted. "Get her off."

"Miss Catharina say she do. She need her when the baby comes. Anyway, she belong to Miss Sarah."

Cornelius shrugged, turned away and supervised the hauling in of the sheets. The great fluttering mainsail began to tighten with wind, and the *Lady Lydia* turned her stern to the frowning castle on the hill. Sally wondered if she'd ever see it again, wondered if it mattered. It didn't now.

But it certainly did to Flossie. The black girl was lying on the deck at her feet, shivering and sobbing. In all of her eighteen years, Flossie had never been off the Schuyler property, never away from her par-

52

ents, never in a boat. An hour before she'd been busy spooning breakfast into a spluttering baby James without a thought in her head, and here she suddenly was—off to a place she'd never imagined going and possibly forever with a mistress who even she knew was "in trouble." Sally was as surprised by the girl's presence as Flossie herself, and she took her down below where, forgetting herself for the first time in months, she concentrated on calming her enough to find out what had happened.

"They was an awful arguing," Flossie finally said. "Massah Jacobus and Mis' Catharina come together down to young massah's house, talking right in front of me and the baby and Mis' Martha. He sayin': 'I tell you, Catharina, I *won't* let her go. They need her here to take care of James, and that girl doesn't deserve her. My mother'd turn over in her grave if she knowed what she done.' She sayin': 'But the girl's *her* property, Jacobus. She's all we have to give her.' And he sayin': 'Why do we have to give her *anything?* God knows, Cornelius has enough.' And she sayin': 'Oh, Jacobus, I jus' have a *feelin'* about it—the girl did save Sarah's life, and . . . Well, I wouldn't feel right about keepin' the onliest thing our daughter owns, would you?' And he turnin' around and walkin' away and she tellin' me to get my things together and Miss Martha standin' there and sayin': 'Oh, I don't know what I'll do without you, Flossie, I just don' know . . .' "

Once started, Flossie went on and on about her own mother starting to wail and her father starting to cry and her being scared, but Sally stopped listening. She knew what it must have cost her mother to go against her father's wishes like that, and the very presence of this black girl was like a shriek of love coming to her across the water from the cold stone fortress which was dwindling now to a tiny speck in the sight. She hugged Flossie and said, "You'll be all right. We'll get along all right, Flossie. You'll see. Now you'd better unpack my clothes and hang them—there, in the women's cabin."

Until now, she'd wondered about her mother. After that one moment, almost lost to her because of her own condition of shock, when she'd cuddled against Catharina's bosom, there had been no show of affection or real understanding. In her levelheaded Dutch way, Catharina had seen efficiently to her comfort, usually through the offices of Rebecca, and provided some advice about her physical condition. If she showed more consideration than Jacobus, it seemed only in the interests of making the best of a bad situation, of keeping things calm until they could get rid of her. But now, now. Could it be that beneath her mother's level head there beat an uncertain heart? Could it be that her mother's coolness even in the parting—she hadn't stood by the door to wave, as she normally would have, but had turned at once to go in to Jacobus who had hidden himself in the library—was largely an act to keep her husband quiet? She ran on deck to get a better look at her disappearing home, and for the first time since she'd come out of shock she had enough feeling in her to cry.

An arm came around her shoulders and Uncle Cornelius' voice, no longer cheery but grumbly with emotion, produced almost the same words she'd used with Flossie. "There, there, little one," he said. "It will be all right, you'll see. Now you come on up on the poop and watch me sail this craft. Get your mind on the business at hand and you'll feel better. That's what I always say . . ."

Despite that visit to New York, Uncle Cornelius was an unknown quantity to her. Then, he'd been just a presence in the house, a jolly Santa Claus figure moving through a Christmas tree world. What she'd learned of him since was not reassuring. As they'd grown older, their father had been more open in discussing affairs in front of them, revealing his bitter belief that Cornelius had gained his wealth by trading with the enemy and his suspicions about Cornelius' seeming generosity to them. "That man isn't capable of making anything but a Dutch bargain," he'd say, meaning a one-way trade. And the way George told it, his dissipation was an effort to put salve on the wounds inflicted by the lash of a hard-driving father. Sally often thought that one reason her father tolerated those visits by Mr. Burr who was so unlike him in so many ways was because of Burr's scornful comments on Cornelius Van Alen. "One reason we've got to get those Federalists out of power is to get that jolly old Dutchman's fat fingers out of the till," he'd say when Catharina was out of earshot. Only her mother ever had good words for Cornelius, and she spoke them guardedly in deference to her husband's opinions and only about the old days when he was a young riverman.

Looking at him now, it was hard to visualize the Cornelius Van Alen whose youthful sailing feats on what was then called the North River were legendary. Beloved by artists for its vistas and poets for its legends, the river could be a bitch to the men who sailed it. Like a great pump, the ocean shoved its tides up the river a hundred miles or more and sucked them back again. The flow could be as strong as

54

three miles an hour in stretches, particularly in the dry summer when it wasn't headed by the runoff of streams above Hudson, and a contrary tide was more than a sloop could contend with in a light head wind. If a tide didn't push an unwary sailor backward, it could set him sideways right across the river where it bounced off a headland. The winds could be tricky, too. Under the bluffs of the Highlands, for instance, was a stretch the Dutch skippers called *weer gat,* or weather hole, and keeping a sloop on her feet there in williwaws out of the west could take the nimbleness of a dancer and the guts of a freebooter. Neel Van Alen, they used to say, could tame that bitch of a river to his uses better than any man alive with the result that his produce got to market faster and fresher and fetched higher prices. A man who could do that had to be quick, muscled, and full of nerve, and he was.

But that was years ago—fifteen or more since he'd left the river— and Cornelius Van Alen, approaching sixty, had sat too long in his counting house and too often at splendid tables. His muscle had melted into fat that rolled in ever larger puffs from generous cheeks, through a number of chins, to a truly impressive paunch. Despite entreaties from his wife and children, he would not wear a wig, and his scalp shone like the fat end of a darning egg poking out of a thin gray shawl, the remnant of hair once as curly and golden as his son's. He still had sailor's eyes, however, bedded in squint wrinkles and as blue as the waters they reflected, and he still had a captain's voice, trained to be heard in a gale. A man who could afford to be fat could afford to be happy, and the jollity that men in his debt like Jacobus Schuyler found infuriating was a natural response to a world that had treated him well.

Having long ago unburdened himself of Calvinist convictions about sin and the fall of man, Cornelius couldn't understand why a pretty thing like this Schuyler girl would want to destroy herself or why Jacobus Schuyler would want to banish her from his sight. All this came through in Catharina's anguished letter to him, and it was underscored when none of the Schuylers but Sally, as he'd come to think of her from hearing George talk, came down to greet the *Lady Lydia.* He might as well have been picking up a piece of freight. But such freight! Whatever else George lacked he had good taste in women. Until Sally came aboard, his memory of her was of a skinny little thing with enormous eyes like wet coals. The eyes were still there, but she had rounded out nicely in all the right places and was, of course, carrying her skirt high over her swollen belly—a condition that Cornelius had noted often rendered young women peculiarly attractive as if they were radiating an inner glow. And if, as Catharina had written in a rather pathetic effort to sell her daughter, the brain under those black ringlets could cope with French and Latin and Greek, she was altogether a girl to be prized. To Cornelius, her condition was mostly a sign that she might be an inheritor of his own risk-taking spirit. Well, their loss, his gain.

In all his growing-up years, in all those years when he'd sailed, or drifted, or sometimes anchored against the tide in the river day after day after day and there'd been little to do but gaze upon the vast lands belonging to Van Rensselaers, or Schuylers, or Livingstons, or Phillipses, or de Lanceys, or Hoffmans, or Beekmans and chew the cud of envy, he'd wished that he had been born a patroon. Not that he admired them much as men. He held them all, his brother-in-law included, in jealous contempt for the fact that they'd never done an honest day's work or suffered from an empty belly. Yet simply by being born with a certain name, they'd acquired an indefinable prestige that none of his striving could ever achieve. He'd come close, he thought, with his marriage to Lady Lydia, his daughter's marriage to a de Lancey. But he quickly discovered that Sir Robert was a knight newly minted for the sake of the money he rendered the crown, and the de Lanceys, who like all patroons could afford principles, left with the losers when the war was over. So his sister's marriage to a Schuyler had meant more to him than he liked to admit, and he'd considered the loans that would bind them to him money well spent. But he could never have imagined that such a risk would yield such a profit, and through such a worthless agent. His son's distressing philandering had brought him something that no amount of money could buy—an undissolvable bond with the Schuylers; whatever his feelings, Jacobus could never deny that the child about to be born was a Schuyler.

While she couldn't know her uncle's thoughts, Sally was moved by his tone and touch. He really did welcome her, accept her as she was without judgment. Why then bury herself below? She followed him up onto the poop, and he commanded a chair for her next to the big tiller which he immediately took out of the hands of his captain. "Now we're going to see how this *sloep* sails," he said, lapsing into

Dutch inflection as he often did on the river. "I hear from your brother, Peter, that you're a sailor, too . . ."

It was an exaggeration typical of Peter since all she'd done really was to take the tiller of his little periagur when they were out together in a breeze light enough for him to trust her. But she did, from Peter's talk, understand more about sailing than most girls, and she had longed all of her life to go aboard one of the big sloops she'd watched gliding the river to some destination that had to be more fascinating than the tranquil manor. Her imagination had taken her on voyages often enough but never, never under such humiliating circumstances. But she'd try not to dwell on that, try, as Uncle Cornelius suggested, to keep her mind on the business in hand. And the wind, on this clear, cloud-puffed April day, was cooperating to provide plenty of business.

Coming strong out of the northwest, it strained the ribbon anchoring her bonnet under her chin, ironed the carefully curled ringlets of hair it could reach into wisps that tickled her cheeks, whipped her skirts so that she had to pin them by clutching her knees. Cornelius had to doff the tricornered hat he still favored lest it be blown overboard and expose his white crown to the sun. Heading south now, the *Lady Lydia* caught the breeze on her starboard quarter and with her huge mainsail and jib eased to port boiled along on a broad reach, the best point of sailing for her. Cornelius ordered the triangular topsail set above the main to see if she could carry it in such a wind, and the added sail caused the sloop's bow, bluff as a Dutch matron's bosom, to bury in the puffs and toss foam like showers of jewels on deck. But she could carry it, and Cornelius laughed and shouted like a boy, "Steady as a church. Steady as a church she is. I knew she'd be. Here, feel her, little one, feel her."

Forgetting her delicate condition, as he evidently had, too, she stepped up beside him and put her hands on the shaft of the tiller, so fat that she could barely get a hold. He took his away, and she was amazed to discover that, beyond a slight trembling caused by the water rushing past the rudder far below, there was no strain imparted to the tiller by all that wind bagged in the *Lady Lydia's* sails. She was as easy to steer as the little periagur, and Sally had a wonderful sense of power at being able to command her with her own little hands. "See?" Cornelius said. "She'll be a good craft, I'm sure, although we'll get the real test if this wind holds in the *weer gat.* . . . Look! Look over there! Sturgeon running . . ."

He was pointing toward the east bank where the river seemed to be spewing thousands of silver arrows into the sun as the sturgeon leaped above the surface in their fierce urge to reach spawning ground. Already men were shoving off from shore in any boat they could find, and Cornelius took the tiller out of her hands. "Let's go after them," he shouted to the crew. "Ease the sheets." When they came boiling through the school, one of the men speared a fish so large that it took the whole crew to bring its flapping carcass on deck. The black cook was upon it in an instant with a long knife, and Cornelius predicted, "We'll dine well this day, little one."

He was right. The fresh air and excitement had given her a true appetite, and she was most unladylike in the way she attacked the steaks of fresh sturgeon and washed them down with the Madeira that Cornelius kept pouring into her glass. It was the first time they'd been alone and could talk and Cornelius began by saying, "Well, a day like this makes me wish I'd never left the river. I feel twenty again."

"You look twenty, Uncle Cornelius," she said, and she wasn't stretching it too much since, despite his bulk, he still moved so nimbly and surely at the tiller that the outlines of the jaunty sailor he'd once been seemed to emerge.

"Now, now, you needn't lie to me," he said. "But I will admit that flattering an old man can be a very useful talent. I really hope we get along together, little one. I want you to like being Mrs. Van Alen."

Whether the wind and wine had gone to her head or whether it was something in this man that demanded honesty from her, she felt impelled to say, "Uncle Cornelius, I don't want to be Mrs. Van Alen. It wasn't my idea, as you must know. I know George doesn't love me, and I don't love him . . ."

"Huh! I'm not surprised. George is hard to love, but what does it matter? In my experience what they call love is a poor basis for a good marriage. Now you take Lady Lydia and me . . ."

"What does she think about this? Does Aunt . . . I mean Lady . . . Lydia want me?"

"She doesn't know yet."

"Doesn't know? But . . ."

"My dear, in business I've learned that a fait accompli is more persuasive than any amount of argument. When we have you under our roof, and Lady Lydia sees what a pretty thing you are . . ."

"Pretty? Like this?" she said and indelicately patted her stomach.

"Yes, like that. A woman is never more beautiful than when she's with child. But that isn't the real point; the real point is that you're a Schuyler, and . . ."

"A Schuyler? My father has as good as disowned me . . ."

"Blood cannot be disowned. You are a Schuyler and never forget it. Your visit last time put Lady Lydia back into the best of social circles, and she's above all a very practical woman which is why we get along together. You've got to be practical, too. This is your only real choice, and you might as well try to like it."

"Oh, how can I? What if George won't have me?"

"He'll have you all right. It's either that or losing his inheritance in a business, the extent of which he'll appreciate much more when he gets back from China. George is a fool, but he isn't that much of a fool. And remember, the business will be yours, too, yours and your children's . . . . Well, we must be getting near the *weer gat.* Come on deck with me and watch some high jinks."

The *Lady Lydia* was scudding along in the shadows where the Highland bluffs shouldered out the rays of the late afternoon sun. The wind was holding strong out of the northwest but hauling due west through the passages of the bluffs in the strongest puffs. When they came on deck, the captain, a thin and silent man named Coffin whose Adam's apple seemed to pop like a cork with the strain of releasing every word, said, "Best anchor here in the lee and wait for the tide, sir. Wind'll die at sunset and the turn of tide'll take us 'round yonder point. It's in the pear tree, you know."

Cornelius was testing Coffin, whom he'd just hired, as well as his new vessel. One of the whalers from Nantucket who'd settled up in Hudson during the war, the man was probably good enough at deep-water sailing but could he cope with the river? At least he'd learned some of the lingo—a pear-tree tide was a full tide at perigee "when the moon hung near in the pear tree;" a low tide at apogee was an apple-tree tide "when the moon hung far away in the apple tree." But his suggestion to anchor and waste a wind like this was disturbing.

"Just jibe her around, Mr. Coffin," Cornelius said.

"Jibe? In this wind? Not enough in crew to manhandle a boom like that. Take the stick right out of her."

So that was it? Either the man didn't know how to sail a river sloop or he was cunningly protesting Cornelius' insistence that, not needing muscle to move freight, a packet like *Lady Lydia* could get along with fewer men in crew. It was a matter of simple arithmetic: the wages of one man would eat up the fares of one and a half passengers at a rate of two dollars a head between Albany and New York. Well, he'd show the man how it was done, what Cornelius Van Alen expected from a skipper. Since time was money, the way to get ahead on the river was to keep your boat moving unless and until nature's hand in the form of an adverse tide and strong head wind was against you; the only time to anchor was when standing still beat going backward. Many's the voyage on which Cornelius Van Alen never wet the anchor, and both passengers and freight shippers scrambled to take advantage of his record times.

"Haven't you heard of a North River jibe, Mr. Coffin?" he asked. "Why I'll bet even this little lady knows how to pull one off. Isn't that right, Sally?"

She nodded, though she wasn't quite sure. She did know that jibing, putting the boat on another tack with the wind at the stern, could be dangerous in a strong breeze. Peter had once broken the masts of the periagur and dumped them both in the water in a bad jibe. The thought of what could happen to a mammoth machine like this made her stomach cramp with excitement and caused the baby to jump in complaint. Her Uncle Cornelius hadn't been sailing in a long while and was old besides. She almost literally held her breath as he took the tiller and ordered the captain forward to help the crew strike the topsail.

Although he'd pulled this off a thousand times in his youth, Cornelius found his old heart thudding with excitement. Many's the time he'd seen a boat dismasted or swamped in the maneuver, and once he himself had come to grief. A great deal depended on how well the sloop would respond to her helm, and the *Lady Lydia* remained untested except on a steady reach. Well, there was nothing for it but to try; the day he stopped taking risks would be the day he died. The fact that he put others to risk, too, never had concerned him; it was what they were paying for or being paid for, wasn't it? But Sally wasn't paying, and she did know more than most about what was going to happen. Glancing at her sitting by his side, he saw that her mouth hung open, her hands were tightly clasped over her middle, her eyes were alight with something like fear or suspense or both.

"You aren't afraid, are you, little one?"

She only managed to shake her head, and he tried to be light. "Nothing to it if you know how, and nobody knows how better than your old Uncle Cornelius," he said. "But duck when I give the order, because I don't want you to lose that pretty head of yours. A while back a slow Dutchman got his neck caught in the sheet coming over and it took his head clean off."

To start rounding the point, Cornelius swung the *Lady Lydia's* bow to the east and then a little north of east, ordering the sheets eased as the wind came behind them. Soon she was by the lee, and the taut mainsail began to show signs of slack. Now. Cornelius pulled the heavy tiller right into his fat stomach and boomed, "Jibe ho! Around we go!"

As the wind caught the sail on the other side, it began to fill, lifted the massive boom like a toothpick and sent it swinging over their heads with a woosh they could feel. Lines snapped and blocks screamed. Cornelius clung to the tiller, pressing it into his belly until it hurt, and muttering, "Up, up, up" like a prayer. If the *Lady Lydia's* head didn't keep swinging into the wind, the full sail would slam itself forward with such force that breaking the boom or mast might be the least of the damage it could cause. But she was a good *sloep,* a lovely bitch. She slid up so nicely that the great sail began again to flutter and landed softly on a cushion of wind coming from the beam. Cornelius quickly shoved the tiller down, letting the sail fill again from behind, while the crewmen scrambled forward to shift the jib.

"Heigh-ho, and away we go!" he sang.

Sally started to breathe again, and Captain Coffin came up onto the poop and doffed his knit cap. "By Christ, I've never seen the like," he said. "I'm proud to work for you, sir."

Cornelius appeared to ignore the compliment. "All right, Mr. Coffin, take the helm. Hold this course about fifteen minutes and jibe her again."

Coffin's Adam's apple bobbed up and down like a float with a fish on the hook, and his voice gurgled when he tried to say, "Jibe, ho!" But he managed to duplicate the maneuver without mishap. While, as in most things in life, it wasn't nearly as exciting as the first time around, Sally thought that she admired her uncle more for the way he could stand impassively by and let another man try his hand with so much at stake than she did for his own skill.

"You'll do, Mr. Coffin," Cornelius said, and then suggested that he and Sally go below for a rest, he for his age and she for her condition.

Only when she got into her bunk did Sally realize how tired she was, not weary as she'd been for months, but nicely tired from the excitement, the fresh air, the good food of the day. Hardly once had she thought of herself or of that scratching life in her belly, and it was like being born again, opening her eyes to find the world fresh as spring's green mist on the trees along the riverbank. Nor did she think of herself now. She thought instead of the great bear of a man whose comfortable snoring could already be heard beyond the partition between their cabins. She still wasn't sure of why he'd wanted to claim her as a daughter-in-law, but she was sure that he did. Being wanted again by anybody stirred some of that nice feeling of being special that had given life its promise. More than that, she thought that she was going to like Uncle Cornelius no matter what anybody had said about him. Perhaps she'd been fortunate to see him at his best, at the helm of his sloop, where he revealed himself to be a man of both nerve and competence, a man you could trust in hard going. If she'd lost one father, she'd apparently gained another, stronger, one, and the thought was as comforting as the sleep that warmly surrounded her.

Chapter *IV*

The Richmond Hill Gang

"Well, she'll never tell it on herself, so I will," Natalie de Lage said.

Theodosia Burr rattled her teacup against its saucer in pretended annoyance and said, "You know I don't care for that flirtatious nonsense."

Young Matty Van Buren, wandering restlessly around the room, picking up and fingering a Chinese vase here, a silver snuff box there, suddenly stopped and started to laugh. "Now that *is* nonsense. A vainer lady never lived—not that you shouldn't be. Come on, out with it Natalie."

"Matty!" Theodosia said and then turned to the darkly pretty, quite obviously pregnant, woman seated beside her on the settee. "Sally, why don't you teach your little cousin some manners?"

Sally shrugged. "Matty's trying, Theo. Give him time. But I'd like to hear the story, too."

"Well," Natalie said, "there we were—all of us going out on the barge to visit that new French frigate in the harbor. Just as we were about to board, Mayor Livingston steps up to Theo, puts his arm around her and says, 'Now, Theodosia, you must bring none of your sparks on board. They have a magazine there, and we shall all be blown up.' "

They all laughed and clapped while Theodosia sat, eyes lowered in a mock show of modesty, before she said, "All right, that nonsense is over. Now tell me, Peter, what do you honestly think father's chances are?"

Peter Schuyler, who had been lolling in a soft satin chair as if it were a haystack, long legs outstretched, cigar in mouth, jumped up and waved his cigar at Theodosia like a pointer and said, "Chances for what, Theo? All ye of little faith think that Mr. Aaron Burr may become vice-president, but *I* think he'll be president. There's talk now of Federalists bolting to Mr. Burr since they know Adams doesn't stand a chance of reelection, and they think Mr. Jefferson wears horns."

"Horns? What do you mean?"

"I can't say—there are ladies present."

"Now, Peter, you know that you can always speak freely in this house," Theodosia said.

"Well . . . all right; it's said that Jefferson is peopling that place of his down at Monticello with little mulatto . . . bastards. The point is, though, I *love* your father, Theo, and I want him to be *president*. But, tell us sister Sally: what's the word from the enemy camp?"

In this year of 1800, Peter's description of the house on Broadway where Sally lived with old Cornelius, Lady Lydia and George, the man who was supposed to be her husband, was scarcely an exaggeration. Ever since General Washington had voluntarily resigned the presidency, the men he'd managed to keep in harness had started going in different directions, like a team when the stage driver drops the reins. And now that Washington had died, almost symbolically in the last month of the last century, the Federalists and Republicans were at each other's throats. Sally's was a Federalist house, and political passions were running so high that, ever since Aaron Burr's name had been put on the *Republican* ticket with Jefferson's, she'd had to learn to lie and buy silence with bribes from the old slave Daniel who drove the Van Alen coach to sneak over here to Richmond Hill for a few relaxing hours with the only real friends she had in New York.

But she wished that Peter hadn't asked her such a question. He alone had to know what she'd been through, was going through. It seemed as if her brother were trying to goad her in the presence of his friends into an open disloyalty to the family with whom her lot had been cast by a God who refused to let her die and a man who was kind enough not to abandon her to disgrace. He probably meant well. Like the rest of "the little band," as the young people who surrounded Burr called themselves, Peter couldn't understand how she could go on living in that house and was forever urging her to move out bag and baggage and join Theo and Natalie here at Richmond Hill. To that end, they never stopped reminding her that in Republican circles Cornelius Van Alen was considered an unpatriotic old pirate and that there was hardly a soul in New York unacquainted with her husband George's drunken delinquencies. As for Lady Lydia Van Alen, it was Washington Irving who had sent the whole group into laughter by saying, "That horror was stuffed in 1775, but nobody's pinched her to find that she's dead yet."

While she could forgive the others who knew only the official story of how she'd come to be Mrs. George Van Alen, she thought that Peter, knowing the truth, ought to be able to guess her reasons for trying to play out the role assigned her. You could call it a guilty conscience, a false pride, a sense of obligation, an instinct for survival —whatever, she was determined to make the best of her life, and fleeing would be a kind of defeat. Another thing that even Peter couldn't know was how much she felt that she owed to Uncle Cornelius. For all his gruff and grabbing exterior, he had another side to him that perhaps she alone had been privileged to see. He had not only begun rebuilding her confidence on that long-ago sail down the river, but he had, she was sure, saved her life when the baby was born.

Although it was a difficult thought to deal with even now, Sally was still certain that, consciously or unconsciously, Lady Lydia had wanted her to die in childbirth. It would have made things so much easier for everybody. When Uncle Cornelius had playfully presented her as "a surprise gift from the river," Lady Lydia had received her with the sniffing expression of a person who's been handed a very dead fish. Sally's presence and condition had, in her words, "ruined everything," since all indications had been that her son George would marry a certain Miss Walton on his return from China, and Miss Walton would not only bring with her a distinguished dowry but pure pre-Revolutionary British blood, compared to which that of a Schuyler, especially a poor Schuyler, was cherry juice. But Lady Lydia *was* practical, as Uncle Cornelius had predicted, practical enough to concoct for the public the story that George and Sally had been secretly married at the manor during the summer and that Sally had naturally come to bear the Van Alen heir under the family roof. This served well enough to bring the Schuyler relatives such as Mrs. Hamilton and Mrs. Church and their friends to Broadway on calls of congratulations but did little to relieve Lady Lydia's overwhelming disappointment in the failure of her plans for George.

Within the house, Lady Lydia made it clear that a sixteen-year-old girl who'd played woman's oldest trick of entrapment on her precious son would have little standing in her eyes. One small way she'd chosen to demonstrate this was to assign to Sally the worst bedroom in the house, on the fourth floor rear. When Cornelius protested that other chambers were vacant and that it might be a hard climb for Sally in her condition, Lady Lydia said, "You know nothing about these things, Cornelius. The stairs will be good exercise for her, and you'll be glad enough to have her that far away when the screaming starts." Cornelius evidently felt obliged to bow to feminine wisdom in such matters, but, if Lady Lydia weren't around, he would unfailingly give Sally a hand when she was puffing her bloated young body up flight after flight of stairs.

The room itself was small and airless with only one window overlooking the carriageway and stable. As the spring nights grew hotter, she would often toss and turn on her hard horsehair mattress in a bath of sweat, induced as much by her fears as her exertions. All she'd ever heard about the birth of a baby had to do with pain, and, during those night sweats, she wondered how bad it would be and whether she could stand it. Beyond a few scratches and bruises and the wounding by George, she'd never experienced pain, and it held for her the terror of the unknown. She couldn't forget Lady Lydia's matter-of-fact mention of screams, and, aside from inconvenience, the location of her room made it probable that nobody would hear her if she were suddenly reduced to screaming with pain. The possibility of having to go through an unimaginable ordeal alone began growing into the worst of her fears. And the dark. Welcome as any slight breeze through her window might be to her perspiring body, it would make the flame of her little oil lamp flutter, setting the shadows to dancing and her heart to racing. If the lamp went out, she'd either have to spend the rest of the night alone in the dark, or grope her way down to the tinderbox in the kitchen. She never had liked the dark, and now she really feared it, as she feared being alone.

Night became such a horror that she finally asked to have Flossie sleep with her in the house—on a mat outside in the hallway since there was no room in her cubicle. Lady Lydia's response was, "I won't have a nigger in the house all night, she'd smell it up worse than a dog."

"Now, Lydia, that's ridiculous, and you know it," Cornelius said. "I think it's a very good idea. Can't you see the little one's frightened? I doubt she sleeps a wink from those circles under her eyes."

"Frightened of what? Of having a baby? Such nonsense. I've had babies and your own daughters have had babies without all this fuss."

"But you weren't stuck away all alone up in the attic of a strange house. I say let the slave girl sleep there."

"And I say no. It's my house, and—"

"I've heard enough of that, Lydia. You know I bought it from you long ago. Now I want that girl up there tonight."

He turned and walked away with Lady Lydia muttering after him, "Stubborn Dutchman, stubborn Dutchman. He knows nothing of these things . . ."

But Flossie did curl up at her door, and Sally slept better. Sometimes she thought that it was her ability at last to relax a little that, one night, brought on the pain. It wasn't bad at first, a few sharp cramps that went away before she could even bother to call for Flossie. She drifted back into sleep but then came awake with a pain that made her cry out involuntarily. Flossie came running, "Your time, mistress? Your time?"

"I . . . I think so . . . . Go get help, Flossie . . . . Get Lady Lydia . . . . Hurry!"

Though the last person she really wanted to see, Lady Lydia had had babies, and she would probably know what to do. Ah, God— there it came again, the pain. She bit her lips to keep from crying out. There was a commotion on the stairs, and Lady Lydia, looking like a white crow in her nightdress and cap, came in; behind her, the huge bulk of Uncle Cornelius, also shirted and capped, filled the doorway.

"Well, now, what's this about pain?" Lady Lydia asked.

"I'll send for the doctor, Lydia," Cornelius said.

"You'll do no such thing. This is no matter for a doctor. It's women's work. Flossie, you run down to the quarters and get

Miranda. She's as good a midwife as any. And you, Cornelius, get out of here at once."

She screamed; she couldn't help it; she was being split apart. Cornelius said, "She's in agony. We've got to have a doctor. I'll fetch him myself."

"Well, you didn't show such concern over me and the girls," Lady Lydia said. "Now you go back to bed, Cornelius. She's just beginning, and this will take hours. Miranda is perfectly capable. Now go. All you're doing is embarrassing the girl. Isn't that right, Sally?"

She was beyond embarrassment, concerned only for the heaving and wracking of her body over which she had no control. If the next pain were worse than the last, she was sure she couldn't stand it. She needed help. "I think I'd like the doctor," she said.

But Cornelius had gone, and Lady Lydia said, "Nonsense. Now you listen to me, young lady. There's no reason to go to the expense and fuss of a doctor when we have a capable slave in the house. You're not suffering anything all the rest of us haven't gone through. Here, chew this when you want to scream. If you keep carrying on this way, you'll frighten the horses."

Lady Lydia handed her a handkerchief, and she clamped it between her teeth. It did help, and she managed to float through the next wave of pain without a whimper. Keeping her silence became the one important thing for her to do, the only way to salvage some pride in the presence of this cold, bony woman. When Miranda and Flossie arrived, Lady Lydia said, "Well, thank goodness you're here, Miranda. It took you long enough. Wake me when anything happens. She's so small it will be hours yet, I'm sure."

Miranda was the cook, and Sally had seen too little of her to know her well. She was shrunken with age, and her eyes had the hooded look of a person who's seen everything. With fingers like feathers she examined Sally's abdomen, then reached up and took the handkerchief out of her mouth. "You like to choke on that thing, honey. Cry out all you want."

"I won't . . . . I won't . . . . I might scare the horses . . ."

Miranda chuckled. "Now where did you get a thought like that? No, you just go ahead and cry. You is small, honey, and it's going to hurt like the very devil's in you. Now you just cry all you want, and push, push hard when the pain comes. I'll help you . . . . Flossie, you keep that water hot on the stove and keep bringing it."

Somehow the night passed, and somehow she managed not to cry, or at least not much. Wave after wave of pain and strain would sweep over her, after which she'd lie sweating and panting as if she'd been pulled from scalding water. She'd never imagined that a body could endure such rage without bursting. Gradually her window paled with light, and between convulsions she was aware of the familiar morning sounds of the city. She could hear the mooing of cattle on their way to slaughter in the Fly Market and the sharp cries of the drovers. Then came the creaking of the farmers' carts. By full light the vendors were singing their songs, "Here ye are! Nice clean Rockaway sand! Sand yer floors!" . . . "Greenwich spring water, two cents a pail!" . . . "Fresh straw! Throw out your ticks! Fresh Jersey straw!" . . . "Oysters here! Long Island oysters!" It seemed incredible, but strangely comforting, that the world could be worrying about floors and ticks while she labored to give it new life. The very ordinariness of the sounds was a kind of promise that she, too, might once again find the ordinary uses of life possible.

But gradually she weakened, felt overcome between spasms by total exhaustion. Miranda grew nervous, impatient. Her hands, more claw than feather, bit into her belly as she tried to help, and she kept saying, "Now don't you quit on me, missy, don't you quit . . . ."

Angry voices rose up the stairs. "Get out of my way, Lydia," Cornelius said. "I'm going to see what's going on up there. It's been nearly twelve hours . . ."

"Stay away from there. It's none of your business. It can take twenty-four hours. Remember Charlotte. Miranda will send for us."

But he came wheezing, flustered. He stuck his head in the door. "Miranda, what's happening here?"

"I don' know. The baby don' come. An' Miss Sally she quitting."

Lady Lydia, shoving by her husband, said, "Miranda, you remember how it was with Miss Charlotte. Tell Mr. Cornelius—"

"But she bigger and showed more this time. Look here . . ."

"Miranda! Not in front of the master!"

"I'm going for the doctor," Cornelius said, and the sound of feet pounding down the stairs echoed up the well.

"He'll kill himself running like that," Lady Lydia said, "and it will be all your fault. You just have to try harder."

When the doctor came he examined her and began at once taking off his coat, rolling up his sleeves and sending Flossie scurrying for more boiling water. "I wish you folks had sent for me sooner," he said and started taking instruments out of his bag. One of them, a knife, flashed in a ray of sunlight, and it was the last thing she saw before pain, more searing than all the rest, brought blessed unconsciousness. When she was again aware of anything, it was the strong odor of smelling salts, and the doctor, bending over her, said, "Good. Good. Well, Mrs. Van Alen, you have a healthy baby girl . . . ."

She said, "I'm still Sally Schuyler . . . ."

From somewhere behind the doctor came Lady Lydia's voice, "She doesn't know what she's saying. She must be delirious."

The doctor straightened up and began putting on his coat. "Yes . . . well . . . in any case the baby was coming the wrong way, and I had to cut her a little and turn it around. But I'm sure they'll both be all right. I'll look in tomorrow." . . .

Yes, she was sure to this day that she had Uncle Cornelius to thank for her life, for that baby. He was considerate, too, in hiding his disappointment that the baby was not a boy. Blond and chubby, she was, according to Uncle Cornelius, "the spitting image of your mother Catharina, a real Dutch younker," which, he said, was good enough for him. The birth of the baby, the physical presence of this doll-like creature that was all hers, gave Sally much more than a release from discomfort and anxiety; it gave her an unanticipated sense of accomplishment and of mission in a life she'd felt hardly worth living. In a strange way, she was grateful for Lady Lydia's odd, antagonistic behavior; it freed her of any feeling of obligation to her future mother-in-law, made the child more truly her own. She asserted her independence by naming the girl Evelina, against everybody else's wishes, because it had nothing to do with anyone in either of the families and because it might confer on her child the gay spirits of the heroine of the novel she'd liked so much as a girl. The birth also freed her in a physical sense so that she could go out with her brother Peter who led her to Richmond Hill, where Mr. Burr, still a senator and often in Philadelphia, welcomed her warmly as a companion to his daughter Theo, who was often alone now that her mother had died. Even then Lady Lydia complained that Theo was too spoiled by all her reading and association with those "godless Frenchmen" her father was always bringing home to be a suitable companion for Sally, but Uncle Cornelius said, "She's often seen at the Hamiltons' table, and that's good enough for me." Back then in '96, it was still the golden age with Washington in the White House and the political divisions that would make of Broadway and Richmond Hill enemy camps were at least invisible.

But now, still nettled by her brother's question, she said testily, "I wish you wouldn't always keep asking that, Peter. You know how I feel about these things. I think people must be going mad to let politics make of them enemies."

"Well, all right, perhaps I did put it a little strongly," Peter said, "but I hope Uncle Cornelius and his friends like Hamilton aren't up to any nasty tricks, because they'll have to answer for them to the next president of the United States."

"Let's drink to that, though I wish we had something stronger than tea for a toast," said Billy Van Ness. A young lawyer from Kinderhook who'd established himself in the city, Billy had brought Sally's cousin Martin Van Buren down to serve an apprenticeship in his office and had naturally introduced him, too, into Burr's little band. "But I'm afraid your father's victory won't be so nice for you, Theo. It'll be a sacrifice you'll have to make to move from Richmond Hill here to the White House. What a dreadful mud hole that Washington is! Some Frenchman, trying to be nice, called it a city of great vistas—meaning there isn't a fit habitation to be seen for miles around. Mrs. Adams was telling me that the palace, as they call their place, is so surrounded by forest that she can't even find a place to hang up the wash —has to string it out in the East Room—and with all those trees she can't get men to cut wood for the fires. She longs for those good old days when she was the vice-president's wife and they lived in comfort here at Richmond Hill. But don't worry, Theo, we'll all be there, the whole little band, to make things merry for you."

Billy was undoubtedly speaking the truth. Richmond Hill with its high, airy rooms, its columned portico, its view of the spires of the village of Greenwich to the south and the river and hills of Jersey to the west, was a residence so fine that it had been commandeered by both General Washington and Sir Guy Carleton when their respective forces occupied New York, and by Vice-President John Adams when the city was the nation's capital. But Theodosia responded with no lament; instead she sprang a surprise. "But *I* won't be in Washington," she said. "I'm getting married."

"You're what?" It was said in astonished chorus.

"Married I said. To a Mr. Alston of South Carolina. A very handsome gentleman who owns acres of land."

"I'm devastated," said Matty Van Buren. "I might as well go back to Kinderhook."

"I'm crushed," added Peter Schuyler, "although I will say it makes me feel better about my own impending nuptials . . . "

"And I . . . I . . ." said Washington Irving, "shall never marry at all, now that the light of my life has been snuffed out."

"Oh, stop it, all of you," Theodosia said. "You can be sure I'll be back to see you all, because I could never, never desert my father. And you can be sure that Richmond Hill will still be open to you, because he'll need you around him even more when I'm gone."

"But it won't be the same, Theo," Irving said. "Oh, Lord, remember when you wanted to go to the hospital and buy a human head to serve up to that Indian chief Brant because you'd read

> 'The cannibals that each other eat,
> The anthropophagi, and men whose heads
> Do grow beneath their shoulders . . .' "

"Mr. Irving, I was only fourteen then . . . ."

"Ah, yes, but a precocious fourteen. Well, and what happens to Natalie? I suppose it wouldn't be right for her to stay under the circumstances."

"I'm going home," Natalie said. "Father's written that it's perfectly safe now that Bonaparte's established order as first consul. I can hardly wait . . ."

"We are lost! Lost! Theo gone! Natalie gone!" Van Buren said, demonstrating his sincerity most effectively by pulling at the blond curls over his ears that he was said to spend hours putting in place. "All the bells of New York will stop ringing."

Irving clapped. "Very good, Matty, very good. Maybe you ought to give up the law and be a writer, as I'm going to do."

"Sally will still be here," Theodosia said. "She can sit in for me as hostess, and it will be very proper since she's . . . uh . . . *much married,* as anyone can see."

This was greeted with general laughter by everybody but Sally and her brother Peter. This reminder of Sally's condition was painful to Peter. Of all the improbable things that had happened to his favorite little sister in the last four years, this was hardest for him to take, or to understand. When she'd come down from the manor, also in this condition, Peter had known the truth, not only from his own strange experience as go-between for Sally and George but from a rather gloating letter Rebecca had written about the whole affair. How he'd wondered could this have happened to a girl brought up as she'd been? Because he'd been responsible for much of the devilry she'd gotten into in a tomboy sort of way, he was even more certain of her innocence, her purity. The only logical explanation of her predicament was intolerable to contemplate, if true, and the first time he'd seen Sally in New York he'd tried to get her to talk about it. Either from modesty or pride, she'd withheld all details of the affair except for a confession that she had no love for George. That had been enough for Peter, and, jumping to conclusions, he'd said, "I'm going to kill him, Sally, I swear it. I'll challenge him the minute he steps off that boat."

"No, don't, Peter. Can't you see it would just make matters worse? We're not even married yet, and—"

"Oh, I'll wait till he makes an honest woman of you, and then I'll call him out."

"And what good would that do?"

"But I don't see how you can live with such a . . . a monster."

"I have to. It isn't all George's fault, Peter. I have thought about it and thought about it, and I know I'm as guilty as he is. I led him on . . ."

"But you're just a child and . . . and my sister. He shouldn't have taken advantage of you."

"And tell me Peter, have you never . . . uh . . . taken advantage?"

For answer, he blushed and she rushed on, "Just remember that any woman is somebody's sister."

"All the same I hate him for what he did to you."

"Don't, Peter, don't. I hate to say this, but I decided a long time ago that George isn't worthy of my hate, and the same should be true of you."

As much as he'd thought he loved his sister before, he'd really loved her then. Instead of embittering her, what she'd gone through had matured her so much that it was he who felt childish for his attitude. He'd had another lesson along the same lines from Mr. Burr shortly after Sally's baby daughter was born. Evidently as a result of

73

something the doctor who'd attended her said, ugly rumors about Sally's marital status began spreading through New York social circles. If he heard them at all, Burr not only ignored them but seemingly went out of his way to parade Sally along with his daughter Theo at his gatherings of notables. In this situation, Peter was torn between loyalty to his sister and loyalty to his *baas,* as Billy Van Ness had nicknamed Mr. Burr in mimicry of his upcountry Dutch tenants. His ringing statement to the little band that he loved Mr. Burr was not hyperbole.

Always restive on the manor where the future outlined for him by Jacobus was nothing more than an endless succession of days like those he'd already lived, Peter at first accepted Mr. Burr's invitation to read the law in his offices as the only escape he'd been offered. But, aside from the necessary drudgery of pouring over musty old casebooks, life with Mr. Burr proved to be a dazzle. To watch him in court or on the floor of the Congress or legislature was a wonder: while others would dwell dully on precedent and principle, Burr would cut through to the heart of whatever matter was in hand with a few sharp sentences, usually winning his point. Hardly a day passed but what some person of note, whether it was Governor Clinton come to discuss politics or Mayor Edward Livingston come to seek support for some civic project, dropped into the Partition Street offices; hardly a dinner was set at Richmond Hill without some exceptional guest like the great Napoleon's brother, Jerome, or the mysterious diplomat Talleyrand. Since Burr had a way of including his clerks or children or anybody who might be around in his activities, Peter had the heady feeling of rubbing elbows with the gods of this earth.

If Burr, the public man, was impressive, the private man became even more so to Peter the longer he knew him. Others wondered how the garrulous Burr, spending so much time in political halls, or in court, or socializing in taverns, ever accomplished any work. But Peter learned the hard way. Every morning when they were in Philadelphia for the session of Congress, for example, Peter was instructed to appear in Mr. Burr's chamber punctually at 5:30 with a good supply of candles, quills and paper. There they'd get out the day's correspondence, draft bills, outline cases, labor over Burr's projected history of the Revolution—in all, accomplish the average man's production by breakfast. Peter was happy to note that his little stepcousin, Matty Van Buren, a scrupulous student of every aspect of success, was as interested in Mr. Burr's working habits as in the style of his furniture and clothes; if he hued to them, Matty, with an almost equal gift of gab, could go a long way. The Dutch in Peter did, however, cause him to worry from time to time over the way Mr. Burr came by the money he needed to maintain his townhouse, his place at Richmond Hill, his horses and carriages and slaves. Burr's enthusiasm was forever leading him into involvement in some scheme or other to gobble up and develop millions of wild acres in the West, and he would pocket loans to that end from men less well-connected and visionary. From his knowledge of such books as Mr. Burr kept, Peter guessed that he could never meet his loans if they were called, and he once worked up the courage to warn the *baas.*

"Oh, I know, I know," Burr said. "But I don't let it worry me. Debt is the worry of little minds. I may be a small man, but I don't have a small mind. You see, I believe in my dreams. If one goes sour, another will take its place. Dream, Peter, dream, and don't let the crippling concerns of little minds, like a trifling debt here or there, hold you back."

If Burr used his money, or other people's, only for high living, such words would have a false ring, but Peter knew, too, that much of it was handed out without thought of return to artists or actors down on their luck, to widows defrauded by the courts, to the orphans he sheltered. This side of Burr was the side Peter loved; he never crossed the road when he saw people in trouble. So his treatment of Sally was perfectly in character, but Peter's uneasy fear was that scandal about her could hurt Burr's political career. Ultimately, he felt obliged again to warn the *baas* that the allegations were unfortunately true. "Well, well," Burr said, "our little Sally's more of a woman than I thought. But she's Mrs. Van Alen as far as I'm concerned. If it's a lie, it's only a technical one. Knowing Cornelius Van Alen as I do, I'm sure she'll be married to that worthless son of his within an hour after he sets foot in New York. I just think it's a shame that a girl of such promise has to be sacrificed to a man like that. It's that confounded, hypocritical righteousness that drove me out of the church. But I remember enough of Scripture to know that it also says let he who is without sin cast the first stone. I don't care what other people think: we'll do what we can for the poor girl, Peter."

How could you not love such a man? As it turned out, Burr had underestimated Cornelius Van Alen's determination to set things right. At Sally's insistence, Peter had been one of the small party who took the pilot sloop out to meet the Van Alen & Son square rigger, *Cathay,* when she was sighted off Sandy Hook. He was to be witness to the wedding which Uncle Cornelius had rather cleverly decided to have performed aboard by the captain before the ship docked, thus adding some substance to the much-doubted Van Alen story of a secret marriage and eliminating the possibility that a preacher might prove as slackjawed as the doctor: employees, as Cornelius said, don't talk about their *baas's* business. Peter was sure, too, that shrewd old Cornelius Van Alen had in mind that Lady Lydia, fearing the transfer from the sloop to the ship, would not wish to accompany them, as it proved. The old man wanted no last minute interference from Lady Lydia, who might be moved to something rash when she actually saw what she still considered Sally's trap snapping shut on her son. But Cornelius did insist upon bringing the baby Evelina with Flossie to attend her; George would have to be a beast not to find the baby's presence all the persuasion necessary.

Getting them aboard the *Cathay* as she rolled and bucked hove-to in a choppy sea was an exasperating business for the captain. The pilot's rope ladder was out of the question, and he had to devise a special sling harness to convey two women, a baby and his fat employer from the sloop to the ship's high deck. It was obvious to Peter that Captain Roberts, a handsome, slender young man little older than himself, felt that a good explanation for all the fuss was in order. It was obvious, too, that the captain found Cornelius' request that he perform an immediate marriage startling and disturbing.

"I'm afraid, sir, that your son is in no condition for a wedding."

"No condition? Where is he?"

"Down below, sir, in his cabin."

"Is he sick?"

"In a manner of speaking. To be blunt, sir, he's drunk as a lord. Has been the whole voyage . . ."

"You mean to tell me, Mr. Roberts, that as master of this ship, you've permitted one of your men to—"

The captain cut him off, saying icily, "I have been reminded continually, sir, that my purser is the 'son' in 'Van Alen & Son' and that I am his employee. You have my resignation now, sir, before I have to perform a ceremony that would subject this lady to—"

"Never mind, Mr. Roberts, I'm sorry that I spoke in haste. He's going to be married, drunk or sober. It's for the lady's good as you can see with your own eyes—that child is George's daughter. Now let's get on with it."

Peter liked the captain for the look of sheer pity his clear gray eyes shot at Sally. In a gentlemanly gesture the captain took Sally's arm to assist her down the companionway and whispered loud enough for Peter, who was following them, to hear, "I won't go through with it, I swear, if you but say the word."

"Oh, no, no. Thank you, captain, but it must be done."

The George Van Alen who lurched to his feet when they all crowded the door of his little cabin was scarcely recognizable. He wore only a dirty shirt, open to the waist, and stained black breeches. Probably for lack of eating, he was a bony replica of his mother, his nose beaked by sunken cheeks, his eyes red and watery, his chin dirtied by at least a week's stubble. His hand shook when he picked up a glass of what looked like brandy, but there was some of his old mischief in the grin he flashed as he held the glass out in toast and said, "Well, well, a welcoming party. To what do I owe this honor?"

Cornelius shoved Flossie, cradling Evelina in her arms, through the door. "To this," he said. "Your child."

George laughed. "And is this fair lady the mother? Well, well . . ."

Cornelius brushed past Flossie, struck George a blow across the face, knocked the glass out of his hand and said, "You know well who the mother is, and you are going to marry her within the hour, before this ship docks. Now get yourself shaved and dressed. The rest of you wait for us in the captain's cabin, and I'll bring him along . . ."

The captain's cabin was commodious, running the width of the ship except for a small sleeping alcove, and better fitted with its rosewood desk, black mohair settee and barrel-backed chairs than most of the offices Peter had seen in the city. Sally sat on the settee next to Flossie and the baby and kept patting her face with a handkerchief to hide the quiver of her lips. The captain sat down behind his desk and started fussing ostentatiously with papers. Nobody could think of anything useful to say, and the silence was broken only by the creaking of the ship's timbers and a little cooing sound with which Flossie was trying to keep the baby soothed. Suddenly, the captain jumped up, went into his sleeping alcove and returned with a portrait of Lady Lydia which he hung on the bulkhead. "My Lord, I almost forgot," he said. "My apologies, but I take it down as soon as we leave port—to keep it out of harm's way, you know."

Sally started to laugh, a little hysterically to be sure, but the captain joined her. "I knew I liked you from the minute I first saw you," he said. "I'm so sorry . . ."

"It's not your problem, it's mine," Sally said, and then to change the subject, "What's that green thing on your desk?"

"Oh, that. That's my good luck paperweight," the captain said. Picking it up, he brought it over to Sally. "A dragon, you see."

"Like the one on the wall," Peter said, feeling they'd found a friend.

"Not exactly. This one's jade. Probably worth a fortune but I wouldn't part with it. Here, feel how cool it is—that's how you know real jade."

Captain Roberts held the dragon to Sally's cheek, then to Flossie's, then to the baby's. The baby grabbed for it, and he said, "Cute devil. Has her father's coloring . . ." Then, apparently embarrassed, he added quickly, "I've got something you might find interesting . . ." He went over to his desk, picked up a rather crude box and held it under Sally's nose. "Smell it—sandalwood. My bosun made it for me. We picked up a deck load in the Sandwich Islands to trade in Canton . . . Oh, they're coming. Are you really sure you want to go through with this, madam?"

"Perfectly sure. The baby needs a father, and, as you noticed yourself, this is the right one. But thank you again, Captain Roberts," she said.

"Aaron. My name's Aaron."

"Thank you, Aaron."

Appearing with his father clutching his arm, George was dressed in a proper stock and waist coat and black broadcloth suit, shaved and combed, but he still lurched with every roll of the ship. Seeing Sally for the first time, he said, "Well, if it isn't little Miss America. Hello."

Sally said nothing. She ducked her head and up came the handkerchief. Peter went to her, and she whispered, "Help me up and hold me, Peter."

With George propped by his father and Sally by Peter, they managed to stand before Captain Roberts while he mercifully rushed through a service. George hiccupped and when it was over said, "And now I get to kiss the bride. Right?" Sally tensed and bent her head so that George got a faceful of hair. He pulled back and laughed, "Shy one, eh? Well, we'll have plenty of time for that later. But now I think I'm in need of a little rest if somebody would shut that baby up . . . ."

Nobody else had noticed that the baby, despite all of Flossie's cuddling and cooing, was crying. Sally went to her and took her in her arms and she stopped. Peter ran up on deck so that nobody could see his wet eyes. The captain said, "I'll just go tell the pilot to take us in." Cornelius went over to his daughter-in-law, put a hand on her head and then kissed her on the cheek. He said nothing. It was all beyond words . . . .

Since then, George drunk had become a more common sight around town than George sober, and, although people were civil to him for the sake of old Cornelius and Lady Lydia, he was no longer welcome in respectable society. Because he had been such a popular and promising young man before he shipped out for China, George's behavior was held by the charitable to be a tragedy and by the uncharitable to be the probable result of some dark sin. Whatever, everybody could see that George Van Alen would never be the man old Cornelius was, and the vultures were already gathering to pick over the corpse of Van Alen & Son when, and if, the old man died. Altogether, George Van Alen wasn't a man fit to be killed, and Peter was glad that he'd been persuaded not to try. He wasn't, as Sally had said, even worth hating, but he could be despised, and Peter despised him. Which was why he found it so incomprehensible that Sally was again carrying his seed. He had to accept her explanation that she wanted, needed, another child after little Evelina's tragic death in the yellow fever epidemic of '98, but he didn't have to like it, and it was certainly no joking matter.

Sally knew well why Peter didn't laugh with the others. He'd never been able to conceal his outrage that she would choose to bear another child by George Van Alen. But then Peter for all of his five more years was so much younger than she in so many ways. He couldn't know, for instance, what it was really like to have and to lose a child. Oh, God! How often had she wished in that time of the fever that Lady Lydia had had her way, that she and the baby both had died then before they got to know each other, before Evelina learned to lisp words that made of her a person, learned to say, "Mommy, I'm afraid," when the shivering seized her, when she was gripped with vomiting and diarrhea and the telltale yellow urine flowed. She was only one of hundreds who died in the city that summer, as they seemed to die nearly every summer, of yellow fever. But she was Evelina and only two. She was an unwanted child who had already made herself wanted which is more than many people accomplished in a long life. No, Peter couldn't understand what the baby had been to her, what she'd do for another. Maybe no man could, although she thought that Mr. Burr did from losing his own Sally.

It was, Mr. Burr told her, the death of Evelina whom he thought of as his own granddaughter that spurred him to push a charter through the legislature for the Manhattan Company to bring water to the city. While nobody knew for sure, it was assumed that the city's worsening water supply brought on the yellow fever. Anyone with eyes and a nose could tell that the Collect was turning into a cesspool, and that the sewage running through the streets must be contaminating the wells under the street-corner pumps from which the people who couldn't afford to buy it drew their water. Sally thought of the Manhattan project as a kind of monument to Evelina, which was why it riled her so to hear them talk around the Van Alen house about how Burr cleverly stuck a rider into the bill to allow the company to lend out money to get around the fact that the city's only two banks favored Federalist clients with their loans. Such talk stirred up enough mistrust among voters who hated any kind of bank that the Republicans lost in '99, but now that water was beginning to trickle through the Manhattan Company's wooden pipes most people were beginning to believe again in Mr. Burr's good intentions.

Not her in-laws, unfortunately. They were poisoned by the bitter comments their friend General Hamilton was forever making about all Republicans, especially Jefferson and Burr. To Hamilton, Republican was a misnomer; he considered the followers of that party literally to be enemies of the Republic. Sally found Hamilton's intemperate views not only insulting to her friends but frightening in view of his possible power. In those last years of the '90's there was so much talk of war with France over depredations on the American fleet that Washington was summoned from retirement to head the army, and he appointed Hamilton to be his general in the field should hostilities break out. Though he made a show of reasonableness in public, even to the extent of working for practical purposes with political opponents like Burr, Hamilton would give vent to his true feelings when he lingered over a bottle in the congenial atmosphere of the Van Alen home. Lady Lydia all but hung the British flag from her window to proclaim her sympathy for "my people" in their struggle with "Godless France," and, now that their ships were roaming the oceans, Van Alen & Son had the bulk of its trade with England, financed by loans from London. So Hamilton knew that he would be pouring his words into friendly ears. And what words they were!

One night at dinner, talking of war with France in which he would lead the American forces, he said, "I can hardly wait for it to come. Were it I instead of Adams in the White House, I would provoke it. I would throttle that fool Jefferson who keeps advising the French to be patient—let the French insult us enough to arouse our people. You see, the truth of it is that Jefferson with his pretended faith in the people is a far worse threat to us than France. If he gets elected, we'll have chaos and anarchy. The farmers and mechanics will arise. We'll be at war with England, our natural ally and best market. Your dollars, Cornelius, won't be worth a dime. But if we fought France now, I could get a disciplined army at my back, and I could unite these states once and for all, suppress all dissidence. Although the Republicans scream about a reign of terror, Adams, with no army and weak knees, doesn't make full use of the power we Federalists gave him in the Naturalization and Sedition acts. Oh, God, how I fear for this country in the hands of that Godless rationalizer Jefferson. And Burr? Burr? He's worse. At least with Jefferson, you know how wrong he is; with Burr, it's impossible to know where he stands. Oh, give me that army, and . . . well, forgive me, ladies, for letting my passion carry me away."

Passion: that was it, that was what Sally found frightening in the general. And, despite his short stature and plain black civilian suit, Hamilton could look the general. He had a high-bridged sharp nose, a little like Lady Lydia's, almost fierce eyes and a habit of holding himself with military rigidity. He was known to act and speak decisively, as if the battlefield authority he'd assumed in youth had also become a habit. She could understand how women, schooled to mastery by men, found him attractive. It was said that he'd virtually snatched her cousin Betsy out of the Schuyler place at Albany when the general, her father, objected to a young man of fighting fame but no family—indeed, he was widely known to be a bastard, though proclaiming his father to be of English nobility. But Sally found it rather chilling to hear Hamilton quote Machiavelli, as he was fond of doing: "I certainly think that it is better to be impetuous than cautious, for fortune is a woman, and it is necessary if you wish to master her, to conquer her by force . . ." Hamilton was nothing if not bold, acknowledging his sordid affair with the Reynolds woman in Philadelphia as if it were his right and knowing that Betsy with all those children on her hands could do nothing about it. What bothered Sally about Hamilton was not so much what he did but his smug, self-righteous attitude. She guessed that it was natural in an ill-born child who by his intellect and boldness had made himself the companion and agent of the rich and powerful. In their eyes a man so sound about money could apparently do no wrong. His greatest champion was now his own father-in-law who, overlooking the near elopement and the later philandering, was, so they said, sending down lumber for Hamilton to build a country estate on the upper part of Manhattan Island that would rival Richmond Hill or Mr. Gracie's place at Horn's Hook. It was not suitable for a man so fiscally unsound as Burr to live in grander style than Hamilton.

One reason that Sally found visiting Richmond Hill so relaxing and comforting was that, compared to Hamilton's frightening passion, Mr. Burr's attitude made politics seem more of an exciting game. Although he and his little band worked hard at politics, holding meetings every night in every ward of the city and buttonholing men for their votes on the streets by day, they took pleasure in it, too. They'd all get together in the long room of Brom Grantling's tavern on Nassau Street and drink and, from what she gathered, play like boys at being Indians. They called their place the Wigwam, though it was known in her Broadway house as the Pig Pen, and called each other sachems. It sounded very silly to her until Peter explained that the organization had an honorable and humorous history. They were all Sons of St. Tammany, a legendary Indian chief promoted to sainthood before the war to compete with St. David, St. George and St. Andrew for whom societies of people who considered themselves British aristocrats were named. A humble upholsterer, William Mooney, got it started again after the war when he saw the same old aristocracy climbing back into the saddle. So it was a place where the mechanics Hamilton feared could meet with men like Burr and his little band in the name of democracy and have a good time at it too.

It sounded like the sort of place where Mr. Burr would feel at home. He had an interest in all manner of men—and women, too. As long as they had brains. "The only thing I can't abide is a bore," he'd often say. She had to admit that it was sometimes hard to know what Mr. Burr stood for since he loved argument for argument's sake and, like the good lawyer he was, would take any side of an issue for the sport of it. When someone in one of their discussions at Richmond Hill tried to pin him down by asking, "What is your philosophy, Mr. Burr? What do you believe in?" he said, "Nothing—or rather a lot of things. I guess I gave up on dogma when I gave up on trying to become a minister like my father and grandfather before me. Take, for example, the sinfulness of man. You know, the Federalists and particularly Hamilton take a very low view of their fellowman, per- haps because they know what goes on in their own heads, and feel he ought to be confined for safety's sake in a straightjacket of laws and social etiquette of their own devising. That's why I favor Mr. Jefferson's belief that all men are capable of governing themselves through reason. But *that* belief supposes a willingness to compro- mise, to change, to do the *reasonable* thing under any given circum- stances. I say, give me a problem, and I'll look for a policy instead of I've got a policy, find me a problem. Even these United States are an experiment—a noble experiment, granted—but an experiment nonetheless, just another way station on man's long march toward a form of government under which the human potential will be real- ized. That's it—the human potential. If you want to know what I believe in, that's it."

Out of her own experience, Sally knew that in this Mr. Burr was sincere. During her growing-up years, he'd been as good as his word about drawing up an educational plan for her, about writing often and dropping in occasionally to check her progress. She'd thought it an odd idiosyncracy having to do with herself or some sentiment about his lost child until she'd come to New York and met Theo and the others and learned more about him. Some said he'd hastened his poor wife's death by keeping the house filled with orphans of both sexes, often children he'd encountered in the course of some sad legal case. Though he'd started a lot of boys on their way, such as John Vanderlyn the artist, he was particularly interested in girls who, he claimed, were held back by errors of education, prejudice and habit. Theo could still remember his excitement when he read Mary

Wollstonecraft's *A Vindication of the Rights of Women* and wrote her mother a long letter from Philadelphia which she shared with Sally. "I wouldn't dare show this to anybody but you, Sally," Theo said, "but I'm sure from the interest he's taken in you you'll understand."

After praising Mrs. Wollstonescraft's thesis that women should be educated to become the companions of men, Mr. Burr wrote: "If I could foresee that Theo would become a *mere* fashionable woman, with all the attendant frivolity and vacuity of mind, adorned with whatever grace and allurement, I would earnestly pray God to take her forthwith hence. But I yet hope, by her, to convince the world what neither sex appears to believe—that women have souls."

Of one thing Sally was sure: if women could vote, they would vote for Mr. Burr. His reputation for enjoying the love of many women was as widely known as Hamilton's. But if Hamilton made his conquests through force, Burr made his through grace. It went unnoted in the enemy camp, except by Sally, that Mr. Burr was also unmarried and therefore doing no dishonor to a wife. In any case, having been so much at Richmond Hill, Sally knew that no woman could ever lay full claim to Mr. Burr; his heart so obviously belonged to Theo. Since this was not widely known, Theo's suggestion that Sally could become hostess of Richmond Hill in her absence was, of course, frivolous. Despite, or perhaps because of, her visible much-married state, it would be considered a scandal as well as political heresy for her to go there after Theo and Natalie departed. It was knowing this that made it impossible for Sally to join the laughter at Theo's remark; it would be hard to give up coming to a house in which women were thought to have souls.

She'd have to say this for her cousin Matty Van Buren: whatever he lacked in manners, he made up in sensitivity. He was immediately aware that neither Peter nor Sally were laughing, and, whether he guessed at the reasons or not, he knew that it was time to change the trend of conversation. Matty attributed his alertness to the undercurrents of talk to his training in his father's tavern where, while serving drinks, he often found himself diverting a discussion that threatened to lead to physical violence. This day Matty pulled a card table away from the wall near the fireplace and began folding down the top and swinging it into place. "Well, no more talk of partings," he said. "Let's not waste this time. Where are the cards? Where are the cards? Get another table. We've eight for whist." Then, running his fingers lightly over the beautiful waxed grain, he asked, "This is one of Phyfe's, isn't it, Theo?"

"You're learning fast for a country boy, Matty. Maybe some day you'll acquire manners enough not to put a lady on the spot. The cards are in the drawer there—under the top."

Just as they sat down to the tables, Sally felt the first familiar twinge of impending birth. "I'm sorry, Theo . . . Matty . . . but I'm going to ruin the game. My time's coming, and I must go home."

"I'll go with you," Peter said at once, and she was grateful, having heard that the second child sometimes came with surprising swiftness.

In the carriage, they seemed shy of each other, silent. To ease a kind of tension building between them, Sally said, "Well, I guess that's the last I'll see of Richmond Hill."

"Why? You heard what Theo said."

"Oh, Peter, don't you see how impossible it will be with Theo gone? It's not only the impropriety of my visiting the house of a dashing widower, but it's this dreadful politics. I'm sure the Van Alens would have found a way to keep me from consorting with a bunch of revolutionaries—yes, that's what they think of all of you— long ago but for Theo."

"Now that I don't understand. Theo's as rabid a Republican as any of us . . . ."

"Ah, but she's also a beautiful woman, and when it comes to that, men rise above politics. Look how she's still invited to the Hamilton house. Even the Van Alen ladies are afraid of her popularity, but you should hear them talk behind her back. When we were coming home from the theater the other night, Charlotte said, 'Did you see that Theo Burr—hanging over the box so that the whole house could see her breasts?' And Amelia said, 'Yes, and I was grateful that my Gwendolyn was detained home with a cold. I wouldn't want her to see a so-called lady behave so in public.' "

"Theo was just calling down to me. I was in the pit . . . ."

"Of course. Of course. But . . ." Here Sally started to laugh. "Just wait till I tell them what a wealthy connection she's made. They'll die . . . ."

Peter could only shake his head. The world of women was much of a mystery to him. He tried another approach. "Well, even with Theo gone, you have me . . . your cousin Matty. Surely, they can't object to your seeing your family, *their* family . . ."

"Dear Peter, you're forgetting that, even though you're my brother, you are *not* a Van Alen, and as for Matty . . . . Well, when he came down to the city Uncle Cornelius suggested that we have him to the house and Lady Lydia gave that little shudder of hers as if someone had dropped an ice down her bodice and said, 'I'll not open my door to a tavernkeeper's son.' I guess it was one more battle Uncle Cornelius didn't want to fight. He just shrugged and winked at me and said, 'I thought he and George at least would have a lot in common.' And Lydia said, 'I don't like to hear you talk that way about my son—and in front of his wife.' And Cornelius said, 'She knows him better than either of us, my dear . . . .' "

"Sally, I don't know how you stand it."

"I've tried to tell you, Peter, that I *have* to stand it. I've had no other choice, have I? At least Uncle Cornelius took me in when . . . when father . . ."

She stopped, because she was likely to break down when she tried to talk about her father, whose intransigence remained the heaviest of her burdens. She didn't have to spell it out to Peter, who had tried his best to reestablish some line of communication between her and her mother, at least, but had failed. Jacobus Schuyler insisted on acting as if Sally had never existed; he forbade any exchange of letters and, according to what Peter had learned, went into a tantrum of rage when Catharina mildly suggested that she'd like to go down to see her granddaughter, Evelina. He'd supposedly greeted the news of Evelina's death as the logical fate of a child conceived in sin. As a matter of survival, Sally had forced herself also to act as if the family from which she sprang did not exist. It was only occasionally when she was with Peter that she slipped.

"Yes, I know," Peter said. "Don't talk about it—unless you really want to."

"No, no I don't. It's just that you, of all people, Peter, should understand why I have to be a Van Alen now. For better or worse, they *are* my family, and, believe me, I'm going to make the most of it—oh, oooh . . ."

"Sally, what is it?"

"Just the pain," she whispered through clenched teeth. "Tell him to drive faster . . . ."

Peter banged on the coach roof with his stick and shouted to the driver, "Gallop! Gallop!" The clatter of their coach arriving at the door on Broadway evidently alerted old Cornelius, who came running out. He gathered Sally up into his arms and carried her, shouting orders to his coachman to fetch the doctor. As they were crossing the threshhold, Sally called back to her brother, "Peter, do me a favor, please. Go out to Richmond Hill and tell them good-by. I forgot to say good-by . . ."

Chapter *V*

The Counting Room

Standing there with the little knot of friends and family by the graveside in the cemetery of Trinity Church, Sally Van Alen put an affectionate arm around her cousin Angelica Hamilton. There was little else she could think to do for the girl since words no longer seemed to penetrate her ears, nor sights her mind. Still outwardly as beautiful as ever at twenty-one, Angelica was now a hollow shell, a crueler casualty in Sally's opinion of men's crazy passion for politics than her father whose body lay there in that flag-draped coffin waiting to be lowered into the earth. You would think that by now, by the fourth year of the nineteenth century after Christ, men would have found a more civilized way to settle their disputes than by killing each other like savage beasts. By going mad, Angelica may have shown herself more capable of understanding the event than all the rest of them, for it was madness, sheer madness.

Up until now, until she found herself standing here among the mourners, seeing with her own eyes the vacant look and inappropriately childish smile on Angelica's face, Sally had not quite believed the awful news. The fact that General Hamilton, so bold and assured, had been killed was incredible enough; the fact that the killing had been done by Mr. Burr was overwhelming. Although she'd seen little of Mr. Burr these past four years, what she'd heard had all been good. Letters from Theo were full of her father's excitement and concern for his grandson, Aaron Burr Alston, whom he called "Gampy," and for whom he was already laying out a course of study even though the boy would only be two this year. Sally had thought that Mr. Burr sounded so much like her own father-in-law that she was hoping to get them together once Mr. Burr left the vice-presidency and had more time in New York; their common interests as grandfathers might override their differences. She'd missed Mr. Burr and his little band although her own son nearly made up for it.

Looking around at the men who'd marched in the cortege and were now quietly grouping themselves among the headstones behind the family for the final rites, she spotted her brother Peter. She was both surprised and relieved to see him here; if he'd had anything to do with this, he would not have dared to come. She guessed that he, like she, was drawn by a sense of duty to their cousin Betsy, the general's widow, and she hoped that she might have a word with him after the services. At least Peter might be able to tell her something of what had actually happened; nobody else seemed to know much beyond the fact that there had been a duel between Hamilton and Burr from which the general died. Sally had lost touch with Peter, too, these years, not so much because of his political associations as because of his marriage to Frances Livingston. Probably prompted by gossip from her Livingston relatives who'd married Jacobus and Rebecca, Frances had made it icily clear the one time Sally called that the less they saw of each other the better. It had been grievous to lose in Peter her one last touch with home, but she had been too proud to force herself upon them, and he had evidently been too much enthralled or intimidated by his wife to do anything about it. She didn't like to think that the rumors she'd heard that Peter was using the Livingston connection politically had anything to do with it, but, especially now, she could almost believe anything.

Apparently oblivious to the fact that the bishop was praying, Angelica was suddenly saying something. "Look," she said, pointing up to a leafy bow above them, "a butterfly. Pretty butterfly."

It was a pretty butterfly, and its flitting, flashing presence made this solemn ceremony with its prayers, its rolling of muffled drums, its sniffling and sobbing, seem even more incredible to Sally. Death was not supposed to arrive either in the summer of a life or the summer of a year as it had now. The butterfly drew Sally's eyes on up into the trees where the leaves were alive with a breeze and on out over the open expanse to the west where the white sails of sloops were riding the river on the same breeze. Sally hugged Angelica and whispered, "Maybe it's your father's spirit," and she thought, she hoped, that the girl's smile was one of understanding.

To make the family feel better everybody said that Angelica's insanity might just be temporary shock, but it had been the second such shock since Angelica's older brother Philip had died in an even more senseless duel a few years before. How many shocks could a person absorb? God knew, Sally had had her own share, and she would surely have more, and she wondered whether she might one day, too, seek refuge in insanity. It seemed such an easy answer to so much: of them all at this graveside, Angelica alone appeared happy and aware of life instead of death. Yet Sally had the certain feeling that she would never be granted this grace, if grace it were, as if in the failure of her own effort to retreat from life she had been fated to face whatever might be in store. This was what she'd tried to tell Uncle Cornelius when he had been so understanding about George.

Old Cornelius had, in fact, been understanding about a great many things, and, if she grieved for General Hamilton, it was more from sympathy for her father-in-law's loss of a friend than from her own feelings. Partly as a result of her being cut off from her own friends and family but more as a result of his reaching out to her, she and old Cornelius had grown close these last few years. She knew how he worshiped Hamilton, and, while she still couldn't agree with him on that, she had to respect his sorrow which, from the size of the crowds gathered silently beyond the fence on Broadway, was shared by most of New York. Where *was* Cornelius? She tried to peer around without being obvious and couldn't see his great bulk anywhere in the cemetery or the crowd beyond. Well, that was like him. He wouldn't want to be here and show that he was soft enough to weep. Though he kept his feelings from others, it had become almost a joke between them that she could read his mind ever since the day the baby was born.

From the moment old Cornelius had heard the carriage clatter up to his door, he had almost literally taken this birth into his own hands. There would be no repeat of the last performance. He carried Sally up to her bed and sent for Dr. Hosack, who by reason of being physician to the Hamiltons and other prominent families, had one of the best reputations in the city, and he insisted that the doctor stay through the whole term of labor. He also insisted that Lady Lydia stay away from Sally and for once personally participated in plying George with brandy until the young man staggered off to bed. Then, himself playing the nervous father, he wandered restlessly through the shadowy house until nearly dawn when Dr. Hosack came down with the glad news that Sally had delivered a healthy boy.

"I don't know why you were so worried, Mr. Van Alen. No trouble at all; Miranda could have taken care of it. But then, this was the second, wasn't it? Where's the proud father?"

"He—uh—didn't feel well."

"I see. It affects some men that way. Well, give him my congratulations—and I guess you deserve them, too."

"May I go see her?"

"Not yet. She's sleeping. I'd give her until noon at least. Well, I'll look in later in the day . . ."

One of the reasons Cornelius had wanted George and Lady Lydia out of the way was that he planned to ask a very special favor of Sally if she had a boy. He wanted her to name him Cornelius. Not that he had any right, any right at all, after the way the rest of his family had treated Sally. Moving up to resume his pacing vigil in the hall in front of Sally's door and telling Flossie to call him when she awakened, he almost decided to forget about his request. It was miracle enough that there was a child at all. Sally had moved down into George's spacious front room right next to the one he and Lady Lydia occupied, and he had reason to know that she slept mostly alone, for George, coming in late and liquored and probably spent, at least had the consideration to crawl into an empty bed in the upper story. He ought to be grateful that Sally had found either the courage or charity to admit George to her bed when he sought it and let it go at that. He did hope that, by reason of all his practice, George could reward a woman's submission in that way, but there was little he could observe in their daily relations to give much substance to that hope. When Sally's pregnancy became obvious, he had tried delicately to sound her out on the subject, but she had shut him off by saying only, "After what happened to Evelina, I think this house needs a child. Don't you agree?"

He did—most emphatically. Though disappointing in her sex, little

Evelina had won Cornelius' heart, not least by evoking nostalgic memories with her resemblance to his sister Catharina. He had refrained with difficulty from pressing Sally to have other children, especially at the sad time of the girl's death, and her decision to do it on her own placed upon him a debt of gratitude. He had other grandchildren, of course, Gwendolyn de Lancey, Amelia's daughter, and the three little Smiths whom his other daughter Charlotte had delivered so far, but none were named Van Alen and none lived under his roof. In any case, and though he tried to hide it, he had little liking for either his own daughters or their children who, like George, took after Lady Lydia in both looks and outlook. It could have been different—should certainly have been different with George—if it hadn't been for the war and his being so busy during their young years that he gave his wife free rein with the children. Well, it *would* be different with this little boy.

Cornelius' thoughts were interrupted by Flossie who came out of the room and said, "Master Cornelius, she awake and she askin' for . . ."

He couldn't resist a little test. "For whom, Flossie? For Mr. George?"

"Oh, no, for you, Master . . ."

With a heart oddly set tripping by this answer, he brushed by the slave girl and went in to Sally. She was propped up against the pillows, her black hair loose and splayed around her head like the velvet setting for a jewel. To Cornelius, her face, pale as pearl from loss of blood, seemed a jewel, and it so riveted his attention that he didn't at first see the blanketed bundle in her arms. She smiled and held it up. "Well, Uncle Cornelius, here's your Van Alen . . ."

"How did you know I wanted one?"

"If you think you can keep many secrets from me, you're wrong. Here, look at him—round and bald as a Dutch burgher. And I do think he's going to have blond hair like . . . like his father. Where *is* George?"

Cornelius could feel himself blush with embarrassment. "Sleeping it off," he said. "He was so nervous that I gave him some brandy, and . . ."

"Uncle Cornelius, I don't believe a word you're saying. You were the only one who was nervous, the only one outside of myself who was even interested in this baby. My guess is that you wanted him out

92

of the way so you could enjoy this moment yourself. Well, I thank you for it, because, just between us, I'm not up to taking George just yet . . . . Here, why don't you hold your grandson?"

Cornelius took the bundle in his arms so gingerly that Sally laughed. "He won't break, you know. For a grandfather, you don't seem very used to babies."

"I'm not, and more's the pity. I sometimes think that . . . well . . . no use crying over lost money, as I always say; keep your mind on the business at hand—and a good business this is."

For the first time he really examined the baby. Still raw-red, bulb-cheeked, neckless, bald, the face poking out of the blanket looked remarkably like his own. For an instant, he suffered a twinge of sad intuition that life after all was a passage from one ugly state to another, making of the hopeful striving in between a form of fraud. He was having too many such twinges lately, and to get himself out of it, he tried testing the baby's reflexes with a tickle of the cheek. They were good; the baby started to cry, and he hastily put him back in Sally's comforting arms. He could hear Lydia stirring in the next room, and, not knowing how long he'd have alone with Sally, he raised the question he was almost afraid to ask.

"You were right—he does look like a Dutch burgher, a little like me," he said. "I suppose you have a name for him?"

"Not really. I didn't know whether it would be a him or a her."

"What does George have in mind?"

"I wouldn't know. We've never talked about the baby except when . . ." Sally paused; two pink pinpoints appeared on her white cheeks. Then she went on, for she felt somehow compelled to let old Cornelius know that this birth was an end and not a beginning. "Well, it's been a good excuse to avoid *that.*"

Fortunately sensitive enough to catch her meaning, Cornelius blushed, too, and stammered, "Sally . . . . I've always meant to tell you that I . . . well, that I'm sorry . . ."

"No need to, Uncle Cornelius; I've always known it."

"As you said, I can't hide much from you, can I? So I might as well come right out with it. Have you thought of naming him Cornelius? I know it isn't my place to ask, but . . ."

"You have every right, Uncle Cornelius, every right in the world. I'll have to admit that I hadn't thought of it, but . . . well . . . it might make my mother happy, too."

"Yes, I'm sure. It was our father's name, you know. Your grandfather . . ."

"Well, then, it's done. Cornelius he shall be."

"I must warn you, little one, that Lady Lydia and George won't like it—they'll think it too Dutch."

"All the more reason," she said.

Cornelius laughed and did an awkward little dance step that shook the aging floor under his feet. "Ah, little one, you don't know how happy you've made me! Now the doctor says you must rest, and I must go abroad and spread the glad news."

As anticipated, both George and Lady Lydia protested the choice of a name. George thought that a man had a right to have his own name carried on by a son, and Lady Lydia thought that something like Robert Wentworth Van Alen after her own father would have been more appropriate. But neither Sally nor Cornelius would yield even when George threatened to absent himself from the christening. Instead, he appeared at the occasion so drunk—"A man can't decline toasts in honor of his nipper, can he? And anyway isn't this supposed to be a joyous event?"—that he had difficulty holding the wriggling baby while the rector anointed him with holy water. Mortified and enraged that his son should show himself in such a condition before the elite group of friends he'd invited to the rites at Trinity and the collation at his home afterward, Cornelius nevertheless felt obliged to overlook it as well as he could until the festivities were over. By then, George had disappeared, and so he invited Sally down to his sanctuary, his counting room, for a private talk.

Although she'd passed its doors daily on her way to and from the living quarters upstairs, Sally had never entered the room where Cornelius and—occasionally—her husband worked. She was surprised to find it as bare and shabby as Lady Lydia's domain was opulent. There were no rugs on the floors, no pictures on the walls. Along the wall by the door was a scarred and stained bench where the clerks—four of them now—did their copying. At each place there was a backless stool, a candle, an inkwell with pens and a box of blotting sand. In the middle of the room stood a similarly equipped table with straight-backed chairs at either end where presumably Van Alen & Son sat facing each other. On the far wall, there were open shelves holding ledgers and sheafs of correspondence and a small brick fireplace. Cobwebs festooned the corners of the ceiling, and

94

balls of dust scooted across the bare wood floor like mice. It was obviously a chamber that knew neither the presence, nor touch, of woman; it seemed also a poor retreat for one of the nation's, or perhaps the world's, leading shippers, and Sally couldn't help saying so.

"There's much you have to learn about business, little one," Cornelius said. "If you went the rounds of the other houses in New York, you'd find nothing better. People mistrust a merchant who uses money for show. Why, I remember a few months back when Hall went under without paying his creditors a cent. One of these poor fellows went over to Hall's place of business to try to collect something and found him with a rug on the floor and a roaring fire though it was fifty degrees or more outside. He was so enraged that he said, 'Why, Hall, you scoundrel, you've been burning *my* money, and took his cane to Hall right there in front of his clerks."

"That will never happen to you, Uncle Cornelius," Sally laughed; though a small fire of the cheapest pine was smoking and sputtering, the room had the dead chill of a place that's never known sufficient heat. "I'd better run up and get my heavy shawl."

"No, don't go," Cornelius said, taking off his coat and putting it around her. "Sit down . . . there, in George's chair. I want to talk while I have a mind to."

Lost in the folds of Cornelius' huge coat, Sally could understand in a new way why he always called her "little one," an endearment she sometimes resented now that she was twenty-one and twice a mother; she felt small and vulnerable, like a child. Though Cornelius' great shoulders and paunch were amply covered with white silk and linen, the effect, since she'd never seen him without a coat before, was to make him seem also vulnerable, as if he stood naked before her. She expereinced a sense of intimacy, more warming than the coat, as she waited for him to speak.

"I . . . I'm not sure how to begin, little one," he said, "except to say that George was a disgrace today beyond what I think you should have to bear. I feel it is all my fault."

"Uncle Cornelius, you shouldn't. I really don't know what might have happened to me with my father feeling the way he does if you hadn't come for me."

Evidently touched by her response, Cornelius cleared his throat a few times before he went on. "Yes, well . . . I . . . well, I'd hoped then

95

that somehow we'd all be happy under this roof, but you haven't been happy, have you?"

It was a question for which there was no easy response. Happiness had become a word for which she'd known no proper definition since that terrible day on the river. Often just being alive and healthy, which she usually was, seemed an elating miracle. Since Cornelius kept no riding horses, she did a lot of walking in nice weather—down Broadway to the Battery where she could stroll under the trees and enjoy the sea breezes and, most of all, the sight of winged ships sailing to and from a beckoning world; through the crooked streets to the east of Broadway where every other window or door opened on a kind of little theater in which you could see people playing their different roles—caning chairs, shaping silver, baking bread, tooling harness; up to the Collect, so stinking now that even the horses wouldn't drink from it but still a place for skating when ice sealed its sewage. She'd made friends, too, especially the Richmond Hill set, and she'd gone back to reading anything and everything, finding somewhat to her amusement that few of the pages were slit in the expensive, leather-bound volumes lining the walls of the Van Alen library. With each of them yielding a little, she and Lady Lydia had established a tolerable relationship that allowed for noncommittal exchanges about news, the weather and such exclusively feminine concerns as whether the new lace ruffs coming over from London called Betsies because they made you look like Queen Elizabeth would stay in fashion long enough to be worth the purchase. Though George was a heart-sore for which she'd found no balm, his escape into self-destruction at least granted her long periods when she didn't have to confront the pain. Above all, with Evelina and now again with little Cornelius, she had a real reason for being, for going on, and she wondered whether she had a right to ask for more. But how to answer the question?'

"Oh, there are good times and bad times," she said.

Cornelius studied her for a moment with those sailor's eyes, as if searching for a mark that would let him know where he was. "Yes," he said, "how true. But you shouldn't know that at your age, so you must be unhappy. I don't blame you. As I say, I blame myself. I don't know what went wrong with George, just don't know. For a while it all seemed innocent enough, a natural sowing of wild oats, as they say. I . . . well, maybe your mother's told you that I sowed a few myself. But the difference is, I guess, that I had to work for what I got, even the oats, and George has taken everything as his right and due. I spoiled him with money, and his mother spoiled him with pride. So he's rotten, and I can see that now. And . . . well, it's hard for me to say, not that I have any religious scruples or anything like that . . . but, well, I think you should divorce him . . ."

Sally was astounded; it was the last thing she'd ever expected to hear old Cornelius say. If she divorced George, it would mean that she would have to leave the Van Alen house, taking little Cornelius with her. Already, the old man's love for the boy was almost pathetic to see, and yet he would make this gesture, a gesture of love for her greater than she'd ever known. Beyond the risk of losing the child, a divorce would bring scandal that could cause untold damage to Cornelius since most of his fellow merchants were Sunday pious to make up for their daily sins in the marketplace. So this was why he'd been so anxious to talk while his rage against George was still high? Otherwise he might never have been able to bring himself to it.

Her response was immediate, instinctive. "No. Never! I made up my mind a long time ago when . . . well, when my life was spared . . . that I'd live through anything that came along and I will . . ."

"Sally, little one, you mean that, don't you?"

"Yes, I do . . ."

"I can't . . . I don't know what to say . . . how to thank you."

"You already have. You took a risk on me just as you take on one of those cargoes you send out to China. In everybody else's eyes I was damaged goods . . ."

"Don't ever say that about yourself, little one, ever. You're pure gold . . . ." Then, as if embarrassed to say more, to go too far, Cornelius came over and took his coat off her shoulders, shrugged himself into it and said, "Well, now . . . . Well, that's settled: at least you know how I feel. We'd best get back and see how the star of the christening is doing. You know you shouldn't leave him too much with Flossie, or he'll be spoiled worse than his father."

More had happened in that little exchange in the counting room than Sally could have suspected at the time. One result was that, having once been invited into old Cornelius' sanctum, Sally felt free to invade it again, beginning with stopping in to give old Cornelius a chance to chuck his favorite grandson under the chin whenever she and Flossie were taking the baby out for an airing. These visits were also welcomed by the clerks who were allowed to put aside their finger-cramping work for a few minutes and gather around to pay court to the Van Alen scion. Sally was rather pleasantly conscious of the fact that the clerks, young men of her own age, were more interested in her than the baby, and, when George wasn't there, the more forward of them would indulge in mild flirtation. She was almost ashamed of how good this masculine attention made her feel; apparently none of what she'd been through showed in her face and figure.

These clerks were, as were the clerks in most of the city's commercial houses, raw Yankee lads, sons of farmers or second or third sons of trading families in New Haven or Providence or Boston come to New York in search of their fortunes. But it was well known around town that the Van Alen clerks were the best of the lot. Cheerless and chilly as it might be, the Van Alen counting room was a favored place among the city's fraternity of clerks, and there was fierce competition to land a spot at its copying bench. Among other attractions, old Van Alen was rich enough to own slaves to sweep the dust and offal from the walk and half of Broadway in front of his house, a demeaning chore that fell to clerks in other houses. More important, Van Alen, as something of a freethinker, considered the morals of his clerks their own affair whereas many employers imposed curfews, required pledges of abstinence or chastity and demanded church attendance, one going so far as to expect a written summary from the hand of every clerk of no less than two Sunday sermons on his desk each Monday morning. If the wages he paid were mean, Van Alen's reason for doing so made sense to able and ambitious clerks. "I don't want you hanging around here very long, for there's no future in doing another man's copying," he'd tell each new man he hired, "and starvation's the best incentive to moving on that I know." The result was that, over the years, scores of Van Alen "graduates" had established their own firms in the city, gone west to Pittsburgh and Cincinnati or abroad to London, Bordeaux, Marseilles, Bombay, Canton where they set up agencies in which Van Alen interests were favored. Knowing they were good fellows, Sally did not feel obliged to assume a haughty air of offense, as most ladies in her position would have done, when occasionally their animal spirits led to indiscreet familiarity. They loved her for it, began calling her "Miss Sally" and speaking to her freely, a circumstance that would one day be more important to her life than she could then imagine.

During her visits to the counting room, Cornelius, charmed into a good mood by seeing the baby, would often relax a few moments and share with her whatever was on his mind. "How are you at figures, little one?" he asked once.

"Mathematics was never my best study, Uncle Cornelius . . . ."

"Well, you see these scribbles here," he said, holding up a sheet covered with numbers. "I'm trying to figure out whether it's worth the while to send Captain Roberts to Charleston instead of Canton. You see, we've had private advice through Ned Turner in London—he used to be one of our clerks, you know—that cotton's up two cents a pound in the market there. If Roberts can make Charleston before they get the news, he can load a cargo at present prices, and we'd stand to make $8,000 or more above the normal margin. On the other hand, he'd be out of the China trade three months, and I'd been counting on another load of tea to pay off my notes at the customs when they fall due. The problem is whether the increased profit on the cotton would be enough more than the tea would bring to make it a sensible gamble."

"Why gamble? Why don't you send somebody else to Charleston and send Captain Roberts to Canton?" she asked.

"Unfortunately, Captain Roberts—you remember him, of course . . ."

She nodded. How could she forget the handsome young man who'd been so kind to her during that travesty of a wedding ceremony? From the upper windows of the house, she'd seen him on occasion coming to the offices when he was in port and wished that she could find a pretext for meeting him again if only to reassure him that she was surviving in reasonably good spirits. But, never having warning of his visits, she hadn't been able to manage it.

". . . is the only captain in my service I trust to be absolutely discreet. News of the price rise would be worth a good bribe from any Charleston cotton broker, a bribe in excess of a year's wages for a captain, and, whatever my suspicions, I could never prove that the news hadn't leaked from one of them instead of some other source. So, you see, I have to send a man I trust absolutely since the whole gamble is based upon my secret knowledge. Besides, Roberts commands the fastest vessel . . . . But, well, it's my problem, not yours . . ."

"But I find it fascinating, Uncle Cornelius. I never knew business involved so much intrigue."

"You don't know the half of it, little one."

"Could I learn? I know a woman's not supposed to . . ."

"Why not? It's one subject on which I agree with your Mr. Burr: I see no reason why a smart woman shouldn't learn what she has a mind to. For a beginning, what would you do about my problem?"

"Send Captain Roberts to Charleston."

"Why?"

"I can't pretend to understand your figures—yet. But what I do understand is that your advantage over your competitors is in having a good man in your pay. If you can't trust most of your captains, can they trust theirs? So use your advantage."

Cornelius sat back in his chair and favored her with his Buddha smile. "You know, little one, I like the way you think. Already you see that business is more a matter of men than of figures. So I'll do what you say. More than that, I'll give you one percent of the profit if the venture pays off as planned."

"And if not?"

"Well, then, you'll owe me one percent of the loss and have to think of a way to make it good. That way you'll learn that loss is as much a fact of business as profit."

Nothing in a long while had put such zest into living for Sally as the anxious anticipation of Captain Roberts' return. Aware of her feelings, Cornelius took her down to the wharf with him when the *Cathay* was reported making port. Though he remembered her well, the captain was coolly correct in his greeting and obviously a little mystified by her presence. After they'd settled down to a welcoming glass of Madeira in the familiar surroundings of the captain's cabin, Cornelius explained Sally's interest in the venture, and Captain Roberts thawed like snow in the sun. He came around from behind his desk to seat himself beside her on the settee. He took her hand in his and with a murmured, "May I, Madam?" lifted it to his lips. Surprised and more conscious than she liked of his warm hand, tanned by the sun and flecked with fine hairs bleached to gold, of his sea-gray eyes when he lifted them to hers, Sally blushed, but she made no effort to remove the hand he gripped more tightly while he explained, "I felt the angel of good luck riding my shoulder this voyage, and now I know who she is. I hadn't got my cargo aboard in Charleston more than an hour before a ship direct from London arrived with the news of the new price, but that hour was enough. I hope you'll have this lucky lady riding on more of our voyages, Mr. Van Alen."

Thus began a new phase in the relationship between Sally and old Cornelius. For the first time since his marriage, Cornelius found that he could discuss news of business, the only thing he really thought about, at tea or over the dinner table. Lady Lydia and his own daughters and, to a large extent, George, too, had always considered the mechanics of making money too dull or vulgar for polite talk, and they found the language of discounts, drafts, bank notes, specie, tonnage, duty and all the rest as foreign to their ears as Russian. Not so Sally. She picked it up as easily as she'd absorbed Greek, and, eyes shining with her interest and admiration for his acumen, she would lead the old man on to boast of his feats and share his fears. He felt a hero in his own home, the place where it really mattered, and again blessed the circumstances that had brought this unusual girl under his roof. He'd have to look into the possibilities of drawing a will that would let her, instead of George, manage affairs until little Cornelius came of age.

On Sally's part, she was discovering that reading between the lines of the stiff letters and precise figures that the clerks were forever copying in the dusty counting room could be as stimulating to the imagination as any novel. Sitting there was like being at the center of a web woven around the whole globe. When a tremor could be felt along one of its sensitive strands—a ship going down in a North Atlantic gale, say, or the collapse of a financial house in Amsterdam, or the burning of a tea godown in Canton, or a crop failure in South Carolina—all the others had to be adjusted to hold the web together. She could appreciate how the instinct and daring for meeting unexpected shifts of wind and tide that Cornelius had learned at the helm of his sloops translated into business success. A man afraid of risks, or inattentive to the subtle signs of change, would make no progress, and a man without skill would go onto the rocks. Her admiration for Cornelius was genuine, but the others took it as a new and sly form of female flattery to ingratiate herself with the head of the household.

They'd been brought up by Lady Lydia to look upon Cornelius as a dull Dutch trader whose fortunes were owing to the house and remnants of a business he acquired by marriage. It didn't seem to matter that they were all completely dependent on him; providing for them was his natural duty in discharge of a never-ending debt. He was the sole support of Lady Lydia, of course, and of Amelia, whose husband had been killed fighting on the wrong side in the Revolution and whose De Lancey in-laws had therefore been dispossessed or had fled. Charlotte and her three, going on four, children were nearly as in need as Amelia since her husband, John Charles Smith, grandly overspent the few legal fees he received to maintain the social and sporting standing—his were the fastest horses in the city—that had caused Lady Lydia to select him as a son-in-law in the first place. George took the position that his father was obliged to support him since he'd forced him to marry Sally and forgo Miss Walton's $50,000 dowry that would have underwritten his independence. Still, with the arrogance of natural children, they saw no need to show appreciation to him. Only Sally, the outsider and even more dependent than the rest, felt obliged to try to please him, within the limits of her stubborn nature, and her success in doing so, particularly with the production of a son and heir, was shaking up the whole family.

Sally was amused to note the effect that what they regarded as threatening statements from old Cornelius with regard to his name-sake's inheritance was having on the ladies of the family. Though imperiousness was the marrow of her bones, Lady Lydia's tone with her became less clipped, perhaps because she was also losing her teeth, and she was actually consulting her about household arrange-ments. Her sisters-in-law, who had ignored her as much as they safely could, started calling on her and suggesting shopping trips or rides in the country. Snide references to country cousins and brides with a bun in the oven disappeared from their conversation. But, behind her back, they howled like cats about the way she was teasing and toying with the old man by keeping that baby under his nose all the time and pretending to be interested in all that dull nonsense about business that no lady could possibly care about. She knew this for sure because of what George said when the inevitable confrontation came about.

From the day of their marriage, yielding to George's occasional husbandly demands had been the most troublesome aspect of her life. She never knew when they'd come or whether he'd be drunk and brutal or sober and solicitous. Whatever the circumstances, yielding was easier than resisting, and she was honest enough not to look upon his demands as an assault upon a virtue she'd forfeited. But she was also unable to take pleasure in an act without love. Its reward, if any, would be the conception of a child, for her unanticipated joy in Evelina had made her yearn for motherhood again. It was only with the birth of little Cornelius that she decided that she should no longer yield. If producing a son was, in fact, part of her obligation to old Cornelius, she had satisfied it; if being a mother was necessary to her nature, she had met that need. Still she'd wondered what weapon she could use to turn George away until old Cornelius had put it into her hands with his surprise suggestion that he would support her in a divorce.

Soon after the baby started sleeping through the night and was removed from her room to a nursery, George came, as might be expected, drunk. Not even starlight paled the squares of her windows, and it was so dark that, when she was awakened from a deep sleep by an awareness of his presence, she thought for a moment that she was seeing a ghost hovering above her in a bad dream. All that was visible was the white blur of his nightgown and cap, but from the black hole where a face should be came a rush of brandied breath and a fierce whisper, "I can't sleep. All these months I haven't been able to sleep for wanting you . . ."

He grabbed the covers and yanked them away. Her gown had ridden up in the tossing of her sleep, and his fumbling hand buried itself in the soft down between her legs, his fingers clawed hurtingly at the tender lips beneath. Startled and disgusted, she reacted with fierce instinct and brought her knee hard up into his groin. He clutched himself and screamed aloud, "You bitch! You little bitch!"

She rolled out of bed, half scrambling, half crawling, until she reached the door. Then she stood and opened it and said, "Get out of here—you're drunk. Get out at once or I'll scream and waken your father."

Her blow had robbed him of lust, had sobered him to sarcasm. "Go ahead and scream. I doubt that my father would wish to interfere with his son's conjugal rights. You know how he loves babies."

With her pulse dropping and the fever of her fear subsiding, she felt suddenly clammy cold and calm. She was almost grateful for his ugly attack; it made speaking the truth easier. "You should know," she said, "that your father suggested that I divorce you . . . ."

"What? Divorce? I don't believe you. Why, that would mean you'd have to leave and take his precious baby . . . ."

"Unless, of course, you left . . . ."

"But I'm his own son . . . ."

"In name only. But don't worry. I promised him that I wouldn't divorce you."

"That I can believe. Oh, it might have escaped me, but my mother and sisters are on to your feminine wiles—taking advantage of an old man's vanity to get your hands on our money."

"Whatever you, or they, think, George, that's not the reason. I don't want to bring any more scandal on this house that might rob my son of his birthright or your father of his joy. Neither of them deserves it. I do deserve whatever I have to endure. I guess my father is right about the wages of sin . . . ."

"Now don't go getting holy on me . . . ."

"I'm not being holy—just practical. A divorce would cause a lot of trouble that I don't want and might ruin you. So I hope you're not too drunk to understand what I'm about to say. I'm willing to go on as your wife for the sake of our son if you're willing to promise—and keep the promise—that you'll never touch me again."

His tone turned to a whine. "Sally, you don't know what you're saying. You know how I've always, from the very first, been affected by you . . . ."

At that she laughed. "Oh, yes, by me—and anything else in skirts. Go to your doxies for that, George. In that at least, you'll have an advantage over me."

"But what will people say if they know that my own wife . . . ?"

"They'll never know from me, George—*if* you give me your promise."

George arose from the bed where he'd been sitting, nursing his hurt. The feeble shaft of light from the hallway where an oil lamp was kept burning against an emergency in the nursery was not enough for her to read his expression, but she could see him gather up the skirts of his nightgown in a comic imitation of a Roman senator adjusting his toga before delivering a speech from the rostrum. His voice rose to an oratorical level, too, and she could only hope that his parents in the next room or Flossie across the way in the nursery were too deaf or too lost in sleep to hear him.

"Very well, Madam," he said. "I shall give you my promise, and, as my mother, Lady Lydia, raised me to be a gentleman, I shall honor it. Nevermore shall your sleep be disturbed by me. I might add,

104

Madam, that fucking a body as lifeless as that of a dead mackerel has been more of a duty than a pleasure to me. I am only too happy to dispense with it. Good night, Madam."

George surprised her into hysterical laughter. She was doubled up with it, as he swept by her, skirts in hand. Even in drink, he'd never spoken so before, and she wouldn't have understood one of the words, if it hadn't been so clear in context. So that's what it was to him—fucking? It was an ugly, Germanic—well, Dutch, too—kind of word that reduced the act to a purely physical function. It reminded her of another word she'd heard her brothers use—shitting. Was that all it was for him, for any man? Her laughter was brought on by a great sense of relief, not humor: she would never have to do it again.

But she had reward for it beyond measure. In those early years of a new century, when Napoleon's armies were changing the map of Europe, when restless Americans were pushing west down the Ohio and Mississippi and into the vast Louisiana territory, all that mattered for Sally Schuyler Van Alen was taking place in a nursery on Broadway. Robbed too soon of motherhood the last time, she was determined not to miss its slightest treasure—a smile, a step, a tooth, a word. At first round and pink like Evelina, little Cornelius did finally sprout a head of tow, as predicted. But the outlines of his features beneath the rolls of baby fat shadowed hers and her father's—thin straight nose, level brows, dimpled chin—and the baby blue of his eyes began darkening to deepest brown, to black. He would be striking-looking, she was sure, and, oh, so smart. His first word came on a morning when old Cornelius was leaving the nursery after his ritual period of play with the baby before going down to work. Little Cornelius, stretching his hands as if to grab his retreating gradfather, said, "Grana. Grana." Since the old man didn't hear it, Sally scooped up her son and went tumbling down to the counting room where she managed to get him to repeat the performance. Old Cornelius did his little jig of delight that threatened the aging timbers of the house and bellowed to his clerks, "Did you hear that, young fellows, did you hear that? Talking—and not yet two! He'll some day be a great head of this firm, won't he?"

If there was a sadness in these times for Sally, it was still that she could not have a similar kind of sharing with her own parents. But before she began losing contact with Peter, he had sadly reported that that would be impossible. Even the legitimacy of this baby had

105

not moved Jacobus Schuyler. One of the more charitable remarks he'd made was, "Huh, another Cornelius Van Alen—one's bad enough." Peter had been bold enough to say that the baby looked like Jacobus, to which his father had replied, "Looks mean nothing, as Sarah amply demonstrated to us." While Peter had said that, in his opinion, Catharina took a very different view of the matter, Sally would have to understand her mother's difficult position. She had to think about Rebecca, who had also had a son, Philip Livingston, and unfortunately Rebecca's husband, like brother Jacobus' wife, came from the poor branch of Livingstons with the result that Rebecca would need whatever inheritance her father might give her. This meant treading very carefully, because, in Peter's words, "father's suffering from hardening of the convictions if not of the arteries. He thinks the world is literally going to hell. It all started, he claims, when Washington died and the country got into the hands of men of little faith. He rants and raves against Jefferson for making deals with a man like Napoleon, so Godless that he seized his own crown from the hands of the pope, and for bringing black bastards into the world. He says that we must cast sinners aside, and unhappily he uses you as an example, saying, 'When thy eye offends thee, pluck it out.' The terrible thing, Sally, is that I think he almost enjoys what happened to you, because it's the best possible proof of his own purity—and that of all the rest who go along with him, as at least Jacobus and Rebecca do, probably out of fear of being cut out of his will as you were. So you see what a position your mother is in? I do what I can to reassure her that you're all right, but father absolutely forbids any direct contact. Of course, he thinks I'm damned, too—or did, until he found I was marrying Frances who, as you know, is from the rich Livingstons at Clermont, which, as I gather, is the only family he, as a Schuyler, ever looked up to."

When she thought about that report, Sally sometimes also thought that it might be just as well that she wasn't seeing much of Peter and getting more such wounding information. For long periods of time, she could almost forget about being a Schuyler until something like this funeral came along. Now that she saw Peter, though, she did long to speak with him. She wondered what he was thinking, but it was hard to read anything from his face, even whether he'd seen her, too. He kept his eyes carefully down, and his mouth carefully straight, and she began to think that the stories about his political ambitions must be true: no New Yorker was visibly more respectful to the memory of the city's first citizen than Peter Schuyler.

Peter did see his sister comforting that poor Hamilton girl, and he, too, hoped to have a word with her. He really ought to drop in to see her on Broadway, but Frances was one of those wives who wanted an accounting of every hour of every day, and a reported visit to Sally would provoke another of her harangues. An unreported visit would be worse, if it ever came to light, confirming all of Frances' wild notions. The people up on the manor had so poisoned Frances' mind that he couldn't really defend his sister without arousing his wife's suspicion that he himself might be immoral. For all her fine connections, Frances was at heart an innocent country girl with little knowledge, and great fear, of the world. On the whole, he liked her that way . . . he would never have to cope with jealousy or defend his political and other views against sophisticated attack. If she was as proud as she was pretty, she had reason to be, coming from such a family. Peter just couldn't risk riling her too much. His future now depended on the Livingstons.

Back in 1800 Peter's prediction that Mr. Burr would become president had so nearly come true that he and other members of the little band were bitterly disappointed when the tie between Burr and Jefferson was broken in the latter's favor after thirty-five ballots in the House of Representatives. It must have been, they all agreed, Hamilton's doing, because he had devoted every effort to persuading the Federalist congressmen supporting Burr to switch to Jefferson. Still, Burr's good showing and his election as vice-president virtually guaranteed a succession in '08, at which time Peter and his friends would surely enjoy the fruits of loyalty. Peter's first inkling that this might not come to pass was a conversation that he overheard at his own wedding between his new uncle-in-law, Chancellor Livingston, Jefferson's minister to France, and old Governor George Clinton. They were discussing federal appointments in New York, and none of the names were men proposed by Burr, because, as the chancellor told the governor quite candidly, "The president has no use for Burr." Over the next few years, Jefferson's disdain for his vice-president became so clear that even Hamilton was heard to remark that "there must be some good in a man who can so clearly see so much bad in

Burr." An astute politician himself, Jefferson checkmated Burr's Tammany support in the city by splitting the New York Republican party with his appointment of Livingston and letting it be known that he wanted Clinton to replace Burr on the ticket this year.

Unknowingly, the president also divided the loyalties of an ambitious young lawyer named Peter Schuyler. As both a Burrite and a member of the large and influential Livingston clan, Peter had felt very confident of a bright future until the Clinton nomination was announced. Things still might have gone smoothly enough for Peter if Burr had accepted dismissal gracefully, but it wasn't within the character of the man. Bubbling over with his usual energy and good humor, Burr summoned a meeting at Richmond Hill to inform his rather glum little band that, with Clinton leaving the office, he, Burr, would run for governor of New York, even without the regular-Democratic-Republican support, now represented by the Clintonians and Livingstonians.

"This must be confidential among us," he told them, "but I have been approached by Senator Pickering of Massachusetts and other leading New England Federalists offering me Federalist support in New York if I run. You see, they're convinced that the settlement of Louisiana will soon tip the political power of this country to the South and West, to those forces of democracy which they hold to favor the terror, atheism and free love that ruined France. If Jefferson's reelected, they plan to secede and establish a New England union. *Very* confidentially, I've been offered the presidency of this new nation if I can lead New York into it. So you see we have a good chance."

The enormity of what Burr was saying didn't immediately strike Peter, but he was politician enough to ask, "Is Hamilton with them?"

"No. Oh, no. If he were, I'd never be asked," Burr said with a laugh. "But don't you see what a thumb this would be in Hamilton's eye? And he well deserves it. You know as well as I do that it was Hamilton's influence in the House that put Jefferson over me . . .."

While he was still with them, Peter found the enthusiasm of Burr and the others for revenge on Hamilton, on Jefferson, contagious. It would be sweet, and of course there was no question that they, the little band, would be Burr's lieutenants in commanding what looked like a more viable union. Though the states of the Northeast with their shipping and mercantile interests were the wealthiest, the presidents and policies were coming from the agricultural, slave-holding

108

South; everybody knew that the selection of Clinton, too old and worn-out to be president, was nothing but a sop to the North and that Jefferson would use all his influence to make James Madison, his fellow Virginian and secretary of state, his successor. Thus, in a very practical way, the political future was limited for at least twelve years for any northerner in the Republican party dominated by the South and West; moreover, the shipbuilding subsidies, high tariffs and monetary policies needed to protect the Northeast's growing industry and trade would forever be running into opposition. And then there were those moral issues. As Burr told his young followers, "With the blood of my grandfather Jonathan Edwards running in my veins, I can't but believe that the Puritan purity on which our struggle for freedom is based is being tainted. If the men of the South owe allegiance to any religious persuasion—which I doubt from knowing Mr. Jefferson so well—it is to the foreign churches of England and Rome. And without the South, we could abolish slavery, an abomination in a free society. Oh, I know that I own slaves myself, but I have always felt it would be a cruelty to free them until their rights are recognized and established by law. I've always said this union was an experiment and, gentlemen, the experiment isn't working . . . ."

Although it all sounded sensible and even right, Peter began having doubts as soon as he left Richmond Hill in company with Matty Van Buren. Usually too talkative for his own good, Matty had sat silently through the whole meeting, staring at Burr with what Peter took to be a look of adulation. But, as soon as they were alone together, Matty said to Peter, "You're not going along with him, are you?"

"Well, I . . . I thought he was pretty impressive. With his popularity among the Republicans, he wouldn't need much in the way of Federalist support . . ."

Matty shook his head. "I took it you had more sense from the question you asked. If Hamilton's against him, he'll kill him among the Federalists here in the city where he should have the most strength. If he does lose and it ever gets out that he was involved in the New England conspiracy, everybody with him will be politically dead, too."

"You don't sound like the Matty I used to know. I thought you were one of his disciples."

"Even Jesus had his doubting Thomas. No, I tell you to stay out of this, Peter. Now that you're in the Livingston clan, I've been hearing your name mentioned favorably for a number of things—Congress, perhaps even the Senate . . ."

It was news to Peter, but he had to believe it. Though he was only twenty-two, Matty Van Buren had been making a name for himself in the few years since he'd gone back up to Kinderhook to practice law. Once admired as the "boy lawyer" for winning his first case at fifteen, he was now, despite his lisp and Dutch accent, considered a wonder in court, and Peter had himself referred cases to him. Like anyone who had sat at Burr's feet, Matty had taken to mixing law with politics. Self-effacing and seemingly uninterested in any office that would interfere with his lucrative law practice, Matty would promote the fortunes of others. For all of looking the dandy with his tailored blue swallowtail coat and dove trousers, his carefully dressed hair, Matty proved himself a man of the people by making the rounds of the taverns in the Albany area where he would listen to the common man's complaints, plump for his candidate and drink so convivially that he was jokingly known as "blue whiskey Van." With his ear that close to the ground, there was little that Matty didn't hear about the politics of the state, and Peter had to respect his opinion.

Still, he argued, "But what if Burr wins?"

"In that unlikely event," said Matty, "he will be obliged to those Federalists, those moneybags and aristocrats who support him because they fear democracy. It might be all right for patroons like you and Billy Van Ness, but it would be the end for a person like me. I was for Burr in the first place because I thought through his Tammany connections he favored spreading the franchise. The more ordinary people vote, the more an ordinary person like myself will have in this country. He's lost me, Peter."

"So you'll be a Judas?"

"Oh, no, I'll keep his secret, if that's what you mean. But right now I'm managing the congressional campaign for my partner, James Van Alen—my half-brother, you know—and we can't afford to lose the Clintons' support, or the Livingstons' either. Anyway, young DeWitt Clinton did some favors for my friends when he persuaded his uncle to clean house of those Federalists and appoint deserving Republicans and I believe in returning favors . . . . Well, I must hurry to catch the night sloop to Albany. I'll be glad to spread it around that you agree with me. They're still looking for candidates."

"Don't say anything yet, Matty."

Matty shrugged and turned away to set off toward the river at his little trot. Peter was fairly certain that Matty was running for more than a boat; the time would come when the favors he was doing for others in his friendly, casual way would be richly rewarded. He realized that if he, for example, had but said the word Matty would have lost no time in pouring it into the right ears in Albany where defecting Burr disciples were in great demand. If it resulted in a plum falling his way, he doubted that he'd ever be allowed to forget who shook the tree. Though he didn't like to think of himself as a snob, Peter had been to the manor born, and he couldn't quite bring himself to being under obligation to the little towhead he'd seen sweeping the floors and rushing beer in the Kinderhook tavern. Looking into his own heart, he suspected that Matty was right in wanting more democracy, but he also suspected that his own enthusiasm for democracy might be more in the nature of a lip service to a theory than a faith in a practice.

So Peter liked to think that it was patriotic principle—a strong belief in saving the union—that prompted his actions. But he took a way out, pleading too much business in the courts, and simply did not participate in the campaign. Pleading further the duties of a new husband, he absented himself from places like the Pig Pen and the club in a side parlor of the City Hotel where he used to meet regularly with Billy Van Ness and the others, and he turned down invitations to Richmond Hill. On several occasions, he crossed streets or ducked into doorways to avoid coming face-to-face with Mr. Burr, fearing the strength of his love for the man. He could only wonder what the others remaining in the little band thought of him, but, while they publicly denounced Matty as a traitor, they never mentioned his name. Perhaps they felt it better strategy not to have another defection known, or perhaps they believed his rather feeble excuses.

It seemed inevitable that, with Hamilton working quietly against him among the Federalists, Burr would lose, but when the election returns confirmed this loss Peter was surprisingly not at all elated about his decision to evade the race. He felt only regret at the loss of friendship and a sense of shame that he'd lacked the courage either to break with Burr openly or support him. No good excusing himself on the grounds that he was only twenty-nine and still had much to learn when Matty, reveling in his own candidate's success, was so much younger.

Feeling this way, Peter was not only surprised but pleased when Billy Van Ness came knocking on the door of his house in Partition Street in the late afternoon of a hot July day—July 12, 1804, to be exact, a date no New Yorker would soon forget. From where he was sitting at dinner alone with Frances, Peter could see who it was at the door and went himself to open it. Billy was distraught, disheveled, drenched with sweat, half-drunk. He pulled Peter into the street and, words tumbling over each other, said, "Hamilton's dead . . . Burr killed him . . . You've got to hide me . . . Don't tell anyone, not even your wife . . . They're after me . . . Oh, God, I'm ruined . . ."

The man made no sense to Peter, no sense at all. What in heaven's name could have happened? Peter himself had been in the raucous crowd at Fraunce's Tavern a week before for the July Fourth celebration of the revolutionary veterans, the Cincinnati Society where Hamilton stood on a table and sang "The Drum" while they all clanked their glasses in time. To be sure, Burr, who was there too, hadn't joined in, but that was to be expected since everybody knew that Hamilton had turned the tide against him by visiting every prominent Federalist and warning them not to vote for Burr. A careless letter quoting Hamilton's private words to Judge Kent—"Burr is a dangerous man and one who ought not to be trusted with the reins of government"—had been distributed, but that was all part of the game of politics, a game Burr knew as well as anyone in the land. His very presence at Fraunce's was ample proof that Burr could hold his head up in defeat as well as victory. And the Burr Peter knew could not possibly be a murderer. He grabbed Billy by the shoulders and shook him.

"What's happened, man? You're making no sense . . . ."

"A duel . . . yesterday morning . . . I was second to Burr . . . now they've a warrant out for murder on him, accessory on me . . . I've got to hide somewhere . . ."

As if cowardice grew by practice, Peter asked instinctively, "Why here?"

"They'd never think to look here. You are cousin to Mrs. Hamilton, and everybody knows you deserted the cause . . . ."

Peter glanced up and down the street, fortunately empty at dinner time. He pulled Billy into the house and slammed the door. He led him into the dining room, saying, "Frances already knows you're here . . . . Frances, Billy's in trouble . . . . Now sit down, Billy . . . . Have you had dinner? . . . Frances, ring for another plate."

Though Billy showed evidence of having had more than enough to drink, Peter went to the sideboard and poured a stiff brandy and set it in front of him. "Calm down, Billy, and tell us all about it. Begin at the beginning. I didn't even know there was a challenge. Why, I saw them together just a week ago . . . ."

After a greedy gulp of brandy, Billy said, "God knows, I tried, I tried. Mr. Burr was incensed over that remark Hamilton made to Judge Kent—you know, about not being trusted with the reins of government. As he says, he is still the vice-president and only a heartbeat away from being president of the United States. He sent me to General Hamilton to get a retraction or an apology, and . . . well, the general wouldn't yield, though I met him a number of times, and Mr. Burr felt obliged to challenge and asked me to be his second . . . . It would still have gone off all right if Hamilton hadn't died, and I'm sure Mr. Burr didn't mean to kill him . . . . But you know what they're saying already? They're saying that Burr's been practicing out there at Richmond Hill till he could hit the edge of a trembling leaf with his pistol. That doesn't sound like Burr, does it?"

"No, it doesn't," Peter admitted. "But go on, Billy."

"Well, it was finally set for yesterday morning, just after dawn, over at Weehauken . . . . There's a place there, a little shelf in the cliff pretty well hidden from the river below and the heights above . . . . It was a fair fight, I swear it . . . . Why, Pendleton, Hamilton's second, even won the toss over me which gave him the right to select positions and give the signal for firing by saying 'Present!' . . . There's a little slope to the land from west to east and for reasons I'll never know Pendleton put his man on the high ground which meant he had to look right into the rising sun which was bouncing off the river with a fierce glare . . . . Well, Hamilton kept delaying the start while he tried his aim with his glasses on and his glasses off and finally decided to wear them, saying, 'In certain states of the light one requires glasses.' . . . A man who intended to fire over his opponent's head, as they're saying Hamilton did, wouldn't go to all that rouble, would he? . . . Anyway after Pendleton called 'Present!' I heard two shots together and saw Hamilton rise up on his toes and do a little twist to the left and fall . . . I think Burr was as surprised as anybody

113

. . . He started to run to Hamilton, saying, 'I'm sorry, general' but I pulled him away because I was afraid something worse might happen . . . . We knew the general wasn't dead since, from our own boat when we were rowing back, we saw him moving in his boat . . . .

"Oh, God, how I wish that he hadn't died, not that I have much love for him . . . . Until then, just an hour or so ago, nobody knew a thing about the duel . . . . We're all gentlemen, you know, and even Dr. Hosack who tended the general kept his mouth shut . . . . Mr. Burr was magnificent—you'd have been proud of him, Peter . . . . I was with him all day yesterday at Richmond Hill, and he breakfasted with a cousin of his from Connecticut and treated with his broker as if nothing at all had happened. But all day and all this morning he was sending his slave Sam to Dr. Hosack for news of the general's condition . . . . They even brought a surgeon from the French frigate in the harbor, a specialist in gunshot wounds, but it was no use . . . ."

Billy paused to take a long swallow of brandy. Then he actually laughed, but it was a bitter sound without joy or humor.

"You know what undid us, Peter? . . . religion . . . you wouldn't believe it . . . it seems for all of his professed piety the general had never been baptized in the true church—he was a bastard, you know —and he called for the Anglican bishop, Benjamin Moore, you know . . . I guess to save his soul he told the bishop, 'I have no ill will against Colonel Burr. I met him with a fixed resolution to do him no harm. I forgive all that happened.' . . . The bishop was so bowled over with getting such a famous convert who turned out to be such a Christian gentleman that he went boasting of it to everyone—and provided evidence for the warrants . . . . You will hide me, won't you? . . . I've done nothing that any gentleman wouldn't do . . . . In fact, you'd have been in my place if . . . if you hadn't let Matty Van Buren get to you with promises of political preferment."

So that's what they thought of him? Billy must be drunk to say such a thing while asking for aid. Peter had a momentary flush of anger and thought of showing him to the door, but an uneasy conscience restrained him. Frances, who'd been listening silently but open-mouthed with astonishment and horror, decided him. "You can't harbor this man here—he's a criminal," she said. "Think of what it would do to our reputation. Turn him out, Peter, please."

Though she was probably just frightened, his wife's lack of charity angered him nearly as much as what Billy had said. "Frances, you can't mean that. Billy's right, you know, I could very well be in his place now . . . ."

"Please, Peter. Think of our son. Why can't he go to that sister of yours? She was a member of your little band—wasn't she?—and she has very little to lose in the way of a reputation . . . ."

"This is no time for such talk, Frances. You know very well that Sally lives in a Federalist house where Billy's life would be forfeit. He's going to stay here . . . . We've an attic, Billy, where not even the servants go. If you can stand to stay up there, I'll personally see to your food and drink . . . ."

The next days were among the most troubled Peter would ever know. While Billy Van Ness paced his attic, he felt obliged, as a Schuyler, to hire a hack and go out to The Grange, Hamilton's new country home on Washington Heights, and present his condolences to a grieving Betsy and her seven children. Betsy was convinced that the general never meant to fire on Burr; how could he when his advice to hold fire had caused the death of their own oldest son, Philip, in a stupid duel three years before? A son and now a husband sacrificed to this insane practice of masculine pride! The general would not have accepted the challenge at all, she said, except that he was convinced that the nation would soon be calling upon him as a strong man to lead it out of the difficulties it would suffer from Jefferson's weakness, and a man who feared to fight a duel would not be regarded as strong. Everything the general did was prompted by his patriotism; he could not retract his statements about Burr because he meant them. He was particularly distressed at the idea of a New England confederacy. "Here, read this. He wrote it the night before the duel," Betsy said, thrusting a letter at Peter.

Peter glanced hastily through paragraphs arguing that a dismemberment of the American empire would sacrifice too many advantages for too little gain. "It will not," Hamilton concluded, "relieve our real disease, which is *democracy,* the poison of which by a subdivision will only be the more concentrated in each part, and consequently the more virulent." The general had gone down fighting and fearing the people, and Peter couldn't help thinking of the irony that young Matty Van Buren had also opposed the scheme for precisely the opposite reason, that it *would* wipe out democracy. He didn't have long to dwell on such thoughts because, even as he was handing the letter back to Betsy, Angelica, the Hamilton's oldest daughter, a willowy girl whose beauty made her the belle of New York, wandered into the room. Incongruously, she was smiling, but there was a vacant look in her eyes. "Mother, when is father coming out from the city?" she asked. "It's such a nice day, and he promised to let me drive his one-horse chair . . . ."

Betsy flashed Peter a look full of misery and warning and said, "By-and-by, darling . . . ." When the girl drifted off again, still smiling, she said, "We humor her. She's lost her mind and can't understand what's happened. I've tried to explain to her, to all of them, that it's God's will, as the general instructed me to do in a letter he left for me. But she asked, 'What God? How can there be a God when father's gone?' and then . . . well, I just don't know what we'll do . . . ."

Betsy was breaking down, and Peter hastily excused himself. But he did feel obliged again to march in the long cortege—the longest, they said, ever seen in New York—behind the general's flag-draped coffin and riderless horse to the cemetery beside Trinity Church where he saw his sister, Sally, standing by the grave with an arm around a staring Angelica. When the soldiers lined up on the other side of the grave had fired their last volley, he managed to squeeze through the crowd for a hurried word with Sally.

"Oh, Peter, you know I didn't like him, but what a terrible tragedy. Look at Angelica—she doesn't know a word we're saying," she said. "You aren't mixed up in it, are you?"

"No, oh, no. I was too busy even to get involved in the campaign. Didn't you know that? My God, is it that long since we've seen each other?"

"Well, I . . . I know I'm not one of Frances's favorite people, so I . . . But this is no time to go into that . . . . Do you have any news of Mr. Burr?"

"Matter of fact I have, and I know I can trust you," he said. "We're hiding Billy Van Ness, and people get word to him. Burr's escaped, rowed off from the foot of Richmond Hill in the middle of the night with only his slave Sam. Muffled oars and everything. Can you imagine—the vice-president of the United States having to behave like a thief in the night?"

"Oh, I'm glad he got away," Sally said. "I can't help it but I still love him. I can't believe he's so evil, as everybody here is saying now."

"Nor I. Foolish perhaps but not evil. There's scarce a gentleman in New York who wouldn't have challenged under the same provocation, and if it had been anybody but Hamilton . . . . Well, I doubt that the rest of the country will feel the same way."

"I hope not. Why do people get themselves into such terrible trouble, Peter?"

Peter was a little startled that his sister could ask such a question so innocently. It was an encouraging sign that she, at least, was putting away the past. "I don't know," he said, "but tell me, how are things with you?"

"Fine, just fine. Would you believe that Cornelius can already do sums?"

"It doesn't surprise me with such a smart mother. Our little Francis already has said his first word—it was 'Mamma' of course . . . . Sally, we ought to be seeing each other."

"You know where to find me," she said, "but now I must help Angelica find her carriage . . . ."

Walking away from the cemetery, Peter met Mayor DeWitt Clinton who not only offered him a hand but said, "Why, Peter Schuyler, it's good to see *you* here, though one must sincerely regret the occasion. But we're well met. Matty Van Buren's been talking to me about you, and I just haven't had time to seek you out. Would you call on me some day?"

"I'd be delighted, Mr. Mayor," Peter said, tipping his hat as Clinton moved off.

So Matty had, after all, put in a good word for him? Well, if Matty had such influence with DeWitt Clinton, who would undoubtedly inherit leadership of the party in New York now that his uncle would be going to Washington, who was he to scorn him. The idea that a tavernkeeper's son—and Dutch at that—was somehow inferior was an unconscious hangover of those attitudes and that way of life he'd rejected in coming to the city from the manor. Here in New York, old ways, old beliefs, old institutions were as likely to be torn apart as the old buildings that each spring were being reduced to rubble to make way for newer, bigger structures. A man in New York was what he made of himself, not what he'd been born. All you needed for proof of that was Mr. Astor, the city's richest citizen, who'd arrived twenty years ago from Europe with only twenty-five cents in his pocket and begun by selling cakes in the streets to keep from starving, or, for that matter, Cornelius Van Alen, who'd turned an ancient river sloop into a worldwide shipping concern. It was time that he too started making something of himself, and whatever he owed to Matty could be paid when that time came. Meanwhile he'd have to remind Frances, who would be most impressed with the invitation from Mr. Clinton, that his sister Sally was a cousin of Mr. Van Buren. Maybe he would be calling at Broadway after all.

Chapter **VI**

The Parting and the Promise

"And did you see the great rotunda at Ranelagh? I think that's what I'd want to see. I read in Boswell that Dr. Johnson said of it that it gave an expansion and gay sensation to his mind such as he'd never before experienced," Sally said.

"Alas, it's gone—torn down and taken away just like everything in New York," Washington Irving replied. "But I didn't know you read Boswell . . ."

"Oh, yes, and Goldsmith and Burke and Sheridan and—"

"You're beginning to sound like Madame de Stael—I met her, you know."

"Well, Mr. Irving, not all New York women are as frivolous as you make us out in your *Salmagundi*. What an insult—advertising your hot-pressed vellum paper as just right for buckling up our hair. Some of us *read*, you know."

"Now, now, Sally. Who said I had anything to do with that scurrilous sheet? Blame those who sign the pieces—Launcelot Langstaff, if you like, or William Wizard, but not Washington Irving."

Sally laughed. "Please, Mr. Irving. You should invent better names, if you want me to believe that. There's hardly a soul in town

119

who doesn't know that you and the Kembles and Henry Brevoort and James Paulding and I don't know who else are cooking it up when you're seen with your heads together at Dyde's Tavern. But now that you're here, tell me: where did you get that preposterous name, *Salmagundi?*

"Now you do surprise me. It's in any dictionary. A salmagund is an appetizer made of raw chopped meat, pickled herring, onions, olive oil, vinegar, cayenne pepper. Delicious with cocktails or beer."

"Well, I wouldn't know. I don't drink those things. But why such a name?"

"It stands for good, strong American tastes instead of the French slop and fricasseed sentiment that so many of our publishers import. Do you know that everywhere I went in Europe, especially Italy, they called me, of all people, the *wild* American?"

"I wouldn't be surprised the way I hear you and your friends carry on. But I do appreciate what you're doing. We all need a little levity, and it is time that we had an American literature. I might warn you, though, to stop teasing us ladies about our nudity."

"And why, Madam?"

"Well, because we might take you seriously and start wearing shawls and petticoats instead of bare bosoms and flesh stockings. You wouldn't like that, would you?"

Irving blushed, and Sally tried to cover up for him by lifting the teapot. "Have another cup? And another *koekje*—sorry, cookie. It's an old Dutch recipe."

"I shouldn't. Look how fat I'm getting. But I will, because I can't resist old Dutch. You know, I was walking down Broad Street the other day and looking at those old Dutch houses with their gables and *stoeps* so scrubbed you could eat off them and thinking maybe I ought to write something about Dutch New York before it's all gone."

"Perhaps you should, but I'm more interested in the future than the past. If I were you, I'd be writing about Mr. Fulton's steamboat. Do you know that she's making three round trips to Albany every week in only thirty-three hours and they've another one building? Think how this is going to change our lives . . . ."

"You're right, you're right, Sally. As a matter of fact I have been playing around with an idea of having a fellow fall asleep in the last century and awake in this one to all the new wonders . . . But, I fear I must go. I hope I may come again. This has been almost like the

120

good old times at Richmond Hill. A shame about Mr. Burr, eh? I always thought him a man of dreams, and they turned out to be nightmares. My respects to your brother, Peter, if you ever see him . . ."

It *was* like old times, and Mr. Irving could be certain that she would invite him again. This time it had been a sudden inspiration and a rather bold one—she, a nominally married woman, having an unmarried and charming man-about-town like Washington Irving in for a tête-a-tête over tea. She'd been window-shopping Maiden Lane, little Cornelius in hand and Flossie behind with a bag to carry her purchases, when she'd literally bumped into him. She'd known, of course, that he'd returned from Europe; what literate person in New York could be unaware of the irreverent new magazine that he and his friends were publishing? But she'd been so out of touch with the remnants of the little band, even Peter, that there seemed no correct way of meeting him again. She'd been flattered that he recognized her at once, doffing his hat—one of the tall beavers that were in fashion in London and gradually being seen in New York—and saying, "Madam Van Alen—Sally! You are looking younger and more beautiful and more . . . more French than ever. In all my travels on the continent, I did not lay eyes on a lady with form so fair or eyes so black." She hadn't been able to prevent herself from blushing with pleasure, though she knew his tendency to use flowery language for its own sake, nor from blurting out an invitation despite the fact that Lady Lydia was out somewhere with her daughters. Regardless of proprieties, it had been perfect timing, for it would have been impossible to try to talk to Mr. Irving with Lady Lydia, who never read anything, putting the trumpet she was starting to use to her ear and asking, "Eh? Eh? *Salmagundi?* What sort of *thing* is that?" Yes, she'd have Irving in again when everybody else was out and maybe use it as an excuse to have Peter and Billy Van Ness and Matty Van Buren if he happened to be in town for one of the Tammany meetings.

It wouldn't be quite the same, of course. There would be no Theo, no Mr. Burr, no Richmond Hill. It was 1807 now, and a lot had happened in the three years since the duel. The place itself had been sold off to Astor for $25,000 back in '04 to pay part of the debts Mr. Burr left behind when he fled New York jurisdiction after the duel. He'd never returned, couldn't return even now, because the warrants and judgments still stood against him. Peter had been right about the

121

fact that the rest of the country did not view Mr. Burr's slaying of Hamilton in an affair of honor with the same horror as the citizens of New York. When he returned to Washington in early '05 to take up his last duties as vice-president, President Jefferson actually had him to a White House dinner. The cynical said that the president was expressing his thanks to Burr for ridding the world of his enemy; the even more cynical said that it was a form of bribery to influence Burr when he presided over the Senate's impeachment trial of Supreme Court Justice Samuel Chase. But from what Peter told her it was Burr's masterful handling of that case that got Chase acquitted against the president's wishes. Some said it was Jefferson's irritation over that trial that caused him to have Burr arrested on charges of treason for his western adventures. Sally could never understand just what Mr. Burr had been up to. Possibly out of embarrassment, Theo had stopped writing, and it was hard to believe what the papers said. Some accounts held that he was planning to separate Louisiana from the United States and make himself president; others suggested that he was going to conquer Mexico and make himself emperor with Theo as his consort and "Gampy" as his heir. Peter said that, from what he knew of Burr's ambition, neither scheme was as incredible as it sounded, but Sam Swarthout, the only one of the band who went west with him, insisted that the men Burr recruited were only meant to be settlers for one of those western land tracts he'd acquired. Sam must have been right, since Burr was acquitted this summer in a trial at Richmond with General Jackson, the Tennessee Indian fighter, testifying for him and Chief Justice Marshall, certainly no friend to Burr, presiding. Sally had been warmed to read that Theo, regardless of her husband's position as governor of South Carolina, had taken rooms in Richmond to be with her father through the whole of the trial. But she was glad that Peter and the others hadn't been involved. Even Billy Van Ness had quietly brought Matty Van Buren down from Kinderhook not long after the duel to get him off the hook as an accomplice and had gone back to practicing law. No, there was no little band, and the Lord only knew what might happen to Mr. Burr now. But if he ever did come back to New York, she'd certainly include him in the invitation to the others.

In the back of Sally's mind was something she'd been forced to think about against her will since that day a few months ago when she'd gone with old Cornelius to the wharf on the North River near the state prison to watch *The Steamboat's* maiden voyage. He'd seemed in the best of spirits, rushing right up to Chancellor Livingston and his brother John and the others waiting to board the boat. Greeting him, John Livingston said, "Bob Fulton has had many a bee in his bonnet before now, but this steam folly will prove the worst yet."

The chancellor, deafer by the year, cupped an ear with his hand and leaned into the little group, asking, "What's that? What's that? What did John say?"

"He said, if I interpret him rightly, that you are crazy, chancellor," Cornelius boomed in the poop deck voice that now seemed incongruous coming from his aging hulk.

"Crazy, eh? Crazy? Huh! John'll be the first to want a share in it by tomorrow. Why don't you come along and see how she goes, Neel? It should interest an old river dog like you."

"It would be interesting, chancellor, but I don't think my old heart would stand the excitement . . ."

"Well, then, what about the young lady here?" asked the chancellor, bowing to Sally with Old-World courtliness. "Helen and Harriet and the others are going, so she'd have plenty of feminine company. You know I wouldn't take the ladies if I thought it unsafe."

"Oh, I'd love to go, but I have a young son at home to see to."

It was only partly a lie. Flossie could well see to Cornelius, and she did want to go, not only for the experience but for a chance to see again the countryside of her youth since the ladies would be going as far up as Clermont at least. But what really held her back was surprise at hearing Cornelius complain about his heart. It wasn't at all like him, and, looking at him carefully she thought that he was pale and sweating far too much for even this warm August afternoon. "Are you all right, Uncle Cornelius?" she whispered.

"Perfectly, little one, perfectly," he said. "I just needed a good excuse. No real sailor would want to set foot on that . . . that contraption . . ."

"Don't you think we should go home?" Sally urged.

"Not on your life, little one. I have to see whether it works."

For Cornelius this experiment with *The Steamboat* was no matter of idle curiosity as it was for the hundreds of other people jamming the wharf, lining the roofs of warehouses and peering from the prison's barred windows. If the thing did work, the business he'd spent a lifetime developing could be in jeopardy. Fortunately, there was every reason to share John Livingston's view of steam as a folly. Nearly a dozen years ago, Cornelius had seen that poor fellow John Fitch run a little steamboat around the Collect Pond in a futile demonstration to get financial backing. One wag, he remembered, said the thing sounded like the blowing of a school of porpoises which had found their way from the river. He'd thanked his lucky stars a hundred times that, being a hardheaded Dutchman, he'd kept his pockets closed. Fitch did get a boat going between Trenton and Philadelphia, but the public wouldn't patronize it, and he'd gone back to Kentucky where, from what Cornelius had heard, he'd killed himself in despair.

But, despite what his brother said, Chancellor Robert R. Livingston could not be laughed off like Fitch. The man who'd sworn Washington in as president, who, as Jefferson's minister to France, had bought all of Louisiana for $12,000,000, was no fool. Whatever this young Fulton fellow had shown him over there in Paris had been so convincing that Livingston had borrowed every cent he could on his holdings at Clermont to build *The Steamboat*. Not only that, but Livingston was turning out to be as shrewd as Astor when it came to business. He'd used all of the Livingston political connections to get a bill through the legislature granting him and Fulton exclusive rights to use steam in New York waters. If this boat of his could plow back and forth between Albany and New York without regard for wind and tide he'd have no trouble at all getting his proposed four dollar fare from people who always seemed to be in a hurry these days. In fact, they'd be the very people who so far had favored the fast Van Alen sloops.

Cornelius had found it odd that an artist like Robert Fulton should be building boats when there were so many real masters of the craft right here in New York, and a look at *The Steamboat* confirmed to his sailor's eye that the man cared little for the ways of wind and water. With only a few feet of freeboard and no sheer to the deckline, the thing looked like nothing but a floating box, thrown up hastily around the engine he'd imported from Boulton and Watt in England. Only the boiler, encased in masonry—no doubt as a precaution against explosion—was under cover. All the rest of the clanking machinery—flywheels, walking beams, cylinders, paddle wheels—affronted the nautical eye. There was a stub of a mast aft on which to hoist the colors and a great stack amidships rising out of the kind of square, ugly house those upstate carpenters tacked onto the decks of

124

canal boats. If she went at all, she'd be noisy, dirty, shaky, and Cornelius could hope that, once the novelty wore off, people would prefer the clean, quiet ways of sail.

While they talked on the wharf, Fulton was scrambling around his boat giving orders and checking on everything. Sweating crewmen were stoking the fire under the boiler with chunks of pine until the stack began spewing smoke and sparks that a breeze off the river spread through the crowd; as if under attack by insects, people were soon jumping and flicking at themselves to protect their clothes from fire. When the steam came up, Fulton himself pulled the lanyard that set the whistle to screaming. The chancellor and his party, making nervous jokes among themselves about trying anything once, went aboard. The great bare wheels on each side of the craft started to churn the water to a froth. Lines were cast off, and *The Steamboat* leaped away from the wharf amid mingled exclamations from the crowd that blended into a jeering cheer.

"Looks like the devil's own barge to me." . . . "More like sailing in a tea kettle." . . . "Hate to see so many pretty ladies on their way to Davey Jones' locker." . . . "Wouldn't ride in that thing for all the tea in China." . . .

Nearly in midstream, *The Steamboat* stopped and then started slipping backward with the tide. The wheels were no longer revolving. An old salt turned philosopher seemed to express the sentiment of the onlookers when he said, "By Jesus, I knew it! The good Lord didn't mean for man to go puffin' and snortin' against the laws o' nature. He give us the wind, and he means us to use it."

A crew of more charitable men jumped into an eight-oared barge and set out to try to give *The Steamboat* a tow. Fulton could be seen waving them off, and the crowd stayed to watch, for the most part in silence now, until the wheels were turning again, and Fulton let out another triumphant blast of the steam whistle. As soon as the boat was moving, Sally tried again to get old Cornelius to return to his carriage. "No, no," he said, brushing off the hand she put on his elbow. "I want to be sure . . . ." And so they stood there until *The Steamboat* dwindled to a dark plume of smoke on the northern horizon.

Cornelius sighed heavily and said to Sally, "We can go now. Mark this day, little one—August seventeenth in the year of our Lord eighteen hundred and seven. From now on, mechanics will take over the sea like they're taking over everything else. You know, I've always said it's hell to grow old, but right now I'm rather glad of it."

"Don't talk like that, Uncle Cornelius . . . ."

"Why not? Why not? You realize what this means, don't you? I've built what little fortune I have on knowing how to outsail the other fellow, and . . . Well, even if I understood this steam business, Livingston's got a thirty-year lock on it."

In the carriage, old Cornelius said suddenly, "I'm tired . . ." and slumped over unconscious. Sally started slapping his cheeks. When he came around again, she said, "You fainted, Uncle Cornelius," but he said, "Nonsense, just a little nap. Man has a right to a little nap on a hot afternoon . . ."

Sally, of course, knew that it was no little nap, and increasingly there had been more of these fainting spells with much wheezing in between. She'd taken to making him go outside and stroll up and down the block with her, thinking it might help his breathing, and the sign that he was in real trouble was that he would rest his great weight on her thin shoulders during these walks. She tried to get him to break down and go to Dr. Hosack or Dr. Mitchill or *somebody*, but he seemed more determined than ever not to admit that there was anything wrong with him. "We're going to have to strike sail or change course, and I've got to be at the helm," he'd keep saying. "Can't trust it to George, and it'll be a dozen years before the younker can take over. Sometimes, little one, I wish you were a man, but then that wouldn't do either, would it? No man could have given me a grandson."

What worried Cornelius, of course, was the fate of his river sloops. They'd never been big money-makers, but the small and steady profit he could count on from their operation was the base of his business. It gave him the courage to sign the heavy notes he needed to take more profitable gambles in ocean trading. Already these profits were going up in smoke as surely as the chunks of pine that fed *The Steamboat's* fires, and it wouldn't be long before he'd have to sell off his vessels at a loss. For all that, Cornelius absolutely forbade his captains to engage in the sabotage by which other shortsighted Dutch skippers were trying to save their livelihoods. Nearly every trip, *The Steamboat's* paddle wheels were "accidentally" shattered by the bowsprit of a sloop whose captain complained that he couldn't get out of the way of such a hellish thing, or they were jammed by debris that mysteriously appeared in the vessel's path. Such tactics simply inspired Fulton to invent a cover for the wheels. Cornelius would have done the same. He'd always argued that turning back progress was as futile as trying to stop the tide the way that old King Canute did in the legend. If it weren't for Livingston's damnable monopoly, he might even think of selling the sloops while they had some value and building a steamboat himself. But that was no way out, either, since, being a Federalist, he might as well be as dead these days as his friend Hamilton when it came to political influence to break the monopoly.

When he shared these thoughts with Sally on one of their strolls, she asked, "Why don't you sell the sloops and buy real estate?"

"Huh!" Cornelius snorted. "That shows how much you still have to learn, little one. No merchant worth his salt would put money into the ground except for the buildings he needs for business. Ties it up too long."

"What about Mr. Astor?"

"Astor! Astor!" shouted old Cornelius, waving his arms in a gesture of frustration. "Astor's nothing but a lucky fool. He'd still be trying to sell flutes out of his mother-in-law's boardinghouse if it weren't for that trick he played on Livermore . . ."

Sally almost regretted her question, because the mention of Astor was sure to raise Cornelius' blood pressure. Cornelius, already wealthy and connected by his own and his sister's marriages to the best families in the state when Astor was still peddling cakes, was both mystified and miffed by the man's spectacular success. Like many self-made men, Cornelius resented, perhaps feared, the reflection he saw of his own crude beginnings in other, younger men like Astor. Just as Cornelius had sharpened his wits and strengthened his body by contending with wind and tide and weather and manhandling hogsheads of freight on his sloops, Astor had developed a cunning and built a body nearly as big as Cornelius' by coursing the wild Iroqouis country in northern New York, paddling and portaging canoes, in search of fur. But whereas Cornelius had turned himself into a gentleman as rapidly as he could, mastering with Lady Lydia's help the English tongue, observing which fork to pick up and which wine to select, pledging allegiance to the aristocratic principles of Hamilton and Jay and Kent, buying a pew in Trinity and riding out in a carriage, Astor went on mangling the language in his guttural German, stuffing his family into whatever cramped quarters he could get for a bargain, drinking beer and walking and caring not a whit for politics or social prestige. Why, even now with his ships competing for the China trade and his trappers spreading north and west clear to the Pacific, Astor would like as not cut a bolt of cloth for you with his own hands if you dropped into his store on Pine Street. He was no gentleman and showed no signs of ever becoming one though he had to be over forty. What probably galled Cornelius the most was that Astor's son, William, *was* showing signs of becoming a gentleman and was a great help to his father whereas his George . . .

Nobody knew how rich Astor was, though once in a while he'd reveal his hand as he had when he plunked down the cash for Richmond Hill where, of course, he'd never think of living. Not many knew, either, how he'd tricked Livermore, a real gentleman, a few years back, and if those who did equate that sort of thing with supplying provisions to keep people from starving in occupied New York, Cornelius would have to conclude that they didn't understand morality at all. Cornelius had the story from the lips of James Livermore himself, and he knew it must be true since it made Livermore look the fool.

It began with the usual Astor luck. Back in those days you couldn't get rid of a beaver pelt for love or money in New York, and Astor had piles of them that threatened to take over his mother-in-law's whole house. So one day he loaded them on a London ship and went with them, riding steerage, of course. He peddled the pelts around London for a handsome profit, and in the course of doing business ran into an old schoolmate from Germany who'd risen to the top of the East India Company. As a kind of souvenir, the man gave him a list of Canton prices and Permit No. 68 to trade in East India company ports. Since Astor didn't even own a periaguar, let alone a proper ship, he didn't know what to do with these papers when he got back to New York. He talked it over with that shrewd wife of his, and, together, they had an inspiration: why not trade them for a share of the profits to someone like Livermore who already had ships trading with the West Indies and capable of reaching the East Indies? Fair enough, but Astor demanded *half* the profit without putting up a cent for the cargo.

At first Livermore laughed, "Now that is a Dutch bargain if ever I was offered one, Mr. Astor. Are you sure you came from Germany?" But after studying the price list—ginseng, for instance, which he could buy at twenty cents per pound in New York was selling for $3.50 per pound in Canton—Livermore dropped by the Astor store and accepted the bargain with a handshake. When the ship returned, her cargo of tea sold at auction for a profit of a dollar a pound. Perhaps thinking to embarrass his partner, Livermore had Astor's share—$55,000 in silver—packed in barrels and carted to Astor's door. Astor wasn't the kind to be embarrassed by getting money in whatever form, and he was quick to learn. He asked Livermore to return the pass—"a souvenir from an old friend, you know"—put the $55,000 into a ship and cargo of his own and with the East India pass went into the China trade. Rather naively, Livermore tried to take the curse off the tale by ending with, "Actually the joke was on Astor. My captain told me that when he got to Canton he found that he didn't need the pass to trade with the Chinese."

For most people the story would end there, but not for Cornelius. It inspired him to build the *Cathay* and go into the trade himself, and he began paying more attention to Mr. Astor's operations. Watching an Astor ship get under way one day, he detected with his sailor's eye that she rode surprisingly high in the water for a vessel supposedly laden with goods for Canton. Since Roberts was sailing the next day, he directed him to catch up with the Astor ship, if possible, and keep an eye on her. When Roberts returned, he brought with him the tale of another incredible bit of Astor luck. At the Sandwich Islands, Astor's ship put into port, ostensibly for food and water, with the *Cathay* at her heels, ostensibly for the same reason. While Roberts, mystified, watched through his glass, natives began floating large rafts of lumber out to the Astor vessel; the crew winched them aboard and lashed them to the deck. Ashore that night, Roberts plied the Astor captain with drink until his tongue began to wag.

"Well, I'll tell 'e," he said. "First trip out here for Mr. Astor, I didn't know whether we could make the China coast without more water and wood for our fires, so I put in here for good measure. When we finally got anchored up there in the Whampoa river, one o' these Chinese traders comes aboard. We still had so much firewood clutterin' up the decks he almost fell over it. He picks a piece up and looks at it and *smells* it and says I'll give you $500 a ton for it. Queer these Chinese, I think, but havin' learned a thing or two from Mr. Astor, I snap it up. Turns out it's something called sandalwood they use to make boxes and things and here we were burnin' it like any old pine. Well, I've been leavin' room for it ever since. It's better 'an ginseng or iron scrap or anything else we bring over."

Roberts had the wit to ask, "And nobody in New York knows of this?"

"Mr. Astor o' course. Aside from him, nobody in the whole East Coast or London or anywhere else I know of has tumbled to it . . . ."

"Then let's keep it between you and me," Roberts said with a wink and ordered up another drink.

So Cornelius was in sandalwood, too, and he often wondered whether Astor knew. He couldn't blame Astor for trying to keep that secret, nor would any other merchant in the city. What bothered him was the man's damnable luck in falling into something like that. Of course, he'd have to grant that Astor had the guts to act upon his luck. But so had he. It had been one of his own secrets of success, if it could be called a secret. Still, when it became apparent that Astor was picking up every bit of swamp and rocky farmland he could find on Manhattan Island, Cornelius decided that Astor's luck was going to his head. Who in his right mind would want to live so far away you couldn't walk to work? In any case, there weren't even cart tracks leading into some of that stuff Astor was buying across the Collect and over on the other side of Murray's hill. Yet Astor was willing to sell at a bargain in town to get hold of it.

Just the other day, Tom Wilson had come into the Van Alen counting room, all agloat over having got the best of Astor. "I've just closed a deal with Astor on that old house right across the Broadway from you, Cornelius—for only $8,000. Why it'll bring me twelve in a couple of years," Wilson said.

For once Cornelius could agree: the old houses on the east side of Broadway were being converted into lucrative boarding houses, stores and taverns at such a rate that Wilson might be conservative; indeed, that was one real estate deal Cornelius might have been interested in himself had he heard about it. Knowing Astor, however, he was suspicious: "Why did he sell to you so low, Tom? It doesn't sound like Astor."

"Between you and me, I think he's losing his grip. I waited until the papers were signed and then I said, 'Thank you, Mr. Astor—that's as good as putting four thousand in my pocket.' Well, he got that little twinkle in his eye that bodes no good for anyone dealing with him and said, 'You are quite right, sir. But do you know what you have done for me? I am going to take your $8,000 and buy ten lots above Canal Street, and by the time you get your $12,000, I will get $80,-000. So *I* thank *you*, sir.' I don't think he's right, do you, Cornelius?"

No, he didn't, and yet Astor had seldom been wrong. Now his little one, his Sally, whose head was proving to be as level as her mother's, seemed to agree with Astor. Could it be that Cornelius' vision, like the rest of his sense, was failing with age? Perhaps he ought to be getting into real estate, but just the thought of it made him tired; he was as uncertain of ventures in land as he was sure of them at sea. And he was tired—too tired, too often these days. He wished that Sally wouldn't keep insisting that he'd fainted when he'd just drifted off into little naps. A man had a right to nap now and then after working fifty years. And he dreaded these infernal walks when he found it so hard to breathe and sometimes had to clutch at this bit of a woman to keep from falling. She was made of iron, though, as he could feel when he leaned upon her, and that was a comfort. But those black eyes of hers seemed to see right through him, and that wasn't always a comfort.

"I'm sorry, Uncle Cornelius," she was saying. "I know you're not so fond of Mr. Astor, and I shouldn't have mentioned his name. But look at the Roosevelts. They're gentlemen and, as you yourself say, as good merchants as any in the city, and they're making a killing developing the Swamp. I think I'm right about real estate."

"Well . . . well . . . I'll think about it . . . maybe next spring when the moving fever seems to set in . . . I just don't know . . . I'm a little afraid . . . Did I ever tell you, little one, that it's hell to grow old?"

In that fall of 1807, the prospects of the house of Van Alen deteriorated as rapidly as the weather. The successful operation of the steamboat was an insignificant smudge on the horizon compared to the gathering clouds of an embargo. True, American vessels were being harassed as both Britain and France sought to keep them from trading with each other, but to a New York merchant like Van Alen the loss of a few sailors to a British press gang or the impounding of a ship in a French port was just a cost of doing better business than ever in supplying the armies of Europe. But to politicans and patriots, these depredations were an insult to the national honor, and when one British warship lying off the Chesapeake seized, among others, an American Indian and a Negro on the grounds that they were defectors from His Majesty's navy, the cry for war began to sound. True to his devotion to peace and belief in neutrality, President Jefferson came up with the idea of punishing both sides in what he regarded as a distant conflict by preventing American ships from trading to any foreign port. With all he owned or could borrow tied up in the *Cathay* and his new ship, *Canton,* already being rigged in the yards at Coenties Slip, Cornelius viewed the prospect of an embargo with the anxiety of a sailor watching a hurricane come down on him (and Sally often thought it a mercy that he did not live to see that black day of December 22, 1807, when Congress passed the President's act.)

After the weather turned foul, Cornelius absolutely refused to go out on walks with Sally on the grounds that he might catch cold. It did seem reasonable, what with his wheeze, but she doubted that he was doing any more good for himself by sitting in that chilly counting room, huddled down into his great coat like a turtle in its shell and looking blue around the lips. When she chided him, he grumbled, "Can't afford to waste money on fires these days—you know as well as I do. Besides, it would spoil the boys." Seeing him struggle with the stairs more slowly each day, clutching the bannister and pausing at each step to catch his breath, she went herself to Dr. Hosack. "What? Old Cornelius ill? I can hardly believe it," the doctor said. "Why, he's never been to me all these years, never even left town when the fever struck. But it does sound serious—small strokes probably. He ought to be bled. I'll come at once if you send for me." Cornelius, of course, would have nothing to do with bleeding. "Killed General Washington from what I heard," he said, "and I can't afford to die. Roberts is due in any day, and we've got to turn him right around or he'll be caught in the ice and fall foul of this embargo that fool Jefferson is talking about. Might be able to get the *Canton* out of the yards, too, if . . ."

One morning old Cornelius didn't make his usual visit to the nursery where these days young Cornelius was always busy at his lessons with Sally's help. Instead, it was Lady Lydia who came. Still in her nightgown, the bridge of the false teeth she'd taken to wearing to restore her clipped speech missing, her thin gray hair grotesquely spiked in paper wrappers, she seemed in a state of shock. "He won't get up . . . he . . . he's dying," she said. "He can't leave me like this.

132

He . . . he says there may be no money . . . do something . . . do something, for God's sake . . ."

With great restraint, Sally refrained from telling her mother-in-law that she'd been doing all she could, had been, in fact, with the possible exception of little Cornelius, the only one in the house aware of old Cornelius' deteriorating health. As in many long and passionless marriages, Lady Lydia had for years failed to see, or hear, beneath her husband's robust surface and booming voice. The idea that anything inconvenient could happen to him was as ridiculous to her as it was impossible to him. George evidently felt the same way; in any event, on his rare appearances in the living quarters or offices, he had other things on his mind. He had used Sally's rejection of him to reject, in turn, all pretense of performing his duties. When he wasn't in some bar or other or the third tier of the Park Theater where he devoted his attention to the prowling prostitutes instead of the stage, he was out racing horses with his brother-in-law, John Charles Smith. Dissipation made him look like a walking cadaver, but relinquishing duty had seemingly restored enough spirit that he was once more considered one of the gayest blades of the city by those he couldn't hurt. If George wasn't aware of his father's failing, it was, as in Lady Lydia's case, at least half the old man's fault. The worse he felt, the less Cornelius wanted to have anything to do with them; he had to husband both his energy and emotions for business.

Taking little Cornelius with her, Sally went at once to the bedroom where a huge and motionless lump lay under the covers. She thought that old Cornelius was already dead and started to take the boy away. Then a voice, wheezy and whispery, came from the lump. "Bring him here—I want to have a last look."

For all her concern, Sally herself had never quite believed that Cornelius could die. But then she'd never heard him speak such words in such a tone. Her first emotion was a kind of anger at him for giving up. "Uncle Cornelius, don't talk like that," she said. "You've just had another fainting spell or something. You've scared Lady Lydia half out of her wits. Here—let me get some light in this place . . ."

The drapes were drawn since Lady Lydia liked to sleep until noon, and when Sally pulled them back, a wintry sun fell across the bed. Old Cornelius' cap had fallen off, and his bald pate looked more bone than skin in the light. He still would not, or could not, move, and only

133

his sailor's eyes, squinting and roving from one to the other of them, betrayed some life. Little Cornelius, who had never seen his grandfather other than fully dressed, on his feet, and full of joking good humor, was awed into silence. Sally, still denying what seemed inevitable now that she could see his lifeless pallor, said briskly, "Well, maybe you'll admit that you're sick at last, you stubborn man. I'm going for Dr. Hosack . . . ."

"No, wait," Cornelius said, his voice so strained that she had to lean over him to hear. "He'll do me no good now . . . the pain . . . in my heart . . . but I must say something to you, Sally . . . I must . . ."

"Cornelius, go back to your room and study," Sally said.

"Let him stay . . . . He might as well know . . . . I'd wanted to do better by you, Sally, leave everything to you—and to the boy . . . . But it is complicated . . . the lawyer . . . . I would have to dissolve the firm . . . . Van Alen & Son cannot exist without the son, he says . . . . That's why . . . oh, I wish you were a man . . . the best I could do was a kind of trust—all the assets to the boy if there are any . . . that's why I couldn't die . . . ."

"And you're not going to die now," she said, taking his hand, but she knew from the cold feel of it that he would, and she was suddenly frightened for herself, for her son, and she was ashamed that all her thought was not for him, the dying one.

"I am . . . I can't . . ." A gasp blew his words away, a shudder shook the big body, tears squeezed from his eyes. ". . . the pain . . . forgive me . . . forgive me . . . for everything . . . Promise you'll see to the boy . . . see he gets the firm . . ."

"Hush. Don't try to talk. I promise. I promise. Don't worry."

He seemed to understand her, but she wasn't sure. He made a choking, gargling sound, terrible to hear. Then, lifeless, his head rolled to one side, mouth open, eyes staring. Beside her, little Cornelius uttered what was more a cry than a word, although she was sure of what she heard—"Grana!" It had been the boy's first word, and he hadn't used it in all the years since he'd become proud of his ability to speak distinctly, but it was the right word. She took her son in her arms, and, together, they wept.

Chapter **VII**

The Fire Without and the Fire Within, 1807–1813

The ringing of bells dragged her out of a deep sleep, out of a night-mare which must have visited her when the first of the metal tongues began crying alarm. In the dream, she had been running and running, skirts afire, without hope of ever escaping a slithering snake of bright orange and red flame that pursued her. Though she knew she was awake, her heart kept pounding as hard as it had in her night-mare, for she heard bell after bell in steeple after steeple joining in the cacophonous clangor. Fire in the night was always a terror in this city with its buildings squeezed together in long blocks across narrow streets. She could already detect the acrid smell from the burning on the breeze that stirred the curtains at her window; sitting up in bed, she could see a rising glow to the southeast that made a black silhouette of the spire of the First Presbyterian Church on Wall Street. It was far away, over on the East River. Her pulse slowed—she was safe, and young Cornelius who was probably sleeping sweetly through the clamor was safe and Flossie, the only slave they had left, was safe, and George—where was George?

Feeling this fire of no immediate concern to her, she lay back, listening for the pound of George's boots on the steps. George always ran out to watch fires; they excited him in some peculiar way. Although he wouldn't join one of the volunteer fire companies on the grounds that the members were lower class, he would take the fire bucket that hung by the front door and get into the lines passing water. Several times people had mentioned to her that they'd seen her husband perform small acts of heroism at fires, such as rushing into a burning house to help an old woman out. She thought that George's reaction to fires had something to do with the great conflagration during the occupation in '76 which gutted all the houses on the east side of Broadway. Though he was only six, George had, according to family stories, worked along with everybody else to wet down the Van Alen house and save it from the flying red embers. She wondered if, in fighting fires, George felt himself the man he might have been, and she felt both sorry for him and almost proud of him. Judging from the number of bells and the glow that was tingeing the clouds and lightening her window, this would be one of the biggest fires in years, one George wouldn't want to miss. She decided to go and wake him, though it was hard to imagine how he could sleep through such noise.

George slept on the fourth floor front in a room just above hers. She had not entered his room at night in ten years, nor he hers. As she went up the stairs, she had a thought that almost turned her back. Could he possibly misjudge her intentions? Several times since Lady Lydia had died, leaving them more or less alone in the house, he had hinted broadly that he would still like to share a bed with her. Just the thought was so chilling to her that she'd surrounded herself as well as she could with people, moving young Cornelius from the nursery across the hall into his grandparents' bedroom next to hers and bringing Flossie in from the lonely quarters to the nursery. She'd thought, too, of locking her door at night but decided that it was somehow beneath her dignity. Under the circumstances, there would be some logic in her going to him if she ever wanted him again. Well, she'd risk his thinking that. But why? What difference did it make if he missed a fire? Did she have some hidden hope that, drunk as he too often was, George would get in the way of a racing flame or falling wall? No—that couldn't be it; she'd never wished death on anyone although she'd been ashamed of her mixed feelings when her father died. She just didn't want to have George fuss for days over missing the fire.

There was no light in George's room, but it wasn't necessary. Up here you could see across most of the roofs clear to the river, and the light from the fire was brighter. It was also easier to tell just where it was, and, even as she tried to shake George awake, she was suddenly aware that the Van Alen warehouse on Front Street and the *Cathay,* loading at the wharf, were probably in great danger. This certainly was one fire George shouldn't miss. "George! George! Wake up! Fire— down by our wharf!"

George rolled over, made a grab for her, and said, "So you've come to me?"

"No, George, no. There's a fire. Get up!"

"Fire . . . who cares . . . want you," he said, pulling her down on top of him. His words were slurred, the smell of his liquored breath nauseating. She easily pulled free, because there was no strength in him, and said, "Oh, God, George, we could lose everything. Get up!"

"Don' wanna get up," he said, pulling the cover over his head.

She could see that any more effort would be futile. There was in any case no time to waste. She'd have to go herself. She ran down the stairs and into her room. She ripped off her nightgown, pulled on drawers and a chemise and was struggling into the first gown that came to hand, an inappropriate low-cut satin, when young Cornelius came into her room. His eyes were wide with fright. "Mother, what are you doing?" he asked.

"I'm going to the fire. I think our ship's in danger."

"Why doesn't father go? He always goes to fires."

"He isn't feeling well . . . ."

"Let me go. You shouldn't go. You're a woman."

She almost laughed, but she said quite seriously, "No, Cornelius, I want you to stay here with your father—in case he needs you."

"He never stays with me . . . ."

"That's different. I'm always with you."

"But Flossie's here."

Cornelius was eleven, but still short. He was looking more and more like her father, like her, except for the blond hair. She kneeled in front of him. "Hook me up the back, Cornelius," she said. "I have no time to argue. I want you here to . . . to be the man of the house. Flossie wouldn't know what to do if anything happened. Now you will take care of her . . . and your father?"

She'd hit the right note. Cornelius was a serious boy, too serious for his own good she often thought, and he seemed to appreciate her confidence in him. "Yes, I will, mother, but I still wish I could go . . . ."

She pressed his head against her breasts. "Yes, I know. I wish you could, too. Don't think I like this, but you are still a boy, and I'm afraid they might not pay attention to you if something has to be done. Hand me my shawl—there, the one on the chair."

She wrapped the shawl around her head and bare shoulders, blessing the fact that she'd been too tired to put her hair up when she went to bed, and stepped into satin slippers matching the gown, also inappropriate but faster than lacing boots. With Cornelius carrying a candle to light her way, she ran down to the door, kissed the top of his head and stepped out into the night. The streets were surprisingly full of people, mostly men carrying buckets, all moving south and east toward the ominous glow. She decided that the fastest route would be down Broadway to Wall Street and then down Broad Street to the waterfront. She half ran, half walked, her feet hurting without adequate cushion against the sharp bricks and cobbles. Some of the men, as she pushed by them, would challenge her. "Where are you going, Madam? It's no place for ladies up there." But she kept her head down and did not respond. They were right: it was no place for ladies, and even as she ran on she had no clear idea of what she could do when she got there.

It was like running toward a weird and awful dawn. The flickering, fiery light grew brighter and brighter. By the time she reached Broad Street, she could see that whole blocks of buildings were ablaze, their tops sprouting long, waving hairs of flame, and that the yards and rigging of ships beyond were dripping fire. She could hardly squeeze through the crowd—lines of men shouting and singing a kind of chant as they passed buckets . . . carters, their wagons piled with hastily seized goods of all description, calling for way as they grunted their loads toward safety . . . knots of beaver-topped gentlemen, canes in hand, watching and speculating about damages. One of these seized her as she passed, "Here you, stop!" he said. "You can't go any closer . . . ."

"Let me go. I have to," she gasped. "My ship . . . ."

"*Your* ship?"

"The *Cathay.* I'm Mrs. Van Alen."

"Oh, George's wife? Why didn't you say so? Take my word,

Madam, it's not safe, and there's nothing you can do."

"But I have to try," she said. "Let me go."

She broke away, and she could hear him telling his companions, "Imagine a man letting his wife out like that? I always took him for a rotter . . . ."

She plunged on, pulling the shawl tighter to guard her head and shoulders from flying sparks. There was nothing she could do to protect her feet and the hem of her skirt from the muck and water, running ankle-deep through the street. Somehow she managed to reach the river, and she could see that the warehouse was already a smoking skeleton. But the *Cathay* still lay at the wharf, and she ran on, ducking under the bowsprits and chains of other ships, many now aflame. Men were rushing around the *Cathay's* decks smothering spurts of fire with wet tarpaulins; others were humping sacks and bundles up the gangplank. Just as she reached the ship's side, Captain Roberts, leaning over the rail, shouted, "Raise the plank! Cut her away!" The gangplank began swinging up, and a man with an axe, its head gleaming pink in the light, started slashing the ropes tied around piles. She yelled, "Captain Roberts! Captain Roberts!"

He was shocked into sailor's language at the sight of her. "My God, Mrs. Van Alen, what the hell are you doing here?"

"I came to help . . ."

"There's nothing you can do. We've got to get this ship out of here. Go back . . ."

She was out of breath, panting, frightened. The gangplank kept creaking up and up. The axe thwacked through another line. Captain Roberts, shielding his eyes and looking at the fire, called, "No, dammit, you can't go back through that. It's reaching the wharf. You'll have to come aboard. We don't have time to lower the plank. I'll throw a rope ladder. Do you think you can make it?"

Still catching her breath, she didn't reply. There was nothing to do but try. The ladder snaked down the side of the ship which was already a foot or so from the wharf. As she reached for it, her muck-slicked slipper slid, and she went down between the ship and the pilings, feet first. Her skirt ballooned and caught a little air, so that her head stayed above the surface. But the cold, black water enveloping the rest of her body felt so like that other time that she was disoriented—going, going . . . . Captain Roberts dropped over the side like a sack, and, landing beside her, took her in his arms. He wasted no words. "I think we can just reach the ladder," he said. "You grab it and pull, and I'll boost." It was no time for niceties, and his strong hand kept digging into her buttocks as he shoved her up the ladder. It was also no time for the sensations she felt from his touch, but they were simply and strangely there.

On deck, he said curtly, "Get down to my cabin," and turned to his mate, "Get the boat over and take an anchor out for kedging. This tide'll drift us out a little, but we'll still have to kedge. I'll handle the fire crews . . . . Look aloft, lads, fire on the foretopsail yard!"

In the captain's little bunk room off the cabin, Sally found a blanket and wrapped it around her shivering body. Above her she could hear the thud of boots, the creak of the winch. Through the stern windows, she could at first see only the dark river, streaked red with reflected flame. But gradually the ship bore around and brought into view the burning quarter of the town. The fires seemed to be sinking a little under the feeble fingers of water that the pump crews arched over them, but a pink haze of smoke drifted across the whole city, ringing the spires of the churches. She hated to think of looking upon the devastation by day; if not lives, certainly fortunes were drifting away with that smoke, among them their own. Despite the blanket, the shivering would not stop, for it was induced as much by her state of mind as her physical chill.

In the four years since old Cornelius died, all he had feared, and more, had come to pass. The old man's lawyer had done him ill in drawing the will. To be sure, such assets as the river sloops, the *Cathay* and *Canton*, the house on Broadway, the warehouse and wharf on Front Street had been put into trust for young Cornelius, but the license to do business as Van Alen & Son had passed to George with the stipulation that he take his own son into the firm. Cornelius had long since purchased the Broadway place from Lady Lydia in return for twenty percent of the company's stock; the other shares, all in his hands, were distributed to guarantee some income for his daughters and Sally—ten percent to each—and give a nominal ownership of one percent to George, with the rest going into the trust. It was stipulated that both Lady Lydia and Sally have life tenancy of the Broadway house, should they so desire, but Sally was effectively anointed head of the household by a deed of the carriage, horses, slaves and all furnishings in Cornelius' personal possession. The will was a pathetic effort to keep alive the one creation Cornelius prized

—his business—when it would have made more sense under the circumstances to order a liquidation and put the proceeds in trust to give young Cornelius the capital to start a venture of his own when he came of age. With some forty-one percent of the stock under their control and the obvious need for flexibility in the conduct of business, it was not difficult for George and his mother and sisters, guided by John Charles Smith, who for once enjoyed the practice of law, to persuade the trustee to invade the trust when times got hard.

Like a careless hand sweeping away a cobweb, Jefferson's embargo wiped the delicate Van Alen web of commerce off the face of the earth. The *Cathay* was caught in port, and the *Canton* was stuck on the way. Sally would not have known the true state of affairs except for her friendship with the clerks. Once his father was dead, George at last assumed a semblance of responsibility, spending at least his mornings, when he was usually in a vile humor, in the counting room. George never discussed business with Sally and made it clear that he didn't want her, or little Cornelius either, disturbing the clerks. But on one of those afternoons when George stretched a drinking dinner at the Bull's Head into a series of trotting races along the Bowery with Smith, a young and worried-looking clerk named Abner Cole stopped Sally in the hall and begged her to come into the counting room. Talking nonstop, he laid out the books before her. Even with no mind for figures, she could understand at once the problem. Like all the other merchants, Van Alen took full advantage of the government's eighteen-month grace period for paying duty; it amounted to a free loan which was intended to stimulate commerce. Thus, instead of paying duty on the *Cathay*'s last cargo from China, the Van Alen firm had put the money into fitting out the *Canton* and supplying the *Cathay* with trade goods for a new venture. With a little luck—and all merchants thrived on luck—the *Cathay* would return with a new cargo of enough value to pay off the old duty and allow for refitting again by postponing the new. When the *Cathay* couldn't sail, however, the money to meet the duty falling due was not in prospect. So it became a question of borrowing or selling off assets. What disturbed young Cole was that, whereas Mr. Van Alen would have "begged, borrowed, or stolen the money," as he put it, to retain his assets, Mr. George was all for unloading the *Canton* which, as Miss Sally must know, wouldn't bring the price of the lumber in her while the embargo lasted. He didn't know for sure whether the idea was Mr. George's or Mr. Smith's, but they'd been talking about it right here in this room, and Mr. Smith had promised to go to the trustee or the court, if necessary. He just thought that she ought to know.

That time she hadn't been able to do anything about it. She'd gone herself to the trustee, the same fusty old Dutch Federalist lawyer named DePeyster who'd drawn the will, and he had told her, "You must understand, Mrs. Van Alen, that with your husband's reputation he would not be likely to get a loan at all, or, if he did, it would be at a rate of interest so usurious that all the other assets of the estate would be further endangered. It is my duty to protect the interests of the boy, and I'm certain the court would agree with me, if it came to that, in feeling that the sale of a vessel that may never be used is preferable to saddling the estate with unfavorable debt. Lord knows how long this fool in the White House will enforce the embargo. He cares not a whit for commerce. Most of us in New York would rather see war than this, and they tell me the shipping interests of Newburyport and New Haven are already ruined beyond hope of recovery. How often I wish that Burr had shot Jefferson, for he had as much reason, instead of Hamilton . . ."

Nevertheless, Sally, remembering her promise to old Cornelius, decided that she somehow had to get involved to save whatever she could of her son's legacy. She took to dropping into the counting room again when she was sure that George was out and talking to the clerks, particularly young Cole. It was he who unwittingly gave her the idea she needed when George and his brother-in-law began talking, as the embargo wore on, of selling the *Cathay* and the warehouse in order to keep up the dividends Smith needed to pay for his horses and the large salary Geroge allowed himself as compensation for being shortchanged on stock. The occasion was the sailing of Mr. Astor's ship, *Beaver,* for China on orders of the White House. The story around was that it had been chartered by a Chinese mandarin, the honorable Punqua Wingchong, who had written Mr. Jefferson personally with a plea that he be allowed to attend the funeral obsequies of his grandfather and take with him suitable gifts for a grieving family. Jefferson, it was said, thought that letting the Chinese gentleman charter a vessel of his choice would be a gesture of diplomatic good will toward China worthy of making an exception to his embargo. The sailing of anything larger than a coastwise schooner was now such a rare event in New York harbor that, George being out,

Sally urged the Van Alen clerks to run down to the Battery and join the crowds watching the *Beaver*'s departure. When they returned, Abner Cole was laughing and shaking his head, "By George, he got away with it. I'll bet if Mr. Van Alen were alive, he'd have thought of something like that."

"Something like what?" Sally said. "I'm sure he would have said that it was just another of Mr. Astor's strokes of luck. You know how he always called Mr. Astor a lucky fool."

"This was no luck, Miss Sally," Cole said. "You know who that Chinaman really was? He was one of Mr. Astor's clerks, a friend of mine from Hartford—Joe Springer."

"But I heard people saw a Chinese gentleman go aboard," Sally protested.

"Oh, that," Cole said, hardly able to speak for laughing. "They rigged him out in some kind of a coat and funny hat one of Astor's captains brought from China and braided his hair in a pig tail. He kept a scarf over his face because, as he said, it was an old Chinese custom not to let people look upon your grief. But don't tell anybody, Miss Sally; it's a secret between me and Joe on account of knowing each other since we were boys. What a trick on Mr. Jefferson . . ."

What a trick indeed. When the clerks told her about plans to sell the *Cathay*, Sally decided that she would try to make good use of the information. She cornered George and promised him that she would personally get a loan to tide the company over if he would hold onto the ship. He laughed at her, "If I can't get a loan, how could you? And a woman, to boot. Don't tell me you are going to try to sell your body like the heroine of one of your novels? It isn't worth that much. But give it a try. All I care about is the money; I have to keep up with my bar bills, you know."

Sally went right to Mr. Astor's shop in Pine Street. She paced the sidewalk, trying to master her nerves. She felt as jittery as if she were trying to sell her body, but it wouldn't do to let him know. When she could see that he was alone in the shop, she went in, pretending to be in search of a few yards of Chinese silk. As she'd heard, he waited patiently on her himself, bringing down bolt after bolt and spreading it out. "None of them quite suits me, Mr. Astor," she said. "Perhaps I should wait until the *Beaver* returns with a new lot—*if* she does."

"She vill, Madam, she vill. I haf yet to lose a wessel."

"Oh, I wasn't thinking of that, Mr. Astor. I was just wondering what

Mr. Jefferson might do when he hears that your Chinese gentleman has the good, old American name of Springer . . . ."

She thought his huge hands, still holding a bolt of cloth, shook; she was certain that his shaggy brows lifted, as if to let him see better who this woman could be. "Madam, are you suggesting . . .?"

"I'm suggesting nothing, Mr. Astor. I *know.* If it is of any consequence, I may be the only person in New York who does, aside from my informant who, I can assure you, will keep his mouth shut."

"And who are you?"

"Mrs. Van Alen . . ."

"Oh, Cheorge's vife? Ach! Vell, vat haf you on your mind?"

"It occurred to me that you might be willing to lend Van Alen & Son $20,000 until this embargo lifts and the *Cathay* can sail again."

She'd have to say this for Mr. Astor; he made a good recovery. He actually chuckled when he said, "I haf never been blackmailed before, especially by a beautiful voman, but . . ."

"This is not blackmail, Mr. Astor, it's a business deal. You know well the reputation of Captain Roberts and the *Cathay* . . . ."

"Ja. And I know too vell the reputation of Cheorge Van Alen. Now if old Cornelius vas alife . . ."

"If old Cornelius were alive, the Chinaman might have chartered his vessel instead of yours."

Astor laughed outright, and she hurried on, "It won't be George who will be responsible for this; it will be me. I'm a Schuyler, you know, and my brother, Peter, is the Republican congressman and well acquainted with Mr. Jefferson."

"Enough, Madam. You haf made your point. I vill send the money around tomorrow."

Just then the bell tinkled announcing the entrance of a customer, and, offering him her sweetest smile, she said, "Thank you so much, Mr. Astor, for showing me all of those things." Incredibly, he winked at her, and she fled, wishing she could dance instead of walk sedately through the street . . . .

It had taken nearly two whole years since Jefferson had lifted the embargo just before leaving office in March, '09, to assemble and store in the warehouse the goods for China and to haul and scrape and retar the hull of the *Cathay* which had become encrusted with barnacles and fouled with seaweed in her time of idleness. In order to make sure that there would be enough money for a successful

144

venture, Sally sold the horses and carriage she'd inherited. Then, with the barn empty, it seemed logical to sell off the back lot, and this time it was she who went to Mr. DePeyster to beg his consent which he gave readily when she, in turn, agreed that he himself be the purchaser. More reluctantly, since it would mean for them starting a new life at advanced ages, Sally sold the slaves, too. She told herself, and them, that she really had no choice, for there would be no proper quarters for them once the property was gone. It never occurred to her, of course, to sell Flossie who'd lived in the house so long as little Cornelius' nurse that nobody, even George, really thought of her as a slave.

In many ways, these economies proved a blessing beyond the money they generated. She'd never liked riding around in the carriage; it made her feel conspicuous because there were still so few in the city, and it often took longer to get where she was going by carriage than by foot. But after Lady Lydia died, taking the carriage out fell to her as a kind of humane chore to be sure that the horses were exercised. As to the slaves, they all, Miranda included, had demonstrated their loyalty to Lady Lydia and Master George, and she'd never felt mistress of the house as long as they were around. She found to her delight that she could hire a couple of German girls to cook and clean for less than it cost to feed the slaves, and she had little trouble persuading the clerks that, in the interests of keeping the firm going, they should take on the usual clerical chores of sweeping the street and polishing the brass knocker and lamps at the entrance. She did regret losing the trees and garden back of the house but not the flies and stench of the stable. If a few outsiders thought that they saw in these changes a decline in the Van Alen fortunes, more might credit them with shrewdly moving on with the times.

Now, just as all her efforts and planning were about to pay off had come this fire. It was no wonder that, huddling in her blanket, Sally went on shivering. She wished Captain Roberts would come down; she desperately needed advice from a man of decision. She'd never told a soul about her deal with Mr. Astor, but she knew now that she could not bear the burden of trying to pay him back alone. Thank God the *Cathay* was saved. Perhaps Mr. Astor, knowing her for a swift ship, would take her in repayment—and hire Captain Roberts. It seemed the only way out, and she wanted to discuss it with him.

But the captain was in no mood for discussion when finally he burst through the door. He was as wet as she and shaking, too, with chill. He brushed by her and headed for his bunk room, saying, "Begging your pardon, Madam, but I must get into dry clothes." Turning to drop the curtain that provided a degree of privacy, he really looked at her for the first time. "But you are shivering," he said. "You must get out of those clothes. I've a Chinese robe here that will cover you decently."

"No," she said, "no, I'll be all right. I'm beginning to warm up with this blanket."

"No, you're not. If I've learned anything at sea, it's the folly of staying wet any longer than can be helped. Now get in here . . . ladies first . . . and hand me your wet clothes. I'll have the cabin boy build a fire, and we can dry them . . . . The wharf's collapsed, and you won't be able to get safely through those fire lines until after dawn. So there's plenty of time . . ."

Meekly, she did as he bid. It was awkward fumbling off her wet clothes in the cramped dark of the little cubicle; she feared any moment that she might stumble stark naked through the flimsy curtain, and she feared even more the odd thrill of excitement that shivered her at the thought. It was unexpected and unbidden like the sensation she'd felt going up the ladder. She found the robe by touch; it was soft silk, and when she put it on, the slithery feel of it against her bare skin gave her a wicked sense of being more naked than if she wore no clothes at all. She wanted to cower there in the dark, but it wouldn't be fair to keep him waiting. It was evidently a man's robe, for the sleeves dangled over her hands and the skirts swept out like a train. She was grateful that it was full in front with a stiff collar, for the fact that, indeed, within its folds the shape of her body would disappear. When she stepped out into the light of the cabin, dazzling now since he'd busied himself lighting candles on his desk and tapers between the windows to augment the dim light from the oil lamp swinging from the ceiling, she could see that the robe was bright red, embossed with golden dragons. He laughed when he saw her. "If it weren't for your hair, you'd look like a Chinese boy pretending to be his father," he said.

Before she could stop herself, she said, "I feel more like a scarlet lady." Then she blushed, almost welcoming the warm rush of blood to her skin.

146

He laughed again. "You *are* scarlet. From the top of your head all the way down to your toes, I'll bet, if I could see them."

He went to a decanter on his desk, poured two glasses of a goldish liquid and handed one to her. "Rum. Drink it down. Next to dry clothes, it's the seaman's best protection against the chill. Now I'll just go change and join you . . . ."

But he was back in a minute, her dripping things in his hands. "I thought I told you to give me these . . ."

"I forgot . . ."

"Well, we'll just hang them to dry," he said, spreading them out around the sides of the little iron stove where the boy had built a cheery fire. Seeing him handle her drawers, her chemise, her stockings was embarrassing and again strangely provocative. It seemed more intimate than a kiss. She'd never let a man even see her underthings except for that first time with George. He sensed what she was thinking. "Oh, don't be embarrassed," he said. "I've seen all these things before—on my mother's wash line, of course."

She had to laugh then, too. But while he was changing, she wondered, not for the first time, what a man of forty and unmarried did for . . . for *that*. Probably just what George and his friends around New York, married or unmarried, did, and she didn't like to think about it. He came back wearing only clean white pants and shirt which, without a stock, fell open down his chest, revealing a sprig of the same bleached gold hair she'd once noticed on his hands. Was he gold all over and why was she even thinking about this in the midst of a disaster? She had to get hold of herself. "Captain Roberts," she said, "I've been thinking . . ."

"It's Aaron; I thought we settled that long ago," he said. "And what have you been thinking? About how lucky you are to be alive? You are, you know. If an adverse current had swung the ship against the pilings, you'd have been crushed to death, and I with you. I still don't understand what possessed you to come down here."

"I was concerned about the ship, the warehouse . . ."

"Why didn't Mr. Van Alen come instead? Drunk, I suppose."

She didn't answer, and he went over and refilled their cups from the decanter. She had hated the taste of the rum, but she had liked the relaxing warmth that spread outward from her throat, her stomach. Still, she said when he handed it to her, "I . . . I'm not used to drinking . . . ."

"You aren't used to falling into the water in March either, are you? Now you drink this. Captain's orders." She started to sip, and he went on, "It must be hell for you living with that man. I just can't see how a beautiful woman like you can . . . can . . ."

There was the same look of puzzlement and sympathy in his eyes that she remembered from the time of the wedding, and, despite the promise to George that she'd so far kept in good faith, she couldn't now bear to have this man think such thoughts about her. "I only *live* with him," she said. "That's all I've done for ten years."

He smiled then, with his mouth, in his eyes. "You don't know how happy I am to hear that. But what do you do for . . . for . . . ?"

"Women have no need . . ."

"Only if they've never really known . . . But what a waste! . . . Then you've never had a lover?"

She shook her head. This wasn't at all what they ought to be talking about. "Captain . . . Aaron . . . we must be serious . . ."

"Serious about what? The fire? It's an act of God about which we can do nothing now. But we can do something about you," he said, and he went over to the door and threw the bolt and began walking around the cabin blowing out candles.

She knew that she should do something about herself, too. Get up. Scream. Pound on the door. But she just sat there, mesmerized. The rum, the heat of the fire, had more than overcome her chill; they filled her with a delicious languor. And although she knew very little about this man, she felt no fear of him. She was, in truth, more curious than frightened. Over the years, with the exception of that time when he'd kissed her hands, he'd always been most correct in her presence, and yet she'd been ever conscious of his eyes silently reaching out to hers and aware of her own peculiar sensitivity to small details about him that would escape her in other men. Yes, she was curious, had been curious for years, to learn what might happen if ever they were alone together like this. All the little signals that had been coming from her body on this strange night warned her of what it would be, and yet she just sat there and watched and waited.

When the only light was the ruby eye of the stove and the faint fire glow from the windows, he came over and sat beside her on the settee and took both of her hands in his. His sea-gray eyes seemed to pick up whatever there was of light, because she could read in them clearly his intense sincerity, as he said, "Sally—I may call you that?—I've loved you since the day I had to do the hardest thing of my life and marry you to that swine. I've purposely stayed away from you, because I thought I had no right to complicate your life. But now that you've come to me, been brought to me by a true act of God, and now that I know for certain that what I'd hoped is true, I feel free to offer you my love, to show you what it's like being loved."

"How can you feel that way?" she asked. "You know so little about me, and what you know is bad . . . ."

"Not true, Sally, not true. I know more about you than you can imagine. Every time I was in port, I pumped Mr. Van Alen for every detail of your life. It wasn't hard to get him to talk because he was so proud of you. But it was often hard for me to take . . . to think of you wasting your life, suffering . . ."

"I have not suffered, Aaron. You mustn't think that. In any case, it's what I deserve . . ."

"And you mustn't think that. It's that father of yours. Oh, I've heard about him, too. I had a father like that, a minister. No, what you deserve is to be cherished, as beauty should always be cherished . . ."

He was leaning close to her and his lips came down on hers, not hard and demanding but soft and searching. He let go her hands and put his arms around her. His lips explored her cheek, her neck. Gently, he bit the lobe of her ear. She ought to stop this. That almost forgotten feeling of her body separating from her mind, her will, was coming on. Ripples of warm and pleasant sensation ran through her. "Aaron, can't you love me without . . . without this . . .?"

"No, no. This is what I have to offer you, what you've been missing, needing . . ."

His fingers were undoing the cloth frogs that bound the robe chastely over her chest. His lips lingered over the pulse at the base of her neck and moved down to close over the rising nipple of her breast. His hand slid in and along the tingling curve of her stomach and down to finger the hair on the soft mound between her legs. The ripples became waves, and she was awash with wanting more and more. "Oh, Aaron, Aaron, no—it's a sin . . . ."

"There is no sin in loving and being loved," he said. "Let me worship you, as you should be worshiped."

He pulled away her robe and kneeled beside her. His lips examined her stomach, her navel. His tongue became a tongue of fire within the petals of her most private part. She was aware of the thrust of his own desire, straining against the tight shank of his breeches. Swept by these waves, this rising tide, from all the safe moorings of prudery, she wanted for the first time in her life to free this strange male organ to work its will with her, for it was now, surely, the instrument of love. With fumbling fingers she undid the buttons, reached in to spring the hard, warm shaft from its confinement, caressed the silk of its tip and fondled the sack where his manhood lay. Moaning softly, not as a beast but as a man in rapture, he spread her legs, cupped the cheeks of her buttocks and lifted and filled her as she'd never before been filled. It was she who moaned now, moaned and cried out, "O God . . . O God . . ." as everything inside her melted, flowed, dissolved in a heat more ravishing than fire.

When her mind began to work again, she knew that she should feel embarrassed, ashamed, but she didn't. He covered her with the robe, still kissing her and saying, "Sally, oh Sally, I love you, I love you. Even in all those dreams on all those nights at sea I could never imagine it would be so good. And now I know that you love me, whether you know it or not . . ."

"Aaron, I . . ."

"Shh, don't say anything now. What you need is sleep."

Though she felt herself more deeply released and relaxed than she'd ever been, she didn't want to sleep. She wanted to talk, for she also felt closer to Aaron now than she'd imagined she could get to any human being. It was the magic of openness, of touch. What could they hide from each other now?

"I should be ashamed . . ." she started to say.

"Ashamed of what? Of being loved?"

"No, of what I did to you. I don't want you to think that I . . ."

"I don't think anything except that you wanted me as much as I wanted you, and I love you the more for it."

"I'm glad, because I did want you. I needed you."

"Didn't I tell you women have a need?"

"I didn't know . . . I've never been so . . . so . . . transported."

"Then you do love me, Sally?"

"I . . . yes, I must . . . . Oh, I wish I were free."

"But you could be. If what you say is true, you are married only in name. You could get a divorce. I'm sure he gives you reason enough."

"Even his father suggested that once, but I promised that I never would."

"Why, Sally?"

"I have a son. You'd like him if you got to know him. He's not at all like his father. He's solemn and sensitive, and a scandal would hurt him very much. Besides, I'm sure we'd lose the business."

"So you'll sacrifice yourself to your son?"

"Yes. Wouldn't any mother worthy of the name?"

He put his arms around her, buried his face against hers and whispered in her ear, "Sally, oh, Sally, I knew you would say that, and the terrible thing is that I love you for it. But we can meet again, make love again—can't we?"

Into his ear, she whispered, "Yes, Aaron, yes. I think now that I would die if we couldn't."

After that, they got up and dressed, her clothes being dry, and sat in the darkened cabin watching dawn pale the tongues of the dying fires and turn the smoke from rose to black. She told him then everything she knew about the business, sharing her secrets and her fears. He didn't like her idea. He couldn't possibly work for Mr. Astor from what he'd heard of him, and he would be sure to lose the *Cathay* for which he had a love nearly as great as the one he'd just expressed for her. Besides, without the *Cathay* and with the coming on of steam —did she know that a steamboat had gone *up* the Mississippi?—the whole Van Alen enterprise would collapse. He didn't want to see that happen any more than she did, and, together, they might be able to save it. Things weren't quite as bad as she thought. The reason he'd been at the wharf at all was that he'd been saving what he could from the burning warehouse and loading it. He had perhaps half a cargo, and he also had another idea. Mr. Astor had interests in a fur station in Oregon, and the *Cathay* could fill out her holds with furs which he knew were much in demand in China. If Astor would agree to extend the loan and accept the services of Captain Roberts and the *Cathay* in carrying his furs as partial payment, they might get back in business. After all, Astor must be as rich as—what was that old king? "Croesus," she supplied—with the profits he got off that cargo the *Beaver* brought back during the embargo, and in a way he owed it all to her. So he should be reasonable.

She'd try Astor, but she really had to go now; her son would be frantic with worry. As she got up to leave, he went over to his desk, picked up an object and handed it to her. "The dragon—remember?" he said.

"But it's your good luck charm . . ."

"I don't need it any more; you're my charm. It's all I have to give you, and I want you to have something to make you think of me when I'm away . . . ."

"Do you think I need some *thing* for that?"

"No, but I want you to have it."

Going back home through the smoking ruins, the piece of jade cool in the clutch of her palm, she should have been weary from her experiences and depressed by the sights around her, but she wasn't. For her, the Phoenix of hope had arisen from these ashes: somewhere, sometime, she would know love again, and the white-winged *Cathay* would be a bird of promise. As proper to a lady in public, she kept her bubbling emotions under what she thought was control, but she noticed that people were staring at her. No doubt she was a sight with her smudged dress and shawl and mud-encrusted skirts. But passersby were not looking at her clothes at all: they were attracted to her face which, in sharp contrast to the faces of the injured and dispossessed moving aimlessly away from the desolation, wore an expression as radiant as the sun rising at her back.

Chapter *VIII*

The New Year in New York

This being the day for New Year's calls, Congressman Peter Schuyler dressed carefully in Sunday black broadcloth, clean white stock and waistcoat, polished black boots, white gloves. He threw a beaver-trimmed black cape over his shoulders, put on his tall beaver hat, picked up his gold-headed walking stick and paused before going out to examine himself in the full-length, gold-trimmed mirror, the only piece of furnishing he'd brought over from the Partition Street house to his room at Mrs. Keene's. People liked their political leaders to look the part, a piece of wisdom he'd absorbed from watching Matty at work. Matty'd flutter into the Wigwam with not a hair out of place, buttons twinkling like stars, not a speck of dust on his boots or thread of lint on his coat, and perch beside some sweating Irish laborer, plastered with the scum of his work, and literally rub elbows as he joined in a drink. "That Matty Van's a real gent—a grand Grand Sachem if ever there was," you'd likely hear the man say as Matty moved on to make another conquest. Since the Irish had started crowding in, far fewer of the old gentlemen of the Livingston stripe could be seen in the new Wigwam than at Grantling's old Pig Pen although, like himself, they were glad enough to have the Tammany vote when elections rolled around. The place was getting to be so Irish that some now said St. Tammany was a relative of St. Patrick instead of an Indian, but they still wore hats with bucktails on parade. When anybody'd complain about the Irish to Matty, he'd say, "Well, you should welcome them just as we Dutch welcomed you English when you came over." That was the sort of jibe that made the Irish love Matty as much for his wit and tolerance as his elegance.

Peter was on the whole satisfied with his own reflection in the glass. There were some ways in which he couldn't match Matty. At thirty-eight, he'd put on a bit too much weight, and his black hair was thinning so much that it was the despair of his barber. "About all I can do for you Mr. Schuyler is a little pigtail like that one of Jimmy Madison's that'll ruin our trade if it becomes the fashion," he'd said. Well, it was all right to look like the president, particularly when you were of his party and in line for some sort of reward for supporting his war. That had been another bit of wisdom he owed to Matty. It had been risky for him, considering his city constituency, to follow along with Matty and break with DeWitt Clinton on the issue of whether to declare war on England. Like most of New England, the New York merchants wanted either peace or war against the tyrant Napoleon instead of this fight with their main trading partner, and Clinton as mayor and their leader had run on a peace ticket that nearly ousted Madison. But Matty from his perspective in Albany had argued that the East-Coast merchants were looking the wrong way: greater wealth lay in the West where expansion was threatened by a coalition of the British and Indians despite Harrison's victory at Tippecanoe, and the rest of the country would support Madison. As usual, Matty had been right, and, with the battle joined, the city was coming around, too: Mr. Astor had put together a group to take $10 million of the government's $16 million bond issue, and just a few days ago five hundred of New York's leading citizens had subscribed to a banquet in the City Hotel to honor Hull and Decatur for their victories at sea. For his war vote, Congressman Peter Schuyler was now considered more a far-sighted eagle than a hated hawk.

As he went down the steps, Peter thought of knocking at Mrs. Keene's door to see if Matty had come to town for the holiday. Shortly after Frances died, Peter had moved into this house on the corner of Wall Street and Broadway, not only for its convenience but for the company, since it was a favorite stopping place for lawyers like

Matty when they were in the city on business. What with going back and forth to Washington, living in a boardinghouse made more sense than to try to keep his own establishment, and he was sure that his son Francis was better off up on the manor with his brother Jacobus and his family than alone in a house with servants. Maybe the boy would come to like country life and stay on to take up Peter's share of the inheritance which promised to be a good thing now that the steamboats were able to get fresh produce into the New York markets. Thinking about the manor, he wondered how Sally's suit was coming along; he'd have to remember to ask her today. Thinking about the suit, he realized that Matty, who was representing Sally's interests, would certainly be at her place, if he were in town, so he passed by Mrs. Keene's room and went out into the street.

The day sparkled, as so often it seemed to do for New York on New Year's. Bells, somberly saluting the birth of 1813, rang out from the First Presbyterian Church at his back, from Trinity across the street, from St. Paul's up the way. Smaller bells jangled merrily from the harness of horses pulling sleighs loaded with holiday visitors. Down the Broadway, men, singly or in groups, mostly dressed like himself, picked their way gingerly over the packed snow from stoop to stoop along the row of the city's most elegant houses. Mufflered boys with sled in tow or skates slung over a shoulder trudged north toward the canal and the hills beyond. Following the boys' progress with the wistful thought that it would be more fun to go with them than into a lot of stuffy parlors, Peter's eye was taken by the marble façade of the new City Hall, more dazzling white than the snow blanketing the park at its feet. Never having been abroad, he couldn't know for sure whether it was "the handsomest structure of its size in the world," as one New York gazette trumpeted, but, standing out in dramatic contrast to the red brick and wood of the buildings around it, the hall was certainly as magnificent as anything in Washington—and fittingly so, for New York was clearly the first city of the land with a hundred thousand or more people. Peter was amused that the Corporation, after they got that bill of more than $10,000 for the copper roof imported from England, faced the north side in plain brownstone on the theory that there never would be enough citizens living above it to be offended. Either the city's Corporation was crazy, or the commissioners appointed by Governor George Clinton to devise a plan for Manhattan were crazy: the map they'd hired John Randel, Jr., to prepare showed avenues, streets, lots, in a perfect grid pattern running from Fourteenth Street as far north as the village of Harlem.

Maybe Washington Irving was right when he called the city Gotham after some legendary English village where the people avoided the king's taxes by acting demented. But the brownstone back to the City Hall was typical New York thinking, for Peter knew that many of the solid brick facings on Broadway and the Battery, Pearl and Partition, were attached to structures of wood. He wondered if something couldn't be made of that thought and decided to pass it along to Irving if he ran into him at one of the gatherings. Irving was the only man around with his tongue stuck far enough up in his cheek to expose the pretensions of New Yorkers. He'd got away with murder in that book of his, *A History of New York from the Beginning of the World to the End of the Dutch Dynasty* which he tried to pass off as coming from the pen of one Diedrich Knickerbocker. Not surprisingly, since they'd rather laugh than cry over the loss of their colonies, the British made more of the book than the Americans; Irving had a letter from Walter Scott himself who reported that he'd laughed until his sides hurt. Peter wished that his father had lived long enough to read it. Though he never had a sense of humor about most things, Jacobus would certainly have appreciated such a spoof on the Dutch. It was a curious thing, though, that the Dutch around New York were rather puffed up about it, actually calling themselves Knickerbockers; they'd been trying so hard for so long to be English that they'd almost forgotten about being here first. These New Year's visits were just about the last of the Dutch customs that everybody observed. Yes, Irving might do a lot with the thought that modern New Yorkers live behind false façades. He could get away with it, because he was as native as anyone else, having been born right here in William Street, and everybody knew that he loved New York. Peter could hardly believe it when he heard that Irving, of all people, had signed on as a colonel to help defend the city. He rather hoped that they'd keep him at a desk somewhere since Irving, what with his dreaming up stories all the time, had proved a failure in the family hardware business and wasn't much better at the law, according to his mentor, old Hoffman, and probably didn't know one end of a gun from the other.

Peter stepped out to cross Broadway, being careful to look both ways since the snow muffled the hooves of horses and many a man he knew had been run down by a silent sleigh traveling too fast. On the west side of the street, he stood rather uncertainly by the fence around Trinity's graveyard as he tried to make up his mind whether to plunge into his duty calls first or stop by Sally's a few doors down. If he went there, he might never get away. Sally, he knew, would draw the most varied and interesting visitors. Irving and his brother Peter were certain to make her house one of their stops; Mr. Astor, who wasn't much for socializing, always made a point of calling on what he called his "liddle bartner;" old Colonel Trumbull would drop by to admire his portraits of Sally and her son Cornelius hanging above the mantels in place of the Wentworth likenesses which had been packed away; that Captain Roberts with his amusing stories about China would be on hand if the *Cathay* were in port; and Matty and Billy Van Ness if they were in town and, of course, Mr. Burr. Strange to see Mr. Burr in this old Federalist house, but Sally had changed it so much that it was hardly recognizable. In addition to putting new paintings on the walls, she'd sold off Lady Lydia's heavy English furniture and replaced it with pieces of the graceful French Empire style that Duncan Phyfe was turning out in his workshops on Partition Street, not far from where Peter had lived, and the food this day would be served on delicate Chinaware brought back in the *Cathay* instead of the old Wedgwood. There was a French atmosphere about Sally's house now that went well with her looks and their heritage, and it could be one reason that Burr after his long stay abroad would feel so at home there that he'd probably stay all day, acting as an unofficial host for Sally—"my Sally," as he called her—since George would be out making his own rounds that would no doubt end up in some bar or cathouse.

Now that Burr was out of politics you had to feel sorry for him and glad that he had a person like Sally to turn to. He'd been pathetic enough when he'd come sneaking back into New York a year or so ago under the name of Monsieur Arnot and with only ten dollars in his pocket, but when the ship bringing Theo up from Charleston to visit him vanished without a trace, he'd seemed inconsolable. Not surprisingly, because he was a good lawyer, notoriety had restored Burr's practice—$12,000 in the first year, some said—almost as soon as news of his arrival got out, but he could still be seen every day standing at the edge of the Battery and looking hopefully south toward the sea. Without Sally, Burr often said, life would have no meaning for him, since even his grandson, Aaron Burr Alston, his little "Gampy," had been taken from him by illness shortly before Theo sailed on the ill-fated *Patriot*.

An urge determined Peter's direction. He hadn't had a cigar since breakfast, and he knew that Sally was the one hostess who would tolerate his smoking. Odd, he thought, Sally's tolerance of smoking, and some said chewing as well, was one of the things that had made Frances so certain that Sally was not a good influence on him, or anybody. It was a thought that made Peter feel guilty, since poor Frances had died in an effort to bear him another child, but he had felt freer and more alive since she'd gone. Nobody but a Livingston was good enough for her company, and the city of New York was nothing but a large swill for the feeding of its ravenous pigs. She couldn't believe that a woman with such a notorious reputation as his sister had upcountry would have the nerve to parade the streets in a carriage even though she said it was only to exercise the horses. It was a good thing in her view that he, Peter, wasn't a common Van Alen. Money, especially when it was earned in a traitorous manner, was no substitute for breeding. And on and on—no wonder his father had considered her a fine daughter-in-law. The damnable thing had been that she was a beauty; the more damnable thing had been that, in the few gropings she permitted in the dark, he had never had a sense of possessing her beauty. Well, he didn't need the Livingstons anymore, and it was a pleasure to be able to go to Sally's without lies or apologies.

Peter took off his hat, plucked a cigar from its convenient storage place in the band, bit off the end and clamped it between his teeth. He'd get a light in Sally's house, for the fires would surely be burning this day. At the door, one of the smiling German girls took his hat and cloak, and he thought about how pleasant it was not to be greeted by a slave. It wasn't that Peter exactly agreed with those abolitionists, most of whom seemed to come from up Boston way where they didn't have slaves anyway, but the idea of one man's owning another gave him an uneasy feeling, and it clearly made a mockery of so much of the rhetoric about democracy of which he himself was increasingly guilty. On the second floor, Peter went right past the parlor, from which there came a babble of conversation, and the dining room, where the clink of glasses meeting in toasts could already be heard, and continued on up the stairs. Before he got trapped in talk, he wanted to have a look at his namesake in the nursery.

Peter Schuyler Van Alen. Just a little more than a year old and giving promise of being a handsome bearer of the name what with Sally's black hair and those sea-gray eyes that must have come from some remote ancestor. Sometimes Peter thought that Sally had named the boy after him and asked him to stand up as godfather at the christening in Trinity just to keep him from prying. He still could not imagine how Sally could stomach George even for the sake of procreation. She ought to have been content with Cornelius who, at going on thirteen, was all that anybody could ask for in a son. Despite his short stature, Cornelius was a real little man, something like Matty Van Buren had been. Cornelius had balked at staying on in school and insisted on going into the company's counting room to take the place of a clerk who'd signed on in the militia. Some said young Cornelius knew more about the business than his father—not, Peter had to concede, a difficult thing to believe.

Flossie was in the nursery, rocking by the baby's pen and busying her hands with sewing. The sight of Flossie, gone to fat and graying at something like thirty-five, was an exception to Peter's feeling about slaves. She reminded him of the good days on the manor when he was young and frequently full of the devil and would tease the life out of her, as he would his own sisters. Flossie was particularly susceptible to stories about ghosts and goblins, and this morning he said, "Morning, Flossie. Happy New Year! Glad to see the goblins didn't get you in the night . . . ."

"Now you stop that, Mr. Peter. I don't believe in that nonsense no more."

"Ah, but weren't those days when you did grand? Do you ever wish that you were still back on the manor, Flossie?"

"No more. Not now that most of them has gone to the Lord—Miz Catharina and Miz Rebecca and my Pappy and Mammy and . . . I do wish, though, I could see Master James."

"He's almost eighteen—can you believe it, Flossie? A big boy, bigger than his father. I wanted Jacobus to send him down here to Columbia, but he's going to Princeton over in New Jersey to become a Presbyterian minister."

"Must take after his granddaddy. Lordy, I never heard such preaching, standing up there on his toes and lookin' down on us sinners. He was a holy man for sure . . . ."

"I'm surprised to hear you say that after the way he treated your Miss Sally."

"I said holy; I didn't say human . . . ."

Peter laughed. "I guess there is a difference, Flossie. How's my boy?"

"He healthy but not as smart as Mr. Cornelius . . ."

"Now, Flossie, how do you know that?"

"I jus' know—the way he smile, smile, smile all the time. Anybody knows anythin' isn't allus smilin'."

Peter laughed again. "My, you're turning into a philosopher, Flossie. But I think a year is a little early to make such a judgment. He's probably just happy because you keep his stomach full. And see that you go on doing so, because I think I'd rather have a happy namesake than a smart one."

Peter went over to the fire and picked out an ember to light his cigar. As he took his first satisfying puff, Flossie said, "You get out of here with that thing, Mr. Peter. You'll poison the baby."

"All right. All right, Flossie . . ."

Going downstairs, Peter reflected on the irony that only a slave would feel free to talk as Flossie did; a servant would fear for her job. True freedom, freedom of the spirit, was not a state that could be established by law. He'd have to use that thought to get Mr. Burr going unless there was some other stimulating topic. But there was. Entering the dining room to get a cup of whiskey punch to go with his cigar, Peter found a knot of men, among them Burr and James Roosevelt, the hardware man, and that Captain Roberts, engaged in a spirited discussion of naval affairs, prompted by the banquet still fresh in their minds.

"I guess I must be losing my stomach for politics, but I couldn't eat a bite when I saw DeWitt Clinton after all his ranting against the war standing up there between the commodores and puffing himself up over organizing such a feast," Burr was saying. "What a waste! Imagine what it must have cost to have that transparency of the battles painted on that mainsail they unfurled behind the dais and that artificial lake with the miniature frigate, not to mention all the wine and food that went down all those throats. Why, we could have fitted out a real frigate for the expense . . . ."

"I don't agree. I think they deserve every honor for going out so successfully against such superior force," said Roosevelt, peering

160

down at Burr through his steel-rimmed spectacles. "I had the good fortune to talk directly to Decatur who told me he owed his victory to the rapid fire the American seamen have perfected. When the survivors of the *Macedonian* came aboard the *United States,* they told Decatur they thought his ship afire from the constant blaze of his guns. He said Hull had almost the same experience when the *Constitution* reduced the *Guerriere.*"

"Granted, granted," Burr said, "but we wouldn't have to face superior force if Jefferson hadn't done his best to scrap the navy by going against his admirals' advice and building those gunboats instead of frigates. I could tell from being in Europe then that his shortsighted policy was much appreciated both in France and England. Why, there was even a joke about it that made its way across the water. You remember when one of those gunboats broke loose in a gale and landed in a cornfield? According to the way I heard it, some wag—a Federalist no doubt—got up a toast: 'To Gunboat Number Three: If our gunboats are no use on the water, may they at least be the best on earth!' . . . Ah, but here's the congressman! What do you think about all this Peter? Are we going to get a navy now?"

"If we do, we're going to have to concentrate on putting boats into the lakes to support our Canadian operations," Peter said.

"I doubt your constituents would like to hear that," Burr said. "Sounds like you're in bed with Matty and his Albany gang . . . ."

"Not at all," Peter replied. "I happen to believe that the main purpose of this war is to open the West, and if we could liberate Canada in the process, so much the better . . . . What is your opinion, Captain Roberts?"

"I'm not much for politics, but while we're talking about the banquet, I think there's a young sailor in New York who should have been right up there with the commodores, though he's not in uniform . . ."

"Who's that?" someone asked.

"Fellow named Vanderbilt—Cornelius Vanderbilt. Big, raw young lad—couldn't be more than eighteen but he's running a ferry service over to Staten Island by day with a fleet of periaguars and coining money at night taking supplies to the offshore forts. But that isn't what I mean. I happened to be down on the Whitehall wharf the day Admiral Cockburn was pounding away at the fortifications at Sandy Hook with so many guns we could hear the thunder of them over the shriek of a northeast gale. Well, a young officer comes running down looking for someone to sail him out to the fort and everybody had excuses, not that I blame them, except for this young Vanderbilt who said, 'I'll take you if you don't mind sailing under water.' He not only took him out but brought him back again in the same storm after the British sheered off, and from the looks of them they *had* been under water. An old fellow standing next to me said, 'By Christ, I wouldn't go out in that for love nor money. Guess Corneel's the only one who could have made it.' It was some piece of sailing, I can assure you, and he ought to be known for it."

While Roberts was talking, Peter studied him. In view of his own corpulence and thinning hair, he was a little envious that the man had changed so little in the sixteen years since they'd met at Sally's wedding. He seemed straighter, thinner, harder, if anything; his skin had a healthy leathered look from exposure to the elements, and his thick mane of hair was sun-bleached to a tone of old gold. But what fixed Peter's attention were his eyes: sea-gray and hauntingly familiar. Where had he seen such eyes before? After his story, the captain excused himself to join the ladies, and Peter went with him. In the hallway, Captain Roberts put a restraining hand on Peter's arm and said, "Not being a constituent, Mr. Schuyler, I hesitate to seek favors..."

"Go right ahead! I know how much you have done for my sister."

"Well, what's been said in there about the navy is right. Thank God for a few small victories, but the British are still going to keep us merchantmen bottled up in port until the war is over. I think our only hope is to go privateering, and I'd like to offer the *Cathay* if you could use your influence to get me some armaments and letters of marque...."

"What do George and Sally think of this? You'd be risking their ship, you know."

"As to George, I can't tell you. It's hard to get to him when he's sober enough to talk these days. But Sally's all for it. She knows as well as I do that they'll lose the *Cathay* to their creditors unless it can bring in some prize money."

"Well, if Sally's for it, so am I. I'll do what I can .... Ah, here she is!"

Seeing them in the hall, Sally came out from the parlor, arms outstretched. It was hard for Peter to believe that his little sister was thirty-three and thrice a mother. Her waist was still so small you could almost circle it with your hands, and her skin as smooth and

unblemished as fine porcelain. The fact that Sally could go on looking so innocent and apparently undamaged by what she believed was
her jaded life—she was seldom seen in church and often in the
theater, for instance—had always galled his Frances. Sally took their
hands in each of hers and said, "Two of my favorite people! Where
have you both been hiding? By the punch bowl, I'd guess . . . ."

Sally gave Peter a sisterly peck on the cheek but bestowed upon
Captain Roberts a smile so intimate and warm that Peter was almost
embarrassed to have seen it. "Well, come in, come in," she said. "Mr.
Irving's here and Matty and Miss Fish—you've met Alexandra,
haven't you, Peter? And I've a surprise for you—George's niece
Gwendolyn and her husband, Mr. Downing. They've just got out of
England on diplomatic exchange, and they're trying to convince Mr.
Irving that he should go there as soon as the war is over, because his
works are so popular there . . . . But look at Gwendolyn, can you
believe she's had five children?"

Like Sally herself, Gwendolyn de Lancey Downing, a year or so
younger, was one of those women whose beauty seemed to deepen
with years and experience. She'd inherited the majestic height of
Lady Lydia and old Cornelius, but her features, noble and classical,
must have come from the other side of her family. It was appropriate,
Peter knew, for Gwendolyn to be the only one of George's family
here since her husband, a genial, florid man, had been named consul
to Liverpool for his Republican services. Irving, looking hopelessly
unmilitary despite his blue uniform coat with its dangling gold epau-
lets, was lecturing the Downings in a voice that, as usual, commanded
the attention of the room: "You are right, but it's a shame—a shame,
I say. To think that I must go to England to live by my pen. But
American publishers have no desire to pay an author here when they
can reprint the works of such as Byron and Scott for the cost of ink
and paper. Sometimes I despair of our ever having a literature
. . . ."

Matty, who had been talking to Alexandra Fish, brought the young
lady over as soon as he saw Peter enter the room. Peter had met her
before, and he was delighted to see her again. Though not a striking
beauty, she had eyes of the brightest blue and a smile of melting
sweetness. Peter suspected that she must have intelligence, too, or
she wouldn't be a favorite of Sally's. She curtsied and said, "My
goodness—a state senator *and* a congressman all to myself. I must be

the luckiest girl in New York. I wish I could think of some way to take advantage of it."

"You might send one of us to get you some punch," Peter said. "I suggest it be Matty since I outrank him. Anyway, your charms are wasted on him. He's a married man, you know."

"I thought you were married, too, Mr. Schuyler."

"My wife passed away . . ."

"I'm so sorry," she said, putting a hand on his arm. That instinctive touch of sympathy, the way her eyes clouded, moved him. He realized that he yearned for a woman's comfort.

"It was a number of years ago," he said. "I'm over it now—the worst of it. But what do you do with yourself, Miss Fish?"

"Too little, I'm afraid. I'm living at home, and I think my parents fear they have an old maid on their hands."

"How is that possible? Why, you can't be more than . . ."

"Twenty-three. My sister was married at nineteen, and . . ."

"Would you believe me if I said I'm glad you weren't?"

She blushed prettily and dropped her eyes. "I wasn't fishing for that, Mr. Schuyler. I . . ."

"It wouldn't matter if you were . . . . Here's Matty with the punch . . . . May I call on you one day, Miss Fish?"

"Yes. Oh, yes."

When he'd handed Miss Fish her glass of punch, Matty said, "I hate to break this up, but, now that you're here, Peter, I must have a word with you and Sally—privately."

Peter wasn't sure why Matty would want him to be in on this conversation since it would probably be about Sally's claims to the Schuyler estate. All things considered, he'd been treated very fairly by his father who had left him a third of the land, mostly of course in undeveloped woodland. He'd been summoned home when Jacobus had collapsed giving one of his increasingly violent sermons, but he hadn't been able to get there before his father died of what the doctor said was apoplexy. He had, however, stayed on for the reading of the will, which also alloted his brother Jacobus a third, and Catharina and her descendants another third. It was not surprising, but sad, that the will contained a codicil in Jacobus' own handwriting and attested by his attorney specifically excluding "Sarah Schuyler Van Alen, my daughter whom I hereby disown for sins in violation of the covenant with God." Peter had felt obliged to report the fact but not the wording to Sally, who had taken it with a philosophical shrug, "I never expected anything anyway." But complications had arisen a year or so ago when the cholera struck, carrying off Rebecca, her husband, her son, and Catharina, who had been nursing them. No matter what her differences with the family had been, this had been a stunning tragedy for Sally. As she'd confessed tearfully to Peter, she had been hoping, with their father gone, to reach a reconciliation even though brother Jacobus, following too closely in his father's footsteps, and his wife, whose brother was married to Rebecca, were doing their best to prevent it. It was only then, with all such hope gone, that Sally asked Matty Van Buren to look into the disposition of her mother's property.

Sally led them down to the counting room where, presumably, they'd be alone, since New Year's, like Fourth of July, was a holiday for all the city's clerks and workmen. However, they found young Cornelius sitting up to the bench, legs twined around the stool, brows drawn together in a frown of concentration, pen scratching busily. Sally was about to send him up for some refreshment when Matty said, "He might as well stay. What I've got to tell you concerns him in the long run, and I can see he's already playing a man's part. Good for you, Cornelius. I started clerking at your age, too—in a law office—and I've never regretted getting a jump on my work."

"You're undermining me, Matty," Sally said. "I wanted him to stay on in school, go to college. I only gave in because of the war, but when it's over . . ."

"Mother, I *like* working," Cornelius protested.

"Well, we'll talk about it later. What's the bad news, Matty? I know it must be bad, because I've had nothing else from Kinderhook these last few years."

"I guess it depends on how you look at it," Matty said. "I'm sure we could go into the courts and claim your mother's share of the estate for your children with a good chance of getting it—but not without a fight. Jacobus is evoking primogeniture to assert that, Rebecca and her family having died in a common tragedy, your mother was left without legitimate heirs and it falls back to him as first son."

"But see here," Peter broke in, "Cornelius and little Peter are heirs in fact—so is Sally, for that matter."

"I know, I know. But since your father specifically and by name excluded Sally from any and all provisions of his will, Jacobus and his attorneys argue with some logic that it was his *intent* to exclude her heirs as well. Either the old man or his lawyer did make a mistake in not so stipulating, so we have a case. The reason I wanted you here, Peter, is that you might wish to join in the suit since Jacobus has no intention of dividing Catharina's share with you or Janet."

"Leave me out of it. I've enough and, as you know, Jacobus and Martha are caring for my son," Peter said. "But I do think Sally ought to fight it."

Sally buried her face in her hands and said in a voice so low that they could hardly hear her, "I won't. If they don't want me to have it, I don't want any part of it. There's already been too much hurt."

Peter went over and put his hand on her head. "I know how you must feel, Sally, but you have to think of Cornelius here or—or little Peter up there. It's their *right.*"

"Please, I don't even want to talk about it. It's New Year's, and we're supposed to be happy, and I have a house full of guests."

"I'm sorry, Sally, but it's the only time I could get away from Albany," Matty said.

"Oh, it's not your fault, Matty. How can I blame you for all that's happened? Just forget the suit."

"Sally, you *can't,*" Peter said.

Sally couldn't help herself; she started to cry. She didn't really care about the land or Jacobus either—he'd been a brother so much older that she'd hardly known him. But the idea of having to go to court to prove who she was, who her children were, gave her a feeling of rage and helplessness that she could express in no other way but tears. Matty and Peter stood awkwardly by, but Cornelius ran to his mother, kneeled in front of her, pulled her hands away from her face and said, "Don't cry, mother, please don't cry. I don't want any old land. I'll take care of you . . ." Then, looking up at the men, he said, "Go away. I'll take care of my mother."

The men quietly withdrew, but out in the hall Peter said, "I still think she's making a mistake."

Matty shrugged. "Well, I've done what I came here for. Now that I'm in New York, I've got to hurry and mend a few fences."

"Me, too," Peter said. "You might as well be off in a foreign country as down in Washington from the way these New Yorkers think."

As he went out the door, Peter heard Cornelius' feet striking the stairs, his still soprano voice calling, "Uncle Aaron . . . Uncle Aaron . . . Mother isn't feeling well, she wants to see you . . . ."

Walking down Broadway toward his next stop, Peter found the pieces of a growing puzzle falling neatly into place. Captain Aaron Roberts. Of course. Those eyes so like his namesake's, that smile of Sally's, that call for his comfort echoing in his ears. Why the devil, the little devil. Not that he could blame her with all she'd had to put up with. Still, it could be embarrassing to a politician if it came out that his godson was a bastard, and his sister a . . . what? Had his father, had Frances, been right about her? All that nonsense about sin aside, how could an intelligent woman who was becoming a leader of New York society, whose son would head one of the city's great merchant houses, take such a risk? And with nothing but a sea captain without, as far as he knew, family or fortune. No question the man was uncommonly attractive, and there was always an air of mystery and daring about those fellows who sailed off to the far points of the compass, braving wind and weather, but sea captains were notoriously errant, morally and physically. Oh, Sally, Sally, what a fool you can be! She must love him very much, but love, from what Peter had seen of it, was a dangerous thing. He was glad that he'd never experienced that kind of fool-making love. Or was he . . . ?

His thoughts turned to Alexandra Fish, who had been so warm and so, when he thought about it, forward. Could a proper young woman from a proper Federalist family *really* . . . . Well, God knows no family had been more proper than the one in which Sally and he had been raised, and yet she obviously . . . A man his age and with his responsibilities shouldn't be troubled by thoughts like this. He had to pull himself together and think what he'd say when he called on James Kent, the chief justice of the state's supreme court whose power and knowledge of the law had to be respected even though he was a Federalist, and he'd have to put in an appearance at Chancellor Livingston's townhouse despite the fact that the old boy was said to be ailing up in Clermont, and then he'd have to drop by the Wigwam for at least a quick drink, and then . . . but, damn, none of that interested him at all. He wanted to have what Sally had got and wanted her courage to grasp it. He'd get through the rest of this day somehow, and tomorrow he'd call on Miss Fish. Maybe this could be the new year of his life too.

Chapter *IX*

The Calling of the Lord

In the summer of '17 when young James Schuyler came knocking at her door on Broadway, Sally thought it part of a benign providence that seemed to be blessing the affairs of all New York these last two years. With Napoleon deposed, peace had come to Europe as well as America, and commerce, on which the existence of Van Alen & Son and other New York mercantile houses depended, was once again thriving; from a low of $500,000 in 1813, the port of New York revenues had shot up to $14 million in the first year after the peace and were still rising. While it had for long been the major shipping center on the eastern seaboard, New York was likely to become the gateway to the world for the whole expanding West now that Governor DeWitt Clinton and his commission had turned the first spadeful of earth for the Erie Canal. What political writers were calling "an era of good feeling" had come in with President Monroe. Though one of the Virginia dynasty, he was married to a Kortwright of New York and would therefore retain a lively interest in the progress of the city. With all this happening, New York's population, which had remained as stagnant as its commerce during the war, was swelling, and there was a slow tide of new construction moving north, flattening hills, filling the Collect, burying the canal, chewing up the trees. To Sally there was no more personal and dramatic sign of a changing, growing city than the work Mr. Astor's people were doing at Richmond Hill to turn its six acres into building lots. For sentimental reasons, she went out to watch the day they inched the stately old structure, groaning and trembling on sliding ways, down to the level of Varick Street so that they could cut away the knob on which it had stood. When she told Mr. Burr about it, thinking it might make him sad, he just laughed and said, "Astor must have found the old plan I drew up for development of the place. I always knew New York was coming my way, and I'd hoped to profit by it, but I guess fortune wasn't my fate."

Fortune did, however, seem again to be the Van Alen fate. After the *Cathay*'s voyage had cleared the house's debt, thanks to Astor's furs and a heavy load of sandalwood, Astor had approached them to join in his consortium to buy bonds to support the war. He had come to Sally instead of George because, as he said, "You haf a leffel head." With that little twinkle in his eyes that some found disconcerting when doing business with him, Astor went on, "You vunce told me you were not blackmailing me but offering a business deal. Vell, I am not selling batriotism but brofit. If ve lose this var, ve lose everything; if we vin, ve gain everything." With a hunch that some of the Astor luck might be coming their way, Sally had used every means of persuasion, including a threat to leave and take Cornelius with her, thereby breaking up the firm, to get George to go along, and the $80,000 they'd subscribed had been redeemed at $120,000 in the year after the war—enough to go into Aaron's scheme to compete with the Black Ball Line in the new and exciting packet service to Liverpool.

Aaron, dear Aaron, what would she—would any of them—have done without him in those dark days of the war? He'd risked his life for them, dodging the British blockade in pursuit of prizes. Though he'd brought back just enough to keep them going, she'd waited out his voyages with an anxiety so acute that she was actually glad when the *Cathay* was caught off Sandy Hook by a British frigate and reduced to such rubble that she had to be beached. All that mattered to her then was that Aaron had survived and that he could no longer put himself in jeopardy at sea. Even the wound he got was in her view a romantic one, a scar that lifted a corner of his thin lips into a perpetually superior and sardonic smile, an expression with which he had every right to greet the world. Seeing more of him than she'd ever hoped these last few years, she'd finally come to know him, to understand why she had trusted him with her love. Unlike old Cornelius, who protested too much, Aaron *was* a simple sailor, a man so in love with the sea that it seemed a happy stroke of nature's art to have painted it in his eyes. He had an artist's devotion to his calling: give him a ship to sail, and he was wholly without ambition or avarice, those twin ties by which most men seemed bound. Claiming little for himself but the right and ability to do his work, he claimed as little from others. There was no sea he was afraid to cross, nor any land he feared to leave. If he was not a man for holding, neither was he a man who held. Life and love were for him acts and experiences rather than prizes or possessions. Not given to introspection or philosophizing, he seldom articulated his attitudes; he simply lived them. From Sally's point of view, Aaron's ability to let go, to cast off when the time came, made possible their love, because she could never be his to possess.

She was most fully aware of this when he came back from China to discover the child named Peter Schuyler Van Alen. "I'm sure he's my son," he said quietly when he first looked at the baby, and her heart flipped with fear of what he might do.

"How can you be sure? I am a married woman, you know," she said, testing.

"Well, he does have my eyes . . . but most of all I know you: you couldn't have done that . . ."

"Oh, I love you for saying so, Aaron. No, I couldn't have done that. But I may have done worse."

His face flushed—with anger? . . . jealousy? "What do you mean? What are you trying to say?"

"I . . . I . . . Well, you remember the night of the fire? . . . I'd gone to George's room to waken him, and he was in such a stupor that all he could remember next day was that I'd been there . . . well, when I knew I was with child, I let him think . . . isn't that terrible of me? I'm so ashamed."

He took her in his arms then and stroked her and said, "Poor Sally, you must have gone through hell."

"I did. You were gone, and I had nowhere to turn. I can only thank God that George believed me, but it's been difficult since."

He jumped up and began pacing back and forth, pounding a fist

170

against the palm of his other hand. "The devil! The devil! If he's doing what you're saying, I'm going to call him out. And then I'm going to take you and my son out of here and start a new life. I can't bear the thought—"

"Don't worry, Aaron. I can manage him. As I told my brother Peter once, the poor man isn't worth challenging. I explained to him that something had got into me that night with the shock and fear of the fire, but that my real feelings had not changed. All I have to do to keep him away is threaten to leave him, and he knows he couldn't carry on without me and Cornelius. It's pathetic in a way."

"It's not pathetic; it's tragic. I'm going to take you away, I tell you, even if I have to do it by force."

"Take me away to what, Aaron, to where? I have another son, you know, Cornelius, and it would ruin his life. And what would it do to your son—our son—if all this came out? It could ruin us too . . . ."

"How? We love each other and want to be together—"

"But we wouldn't be together, would we? Little more than we are right now, I'd guess, because you *must* go to sea. I know that, and I respect it, just as you must respect that I have to be a mother to my sons."

He stopped his pacing, kneeled before her and buried his face in her lap. "Oh, God in heaven, how I love you, Sally! I think you know me better than I know myself. It's true . . . I could never give up the sea—"

"I know that; it's in your eyes. And I think I love you for that, too. You are a rare man to want no more than to use the talent that's been given you. I'm only sorry about . . . well, about the name . . . ."

"The baby's name? What's in a name? I know he's mine, and I'll watch over him like a hawk."

"When you're here . . ."

Then he was laughing—a full, rich laugh. "Oh, Sally, Sally, you're priceless. What is it I've done to deserve you?"

"Nothing but being you. Now, come with me—up to my bedroom. Flossie's out taking the baby for a walk, and Cornelius is in the counting room, and George is God-knows-where, and we've been wasting a lot of precious time with talk . . ."

And so it had been settled, and so it had continued. When he was in port, "Uncle Aaron" was around the house more than Father George. Young Cornelius found him fascinating and would spend hours plaguing him with questions—not the questions of a romantic boy about life at sea but shrewd inquiries of a budding merchant as to where such and such an item could be found and what it would fetch in such and such a port. Sally could understand her son's interest as a kind of romanticism because of her own fascination with the intricacies of commerce, but it did seem unnatural in a boy so young. Coming out of one of his sessions with Cornelius, Aaron siad, "I swear that boy was born old, but, considering everything, you're lucky to have him. The day he takes over the firm, Astor'll have to look sharp to stay alive." For Peter, Aaron was simply a source of play —a real live hobby horse. For George, Aaron's attentive presence provided welcome relief from such occasional husbandly duties as escorting Sally to the staid second tier of boxes at the Park Theater when one of those interminable Shakespearean tragedies she liked was playing. For society in general, Captain Roberts' personal loyalty to members of the Van Alen family who had so long employed him was little more than might be expected of a good servant.

If Sally and Aaron were committing a sin, they tried not to think about it and seldom discussed it. When Sally did bring it up on one occasion, Aaron said, "My idea of sin is something that hurts somebody else. Who's being hurt?" In the circumstances of their lives, it was a very reasonable and comforting thought. Their love was not depriving George of the traditional comforts of a wife, as adultery might do in other cases, nor even of self-respect in view of their discretion and George's own sacrifice of respectability to profligacy. As to the boys, Aaron was not only a surrogate father but his supporting love undergirded Sally's own ablity to love them. She could see it clearly in Peter, growing up so sunny in contrast to her serious Cornelius. Poor Cornelius. Unwittingly, she'd overloaded him with that desperate love of the loveless, and her fear now was that Aaron had come into her life too late to lift the burden from his shoulders.

Whatever the emotional effect, Aaron's involvement in their lives was a great help to Cornelius in a practical way. At sixteen, at a time when he should have been thinking about going to Columbia or perhaps Yale, Cornelius had already moved off the high clerk's stool and into his grandfather's empty chair at the partner's table. The move was more than a physical matter of making way for the clerk returning from service on the Canadian front. Although, as head of the firm, George was required to sign all the important papers, he had taken, as he had with his father before, to letting young Cornelius handle most affairs. "Good training for the boy," he'd say to anyone who questioned him, and to friends he'd confess, "I find poring over all those letters and ledgers a dreadful bore. In any case, what's the use of having money if you have to work all day?" So it became common when other businessmen would approach George Van Alen at the theater or race track or City Hotel for George to say, "Ask my son; he has all the answers." But Cornelius didn't have all the answers, though he had all the facts at his fingertips, and he relied on advice from Sally and increasingly Aaron to steer his father and the firm in the right direction. It was Aaron who came up with the answer to the problem created by the loss of the *Cathay*.

"Forget the China trade," he said. "We're getting too much competition from Astor and the Boston houses who have picked up on my idea of loading furs in the Northwest. What we ought to think about is what Isaac Wright & Son and the Thompsons are planning with their Black Ball Line of packets. They've already got the *Pacific* and *Amity* in service and the *William Thompson* and *James Cooper* almost off the ways. They're going to have a sailing for Liverpool the first of every month, regular as a clock . . ."

"But with all those ships, we couldn't get any business, Uncle Aaron."

"We would, and I'm sure of it," Aaron said. "You'll be surprised at how many people will want to go over to Europe now that peace has come and even more surprised at how many people over there will want to come here and take advantage of the way America is growing. And then there's all the material we haven't been able to get these last five years—Irish linens, British woolens, Swiss clocks, French wines. Believe me, merchants will be standing in line for this kind of service. And you're forgetting that with Downing back at his post in Liverpool and his own daughter staying right here in the house, we could expect some favors."

It was a good point. Sally had been surprised and flattered when the Downings came gravely calling just before they left and asked if their ten-year-old Amelia could stay with her. They thought British schools good for the boys, but they felt that the New York atmosphere was—well, freer and more encouraging for a girl. They'd thought of leaving her with her grandmother for whom she was named, but Amelia, too long a widow, was growing as crotchety and set in her ways as Lady Lydia had been and would probably make a little girl's life miserable. The Smiths were out of the question, because they were mixed up with that worthless, racy set. But they were pleased with the people Sally knew—that Mr. Irving, the only American author anybody'd ever heard of on the other side of the water; and Mr. Van Buren, a "real comer in the party," according to Downing; and Mr. Astor and Congressman Schuyler. "You have the liveliest salon in New York. I'd be proud if Amelia grew up to be like you," Gwendolyn had said, and Sally had been so deeply touched by the compliment that she couldn't say no. In truth, it was a pleasure having a little girl around the house, someone to take shopping who could get excited over the laces and ribbons and scents and things that were part of being female. Sally supervised the girl's studies at home, much as Mr. Burr had done for her, but sent her out with Flossie as chaperone for the piano and dancing lessons which she wished she had had. She'd never thought of any business advantage in caring for Amelia—only that it was a joy, having been lost to so much of her own family and so unwelcome to so much of George's, to feel that she was part of larger family again. Still, Aaron was right: she had no doubt that Henry Downing, as consul, could and would be influential in seeing that business went to a Van Alen line.

"How could we afford the ships?" Cornelius wanted to know.

"Sell your bonds," Aaron advised. "I stopped by the Tontine Coffee House the other day and heard them bid at $120 on the exchange. Astor was selling, and I don't doubt many of the others. Sell your sloops, too . . ."

Sally balked at this: "Uncle Cornelius always said the sloops were the foundation of the business. We're still making money on them, aren't we, Cornelius?"

The boy nodded his head, but Aaron said, "For now, perhaps, but not for long. There are more steamers on the river every year. You could go into steam, of course, but you'd have to be licensed by the Livingston monopoly and give away much of your profit. I'd thought it might change now that the chancellor and Fulton are dead, but the law's still on the books and their friends still in the legislature. On the other hand, the ocean's free, and it will be a long time, if ever, before one of those steamers can cross it. I can't imagine riding out twenty-foot waves in a clumsy firebox, and you'd have to ship so much wood to burn there wouldn't be room for paying cargo. And don't forget we could use those good sailing men, like old Coffin, as skippers on the packets. I could command one, of course, but . . ."

Just that thought, if nothing else, tipped the scales for Sally. Aaron could still have his sea and be back in port every two months instead of every fifteen or eighteen months. "I think it's a good idea," she said. "What do you think, Cornelius?"

"Well, if Wright & Son is going into it . . ."

"Good! Then it's settled," Sally said, clapping her hands. "Now, how do we convince your father?"

"We'll just tell him that he could travel free to Europe—he's always wanted to go."

Young Cornelius was so without humor that they had to accept his suggestion as a serious one, and it turned out that he understood his father almost too well. Not only was the thought of going to Europe whenever the spirit moved him persuasive to George, but he insisted that each packet be designed with a spacious owner's cabin for him to use or loan to special friends in return for favors. Cornelius thought it a waste of space that could turn a dollar but probably worth it in terms of both getting his father's agreement and having him far removed for long periods of time. If Cornelius had had anything he could think of as a father, it was his grandfather; George was a figure he had feared and hated and finally come to despise. He could tell that his mother despised his father, too, and it was a cruel and awful blow when she began to swell with his brother, and he had to try to imagine what his father had done to her. He was sure it had something to do with that terrible night of the fire, for he had heard her go up to his father's room and then seen her go rushing wildly out and then waited and waited and waited the whole night through. Thank God for Uncle Aaron, for his saving his mother from drowning, for his saving the ship. From that night on, he had been struggling against wishing for his father's death which must be a mortal sin and against hating his own brother who was the cause for this sinful wish. If only he could have his mother to himself . . . anything to get his father away from her and away from the business which he'd ruin if he could . . .

The first of the packets, to be christened *Evelina,* was nearly finished when James Schuyler unexpectedly knocked on the door of the Van Alen house in Broadway. Since one of the clerks, peering out, identified the caller as a gentleman, Cornelius went to the door himself. Standing on the stoop was a tall, handsome fellow, a number of years older than himself, with broad shoulders and a broader smile, curly black hair and black eyes. "I'm James Schuyler—Cousin James," he said. "You must be Cousin Cornelius. Is Aunt Sarah at home?"

Cornelius ignored the hand the young man was holding out. "I think you'd better go away . . ."

"Why? I've just been called to assist the pastor at the First Presbyterian Church over across the way, and I'm in need of lodgings. I saw your house was so close that I . . ."

"How can you come here when you know how your father has treated my mother?"

James didn't seem ruffled in the least. "Oh, come now, Cousin Cornelius—don't tell me you believe that the sins of the father should be visited on the son? I never paid much attention to what my parents were saying, and anyway I've been away at Princeton these last four years. You know who you look like? You look like Grandpa Schuyler except for the blond hair. I think it's time we cousins got to know each other."

There was something engaging about this cousin, almost a radiance, that Cornelius found hard to resist. It might have been that his hair and eyes were so like his mother's, his Uncle Peter's. He responded with his own tight imitation of a smile and held out his hand. "Perhaps you're right. You'll find mother upstairs in the parlor. I've got work to do, but maybe I'll see you later . . ."

"I hope we'll see a lot of each other," James said, taking the stairs two at a time.

Sally was as surprised at this visitation as her son. Could it mean a change of heart at the manor since she'd declined to sue? She doubted it, but she asked, "Did your father send you to me, James?"

James laughed. He had an openness, a frankness, she had to admire. "Oh, no! Not to the notorious Aunt Sarah . . ."

"Well, if we're going to get along, James, you'd better call me Sally. I've been a Sally for a long time."

"Too bad. Sarah's such a beautiful, biblical name, and, begging your pardon, ma'am, it suits your beauty. They never told me about that."

"I suppose not. After all you've doubtless heard, what brings you here? I would think a minister . . ."

"Well, ministers have to be practical, Aunt Sally, in view of not being well paid. I thought that, your house being so near the church . . ."

"I'd take you in? Well, why not? We do have the room, but living with us might be a test of your faith."

James laughed again. "I'll make a bargain, Aunt Sally: I'll save your souls in return for room and board."

It was Sally's turn to laugh. "That sounds like a Dutch bargain to me," she said. "I'm not aware that our souls are in need of saving. You must have been listening too much to your grandfather."

"I was teasing, of course. But I had a hunch about you, so I left my things on the stoop. I'll just go and get them . . ."

Sally had a hunch about James, too. Minister or no, he seemed so strong and full of good humor and youthful animal spirits that he might be what she'd been wanting for Cornelius—a male friend, a sort of brother. Cornelius had left friends behind when he had quit school. The clerks didn't serve the purpose, because, as could be expected, they were too deferential to the heir to the house of Van Alen. Peter, being ten years younger, was only a nuisance to Cornelius. What Cornelius needed was someone to play and argue with, someone with whom he could share the questions and confidences of young manhood from which a mother was necessarily excluded by reason of age and sex. If James could provide that for Cornelius, he would prove a true godsend.

After he'd been around a while, Sally began to think that, if James did save their souls, as he put it, it would be more because of what he was than what he said. Like generations of Schuylers growing up on the manor, he'd developed a love for outdoor exercise, and he teased, dragged or argued—"A sound mind in a sound body"—Cornelius into joining him on nice days for swims in the river or a game of pickup ball with the Columbia students who clustered about Battery Park. Seeing her son for the first time have some healthy fun was enough to earn Sally's gratitude. Never having had a sister, James was enchanted with Amelia Downing and would help Sally with her lessons, "enriching" them with some of the more romantic Bible stories. James was fascinated with Flossie, who never tired of telling stories of his every burp as a small baby. He even got through to

Uncle George with his knowledge of horseflesh and once drove Smith's trotter to a highly profitable victory in a race on the Bowery after which his order for lemonade at the Bull's Head had to be respected. As for Sally, she most enjoyed the fact that James' education had given him an interest in literature equal to her own, and the table discussions were enlivened by their trading opinions and reading to each other from their favorite books, discussions that occasionally inspired Cornelius to try to make up in reading for his own lack of schooling.

As if by silent and mutual understanding, they seldom talked of religion beyond the occasional amusing anecdote James would relate about his work in the church. But at dinner one day, when Uncle Aaron happened to be present, Sally brought up a poem called "Thanatopsis" that she'd just read in the *North American Review;* it was by a young Masachussetts lawyer named William Cullen Bryant. "You know, Washington Irving was always afraid that we'd never have an American literature," she said, "but he's wrong if we have poets like this. Listen to this passage . . .

> '. . . Earth that nourished thee, shall claim
> Thy growth, to be resolved to earth again,
> And, lost each human trace, surrendering up
> Thine individual being, shalt thou go
> To mix forever with the elements,
> To be a brother to the insensible rock
> And to the sluggish clod, which the rude swain
> Turns with his share, and treads upon. The oak
> Shall send his roots abroad, and pierce thy mould.' . . .

"Isn't that beautiful—and isn't it a beautiful thought? I think it would be wonderful to become a part of the whole universe instead of just being me."

"It scans well, I'll agree," James said, "but, Aunt Sally, don't you realize that it's pagan nonsense—nothing but nature worship? You can never get away from being you, because God gave you a soul, and when you die it will be resurrected if you believe in Christ and follow his commandments."

"But isn't God in nature?"

"Of course, he is," James agreed. "He created it. But the Bible tells us that, in breathing a soul into man, God made us different and apart from nature, gave us command over it . . . ."

"You ought to try rounding the Horn in a blow, young man," Aaron said. "No, I agree with your Aunt Sally, I think it's beautiful, and I can think of nothing better than to become part of the sea when I go."

"Then you don't believe in the word of God, Captain Roberts?"

"Not the way I've heard it preached. Maybe my eyes have been opened by seeing too much of the world. You know there are China-men who believe in the word of Confucius, and in Bangkok in Siam there are more temples to Buddha than there are churches in New York. Are all those people wrong?"

"Yes, there is only one true God," James said.

"That may be, but, you know, I'm more interested in how men act than what they believe. I've seen good and bad with every religion," Aaron said, "but I never trust a man who has too much of it. I learned that when I was a boy growing up in Connecticut. Before I was old enough to sign on a ship and get away from there, I worked as a clerk in the store of a very devout deacon, my father's favorite disciple who took me on, I'm sure, just to curry favor with the parson. You can get an idea of what it was like working for him when I tell you that one morning he called down to me from his living quarters above the shop, 'Have you watered the rum, Aaron?' 'Yes, sir,' I said. 'Have you sanded the sugar?' 'Yes, sir.' 'And dusted the pepper?' 'Yes, sir.' 'And have you chicoried the coffee?' 'Yes, sir.' 'Well, then,' he said, 'come up to prayers.' I ran right out of there and never went back. I don't know whether that man taught me more about religion or Yankee trading, but I've been grateful on both scores."

Even James had to laugh, and the talk drifted on to other, safer, subjects. But later Aaron expressed some concern. "I tell you, Sally, that young man's so narrow-minded his ears touch," he said. "For all of his pleasant manners, I think he's just waiting to pounce on you."

"Me? Why me? I may be his wicked Aunt Sally, but he knows that I have a mind of my own, and there's nowhere else in town where he could find free board."

"You see, you're proving my point by calling yourself wicked. You haven't talked like that in years, even in jest. Next thing you know you'll be going to church with him on Sunday instead of . . ."

"Never. You know me better than that, Aaron. I think you're mak-ing too much of this. After all James is only here because he's my

179

nephew, and I do think he's good for the children. I'm sure you don't object to his taking *them* to church."

Aaron laughed. "You've got me there, Sally. I guess preachers do have their uses. I wish it were Sunday right now . . ."

Not the least of the blessings Sally saw in James' presence was that time every week when she and Aaron could be fairly certain of having the house to themselves. Quite naturally, James had offered to take the young people with him to the Presbyterian Church, and Sally had approved enthusiastically. It would be an experience for them that she had failed to provide more by default than intention. Dropping the pew rent at Trinity had been one of her economies at the time of the boycott since she'd never liked the place where Lady Lydia had dragged her only to see and be seen by the "best people," and, what with a baby at home and Cornelius content to spend his time in the counting room, she'd never gotten around to going anywhere else. She wasn't surprised that Cornelius enjoyed the intellectual stimulation of discussing the sermons with James; that Amelia liked an occasion to put on her best buttons and bows; that little Peter, though a squirmer, felt important sitting in the first pew and looking up at his handsome cousin in the pulpit. As for the rest of the household, George, on those Sundays when he wasn't too distressed to rise from his bed, would be off to the races or somewhere; the German girls were encouraged to go over to the Lutheran Church, what they called the "Swamp Church," in William Street where they could safely display themselves to boys of their faith; and Flossie was granted her weekly hour or so of freedom to commune with her own in the little black Methodist church. So, with the empty house echoing to the bells ringing out from a dozen spires, Sally and Aaron would seek their own state of grace in her bedroom.

To indulge themselves thus when so many of New York's citizens were going solemnly to worship spiced their affair with a sharp pinch of defiance. It made her feel deliciously free of crippling conventions. When Aaron was in town and she knew he'd be coming, she would find herself, as she did this morning, tingling with anticipation from the moment she awoke. What would he do and say today? What new and exciting caress would he invent? What caress would she dare? Just thinking about it brought a pleasant flood to the valley between her legs, and she arose reluctantly to go through the motions of dressing, making conversation at breakfast, waiting for the magic

180

hour. When the young people left, she went to the window and watched. Soon she saw him come rolling down the sidewalk with that peculiar gait that he said came from bracing against the roll of the deck, tipping his hat and smiling at the church-going ladies in their shawls and poke bonnets. She wondered if any of them could ever imagine the beautiful business he was so briskly about. She ran down to the door to greet him, and he swept her up into his arms, twirling her in a little dance step. He was so eager that he lifted her and carried her up the steps, taking them two at a time. The flood was returning. *Hurry, love, oh, hurry.*

But this day he did not hurry. Once he got her into the bedroom, he kept her in exquisite suspense. He helped her to undress, pausing to kiss each toe as he removed her slippers and stockings, nibbling the nape of her neck as he unhooked her bodice. When she lay naked on the bed, goosefleshed with excitement, he caressed her lingeringly, more with his eyes than his hands. "I want to fix the look of you in my mind, memorize every lovely inch of you," he said. "The *Evelina* is ready, and I must sail within the week." She liked being naked to his eyes, hiding no blemish from him. He went out of his way to kiss the few she had, saying they made her more bewitching because they made her unique. She wanted to be open to him, and she was. He buried his face in the damp of her valley. Now she said it aloud, "Hurry, love, oh, hurry."

Just then she heard a creak of the stair, a thump in the hallway. Fear snaked up her spine. "Oh, my God, Aaron, someone's here . . . ."

Fortunately, he was still dressed. While she covered herself with a quilt, he ran to the door and pulled it open. Flossie nearly fell into the room. "What are you doing here, Flossie? I thought you were in church," he said.

"I didn' go. I was took with the cold. I come to see whether Miss Sally have some epsom salt . . . ."

She had never admired Aaron as much as she did in that moment. "Oh . . . oh, yes," he said. "You must have the same complaint as Mrs. Van Alen. She fainted dead away in the parlor, and I carried her up and put her into bed. There are no salts here, but I tell you what: you come with me down to the dining room, and I'll give you a tot of rum, same as I'm going to get for your mistress. It's what we sailors do for the cold."

He turned, winked at her and went out the door with Flossie. When she could hear them on the stair, she jumped up and fumbled into her clothes. The cold bath of shock had dampened desire, and she was left only with the hissing ashes of frustration and fear. She wondered how much Flossie could have heard, or seen. Her cry? The clothes scattered on the floor? She would never know, because she would never dare to ask. In order not to create suspicion that might not exist, she would have to act above suspicion. She was ready for the rum when Aaron brought it. She had a different kind of gooseflesh. "Do you think she knows?" she asked.

"I don't know, but she looked . . . she drank that rum down faster than you're doing. I guess we'll just have to live with it."

"As with so many things. Oh, damn, damn . . ."

"Why, Sally, such language."

"I could say worse. It isn't just Flossie. I don't worry about her . . . But you don't know how much I wanted you—"

"Oh, I think I do. And I you. But there will be another time."

"Not for two whole long months. Oh, Aaron, Aaron, I'm shameless in wanting you. I just hope my soul doesn't burn in hell for it."

"There you go again. I'm sure that preacher's getting to you. If I were you, I'd throw him out of the house."

"I can't. He's so good for the children . . . ."

"Everything for the children! Much as I admire you for thinking that way, it grieves me. It's you I care about—you, Sally. I'd hate to think that you feel our love is somehow . . . well, defiling . . ."

"I don't. Oh, I don't, Aaron. It's just that it is so wonderful I can't believe that I deserve it, that I won't sometime have to pay for it . . . ."

"Stop talking that way, Sally, You've got to learn to take life as it comes, when it comes, the way a sailor takes weather."

"It's not that easy for a woman. Oh, how I sometimes wish it were, but it isn't. We literally must bear the consequences of our acts."

"I've never thought about it that way . . ."

"I'm sure you haven't. And why should you? I think one reason I love you is that you are so much the man, so free. All I ask is that you come back to me again, and again . . . ."

"You know I will."

"Yes, I know, Aaron. So you'd better go now and let me pretend to be ill."

When he'd gone, she picked up the little jade dragon that lay always on the table by her bed and held it against her cheek. It felt so cool that she wondered whether she didn't actually have a fever. If so, it was a fever of frustration. Forcing her yearning body to lie there all day in a charade of illness would be hell, and she was in a touchy mood when young Cornelius came bursting into the room. "Mother, mother, what's wrong? Flossie says you're sick—"

"Nothing much, Cornelius. Just a touch of cold, I guess."

"But she says you fainted. She says Uncle Aaron had to carry you up to bed."

"Yes . . . well, maybe I'm just tired. You'd better go and let me rest."

"Let me stay. Let me take care of you. You've never been sick . . . ."

There was such concern in the boy's voice, his expression, that she felt a sharp twinge of guilt over her deception. "No, I'll be all right, Cornelius," she said. "I'm ever so much better already. Uncle Aaron gave me some rum to take away the chill. How was the sermon?"

"Wonderful! Cousin James preached, and I . . ."

He stopped in some kind of evident embarrassment, and she had to prod him, "You what?"

"I . . . I accepted Christ as my savior."

Although he'd got the words out with a tone of pride, the boy's eyes were fixed on his boots, and he was blushing. He was obviously uncertain of her reaction, and at this, of all times, he had good cause. "I don't understand," she said, stalling for time to bring this matter into focus. "You were baptized at Trinity . . ."

"But that's different, mother. I was just a baby, and I was never confirmed. Cousin James says that when you understand all about how Jesus died to save us from our sins, you have to publicly confess your faith, and . . ."

"I wasn't aware of your sins, Cornelius . . ."

"Oh, Mother, *everybody* is a sinner. Don't you know that? Cousin James says it is the doctrine of original sin, and the only salvation is in Christ."

"Cousin James says quite a lot, doesn't he?"

"You should have heard him, mother! When he got done preaching, got done telling us how the love of God could live in our hearts and transform our lives, he asked anyone who wanted to to come down to the pulpit and publicly accept Christ, and I just had to go,

I had to . . . . There must have been a dozen of us, women as well as men . . . . He's going to have a class for us, and we're all going to join the Presbyterian Church. Maybe you could get in it. Would you? Would you?"

"I don't know, Cornelius. I'm too sick to think about it today . . . ."

If she hadn't felt sick before, she did now, and she wondered why. Nothing should be more comforting than to have a son find his way into the confines of a respectable church; James's influence was more far-reaching and, she supposed, better than she could have imagined. She could tell that Cornelius was taking this seriously, as he took everything seriously, and it was probable that the strictures of the church would keep him out of trouble, as he struggled with the passions and temptations of becoming a man. So why, then, did she feel this way, feel a kind of dread? No doubt it had to do with the bruising faith of her father, though James insisted that the faith into which he was leading Cornelius was very different. She hoped so. Lord, how she hoped so. She didn't know whether she could endure being rejected by a son, as she had been by a father, in the name of God.

Oh, Aaron, Aaron, come back and love me.

Chapter X

The Play's the Thing

It happened when George was in Europe, when Aaron was at sea, when Peter was down in Washington, and it seemed innocent enough at the time. Now that they were truly sisters, Sally and Alexandra Fish Schuyler were seeing a lot of each other. Several times a week they would have tea together either at Sally's on Broadway or the new and elegant house that Peter had built for his bride on Beach Street near St. John's Park. It was all of marble, one of the first such private residences in the city, and Sally usually tried to be at Alexandra's on Sundays, because it amused her to see the lines of curious citizens, some of them richly dressed and provident enough to hire hacks to get to the scene, who walked up and down staring at the oddity. For some peculiar reason, Peter had insisted that the back of the house be of marble, too, although only the neighbors on the other side of the yard could see it. She still wondered where he'd got the money and why he had spent it so lavishly, since cabinet officers were notoriously underpaid, but he argued that an imposing residence would be worth its weight in marble in keeping his name in the public eye should he decide to try for the Senate, and apparently he was right. But they were at Sally's when Alexandra brought up the fact that a dramatization of *The Spy,* a novel by her new neighbor, James Fenimore Cooper, was playing at the Park.

"Oh, I wish I could see it, but I'm afraid that it will be gone from the boards by the time Peter gets back. Even then, I'm not sure he'd take me; he doesn't think it's right for the wife of a politician to be seen in the theater," she said.

"That doesn't sound like Peter," Sally said.

"He's very ambitious, Sally. Sometimes it frightens me. He says that ever since Matty managed to get suffrage for almost all white males written into the new constitution last year, there's no office in the state to which a good Tammany man can't aspire. So he says we have to be very careful not to offend the common morality."

"Heavens! Even Lady Lydia used to go to the theater, and I never knew anyone more concerned with her social reputation," Sally said.

"I know, but that was a different generation. I can remember my parents saying that they actually saw General Washington laughing in the old John Street theater when he was here as president. I don't think the real aristocrats took their religion as seriously as the present class of merchants."

"You should have known my father—Peter's father."

"Yes, I've heard about him, and maybe that's where Peter gets some of his ideas, but you know as well as I do how most people, especially up in the country, feel about the theater."

Sally sighed. "Yes, I should know. My own Cornelius wouldn't be caught dead in the theater—he says it is infested with wicked women, though how he would know one, I'm not sure. Anyway, it pains him whenever Aaron and I go. But I won't yield to him. I'm sure he gets his ideas from James, and I won't give up the glory of Shakespeare for the good opinion of some narrow mind . . . . That gives me an idea. Why don't you and I go together to *The Spy* tonight? I haven't had time to read the book, but they say it's the best thing done in America so far, and I'd like to see it."

"Oh, Sally, without an escort? We couldn't."

"Why not? We could sit way back in the box, and the chances are nobody would notice us—or they'd think our husbands were out to the bar. Nobody'd need know. Your servants know you are over here, and Cornelius will think I've gone to your house . . ."

It didn't take much more argument for Sally to persuade Alexandra, if for no other reason than the fact that the young woman was dreadfully bored. She hadn't been able to give Peter any children though, heaven knows, not for lack of trying. She was often embarrassed about that part of her marriage, because she liked it too much, and she was sure that it wasn't right. Peter kept insisting that her pleasure was perfectly normal and said more than once, "Look at Sally." She'd looked and looked at Sally, but she didn't understand what he meant. Though Sally was still beautiful at forty-two, she seemed small and delicate like a French doll, and, if it weren't for her children, it would be hard to imagine her ever doing the things that she and Peter did. Alexandra wished that she could talk to Sally about her relations with Peter and what they did to her, but she could never seem to bring the subject up. It wasn't that she was afraid of being laughed at or scolded since Sally, being so much older, had always been like a loving aunt to her in giving advice on other matters. What kept her silent was the fear that, by disclosing her happiness with Peter, she would add to the hurt that Sally must suffer from that dreadful drunken husband of hers. How Peter could imagine that Sally would enjoy that man's advances just showed that the poor dear was innocent of women for all of his having been married before. She only wished that Peter would take her to Washington with him where they could be together more often instead of leaving her here in New York where there was nothing to do at night but read or practice on the harp he'd given her for a ninth anniversary present. She tried her best to believe in his logic: "You must understand, dearest, that my cabinet position is only temporary. I'll go out with Monroe in '24, if not before, and it would be folly to put money into an establishment in Washington. I have to keep a presence in New York—and what more charming presence than you—because this is where I'll need the votes. I'll be home here as often as possible, I promise you." He tried, but it wasn't very often, and, considering the difficulties and dangers of the trip, his visits could be as much of a worry as a pleasure to her. He laughed off her fears. Once in the spring when mud made the roads almost impassable by stage and she tried to persuade him to stay, he said, "Oh, it isn't so bad. Coming up on the New Jersey turnpike, we spotted from our stage a hat in the middle of the road, and the driver stopped. I got out to retrieve it and—lo and behold —a voice came from the head beneath it: 'Thank you, governor, but I've a good horse under me and am getting along very well, considering.'" She had to laugh with him, of course, but, oh, how she wished for an end to this lonely life, for something exciting to happen.

Walking up Broadway in the twilight, Sally and Alexandra were giddy with the sense of adventure, whispering together though nobody could hear, like children on a forbidden lark. Sally had had the prudence to send one of the clerks to buy up all the tickets for a box in the second tier. So instead of mingling with the crowds at the theater's entrance on Park Row, they cut through Ann to the back entrance on the theater alley, adding another pinch of spice to their game. The guard at the door to the box seemed surprised to see two ladies alone, and Sally said, "Our husbands are up at the bar. I'm sure you will be good enough to admit them when they come down—if ever. They care little for the theater."

When they were inside and giggling, Alexandra said, "Oh, Sally, you are so good at deception."

"I've had a lot of practice," Sally replied without much thought.

"What do you mean?"

It was a bad slip. "Oh, nothing. When you become a mother, Alexandra, you'll discover that it isn't always possible to tell your children the truth. And I'm sure you don't share *everything* with Peter."

"But I do, I do . . ."

"Then you must have a wonderful relationship."

"Oh, we do. I . . . I so . . . yearn for him."

Sally could tell by the young woman's color what lay behind her words, and she patted her hand. "You're a very fortunate woman, Alexandra. But then I always thought Peter was special. I just hope he isn't getting too . . . too respectable with all of his political ambition."

To Alexandra it seemed the moment, with their sharing of this adventure and coming so close to the subject, to break through. She said, "Not in *that* way . . ."

But Sally just squeezed her hand and said, "Good . . . . Now tell me about Mr. Cooper. Have you met him?"

It was a clear sign to change the subject, and Alexandra went along. "Not yet," she said. "I did call on Mrs. Cooper when he was out. Do you know what she told me? She said that Mr. Cooper started writing novels on a challenge from *her.* He was ranting and raving about how poor some English novel was, and she said, 'Well, if you think you can do better, why don't you try?' I guess his first one wasn't very good, but he got the idea for this one from a story old Governor Jay told him about spying up in Westchester during the Revolution. So it should be exciting . . . ."

The bare benches on the floor of the house were filling up entirely with men, many of them clapping each other on the back and evidently exchanging jokes from the sound of their laughter. A smattering of women with their husbands and sometimes older children could be seen entering the boxes around and across from them, and there were women, too, in the boxes above, doubtless the wicked women of whom Cornelius had been warned. They didn't look wicked, but their free and easy manner with the men around them was in sharp contrast to the sedate behavior of the ladies in the second tier. Sally and Alexandra eyed these women with some interest, and Alexandra said, "Look at them—the way they flirt. I can't imagine a life like that."

"Nor can I. But I feel sorry for them, poor dears—and sorrier for the wives of those men."

She was speaking for herself, of course, but she didn't elaborate; she was sure that Alexandra, like nearly everybody else in New York, knew well that George Van Alen was a steady patron of the Park Theater's third tier, where he was never far from the bar in the gallery just outside the boxes, and only too open to solicitation by any of those women who took his fancy. During their long truce, George had taken to telling her about his adventures in a pathetic effort to arouse her interest or jealousy. She had humor enough to find one of his revelations amusing. It seemed that there was a perfect whispering gallery in the third tier; something about the arch of the proscenium made it possible for every sound uttered in the box on one side of the stage to be heard in the box on the other. Knowing this from long experience, George and his friends would take one of those boxes. When they would see across the way a man they knew to be innocent of this acoustical peculiarity sitting down with his doxie of the evening, they would whisper reminders that he ought to be home with his wife. According to George, this produced a better show than anything on the boards: their victim would usually look nervously around, get up and open the door, try to peer into the next box, lean dangerously over the rail to study the crowd below, glance imploringly at heaven and finally flee, leaving an irate woman to fend again for herself.

When the ushers began snuffing candles to dim the house lights, and the curtains parted, Sally and Alexandra left the shadows at the back of the box where they'd been sitting and moved forward for a better view of the stage. They were so absorbed in the drama, as they supposed others to be, that they didn't give a thought to being observed. Sally was particularly excited to encounter a story exploiting the same confusion of loyalties that she'd known in her own family, and it made her wonder whether old Cornelius could also have been a Harvey Birch who carried the secret of his intelligence service to the grave with him. On the way out, she was expounding this theory to Alexandra and was totally surprised to find two gentlemen, dressed for the evening in black, at the door of the box. One bowed and said, "Ladies, will you permit us to escort you home through the dark?" Sally almost agreed. She'd only had a glimpse of the man's face before he bowed, and he wore a waxed mustache; as far as she knew, the first and only man in New York to sport such a facial decoration was her neighbor, "Dandy" Marx, who'd been to her house on New Year's. But when the man looked up again, she realized her mistake: he was very young and quite obviously not an Israelite. "No, thank you," she said. "Our husbands have gone to get the carriage."

"Begging your pardon, Madam," he said. "But I happen to know that your husband is in Europe and that this lady's husband is in Washington . . ."

For the first time in an evening that so far had been good clean sport, Sally was apprehensive. But she had not lived so long with Lady Lydia for nothing, and she drew herself as tall as her inches would allow and said, "Sir, you are misinformed." Taking Alexandra in tow with her hand, she started to sweep by, but the man would not be evaded.

"I am not in the habit of being misinformed," he said, following along at her side as she made her way for the stairs. "I am a gentleman from the *Post,* and . . ."

Oh, my God, a newspaper reporter. Sally forgot about being a lady. She ducked her head and, dragging Alexandra with one hand and using her reticule as a weapon with the other, fought her way through the crowds to Park Row where they managed to escape into one of the waiting hackneys. Alexandra was upset. "What will I do, Sally?

What will I do? If this gets into the papers, it will embarrass Peter terribly."

With more conviction than she felt, Sally said, "Why would it get into the papers? The gentlemen were only having some sport with us."

Sally had, however, no previous experience with a reporter scorned, and the next day's paper carried this small but stinging item:

"At the Park Theater last night we spotted two unescorted ladies in second tier boxes, and we at first thought that the management had grown lax in allowing the *demi-monde* to invade the precincts of respectability. Upon closer inspection, however, we discovered that one of the ladies was the wife of a very high-ranking government official and the other the wife of a prominent merchant, both of whose husbands were out of the city attending to business. We are hard pressed to say whether our first supposition or the actual truth is more shocking. What is the world coming to in this year of eighteen hundred and twenty-two when respectable women go out to places of amusement at night alone?"

Sally was furious, and Alexandra was crushed. Her only hope was that the item would somehow escape Peter's attention, but the hope was vain. Several sharp-eyed "friends" clipped it and sent it to Washington. In a fury, he took the first stage home. Such a foolish thing did not sound like his Alexandra, and he wasn't too surprised to discover that it had been Sally's idea. He had for long been uneasy about Alexandra's close association with his unpredictable sister, but he had let it go on since it was apparently her only source of contentment in New York. As soon as he learned the truth, he went around to Broadway to call on Sally. He found her drilling her niece, Amelia Downing, now an uncommonly pretty girl, in Latin conjugation. Although Sally guessed why Peter had come, she pretended it was a normal social call.

"Well, Peter, I didn't know you were up from Washington," she said. "We've had the most exciting news. Miss Emma Willard has started a college for young ladies up in Waterford. High time, I say. So we wrote Amelia's parents in Liverpool about it, and they've replied that they'd like her to go and we're drilling her for it. You should sit and listen; it still may not be too late for you to learn some Latin."

Peter wasn't amused. "I must speak to you alone, Sally."

When Amelia had left the room, he asked, "Do you have any idea what you've done to me?"

"What on earth are you talking about?"

"You know damn well what I mean—that business in the theater. You've made me the laughingstock of Washington and no doubt New York, too."

"I?"

"Yes, you. It would never have occurred to Alexandra to do such a thing but for you."

"But, Peter, we didn't *do* anything. We just went to see a play—and a very respectable one as you'd know if you ever read anything but official papers."

"Sally, whatever else you may be, you are too intelligent to talk like that. This is a very serious matter . . . ."

"And I should think you too intelligent to take this matter seriously . . . ."

Sally looked hard at her brother as if she'd never seen him before, and, in truth, she hadn't for years. His was a figure so familiar to her that its slow changes were scarcely visible. Because he was balding and the hair at the back of his head and the mutton chops fringing his jawline were gray, he looked more than five years older than she. The black eyes that were liquid mirrors in her face were burning coals in his. The thin lips they also shared, which curved to her every emotion, were set by him in a line of rigid determination. Although he'd put on weight, his body, clothed always in formal black, was erect and supple, still that of a man who spent as much time as he could in the saddle. Altogether, he had the look of gravity and intensity expected of leaders of men, and she wondered if he practiced in front of a mirror to achieve it, as Matty Van Buren was said to do. Whatever, he seemed at this moment nearly a stranger.

"The matter I assure you is serious enough to have come up in a cabinet meeting," he was saying. "John Quincy Adams, who is not given to joking, said, 'Gentlemen, from what I read in the papers, I am glad that I am secretary of state and have to deal only with the Russians and can leave the insubordination of women in this country to other secretaries, such as Mr. Schuyler.'"

"If he wasn't joking, you have to be, Peter," Sally said.

"How can I get through to you, Sally, that this is no joke, no joke at all? I think I have been very understanding about your private affairs through the years, but when you provoke a public scandal I can't tolerate it. There is going to be a real scramble for the presidency next time with the Democratic-Republican Party so split between those who favor Jackson and those who favor Adams that they're looking hard for a compromise candidate, and . . ."

"You mean *you* may have a chance to be president, Peter?"

"I do. Or at least I did. I'm taking Alexandra to Washington with me to see that there will be nothing else like this. But if it ever comes out that you and Captain Roberts, that my godson . . ."

"Peter! What are you accusing me of?"

A mixture of fear and anger rose in her throat. Like her brother's looks, her arrangement with Aaron had become so familiar, so much a part of her life, that she no longer really thought about it. The fact that she couldn't detect the slightest suspicion among the sharp-eyed children with whom she lived was reassurance enough that they were being wholly discreet. Only Flossie had anything like evidence of more than the most proper relationship between them, and she hadn't given a hint of understanding what she'd seen although Sally had to concede that, for all of their living together these many years, she seldom knew for sure what went on behind that impassive black face.

Now her brother was saying, "I'm not accusing you of anything, Sally. I am stating what I've been sure was a fact for a long time. I've tolerated it, even condoned it, out of consideration for all that you've been through. God knows, I'm no saint either, and I certainly wouldn't want to follow in father's footsteps. But you must understand what it would mean to me . . . to you, too, and your son, my namesake, if I were chosen . . ."

"What are you really trying to say to me, Peter? I think we've been honest with each other up to now, so . . ."

"I'm asking—and I'll plead, if you like—that you give Captain Roberts up—at least until I've had my chance."

"Peter, you don't know what you're asking. That would be two whole years, and he's all I have to live for."

"Nonsense. You have two sons."

"You needn't remind me of that. The truth is, if it hadn't been for them I'd have run off with Aaron long ago."

"Well, then, you must appreciate what knowledge of your . . . your relationship would do to them. I don't know which of them it would hurt most—Cornelius with his Presbyterian righteousness or Peter who thinks he's somebody else. That they would be hurt, make no mistake. Actually, I agree with you that this theater business was trivial in itself and innocent on your part, but the reaction to it shows the temper of the people. You know I can't hold a candle to you in brain power, but I am a good politician, and the essence of politics is to understand the people. With all this revivalist religion around, not only Caesar's wife but his sister, his brother, his children and his godchildren have to be above suspicion. I know General Jackson for a good man, but the story that he lived with his wife before they were married may kill him politically, if enough people believe it. I can't tell you what to do, Sally—nobody has ever succeeded in that—but I do plead with you to think of all the rest of us. Now I'd better leave you to go back to helping Amelia, though from what I've seen I doubt that all this education of women is a good thing . . . ."

Sally's first reaction when he left her was rage. The prig! The prude! Her own loving brother who she knew from Alexandra's shy confidences shared her needs of the flesh and who she thought from years of discussion shared her contempt for hypocrisy! Oh, how ambition altered men as she'd seen so clearly with Mr. Burr! How could he ask her to give up Aaron, to lose her sustaining love, for the sake of his political hopes? Had it been anyone else, anyone else at all, she would have laughed in his face or screamed her fury, or both. But Peter had been her stay against consuming self-contempt even before Aaron, and she owed him the courtesy she'd shown by not so reacting to his plea. He'd come to her in a moment of his own anger, and perhaps he'd think better of it. But she doubted it: a man with a chance to be president could not really afford concern for the state of his sister's heart, or for that matter his own. As she calmed down a little, she began to feel the real weight of the burden he had put upon her. He was probably right that knowledge of her indiscretion would hurt him badly with a self-righteous public; he was certainly right about what it would do to the boys. The thought of how it might affect her sons was always with her, but she had calmed her conscience with the kind of rationalization that springs from desire: denying Aaron's wish to claim her totally was sacrifice enough; the love and respect the boys had for Aaron would ease the blow, if it ever came; God was showing his blessing by letting them get away with it, and on and on.

But thinking about Peter's situation gradually brought her up short. She'd been skating on very thin ice, and she knew what that was all about: once the crackling started, anything could happen. All of Peter's enemies, not to mention his "friends," would be probing his life and the lives of those around him, and the slightest suspicion of impropriety or irregularity would be invested with innuendo far beyond what had appeared in the little item about the theater. She could just imagine, for example, what her brother-in-law, John Charles Smith, might suggest to the press. He had been furious ever since Cornelius, having reached his majority and entered into his full inheritance, had cut the dividends drastically to build steamboats in anticipation of putting Van Alen & Son back onto the river, once Corneel Vanderbilt succeeded in breaking the Livingston monopoly, as they were sure he'd do. In fact, she'd helped Vanderbilt in one of the craziest, most exciting ventures of her life, and it had really been Aaron's doing. She was sure that Peter didn't understand at all this aspect of her relationship with Aaron. From his last remark about educating women and from a few things Alexandra had dropped, it was clear that Peter, whether as a result of the conforming warp of politics or a reversion to his upbringing, thought that the proper posture for a woman was on her back. Not so Aaron, bless him. He took her interest in the business seriously and respected her authority, and they spent much more time worrying with Cornelius in the counting room than they did in bed. But even if Peter knew this, it wouldn't matter, for a woman bold enough to do what she had done for Corneel Vanderbilt would be thought by many as bad as a whore.

It all started one night when Aaron brought a tall, tow-headed, powerful-looking young man in his twenties to the door. He had the fiercest blue eyes she'd ever seen, and his Dutch-flavored tongue was as rough as the sailing clothes he wore. "This is Corneel Vanderbilt . . . He needs a hiding place . . . . Let us in, please, Sally, and I'll explain later," Aaron said between gasping breaths that revealed they had been running.

Vanderbilt was bold. When she let them in and bolted the door behind them, he said, "You're Dutch? You remind me of my mother, but you're a lot prettier."

"Part Dutch, and you're welcome if you come with Captain Roberts," she said. "What's this all about?"

"I know I must have told you about Corneel here, Sally—one of the best sailors in the harbor," Aaron said. "Well, he's decided to learn steam and has been running the *Bellona* for the Union Line owned by Thomas Gibbons over in Elizabethtown, New Jersey. It's a ferry service from the Battery pier to New Brunswick, and there's competition with the ferries that the former governor of New Jersey, Ogden, operates under a license from the monopoly to come into New York waters. They've managed to get a warrant out for Captain Vanderbilt's arrest, and when we were walking together from the pier to his room on Washington Street we saw the deputies at the door, so I brought him here. Can he stay the night? He'll be sailing again in the morning."

"Well, I suppose so. But won't they catch you at the pier, captain?"

"Hell, no! . . . 'scuse me, ma'am . . . they've been trying ten days running and haven't laid a hand on me," Vanderbilt said. "You see, I've got my crew trained. They get the passengers aboard and get up a good head of steam and when the sheriff's men are done looking around and can't find me aboard and walk down the plank, they haul it in and cast off and I make a flying leap aboard from wherever I've been hiding. Makes for good sport."

Sally laughed. "I should think so, but you can't go on like this very long, can you?"

"By God, I'll try until this damned monopoly is broken. Strikes me it ain't either fair or legal. Keeps a good man down. Mr. Gibbons is a good man, and unless I can get him passengers out of New York his whole Union Line of stages and inns and boats running all the way to Washington wouldn't be worth a damn."

Sally took an immediate liking to this young man with his fierce eyes and profane speech. She sensed in him a hardness of mind as well as body, and she thought that he must be very like old Cornelius must have been in the days when he was jibing his sloops up and down the North River. He didn't seem a man for the parlor, so she led him into the counting room where young Cornelius was working late, as usual. Though they were only a few years apart, the contrast between her son, finely molded, almost delicate, immaculate in black suit and white neckcloth, and Vanderbilt was great; yet within minutes, as Cornelius began pumping the Dutch skipper about the business he was in, she had a feeling that their minds might be very much alike.

Like her own Cornelius, Vanderbilt was interested only in work. At

196

the age of eleven, he'd managed to persuade his mother to give him all the money she'd saved over the years from the earnings of an improvident father—one hundred dollars, kept in the kitchen mantel clock. With that, he got his first periaguar, a little rowing-sailing boat, and began ferrying passengers between his native Staten Island and New York. Within a year, he'd acquired two more periaguars with other young skippers to man them, and by the time war came along he was in a position to run his ferry service by day and a military supply line by night. The money rolled in, and he traded his peria-guars for three coastal schooners. In the next two years, he did so well that he had $9,000 cash in hand. "People thought I was sitting pretty for a younker of twenty-three," he said, "but I could see the handwriting on the wall so I sold everything and hired out to Gibbons for a thousand a year to get the hang of steam. Then people thought I was crazy. But when the *Savannah* made it across the ocean last year, I knew for sure I was right. 'Course Captain Roberts here don't agree . . ."

"No, I don't Corneel. The *Savannah* was just an experiment. She has folding wheels and used her sail most of the way, as you know," Aaron said. "Neither fish nor fowl in my view."

"Well, by damn, I know steam is comin' not only on the rivers but on the ocean and on the land, too," Vanderbilt said. "They've been tryin' it on a railway in England, and they'll soon figure out a way to use it here. I'm saving up to get into it—me and Sophie, that's my wife. She's got the younkers over with her in New Brunswick where she's running Bellona Hall for the Union Line, so we ought to be ready when we get this monopoly busted . . . ."

Captain Vanderbilt not only hid out with them that night but every other night for a week or more. It was, he said, a perfect place, because nobody around the New York waterfront would ever think of looking for Corneel Vanderbilt in such a magnificent Broadway establishment. He couldn't thank them enough; all he could offer was a free ferry ride to New Brunswick any time they wanted it. Both Cornelius and his mother were quick to accept the offer. The young Dutchman's talk about how the fat, lax Livingston monopoly and its licensees could be driven off the river by a little lean competition intrigued them, and they wanted to see for themselves how a steam-boat operated. Cornelius, with no experience of boats and little inter-est in them, spent most of the ride over to New Brunswick calculating how much wood the fires consumed compared to how many fares had been collected. Sally, however, was fascinated with the vessel itself, and she persuaded Corneel to take her down into the steamy engine room to watch all the levers churning and up onto the cabin top where he, or one of his crewmen, stood and steered with a huge tiller not unlike the one on the old *Lady Lydia.* When she confessed that she'd once sailed a large sloop, he persuaded her to try her hand on the *Bellona.* Compared to sailing, it was child's play, and she said, "Doesn't this get rather boring, Captain Vanderbilt?"

"Aye, though you do have to mind the wind and tide a bit when making for a landing. But I find it good for thinking."

"And what do you think about—or is it wrong of me to ask?"

"No, no. Right now it's about how to outwit those damned deputies. They've taken to boarding me as soon as I enter New York waters instead of waiting at the Battery. So far I've got away with my disappearing act. I built a little closet just forward of the engine room —looks like a fixed bulkhead but it slides. When we spot the sheriff's boat, I stow myself away in there and all they can find when they come aboard is my crew. That's why I haven't been to your house the last few nights—I've been sleeping there. It's a little hard standing up, but . . ."

"I must say you'll go to any lengths, Captain Vanderbilt. I hope your employer appreciates it."

"He does, and so does Ogden. He's so tired of paying all those deputies to catch me, he tried to hire me away for $5,000 a year. But damn if I'd do that. Mr. Gibbons has been good to me, and I'm going to see him through this. I don't know yet how I'm going to get back into New York today. They told me on the waterfront that the deputies have warrants for my crew, too, but seeing you steering there so good, ma'am, gives me an idea . . . ."

Vanderbilt's idea was so outrageous that she couldn't at first believe that he was serious. He would leave his crew behind in New Brunswick and do all the work himself. When he saw the sheriff's boat approaching, he would turn the tiller over to Sally, go below and stop the engines and hide in his closet. Since they had no warrant for her, they couldn't arrest her, and it would be a great joke on them, besides, to find nothing but a tiny lady running the *Bellona.* Would she do it? If she had trouble believing that he was serious, it was almost harder to believe what she heard herself saying, "Why not? If it weren't for that monopoly Van Alen & Son would probably still be on the river. You're too young, captain, to remember when our sloops dominated the trade."

"Aye, but I'm not surprised with a good Dutch name like that. I knew you were a lady after my heart the moment I saw you."

Before the *Bellona* left New Brunswick, Captain Vanderbilt took the precaution of explaining his plans to the passengers. Those who weren't for it were invited to spend the night at Bellona Hall and take the next day's ferry. But all of the passengers were enthusiastic over the sport of outwitting the law—all, that is, but Cornelius. "What if they do arrest you, Mother? It would be a disgrace, and I don't think it's proper for a lady like you to do a thing like this. Please, don't; I beg you."

"Ah, Cornelius, don't you have any sense of fun?" she asked. "Can't you just see their faces when they confront me? In any case, don't you agree we should do what we can to help the captain break this monopoly?"

"Yes, I do. But let me do it. It just isn't right for a woman . . . my mother . . ."

"Cornelius, Cornelius. Sometimes I wonder if you even know your mother. I'm not made of glass; I won't break. Can't you see that the whole joke depends on my being a woman? Besides, I know something about handling boats, and you don't. If you're ashamed of me, you can pretend you don't know me, but I'm going to do it. I haven't had such an exciting adventure for years."

While Cornelius sulked in the cabin, Sally stood on the roof beside Captain Vanderbilt, the wind whipping her skirts and rouging her cheeks. From time to time he would turn the tiller over to her and study the waters ahead through a glass. As the outlines of the Battery and the round, squat fort at its tip grew ever more distinct on the horizon with no sign of boarders, Sally was surprised to discover how disappointed she felt. Then Vanderbilt cried, "The bastards are there—over there! Can you make out that rowboat just off the port bow? It's them all right. Now listen, ma'am, I'm going below. When you're just upon them, tap the roof twice with your heel, and I'll disengage the wheels. It wouldn't do to run down the law, though I'd like to. When you get rid of them, tap three times, and I'll get us under way again."

As Sally steered, a little less confidently now that she was alone, the

Bellona bore down on the rowboat at what seemed an alarming rate of speed. A man was standing in the bow making gestures for her to stop, and she tapped twice with her heel. She could hear a clanking below as the gears were disengaged, and the paddle wheels stopped turning. But the ferry still had enough way on that she had to use all her strength to swing the heavy tiller in an effort to avoid the rowboat that was pulling clumsily across her bow. Vanderbilt more nearly got his wish than she would like to remember. There was a thump, sounds of splintering wood as the rowboat slid along the side, loud cries and curses. The first deputy aboard howled, "Who's running this tub? You like to kill us."

"I am," Sally said, "and you're no seaman to come across my path."

"By the saints, no wonder we almost drowned," the deputy said to the two men who came over the rail behind him. "There's naught but a woman at the helm. 'Tis another of Vanderbilt's dirty tricks. Where is he? Where's the captain, miss?"

The noise of the collision had brought most of the passengers out on deck, and they were surrounding the deputies, looking up at her expectantly. She noticed rather thankfully that Cornelius wasn't among them. She must be a sight: hair disheveled and skirts lifted by the breeze to show a length of leg, face flushed with excitement and embarrassment. How had she got herself into this? Well, at least her son wouldn't have to hear his mother lie. Then she had an inspiration. "I am the captain *now,*" she said, as if that one emphasized word were saving.

A number of emotions seemed in struggle to take command of the leading deputy's round, whiskey-purpled face. Finally, a cunning smile won out. "Now, miss, you and the captain have had your little joke, and we've had our bath," he said, shaking the leg of his trousers that had been soaked when the rowboat evidently shipped water, "and now let's get down to business. We have warrants here for the captain and the crew—Higgins and Shufelt. Where are they?"

"There's nobody by that name aboard," she said.

"We'll just see about that. Mike, search the vessel. I'll talk to the passengers."

Feeling a little weak and more than a little apprehensive, Sally clung to the tiller for support while the deputies went about their search. Though she couldn't hear what most of them were saying, she could tell by the way they were shaking their heads that the passengers were supporting her; a number of them were having obvious difficulty to avoid laughing outright. Finally, the deputies got together in a little knot by the rail, conferring in whispers. Then the leader jumped up beside her. He tried pleading, "Be reasonable, miss. We're just trying to do a job," he said. "No harm will come to you if you tell us who's running this boat."

"I think that should be obvious," she said.

"Now, miss, you know, and I know, that no woman has ever run a steamboat . . . ."

"There's always a first time for everything."

"Well, then, seeing as how you damaged our boat, why don't you just show us how you do it and run us into the Battery?"

She hadn't reckoned with this, and she had a gulping moment of panic. But she raised her voice so that the passengers could hear her and said, "I will not! You boarded without proper papers. Now get off!"

It worked. One of the male passengers called up, "Is he giving you trouble, ma'am?" Another shouted, "Give us the word, ma'am, and we'll make them swim for it." The deputy's eyes darted nervously around, assessing the odds. They were very unfavorable, and he whispered, "You win *this* time, miss, but . . . ."

When they'd cast off in their half-awash boat, she tapped three times, and, miraculously, the *Bellona's* wheels started to turn. Looking back over the stern, she saw the deputies' boat rocking drunkenly in the *Bellona's* wake; two men were bailing frantically while their leader shook his fist at the retreating ferry. Her own laughter of relief was drowned out by that of the passengers. Words like "Good show!" and "What a plucky woman!" drifted up to her. Within minutes Captain Vanderbilt was beside her. Impulsively, he hugged her and said, "By damn, you have guts. You're a real Dutch mother like my own. I think your son should be proud of you." Sally said, "I wonder . . ."

Apparently the enthusiasm of the other passengers was catching, for, although he said little to her, Cornelius was the first to boast of his mother's feat when next they met with Aaron. What he'd learned from it, he said, was how strongly most people felt about the monopoly which meant that it was certain to be broken either in the legislature or the courts. That being the case, he proposed that Van Alen

& Son make plans to go into steam, an enterprise in which Vanderbilt, because of his admiration for Sally, might be a valuable ally. They all watched with keen interest the young Dutch skipper's next moves. A week or so after outwitting the deputies with Sally's help, he surprisingly let them serve him in broad daylight of a Sunday while he was loitering on the Battery pier. Summoned to appear before Chancellor Kent in Albany, Vanderbilt calmly revealed that on that Sunday, a day when the Union Line didn't operate, he had hired out to another firm which was licensed by the monopoly and was therefore violating no law. Chancellor Kent was said to be furious that such a spurious case had been brought before him and dismissed it out of hand. Meanwhile, the New Jersey legislature passed a law calling for the arrest of any New York deputies who sought to serve warrants in that state's waters. Corneel Vanderbilt turned this to good use by hauling in the gangplank and casting off at once the next time a deputy boarded him at the Battery. "Scared the hell out of him. Thought I was going to take him over and have him arrested on the Jersey side," he told the Van Alens. "They've let me alone since, and I guess they'll go on letting me alone now till Mr. Gibbons' case against them gets through the courts. He's hired Daniel Webster himself to argue it, so he's sure to win."

Aaron couldn't get over Sally's temerity, and he started begging her to come to sea with him. There was no reason why she couldn't with all propriety use the family stateroom, as George did, and he was sure that they would have a glorious time together when he showed her what a real sail was like. She'd find London fascinating, and she'd fall in love with Paris if they could work out a trip over there, perhaps by taking Gwendolyn Downing along as chaperone. Cornelius was a man now, and Amelia a young lady, and, with Flossie to help them, they could look after little Peter for a few months. It all sounded plausible and very appealing. What Sally got out of her experience on the *Bellona* was the realization that she had the nerve for almost any adventure, and she had been very seriously contemplating a voyage with Aaron when the incident in the theater took place. It would have been chancey at best, however she disguised her motives as a visit to Amelia's parents or a trip for the sake of her health, but Peter's knowledge and attitude now made the venture foolhardy in the extreme. He would conclude that she *was* running away with Aaron, and there was no telling what reaction his ambition might motivate him to take in self-protection.

The more she thought about how that little lark with Alexandra had stirred up her pleasant and placid life into turmoil the more incredible it seemed. Why, oh why, was virtue held to be the exclusive province of women? Men could get roaring drunk, deceive their wives, cane each other in the streets, kill each other in duels, cheat each other in trade, and yet be held in high esteem, as the statues rising to the memory of Alexander Hamilton so clearly demonstrated. Yet she didn't envy men, because she often thought that such stupid and dangerous behavior was as surely forced upon them by society, as contrary to their natures, as the prim and proper deportment expected of her for being female. What she resented was the prevailing thought that women were not capable of making intelligent decisions, of mastering academic subjects, of going out without escort, of handling horses or boats, of displaying passion, of . . . well, almost of living at all outside the confines of the home. The Germans had a catchy phrase for it which her maids often used in complaining of the fate that lay ahead of them: *kinder, kirche, küche*—children, church, kitchen. Ironically, only the women who were despised, like the actresses on stage and those lost souls roaming the third tier of the theater, like the poor country women who peddled their produce in the markets while their men worked the fields, were granted the freedom to go about their business as any man could do. Sometimes she thought that her slave, Flossie, was freer than she, and she wondered whether the legal freedom she would have to grant her in 1827 under the new state constitution would improve her lot. During the constitutional convention, she'd twitted Matty about giving women a vote while he was working for platforms to free the slaves and enfranchise men without property, and he'd been horrified at the thought. "Whatever I think of women—and I assure you I believe the world could not get along without them—it would be political suicide even to suggest such a thing," he'd said and added with a wink, "and when it comes to politics, as you know, I am not suicidal." So the world was the way it was and wasn't likely to change, and she was being asked once more to pay the price of being born female.

In the end, she decided to take advantage of being a woman and let Aaron tell her what to do. He understood and appreciated her impulses to throw over the constraints her sex put upon her, and he also understood better than she the male mind which, of course, was what Peter, the politician, meant by the mind of the people. Trusting in his love for her, she could trust Aaron's judgment. The next Sunday he was in port, she had a surprise for him when he came rolling down Broadway in anticipation of a tryst. The day being pleasant she was waiting on the stoop, and she had taken great care to dress as if for a fashionable outing. She wore the pink silk gown and matching Restoration hat with its flowing ostrich plumes that he'd brought her as a present from London and her own best white velvet spencer, trimmed with swansdown. He seemed pleased, if a little puzzled. "I knew that would look beautiful on you," he said, "but why now? Don't tell me we're going to church?"

"I hadn't thought of it, but it might be a good idea. There's something that I've been praying over for weeks in my own way that I must discuss with you. So I thought we might take a little walk in the Battery," she said.

"Must we walk? I've still got my sea legs."

"Oh, you can lean on me. Old Cornelius used to do that all the time. It's such a nice day, and I've been cooped up in the house . . . ."

What she couldn't tell him was that she feared the temptation of being with him in the house, of wanting nothing but to make love again and forget everything else. Whether he sensed that or not, he rather grumblingly agreed, and they set off down Broadway, smiling their way through the church-going traffic that ran counter, as usual, to their course. She said little except to comment on a hat here or a dress there until they passed the Bowling Green, deserted on the Sabbath except for a few old men dozing in the sun, and entered the park. "Now I'll take pity on you," she said, leading him over to a seat on the water's edge where a soft southwest breeze came clean over the sea, ruffling the feathers of her hat and filling the sails of a packet moving sedately toward its berth in the East River.

Studying it with shaded eyes, Aaron said, "It's the *Columbia*, I'm sure. I showed her a clean pair of heels two days ago, and I'll bet old Delano, her master, is still cursing me. They'll never cut into our trade, if they can't meet their schedule."

"I'm sure I've told you how grateful Cornelius and I are to you and the other captains for that. Henry Downing writes that he doesn't even have to use his influence to see that the Van Alen line is favored," she said.

Aaron laughed. "Well, if he does, he's certainly discreet about it, and it's just as well. I hear Secretary of State Adams is so pleased with him that he might recall him for a high post in the department if he's elected president."

She'd been wondering how to get into the subject on her mind, and here was a God-given opportunity. She plunged right in, telling him everything but trying to be light about her lark and Peter's stuffy reaction. She was rather hoping that he'd just laugh it off, but he didn't. When she'd finished, he said, "Sally, Sally. You certainly get yourself into things, don't you?"

"But it was innocent and really humorous—don't you think? And as for Peter, he has no proof; nobody has . . . ."

"What about Flossie? You know, Peter's been so interested in the boy . . . our boy . . . that he's spent a lot of time in the nursery with Flossie, and . . ."

"No! I'm sure she'd never say anything to hurt me even if she thought anything. She's my own slave—"

"But not for long. In any case, he *knows,* and I'm not surprised. It won't be long before other observant people will know, too. Whether for good or ill, the boy is looking more like me all the time . . . ."

"For good! Oh, for good, Aaron! I love what I see of you in him. But what do we do about it?"

"What I'd like to do is make a clean breast of it. Tell young Peter, tell the world. I'm proud of you, of him. Maybe he could learn to be proud of me."

"He could, I'm sure, but there's Cornelius to think about and . . . and my brother . . . and . . ."

". . . your reputation. You're right, Sally: it's selfish of me to make such a suggestion. If Peter really has a chance to be president, there's a lot more at stake here than our own feelings. For all his good service, Adams doesn't really appeal to the people, and I'm afraid of Jackson. When he went into Florida and hung those Englishmen without orders, he proved himself a real man on horseback as far as I'm concerned . . . ."

Hurt that he could think of anything but their relationship, she said, "I didn't know that politics were of such concern to you."

"Normally they're not, but when it comes to who's running the country . . . well, when you're out there with nothing but the flag for protection, you get to feel that it is important. Your father-in-law understood that in his way. He was a loyalist and then a good Federalist, because he knew that people with such principles would protect commerce, the one thing he cared about. There aren't any Federalists left; but at least Peter is enough of a New Yorker to want to see the city prosper—and you and me, for that matter, along with it. Besides, I like him, as I know you do, too. Up to now, he's certainly been understanding about a knowledge that could have provoked a challenge or any number of other unpleasant results. I'm afraid that what we do has suddenly become involved in issues that affect too many others, as you've known all along . . . ."

"What do you mean by that?"

"You've repeatedly sacrificed your own desires, your own will, to your children, and I've loved you for that. But I've made no sacrifices . . . ."

"Your son. You've given up your son . . . ."

"Only for what I've come to see, as you saw so clearly, was his good. And now that his namesake might reach the White House even greater good may be in store."

"Then you agree with Peter?"

"Well, unfortunately he's right about public reaction. Men love to discover what they think is evil in others to excuse their own, and they'll be sniffing his trail like hounds to get a whiff of it. I don't think we can take a chance. I could take over the office in Liverpool as Abner Cole has been asking me to do so that he can come back here and start his own business. It would be a great sacrifice for me, but after a few years . . . ."

"A sacrifice for *you*? I suppose because you couldn't have your beloved ship?"

"No, and you know that. You're just upset. Because I couldn't have my beloved. I know it would be hard for you, too, but . . . ."

"Hard? Oh, God, Aaron, I might as well die."

"Don't say that, Sally. We used to be apart nearly that long when I was in the China trade, and our love survived. Believe me, this will be the best way now for all of us."

She knew he was right, which made his reasonable proposition hurt the more. She hadn't wanted him to be reasonable, logical; she had wanted him to come up with some strange and magical solution to their dilemma that was beyond her own power of thought. She should love him for being unselfish, but she didn't. What she'd loved him for was that he had the nerve, the audacity, to fly in the face of all morality and convention to meet her needs. Couldn't he see that her one need now was to be loved beyond reason?

"You couldn't say that if you loved me," she said.

"But I say it *because* I love you," he argued. "Up to now, it's you who have been wise for both of us, but this time I must be. There just is no other way out."

"I was so sure that you'd think of a better way, Aaron," she said peevishly, leaving words between them that would linger bitterly. "Well, I hear the bells. Church is over . . . ."

Chapter **XI**

The Agony and Ecstacy

He was thirteen and mortified as only a thirteen-year-old boy can be. Why couldn't *anybody* understand how he felt? Up until the minute they started to board, he had been having the time of his life. Going upriver, he'd been so excited that he'd stayed up half the night; he could get away with it, because his mother, sleeping in the women's quarters, couldn't see his empty bunk, and Cornelius always slept like a log anywhere—"the sleep of the just," Cornelius would call it. He would lie for a while on deck, trying to summon poetic thoughts about the universe which did seem infinite, stretching away star upon star upon star in the clear November night until the eye failed and the mind lost comprehension. When his teeth began rattling from the chill, he'd go down to watch the stoker, half-naked and running with sweat, chuck hunks of wood into the fire under the boiler and warm himself on the blasts that came each time the furnace door was opened. It was too noisy there from the clank of machinery for much talk, but the man would wave and wink at him in a friendly way, and he would try to imagine what it would be like tending fire hour after hour and decide that he was lucky to be who he was. He felt differently about the man at the helm, though. Steering a steamboat by day wasn't much of a trick, since even his mother had done it, but you really had to know what you were doing at night. Although the water picked up some light from the stars, its shape was distorted by shadows from the hills, and there were snags and rocks and shallows that only the most alert and practiced eye could detect. He'd stand by the tiller an hour at a time, trying and failing to see the objects the helmsman pointed out ahead, and envy the man his eyes. Probably he could train his own, the way he could train his brain to read Latin and do geometry, but he'd wondered whether he ever would since there were so many, many things he wanted to learn and do. Moving alone from place to place around the darkened boat which itself was moving through a dark and mysterious vale toward new sights and experiences, he had finally been seized with an uncontainable yearning to go everywhere, do everything, be everybody, a yearning that erupted into a conviction that there was nothing here on earth or on those stars above beyond the reach of Peter Schuyler Van Alen. He had carried the conviction like a dream when he crawled into his bunk among those snoring, unimaginative fellow passengers for whom he had only scorn, and it was still on the edge of his consciousness in the morning when the blow fell.

They were all gathering on the piers at Albany where the fleet that had started on Lake Erie a week before was assembling to sail down the Hudson River to New York and out into the Atlantic Ocean. Because of his uncle, Peter Schuyler, who was a senator in Washington, he and his mother and Cornelius had been invited by Governor Clinton to come up and be part of the party to make what the newspapers were calling "the most historic voyage in the three hundred and thirty-three years since Columbus discovered the New World." Excitement had been mounting in the city ever since just before noon on October 26, 1825, when the boom of guns from the Battery signaled that the *Seneca Chief* had moved from the lake into the Erie Canal only eighty-one minutes before. That was how long, Peter figured by reading the accounts, that it had taken batteries placed eight miles apart the length of the state to pass the news along with firing after firing. There wasn't a schoolboy in New York who hadn't been tutored on what the opening of this waterway would mean to the city. All the products of the villages and vineyards, corn fields and cow pastures, forests and fur traps, mines and mills that enterprising settlers were establishing in the boundless interior of the continent could be floated in bulk to New York for transshipment along the East Coast or abroad, and the wines and spices, glass and metal, books and weapons, cloth and perfumes, machinery and medicines coming into New York could be floated west in return. Already the largest city in the nation, New York would now be clearly the richest, and every organization from Tammany to the volunteer fire fighters to the butchers' guild was planning to turn its members out for the marching, music, fireworks and cheering that would greet the flotilla on its scheduled arrival off the Battery on November fourth. There wasn't one of his classmates who didn't envy Peter for his chance to be aboard; he would of course be riding in the *Seneca Chief* with his uncle and the governor and his cousin, James Schuyler, the governor's pastor, and he would go with them all the way out to the sea where the governor would pour a cask of fresh lake water into the Atlantic salt.

Cornelius broke the bad news with that tight little smile of his that Peter had come to hate. "You're going with mother and Aunt Alexandra on the *Matilda*," he said.

"But I *can't*," Peter said. "That's just for women and children. It's a *safety* barge."

"I know," Cornelius said, still grinning, "but there are too many important people wanting to go on the *Seneca Chief*. I only got on myself because I'm an elder, and Cousin James insisted that he needed me to help with the service of blessing when they mingle the waters. You'd better hurry—they're loading now."

"Cornelius, *please*. Couldn't you get me on a real boat at least?"

"Oh, grow up. The *Chief* is just a canal boat, and it's going to have to be towed by the *Chancellor Livingston* just like your barge. I'd just as soon go with mother myself if it weren't for my duties. Now, hurry . . ."

In all the confusion, there was little else he could do. There was no way of getting to Uncle Peter, the only person who might save him, because he was on the deck of the *Chief* with all of the notables surrounding the governor. Whistles were already shrieking and mates crying, " 'Board!" He might be left behind which would be worse, but only a little worse, than going on a safety barge. He ran off in search of his mother and found her waiting by the gangplank leading to the deck of the *Matilda*. "Heavens, hurry, Peter! Where have you been? I was afraid you were lost."

"I thought I was going on the *Chief* with Cornelius, and . . . and all the men."

"There just wasn't room. Anyway, your Aunt Alexandra and I need a man to look after us. Now, hop—they're casting off."

She was trying to make him feel better by calling him a man, but why couldn't she see that it was no *use?* The *Matilda* which was nothing but an old barge with a cabin to get in out of the sun or rain looked like a floating flower garden with all the ladies in their feathered silk hats, and the few children among them were much smaller than he. He was half a head taller than his mother, or brother, and growing so fast that his bony wrists dangled out of the sleeves of the Sunday suit he'd got last year, and his trousers left a gap above the tops of his boots. It was a little hard to be proud of a body that his brother called "a bag of bones," probably out of jealousy of his height, but he could run faster and throw harder than most of the boys who hung around Battery Park when school was out, and he was sure that he could do Cornelius in if it ever came to that. About the only physical feature that gave him hope of ever being handsome was his hair which was black, wavy and shiny as his mother's used to be before it was dulled with specks of gray. There were people who said he was getting to look like Uncle Aaron which was odd since they weren't really related, but he didn't mind; Uncle Aaron had had the eyes of a man who could read the stars and see through the winds, and the mouth, particularly with that scar, of a man who feared nothing and nobody. Uncle Aaron, he bet, would *never* have let himself get trapped into riding on a safety barge with a lot of women. The barges, of which there were two in this flotilla, had been the clever idea of some shipping owner who thought that he was losing the custom of timid women after a number of steamboats blew up. Towed sufficiently aft of the steamer to be out of harm's way, a barge made for slow going, and there wasn't a man worth his salt who would give up the thrills and advantages of speed for a ride in a barge, which accounted for Peter's feelings of humiliation.

Once aboard, he looked around for a place where he could be inconspicuous, but his mother took his hand. "Alexandra's saved us seats—there, right up forward. Come sit with us, Peter," she said.

"Oh, mother . . ."

"What's the matter? You were so excited coming up, and now you look sick."

211

"When we get to the city, all my friends will see I'm riding in a *safety* barge, and . . ."

Sally had the grace and good sense not to laugh. "Oh, so that's it? Well, let me tell you this will be a lot more comfortable and we can see a lot more without all that smoke pouring down on us. We won't get to New York until morning, and maybe we can do something about sneaking you onto the *Chief* later on. But for today, I'm glad you're with me. There's something I want to show you . . . ."

Just the promise of redemption brightened his spirits. "What?"

"Well, I won't tell you—it'll be a surprise."

Peter knew that his mother had grown up on a manor along the river near Kinderhook and that she had had a horse of her own, for which he envied her, and that she had skated clear across the river and back, for which he admired her, but he knew little else of her life as a girl. There was talk about some trouble between her and his grandfather Schuyler, but whenever he asked Uncle Peter or Cousin James about it, they would brush him off. His mother herself would only say something like, "Oh, that was all so long ago, and it doesn't matter now." Actually, Peter rather liked the mystery surrounding his mother's early years, because it allowed an imagination stuffed with reading every romance he could get hold of to play with all sorts of dire and dramatic possibilities. When they'd passed Kinderhook and his mother started excitedly pointing out to him the place where she'd been born, he was not disappointed. The stone house frowning at them from the top of an open slope leading down to the river was very like he'd pictured one of those Scotch castles in Macbeth or the books of Sir Walter Scott, and the impression was enchanced by a mist, drawn from the river by a sun that was warm for November, in which it seemed to float. He could clearly see his mother as a beautiful young princess, entrapped behind its gray walls, until his Grandfather Van Alen, as courageous a sailor as Uncle Aaron from what he'd heard, came to rescue her. He would very much have liked to ask his mother if that's the way it had been, but he was afraid that she'd laugh at him, so he said, "Is this the surprise?"

"Well, yes, in a way. You see all that land, miles and miles of it? A third of it will be yours—yours and Cornelius'."

"But I thought it belonged to Uncle Jacobus and Uncle Peter."

"The surprise is that Uncle Peter, thanks to Aunt Alexandra, has just agreed to sell his share to us. He told me this morning while we were waiting for the boats."

While Sally hoped that the "surprise" would take her son's mind off his childish misery, she had no idea whether owning part of the old Schuyler place would have any meaning for him, and she wasn't even sure of her own motives in arguing Cornelius, much against his will, into joining her in the purchase. On the surface, it seemed logical enough—a way of helping out a brother who'd been good to her and a way of keeping the land in the family. It had been Alexandra who, having no associations with the manor and therefore no feeling for it, had quite naturally suggested the sale to relieve the senator of the debts he'd accumulated in trying to maintain both his marble-faced house in the city and a suitably handsome Georgetown establishment. Since he'd planned to let his son Francis develop and ultimately own the land, Peter had agonized for months before he had come around to Alexandra's point of view, and he and Sally had just this morning sealed the deal with a handshake.

Now that she had it, Sally was conscious of the fact that beneath the surface, somewhere in her depths, lay a motivation that had nothing to do with logic. It had, instead, more to do with a tragedy from which in three long years she had not yet recovered—and might never recover. For the sake of the boys, for the sake of her brother Peter who'd taken on himself more of the blame than he deserved, she had been playing the role of merry widow, filling her house, as always, with the brightest minds of New York, seeing the latest plays, reading the latest books, pretending an interest in the business that Cornelius was so ably taking over and transforming. Yet she had only to close her eyes, day or night, to see again in all its stark black and white reality that little item that, appearing in the papers on a cold winter morning in '22, had stopped her heart.

By long habit developed through the years of living and working in a commercial house, Sally always glanced at the shipping news first. This news was at such a premium in New York where so many men made or lost fortunes by being alert to slight shifts in the prices on European markets, political upheavals, disasters at sea, currency variations and the like that the enterprising New York papers would despatch reporters on fast schooners to get the latest European intelligence from passengers of incoming packets and print it before their competitors. These accounts were often little more than a headline and paragraph on the front page to be followed up at leisure and in more detail after the ship docked, but the information could be enough for a quick-thinking merchant to turn a dollar in the meantime. The item that shook Sally to the depths had run under a headline, OWNER AND CAPTAIN LOST AT SEA:

"The mate, Mr. Coster, of the *Evelina*, flagship of the Van Alen line of packets, told this reporter that the ship's owner, Mr. George Van Alen, and her captain, Mr. Aaron Roberts, who is well known in this port for his daring adventures as a privateer during the late War, had been swept overboard in a storm in the Irish Sea, where waves rise in monstrous proportions. It is hoped that more intelligence on this tragic occurrence will be forthcoming when the *Evelina* makes port."

Sally couldn't remember how long she stared at the item, how many times she read it over before pure shock gave way to something like panic. She had to get down to meet that ship before Coster talked to anyone else. Fortunately, under the circumstances, one of the ways in which she helped her son Cornelius with his workload was to scan the papers and inform him of any news that might affect the business. He'd hear of this soon, of course—from the next customer who dropped in—but, if she hurried she just might have time enough to learn what really had happened before she had to face Cornelius. Taking the paper with her, she put on her heaviest fur wrap and muff, ran into the street and flagged down a hack. When she reached the docks, she found that a pilot schooner was just putting out to meet the *Evelina*, which was hove to outside the Narrows. Not willing to tell her name or mission, she begged, then finally bought, her way aboard, much to the annoyance of the old pilot who considered women at sea bad luck.

The boat, designed for speed and to move in the lightest of airs, carried a great spread of sail above her narrow open-decked hull. Sally was grudgingly allowed to huddle in a corner of the little cockpit in the stern, where the crew also crouched to work the helm and the sheets that ran aft from the booms through blocks. There was little protection there, however, as the boat, heeling sharply to the winter wind, smashed into choppy seas. Water boiled along the lee combing and came over the windward side in sheets of icy spray. Except for her muffed hands, Sally was soon miserably wet and cold. But both the drenching and the bustle when the little schooner would flip, sails rattling and blocks squeaking, from tack to tack were exactly what she needed to keep her mind from dwelling on all the dark possibilities of what she might learn. The one question most urgently demanding an answer was why was Aaron on the *Evelina* at all? He'd taken over the Liverpool office as planned and was supposed to stay there until Peter's political fortunes were assured, one way or the other. Why, then—why? She could only hope that this Mr. Coster would have an answer. When their schooner emerged from the Narrows and took the full force of the wind Sally thought for an instant that she would meet the same end as Aaron: before the men could ease the sheet, the boat heeled so far that water poured into the cockpit, running chill over the tops of her boots and down around her ankles. Involuntarily she cried out, and the old pilot said, "Told you this was no place for women, should have waited until we got the *Evelina* in. What's your all-fired hurry?"

Under these circumstances, being coy made little sense. "I'm Mrs. Van Alen."

"Oh, ma'am, I should have knowed," the pilot said, taking off his hat and baring a shiny skull to the cold. "My apologies, ma'am. Here, have your money back, I'm sorry about your husband but, if you'll forgive me saying it, more so about Captain Roberts, as fine a man as ever sailed from this port."

As far as she was concerned it was the judgment of the world on the two men whose lives had so suddenly ended. When they managed to get her aboard *Evelina* and Mr. Coster joined her in the captain's cabin he gave her, innocently enough, a greatcoat that Aaron had worn to replace her wet furs. She very nearly broke down, very nearly, but she knew she couldn't afford to waste these moments in such self-indulgence. "Just tell me everything, everything you know, please, Mr. Coster."

Mr. Coster, solid, strong-faced, the kind of man Aaron would want by his side, seemed very uncomfortable. He wouldn't sit, kept twisting the hat he'd taken off in his hands. "I don't know as I should, ma'am."

"Mr. Coster, I am, after all, the owner's widow and the new owner's mother. I have a right to know. Why was Captain Roberts aboard? It was my understanding that he was to stay and manage the company's affairs in Liverpool."

"Mine, too, ma'am, mine too. I was going to command the *Evelina* first time and looking forward to it—"

"Well, what *happened?*"

"I'm not rightly certain, ma'am. In the last hour before sailing Mr. Van Alen comes up from London in a private carriage, horses frothing as if he'd raced them the whole way, and goes into Captain Roberts' office. They had words from what the clerk tells me but none he could rightly hear. Next thing I know Captain Roberts is bringing his duffle aboard and telling me, 'Mr. Van Alen has decided to sail to New York, and I feel obliged to look to his comfort.'

"I don't mind telling you, ma'am, I was right miffed and took some pleasure when the blow comes out of nowhere that first night and hits us like a hammer. We lost the foretopsail and main gallant before we got her reefed down, and the Irish Sea, being shallow, was throwing up waves higher than a church steeple. The *Evelina's* sound enough, and she was riding them like a cork excepting for an occasional wash of white water, but she was tossing the passengers around like dice in a box. Captain Roberts and I are standing watch together near the helm, so when we have a chance to talk I says, 'Is this your idea of keeping the owner comfortable, captain?' Most times the captain would have laughed at that but he says, sober as a judge and as if he could read my mind, 'Don't worry, Coster, you'll get your ship soon enough. Go below and fetch the owner, I want his permission to turn back.'

"Now a captain needs no such permission, and I was afraid of bringing Mr. Van Alen up on a deck awash since, begging your pardon, ma'am, I knew I would find him unsteady on his pins and not from the sea. But you don't argue with your captain in a storm, so I just about drag Mr. Van Alen, mad as a wet hen and frightened too from the looks of him, up on deck. He lights right into the captain, 'What the hell are you trying to do, Roberts, kill me? I guess you don't want the whole world to know about you and that—' "

Coster who had been warming to his story stopped dead and turned red in the face. "What were you going to say, Mr. Coster?"

"It ain't right for a lady, ma'am . . . ."

"Mr. Coster, *please,* I have to know everything."

"Well, ma'am, what he said was, 'that whore.' So then the captain gestures at me and the helmsman and says, 'This is no place for such talk, George. Come over by the rail.' He puts an arm around Mr. Van Alen to steady him and leads him back by the taffrail. Well, it's so dark and with the wind whipping spindrift like shot into my eyes, I can hardly see them. We were taking waves, as I say, but nothing the captain wasn't used to, so I didn't worry until fifteen minutes or so went by. Then I hear this sound like a wail, a little different from the howl of the wind, and I get this odd feeling, and I know before I even go back to look that they're gone. I just can't believe it—if there's one man who ain't careless at sea, it's Aaron Roberts. So I heave to, have a search made of the ship and even manage to get a boat out in all them waves when we had some light at dawn. But there's never a sight of them—nothing but the angriest sea you ever saw. All I can think about is how Captain Roberts always said to me, 'When I die, Coster, I want to be part of the sea.' . . ."

Coster's voice started to break. "What are you trying to tell me, Mr. Coster? Are you trying to say this wasn't an accident?"

"I rightly don't think it was, ma'am. I've served with Captain Roberts through hurricanes and battles, and he had the best sea legs I've ever known. No wave would tumble him, not likely—or anyone with him, unless . . . just my thinking, ma'am . . ."

Struggling for control, Sally said, "Well, thank you, Mr. Coster, for being so truthful. I'm sure you understand that it would not be good for the company if such a story gets out. Let's keep your suspicions between you and me, and perhaps it would be best if young Mr. Van Alen handles the reporters."

"Never you fear, ma'am, I wouldn't want it thought that Captain Roberts . . . . well, he's the best I ever shipped with and—"

"I know, Mr. Coster. We'll all miss him, but I'm sure you will take his place creditably in the *Evelina*. Now I must be keeping you from your duties on deck . . ."

Relieved, Coster clapped on his hat and almost ran from her. It was not a moment too soon, because she suddenly lost all control. Still wet and cold in spite of Aaron's coat, she was a mass of such misery that for a second time going on living seemed worse than dying. But unlike that first time, she knew even as she rocked and shivered and cried that she would have to live, and gradually, with the sounds of the ship being warped into the wharf penetrating her shell of sorrow, she began to think again. The boys must never know—nobody must ever know. She felt confident that she could trust Coster, to protect Aaron's reputation, and the story that Cornelius as head of the firm and head of the family would put out would simply confirm that stark little item: it was a freak if believable accident, the kind that unfortunately kept claiming lives from among New York's shipping fraternity. Only she would ever know and have to learn to live with the knowledge that Aaron had found that "better way," about which she had so carelessly taunted him, of solving their problems. It was all too obvious from Mr. Coster's story that George had at last come to suspect, or to know, their secret and had been on his way back to make trouble. Could it be considered a gallant act that Aaron had taken George with him—or was it simply murder? Oh, God! In any case she was the cause of it all, and who would, who could, forgive her? For the first time in a long while she wished that she could find and believe in a forgiving God . . . she still stood condemned by the only God she'd ever heard about—the God of Jacobus and of James and of Cornelius, her son. Yes, condemned to go on living—and to what purpose . . . ?

Cornelius was not hypocrite enough to weep for his father, but he did mourn the loss from the business of Uncle Aaron. Young Peter also seemed more concerned about Uncle Aaron's death, more shocked than saddened that so brave and expert a seaman could be killed by the sea he'd loved and, up to then, conquered. Taking his first experience with the reality of personal death harder than his brother, Peter had for a while gone into a funk that mercifully called on her to demonstrate a belief she scarcely had in the need for the living to go on. As a matter of the necessary propriety to uphold the Van Alen name in the community, she consented to let Cousin James hold a joint memorial service in his church. She thought that he was rather unkindly vague about the probable destination of the souls of the departed, concentrating instead on the comfort a loving Lord would give the bereaved. Whether it was the doing of the Lord or not, her comfort, such as it was, came from the fact that the church was packed, not with its fashionable congregation whose members had long ago written George Van Alen off as a black sheep, but with seamen who had walked the long way from the waterfront up Fifth Avenue in the cold to pay their respects to a captain they had admired. Aaron would have appreciated their tribute. *Aaron* . . . how could she reach him, would she reach him? Yes, of course, her own prayer became lines from that poem of Mr. Bryant's that Aaron had liked so for its picture of the dead returning to the bosom of the nature that had nurtured them, and for its promise that . . .

All that breathe
Will share thy destiny. The gay will laugh
When thou art gone, the solemn brood of care
Plod on, and each one as before will chase
His favorite phantom; yet all these shall leave
Their mirth and their employments, and shall come
And make their bed with thee . . .

Gradually, gradually, she had learned again by living how to live, by pretending to become something of what she pretended, but now she wondered whether buying that land for which she really had no use wasn't a subconscious effort to reach back into a time of innocence, wondered if she didn't look on the very opportunity to acquire it as a kind of forgiveness. Interestingly, the graves of her parents lay in that section of the land she now owned, as did a grassy knoll under a great oak tree where she'd lost her innocence. But the boy beside her couldn't know all this, and she hoped that he never would . . . .

All innocent of anything but romantic notions, Peter studied the expanse of countryside that his mother pointed out. Much of it was still covered with forest dressed in the dying reds and oranges of fall. Indians could live there, had lived there; he could blaze trails, camp in the woods. "Then we can come here in the summer instead of Greenwich?" he now asked his mother.

There was nothing for a boy of eleven or twelve to do in a little place like Greenwich except to hang around the wharves and watch the ferries come and go—or read. He'd read everything he could lay his hands on, and just this last summer he'd discovered a new hero who, almost without his knowing it, was changing his life. He was Lord Byron. Peter was first fascinated when he'd read that winter of the poet's death from exposure while serving in the field with the Greek revolutionaries for whom virtually all Americans from President Monroe on down had deep sympathy. But the only poet Peter had ever seen in the flesh was William Cullen Bryant, the new editor of *The New York Review* and *Athenaeum* who'd come to one of his mother's literary evenings. If his coat had been black instead of blue, Mr. Bryant could have passed for a parson with his slight figure, pale complexion, domed forehead and serious expression. He wasn't a figure to inspire a twelve-year-old boy, but Lord Byron certainly was.

So vigorous that he'd swum the Hellespont as a young man and so handsome that he'd known the love of beautiful British ladies and sultry Italian countesses, Lord Byron made the poet's life seem the most romantic a boy could imagine. And his lines! What New York boy who'd wistfully watched the tall-rigged ships heading out to exotic places wouldn't thrill to this?

> Once more upon the waters! yet once more!
> And the waves bound beneath me as a steed
> That knows his rider. Welcome to their roar!
> Swift be their guidance, wheresoe'er it lead!
> Though the strained mast should quiver as a reed,
> And the rent canvas fluttering strew the gale,
> Still must I on; for I am as a weed,
> Flung from the rock, on Ocean's foam to sail
> Where'er the surge may sweep, the tempest's breath prevail.

Peter had started writing poetry immediately after he got involved in reading Byron, and, even as he sat in humiliation between his mother and his aunt on the barge, his mind was playing with lines that had come to him as a result of his night on deck. He had got as far as:

> Roll, mighty river, roll
> Under skies bejeweled with stars
> Like diamonds in a velvet bowl . . .

None of the rhyming words he knew like "ours," "bars," "tars," "spars" yet gave him an idea for another line, but he was sure that it would come to him in time. Meanwhile, he was upset by his mother's answer to his question. "I've been thinking about that," she said, "but I'm afraid Cornelius would never want to be so far from his work."

"Why do we always have to do everything Cornelius wants? Why couldn't just you and me come up here?"

"I hate to leave Cornelius for so long. Since your Uncle Aaron died, I'm the only one he has to rely on for advice."

"But I thought Cornelius was so smart."

"He is when it comes to facts and figures, but he's spent so much time in the counting room that he knows very little about people. You

220

remember the trouble with Mr. Barker? Well, I could have saved him that with just one look at the man, so I've since been arranging to meet everyone he insures."

"I think Cornelius deserved it—he was trying to cheat Mr. Barker, too."

"Peter! How can you imagine that your brother, an elder in the church, would cheat? He was just so busy that he hadn't gotten around to delivering the policy."

Peter sighed. His mother could never see any wrong in Cornelius, just because he worked so hard, but that business with Barker had a funny smell. Ordinarily, Peter was bored to the point of writing poetry in his head by the incessant table talk about business between his mother and brother. But he was interested when Cornelius started complaining about Mr. Barker, because, from the sound of it, his perfect brother had at last made a bad mistake. In the old days, marine insurance was a chancey business with ships sailing irregularly at the whim of captain or owner often to secure some sudden commercial advantage without regard to other considerations. Pioneers of the trade like old Cornelius Van Alen and Jacob Astor scoffed at insurance, regarding the loss of a ship and all hands as part of the gamble they were taking. But with the growth of regular packet service—there were a dozen ships sailing on monthly schedules to England alone, among them the Van Alen's, and more to Le Havre, Havana, Vera Cruz, Savannah, New Orleans—it became possible for minds like that of young Cornelius Van Alen to calculate the odds against disaster and fix premium rates that would enrich the insurer while protecting the insured. When this dawned upon Cornelius he was as excited as Peter would be to find a rhyming line, and he immediately put Van Alen & Son into the insurance business, saying it was like "finding money in the streets."

By covering only those owners and captains with good records, Cornelius made his own words come true until he ran afoul of old Mr. Barker. While, as Sally claimed, her feminine instinct might have warned her against Barker, a man with too glib a tongue and too shifty an eye, Cornelius' calculating logic led him into a trap. One of New York's newly minted rich, Barker had created the stuff of legend among his fellow merchants by his shrewdness and vindictiveness. Somewhat in awe of the old merchant's reputation, Cornelius nevertheless had a few reservations about his proposition. Barker wanted to insure his vessel *Indies* already outward bound on a catch-as-catch-can trading venture in the ports of Bombay, Ceylon, Calcutta and Canton. Because of the length of the voyage and the uncertainty of the value of the cargoes, it was difficult to calculate a suitable premium. But Barker waved away Cornelius' doubts. "I'd be satisfied with ten thousand if she's lost," he said, "and I'll pay double your premium on that if you'll cover me." It was a bargain hard to refuse, and when Cornelius agreed, Barker said, "I don't have the premium money in hand and will have to raise it. But you draw up a policy, and I'll be around presently to settle with you."

It was months before Cornelius saw Barker again. He had drawn up the policy but left it unsigned, pending payment of the premium, and, indeed, he'd almost forgotten the whole matter when Barker came bounding in, all smiles, and said, "Well, Mr. Van Alen, I've heard of the *Indies,* so we might as well forget that policy." Cornelius was stung. When a merchant "heard" of his vessel, it meant that she'd been sighted making for port by one of the fast coastal schooners. The double premium would now be sure money in Cornelius' pocket, money to which as an insurer he had a clear right by the nature of the business. "Mr. Barker," he said, "I took your word and have gone to the trouble of drawing your policy and was just waiting for your payment to sign it. If it's said that you went back on your word, you'll never get another insurer in this city." Barker's smile vanished. "I thought you might take that line, young man," he said. "You're a chip off your grandfather's block, making such a Dutch bargain. But here's your money—just to prove my word." Cornelius took the money, hastily signed the policy and gave it to Barker who stomped out angrily. When the next day, the newspapers published an account of the *Indies* going down in an Atlantic storm, it was only too obvious what Barker had heard of the vessel, and the story went around the exchange on Wall Street as an amusing incidence of "diamond cut diamond"—amusing, that is, to all but a badly shaken and taken Cornelius Van Alen.

But Peter, no diamond himself, thought the story amusing, too. Given a little less greed and sense of righteous indignation, his brother might have avoided the trap. Peter couldn't understand why his mother didn't agree with him, why she put up with so much from Cornelius. For instance, Cornelius was an awful prig. If his mother forgot herself in excitement, as she often did, and said something like

"My God," Cornelius would say, "Please, mother, don't take the Lord's name in vain," and she'd always say she was sorry. Cousin James had got Cornelius to take the pledge and join the Temperance Society he'd started in his new country church way out Fifth Avenue, and whenever his mother served wine to her guests Cornelius would embarrass her by ostentatiously turning his glass upside down. Peter would leave his up and get it filled by winking at the maid who was serving, but often as not Cornelius would see it and say, "Mother, you're not going to let a child drink alcohol," and his mother would meekly tell the maid to take it away. The very worst thing Cornelius did was when Amelia was down from college visiting, and Cornelius caught him looking through the keyhole and watching her undress; she was just about to take off her chemise, and his cock was so hard it hurt when Cornelius snuck up behind him and grabbed him by the ear and dragged him right into his mother's room. She was getting ready for bed herself and was in her nightgown, and it was hard to tell who was more embarrassed at first. Peter wasn't sure whether his mother was struggling to keep from laughing or crying, but she said, "I should think you would have taken care of this yourself, Cornelius," and Cornelius said, "He never listens to me because you spoil him, and anyway I thought you ought to know what kind of a boy he's turning out to be." His mother sighed and said almost to herself, "Oh, I wish Aaron were still alive," and then to him, "Peter you *should* be ashamed of yourself. Now go to your room and stay there and think about it for the rest of the week. Cornelius, I think you should bring Cousin James down to talk to him; he seems to have done you so much good in these things."

Actually, Peter would rather have had his mother talk to him, but he guessed that ladies didn't talk about things like that. He wondered why she'd send for Cousin James when he knew that they argued so much about religion. If his Uncle Peter hadn't been in Washington, maybe she'd have sent for him instead, and he had a feeling that Uncle Peter would be understanding. Even though he was gray haired and getting stout, Uncle Peter had an eye for the ladies and was always kissing them at gatherings—"Good politics whether they vote or not," he'd say with a wink—and once when he didn't know that Peter was watching, Uncle Peter stroked Aunt Alexandra's behind and made her blush and look at him in a way that caused Peter's cock to swell. This seemed to be happening to him all the time lately, and, although he knew from talking to other boys at school that it happened to them, too, it would have been comforting to have somebody like Uncle Peter say that it was all right—and more comforting yet if his mother could have somehow let him know that she wasn't ashamed of his becoming a man. The awful part of it was that, lying alone in his room with nothing to do, he couldn't think of how bad he was but kept imagining what he would have seen of Amelia in another minute or two and ended up taking his hard cock in his hand, as some of the other boys said they did, and getting the most wonderful sensation he'd ever known. All that he could think about then was how much more wonderful it was supposed to be with a girl. One of the boys at school had already lain with a whore and had told them that there wasn't any feeling in the world like sliding your cock right up into a soft and slippery cunt, and he had been sick with disgust at such an unromantic description of what he liked to think of as an act of beauty. Still, it had haunted him and aroused his jealousy that another boy should know so much about the mysterious female body when he, Peter Schuyler Van Alen, wanted to know everything about everything, and had finally afflicted him with the consuming curiosity that drove him to his knees beside that keyhole. He wondered whether he could ever face Amelia again, though he doubted that Cornelius out of shame and his mother out of delicacy, would ever tell her what happened. The thing was—the thing he wished that he could let his mother know—that he had no lust, no lust at all, for Amelia but only an arousing lust for knowledge, for experience: he just wanted to *see* what a cunt looked like. Was this a sin? Probably, since lust itself was a mortal sin, as he'd heard Cousin James say often enough from the pulpit without, until now, really understanding the meaning of the word.

Peter was in a very confused state, at once remorseful and elated over the discovery of the power of lust, when Cousin James did arrive. Still handsome, still affable, and certainly knowledgeable since he'd been married for years and had a daughter of his own, Cousin James pretended not to be shocked. "Well, Peter," he said, "I guess it's natural in a boy your age to be curious about such things, but you must understand how shameful it is to spy on a lady, particularly one who is almost your sister. That is truly wicked, because it smacks not only of lust but of incest, two of the worst sins in the Bible. I'm sure you remember the trouble David got into from looking upon a woman unclothed in her bath, and I'm sure you have heard me speak often enough of how our Lord said that a man who lusts after a woman in his heart has already committed adultery."

Peter tried a defense. "I . . . I didn't lust after her . . . I . . . I just wanted to see . . ."

"But why did you want to see? I'm sure I know what it did to you, and I can only hope you didn't spill your seed on the ground, another grievous sin. Hell's fire awaits those who so sin unless they confess and repent. Did you do that?"

Peter couldn't bring himself to confession, but his silence was damning, and Cousin James said, "Oh, my boy, kneel with me, and we'll ask God's forgiveness . . . ."

There seemed nothing else to do, and Peter kneeled beside Cousin James, burying a face flushed with embarrassment in the covers of his bed. "Our heavenly Father," Cousin James prayed, "look upon this sinner with compassion and pluck from his heart the evil of lust. Thou knowest this sin to be a special temptation of Thy son, Peter, for he is cursed with the blood of his parents . . ." Peter wondered what Cousin James meant and wanted to stop the prayer and ask but didn't dare. ". . . but Thou hast promised, too, that the sins of the father be not visited upon the son who like Thy servant Cornelius seeks Thy forgiveness and support. As he has prayed for the salvation of his brother . . ." That was news to Peter, too, and the thought of his brother praying for him, probably right in front of Cousin James, upset him: didn't Cornelius ever have a hard-on? ". . . so do I now. Grant, oh Lord, to Thy son, Peter, a pure heart in a pure body, we pray in the name of the Father, the Son, and the Holy Ghost. Amen."

Getting to his own feet, Cousin James pulled Peter up with him and, lifting his chin, looked him in the eyes and said, "Don't look so upset, Peter. We are all of us sinners who sometimes need God's help. For men lust is something like a bird—you can't keep it from flying over your head, but you can keep it from nesting in your hair, and you must. God gave men a sexual urge so that they will marry and produce children and care for their families, and he has commanded the man who would serve him to use it only for that purpose. When you get married, you will discover, as I did, that God in his wisdom denied the sexual urge to good women so that they will cleave to their husbands and love their children. The body of a good woman should be thought of as a pure receptacle for a pure seed and not as an object of lust. As for the other kind of women, they should be avoided like the plague—indeed, many of them carry a disease that can cripple your manhood or result in slow and painful death. When you are tempted by lust in any way, pray for God's cleansing. Now I can only say, as our Savior did, go and sin no more. Can you do that, Peter?"

"I . . . I'll try . . ."

He had tried and for the most part succeeded. There were so many other things to think about, especially after he began writing poetry, that he was less troubled by lust. In a way, he had to thank Cousin James for telling him about the feelings of good women, because it made it easier for him to follow his natural inclination and idealize them. In his mind and in his poetry, he could reach for images of perfection and purity—stars and snow, crystal and gold, for example —to describe the girls who attracted him, like the one with the saucy red ringlets and dimpled smile who lived down by the Bowling Green. The possibility, the probability, that a girl's thoughts could be as clean and beautiful as her looks was far more enticing to his imagination than any crude description of rutting. He was jealous when he came upon a poem by Lord Byron that caught what he wanted to think about girls so much better than he could:

> She walks in beauty, like the night
> Of cloudless climes and starry skies,
> And all that's best of dark and bright
> Meet in her aspect and her eyes . . .

Such lines were probably more effective than prayer in purifying Peter's mind and certainly more effective than the proposal that Cornelius made, once he'd served his punishment. "I think Peter ought to go to work, mother," he said. "I was clerking at his age, and it kept my mind occupied with better things. We could well use him in the counting room."

The counting room of Van Alen & Son was the last place on earth where Peter wanted to spend as much as an hour. He found the chill and inky dry smell of it repulsive, and the long columns of figures and lists of goods bought and sold were mentally stultifying. Her interest in the business was another thing he couldn't understand about his mother; he had to conclude that it must have been more exciting in the old days when Grandfather Cornelius sent ships to China. Uncle Aaron's tales of lying in the Whampoa River while the Grand Hoppo, clad in silk and heralded by the ringing of brass gongs, came alongside in his barge to measure the ship and collect the cumshaw that was the price of doing business in China had enough exotic flavor to arouse some small interest in Peter. Not so his brother's talk of fares and duties and premium rates and the like. So he actually trembled as he awaited his mother's reply.

"You know, Cornelius, I've always regretted that you did go to work so young, that you didn't go to college. I appreciate it more than you can know, for I don't know what would have happened to all of us otherwise, but I do want Peter to have the opportunity you missed," she said.

"I don't think I missed anything, mother," Cornelius said. "The worst clerk we have spent a year at Columbia and thinks he knows more than I do as a result. And look what's happened to Amelia. The other day she was arguing against Christianity with Cousin James by quoting out of Voltaire. I don't think she even believes in God anymore."

"Well, now that you mention James, wasn't it at Princeton that he found his faith?" his mother asked.

"You know as well as I do that James got his faith from Grandfather Schuyler. He's told me himself that without such grounding he might have been spoiled by his studies, but as it was he was able to use them to reach a better understanding of the true word," Cornelius said. "You've been letting Peter get away without even going to church here. What would happen to him at a college?"

"I don't know, but I'd like him to go. I've seen some of his poetry, and I think he might become a writer . . . ."

"A writer? There's no money in writing. I suppose you expect me to support him the way Mr. Irving's brothers have done? Well, I'm not about to do it. We've had enough drain on this firm with father and his useless sisters, and I think Peter ought to start pulling his own oar."

"There is almost nothing I wouldn't do for you, Cornelius—and much that I've done that you'll never know about—but I must have my way in this," his mother said. "People are different. You've a natural head for business, thank God, but Peter doesn't. It would be a waste of his talents to put him up to that copying desk. You let me

227

worry about Peter; you have enough to do."

Peter really loved his mother for that, not that he didn't love her anyway. More than anything else she could have said or done, it showed that she did not consider him a hopeless sinner. He was more embarrassed than pleased, though, when evidently to test her own judgment, she summoned him to one of her "blue stocking" affairs, as they were called after the gatherings of literary ladies in London where one of the prominent male guests appeared in blue hose, and asked him to read some of his poetry. He knew most of the men from hanging around the bookshop of James Eastburn & Co. on the corner of Broadway and Pine just to see them come and go and overhear them exchange the time of day. There was Mr. Cooper, a large man with the look and manners more of a country squire than a writer; the lean, intense Mr. Bryant; Gulian Verplanck, whom Mr. Cooper always called "an honor to the Dutch"; Fitz-Greene Halleck who'd written a novel called *Fanny* that poked fun at rich New York belles; John Vanderlyn, a Dutch artist from upriver who was supposed to have kept his mother's friend, old Mr. Burr—"Grandpa Aaron"— alive while he was in Paris; Professor Samuel Morse who taught design at Columbia; and some ladies and other men he didn't know. Most of the men were members of Mr. Cooper's bread and cheese club that met every so often for lunch in Washington Hall up the street; when a new member was proposed, the others voted by popping a piece of bread or a piece of cheese into a bowl—a single piece of cheese being enough to ban a man. When she'd first invited them to her house, his mother had explained to Mr. Cooper, "I'd love to join your club, but I know if a woman were ever put up, you'd have more cheese than bread on your hands, so I'm starting my own. I have neither cheese nor bread, but my father-in-law over the years laid down the best cellar of Madeira in the city, which should make you content."

Evidently it did, for they'd come back again and again and, therefore, they listened to his halting delivery of florid, sing-song lines with the charity of friends. Mr. Cooper clapped and said, "Capital! Capital! A prodigy. I was over thirty before I wrote a line." Mr. Bryant chimed in, "Ah, but you're no poet, Cooper. I was only thirteen when my father got my first work, 'The Embargo,' published, and I've been living it down ever since. It's the right time to write poetry, young man, and yours shows promise, but don't hurry it into print. I'll bet

Halleck here was writing verse at your age, weren't you, Halleck?"
Halleck laughed, "You choose your words carefully as a poet should,
Bryant. Yes—verse, not poetry, alas." In the end the cheerful consensus was that Peter might indeed have the makings of a writer and that
he should get as much education as possible. Both Mr. Cooper and
Mr. Bryant expressed regrets at having dropped out of Yale, the one
as a result of a prank and the other out of poverty. Thinking of his
own lonely youth in the rocky farmlands of Massachusetts, Bryant
said, "Wherever you go to college, young man, you've got an advantage over all of us here by being in New York. Ever since Irving set
up shop—you'll excuse a favorable reference to the defamer of the
Dutch, won't you, Gulian?—it's become the honeypot for America's
literary bees. I confess that my opportunities were better in Boston
where my poetry was first recognized and published, but the minds
on which I wished to hone my own were here in New York. Most of
them are right here in this room, including those behind pretty faces
like your mother's. So you're lucky, young man, to have the stimulus
for a literary career, and, if I may say so, the wealth with which to
pursue it."

After that evening, there'd been a tacit understanding between him
and his mother that he *would* pursue a literary career, and yet the very
imagination that made this feasible kept taunting him with life's other
infinite possibilities. He could easily learn the mysteries of the sea,
as Uncle Aaron had done, by signing on one of the Van Alen packets
as a hand. Then there was this tricky and challenging river. Captain
Vanderbilt was always offering to teach him to pilot one of the steamboats that he and Cornelius were having built now that Mr. Webster
had persuaded the Supreme Court to rule against a state's right to
grant monopolies in interstate commerce in the *Gibbons* vs. *Ogden*
case. "You're a big enough younker and you ought to come by it
naturally seeing that you are your mother's son," the captain would
say. And then there was always the West which tugged like a mighty
magnet on the metal of adventure in every normal American boy's
spirit. There was danger to be sought and fame to be won in exploring the wilds and fighting the Indians; there were fortunes to be made
in trapping fur, developing land, discovering minerals. He could be
on his way any day by just knocking on Mr. Astor's door. When Mr.
Astor moved to Broadway and set up his shop across his backyard on
Vesey Street, his mother started taking Peter with her to call of a nice

afternoon. They were sure to find Mr. Astor sitting in the fancy, arched piazza between his house and shop, enjoying his after-dinner glass of beer and game of checkers. Mr. Astor seemed to light up at the sight of his mother—"my liddle bartner"—and for Peter's sake she would prod him into spinning a yarn about his adventurous days of seeking fur in Iroquois country. Once when the clerk he usually played checkers with was sick, Mr. Astor asked Peter to take him on. He was embarrassed at how easily he beat the big man, but Mr. Astor seemed delighted. "Vell! Vell! A smart boy! But no vonder with such a mother. Vould you like to go Vest? I could use you in my American Fur Company." His mother cut in, "Oh, no, Mr. Astor, he's going to be a poet." Peter blushed when Astor shouted, "A boet? You call dat man's vork? I am surprised at you, bartner—there is no money in boetry. No, you come to me, young man, ven you get over such nonsense." There was politics, too. He'd rather despised Mr. Van Buren for being so small—no bigger than Cornelius—and dainty and smelling of cologne almost like a woman until he'd seen him one night at a political parade, standing on top of a carriage and waving at the cheering crowds with some kind of inner light in his eyes brighter than the torches surrounding him, and he'd caught a glimpse of a power that might well be more rewarding than conquering the sea or taming the forest.

Yes, the possibilities remained infinite on that November day, and just thinking about them increased his humiliation at being sandwiched between his mother and Aunt Alexandra on that barge. The magnificence of the scenery was lost upon him, and he was grateful when night began to fall on his disgrace. Rather than bunk with the children, he would stay on deck and perhaps regain some of the rapture of the night before. But a second sleepless night was too much for his young body, and when he stretched out to look at the stars he fell right into the sky and was surprised to be awakened in broad daylight by his mother shaking and calling, "Hurry, get up, Peter. Your Aunt Alexandra is arranging to send you over to the *Chief.*" Peering around he saw that the fleet was dead in the water; a boat was alongside their barge with an officer distributing orders from the governor for the line of parade past the city. Aunt Alexandra was saying, "Wait a minute. I want you to take my nephew with a very urgent personal message to my husband, Senator Schuyler."

Before he was fully awake, he was in the rowboat with an envelope in his hand. Minutes later he was being rushed to the deckhouse of the *Chief* where his Uncle Peter and the other dignitaries were enjoying after-breakfast brandy and cigars. Cousin James and Cornelius were sitting off in a corner, their glasses turned down, and Cornelius frowned when, disheveled and awkward, he stumbled in with the envelope held out like a ticket in his hand. Trying to ignore the presence of Governor Clinton and the other gentlemen, some of whom were congressmen and mayors of towns along the canal, he went right to Uncle Peter saying, "An urgent message for you from Aunt Alexandra." His uncle, trying to puff a cigar into life, grabbed the envelope, tore it open, glanced at the message, and, smiling, said, "Yes . . . Yes, it's urgent indeed." Then he got up, put an arm around Peter and said, "Gentlemen, I want you to meet my godson and namesake, Peter Schuyler Van Alen. My wife thinks it appropriate that he be with me to witness today's ceremonies, and, by your leave, governor . . ."

"By all means," the governor said. "If he's your namesake, Peter, he's sure to be a politician, and he ought to see some of the rewards of being in politics. Matter of fact, young man, do you see that keg over there? . . ." Peter's eyes, following the governor's gesture, found a water keg, sitting in the middle of the cabin. Once an ordinary barrel, it had been stained, decorated with paintings of birds and flowers, and rather crudely lettered WATER—LAKE ERIE. ". . . I'm going to have to pick that up and dump it into the ocean, and it's rather heavy for an old man like me. So I could use a pair of strong, young arms to help me. Would you do it?"

Would he do it? His emotions were so confused by being catapulted from a sleep begun in a kind of misery to an awakening in a kind of glory beyond his hopes that he could only nod dumbly. His uncle, sensing his feelings, said, "Well, Peter, if you're going to help the governor, you'll need your strength, and I'll bet you haven't breakfasted. I'm sure the captain's wife still has some of those ham and eggs and good hot biscuits left in her galley. Why don't you run along and see?"

The captain's wife, a stout and cheerful woman who made her home aboard the *Chief*, was feeding her own brood when Peter came in and assured him that there was always room for one more. Food had never tasted so good to him as on that morning, and he decided that it had something to do with coming fresh from the farms along the canal. When they'd eaten, one of the children led him down into the hold where the *Chief*'s black crew were busy currying the four matched grays that were used to pull the boat along the canal. The horses seemed nervous, stomping and shaking and rubbing against the bars of their stalls. The men would walk them, one at a time, back and forth along the keel. "Cap'n say they got to get used to ridin' the river now, but it like to wear us out," one of the crewmen complained. The stable stench was powerful, and Peter decided that firing a steamboat's boiler might not be the worst job on the river.

By the time he got back on deck, the *Chief,* jerking like a reluctant dog at its leash to the *Chancellor Livingston,* was abreast of the city and moving through a welcoming fleet of vessels of all shapes and sizes. Yards of the big three and four masters, riding at anchor, were aflutter with flags, and crews, lining their decks, waved their hats and cheered in unison. The voice of the city itself was a discordant medley of bells, guns and fireworks. Peter hurried into the cabin where the dignitaries, still sipping their drinks, were commenting on the scene. "This is a day that will go down in history, governor, and it's all your doing," his Uncle Peter was saying.

"Ah, yes, I wish your friend Matty were here to see this. He did his best to see that I'd get no credit," the governor said. "Look at those crowds at the Battery. It's a wonder it doesn't break off and sink."

"You'd better pray that it doesn't. They're votes, Governor, votes," his uncle said.

The governor and the other men, politicians all, laughed, and the governor said, "Speaking of prayer, would you favor us with one, Reverend Schuyler?"

All the men arose and took off their hats as Cousin James with Cornelius beside him moved into the center of the cabin by the little keg. "I have asked an elder of my church and a prominent merchant of New York, Mr. Cornelius Van Alen, who also happens to be a nephew of Senator Schuyler to read a verse of Scripture," James said.

In a heavy whisper, audible to all, the governor said to his Uncle Peter, "This is beginning to look more like a Schuyler day than a Clinton day. If I didn't know you better, Peter, I'd think you arranged it. I just hope the gentlemen of the press won't forget who built the canal."

Peter thought that his Cousin James and Cornelius looked annoyed, but he enjoyed this kind of banter as did the other men, some

232

of whom couldn't help snickering. These men with all of their responsibilities were after all very human, and knowing it made Peter
feel again that there was nothing out of his reach. Cornelius cleared
his throat to gain attention and began droning out the words from
Genesis in a thin, reedy voice:

"So God created man in his own image, in the image of God he
created him; male and female he created them. And God blessed
them, and God said to them, 'Be faithful and multiply, and fill the
earth and subdue it; and have dominion over the fish of the sea and
over the birds of the air and over every living thing that moves upon
the earth."

When Cornelius had finished, James said, "Thank you, brother
Van Alen." Then he kneeled by the cask, put his hand on it and said,
"Oh, God, Thou who hast commanded thy servant, man, to subdue
the earth, bless now this mingling of the waters of the land with the
waters of the sea by the mightiest work of man. Bless Thou, too, Thy
servant, DeWitt Clinton, whose steadfast faith and unceasing effort
brought this miracle to pass . . . ."

Peter heard his uncle tell the governor in a whisper too low for any
other ears, "Well, at least God will know who did it," and the rest of
Cousin James' words were lost to him as he tried to choke down
laughter. When they'd passed the Narrows, they carried the keg out
to the bow where he and the governor lifted it to the rail and poured
the water of Lake Erie into the Atlantic. The captain of the *Chancellor
Livingston* signaled the event with blasts of his whistle, echoed
throughout the fleet. Everybody cheered, and somebody struck up
"The Star Spangled Banner," that Francis Scott Key had written in
the dark days of the last war: "Oh, say can you see by dawn's early
light . . . ?" It, too, was picked up in chorus and echoed from boat
to boat. Amidst all the confusion a newspaper reporter came over
and asked Peter for his name, and he knew right then and for sure
that being Peter Schuyler Van Alen was no ordinary thing, and that
night when the city erupted in an explosion of fireworks greater than
any since Washington's inaugural he felt that the celebration was in
some measure for him.

Too exhausted to mingle with the crowds in the streets, he stood
with his mother at the window of the old house on Broadway and
watched. His mother said something very strange, considering that
she couldn't know his thoughts, "This reminds me of when I was a

little girl down in Battery Park watching the fireworks and saw General Washington looking out from a window on the Bowling Green. I can remember wondering what his feelings might have been on such an occasion, and I think I can appreciate them a little tonight. With both you and Cornelius playing such prominent roles in the event, I'm bursting like those rockets with pride in what I've created." Then she suddenly hugged and kissed him, something she hadn't done in a long while—really since that night he was caught peeking at Amelia—and said, "Oh, Peter, I'm so glad we managed to get you off that awful barge and up where you belong. If you want to know the truth, the barge wasn't much fun for a lady, either."

Chapter **XII**

The Senator's Silk Stockings

Washington was a very different place in the year of 1829 than it had been when President Monroe still wore small clothes and silk stockings to formal gatherings. Everybody wore floppy pants and boots, often enough encrusted with mud, and he'd actually seen some of the new president's closest friends spray tobacco juice on the White House rugs when they couldn't get close enough to a window or fireplace in time of need. Although he'd had to accept the realities of politics and withdraw his own name in favor of General Jackson back in '24, Senator Peter Schuyler often wondered from what had happened in the five years since whether Washington was the place for him. About the only place north of the Potomac where you could find the ancient aristocratic fashions and virtues alive was in the tall, old Federalist houses of New York. The rich merchants and patroons who inhabited them and pursued the dignified ways of their fathers were sneeringly called "the silk stockings" by his Tammany friends. But to Peter Schuyler, whose ideal of the public man had been formed by a boy's awe at the sight of a majestic and solemn George Washington, a young man's fascination with a brilliant and elegant Aaron Burr, a mature man's admiration for a mild and dignified

James Monroe, silk stockings were no bad thing.

It hadn't been too difficult for Peter to be a loyal Democrat, as the Jackson followers were now proclaiming themselves, while DeWitt Clinton, a true gentleman if ever there was one, was governor and at least nominal head of the party in New York. But when Clinton died the year before and the party recalled Matty Van Buren from his seat in the United States Senate to be governor, Peter had been aware that a new order had arrived. People called Matty "the little magician" for the way he was able to deliver the winning New York vote to Jackson, but Peter knew that there was no magic at all to what Matty had done. He and his "Albany regency" had ruthlessly replaced public servants throughout the state with men whose loyalty was certain and who would expend every effort to get their friends, often the newly enfranchised and impoverished who had nothing to lose, to support the cause. While opponents angrily called this the "spoils system," Matty blandly argued that, in a democracy where all men are equal, one man had as much ability and right as another to perform public service; indeed, said Matty, change for change's sake was essential to keep government out of the hands of an entrenched bureaucracy or aristocracy. Matty had a way of rationalizing to make the expedient seem to be the good that infuriated Peter, and it was all but impossible to know what position he'd take on any given matter. This made for difficulties when Peter was serving as his supposedly loyal colleague in the Senate. When once an exasperated Daniel Webster challenged Peter to get a public avowal of belief—any belief—out of his fellow Democrat from New York, Peter tried a trick. Right in front of Webster, he said, "Matty, it's been rumored that the sun rises in the east. Do you believe it?" Matty responded with a smile and a quick wink at Peter that Webster couldn't see, "Well, senator, I understand that's the common acceptance, but as I never get up until after dawn I really can't say."

Nevertheless, here was Senator Peter Schuyler, full of misgivings, stepping off the ferry at the Battery pier to pursue a delicate mission entrusted to him by the new secretary of state, Martin Van Buren. Whatever he thought about Matty, Peter was, as he'd foreseen so long ago, deeply in his debt, and he had no illusions about remaining in the Senate if he ever crossed the little magician. When he'd abandoned the state house after only a few months to accept appointment as what everybody called Jackson's "prime minister," Matty had left behind plenty of loyal lieutenants such as Ben Butler and Silas Wright to keep the bucktails of Tammany in line—no difficult feat since it was anticipated that, with Matty's elevation to the right hand of power, a national regency was in the making. Already there were Van Buren men in Washington like C.C. Cambreling in the House and Charles E. Dudley, Matty's successor in the Senate, and—well, to be honest—Peter Schuyler whose heart was not yet worn on his sleeve. Already, too, Jackson seemed to be borrowing Matty's magic tricks. He'd started right away firing people who'd served the government for a generation to "clean out the Augean stables," as he put it, and replacing them with known supporters. In a suspicious echo of Matty's reasoning, Jackson had declared in his first message to the nation that the duties of public office were so "plain and simple" that any intelligent citizen could perform them. One Jackson appointment, no doubt at Matty's behest, had made Peter's head whirl with a kind of political vertigo—Sam Swartwout who'd followed Burr in his crazy western adventure and presumably committed political suicide was resurrected as collector of the Port of New York, the most lucrative position in the nation. Although it was more understandable since he was senator from Jackson's own Tennessee, the appointment of Major John H. Eaton as secretary of war was another that made Peter cringe, for, like everyone else in Washington, he'd been aware of the scandal of Eaton's relations with his wife, Peggy. It was certainly an irony, if not an injustice, that he, Peter, now found himself an agent of the effort to save Jackson from that folly.

Peter's assignment was to persuade his sister, Sally Schuyler Van Alen, to return with him to Washington and act as hostess for her cousin, Secretary Van Buren, at a ball he was planning to give to introduce the foreign ambassadors to the high-ranking members of the new administration, including President Jackson himself. As a widower, Matty thought it socially more correct to have a female relative at his side for the occasion, and he could think of none more appropriate than Sally, whose literary evenings had earned her a reputation as New York's most brilliant hostess, and whose beauty, like her hair, had taken on the rich and mellow quality of old silver. There was, as usual and as Peter well knew, a more cunning aspect to Matty's thinking. Being a sophisticated New Yorker who had more than once shown her disdain for convention, Sally would be likely to welcome Peggy Eaton into society in a manner that would impress the president and put down the provincial ladies of Washington who were causing so much trouble. Whether Matty knew or suspected more about Sally than he let on, his judgment in this matter was, in Peter's estimation, almost uncanny. Although he had not detected the slightest whiff of scandal about Sally since that terrible disaster at sea that made her, in effect, a double widow, Peter was hopeful that his sister would be charitable in matters of the heart; she couldn't afford to take any other view and still live with herself. And she was doing an amazing job of that . . . nobody around her but himself would ever know the depth of her suffering, the reason for it . . .

He'd come all the way from Washington to see her the moment he'd heard about it—too late, thank God, to attend a funeral that he would have found a sham in view of all that he knew and in view of Cousin James's ill-concealed distaste for George's high living and Aaron's freethinking. It was a damned shame, but some skipper or other was always being lost at sea. The unnerving thing, as far as Peter was concerned, was that it had happened when it did and that both men in Sally's unholy triangle were involved. He knew that Aaron had gone to Liverpool expressly to eliminate any scandal that might hurt his political fortunes, and he wondered why he had been returning so soon and with George. It was a question that would probably always remain unanswered, but it was a question that left him with a sense of guilt that, except for his request to Sally, this might never have happened. By the time he reached her, Sally seemed remarkably resigned, but the pain she'd been through showed in her face—in small circles under her eyes, in more gray than he remembered in her hair, in a smile that lifted her lips without lighting her eyes.

When he tried to express more than his regret, to stammer out his guilt, she said, "Peter, for the love of God, don't try to take this on yourself. It's enough that I have to bear it. Oh, God, Peter, only you know what I've really lost, but nobody else ever, *ever* must know. It's my fault—the whole mess I've made of my life, of other people's lives. Maybe father was right that there is evil in the world, and it's in me —"

"No, that's not true, don't say that, Sally—"

"Well, you've always been good in not blaming me, Peter, so I don't want you now to blame yourself. *Please.*"

Later when he was elected to the Senate after dropping out of the presidential race, she went further in trying to ease his conscience. "Well, I guess it wasn't *all* for nothing, was it?" she said. "The boys are so proud of you."

The second part of her statement, he hoped, was true, and to assuage that slight sense of guilt he couldn't shake, he tried whenever he could to stand in as a father to young Peter and an adviser to Cornelius.

It was a little hard to like Cornelius, who seemed to have inherited the worst traits of both grandfathers—the avaricious drive of old Cornelius and the puritanical piety of Jacobus—but Peter was an intelligent and engaging boy, full of mischief and grand dreams. He seemed to have inherited some of the adventurous nature as well as the good looks of his real father, and Peter was slightly ashamed that he could feel free to point with pride to his godson only after there was no danger of his parentage coming to light. Young Peter was in Princeton now, and doing well from all he heard, and he would have to get around to finding a suitable position for the boy when he graduated. This godson was, in fact, proving a godsend in a way that he could never have foreseen. For reasons nobody could explain, Alexandra had been unable to bear children, and, when he'd had to sell his half of the manor to the Van Alens to maintain his marble mansion in New York and his house in Georgetown, his own son, Francis, claiming he'd been disinherited, had pulled up stakes and vanished into the West. It was a pity, but it was part of the wages of politics which were nearly as high as those of sin.

Just like this distasteful mission for Matty. Peter hated to ask another favor of his sister, and, as he trudged up Broadway toward her house, he wondered how best to put it. Should he be honest or indulge in Alexandra's female circumlocutions? Alexandra couldn't care less about Matty's machinations. She thought it would be good for Sally's health to get her away from what she called that "madhouse on Broadway," and, seeing the city with fresh eyes, he rather agreed. The gaslights hissing away on either side of the street as far as the eye could see were holding back the restful curtain of an early November dusk, and he thanked the Lord that the lines had not yet been laid to his own quiet road. People who would normally seek the light of home were crowding the walks in search of diversion, and the street was a tangle of carriages, raising as much dust and creating as much noise by night as by day. He could see the grunting pigs and snarling stray dogs, whose scavenging had been mercifully invisible in the dark, attacking the uncollected piles of garbage and excrement householders had pushed into the middle of the street. These piles were called "Bloodgood pies" after the unfortunate politician who headed the sanitation department and whose name would now be anathema on any ballot. For all its being the biggest and wealthiest city in the land, nothing seemed to work well in New York. But most New York citizens were good-natured about their problems, and Peter could well remember the laugh Matty drew when, campaigning in the city for governor, he called his opponent's speech "flat as Manhattan water." Still, Peter blessed the stars that had led him away from city politics and given him cause to retreat from time to time to the fresh country atmosphere of Washington. Yes, it would make sense for Sally to get away, too, and he wondered again why she hadn't done something about building a summer retreat on her property at the manor instead of staying in that makeshift hotel in Greenwich which was almost in the city these days; perhaps she had no taste for facing brother Jacobus who reportedly grew more and more like their father every year.

Peter thought it might be as wise, however, to conceal Alexandra's other motive as Matty's. Alexandra wanted to get Sally down to Washington, because there were so many eligible bachelors and widowers, including President Jackson and the British and Russian ambassadors who would be honored guests at Matty's ball. Knowing, as Alexandra didn't, how his sister's heart had been lost at sea, Peter had scoffed, "Don't you think she's a little old for that sort of thing? She's forty-nine, you know." Alexandra had bridled, "Just the right age, I'd say. Unless you're one of those old men like Secretary Eaton who lusts after young girls." And Peter had lost his temper: "Don't *ever* make such remarks again, Alexandra. You know how the president admires Mrs. Eaton." And Alexandra had replied in kind: "And I know what *you* think of the president and his common friends. I should think you'd have more pride than to ask your sister, not to mention your wife, to acknowledge such a woman. If Sally weren't Matty's cousin, it would be a disgrace. I'm sure she won't come at all if you tell her the truth, and I would warn her away myself but for the fact that I think a change would do her good, and I would like to see her find a nice man." At that point, Peter had given up; women would never understand politics.

240

Women did, however, understand other matters quite well with the result that Peter's mission turned out to be far easier than he could have imagined. After he'd delivered Matty's invitation, Sally said, "What serendipity! . . . A nice word, don't you think? I just found it in Mr. Webster's new dictionary, and it means the gift of finding valuable or agreeable things not sought for . . . . I don't know why Matty would want me with all the charming ladies I hear there are in Washington, but I have great need for a favor from him, and one thing I know about Matty is that he will return favors for favors. Yes, I'll go with you."

Peter was wary. Though he seldom stirred from his counting room, young Cornelius Van Alen was proving from all accounts to be far more daring than his grandfather had ever been; it was hard to know from day to day what new and risky venture—insurance, canal construction, coal mining, rail-laying, road building—might have caught his eye with promise of quick gain and therefore attracted Van Alen & Son investment. Since Cornelius seldom made a move without his mother's assent, her need for a favor from the secretary of state bore investigation. Matty would not be grateful for being put under some embarrassing obligation. "What in the world can Matty do for you, Sally?" he asked.

"I had a letter last week from Amelia—you remember her, don't you? She's like an adopted daughter to me, and I'm distressed about her situation. She had nowhere to go but back to her parents in Liverpool after she graduated from Miss Willard's, and the poor thing's been wretched there. She's got more beauty and wit than any young woman I know, but she's afraid she'll be an old maid, and she's not far from wrong. She absolutely refuses to marry an Englishman, and she says the only Americans she meets are dull commercial fellows who can talk only about the weather and the price of woolens. So I've an idea that Matty could use her father in the department in Washington. There's no more deserving Democrat, you know, than Henry Downing. As I understand it, that's what kept President Adams from bringing him back."

Peter was so relieved that he laughed. "By George, I'm sure Matty would agree to that. If he doesn't perhaps I could do something for Henry. But I still say that young lady's trouble is that she's overeducated."

"Honestly, Peter, sometimes I think you have turned into a stuffed shirt. I hope Matty isn't so full of prejudices."

"If you mean, does Matty stand on principle, have no fear. As to that, he's the same old Matty," Peter said. "But I know you'll enjoy being with him since I have to admit that he does have a certain style, and he's without doubt the second most powerful man in America. He's hardly out of the president's presence. They ride together every day, and a comic sight it is—the president tall and straight and so easy in the saddle that he seems part of the horse and little Matty bouncing up and down like an India rubber ball. They even say Matty attends the general to his bedroom, his health being frail, you know, and Matty and a few others dine so regularly at the White House that they're called 'the kitchen cabinet.' So in a way, you'll be first lady of Washington since the general sent his niece Emily Donelson back to Tennessee in a huff when she wouldn't receive Mrs. Eaton."

Peter thought that was a subtle way of getting the message across, and he was gratified with Sally's quick response, "One of the reasons I want to go to Washington is that I'm anxious to meet this Mrs. Eaton from all I've read of her. I do hope Matty invites her."

"Oh, he will. Matty's very democratic with a small 'd' as well as a large one," Peter assured her.

No use going into all the background now; she'd learn it soon enough. The affair was nearly incredible, and it had so paralyzed the new government that it was being called "Eaton malaria" after the disease that was likely to prostrate any government people too poor or too ignorant to get out of the Potomac swamps in the hot months of summer. If he weren't suspicious of Matty's motives, Peter might give him credit for entertaining a natural sympathy for the young lady who, like himself, had grown up hustling beer to the customers of her father's Franklin House, one of the capitol's most popular taverns. Matty would understand, too, how, in the process, Peggy O'Neil had acquired wit and conversational skills exceptional in a woman and how such public display of her red-haired beauty had resulted in many unusual romantic adventures. One man, to whom she denied her hand and presumably the more enticing parts of her body, killed himself as did the man who won her, John B. Timberlake, an obscure seafarer who chose death over dishonor when word reached him abroad that Mrs. Timberlake and the bachelor senator from Tennessee, John H. Eaton, were traveling openly together and sharing the same hotel rooms. Washington took such rumors in stride since it was considered only natural that a vigorous man like Major Eaton would satisfy his appetites with a barkeep's daughter. The sin took place when Eaton actually married the girl, and it was compounded into an intolerable affront to all decent society when the major's old friend, Andrew Jackson, appointed him secretary of war.

Everything about "Old Hickory" horrified a Washington that for a generation had been ruled by the genteel ways of the Virginia aristocracy. Jefferson's indulgences at Monticello were, as a gentleman's should be, out of sight and therefore out of mind; Dolly Madison's flamboyance as a hostess that once led to inebriating even her lady guests by serving spiked ice was forgiven for her coolness under fire when the White House was burned; the gentle Monroe's wife had the glacial reserve of established New York wealth. As his father's son, a professor at Harvard, minister to Great Britain, secretary of state, and then president, John Quincy Adams had neither need nor interest in proving himself socially in Washington and much preferred to spend his time dreaming up scientific expeditions. Nobody believed for a minute the Jacksonian charges that Adams had acted as pimp to the emperor of Russia, and the story that a lady had spied him taking his early morning dip in the Potomac in the buff was more amusing than scandalous since nobody could imagine that the sight of the president's chunky body would arouse the slightest flutter in a female breast. But Jackson! White of hair, stern of face, erect of bearing, heedless of protocol, direct of speech, he was clearly capable of having hung supposed enemies without trial, killing a man in a duel and sleeping with his wife before their marriage, as charged by the National Republicans who favored the reelection of Adams. When his rowdy followers did nearly as much damage to the White House in celebrating the inaugural as had the British invaders, the guardians of Washington's manners and morals decided that this old backwoodsman would have to be disciplined to civilized behavior—and the instrument of their chastisement would be Peggy Eaton.

What Washingtonians failed to understand was that the very code of honor that drove Jackson to be brave in war and ruthless in personal confrontation also required of him a romantic and boyish gallantry toward women. He was endowed with the American frontiersman's respect, almost amounting to awe, for women—all women, who, regardless of their state of virtue, were a rare and priceless commodity like gold or diamonds. His love for his own wife, Rachel, had been idolatrous, and he had come to Washington sad of heart and convinced that the campaign slanders about their premarital relations, rather than a weak heart, had driven her into the grave. The fire behind the smoke in the affair was their perfectly innocent ignorance that, owing to poor communications and casual justice, Rachel's decree of divorce from her first husband had not been granted at the time of their marriage which was thus annulled, but he had married her a second time to stop the stupid talk. Among the few from Washington to attend Rachel's last rites at the Hermitage were his colleague from Tennessee, Major Eaton, and his new bride, Peggy. Rachel's death had taken whatever joy and sense of triumph Jackson might have felt about going to Washington out of him, and he so hated to leave her there in the ground that he spent much of his last days weeping over her grave. On one of these occasions, Peggy Eaton came to him, cradled his white-shocked head against her soft breast and mingled her tears with his. It was more than probable that a lonely and ill president was half in love with this beautiful and sympathetic woman when the moralists struck.

As might be expected, the Reverend J. M. Campbell, the president's own pastor, and a spiritual ally from Philadelphia, Ezra Stiles Ely, were the first to endeavor to save the nation's soul from Peggy Eaton's corrupting influence. Campbell's interest had been aroused when, shortly after the Eaton marriage, he attended a ball at the British Embassy where a guest, seeing Peggy pass, said, "Well, she's high and mighty now; she's forgotten the time when she used to sleep with *me.*" Set off like a hound by this whiff of evil, Campbell enlisted Ely's aid and together they drew up a long and damning document about Peggy's love affairs which they presented to President Jackson soon after the inaugural. Enraged at such allegations against "his Peggy," the General put his own hounds on the traces. For a whole summer, risking real malaria, they checked out every charge, including registers at hotels where Major Eaton and the then Mrs. Timberlake were alleged to have stayed. They found no hard evidence of misbehavior, and Jackson in early fall summoned the men of the cloth to appear before a full cabinet meeting and informed them that Mrs. Eaton was "chaste as a virgin" and that, were he Secretary Eaton, he would call them out and despatch them to the nether world where, despite their profession, they were surely bound.

Too aroused to take the president's advice which would have

meant going through the delay and ceremony of a duel, Eaton and his wife called upon the Reverend Mr. Campbell shortly after the cabinet meeting and demanded public apology. When the minister stuck to his brief, Eaton tried to despatch him with his fist, but Peggy stepped between them, taking the blow on her own jaw. She went down, opening her head against the sharp edge of the minister's desk, and the sight of his wife's blood drove all thoughts of a fight out of Eaton's head. He rushed her home to bed where, later that night, the president came calling and learned that he—and Peggy—had a very staunch ally in Secretary of State Van Buren.

With some difficulty, owing to bandages around her head and aching jaw, Peggy told the president, "Mr. Van Buren was here just before you, and he told me something he made me promise not to repeat, but I must because it expresses my own sentiments so exactly. He said that he had been reading and reflecting on the characters of the great men of our history and had come to the conclusion that General Jackson was the greatest man who had ever lived—the only man among them without fault. I just couldn't help telling you that, because you have certainly been so with me."

As quick to tears as wrath, the general had to dab at his eyes. "Ah, little Van," he said. "That man does love me, though he tries to conceal it. But I've always known, because I have an instinct for telling friends from enemies. Still, I'm glad you did tell me. Now you rest and get your pretty face back in shape, because it will have to grace the foot of my table when I give my cabinet dinner."

That dinner, for which all Washington waited as a signal that the social season under a new regime had officially begun, was, however, delayed when forces more formidable than those of the faith began piling tinder under the stake on which Peggy Eaton was to be burned. Returning from their South Carolina plantation where they had summered in splendor, Floride Calhoun and her husband, Vice-President John C. Calhoun, found cards left by Secretary and Mrs. Eaton. "I shall certainly not call on that . . . that woman," Floride fumed, and her husband, who regretted for the sake of the country and himself that he didn't occupy the White House instead of Jackson, agreed. "Your decision is a great victory for the moral standards of our country, my dear," he said. The Calhouns' deliberate snub strengthened the moral fiber in the backbones of other Washington ladies, including a number of cabinet wives, and the president, not wishing to hurt Peggy's feelings with a scene, put off his dinner, thus bringing about the paralyzing fever for which the little magician from Kinderhook was conjuring up a cure.

He, being a widower, had nothing to lose and everything to gain by stepping into the social void and organizing his own large ball for foreign dignitaries which the elite of Washington could not decline to attend without offering international affront. Moreover, Matty had persuaded the bachelor ministers of Britain and Russia to follow his ball with cotillions of their own. As wife of a member of the cabinet, Peggy Eaton would be prominent at all of these parties, and as a woman of demonstrated allure, she would most certainly be popular. Far more than his efforts to purchase the department of Texas from Mexico, Secretary Van Buren's skill in manipulating that even more foreign territory, the female of the species, was said to be earning Old Hickory's open-mouthed admiration. If Vice-President Calhoun and his wife were saving the country's morals by their Presbyterian disdain, they were fast losing whatever chance they might have to occupy the White House.

All this was revolting to Senator Schuyler who thought that power should derive from principle, and he was not anxious to share his knowledge of the true situation with his sister. Her scorn of hypocrisy would no doubt make her sympathetic to Peggy Eaton as a woman beseiged, but he was by no means sure that she wouldn't be equally scornful of the way Matty was manipulating the situation to his own advantage and therefore refuse her assistance. So it was welcome when the arrival of young Cornelius interrupted further discussion of Mrs. Eaton. Abrupt and intent on his own business as he always seemed to be, Cornelius barely acknowledged his uncle's presence, went right to the fireplace where he knelt and started blowing. "I'm afraid it doesn't burn well, mother," he said between gasps. "Old Mr. Wilkins may be right, and we should have listened to him."

Peter noticed then for the first time that the fireplace contained a smouldering, smoking grate of coal instead of a crackling wood fire. Cornelius' efforts only produced more black smoke that curled out and around the marble mantel. But his mother said, "I wouldn't be discouraged yet, Cornelius. It's your first try. There must be a better way of burning it, and don't forget that Mr. Wilkins was talking about Rhode Island coal, not ours."

"But it's all anthracite, mother . . . "

"Maybe you'd let me in on this," Peter said.

Sally said, "You'll have to forgive Cornelius, Peter. He has a lot at stake in whether this coal burns or not. You see, we've invested rather heavily in Delaware and Hudson Canal stock, and the purpose of the canal is to bring coal into the city from the Pennsylvania mines."

"Oh, then you must be the people who are running that steam engine on rails?"

"Yes, isn't it exciting—the first in the United States!"

"I know. I saw it last May at Abell and Dunscombe's Foundry here when it had just been imported from England. An odd-looking thing. What did they call it—*Stourbridge Lion?* Does it really work, Cornelius?"

"Certainly, sir. We have it hauling coal cars from Carbondale to Honesdale, but it ought to run on coal instead of wood and so should our boats, if we could get this stuff to burn better," Cornelius said.

Peter shook his head. "I swear you people are on to something new every time I come up here," he said. "I was just thinking as I walked up from the ferry about how I liked the old ways better. I guess I'm a silk stocking at heart."

"You sound like Mr. Wilkins," Sally laughed. "When Cornelius told him that he was going into coal, Mr. Wilkins said, 'Don't do it, don't do it, young man. The stuff's no good. I tried it way back in '16 when the Rhode Island Coal Company was peddling its wares. I am willing to testify that, under favorable circumstance, this coal is capable of ignition, and I am willing further to testify that, if Rhode Island is underlaid with such coal, then at the general conflagration which our ministers predict, it will be the last place to burn.' "

Peter joined Sally in laughter, but Cornelius said, "It really isn't funny. Think what coal could mean to thousands and thousands of people right here in New York—easier to carry, easier to store, longer in the burning. And think what it would mean to us! I hope, Uncle Peter, that you'll see to putting coal in the tariff schedules to protect us from the British imports."

"That's a touchy subject, Cornelius. I don't know whether the South would stand for more. Down there they're calling last year's bill the tariff of abominations, and in South Carolina and Georgia they're talking about nullification—saying that a state can disobey any federal law it deems unconstitutional. It's said that Vice-President Calhoun is actually author of the doctrine. It reminds me of the time Mr. Burr got involved with the New England separatists, and it frightens me," Peter said.

"I don't know about all that. I just know that if you want us businessmen to put our money into building this country, you've got to protect us," Cornelius said. "I should think that a senator with most of his votes coming from the city of New York would understand that."

"You know, you do sound like your grandfather Van Alen, Cornelius. A senator is supposed to take a larger view," Peter said.

"What I think," Sally interrupted, "is that we should all stop talking politics and tell Cornelius about the exciting invitation I've had from Cousin Matty . . . . "

Peter could hardly suppress a laugh. Not talk politics? Was Sally really that innocent of the true nature of her invitation? Apparently, for nothing she said during the long trip down to the capital would indicate otherwise. It was an arduous journey—by boat to New Brunswick, by stage to Trenton, by boat to Philadelphia on the first day; by boat to New Castle, by stage to Frenchtown, by boat to Baltimore, by stage to Washington on the next. Peter had learned stoically to endure the joltings and rockings, the mud baths and soakings of this trip by keeping his mind on those long, long thoughts appropriate to a statesman. But it was all new to Sally, and she was as tiringly alert to every fresh sight and experience as a young girl. In Philadelphia, for instance, when he yearned for nothing but a stable bed and a restoring bottle, she insisted on using the last faint twilight to have a glimpse of Independence Hall before they retired to their hotel. At Baltimore, she demanded to sit up on the box between Peter who wanted to smoke a cigar in peace and an astonished driver. "Ain't never had a woman up on the box," the driver complained. "Sight of skirts might frighten the horses."

"I'll hide my skirts under your fur robe if I may, Mr. . . . uh . . ."

"Tolly, ma'am. Don't think you'll like it. Have to chew to steady my nerves."

"That's all right as long as you spit to leeward," she said.

He thawed a little. "Must be used to water, ma'am . . ."

"Oh, yes, I've sailed a sloop and piloted a steamboat on the North River, and . . ."

"On the North River? Sailed there a mite myself afore I took to driving. Well, then, come up, come up, but mind you hold on. Road's a bit unsteady this time of year."

Tolly's description of the pike to Washington was such an understatement that they might have guessed, if he hadn't confessed it later, that he was a Vermonter. In addition to the four horses in harness, Tolly was driving a dozen or more cattle to the meat markets of the capital. A heavy November rain had fallen the night before, and the road was a greasy brown river with here and there a deep pond, its thinly iced surface winking in the sun. With a "Gee!" and "Haw!" between expectorations and a deft tug of the reins on the snaffle bits, Tolly kept his trotting team weaving through and around these obvious perils, but when the leaders sank to their withers in a slough of soft mud, Sally involuntarily gasped. "No cause for alarm, ma'am," Tolly said. "Long as I can see their ears, I know they'll pull the coach through slick as soap." The coach did slide, buried to the hubs in muck, but it lurched so violently that Sally would have pitched off her perch if Peter hadn't grabbed her. At the same time, three of the cattle went down in a muddy mess, and Tolly rose to his feet, teetering like a sailor on a tossing deck, to prod them to their feet again with flicks of his long whip.

"You'd better get back inside, Sally," Peter said, but she refused. "I wouldn't miss this for anything. I admire skill in any form and never more than Mr. Tolly's. Besides, I want to see the capitol as you've described it . . . ."

Peter wished now that he hadn't been so glowing in telling Sally that on a sparkling day such as this, the great white capitol of the United States would rise out of the horizon like a glistening vision of the heavenly throne. In truth, the sight always inspired him with feelings of awe and gratitude that he was privileged to sit under its dome and deliberate the fate of a nation that in his more idealistic moments he considered the hope of Western civilization. It was the reason he chose to ride the last leg outside except in the very foulest of weather. It had never occurred to him that Sally would be so unladylike as to join him although he should have known better, remembering those childhood days when no amount of teasing, threats or physical discomfort could shake her from his heels. By rights, they both should be inside and Flossie, who'd come along to tend her mistress's wardrobe, should be up here on the box. While

Flossie was free now by New York law and looked quite the lady in Sally's cast-off chinchilla hat and cape, he had no doubt from the expression on her face that the lady who had got on at Baltimore was scandalized at having to ride with a nigger and would probably make a scene of it when they reached their destination.

Thinking of that hat of Flossie's, Peter was reminded of a disquieting conversation he'd had back in the spring with young Peter. The very next Sunday after Sally had given her the hat, Flossie had worn it proudly on her walk out to church. It was the time of spring thaw when the water running off City Hall Park made a knee-deep freshet at the corner of Broadway and Vesey. Just as Flossie was about to cross the board that bridged this dirty stream, a man grabbed her hat and flung it into the water, saying, "I just paid eighteen dollars for a hat like this for my sister, and I'm not about to see any nigger wench flaunting one." The hat started to float down the gutter, and, while people around her laughed, Flossie plunged right in after it, soaking the skirts of her best dress in filthy water. She got back to the house in tears, and young Peter, telling his uncle about the incident, said, "There would have been some broken heads if I'd been there. I can't imagine anyone treating Flossie that way just because she's black. I think what we do to those people is the blackest spot on American honor—and I'm not just playing with words. If I were a senator like you, I'd do something about it."

"What would you suggest, Peter?"

"I'd abolish slavery everywhere and . . . and give them the vote."

"You know, Peter, I've been hoping that you might consider a political career when you get out of Princeton, but there won't be much future for you if you talk like that," he told his nephew.

"Are you serious, Uncle Peter? I can't imagine calling myself a statesman and not denouncing this evil."

"To be a statesman, you must first be elected, Peter. Those men laughing at Flossie in the streets are the voters of New York, and when you consider how they feel in the South . . ."

"But, Uncle Peter, you grew up with Flossie just as I have. Can you say she's less of a human being for her color?"

"That's just it—the only black you know is Flossie, and even she can't read or write. If you could travel below the Potomac, you'd know that most of them are as ignorant as—"

"And whose fault is that? I can tell you from talking to my fellow

250

students that, except for some of those from the South, our generation won't stand for this."

"Then God help us all, Peter. Our real statesmen who believe in making this Union of ours work—men like Mr. Webster and Mr. Clay and, yes, even myself—labor for compromise. But they say that any man worth his salt is an idealist in youth, and I can applaud your thinking on that basis. You'll grow out of it . . . ."

"Then God help me!" young Peter said and slammed out of the room.

It was good to get back to Washington where his fellow legislators, North or South, understood these things. Once in a while, tempers would erupt into fisticuffs on the floor or a more or less ritual duel, usually when some member had had too much to drink, but for the most part compromise, the real art of government, would prevail. So this day Peter found the first sight of the capitol warming and was not surprised when Sally gave a little cry of delight and said, "Look, Peter! Oh, it *is* a vision!" But the last mile or so between them and the vision proved the most difficult part of the trip. Even the skillful Tolly could not negotiate the slippery, rutted road, and they all had to get out to lighten the coach, and the men had to tear and muddy their clothes by pushing to help the horses drag it up through the underbrush. When finally they arrived at the macadam ringing the capitol Sally teased, "Is this how a senator always arrives at his place of business? It isn't very dignified."

"I'm afraid it's a hazard of the profession," Peter said. "It could be eliminated, though, if the president agreed with some of the rest of us to spend money on public roads. He says it's a matter for the states, and the farmers of Maryland aren't interested in making life easy for senators from New York or anywhere else. Now *that's* something you might talk to his prime minister, Matty, about . . . ."

Peter did not see Sally again until the night of the ball. He was kept amply informed of her activities by Alexandra, who accompanied Sally on the ceaseless rounds of calls that absorbed the days of Washington ladies and disturbed the nights of its men. He was sure that the country would be better run if its servants and their wives didn't indulge in so much talk, but there was no other diversion in a city that, despite a few marbled edifices, had the transient, ramshackle character of a frontier trading post. According to Alexandra, Sally was the hit of the circuit with her reports on the new plays opening in New York, the new books being published, the new fashions showing in shops. Since she was also knowledgeable about such current, burning issues as the tariff and the national bank, men found her conversation as congenial as women. By the time Sally stood beside Matty under the draped flags of a dozen nations to receive guests arriving at the ball in Gadsby's Hotel, she was herself considered one of the main attractions of the event. Looking at her, Peter thought that Matty had been inspired in his selection of a hostess if for no other reason than the fact that her petite figure made the dapper little secretary of state seem almost tall.

In Alexandra's words, Sally would have had to be "deaf, dumb and blind"—none of which adjectives could apply to her—not to have picked up all there was to know, and more that was conjectured, about the notorious Mrs. Eaton during their visits to the gossip mills. Whether Matty also briefed Sally as to his diplomatic maneuvers, Alexandra didn't know, but she did pass along almost verbatim Sally's account of the private audience Matty arranged for her at the White House. Sally had been surprised to find the scourge of the British at New Orleans and the Indians of Florida so frail and so courtly. He'd bent low over her hand, groaned involuntarily in straightening up and apologized, "Forgive me, madam, but my body yet bears the metal or flint of some savage whose aim I misjudged." Sally had been shocked when, after she'd dropped the names of some of her literati friends in a mistaken effort to impress, the president had said, "I don't think much of book-writing fellows; they're always looking to put their snouts into the public trough like that Erwin we've got on the payroll in London." Matty had winced at his idol's mangling of Washington Irving's name and had hastened to inform the president that his cousin was also friend to many of New York's leading business men such as Mr. Astor. "Astor, hay?" the president had said. "Now *there's* a man to keep an eye on. Hoodwinked Jefferson for fair, I hear, but you can tell him, Mrs. Van Alen, that he's got a very different kind of man in the White House now. When I get through with my banking reforms, those New York fellows aren't going to own all the money in the country." At that, Matty had adroitly shifted the conversation once more, informing the President that Mrs. Van Alen had called upon Mrs. Eaton and "found her charming." Old Hickory had really brightened then and had said, "You did? Well, then, madam, you and I share the same judgment

252

of character for which I'm very pleased. There are ladies in this town who judge themselves too good for a barkeep's daughter, forgetting that their own forebears were most likely debtors or indentured servants. They say my election has brought democracy to this country, and we'll yet teach them the meaning of that word. Won't we, Van?"

However much Sally might have understood about what was going on, her instant reaction to the first incident at the ball could not have been better suited to Matty's purposes. Peggy and Secretary Eaton were near the head of the column forming to go through the receiving line and meet the foreign diplomats when Floride Calhoun, arriving on the arm of the vice-president, started to push haughtily in ahead of the Eatons. Peggy resisted with a stiff shoulder, and a small struggle was developing when Sally plunged into the line, took both of Peggy's hands in hers and said, "Mrs. Eaton, what a beautiful gown! No wonder you couldn't adequately describe it to me the other day—it's the perfect shade for your red hair. Now come right with me to meet Baron Krudener, the Russian minister. He's been dying of impatience for this moment." Not only was a scene averted, but as a result of getting first through the line, Peggy led off the ball, whirling away in the new waltz step to the delight of at least all male eyes.

Toward the end of the affair, Matty sought Peter out, shook his hand and said, "Thank you, Peter, for your good offices in bringing Sally down. There may come a day when you can say that your sister, thanks to you, saved the country."

"Or made a president?" Peter teased.

"Now couldn't that be the same thing?" Matty asked. "Did you see the look on Calhoun's face? It was worth all that this ball cost me. I've already promised Sally to bring Henry Downing back to Washington. Is there anything I can do for you?"

"Not that I can think of."

"Well, I won't forget, Peter . . . . "

No, you could say that much for Matty: he wouldn't forget. Peter just wished for perhaps the thousandth time in his public career that the patroon in him, the Puritan in him, would allow him to enjoy, as Matty so obviously did, the sweet fruits of being clever. Yes, he, Peter Schuyler, was a silk stocking at heart, and he decided then and there that he would withdraw his name from the next election and go back to New York and practice law. He was, after all, fifty-four, and there might not be much time left to him to earn enough money to pay off his debts and leave his widow in some kind of comfort. It was a decision long in coming, and the feeling of relief that it gave him made him know it was right. He could stop pretending to be a democrat, stop demanding sacrifices from those around him, like his sister and his son, stop putting his aging body through the jarring discomforts of constant travel. He would miss that heart-lifting glimpse of the capitol, that sense that in the sometimes lofty debate under its dome the future of the nation and the world were being decided. But no matter; there would be compensations. What Matty *was* forgetting in his grasp for the trappings of power, what he, Peter, had been learning almost unconsciously, was that the real power to change America lay in the vaults of those silk-stockinged men of New York. It was money. That solemn young man who'd been trying to puff into life the stubborn coal laid in a fireplace that had warmed wealth with wood for three generations knew what he was about, and, if he played his hand right, Cornelius Van Alen could be his first client. His last public act which would infuriate Matty and the president by arousing the South would be to introduce a new and tougher tariff covering coal. But that didn't matter, either, for this night he'd paid off his debt to Matty, and he would incur no more.

Chapter *XIII*

The Ties That Bind

Instead of taking the omnibus up Broadway, he chose to walk in order to think. His mother's invitation—a note on paper fancily embossed with the legend, Mrs. George Van Alen, Lafayette Place, New York City, and delivered to the office at the *Post*— was ominous. "Please come to tea this afternoon, Peter," it read. "All the family will be here, and we have a matter of some importance to discuss with you." Who did she mean by all the family? He could be sure that his sister-in-law, Augusta, would be one of them since she and Cornelius shared his mother's new house—or was it the other way around? And Uncle Peter, who'd become a kind of lost soul after his wife's death, was almost always there. He'd heard that Amelia Downing was in town which might account for the tea if it hadn't been for that important matter, whatever it was. Knowing that his mother was not given to alarm or using words lightly, it was this part of the message that made him uneasy. Depending on the importance of the matter, Cornelius would be there, too, and the less he saw of his brother these days the better he liked it. If it had anything to do with Van Alen & Son, Inc., one or two of the Smith cousins would be on hand, and of course Cornelius could hardly turn around without consulting

Cousin James Schuyler to see if he was right with the Lord.

It turned Peter's stomach to hear his brother assign every stroke of good fortune to "the leading of the Lord" such as the one he'd just pulled off by unloading Delaware and Hudson stock at $125 just before it dropped to $68 as a result of everybody's panic over Jackson's threat to do away with the national bank. Peter knew very well that Cornelius sold because he didn't think there was much promise in coal and because he needed the money, besides, to back his father-in-law, Captain Vanderbilt, in buying the *Cinderella* for the Peekskill run when the *General Jackson* blew up. Often Peter wished that he could sit in on a conversation between those two Corneliuses. He doubted that his brother could get away with passing that pious stuff off on the captain whose words were as sharp and foul as a poisoned arrow. He'd have to say this for Captain Vanderbilt: the man made no pretensions to anything but the desire to get money, by hook or by crook. People said that the captain was a lot like his own grandfather Cornelius, and wondered why more of that kind of honesty hadn't rubbed off on his brother who was supposed to have been so close to him—and why, too, he himself had inherited so little of that fierce desire to accumulate wealth that seemed to run in the Dutch blood.

He'd tried to explain this to his mother and brother and uncle when he was getting out of Princeton and deciding what to do with himself. By then he'd had several poems published by Mr. Bryant who offered him a job on the *Post* at $10 a week. "Chicken feed," Cornelius had sneered. "I could give you $1,200 a year to start—and much more if you take to the business."

"I don't care about money . . . . "

"No, of course, *you* don't care about money," Cornelius said. "All you've done is spend it."

"Your brother has a point there, Peter," his uncle said. "I didn't care about money either when I went into politics with, I dare say, some of the same motivations you now have, and I've paid dearly for it. I'd be a pauper today if I hadn't learned the law."

"That's something you really ought to think about, Peter," his mother said. "Mr. Burr has offered to take you in with him, and for all his peculiarities, they say he's got one of the best practices in the city."

"But, mother, I thought you wanted me to pursue a literary career."

"Well, Mr. Irving and Mr. Bryant, too, were lawyers . . . . "

"And poor ones from all I've heard," he argued. "I don't see how you can do anything well unless you have your heart in it. Don't worry about me; I'll get along."

"Yes, of course, living here free, drawing dividends on stock to which you contribute nothing," Cornelius said. "Even Cousin George Smith has decided to put his shoulder to the harness, and yet my own brother . . . "

It was more than he could take. "I'll seek other lodgings tomorrow."

"Now, Peter, please," his mother said. "Cornelius doesn't mean it that way."

"Oh, yes, he does . . . . "

The very next day he had found lodgings—with a Mrs. Mason on Chatham Street near Duane where he got room and board for $2.50 a week. It was a poor place compared to the tall house on Broadway, a small and viewless room above a saloon, but Mrs. Mason loaded the pine board at which they all ate with plenty of plain food, and there was one fellow lodger well worth knowing. Though just about his own age, Horace Greeley looked a dozen years older. His hair was so light as to suggest the white of middle age; his big body was stooped from bending over fonts of type; his nearsighted eyes were watery with strain. During the dreamy four years that Peter had spent listening to lectures in Nassau Hall or discussing the range of human knowledge and the delights of the female form over innumerable pints in the Nassau Tavern, Greeley had been setting type and writing political editorials for *The Northern Spectator* in East Poultney, Vermont. When the paper failed, he had come to New York where he was laboring twelve hours a day in a printing shop for a paltry six or seven dollars a week with one improbable goal in mind—to start his own paper. Greeley had no other appetite than that for work— and a running response to Mrs. Mason's big brass dinner bell. He would never join Peter and some of the other young men in the tavern downstairs and, perhaps because of his damaged eyes, took no notice of the ladies strolling along Chatham Street. Peter hadn't been surprised when the ambitious Greeley and his friend Story launched the *Morning Post* this year, and, unlike a gleeful Mr. Bryant, he had been rather sad that it went under in a few months. Perhaps if he'd charged only a penny like that fellow who started the *Sun*—but then Greeley didn't want to print that tripe, either. Well, Greeley still had the printing of a couple of other journals, and he was talking now about trying a magazine to be called the *New Yorker* which made more sense in view of the competition and might provide an outlet for some of the things Peter was writing that had no place in a daily paper.

Getting to know Greeley had made Peter ashamed of his own soft life, and he had offered to give up his Van Alen & Co. stock, thinking that living on wages would inspire him to greater effort. His mother had argued him out of it. "I guess I can understand why you wanted to move out of the house—it's probably high time. But don't do this, Peter. Don't let pride make a fool of you," she said. "Mr. Irving would never have got his start without the help of his family, nor Mr. Cooper either. You're my son, too, and you have a perfect right, no matter what Cornelius says, to share in a business for which I've made many sacrifices. Besides, I wouldn't be on the board but for you, and the time may come when I'll need your support again. For all that I admire Cornelius and am grateful to him for his industry, I'm discovering that there are some matters on which we don't agree, and, frankly, I don't trust your cousin George; he's too much like his father. With you and Amelia and myself holding thirty percent of the shares, we might prevent a disaster if the Lord turns out to be wrong."

That last phrase, he was sure, was his mother's wry way of telling him that she was as wary of Cornelius' piety as he. But she'd learned to live with it, because, as she'd once told him, she understood his need for it. With what remained a puzzling slip of her tongue, she said that time, "You were too young Peter ever to really know *his* father, but poor Cornelius had to bear with his intemperance and other shortcomings. He was never young. He had to pick up the burden his father dropped. So—don't you see?—Cornelius is just reacting against *his* father's failures, and it may be a godsend that he's found a faith to help him. Try to be patient with your brother; we all owe him much."

In monetary terms, his mother was undoubtedly right. His experience in the insurance business had so far convinced Cornelius that it was easier to make money with money than with ships that could sink or wear out and goods that could spoil or lose their value. So he sold off the packets and invested the money in enterprises where the risk was minimal, where, if possible, profit was protected by monopoly such as in C. V. S. Roosevelt's plate glass importing business or Eugene Grousett's wine concern. Peter thought this last venture somewhat of a violation of his brother's temperance principles, but the appeal to his business principles was evidently too strong a temptation for Cornelius to resist. Grousset had a corner on "Marseilles Madeira," an imitation of the real stuff which was manufactured in France by his brother, Grousset de Granier, for six dollars a quarter cask and sold on the New York market for eighteen. The profit was obviously huge and assured by Grousset's ability as a salesman. At a banquet in the City Hotel when guests were invited to place bottles of their own choice wine on the table to enhance the celebration, Grousset had a few bottles of his Marseilles Madeira, carefully dusted to denote age, brought up from his Broad Street store. These bottles had come into his keeping, Grousset told his tablemates, as a descendant of generations of wine merchants and their contents were two centuries old and too priceless to sell, but he would let them judge for themselves. To stretch the precious fluid, only a cordial glass was poured for each of the tasters who pronounced it the finest Madeira of their experience, little knowing that the rowdies of Five Points were even then gorging on it at ten cents a bottle. Except for a few, among them Peter who learned of the trick from one of Grousset's clerks, the *bon ton* of New York thereafter began looking upon Grousset as a connoisseur to conjure with, regardless of the run of his business. When Peter relayed this story to Cornelius, hoping it might give him second thoughts about being in bed with such a trickster, his brother said, "People who drink deserve what they get." It was hard to get through to a brother like that, but then it was harder still to complain when dividends on Van Alen stock kept rising by the year.

Peter's share in the Van Alen enterprise had come to him after his Uncle Peter had decided to drop out of the next election for the Senate and return to New York to become the company's attorney. Whether Uncle Peter had wanted to grant his namesake a competence or free Cornelius' hand, or both, was hard to know, but he had advised that Cornelius exchange ten percent of the company stock in return for a release from Peter of any claims that he might make against the rather murky will that old Cornelius had left behind. Uncle Peter had been jolly about it all, saying that even in the best of families disagreements come about that make lawyers rich and their clients poor; that, in this case, Peter, not having yet been born, was excluded from a will in which he undoubtedly would have been named and would appear to have some legitimate rights to the stock and other assets assigned to Cornelius; that, in view of Peter's disinterest in the business, a share equal to those distributed to his mother, the Downings and Smiths would seem to be fair and within the intent of the legator. At the same time, Uncle Peter persuaded Cornelius to let him have an act of incorporation put through the legislature so that Van Alen & Son could issue stock at need and absolve shareholders from personal liability in the event of corporate failure. The corporation was set up with an issue of 10,000 shares of which Sarah Schuyler Van Alen held 1,000; Peter Schuyler Van Alen, 1,000; the Smith family, 1,000; the Downing family, 1,000; and Cornelius Van Alen, 6,000. The charter provided for a board of five directors, with cumulative voting privileges for shareholders, with the result that while Cornelius could certainly dominate the board, he could not prevent the election of one or two directors representing minority shareholders. The first board consisted of Cornelius himself, his mother, Uncle Peter, Cousin George Smith, and William B. Astor; officers were Cornelius, president; Uncle Peter, secretary; and George Smith, treasurer.

Oddly, considering his long reliance upon her advice, Cornelius had not wanted his mother officially on the board, preferring Cousin James Schuyler for whom he cast his 6,000 votes. His reasoning was typical Cornelius: "You know I've always listened to you, mother, and always will, but businesses just don't have women on the board, and we might suffer for being thought odd." While she was hurt, Sally was inclined to go along with Cornelius, paying once more the familiar price of being a woman. But Peter got together with Amelia Downing who held proxies for her brothers, all of whom had remained in England, and, by using the cumulative privilege to cast five votes for one candidate instead of spreading them out, they gave Sally 10,000 votes against Cousin James' 6,000 from Cornelius. While she was cautious in expressing her gratitude for the sake of Cornelius' feelings, his mother had revealed it in many ways, not least in her pleading that he hold onto his stock. He found it hard to imagine a time when his mother would go against the sainted Cornelius, but her hints that this was possible were enough to make him abandon any such quixotic gesture as throwing away his holdings in Van Alen & Son, Inc.

No doubt the meeting this evening was some sort of informal family conference on business matters, Peter decided as he jostled his way through the crowds on Broadway. If this were so, he wondered why he'd been invited since nobody listened to his advice for good reason. He'd been against loaning Captain Vanderbilt the money to buy the *Cinderella* and fight it out on the river with Daniel Drew, and of course he'd been wrong: he'd overestimated Drew's cunning and underestimated the Captain's nerve. One of Peter's first assignments had been to try his hand at sketches of New York's more colorful merchants, a subject for which Mr. Bryant felt Peter would be well suited with his Van Alen connections, and he'd picked Drew as his first subject, as much for an excuse to hire a horse on a pleasant day and ride out to the Bull's Head on the Boston Post Road at Twenty-sixth Street as for any other reason. He'd never been there although Drew's tavern had been a regular haunt of his father and Uncle John Smith when they were racing their horses and was still the headquarters for the drovers who herded their cattle down from the country and auctioned them off to the butchers in the city markets. By the time Peter went on his mission, Cato, a genial black man, had opened an establishment several miles farther north where the quality of the juleps and ginslings he dispensed was drawing the trade of gentlemen horsemen away from the Bull's Head. Still, the place was crowded with drovers and butchers whose thirst was assured by a perpetual haze of dust raised by the hooves of the milling, mooing cattle. Peter took an instant dislike to mine host, a shriveled, shifty-eyed, whining sort of man whose only answers to questions were pieties that would embarrass even Cornelius or Cousin James. How had Drew managed to rise from a simple drover to a man who owned a prosperous tavern and stockyard, steamships on the river, real estate? "The Lord has suffered his servant to prosper," was all that Drew would admit.

Back in the city, Peter did use his connections by going to his old friend Mr. Astor. "Drew—dot scoundrel!" Astor said. "Talk to my brudder Heinrich." Peter found Heinrich Astor, old and retired from half a century of laboring in a bloody apron behind the counter of his meat stall in the Fly Market, more than willing to talk to a Van Alen. Heinrich, who'd come over with the Hessians and deserted to ply the trade he'd learned in Germany in the lucrative market of an occupied and starving New York, had often been supplied by Cornelius Van Alen's sloops. "Your grandfather was an honest man, but that Drew!" he exploded. "You know how that pious hypocrite came by his money? He'd drive his cattle night and day until you could count every bone on them and they were near dead of thirst. Then just before he reached market, he'd let them drink until they were sleek and bloated and twice their real weight in meat. He caught me a few times with that watered stock until I got onto him. When I told Jacob about it, he just laughed and said, 'Sounds like a lot of the paper stock traded down on the exchange.' Write that about Drew, young man, though he'll like as not horsewhip you for it."

Peter hadn't written that, or anything, about Mr. Drew. Mr. Bryant had decided that, the probabilities of a hiding or libel suit aside, he didn't want to devote precious space in the paper to such a man. Indeed, he'd called off the whole series for fear that too many similar practices would come to light and disillusion his readers about the men who were building New York. "While I hold no brief for Mr. Drew, I'm afraid business is no matter for the fainthearted or high-minded," he'd said. "Only the ruthless survive. I happen to know that your friend Mr. Astor picks up much of his property through foreclosures on loans. Still, it's the money such men acquire that makes possible the progress we need. I understand that Astor, for instance, is planning to provide us with a new hotel which the city could well use, and if Drew's ventures on the river are cutting rates for the average man so much the better. We've enough on our hands reporting the corruption of men who claim to serve the public without delving into men's private affairs." Peter wasn't sure whether he agreed with his editor, but had been happy enough to give up the assignment in favor of a more interesting series on the city's religious leaders that had brought him to Rachel . . . .

Rachel. Would she forgive him for not meeting her in the bookstore as they'd planned, or half-planned when they parted in the park? Probably. It was part of the intrigue of their relationship that neither of them knew whether the other would show up at their supposedly accidental rendezvous. He had the damnable uncertainties of his job as a reporter to contend with, and she had to elude the watchful eye of her father. He'd especially wanted to make it this afternoon to see if she'd say anything about what had happened in the dark. Probably not. Part of her charm was her shyness. When they met they would actually talk about the books they were fingering, exchanging other messages with their eyes. Those messages, though, were clear enough. They'd begun when, while interviewing her father, she'd been called to serve them a strange sweet wine. She'd stayed on, sitting in a corner of the room to listen, and whenever he'd look up he'd see those eyes. Not flirtatious but curious, interested. They were dark, as was her hair, her skin. She seemed as exotic to him as the religion her father was expounding, an exposition he had great difficulty concentrating on in the light of those eyes. When once she got into the conversation to act as a sort of interpreter between her father and himself, she showed a rare intelligence and, more to keep her talking than for any other reason, he said, "You must read a lot, Miss Seixas. What bookstore do you favor?" She'd named one on Broadway not far from the synagogue on Mill Street, and he'd haunted it until he found her there.

Peter didn't know for sure whether he was in love with Rachel, or she with him. He did know that he continually hungered to see her, to be with her, that her dark beauty was with him days as well as nights. That she was Jewish only added to her attraction for him; entering her mind, her spirit, had the effect of discovering a new, a strange land, as would claiming her most certainly virginal body. Knowing her, wanting her, made him at last grateful for the romantic spirit that had also kept him innocent as an offering to a great love when, and if, he found it. Could this be it? Maybe he ought to mention her to his mother tonight, in case . . . But he was getting off his train of thought as he generally did when Rachel intruded . . . What was it? Oh, yes, that Drew fiasco that proved he had no head for business . . .

What he'd seen of Drew, however, caused him to warn his mother and Cornelius about backing Vanderbilt. The captain had already lost a great deal of money in a rate-cutting competition that drove the Stevens brothers' boats off the Peekskill run and more yet when the *General Jackson,* uninsured, blew up. It was then that Drew launched his *Water Witch* to take over the trade, apparently confident that Vanderbilt no longer had the resources to challenge him. Drew had evidently been unaware of, or forgotten about, Vanderbilt's Van Alen connection: a friendship going back to the days when Sally Van Alen helped Vanderbilt outwit the deputies had been recently cemented by Augusta Vanderbilt's marriage to Cornelius Van Alen. But then it had been a quiet wedding with no public announcement in keeping with the quiet style of young Cornelius Van Alen whose operations in a dusty counting room in an old pre-Revolutionary Broadway house went virtually unnoticed now that no ships flew the Van Alen flag. Indeed, if the name Cornelius Van Alen had been mentioned to Drew, he'd probably have responded with, "Oh, I thought he died long ago." Whether his mother and Cornelius ignored his warning and backed Vanderbilt out of family sentiment or shrewd business judgment, or both, they'd prospered. Putting the *Princess* which he bought from his old employer, Gibbons, into service, the captain started cutting rates until they reached twelve and a half cents. Nobody, least of all Peter, knew how much money Van Alen & Son risked in the year that Drew hung on, but it was rumored that Drew lost $10,000 before he finally sold out to Vanderbilt. Now plans were being made for a Vanderbilt assault on the Hudson River Association's lucrative line to Albany, and perhaps this was what the family wanted to discuss.

Well, he'd know soon enough. Meanwhile, he found himself caught up in the mood of a bustling Broadway, so different from the dark and silent street he'd known as a boy. It was still only late afternoon, but a December dusk was already gathering, and gaslights were flaring into life along the sidewalks and in the shops and public buildings. Since it was coming on to Christmas, storekeepers were staying open until all hours in hopes of luring homeward-bound clerks and mechanics with an eye to buying presents. He began to think about getting something for Rachel and then wondered whether a present at Christmas would be appropriate for someone of her religion. It would be too bad if it weren't, for Christmas had always been a special joy in the Dutch tradition with its jolly, gift-giving saint. One of the men in Mr. Cooper's bread and cheese club, Clement Moore, had caught the spirit of the whole thing in his poem, " 'Twas the night before Christmas, and all through the house, not a creature was stirring, not even a mouse . . . " Peter had wanted Mr. Bryant to run the poem again this year, but the editor had favored him with one of those stern, piercing looks and said, "I don't believe in presents. We never exchange them in our house, and I don't want to encourage such wasteful frivolity, especially among the poor." For a poet, Bryant could sometimes be shockingly unromantic, but then his attitudes might come from a poor and Puritan childhood. The more he saw of life, the more Peter was convinced that most people never quite outgrew the children they'd been.

His Uncle Peter, for instance. While he was in Princeton, Peter had been boasting proud of his uncle's record in the Senate as a defender of democracy. Then suddenly Uncle Peter had done a switch, favoring higher tariffs, the national bank and everything else that the new Whigs, that strange collection of old Federalists and disenchanted Democrats, wanted. Peter himself had been in the Park Theater the night that the pit erupted in a riot of delight and derision when an actor in an English comedy innocently tossed out the line, "Wigs are out of date." When he'd told his uncle about it, the senator had said, "Perhaps. Perhaps. But if so, it's a shame. They believe in the old values, the kind I grew up with." He'd tried to pin his uncle down on what those values were and had brought forth an ad hominem argument: "We used to have giants in the land, Peter—Washington, Jay, Jefferson, Madison, Monroe, DeWitt Clinton—men of breeding and learning who really rose above party to serve their country. What giants we have left—Webster, Clay, and, yes, John Quincy Adams who's put service before pride to return humbly to the House—are Whigs. It's made me realize that my father was right after all when he used to say that there was a natural aristocracy, an ordained order of mankind. We Schuylers were born into that aristocracy, Peter, whether we like it or not, and we must preserve the lands and wealth on which giants thrive. Government is no better than the men who govern, and good men don't grow up in taverns."

That had been Uncle Peter's bitterest reference to Cousin Matty Van Buren who was now vice-president and sure to go into the White House and should therefore be the pride of the family. But then, of course, Cousin Matty wasn't related to Uncle Peter but only to his mother, and he gathered that the Schuylers had always looked down on the Van Alens. Peter didn't know just what had happened between his uncle and Matty who'd been hand in glove for so long unless it had been his uncle's tariff bill favoring Northern commerce that had caused such a ruckus about nullification in the South that President Jackson had had to threaten to call out troops to preserve the Union.

He didn't like to think that his uncle had been motivated by a desire to help Cornelius in the coal business, but the fact that Cornelius had hired the senator to represent the firm's interests as soon as he got back from Washington was suspicious. It was a nice irony that Cornelius had dumped the Delaware and Hudson stock after all that trouble, but business was full of such ironies. So, in fact, was life. His mother who'd grown closer than ever to Uncle Peter since Aunt Alexandra died was nevertheless fond of Cousin Matty and still talked about her trip to Washington where she was hostess at his ball as one of the high points of her life. "I don't care whether people call him the Red Fox or the Little Magician or what, I like him," she'd argue with Uncle Peter whenever Matty's name came up. "I should think anyone with Dutch in his veins would be proud that one of us is finally getting into the White House. And as for your principles in politics, I've seen little but harm done in the name of principle. Frankly, I just think you have a guilty conscience about Matty, Peter. But then I love you both which always seems to be a woman's problem. Now let's talk about something else . . . ."

Peter more than agreed with his mother; he found Cousin Matty the most fascinating of his relatives, and he only regretted that he'd seen so little of him in recent years when he was old enough to appreciate him. Uncle Peter could talk all he wanted to about principles, but all you had to do was look around you right here in New York to see evidences of the changes taking place because of Cousin Matty and his "Albany regency." Passing City Hall Park, Peter could see the old jail, largely dark now, since a law forbidding imprisonment of debtors which Matty had long favored had gone into effect. That black man, pausing to study the notice of attractions in Scudder's Museum up ahead, was a free man as a result of the constitution Matty had helped draft; next year that fellow swinging his lunch box to scare off the horses as he picked his way across the street, a real Hibernian by the looks of him, would be able to vote for the first time for a mayor of New York because of a change in the city's charter pushed by Matty's Tammany friends. This was what democracy was all about in Peter's mind. He was still only twenty-one and still full of that feeling that he could do everything, be everything, and he suspected that other people felt that way, too. If nothing else, Cousin Matty, like President Jackson, was living proof that there were no limits to what a man could make of himself in a real democaracy, and, from all he could tell, Cousin Matty wanted to give other people the same chance, too.

But what intrigued Peter most about Cousin Matty was his style. With all his seeming to favor the common people, he was evidently a most uncommon man. When Washington Irving had come back from Europe last year, all he could talk about was the way Cousin Matty as minister to the Court of St. James had impressed everybody in the highest circles with his manner and charm. "All those people who used to think of us as savages have changed their minds," Irving said. "There wasn't a man in all of London better turned out or with a quicker wit in conversation." As Cousin Matty's first secretary, Irving was run ragged, accompanying him to balls and receptions at night and visits to historic and literary shrines by day. "Seeing what good he was doing for our country, I was devastated when word came through that the Senate had rejected his nomination as minister," Irving said, "but he was so happy that he actually danced a jig. When he saw the look on my face, he said, 'Mr. Irving, you've taught me a lot about literature these past months, so let me give you a lesson in politics. It was my idea for John Eaton and me to resign and break up the cabinet, so that President Jackson could get rid of the Calhoun supporters among us. The president was gracious enough to reward me with this post and Eaton with Spain. Now Calhoun, the fool, has played right into my hands. By casting, as vice-president, the vote that broke the tie and rejected my appointment, he's made himself a lightning rod for all the resentment of my many friends, including the president. They'll be out for revenge when the convention is called and be sure to nominate me in Calhoun's place.' Well, I say your Cousin Matty is as good a prophet as he is a diplomat." Yes, Cousin Matty was intriguing, and he would have to persuade Mr. Bryant to send him to Washington to see more of him.

Peter was so lost in thought that he inadvertently stepped off the curb and was nearly run down by an omnibus that careened into the gutter to get around a slow cart in the middle of the road. He heard the rattle of its wheels and jumped aside while, with a great deal of cursing, whoaing and tugging on the reins, the driver managed to get his four horses stopped. Peter, embarrassed, tried to make amends by giving the boy at the entrance step a shilling and climbing aboad. It was probably a fortunate occurrence since it was getting late, and he was getting chilly, and his mother's new place was still blocks beyond the end of the line at Bleecker Street. It was also one of those occurrences that made you reflect on the chanciness of life. If there had been an early snowfall and the vehicle a silent sleigh instead of an omnibus, he wouldn't have been warned in time to jump and would have gone down under the horses' hooves despite the driver's skill. Looking around at the other gentlemen riding uptown, Peter reflected that it was the clatter and dust raised by these omnibuses as much as anything else that had finally convinced his mother to abandon the old house on Broadway to purely business purposes and follow the northward migration of the wealthy, and of course it was the convenience they offered in getting back and forth to work that made it sensible for Cornelius to go with her. Peter supposed that someday they'd lay track on Broadway as the New York and Harlem Railway was doing on the East Side. It would ruin sleighing, but at least these fellows would have to keep their horses in line instead of weaving in and out like drivers at a racetrack.

Peter had been happy about his mother's move, not only for her but for himself. In a way he hadn't quite anticipated, it had cut his ties with home. There was nothing whatever about the pseudo-Grecian style of the new Colonnade Row on Lafayette Place to arouse nostalgic sentiment as did the old brick house on Broadway with its faint reek of ink and tea and, when the wind was right, the sea. The terrace on Lafayette Place had a fluted colonnade running the whole length of the row in front of the second and third story windows, fancy wrought-iron rails and fences on the first floor, and a heavy carved cornice. Its construction had inspired the new *Knickerbocker* magazine to superlatives: "It is universally allowed to be unequaled for grandeur and effect, the most imposing and magnificent in the city." More impressive than its looks to his mother had been the facilities; the houses behind the magnificent façade were among the first in the city to have a water closet *and* a bath. "I don't think either the steam engine or the gaslight can compare with these conveniences in improving the quality of life," she joked, and Peter, who'd often use the pretext of a family visit to while away an hour in the tub instead of going to the public baths, could well understand her feeling.

Once they decided to move, his mother and Cornelius could hardly have gone anywhere else without offending their fellow director, Bill Astor. It was the newest of the many real estate ventures that were earning old Jacob Astor the nickname of "landlord of New York." This time, instead of foreclosing on widows to get the property, he had sliced away half of Vauxhall Gardens, a green and flowery oasis where Peter had often gone with his friends of a summer evening to eat ices, listen to band music, watch the fireworks and spy on older couples kissing in its leafy alcoves. Typically, Astor had bought the whole area way back in 1804 for $45,000 from Jacob Sperry who had used it to grow plants and flowers for the New York market. Nobody could imagine living there then since it was four miles—a good hour's walk—from the city, and so Astor had leased it for twenty years to Delacroix for his pleasure gardens. By the time the lease ran out, Bleecker, Bond and Great Jones Streets to the south were filling in with fashionable dwellings, and Astor seized the opportunity to lay a broad street several blocks long right through the gardens. He named it for the French hero of the Revolution who had just set New York on its ear by a triumphal return and began selling lots. What he got for them, Peter wasn't sure, but he did know that his mother and brother had paid $25,000 for their house, and the assumption that Astor's investment had, as usual, doubled or tripled was fair. Well, at least half the gardens remained, and his mother could enjoy for a while a green vista between her house and the Bowery which was another reason she'd chosen the place.

Arriving at his mother's door, Peter was greeted by Flossie, the only real touch of home there. Before he'd let her take his cape and hat, he gave her a hug and said, "I swear you're looking younger every day, Flossie."

"And I swear you's learnin' to lie better every day, Mr. Peter," she said. "You'd better hurry on up. They's all waitin' in the drawin' room."

"Do you have any idea what this is all about, Flossie?"

"I don't know, but Mr. Cornelius he come home early from the office so it must be somethin'."

Going up the stairs with again a feeling of apprehension from the knowledge that Cornelius was there, Peter tried to keep his mind on Flossie. He'd never understood why, being free, she'd chosen to move way up here and virtually cut herself off from her church where, for a few hours a week, she could escape into what Peter imagined was the sustaining world of her own people. In this house, she was virtually useless, what with the German girls to cook and clean, and it was so much smaller that she had only a cramped chamber up under the eaves. Peter had gone so far as to get her a job offer from Mrs. Mason, but she'd turned it down, saying, "Oh, I couldn't leave Mr. Cornelius, he my baby." And he'd said, "But I'm your baby, too, aren't I?" And she'd ducked her head and looked away in embarrassment when she'd tried to explain, "But he the *firs'.* " Peter had been hurt more than he liked to remember by that, but it had recalled many galling moments of childhood when a scolding Flossie would say, "Why do you get in such deviltry? Why can't you be a good chil' like your brother?" With her simple faith, Flossie took both pride in and credit for Cornelius' piety as well as that of Cousin James whom she'd also tended in his first months. It didn't seem to bother Flossie that both James and Cornelius would proclaim in front of her that slavery was the ordained fate of the "sons of Ham" or that Cornelius would often fume, "These people who talk loosely about abolition don't really understand business. Where would Arthur Tappan get the fine cloth that's making him rich here in New York without the cotton the slaves pick? The whole cotton and tobacco economy of the South is based on slavery, and those of us up here who finance it would go under if the institution were abolished." No matter what he said, Cornelius could evidently do no wrong in Flossie's eyes, and, although he didn't like to think about it, Peter often wondered whether his own talk about freeing the slaves wasn't a futile effort to compete for the affections of this simpleminded old woman. His mother, who'd usually sided with him against Flossie in childhood disciplinary matters, sensed this and said once, "Don't let her worry you, Peter. She had the fear of God thrown into her by my father when she was a child, and she's never grown out of it. She'll never understand you, just as she's never understood me. But she's a good soul, and she does love Cornelius, and he needs all the love he can get." As if Peter, too, didn't need love, but he'd relished the hint in his mother's words that *her* love for him might be greater than it was for Cornelius.

Peter was still not used to the harsh light of gas jets burning indoors. Only a few of the newest and richest houses, like this of his mother, were fitted for this so-called "convenience," and a number of them had already blown up. As he entered the drawing room, Peter noticed with a certain amusement that his mother's gilt and white decor was marred by signs under each jet, warning in Cornelius' careful clerical script, "Turn off gas!" Peter doubted that the

270

dangers from gas would inhibit the spread of its use any more than the regular scorching and drowning of passengers in steamboat explosions discouraged that industry's growth. There were those who protested that the loss of any human life was too much to pay for progress, but their pleas went unheeded by most people who were sustained by that universal human assumption that their own lives would never be among those forfeited. He'd tried a cautionary piece on the use of gas for Mr. Bryant who had balled it up and tossed it into the wastebasket, saying, "Ah, Peter, let there be light! For every soul cast into outer darkness, a thousand of the living will be able to make better use of their only leisure hours in the day. Think what it will mean to us who write and publish when people can use those hours to read comfortably." Of course, his editor made all kinds of sense, and yet too much light could banish illusion. He'd been particularly conscious of this when he'd gone this past summer to the old Park Theater, newly lit with gas, to see Tyrone Power's American debut in *The Irish Ambassador* and found the artifice of makeup intrusively visible. He was conscious of it now: the revealing lines of emotional tension stood out too clearly on the faces of the family members gathered in that gaslit room, and he knew that the subject under discussion was unpleasant and divisive.

Cornelius, standing with his back to the door, was saying something in a voice too low for him to catch; his mother, who could see him come in from her place on one of the settees flanking the fireplace, put a cautionary finger to her lips and then called across the room, "Hello, Peter! I was beginning to fear that you couldn't come."

"I started to walk, but then I took the omnibus—it was so cold."

"Well, then, you'll want tea," his mother said, fussing with the things on the table in front of her. "The others have had theirs . . . ."

"No tea, thanks, mother. But if you have any wine?"

"Well, yes. We brought the last of your grandfather's cellar up with us—for guests, of course. I suppose we can consider Peter a guest now, can't we Cornelius? Augusta, be a dear and run and tell the girls to bring up a bottle of Madeira."

"Might add a glass for me," his Uncle Peter said.

"Me, too," Amelia Downing joined in.

"Mother, this is no social occasion," Cornelius protested.

"Go on, Augusta. This is my house, too, Cornelius," Sally said.

The cast of characters was very much what Peter had expected except that there were no Smiths present, which probably meant that there was no business afoot. While they waited for the wine, there was a spurt of nervous small talk—Uncle Peter wanting to know if it had started to snow yet, Amelia asking Sally where she'd got the lace trim for her bodice, Cornelius complaining that the omnibuses were so full he'd had to stand the whole way home. Cousin James who had assumed a commanding position by leaning against the fireplace mantel as he had a tendency to do in these gatherings seemed to be picking up a thread of past conversation when he grabbed the floor with his pulpit voice and said, "Speaking of unsuitable matches, I still think that your Mr. Burr's marriage to Madam Jumel is a sacrilege, a profaning of the sacred vows. I can't imagine how he found a clergyman to perform the ceremony."

"Now, James, Mr. Burr was just lonely," Sally said. "He's complained so of his loneliness to me all these years that I was happy to see him find somebody."

"Lonely? Please, Aunt Sally, sometimes I think you are impossibly naive. He's just after her money. I hear he's already been selling off her assets and putting them into one of those impossible land schemes of his in Texas. You'd think at his age—what is he? at least seventy-seven—he'd give up trying to get rich."

"Mr. Burr always was a big dreamer," Uncle Peter said.

"Schemer more like. Next thing you know he'll turn that beautiful old house of hers on Harlem Heights into a saloon for the money which would be another sacrilege since General Washington used it for his headquarters. No, I tell you it's only money he wants, or why wouldn't he marry some decent woman instead of one who's not welcome in any respectable New York house?" Cousin James persisted. "If we're here to talk about the sacred institution of marriage, we couldn't have a better example of using it to the wrong ends."

Though he was a little confused as to the context of this remark, Peter was angered by Cousin James' self-righteous judgment on a man he, too, had come to love. With some thought of trying to put together a story about this fabulous and perplexing figure, he'd taken to dropping into Burr's office from time to time and nudging the old man into reminiscences about his days of glory. Sometimes these visits would be interrupted by a client coming to pay his bill, and Mr.

Burr would casually toss the money without counting it into a little well in the center of the library table around which his clerks sat poring over their casebooks. More frequently, though, the caller would be a down-at-the-heels, down-at-the-eyes man or woman in need of "just a little something" to tide them over. and Mr. Burr would as casually reach into the well and, again without counting, press money into an outstretched hand. The clerks would shake their heads, and, behind Burr's back, one of them told Peter, "He never keeps a cent, and we're lucky if he has our pay in hand on Saturday. But it's hard not to love him for it. You know the high and mighty still cut Mr. Burr dead in the street, as if they can't remember his name, and yet when they're down and out they come to him, and he always remembers *them.*"

Thinking about this, Peter said, "What difference does it make if Mr. Burr did marry for money? There isn't a more generous man in New York, and he deserves a little luxury in his old age."

"You see?" Cornelius said. "I don't know where Peter gets such cynicism, but now I suppose he's going to tell us that his own folly is also perfectly acceptable."

"My what?" Peter asked. Though he didn't know yet what the subject was, he was sure that the meeting was at last beginning. Augusta had returned, followed by a girl bearing wine, and Peter poured himself a glass and took a generous swallow.

"You ought to know very well what I'm talking about—that Israelite girl you've been seeing," Cornelius said.

Rachel. So that was it? What a way to describe someone so darkly warm and mysterious. And was "seeing" the right word either? Since he'd met her in her father's house, he'd run into her again apparently by chance about four—yes, exactly four—times in one or the other of the bookshops they both frequented and then once more, but not by chance, in the Battery where he hadn't been able to see much more in the darkness but a faint starshine in her eyes but where he'd felt the warmth of her breath on his cheek and the softness of her lips against his and . . . But his mother was speaking.

"I want you to know that this gathering wasn't my idea, Peter, but I thought that you should have a chance to defend yourself. Cousin James has come to us with a story about you and this girl, and he's got Cornelius and your uncle all upset, and . . ."

"Aunt Sally, it is no story," Cousin James said. "Peter, Rabbi Seixas himself came to me in great turmoil—I guess because he knows me from our being together on the platform at a number of patriotic occasions—and said that you and his daughter are engaged to be married. He's very distressed at the idea of his daughter's marrying outside of the faith and thought that I, as a man of religion, would understand and be able to do something about it. Since I never see you, I naturally came here, and . . ."

"Well, I told James that I didn't think this could be true. I can't imagine you going so far as to propose marriage without telling me about it, letting me meet the girl. It isn't true, is it, Peter?" Sally asked.

There was a disturbing note of anxiety in his mother's voice. No, it wasn't true unless telling a girl that you couldn't live another day, hour, minute or second without seeing her was proposing marriage. But he and Rachel had not yet talked about anything as mundane as marriage, hadn't even thought about it: they were too busy falling in love. There was something very odd in the air, but he said to reassure his mother, "No, it isn't true . . . ."

"Then either you or the rabbi is lying," Cousin James said. "What the rabbi actually told me—and it hurt him as a father to have to tell it—is that, fearing for his daughter's safety, he sent his son to watch over her when she went walking. The boy saw you and the girl in an . . . uh, embrace . . . and reported it to the father who was of course duty bound to confront his daughter. It was then that she told him of your marriage plans . . . ."

All Peter could think of was Rachel, shy Rachel—trapped, spied upon, frightened. What hell she must be going through. He couldn't let her down. "Well, if you put it that way, you're right, and is it a crime?" he said, glaring defiance at each member of the family in turn. His mother was shading her eyes with a hand, as if to hide her feelings; Amelia was flushed with embarrassment. "Honestly, Peter, I didn't want to be here, but . . ."she said with an apologetic shrug.

"I see nothing wrong with you being here or anybody else in the family," Cornelius said. "It's not only the family he'll hurt with this liaison but the business, too. I'm sure he's never thought in his unholy lust about what this will do to the good name of Van Alen among Christian businessmen. He never does give a thought to the business—"

"Now, that's going a little strong, Cornelius," Uncle Peter said. "I think it's normal enough for a boy Peter's age to have an eye for a pretty girl. I can still remember the little Irish girl who lived down the block from my boardinghouse when I first came to New York— ah, well. The thing is, Peter, that marriage is a very different proposition from having a little—uh, flirtation—don't you know?"

"This is no flirtation. I *love* the girl—"

"Bravo, Peter! I wish somebody'd said that about mè," Amelia said.

Amelia's outburst startled everyone; it was so unlike her. She was held to be the family cynic, proof positive to the male minds at least that educating a female was a terrible mistake. Despite the fact that she'd been in the very center of the Washington social swirl, owing to her father's position in the State Department, she'd remained unmarried. When Amelia's curious state came up for discussion in the Van Alen household, Sally was very likely to say, "She just hasn't found anyone good enough for her," and Uncle Peter would humph, "What man wants a woman who challenges everything he says, and . . . and *laughs* at him?" For anyone with even a slightly lascivious turn of mind—Peter, for example—Amelia's presumably virginal existence seemed a great waste since she'd inherited her mother's Grecian stature and profile with all that implied about the body under all those yards of concealing cloth. But until that moment, Amelia had given no hint of a starving heart. Indeed, she'd exulted in her freedom from woman's normal fate. When her parents had died, she'd turned their big old Georgetown house into an exclusive boarding-school for girls. She'd travel as far north as Boston, as far south as Charleston, as far west as Pittsburgh, in search of students. Whenever and wherever possible, she would speak, usually to small and subversive gatherings in somebody's parlor, about the coming of the real revolution—the rise of women. She'd insert herself into meetings and tweak the noses of men on the platform with questions from the floor—of Cousin James at a Sunday school rally, she once asked, "Why shouldn't a woman be an atheist when you claim God is a man?" . . . of William Lloyd Garrison at a meeting of the New England Anti-Slavery Society: "Why talk of freeing Negroes when you haven't freed your wife?" . . . of Daniel Webster on the floor of the Senate: "How can you say the whole country favors your measure when half its citizens, we women, can't vote?" Privately, Amelia's reaction to the pretensions of man, including romantic love, was

275

laughter. "If I didn't laugh, I'd have to cry, and I think a person looks so ugly crying," she'd say. But she didn't seem to be laughing now, and Peter was grateful to her for it.

"Really, Amelia," Uncle Peter said, "even you ought to know that love is for a season and marriage is for life. I have to agree with Cornelius that this could ruin Peter's career. Suppose he decided to go into politics? You know better than anyone how such a marriage would be received in Washington. Am I not right?"

"Unfortunately, yes," Amelia said.

Cousin James had stayed out of the pulpit as long as his nature would allow. "We're all straying from the point," he said. "This is a religious matter. Whatever your present practice, Peter, you are a baptized and professing Christian—I admitted you to the church myself—and I must warn you that it is a serious breach of your faith to marry a Jew. They are the people who crucified the Christ . . ."

Even as he listened, a professional part of Peter's mind was making a decision. Cousin James had been next on his list for a portrait of religious leaders, and he would no longer attempt it. He simply didn't understand the man. Among other puzzling aspects of Cousin James was that he seemed to grow handsomer with the years; at thirty-seven, he retained that ready smile and abundance of animal vitality that made it hard to dislike him even when he said things to shrivel your spirit. He kept in trim by riding the saddle horse he stabled behind the manse and would on occasion show up at Cato's to race his mount and demonstrate that God loved clean-living horsemen. The horse was of course a gift of one of the wealthy parishioners Cousin James had begun attracting when the late Governor Clinton blessed his church with his presence. The church's country location out along Fifth Avenue provided the best of excuses for even the pious to take a pleasant carriage ride of a Sunday morning, and in the newsrooms around town the Reverend James Schuyler's flock was known as "the carriage trade." His influence was thus held to be much greater than the size of his congregation would suggest, and men like Willard and Jennings, mine hosts at the City Hotel, were blaming him for a deplorable trend among distinguished citizens to turn their glasses down at public banquets. While he railed against sins of the flesh—some said the visible adoration he received from women in the congregation kept him in mind of these—Cousin James seemed less concerned with sins of the spirit. Thus, his message to his prosperous flock was generally a comfortable one: as God's chosen which he defined implicitly as being male, white, Christian, Presbyterian and citizens of New York, in approximately that order, they were entitled to dominate the earth and all creatures thereon and to enjoy the fruits of their domination. After a number of extensive interviews with Rabbi Seixas for his article, Peter thought that Cousin James might get an interesting argument from the rabbi as to who was chosen and by whom, but then he doubted from knowing both of them that either man could convince the other. What troubled him most about James was that, while he kept insisting that Jesus had turned the hard stones of law served up in the Old Testament into the soft manna of love, his own words still could kill when it came to most matters of the human heart, such as this.

". . . What's more, the rabbi feels even more strongly about this than I do," James was saying. "He assured me with tears in his eyes that he would have to turn his daughter out of his congregation and his home if she persists in marrying you."

"If I have my way, we'll do the same," Cornelius said.

"Oh, stop it! Stop it, all of you," Sally said, her voice breaking. "I would never have asked Peter here if I thought you'd talk like this."

Peter suddenly sensed that his mother's distress might be worse than his own. "What would you have me do, mother?" he asked.

All the rigid control he'd come to expect of her, all the calm intelligence with which she'd handled most crises in their lives, was gone. Struggling to talk against an urge to weep, she said, "I don't know. I just don't know, Peter. Oh, God, why must I always be in the middle? I only know that you ought to be sure you love that girl more than most men can love to do what you're doing to her. If James is right, you'll bring the wrath of her father upon her, and that is just . . . just . . ."

She couldn't go on; she buried her face in her hands; her shoulders shook. All of them but Uncle Peter seemed frozen by shock at seeing Sally come apart. Uncle Peter went to her at once, put a comforting hand on her head, and said, "You see, Peter, how distressing this is to your mother . . ."

He'd had enough; he waited for no more; he bolted from the room. The wine, though the best from his grandfather's vanishing cellar, was sour in his stomach, and he was appreciative of the water closet where he threw it up. At the door, handing him his things, Flossie said, "Looks like they was hard on you, Mr. Peter. You up to some devilment again?" He didn't answer her.

Out on the street, walking the length of that colonnade behind which the windows of the rich and righteous flared gassy bright, he became conscious that the night was powdered with snow. It was cold and getting colder and wouldn't be warm again until spring. It was very like the weather in his heart.

Chapter *XIV*

The Panic and the Palace

When on the morning of Monday, March 6, 1837, the new granite building of the banking house of I. and L. Joseph at Wall and Exchange Streets collapsed in a shower of stone and glass, crowds of businessmen and their clerks on the way to work gathered in the street to look in a kind of awe at the rubble. For months now increasingly strong financial tremors had been felt throughout the whole New York commercial community, but it had not been anticipated that it would have any effect on the solid masonry of the institutions lining Wall Street. As if to ease the fear in their hearts that this was some evil portent of things to come, a number of onlookers tried feeble jokes to explain the occurrence such as: "Must have built the foundation out of paper like their business" . . . "Probably hired Hibernians right off the boat to save the wages of good Americans." But one observer—a short man with thin face, severely straight in lip and brow—saw no humor in any matter having to do with money and said, "It's an act of God, a punishment for unwise speculation."

"Come on now, Cornelius," the man next to him said. "We're all in this thing. Don't tell me you don't have some flimsy paper out, too."

"No, I don't. I learned my lesson in the fire."

"Oh, yes, you were the one who paid, weren't you? I've always wondered how you did it."

"I guess you could call that a *gift* of God," Cornelius said and walked on toward his offices in the old brick house on Broadway which was still as solid as the day it was built in 1760.

Looking after him, the other man said to nobody in particular, "Odd fellow, that Cornelius Van Alen. Always talking about God, but then he's an elder in the Reverend Schuyler's church. Maybe there's something to this religion."

It had been the talk of New York when Van Alen & Son had managed to pay off every dollar to those insured with them after the great fire of '35. It was a burning more terrible than the one that had gutted the city during the Revolution. Starting on Merchant Street on the evening of December 16 when the thermometer stood at ten below zero, the fire rode the wind through the whole southeastern corner of the city, some fifty acres. Several days of these strong northwest winds had so lowered the water in the slips along the East River that suction hoses could not reach it; what water could be found froze in the hoses. Buildings were blown to try to starve the fire into submission, but it leaped over their remains for fresh fodder. For two days and nights it burned with such fury that its glow was seen as far away as Hartford to the north and Philadelphia to the south. Merchants struggling to save some of their goods paids as much as $200 an hour for the hire of a cart to haul them to safety, but to little avail. In the end, damages amounted to $30 million, a sum beyond the capacity of insurers to pay.

At first, Van Alen and Son seemed no exception. It had been natural for Cornelius with the assent of his board, particularly that of Cousin George Smith whose inherited talents for carousal and gambling had welled up into the oil of salesmanship, to branch out from covering ships to insuring the warehouses, shops and homes of the ships' owners. Although he had invested the premiums prudently in other enterprises, some of them, too, were destroyed by fire. Thus, when the directors of Van Alen & Son gathered in the gaslit parlor on Lafayette Place on a night not long before what promised to be a cheerless Christmas, Cornelius was forced to report that, by selling off all the corporate holdings, including their interest in the Vanderbilt vessels plying Long Island Sound, they could pay out only fifty cents on the dollar.

There was some good news. "My father-in-law is quite willing to give us cash right now, and there's a bill in the legislature to have the state advance cash loans against our assets," Cornelius said.

George Smith, tall and big-boned like his Van Alen grandfather, but darkly and weakly handsome like his father, was the first to respond. "But what you're saying is that we're ruined. God, I knew I should have stuck to the horses."

"You don't need that sort of language to make your point, George," Cornelius said. "We're not completely ruined. We do have some policies out on ships that should go on paying premiums, and —"

"But that's peanuts. I know the books as well as you do, Cornelius, and it wouldn't even cover salaries," George said. "I couldn't live a month without dividends, and I doubt you could either. There has to be a better way if we all think about it . . . . Wait a minute? What about this? Why don't we distribute some of the sounder stocks we're holding to the officers as a Christmas bonus in lieu of cash? That way we'd cut down on the company assets and only have to pay out five or ten cents on the dollar like a lot of other companies are doing. Nobody'd be the wiser. Uncle Peter would just have to predate the minutes of this meeting. You could do that, couldn't you, Uncle Peter?"

Peter Schuyler had only been half listening. He'd been staring into the fire and musing on the paradox of how the same flames could be both so benign and so terrible. He didn't answer at once. Whatever they did made little difference to him. He still had his marble house left, though it was graying from the smoke and looked increasingly incongruous in a declining neighborhood, and he could always get back into general practice. Burr, who was trying to work again after getting over that foolishness with Madam Jumel and divorcing her, could certainly use him since the old man was getting on toward eighty and quite feeble from what he'd heard. There was no reason to worry about leaving anything to anybody; for all his effort he hadn't been able to locate his own son Francis, and ever since that business about the Jewish girl his godson, Peter Van Alen, had turned into such a radical that Bryant had had to fire him. Nobody knew quite what young Peter was up to now although once in a while a poem of his would be published in the *New Yorker* or the *Knickerbocker* and a while back his name had embarrassingly appeared in the papers when he got mixed up with trying to help that crazy abolitionist Arthur Tappan save his furniture from being burned during that riot after they let the niggers into Chatham Street Chapel. He knew that Sally kept seeing Peter, but the boy had sense enough not to show up here, and she had sense enough not to talk about him; just the mention of Peter could upset Cornelius for weeks. His hopes that Peter Schuyler Van Alen might carry his good name on in politics were long gone, and leaving anything to him would be a waste.

"Uncle Peter, what do you say?" George asked again.

"Eh? Well, ingenious but probably illegal. When you've danced to the tune, you have to pay the piper."

But Cornelius was evidently intrigued by Cousin George's suggestion; sometimes the man amazed him with his shrewdness which accounted for why he put up with his evil habits. "Would it be all that illegal, Uncle Peter?" Cornelius asked. "Isn't this what you might call an adjourned meeting since we would have met on the fifteenth but for the weather?"

"I'll tell you what—let's put it up to the Supreme Court," George said.

"The what? What nonsense is that?" Peter asked.

"Shows how out-of-date you are, uncle. That's what they call Madeira out at Cato's. We still have some of grandfather's good bottles, don't we, Aunt Sally?"

"There will be no drinking. This is not a social meeting," Cornelius said. "What about the rest of you? You've all been quiet. What do you say, Bill?"

It wasn't unusual for Bill Astor to be quiet. A fleshy, squinty man with a generally vacant expression on his face, he had no use for talk not related to the affairs of the business he was handling more and more for his father, now that old Jacob spent so much time at his country place at Hell Gate or abroad. "If you'd taken my advice and gone into real estate, you could mortgage. I'm sure father would have been delighted to help," he said, "but as it is . . ." He threw up his hands in a gesture of helplessness.

"Mother?"

Of them all, only Sally knew, or could sense, what Cornelius had really been going through these last few days. He hadn't wanted to talk about it, but the pain and fear had stood in his eyes. She'd been reminded of the few times he'd been sick as a child and would retreat into himself, acting silent, stoic, surly. At such times, it was best to leave him alone, and she had done so this time, too. But one night she'd heard noises and, getting up to investigate, had found Cornelius in his study, on his knees beside his desk. He had been praying aloud, "O God, O God, what have I done to deserve this? What sin have I committed? . . ." She had tiptoed away and lain awake the rest of the night thinking. Her thoughts went nowhere, for she no longer understood the business or had much interest in it. It had been a different proposition in the days when old Cornelius was dealing in ships and men and things that people wanted or needed; while her son's shuffling of papers had been bringing in much more money, there was an unreality to it all that made her feel at times as if they didn't deserve whatever it was that they were getting. So she had agreed with Bill Astor's proposals that they ought to be buying real estate, because at least you could go and look at it even if it were still under water as were many of the Astor holdings along the rivers. It took no special genius for anyone living in New York to know that almost any square of land, however unpromising it looked, would eventually grow buildings. Just in this year of the fire alone, some 32,000 immigrants, more than the entire population of the city when she'd first seen it, had arrived from Europe, and they would all need places to stay, places to work. And the way that shrewd old Jacob Astor managed things land could be made to sprout a crop of buildings from which you could reap rents for next to nothing; a little friendly or financial persuasion would induce the city to level a site and put in streets or fill in the shallows along the river, and then a building speculator would be only too happy to lease the land for almost any terms over a period long enough to recover his costs and make a profit. But, perhaps because it was such a simple process that took mostly patience and little in the way of work or cleverness, both Cornelius and George were as scornful as their grandfather had been of the slow yield from land, and surprisingly her brother Peter joined them: "You were probably too young, Sally, to be conscious of what it's like to be land poor, as we always seemed to be on the manor. You see, I don't think even Bill here is old enough to appreciate that his father always had ready cash coming in from the fur trade while he was waiting for his land to bring in rents. We're not in that kind of position yet." So, outnumbered and oversensitive about being a woman in what was considered a masculine preserve, she'd largely held her tongue in company councils. The very fact that he was asking her opinion now was as indicative of Cornelius' state of stress as his seeming willingness to go along with George's clearly dishonest scheme.

"I'm sure you're not in your right mind, Cornelius, even to think of doing a thing like that," she said. "I agree with Peter that we have to pay the piper, and I'm only sorry that we can't give those poor people all that we owe them. Your grandfather was accused of a lot of things in his time but never of not meeting his obligations. That's one reason I've always been proud of the Van Alen name."

"Hear! Hear!" Peter said. "And don't forget the Schuyler name, too."

"I don't think either of you understand," George cut in. "I get about, and I know that we'd be doing better than most of the other houses if we paid as much as ten percent. The public would never blame us—"

"You don't live with the public, George, you live with yourself," Sally said tartly. "What Mr. Astor just said has given me an idea: would your father take a mortgage on several thousand acres up near Kinderhook, Mr. Astor?"

Though his face remained impassive, little lights of interest flickered in Bill Astor's small eyes. "I'm sure he would . . . ."

"Mother, I don't want you to do that," Cornelius said. "I know what that land means to you. This has all been my fault, and—"

"It's not your fault entirely, Cornelius. I've been guilty, too—of silence. For a long time, I haven't liked the way our company has been getting out of dealing in something that . . . well, that you could see and feel, that would be useful to people—for the sake of quick profits on paper, but I've said little about it, bowing to masculine superiority in matters of business. Don't you remember, Cornelius, when your father—and yours, too, George—wanted to sell off our ship and I stepped in and saved it? Not many people know about that, but *your* father will remember it, Mr. Astor. Well, I was younger then, and it must be a sign that I'm getting old that I've kept so quiet. But I can't keep quiet now. If Mr. Astor will give us enough money on that land, I want us to pay off every last cent of that insurance and then see where we go from there."

"I think you're going a little too far already, Sally," Peter said. "I wouldn't have let Alexandra persuade me to sell you that land if I hadn't thought that it would stay in the family."

"We're not necessarily going to lose it. All we have to do is meet the interest payments. Isn't that right, Mr. Astor?"

Bill Astor nodded and said, "I'll talk to father right away. I'm going out to Hell Gate for the Christmas holiday and I'll let you know when I get back. I think, however, that I should resign from the Van Alen board since there might be a conflict of interest—in any case, my advice has seldom been taken . . . ."

Such was the gift of God through which Van Alen & Son managed to meet all the claims against it growing out of the great fire. It proved in the end to be a true gift on Sally's part, for in the fall of '36 when the interest on the Astor mortgage fell due, there was not enough money left in the Van Alen till to meet it. By then, the Van Alens were seeing little of Bill Astor, despite the fact that he was a neighbor on Lafayette Place, and even less of old Jacob. The Astors were busy erecting what was to be the finest hotel in America on the site of the former Astor home at Broadway and Vesey, and Jacob had taken to spending long periods abroad. Since it had been her idea in the first place, Sally went herself to the Astor office behind Jacob's new house on Broadway to explain their circumstances. The place was very like a vault, a square block of solid masonry with barred windows, and Sally felt a kind of chill on entering it. Mr. Jacob Astor, it appeared, was still out of the country, but Mr. William Astor would see her. He was as cordial as his phlegmatic spirit would allow until she got around to asking him for a few more months to meet the interest payment. She was conscious of being too feminine and gushing as she tried to tell him why he should be patient, but she couldn't help herself; his blank, impassive face made her feel like a schoolgirl reciting before a critical master.

"Well, you see, Mr. Astor . . . I know we've been out of touch . . . but I'm sure you're aware that by paying off our obligations, Mr. Van Alen has earned a very great reputation in the city . . . . He's been asked to serve on the board of the Manhattan and several other banks, you know . . . . And, well . . . I know you've heard of Dr. Nott and his new invention to make that stubborn anthracite coal burn in the steam engines of boats . . . . I think they call it forced draft or something . . . . Anyway, you must know that he demonstrated it successfully on the *Novelty* that sailed all the way up to Albany on coal this last June . . . . And, well, it struck us as just the right sort of thing for Van Alen & Son to get involved in since you know how interested we were in the anthracite coal years ago . . . . And, well, we decided to go into the manufacture of steam engines, not only for the boats but the railroads . . . . They've chartered the Erie, you know, and the Baltimore and Ohio is already running passenger service to Washington . . . . And so we've issued stock to build a factory and with Mr. Van Alen's reputation the stock is selling very well on Wall Street, and . . ."

She finally ran out of breath, and Bill Astor said, "That's all very good news, Mrs. Van Alen, but I don't see what it has to do with the matter in hand. You did bring your payment, didn't you?"

"No . . . . You see, when we've sold enough stock, we'll be able to get started on the factory and have some left over to cover the interest. It should only be a matter of a month or so, possibly only a few weeks, and I thought that . . ."

"But this is the date that the money is due. You should have made other arrangements, Mrs. Van Alen."

The chill she'd felt on entering the building was settling into her stomach; she even shivered a little. Perhaps it was her imagination that those little eyes looking out at her over rolls of cheek were lighted by the same steely smile she'd so often heard men complain of in Jacob when he got the better of a deal. Astor was right, of course, and Cornelius had urged taking a mortgage on the Broadway place or the Lafayette Place house or going to Corneel Vanderbilt for a loan, but she'd argued that it wasn't necessary: the Astors were old friends who would be understanding about their plight; with all their money, what would a month or two matter?

"I wish I could see your father," she said. "I'm sure he'd . . ."

"That's impossible; my father is still abroad. But he left very explicit instructions about this mortgage. Here's a note in his own hand. I wouldn't show it to you except from our long association I don't want you to think that I am acting alone."

By now her hand was shaking so that she had difficulty reading, and even more difficulty absorbing, the words. "Watch out for that Van Alen woman," Jacob had written. "She blackmailed me once, and I don't want her to do it again. Be sure to collect that interest on the date due or foreclose. It might be a good chance to get some of that

286

river property those old patroons have been sitting on and which I've always wanted."

She would have burst into tears right there except that she felt the sight would give this cold young man too much satisfaction. She did, however, say, "I always thought that we were friends, I just don't understand . . . ."

"I'm sorry, Mrs. Van Alen. My father's taught me that there is no such thing as friendship when it comes to business. I know he always admired you, but . . . well, you see how it is. Now excuse me, I have other affairs to attend to."

For some time after that, Sally felt numb, as if the chill in that money vault had gone right to her heart. Not so her brother Peter. "Schuyler land in the hands of an Astor! I think father was right after all: the world *has* gone to hell. I never told you out of respect for your so-called friendship, but Astor's name was always coming up when I was in the Senate for the way his fur company defied the law by feeding whiskey to the Indians—not giving it but *selling* it and then when they got the poor savages drunk they'd strike a grinding bargain for their furs. Nothing ever came of the reports the honest army officers were sending in because too many important people like my colleague Benton and that territorial governor Cass were said to be in debt to Mr. Astor. But I always suspected that he was a man of no principle, and now *you* know it, too." Cornelius, who'd never shown any interest in the land on the manor, argued, "It's not a matter of principle at all; it's a matter of business. We defaulted, and he's going to foreclose. I'm not sure that I wouldn't do the same, and I warned you. I feel sorry for your sake, mother, though I never did understand why you wanted to hold onto a place like that with the memories it must have for you. I went along on buying it just to help Uncle Peter out, and to me it's no great loss. We'll just show Astor how wrong he is in not sticking with us."

She'd never been sure just how much Cornelius knew or understood about the cause of her exile from the manor. Always a bright boy, he'd undoubtedly picked up hints from things he'd overheard them saying, and no doubt, too, he'd wormed some version of the affair out of Cousin James. Often she'd thought of telling him about it, but some intuition had always held her back. It was evident that whatever he'd learned, or suspected, had worked to her advantage, adding to his disdain for his father and the kind of man he'd been.

It wasn't entirely fair to let it go at that, but she was selfish enough not to want to disillusion her own son by a kind of confession he would never understand. The longer she lived the more convinced she became that many things in life are better left unspoken when you're sure they won't be understood. Sadly, Cornelius, with a penchant for seeing everything in black and white so like her own father's, would not appreciate the range of colors that blended in her memories. If she could never forget the black of that hole in the ice, she could never forget either the soft green of the springs of her childhood when she was her father's little French gem, or even the bright gold of that summer when she'd wanted so much—and got George. If, as some held, the joys of anticipation were greater than those of realization, then those years of her life on the manor were the most joyous of all her years. It was some such thinking, feeling really, that made her want to hold on to some of that land, whether she ever went back to it or not, and it was this that was her loss.

She felt guilty, as she tended to when she thought too long and hard about Cornelius, for the fact that She seemed to have no such sweet memories of a place of anticipating, a place of becoming. When they'd moved out of the Broadway house Cornelius' only concern was whether commuting by omnibus would take too much time out of his day, and he'd set carpenters to work at once converting the rooms in which they'd all lived so long into storage and office space. Sometimes she thought that Cornelius was an animal perfectly adapted to a city where on the first day of every May the roads and sidewalks were so cluttered with the bedsteads and bureaus and chairs and china of people moving from one house to another, from one block to the next, that it was both difficult and dangerous to go for a walk. Perhaps there was no sense to sentiment about lands or buildings whose measure of value was in dollars per square foot, and the Astors who ruthlessly moved either themselves or their tenants to increase that value were also animals with the right instinct for survival in the city. Her son Peter was different, though. He'd said he was glad when they moved, but his poetry echoed the Sunday sound of church bells on Broadway, reflected dawnings when the rising sun was webbed with the rigging of tall ships, reeked with smells of old tea and new ink. He did have a feeling for his place of becoming and would probably understand hers.

While the falling-out between her sons was in many ways regretta-

288

ble, Sally had to admit that it added a touch of intrigue and excitement to her life. Peter had refused to return to Lafayette Place after that dreadful night when he'd been called on the carpet about that girl Rachel, and she'd taken to meeting with him in public places, usually for tea at Delmonico's in William Street. Though it was probably not right to feel so, these meetings held for her some of the same magic as those trysts with Aaron, not least of it lying in the sympathetic, sea-gray eyes of the son, so like those of the father. She would find herself between encounters saving up things to tell him, questions to ask, feelings to share, thoughts to explore. He seemed to do the same, and, after the initial first few minutes of shyness which she'd bridge with motherly fussing about how he ought to eat better and get his shirts laundered more often, they'd chatter the afternoon away about everything and anything, almost like lovers. One area into which she did not pry was his relationship with women, despite some disquieting rumors about a young actress at the Bowery Theater which of course Cornelius had heard and relayed to her. She was selfishly happy with the evidence in his way with her that he'd found no other feminine ear into which he could pour his deepest feelings. He had apparently loved Rachel, loved her enough to give her up. The only time he'd been willing to talk about it, he'd said, "I thought and thought about what you said, mother, and I decided that I didn't love her enough to put her through what you'd gone through." She'd wanted to hug him then, but she'd contented herself with covering his hands with hers and saying, "Peter, for what it's worth, I think you loved her *more* than enough."

As with Cornelius, she often wondered how much Peter knew about what she'd gone through. He had come along so late that much of it seemed, even to her, like distant history, and it had been easy to brush away his occasional questions. Apparently he had accepted the official version that her father had disowned her for marrying against his wishes and had embellished it with his own romantic notions of her as a princess immured in a stone tower until Grandfather Cornelius whisked her away in his sailing boat. If there was a bad man in the story, it was her unfeeling father whose piety, now reflected in Cornelius, had become a source of evil for Peter. Thus, he was sure that Rachel's father, pious in his own way, would put her through the same kind of hell. Sally had no wish at this late date to tarnish the fable with truth. There had been times, however, and

289

there were still times, when she longed to tell Peter the truth about his own begetting—that he was a child of love. One of her worst temptations had come when Peter, still very small, had run crying to her and saying that Cornelius, in brotherly rage and jealousy, had told him that he was "a mistake." He was too young then for truth, but, thank God, she'd been inspired to reveal a version of truth and had said. "You were not a mistake, Peter. You were born of fire, and you will have fire in your soul." It had lighted his romantic imagination, and she had nearly wept when, years later, she saw a poem of his beginning: "Born of fire, he's yet aflame . . ." But the time had never seemed right for truth; she'd simply lacked the courage to look upon her son's shock and possible hurt, to risk losing his love and respect.

The more she got to know Peter, the more she thought that he was developing into a man who would be capable of absorbing and understanding what she'd really been through. But, sadly, the split between the brothers made it even more imperative that Peter's heritage not be brought into question. Almost daily, Cornelius fumed about having to pay out the dividends which enabled his brother to pursue what he considered a useless and embarrassing life. Those of Peter's writings that Cornelius read out of necessity after some fellow businessman had commented on them struck him as dangerously radical—filled with inflaming sentimentalism about the plight of overworked slaves, underpaid mechanics, dispossessed Indians, despised Irishmen and, worse, with snide attacks on the sincerity and charity of Christians. So when they planned the first public issue of stock, Cornelius suggested buying Peter out. To disguise the real target, he included the Downing interests, too, claiming that, like Peter, Amelia knew nothing and cared less about the business and that her brothers were from all reports more British than King William himself. In an effort to keep family control, the issue was limited to 9,000 shares in blocks of no more than 100 to any individual buyer. It would be difficult, of course, to govern the eventual distribution of outside shares, but the family control seemed assured since the corporation's charter required only a plurality to carry any vote. Once the company started making money on its new and promising venture in coal-burning engines, Cornelius planned to make his control more secure by issuing stock as bonuses to the officers, but until then it became imperative that the family act in consort to support him. If even one family member, holding a thousand shares, went to the trouble to line up enough outside votes his policies could certainly be challenged or possibly defeated; if two or more family members got together, their task would be that much easier. "You see, we really can't afford to have people with wild notions like Peter's, or Amelia's, in our councils," Cornelius argued. Sally was reluctant to see Peter lose his stock for many reasons. With the land gone, it seemed his only tangible tie to the family, and she had to agree with Cornelius that Peter knew nothing about money with the probable result that he would quickly fritter away any cash settlement. But she feared that Peter would jump at an offer if only further to disassociate himself from his brother. So she resorted almost to pleading to persuade Cornelius that they needed all the cash they could raise for their new enterprise and that using it for what amounted to the purposes of internal politics would make a mockery of her own sacrifice of the land. What troubled her was the thought, terrible as it was, that Cornelius could, and probably would, challenge Peter's right to ownership of the stock should he ever discover that his brother was not a legitimate descendant of old Cornelius Van Alen.

In this respect, Sally was grateful to her brother Peter who had shown no inclination to betray her secret. With their business association, he'd grown close to Cornelius, and it was evident that he was disappointed in his namesake. Yet she was confident that she could trust Peter to keep his silence. For all his political compromising and sometimes petty moralizing, her brother Peter was very like her. However they might differ on intellectual matters—he never read fiction or poetry and couldn't abide the theater unless it was a silly comedy, for instance—or personalities—he considered Matty Van Buren vain and unprincipled and Amelia Downing "too bright for her own good"—they shared a common physical and emotional makeup. There must have been some ancestor, possibly the French grandmother they'd never known, from whom they'd both inherited what she could only think of as a kind of animal spirit that had made them rebel against their father's intolerant piety and placid patience with an unchanging order of life. Often she felt sorry for Peter who, like a failed revolutionary, seemed these days to be living in a state of disillusion about everything. His rebellion, she thought, had never gone quite far enough; he'd been like a ship under full sail snagged on its own mooring. Still, his yearning to set sail had once been real enough, and he'd retained an understanding for those who had managed to cast off and therefore suffer the storms. In Peter's eyes, she seemed to be one of these, and perhaps she was. In any case, she had no fear that he would create another storm for her to endure, for, all else aside, he loved her, as she loved him.

When she did get around to telling her son Peter about losing the land during one of their afternoons at Delmonico's, he was surprisingly light about it. "Well—there goes my chance to become a country squire writer like Mr. Irving. You know, he's redone an old Dutch farmhouse up near Tarrytown that he calls Sunnyside."

"A good deal more is gone, Peter."

"I know, mother, but does it really matter?"

"Peter, I can hardly believe it—you sound like Cornelius. I thought that you would have more . . . more sentiment . . . or at least understand mine."

"That's just it, mother: it is pure sentiment. If you'd ever really wanted to go back there, you'd have gone long ago—at least built a summer home instead of going to Saratoga all the time. Oh, I know, there was a time when I wished we would go there—just you and me —and build a little log cabin and I could go looking for Indians in the woods. But I know now that there are no Indians in those woods, just as surely as you know that there *are* ghosts. I think we're all better out of it. Life is the future, not the past."

"Oh, you *are* young, Peter. I used to think that, too . . ."

"You still do, deep down, or you wouldn't have done this. And I like that—it's one of the things I've always admired about you, mother. I can remember when Uncle Aaron and father died and I thought the world had come to an end and wanted to stay home from school and hide. You just marched into my room, yanked the covers off me and said, 'Get up and go to school. No matter what happens, we have to go on living.' You know, sometimes I've thought I wouldn't even be here if you'd let the past get in the way of the future."

She looked at him closely. What did he know? What did he know? But, having paused, he was unconcernedly stuffing his mouth with one of the sweet French pastries with which she always tried to fatten him up at these meetings. Then she realized that what he said made more sense in the light of what he was supposed to know; having another child by George would certainly have been burying the past.

"Well, you do make me feel a little better," she managed to say, "and perhaps you're right . . . ."

"I know I'm right, mother. It isn't just a matter of you or us, either. Just look around you: this whole city, this whole country is full of people turning their backs on the past, pulling up stakes and moving on. It's what America is all about. As my friend Horace Greeley said in his *New Yorker*, 'Go west, young man.' I'd go west myself, if . . ."

Her heart started to pound. For some reason she'd never thought of such a possibility. The West had a way of swallowing people, as it had her nephew, Francis. "You wouldn't, Peter!"

It was his turn to put a hand on hers in comfort. "No, don't worry, mother, although I did hear from Cousin Francis. He's in Chicago now, and apparently he read one of my poems that was reprinted there in the exchange. He says the city is growing wildly and needs another good newspaper so he urged me to come out—"

"You heard from Francis? Wait until I tell your uncle Peter!"

"Don't. Please don't, mother. Francis begged me not to let his father know about him. He's apparently doing well speculating in buying government lands, and he's changed his name to Livingston so he won't be connected with the former senator. I don't know quite what he's up to, but he implied that a connection would be embarrassing to them both."

"Well, then, I don't see why he even wrote to you. He must know you're close to his father."

"He wants to start this paper, back me in it. Apparently men who can write a decent sentence are scarce as hen's teeth out there. The only thing I wish I could tell Uncle Peter is that Francis no longer holds it against him for selling that land to us. He says it's the best thing that ever happened to him since he owns ten times as much now. He told me if I had a piece of the Kinderhook place, I ought to sell and buy out there where the land's so rich that you sink to your knees in topsoil. Still, somehow I don't like the smell of what he's up to, and anyway the real reason I wouldn't go is that I want to start my own paper right here in New York where this country begins . . . . But please don't tell Uncle Peter. I think he's almost forgotten that he had a son, the way you once told me you could almost forget you had a father—"

"Yes, I guess you're right," she said, but it was a subject she didn't want to dwell on, so she changed it. "Are you serious about starting a paper? Where would you get the money?"

"You're always telling me how thin I look . . . . Well, I've been saving out of my dividends and have enough cash for a start at least. Look at James Gordon Bennett. He got his *Herald* going last year with only $500 in cash, and he's still in business. Then I thought I might offer my stock to Cornelius. I'm sure he'd want to buy me out just to get me out of his hair."

"No! Don't do that, Peter, whatever you do."

"Why not? I couldn't care less about the making of steam engines or whatever it is that you're involved in now, and it's a near thing we didn't lose it all with his insurance schemes. While I still have some money, I'd like to put it into what I believe in."

"But you know how chancey newspapers are, and if you failed you'd have nothing. It was really as much to save your income so you could go on writing as for any other reason that I sold that land, and now—"

"I appreciate that, mother, and I'm sorry, but I don't know where else to turn."

"If you're really sure you want to do this, Peter, I'll lend you the money. I have some of my own, you know, and no use for it since Cornelius insists on paying for the household."

"I'm not sure you want to be part of the paper I plan, mother— and I *know* Cornelius wouldn't. If he thought you were involved in it, he'd feel he was harboring a traitor under his own roof."

"Well, I suspect Cornelius would consider it more sensible of you to be a publisher than a poet."

"Not when he reads what I write. The reason I want to start a paper here in New York is to be a voice for the immigrants and Negroes that Cornelius and his merchant and banking friends exploit with their low wages and high prices and rents. You should see these poor people, mother—making a dollar or less a day, *if* they can find work, and paid in paper that Cornelius and his banker friends issue that's so worthless they call it *shin plasters.* If you weren't a lady, I'd take you for a walk with me through the Five Points—you know, that area around Baxter, Worth and Park Streets. There may be a hundred people in a house built for ten. They have to use the hallways for necessaries and fight off rats big as cats. Their starving children have stomachs like watermelons and eyes like little mirrors of misery. You would be sick, mother . . . ."

His voice was rising so that diners around them stopped their own talk and stared. Sally put a cautionary finger to her lips and broke in, "Calm down, Peter. I know how such sights must strike you, and I think you're right: they would make me sick. But will writing about them do any good?"

He slumped a little in his chair and spoke in tones so low that she could hardly hear him. "I don't know, mother, but I have to try . . . it seems writing is my only talent . . . ."

"Have you thought about politics? I'm sure Uncle Peter would help you all he can, and with Cousin Matty going into the White House and having all those locofoco friends in Tammany . . ."

"Yes, I've thought about it, but politics is so . . . so slow and full of compromises, as even Uncle Peter will admit. Besides, I don't know whether I'm a locofoco or not. Maybe I'm too much of a writer, but I find the word pretty silly."

Sally allowed herself a laugh; this was the sort of thing on which she and Peter agreed. "So do I, but then I always thought calling themselves sachems and bucktails and whatnot was silly too, like little boys playing some game. I wonder where they got this name?"

"You don't know? Well, you're not a smoker, so you're probably not aware of these new sulphur matches called locofocos. Anyway, it started at a meeting last year—I guess we could call it a pow-wow— in the Wigwam. There was a tremendous falling-out between the so-called conservative Democrats who are upset by Jackson's policies —and I guess Cousin Matty's, too—and the others. The conservatives thought they'd won the day and turned all the gaslights out to end the meeting, but their opponents had got wind of the tactic and each produced a candle and a locofoco to light it with so the meeting could go on. I mean the whole thing *is* so much like boys playing games that I don't think I could have kept a straight face."

"Peter, I have an idea . . . you don't think being president is a game, do you?"

"Well, no . . ."

"I've been invited to dinner in the White House in the spring after Matty moves in, and I want to take you with me and let you talk to him. He might have some better ideas for you. Could you put off your plan until then? You know, Matty likes writers. He's such a friend of Mr. Irving's . . . ."

"Oh, yes, the squire. Irving's lost me by the way—sitting up there at Hell Gate and taking down all that gush about Astor's fur trading that he published in *Astoria*—no doubt to get the money to buy Sunnyside. You're the one who ought to write the real story of Astor after what you've just been through."

"That's beside the point, Peter. Would you wait and go with me?"

"I've always been intrigued by Cousin Matty, I'll admit, but I still think you're just trying to get me off doing what I know I ought to do, and I don't know why."

"You're still so young, not even twenty-five . . . I think you should explore all the possibilities. It's such a big step that I want you to be *sure* if only for my sake. After all, I'll be backing you . . ."

"Then you really will help me?"

"Of course, if you'll wait . . ."

"Yes—but don't think I'm going to change my mind." . . .

Sally went away from that meeting wondering, not for the first time, what it was that made her so rash and impulsive. Why would she offer to support Peter in a venture that was sure to cause more contention between her sons and make Cornelius miserably unhappy with her if he found out about it? In all honesty, it had little to do with Peter's causes although doing something about the general suffering of men did appeal to the romantic side of her nature. She was just being a mother, trying to keep Peter from selling his stock and cutting what she felt to be the umbilical cord to the family—to her. She couldn't bear the thought of losing Peter, of having him go west or, worse, go broke and sink down into the slums. Her delaying tactic had been a matter of impulse, of intuition rather than thought. He was young, and maybe something else would come along, maybe Matty would prove to be the "little magician" he was said to be. Politics would be so much easier to handle, because Peter was right: he'd have to learn to compromise, to be realistic, as she'd had to learn, as everybody had to learn. Still, half her heart hoped that Peter, this child of her love, would be different, that he would put his ideals to the test, and she knew that, if he did, she would surely back him at any cost . . . .

Sally was planning for her trip to Washington when the house of Joseph fell into the street. Eleven days later, on Friday, March 17, physical collapse was followed by financial collapse when the New Orleans house of Hermann & Co. which owed the Josephs some two million dollars stopped payment. From then on each week, each day brought fresh news of failures among the city's speculators and merchants. A real shocker was the announcement that Arthur Tappan & Co., the cloth merchants, would close its doors because it was unable to meet outstanding debts of $1.2 million; despite his crazy notions about freeing the slaves, Arthur Tappan was considered a sound man of the most notable Christian piety. Soon all the banks were in trouble and, beginning with the Dry Dock, began stopping payment. Terrified depositors jammed the still-open banks from morning until late at night, demanding their money in specie with cries of "Pay! Pay!" Women fainted and men bloodied each other's noses in the lines; extra guards had to be hired to keep order and then protect the property when the doors were finally closed. It was pandemonium, and Cornelius Van Alen was coming home later each night after sitting on the board of one distressed bank after another.

Augusta was ill, as she'd been so often since the birth of her first child, Sophie, and so Sally would stay up to see that her son got a glass of hot milk to calm his nerves and an ear into which he could pour his frustrations. In view of her impending trip to Washington, the rage he expended on the Jackson administration and, by implication, that of his successor, Cousin Matty, was unsettling. As the panic spread, Sally for once found herself thinking that Cornelius might have been right when he called the fall of the house of Joseph an act of God; it seemed incredible that such widespread disaster could be the work of mere men, men as weakly human as she knew General Jackson and Matty to be. But in her son's theology God's punishing agent was the devil, who went about his business on earth in the guise of a slim, frail, white-shocked old man named Jackson, and Matty was fast growing horns too.

As Cornelius explained it, panic had become inevitable when Jackson's veto of the bill rechartering the Bank of the United States allowed that institution to expire in '36. The bank, headquartered in Philadelphia and containing the federal government's deposits, had branches in every state and had for twenty years controlled the country's currency. Since the bank was a private institution enriching a comparatively few stockholders, Jackson viewed its operations as out of step with a democracy where access to the privileges of banking should be in as many hands as possible. He not only vetoed the bank's recharter but ordered that federal funds be widely redis-

297

tributed into what came to be called "pet" banks. With the brake off banking and the rage to buy cheap government land in the West going full tilt, an inflation in loans and paper currency spread across the country. Jackson tried to counter this with something called the specie circular directing that only specie be accepted in purchase of government lands, and at the same time bank failures in England and on the continent resulted in a call for specie to pay off their loans to American businesses and banks. And so the run on the banks for silver and gold until on one May day $600,000 was withdrawn in New York alone, and the frightened banks suspended payment in specie. Businessmen unable to meet their obligations began closing their doors and firing their workers. Hungry and angry people were jamming the almshouse and crowding the streets. After one rally in City Hall Park, the crowd, shouting "Bread! Bread! Bread!" streamed down to the riverfront, tore open a flour warehouse and whitened the streets around with its contents as in a spring snowstorm; men shoveled it up with their hats and women made sacks of their skirts before they were driven away by the militia . . . "You see, mother, if Jackson had just let Mr. Biddle and his bank alone, we'd be all right. Money ought to be in the hands of the people who understand money not a lot of country bank clerks and spendthrift politicians," Cornelius would argue. "I'm afraid our Cousin Matty may be as bad as Jackson. So far he's done nothing, nothing. I was at a meeting at Delmonico's the other day, chaired by ex-mayor Philip Hone, where we all decided to send a delegation to Washington to ask the president at least to rescind the specie circular. When you see him, you should put a word in too. Luckily we've got most of our money in a sound factory, but if this goes on much longer, nobody will be able to buy our engines."

Her son Peter was as disturbed as Cornelius, but for different reasons. Instead of sitting in the boardrooms of banks, he was mingling in the streets with the desperate people who couldn't get their money or had lost their jobs. "I tell you, mother, it's the fault of the banks. Right here in New York, they're sitting with more than five million dollars in public funds alone, not to mention their depositors' money, in their vaults and all they'll issue are those shin plasters," he told her on their way to Washington. "They've bribed the legislature as usual to let them hang onto their specie so they won't lose their own shirts. When this blows over, if it blows over, the banks will own more of the country than ever before. You'll see. I can't wait to get back and start my paper and tell people what's really happening."

All this was distressing news to Sally. Since the fall when she'd impulsively made Peter promise to wait, that something she'd hoped for to deflect him from his plan had apparently begun to happen. He had met a young writer from Richmond named Edgar Allan Poe in Gowan's bookstore on Broadway and had immediately fallen under his spell. Poe had grandiose plans for starting a national magazine that would publish the best in American writing, and he had flatteringly urged Peter, on the basis of some of his poetry he'd read, to join him in the venture. Whether Poe, so new to New York, knew that the Van Alen name meant the possibility of money was uncertain, but he surely was aware of it when one afternoon Peter insisted that, instead of their usual tea at Delmonico's, they visit the Poes. She'd come down in the carriage that Cornelius had finally acquired to save him from the stressful, time-consuming omnibus ride to his office, and she was, as always when meeting Peter, dressed richly—a sky-blue silk gown with the new hooped skirts, a diamond choker and a diamond-studded comb atop her gray hair that was still thick enough to loop into the high coiffeur her French hairdresser called *a la giraffe,* after the strange long-necked beast that was on exhibit in Paris's *Jardin des Plantes,* plus a fur wrap and muff to ward off the cold. She felt awkwardly overdressed when their carriage stopped in front of the little frame cottage on Carmine Street, near St. John's Church. Her feelings must have shown in her expression, because Peter said, "I should have warned you. Mr. Poe has no money, no money at all. Even the editors who use his stuff can't, or won't, pay because of this depression. They get by, because his mother-in-law, Mrs. Clemm, who's his aunt too, by the way, takes in boarders."

Inside, the house was shabby but clean and full of the good odor of some sort of hearty stew that Mrs. Clemm, a stout and cheerful woman, was cooking for her family and boarders. From the minute she met Poe and his shy and shining young wife, Sally forgot her own inappropriate glitter or the poverty evident in her surroundings. The girl first caught her eye. She couldn't be more than sixteen, if Sally was any judge, and she was slim and delicate with skin as translucent as fine china and large intense eyes. Poe, who had summoned his Virginia from the kitchen to meet them, dismissed her again gently as one would a child and turned his full attention on Sally. He was a stunningly handsome man with dark hair and mustache, broad brow and riveting gray eyes that teased or caressed her own as he talked. "Peter's *mother?* But for your hair, I would take you for his sister. You grace our humble home with your presence. Won't you sit and have some tea? Mother, Virginia, tea for the lady! And wine, if we have any, for Peter and me."

As he led her over toward a black mohair settee, Sally saw Mrs. Clemm deftly slip a shawl across a break where the stuffing poked through, but Poe handed her to her seat as grandly as if it had been a golden throne. He kept her hand in his and actually dropped to one knee, cocking his head and squinting as if to see her better. "You do," he said. "Yes, you do. You look just like my Helen, a great lady of Richmond for whom I wrote a poem. Have you come upon it? It goes like this . . . ." And without a trace of self-consciousness he began to recite:

> "Helen, thy beauty is to me
> Like those Nicean barks of yore,
> That gently, o'er a perfumed sea,
> The weary, way-worn wanderer bore
> To his own native shore.
> On desperate seas long wont to roam
> Thy hyacinth hair, thy classic face,
> Thy Naiad airs have brought me home
> To the glory that was Greece,
> And the grandeur that was Rome.
> Lo! in yon brilliant window-niche
> How statue-like I see thee stand,
> The agate lamp within thy hand!
> Ah, Psyche, from the regions which
> Are Holy-Land!"

"It's beautiful, Mr. Poe, truly beautiful," she said, "and more than I deserve in the way of flattery."

"Not so. Not so. Ah, that we weren't a generation apart, but then without you there would be no Peter. Has he told you of our venture?"

"A little . . ."

Poe let go of her hand, got to his feet and began pacing as he talked. "I've been telling Peter he's a fool to try to publish another paper in New York. He's far too good a poet to waste his talent on

300

polemics about poverty and such. I'm not much for the Bible, but I believe it when it says the poor shall be always with you. I am, as you can see, poor myself. But what I've been telling Peter is that men—or women—capable of creating beauty are the rarest flowers of earth, and our business should be to bring them to bloom. Wouldn't you agree?"

"Oh, yes . . ."

"I knew you would. Poetry speaks to a woman—and especially one such as you. Well, Peter?"

"I don't know," Peter said. "I still have to think about it. I brought mother here to meet you because if I do anything, it will have to be with her help."

"Yes, I can see that," Poe said, and Sally thought that a calculating look came into his eyes, but he quickly reverted to flattery. "I've heard, Mrs. Van Alen, that you are among the first patrons of the literati of New York, a friend to Irving and Cooper and Bryant, and I am hoping that you will be as generous with a new generation. I, for one, would be glad to worship at your feet, dear lady, for a chance to realize my dreams . . . ."

"I really don't think that would be necessary," Sally said, "but I would like to see Peter stay with his literary work."

She also, and selfishly, wanted to see more of Poe. It had been a long time since she'd met a man who excited those physical yearnings she thought were forever part of her past. But a current seemed to leap across to her from his eyes like that on the telegraph that her old friend Professor Morse was demonstrating to anyone he could lure to his cluttered quarters. Like Poe, she too regretted that they were of different generations, impossibly different since she was the woman. Men could rob the cradle at will, as Poe himself had done. She looked a little enviously at the poet's cousin-wife, Virginia, who, having served tea, was now sitting quietly off by herself and staring at her husband with the unsubtle adoration of a schoolgirl. Still, she had a feeling that Poe was sincere, that when it came to women he could reach up as well as down. The efficient Mrs. Clemm, for instance, made clear her admiration, perhaps love, for him in the fussy things she did to smooth his way. She had no doubt that Poe would love and be loved by many women, and she was half-afraid, half-thrilled, that, given the opportunity she might be among them, even if their meeting would only be in the mind. It was a ridiculous thought, of course. Women of her age—could she really be fifty-seven?—who'd managed to survive life's many fevers were supposed to sit somberly in black in the corner of somebody's parlor.

But however ridiculous, the thought was also enlivening, and one of the reasons Peter's pronouncement now about getting back to New York and starting his paper to help the poor upset her . . . .

"But what about your venture with Mr. Poe?"

"He drinks too much. You saw him on one of his good days, as I had up until then. But not long ago I ran into Poe staggering down Broadway with eyes so glazed that he didn't even recognize me. I managed to get him into a hack and take him home, and Virginia cried when she saw him, and Mrs. Clemm just sighed and said, 'Not again . . .' So I knew it was far from the first time."

"But I don't see how he can write so beautifully if he drinks like that."

"Well, I thought that too, so I talked to my friend Horace Greeley about him. You know Greeley's been running some of Poe's pieces in the *New Yorker,* and I expected a high opinion of him. But Greeley said, 'Poe is a brilliant writer when neither too drunk nor too sober. He might be somebody if he were not an incorrigible rascal and vagabond. That chap will be getting into scrapes all his life until the sexton gets him into one that he can't escape.' "

"I can scarcely believe that . . ."

"I'm afraid you must, mother. Greeley's a man whose judgment has to be respected. Anyway, Uncle Horace—that's what everybody calls him—went on to warn me that this was a terrible time to start a magazine. He's in such straits himself that he had to give Poe a sixty-day note for his last piece, even knowing how much the poor fellow needs money. But he does think I might make a go of it with a paper that would be cheaper to print and distribute. So I'm going to try."

Sally gave up. "All right, Peter—only don't forget that Cousin Matty might pull a rabbit out of his hat." . . .

Getting to Washington was much easier if less exciting this time since the last leg of the journey was on the Baltimore and Ohio Railroad. The papers had made much of the fact that Jackson, going back to the Hermitage, was the first president in history to depart from the capital by train and even more of the fact that President Van Buren's inaugural address had arrived in New York's newsrooms by means of train, boat and horseback in only twenty-four hours. It was Sally's first ride on a railroad, and although the carriage in which they sat was nothing but an old stage with new metal wheels, the way it rocked along past wagons bogged down in the spring mud seemed a marvel. It was so much warmer down here than in New York that they had to keep the windows open, and she didn't much care for the smoke and cinders that put grit between her teeth and smudged her clothes, but it seemed a small price to pay for not having to get out and walk through the mud to lighten the carriage. What with the speed and smoke, she couldn't share with Peter the sight of a shining capitol that had so thrilled her before, but she wondered if, with his disdain for politics, he could have seen it with the same eyes anyway. There still wasn't much of a city at the end of the track as they'd been forewarned when, riding along through a stand of forest, Peter had innocently asked a fellow passenger, "When do we get to Washington?" The man laughed and said, "You've been here these past fifteen minutes, young man." In any case, they had accepted Amelia's invitation to stay at her school in the village of Georgetown, a short hack ride to the northwest.

The building was a large red brick Georgian structure very similar to their Broadway place but with a garden and stables in back, as they'd once had. What had been slave quarters over the stables had been turned into dormitory space for the boarding girls, as had the two upper stories; Amelia had her own comfortable rooms on the ground floor, but they all ate in a large basement room next to the kitchen, where Peter found himself a rather pleasantly embarrassed object of unblinking scrutiny by forty or so young female eyes. "I hope you don't mind the girls, Peter," Amelia laughed. "They've been so excited at the idea of having a *man* in the house. I didn't tell them that you were handsome too . . . I thought I'd keep that as a surprise." Looking at his cousin in the candlelight she used instead of gas, Peter was struck by how much more attractive she was at thirty than all the unformed girls surrounding her. He began to think that he would have a good time quite apart from meeting the famous Cousin Matty. After dinner when they sat in Amelia's small parlor, also lit by candles and a coal fire in the grate, she offered him a cigar —"an old friend of father's in the State Department gets them direct from Havana"—and brought out a bottle of brandy with three glasses, astonishing them by pouring one for herself and Sally too.

When Sally hesitated, she said, "Join me, please. It's my only vice, but I need it after a day with twenty chattering girls. Try it, you don't have the little Puritan here to look cross-eyed at you, Sally. How *is* Cousin Cornelius, by the way?"

"Fine. But he's very worried about economic conditions . . . ."

"And Augusta?"

"Sick as—"

"You were going to say 'as usual,' weren't you? Cornelius isn't my favorite person, as you know, but it's a bad break that the only girl he ever got up the nerve to . . . well, that she turned out to be one of those sickly ones."

"It's not her fault, Amelia," Sally said. "I don't think she ever ate right as a child. You should have seen how thin she was when I managed to get her out of that dreadful slum on Stone Street where the Vanderbilts were living and bring her home with me. Twelve children crowded into that little place, and I thought poor Sophie must be losing her mind even then, which was why I took Augusta off her hands. I never thought that she and Cornelius . . . well, but she is a sweet thing."

"What did you mean about Sophie's losing her mind?"

"I shouldn't have said anything, but Augusta is worried about her mother. You know, she's been through so much—running that hotel over in Jersey while she was having all those children and then living there in Stone Street. Even though she's in easier circumstances on East Broadway, she still has that boy Cornelius who has the epileptic fits and then Corneel is never around . . ."

"He wouldn't be. I can't understand a man like that with all his money putting a woman through such hell."

"He didn't have money then. He's just beginning to make it now from what Cornelius says, and he wouldn't be doing that if he hadn't saved so much. He's worked hard all his life, and he can't understand why other people can't work just as hard . . . ."

"Huh!" Peter broke in. "From what I hear Corneel Vanderbilt spends half his time racing his trotters out at Cato's and the other half playing whist—that is if he isn't involved with some—"

"Please, Peter, Corneel's a friend of mine," Sally said.

"Just like Astor?"

"Now, you two, let's not argue," Amelia said. "Oh, I do envy you going to the White House for dinner! That Cousin Matty of yours fascinates me—not that I agree with all of his policies. But he's got Washington on its ear. They say he's turning the White House back into a palace. I don't know how he does it without a woman around, but he's been redecorating—getting rid of those old tobacco-stained rugs, replacing all that black mohair with flowered damask, setting the table with the best of china and golden spoons. They say he has an almost feminine touch with such things . . . ."

As she listened, Sally's mind drifted back to a picture of the young Matty, just down from the rough, timbered tavern in Kinderhook, wandering around Richmond Hill and fondling the soft textures of cloth, the shining surfaces of fine wood . . . Peter broke in with, "Spending money like that with the country starving? I'm not sure I'm going to like Cousin Matty."

"Oh, you will, you can't help it," Amelia said. "Everybody does. Even more than the golden spoons, what shocks Washington is that Matty spices up his dinners by inviting his worst enemies, like a good cook using hot pepper. Old Jackson, you know, wouldn't have anybody around him that he didn't absolutely trust. But I noticed in the papers that Henry Clay is going to be at your dinner, and I wouldn't be surprised if there were fireworks. Not only is your Cousin Matty sitting in the house that Mr. Clay thinks ought to be *his,* but he humbled Clay in the Senate in a way you couldn't believe unless you saw it. I was there since I go to the Senate galleries as often as I can. The performances they put on there are better than anything in the theater—as it certainly turned out that day. Your Cousin Matty, as vice-president, was presiding in the chair, and Mr. Clay arose to speak to the issue of allowing the Bank of the United States to expire, to which act he attributes all of our economic trouble—"

"So does Cornelius," Sally said.

"Well, he would have enjoyed hearing Mr. Clay. After rumbling around about monetary matters, which I don't think he understands better than anybody else, Mr. Clay went right up to the rostrum and spoke directly to Mr. Van Buren, imploring him to take a message to the president from the people. I can't remember all of the words, but it went something like . . . 'Depict to him, if you can find language to portray, the heart-rending wretchedness of thousands of the working class cast out of employment. Tell him of the tears of helpless widows, no longer able to earn their bread, of unclad and unfed orphans, who have been driven by this policy out of busy pursuits, in which but yesterday they were gaining an honest livelihood. Tell him that he has been abused, deceived, betrayed by the wicked counsel of unprincipled men around him. Tell him that in his bosom alone, under actual circumstances, does the power reside to relieve the country, and that unless he opens it to conviction and corrects the errors of his Administration no human imagination can conceive, no human tongue express the awful consequences which may follow —' "

Peter interrupted. "There, mother, do you hear that? Clay's saying all the right things, but for all the wrong reasons. The villain isn't Jackson, it's the banks. That's why I couldn't tolerate politics."

"Unless maybe you took a lesson from your Cousin Matty, Peter," Amelia said. "Mr. Van Buren just sat there listening to Clay and blinking like a fat owl—he is getting fat, you know, so you'd better prepare yourself for it if you haven't seen him in a while—until Mr. Clay had spoken his piece and returned to his seat. There was such silence in the chamber while everybody waited for Mr. Van Buren to respond that you could actually hear Mr. Clay panting to recapture the breath he had spent in his oration. The silent tension increased when Mr. Van Buren put down his gavel and motioned to a senator to take his seat. We all thought as he stepped down into the aisle that he would speak, but instead he walked right up to where Mr. Clay was sitting, bowed and said with that little lisp of his, 'Senator, would you favor me with a pinch of your excellent snuff?' I wish I could have seen better the look on Clay's face, but I did see him fumble in his pocket and hand over his snuffbox. Mr. Van Buren took some, delicately sniffed it into his nostrils and handed back the box with a bow. Then he walked right out of the chamber."

Both Sally and Peter had to laugh. "You know, I think I might like Cousin Matty after all," Peter said. "The man clearly has some wit and style."

"Why haven't you been to the White House, Amelia?" Sally asked. "I'd think with all the contacts you have—"

"I don't think even the tolerant Mr. Van Buren could stomach me," Amelia said. "Perhaps you haven't heard, but I've decided that women will never be free until the slaves are freed so I've joined the local abolition society. There aren't many of us, as you can imagine, and we're ostracized. Look up and down this street, and you'll see slaves polishing the brass on every door but mine. I'm afraid it's going to cost me my school too. I've had notices that most of these girls won't return when the term's over. Don't be surprised if you see me back in New York."

"You can stay with me," Sally said quickly.

"*And* Cornelius? He'd find me harder to take than Mr. Van Buren does. Well, you'd both better get your sleep to be ready for the big event."

It *was* a glittering affair. Lights from the chandeliers *did* wink back from gold spoons and gold-rimmed plates and etched crystal and polished mahogany. The president, remembering gratefully her services at his ball a few years before, sat Sally at the foot of the long table as his temporary hostess. He *was* fat and very like an owl—but an elegant owl, swathed in black velvet, a diamond pin flashing from his cravat, his gray hair and chops carefully combed and curled. Mr. Clay and his lady were among the guests, most of whom were foreign ambassadors with difficult names to catch, as was a figure even more surprising to Sally, ex-mayor Hone of New York, whose views as relayed by Cornelius were rabidly anti-Jackson and, by inference, anti-Van Buren. The president announced that they would all be enjoying the first offering of his new chef from Paris, and, through a turtle soup, a sole swimming in sauce, a duck à l'orange, a crêpe suzette, a liquered ice, the talk was mostly of food, each ambassador or his lady being asked to describe his country's delicacies. Sherry had been served at the reception before dinner, and Madeira was poured liberally as they ate. While he enjoyed the food and especially the wine, Peter, bored by the ladies on either side who kept talking across him in an incomprehensible mixture of French and Spanish, couldn't help but compare this scene to the sights of men and women in New York battling in the streets over sacks of spilled flour. He felt his mood turning sour and was almost jealous of his mother who, with Mr. Clay seated on one side and Mr. Hone on the other, seemed to be having an animated good time of it . . . .

Suddenly the president singled him out. "Down there, in the middle of the table, is Mr. Peter Van Alen, a distant cousin of mine, though you'd scarcely know it from his great height and good looks," Van Buren said. "He was a member of the Cliosophic Society of our Princeton College and so was at Mr. Burr's funeral. Would you tell the company what you told me about it before dinner, Peter? The ambassador here knew Mr. Burr in France and is interested."

Stammering a little from the embarrassment of the attention thrust on him, Peter managed to get out the story of how the September before, Burr's body had been taken down to Princeton by him and a few other alumni of the college debating society for a proper funeral. "His father, you know, had been president of the college and he one of its best students and always interested in it, particularly in the Cliosophic Society, where he said he learned how to debate public issues," Peter said. "Dr. Carnahan, the president of the college, gave the eulogy, and the Mercer Guards played martial music and fired over the grave in honor of Mr. Burr's services in the Revolution. We members of the society marched as pallbearers and all of us voted to wear black armbands of respect for thirty days—"

"There! You see how we in America honor our dissidents, and may we always do so," the president said.

"Peter, tell the president about Theo. I think he'd like to know," Sally said.

"Well," Peter went on, "the Reverend Van Pelt who attended to him in his last hours was there and gave a prayer. I talked to him later, and he said that Mr. Burr was in straitened circumstances and died in a boardinghouse in Port Richmond on Staten Island. But it had a view of the harbor, and just before he died Mr. Burr asked to be helped to the window, from which he looked out over the sea and said, 'Ah, if I could only see Theo coming to me over the water there, as they said she walked into it from the ladder when her ship went down.'"

Peter noticed that the president's eyes filled, and he had to reach for a handkerchief to dab at them and blow his nose. He liked him better than at any time, and he didn't want to leave such a sad note hanging in the air, so he said, "But you'd like to know, sir, I'm sure, that Mr. Burr never lost his sense of humor. When Mr. Van Pelt asked him if he expected salvation, he said, 'On that subject I am coy, but I will tell you that if I get to heaven they'll accuse me of taking possession of the moon, and informing my friends that I intend to divide it among them.'"

This story did bring the relief of laughter, and just then a servant came running into the room and whispered in the president's ear. It was quite evidently some emergency, and all talk around the table stopped while everybody watched the president nodding acceptance of the message. When the servant had gone, the president smiled and said, "I am to inform you, ladies and gentlemen, that if you become aware of a burning odor, it is not due to the ineptness of our new chef. It seems a fire broke out in the kitchen but that it has now been got under control by means of copious buckets of water."

At that point, Mr. Clay arose, put a hand over his heart and said, "Mr. President, as you know, I am doing all I can to get you out of this house, but I swear that I do not want to burn you out."

The president bowed in response, and the dinner broke up in general laughter. When the ladies had retired, port and brandy were put on the table and cigars passed around. Feeling surer of himself than usual for having spoken his piece and perhaps even more by the brandy on top of the wine, Peter asked, "Mr. President, what do you propose to do about all the starving? I've seen them in the streets of New York and—"

The president responded with a frown. "I don't think these gentlemen are interested in our domestic affairs, Peter," he said. "But since you ask, let me quote you the motto of a paper in which I believe some of your own writings have appeared, Mr. O'Sullivan's *Democratic Review*, which is: 'The best government is that which governs least.' There isn't much a president can do when men are seized with the fever of greedy speculation. I've summoned Congress to meet this month, and perhaps they will see now the harm they created with their bill to send the excess federal revenues out to the states and thereby virtually nullify the effect of Jackson's specie circular. I don't know. But I doubt that they'll see the wisdom of *my* bill to establish a treasury bank where the people's money belongs. Too many of their leaders are obliged to private banks, like the distinguished Mr. Webster, whose arguments in favor of retaining the Bank of the United States were somewhat colored by his being a director and, as I understand, a heavy borrower from that institution. I don't know what *I'm* to do if Congress doesn't act, but . . . well, Mr. Ambassador, I understand that the climate of your country is most pleasant at this time of the year . . ."

On the way back to Georgetown Peter was silent until his mother finally asked, "Why so thoughtful, Peter?"

"I don't know, I guess I'm just a little confused. I like Cousin Matty, but he seems so . . . so impotent, somehow . . . mother, I *am* going to start that paper."

She squeezed his hand. "I guess there were no rabbits in his hat after all," she said. "Well, just don't tell Cornelius that I'm helping you . . ."

Chapter *XV*

The Apple of Eve

"Cousins. Cousins. Must we be cursed because we are cousins?" Peter Van Alen asked, his voice rising in exasperation. "My mother married a cousin. Mr. Vanderbilt married a cousin—"

"That's because they're what grandmother would have called dumb Dutch," Amelia Downing said with a laugh.

"But you're as Dutch as I am—"

"No, I'm not. Not by a long shot. I've just a touch of Van Alen— like what they'd call a touch of the tarbrush down South. I'm mostly Wentworth and Downing and—"

"Well, that's all the more reason we should marry. You're hardly even a cousin. You're only a second cousin, or maybe a second cousin once removed, or—"

"It's still too close. We English don't believe in marrying relatives except in the royal family, where like the Dutch they're afraid to dilute the blood. Instead, they make it so thick it won't go through the brain and go mad like King George . . ."

They were walking around and around Castle Garden, a promenade and concert hall that had been fashioned out of the old Fort Clinton at the tip of Battery Park—and around and around, too, an old argument between them. In ironic accompaniment to Peter's ever-rejected proposal of marriage, the band in the pit of the circular open-air theater was serenading them with the strains of "Home, Sweet Home." It was a soft September evening, and the calm water to the west glowed like burnished copper in the light of the setting sun; a single star shone in the eastern sky above the dark shoulders of Brooklyn; late homing ships began hanging out their red and green lanterns. It was the dying of a day, the dying of a season, and Peter had the uneasy feeling that it might be the dying of a love, too.

"That's not your real reason, and you know it," Peter said to Amelia, whose regal bearing and classic features, and wearing summer white, seemed to him a Greek goddess come to life. "What is your *real* reason?"

"I'm too old for you—"

"Five years, only five years. That's absolutely nothing."

"Maybe—if I weren't the woman. Women are the weaker sex, you know, and I'd die and leave you alone. Or worse, turn into a hag and you'd be looking around at all the young girls and I couldn't stand that."

"Untrue, and you know it . . . You're the only woman I've ever met that—"

"What about Rachel?"

Silence.

"I always thought you shouldn't have given in to your family on that. You were just the right age, both ripe for the kind of love you deserved and still do . . . . Much as I love your mother, I think she was wrong about that."

"Rachel's married, you know—to a rabbi just like her father. She has three children, I hear, and—well, I'm afraid she'd never have been as happy with me, or my family . . ."

The band had shifted to an achingly romantic aria from some Italian opera, but Amelia didn't seem to hear it. "And what makes you think *I'd* be happy with you, or your family? Your brother Cornelius would have a fit if you married a radical sort like me. Bad enough that I still hold proxies for my brothers and embarrass him at stockholders' meetings with my questions . . ."

"I don't think it much matters now what Cornelius thinks."

"No, perhaps not . . . he was actually livid when you published that story about how his father-in-law, the commodore—you knew Van-

312

derbilt had promoted himself from captain, didn't you—is taking bribes from the packet companies with U.S. mail contracts to Europe in order to stay out of competition with them. He kept waking old Uncle Peter out of his doze and asking him if there wasn't some legal way he could force you to sell him your stock."

"I don't doubt it. He's probably in it up to the eyeballs himself. You know, ever since the *Sirius* and *Great Western* proved you could cross the Atlantic under steam back in '38, he's been gradually getting the company back into shipping, what with his engines and all."

"Oh, I know it. *I* go to the stockholders' meetings. They're really something to see now that the commodore is on the board. You have the commodore swearing and Cornelius praying and George Smith boasting and Uncle Peter snoring. Your mother and I can hardly keep from laughing. You really ought to go."

"And you really ought to stop changing the subject. I've decided I'm going to quit asking whether you'll marry me . . . I'm just going to ask you *when*—"

Just then there was a commotion out in the park, and another band, mostly drums and blaring trumpets, set up a jarring countertune to the operatic air coming from the pit. They could see that the new band was heading a procession, torches already flaring in the gathering dusk. Behind the band was a flat-bed wagon on which was a miniature logcabin and casks at each corner from which men were doling out drink to the crowd. It was a frequent sight in this election year of 1840, and just now annoying to Peter . . . "I hope those Whigs lose some votes for drowning out this beautiful music in the Garden."

But Amelia, apparently welcoming the intrusion in their conversation, said, "Let's go over and see what's going on, Peter. We might get some of that hard cider. I love it."

"You drink too much for a woman," he grumbled.

"There, you see—that's it. That's *it*! That's what I've been trying to tell you, Peter. I don't want *any* man treating me as if, just because I'm a woman, I'm something less than human—or *more* than human would be more like it. I'm just not the marrying kind, and you ought to be happy with what I am."

Before he could answer she grabbed his hand, and he reluctantly followed her along the causeway toward the growing crowd in the park . . . Happy with what she is, he thought. Didn't she know that

313

he'd been so genuinely happy that he wanted it to go on forever? How could she have so knowingly involved him and now turn him down? It had, after all, been her doing . . . it would never have occurred to him that there was a woman like her in all the world if she hadn't revealed herself to him the way she had. He'd come to think of the Bible as a fable, but he was beginning to believe that the story of Eden held at least the truth of poetry. She was no Greek goddess after all, this Amelia, this cousin, this lover . . . she was the Eve who had opened his eyes . . . .

Love, they said, was luck or fate. Whichever, it had come to Peter through circumstances he could never have invented. On that Saturday in the previous spring when he closed his little basement office on Ann Street in Printing House Square and set out for a walk up the Bowery, he was indeed seeking some sort of adventure. But he had no clear idea of where or how the evening might end—only a vague hope that one of the young ladies playing the Bowery Theater would prove enticing enough to warrant going through the old ritual of trying to meet her at the stage door and, with luck, turning her pliant by a supper of oysters and wine. It had been a long time since he had enjoyed such a dalliance, and his memories of even the successful ventures when he'd managed to bed all too briefly a girl he hardly knew were not bright. Still, since he had no taste for going to prostitutes, it seemed the only decent way to respond to the urge that was always with him. By reason of their profession, the ladies of the theater were simply more available, more independent and open to flirtation than the young women of a polite society on which he'd virtually turned his back through both lack of time to waste at balls and teas and a profound lack of interest in the concerns and conversation he'd encounter there. And always, too, in the back of his mind, was the possibility that an aspiring actress who caught his eye would turn out to be a person he could live with . . . Edgar Poe's mother, after all, had been an actress, and Fanny Kemble was entertained in the best parlors in New York when she was playing in America.

Tonight's outing was possible only because one of his few advertisers, Fernando Wood, who ran a saloon for dock workers over on Rector Street near the North River, had come in to pay off his bill in cash. Peter hated to take Wood's money, since he knew where and how he'd gotten it . . . through the week Wood would let the thirsty stevedores charge for whiskey at three cents a glass because he'd made arrangements with their bosses to pay them off on Saturday in his saloon. When the time came to pay out a man's seven or eight dollars in weekly wages the boss would ask, "What have you got against him, Fernando?" Whatever the figure—and Peter understood it was often padded—Wood got paid first. A man who protested might have his memory jollied by a free glass or two dispensed by the amiable Mr. Wood. A man who protested too much might find himself out of work. Wood was now turning his profits into political advantage, and in Peter's mind he was as bloodthirsty a leech on the working classes as a pinch-penny employer like his brother Cornelius. Feeding whiskey to the Irish, Peter thought, was in a class with Astor's old trick of getting Indians drunk. Sheer survival, though, forced Peter to take whatever advertising he could get, and Wood's use of the *Call* was a kind of ironic compliment to Peter's effort to be the spokesman for the workers.

As he started his stroll toward the Bowery with what he considered soiled money in his pocket, Peter thought again, as he did at the end of every hectic week, about giving up. With only two other young, half-starved men to help him, he'd been working around the clock for some two years now to get out a four-page sheet that, at a penny a copy, sold to only a few thousand people. Since his views were anathema to the affluent advertisers he'd been forced to go again and again to his mother for more money. At first he hadn't known where she was getting it, but he'd finally forced her to admit that she'd put what savings she had into a few pieces of burned-over real estate after the great fire. For a while income from leases on this property was enough to bail him out, but lately she'd begun mortgaging it. Money wise or not, Peter could easily see that one day they would reach the point where she could not help him and meet the interest and would once more lose her land. It was a sacrifice he had no right to ask of her, and the bitter irony involved was that she'd bought the land, as she said, to have something to leave to him. If he stopped publishing his paper, he would almost automatically be a rich man someday, and —he had to face it—the temptation to secure such a future for himself was growing.

It would have been a temptation easier to resist if at least his work were paying dividends as readily as his stock. Cornelius' timing in getting Van Alen & Son into the engine business had been perfect . . . bad times or no, men were managing to build railroads around all the major cities to bring produce and people to the market and constructing steamships to overcome the vagaries of the wind in crossing the oceans. Van Alen & Son was rising like Noah's ark on the waters of real wealth that a country of seemingly infinite natural resources rained upon the just and unjust alike. There was a feeling in the country that a man with get up and go could do anything, and no amount of temporary suffering could offset it. So it was "every man for himself and the devil take the hindmost." Nobody seemed interested in Peter's philosophy about being your brother's keeper. More charitable than most, a man like Greeley would at least send his brother west; Peter's own brother Cornelius would gladly send him to hell. Gradually there had come a galling awareness for Peter that the people he wrote for, if they read him at all, didn't recognize themselves—however miserable their present condition, there was at least a chance, they felt, that "they'd get theirs" and, therefore, a reluctance to tamper with a system holding out such a glittering promise. As for those he wrote against, they could afford to ignore him: an exposure of illegality or corruption could easily be taken care of by a sprinkling of money around the city's common council, or the state's legislature, or the courts, or the nation's congress.

Thinking on all this, Peter was especially angry, frustrated and unsure this particular Saturday night. He did, however, have a small sense of satisfaction about an editorial appearing in this day's issue of the *Call.* He had written it right on the stone to fill a hole where some hoped-for advertising had dropped out. It was scribbled on little scraps of paper that the printer grabbed out of his hand as each sentence was finished. He couldn't tell whether the inspiration for the piece came out of an as yet unconscious thought of spending an evening on the Bowery or whether his plans for the evening were a result of having written the piece . . . it was only later that it would all seem part of some mysterious process—luck or fate. The thought and the words had come to him so easily that they still stood clearly in his mind as he walked along . . .

HURRAH FOR MOZE AND LIZE

If you've ever walked the Bowery—and, if you haven't, you should—you'd know them on sight, this lad called Moze and his lass called Lize. They are the Bowery B'hoy, in the parlance of our new friends from Ireland, and the Bowery Gal. They are as much a part of the scenery of this most fascinating of New York streets as the Cheap John shops, the pawnbrokers, the saloons, the chestnut vendors, the flag-faced old theater.

It is to be regretted that some of our so-called respectable citizens regard Moze as a menace and his Lize as a common girl of the streets. One has only to see them in all their splendor to acknowledge that their dress is as fine as that of any lord or lady of Gramercy Park. Observe Moze with his tall beaver hat, its nap carefully brushed to a part; with his well-greased soap curls at the temples; with his scarlet silk neckcloth and black frockcoat. If beneath Moze's turned-up pantaloons you see a pair of sturdy boots instead of polished pumps, consider that they serve him to stand in the blood of the meatmarket, where he likely toils twelve hours of every day or to wade in the water at fires, which he fights for our benefit.

But Lize, ah Lize! I can do no better than to quote the admiring words of a fellow writer upon his first glimpse of her: "Her bonnet was a perfect museum of ribbons and ornaments, and it sat jauntily on the side of her head. Her skirts came to the shoe tops and displayed her pretty feet and well turned ankles, equipped with irreproachable gaiters and the most stunning of stockings. One arm swung loosely to the motion of her body as she passed along with a quick, lithe step, and the other held just over her nose, her parasol."

A most charming couple they are, this Bowery B'hoy and his gal. Is it any wonder then that the elevated nose of a so-called respectable gentleman sometimes prompts Moze to his cry of "Lam him!" and an effort to lower that snooty proboscis with a fist? We might point out that Moze's very cry is indicative of a cultural inheritance, for it undoubtedly derives from the phrase "Lambe them, lads; lambe them!" in Sir Walter Scott's *Peveril of the Peak,* which in turn derives from the unfortunate fate of a Dr. Lambe whose head was stove in in the time of Charles I.

We must not forget in any event that a readiness with the fists was the talent that enabled one of them, big Bill Harrington of our own Central Market, to bring honor to our city and our country by dethroning the British champion in the ring. So we say, "Hurrah for Moze and Lize!" They're New Yorkers of a proud breed, and you might try a bow instead of a snub the next time you meet them on the street.

Thinking about this, Peter was eager to follow his own advice as he entered the Bowery. But even though the long, meandering street —a cowpath in the days when it crossed a *bouwerie,* or Dutch farm— seemed to contain every mobile inhabitant of the multicolored, multitongued East Side, there wasn't a Bowery B'hoy in sight. It was, of course, Saturday night when like the shopkeepers here whose gas flaring windows made day of night the boys would still be working at their market stalls. The theater's doors had opened nearly an hour ago, at six, but Peter was in no hurry. There would be three plays tonight, and only one, the second on the bill, a burlesque of *Don Giovanni,* suggested any real possibility of entertainment. So Peter shuffled along at the pace of the crowd, idly windowshopping, until he came to the open door of a Cheap John store where, judging from the crowd inside, the vendor must have been one of the stars of the trade. Peter often thought that a smart theater manager would put one of these Yankee bummers on the stage instead of the stupid British comedies they imported.

As Peter hesitated at the door, the vendor, a short, stout man with a red face, twangy voice and toothy smile, who walked a long counter in front of a wall of shelves laden with every conceivable kind of merchandise, spotted him and called out, "Come in, come in, gentleman, and see the only truly American Cheap John, the benefactor of his country, the George Peabody of New York."

Likening himself to the famous Massachusetts financier was brash for even a Cheap John, and Peter decided that the performance might be worth watching. As he walked in, the Cheap John said, "All right, gentleman, the sacrifice will now proceed. Who gives two dollars for a superb, eight-bladed knife, the handle made of true father-of-pearl, with ends of solid silver an inch long? Show me the man who gives it, and I'll show you a damned fool. We are only asking a dollar and a half. Here . . . examine the finish closely . . ."

The Cheap John pretended to toss the knife into the crowd, and several men ducked. He laughed and said, "You needn't dodge. These knives are regular lifepreservers. You couldn't kill a man with one of them in the most savage and blood-thirsty fury. No chance of cutting your fingers with these knives—nice reliable family article— who'll buy? Who'll buy a knife with all the merits of a knife and none of the failin's, such as accidentally cuttin' people. How much am I offered?"

Peter thought the show worth some price, so he said fifty cents. This time the Cheap John did close the blades and toss the knife to him, saying, "Sold again!" in tones of resignation that brought a laugh from the crowd.

He then flashed a pair of stockings. "I have a whole invoice of these, gentlemen. Made in England for the Emperor of Siam and

stolen from his caravan at great risk. Only two dollars for four pairs!"
The invoice quickly sold out—at fifty cents for four pairs—and Cheap
John decided that it was time to let his customers in on some secrets.

"You wonder how we can sell so low?" he said. "Why, it's because,
'ceptin' rent, nothin' costs us anything, 'ceptin' paper. Paper costs are
enormous, because that's cash, and we use up lots of it for wrappin'
things. But the things we wrap up, them we never buy on less than
four months, and when the four months have passed, so have we—
we have passed on. That's how we can sell so low, and save your
money. So be your own best benefactors and 'do good by stealth,' as
the poet says. Now, don't go, gentlemen. Aside from all these bar-
gains, gonna have a free lunch at ten-thirty—just brought in another
dog for the soup . . ."

The old dog-in-the-soup joke reminded Peter that he was hungry,
and he went out into the street looking for a place to eat. From the
swinging doors of the Atlantic Garden came a good aroma of beer
and sauerkraut and spicy sausage. The place was fogged with smoke,
and there was an ear-buzzing cacophony of guttural German. There
were nearly as many women as men, and some tables held whole
families, right down to a babe propped in its mother's lap. The mood
was cheerful. Snatches of German song broke out from time to time
to the beat of clanking steins. Peter found a corner table and flagged
down a waiter who was rushing by, sloshing beer from his tray as he
wriggled between tables. Remembering that his plans called for what
might be an expensive supper, he ordered only a strudel and stein
of beer to hold him over. As he ate and listened to the incomprehensible German talk around him, Peter wondered if there could be
another city, another country in the world where so many people
from different cultures were trying to live and work together. He was
sure that there was not, and he felt equally sure that this was, somehow, the true glory of America . . .

It had been this feeling that had made Peter risk upsetting his
mother when he blasted her old friend Professor Samuel F. B. Morse,
who had left Columbia for the new New York University during his
campaign for mayor as a representative of the so-called Democratic
American Association. The professor's opposition to Bishop
Hughes' demand for money for Catholic schools was, as he had
pointed out, neither democratic nor American . . . if we're willing,
eager even, to accept a man's labor we also ought to accept his

319

religion . . . Morse's political involvement was one of those paradoxes of personality that Peter still had difficulty understanding. The man was undoubtedly brilliant. Though an artist by profession, he had been toying with an electronic telegraph for years and had finally demonstrated a working model at the university, a demonstration that Peter, as a newspaperman, appreciated more than most in the audience—if and when it could be put to use between cities, between continents, it would revolutionize communications. How could a man whose work was so likely to change the world lend himself to a movement whose only purpose was to resist change? Peter didn't put all that into his editorial, of course, but it would have made little difference since, although Morse was defeated, there was no evidence that Peter's arguments had been heard. They were going ahead with forming an American Protestant Union and a Native American Party, and he'd heard that the publisher James Harper would be their candidate for mayor at the next elections. This was even more incomprehensible to Peter. He could find some excuse for Morse . . . an artist and tinkerer might be unread in history or philosophy, but if this were also true of a publisher, well American letters was in more trouble than anyone including himself supposed . . .

Such thoughts did not improve Peter's mood as he went on toward the theater. There was so much to rage against in the way of ignorance, foolishness and cruelty in the world, and his own efforts to do so were so feeble, apparently futile. He wondered why he had been cursed with this damned urge to set things right . . . he wished that, instead, he had inherited his mother's apparent gift of accepting things as they were . . . oh, it wasn't that she was insensitive—far from it—but that she had a strange fatalism in her attitude, along with an almost irritating tolerance. It went all the way from seldom fussing about a rainy day because the weather's bound to change, to liking a pirate like Commodore Vanderbilt because she admired his courage. Often he thought it would be a blessing to be able to look out on the world with her bright, black eyes instead of his own cloudy gray ones. This difference between them was hard to talk about, difficult to put into the right words, but he did occasionally make a stab at it, which his mother would blunt with some comment like, "Don't fret, Peter. You're still young . . . things look differently when you get older. Believe me . . ." Age could, he granted, be a factor. Even now, he had to laugh when he remembered the boy named

Peter Schuyler Van Alen who thought he could be everything, do everything. Sex might have something to do with it too. Not only his mother but most other women he otherwise considered wise seemed capable of a kind of almost serene acceptance of reality in or out of bed, as if their physical natures determined their thinking. But wasn't it also true of men? Didn't that organ over which they had so little control endow men with an unconscious desire to cut and thrust, to conquer and create, and give his spirit a willful impatience like what he felt in his loins? Well, it was an interesting thought on this night when he was specifically intent on appeasing the appetite of his own greedy organ.

The Park with its scenes from Shakespeare hung around the balconies was the theater for a man in search of culture, but the Bowery was the place to look for pleasure. Whether or not he found a girl of promise or a play of interest, Peter knew that he would enjoy just watching the crowd. Although, being alone, he would have been content to sit in the pit, the theater was so full that he had to pay fifty cents for the last seat in the boxes on the second tier. Just as Peter, crunching his way noisily across a carpet of spent peanut shells, reached his box, the big green curtain fell on the end of the first play. Evidently he hadn't missed much, because yells of "Cheese it!" and "That's too thin!" came from instant critics all over the house. When the gaslights went up for intermission rowdy young men in the jammed fourth tier exchanged whistles and catcalls with their slightly wealthier friends in the pit. People who had thoughtfully provided more for themselves than peanuts broke out ham sandwiches and links of sausage; a family party near Peter dined more elegantly on chops, which after they'd munched them to the bone they flung playfully at unsuspecting heads below. The whole atmosphere was noisy and joyous and totally free of the wickedness that the city's preachers and some of its best people still claimed to be found in the theater. The *Don Giovanni* that followed intermission, for example, was innocent farce, a little too broad, Peter felt, but right for the audience. And Peter did have to admit that the clown playing Leporello showed great physical dexterity, especially in a scene where, shoved out of a second story window by the Don, he rode the top of a ladder in a great arc clear to the footlights. But what the crowd loved most was a banqueting scene in which Leperello and an old woman fought over a bowl of wet macaroni and finally ended up flinging it strand by strand into the faces of the orchestra and the nearest customers in the pit. One man, taking offense at this, rose and turned his back on the stage, and brought on shouts of "Trollope! Trollope! Trollope!" that forced him meekly back into his seat. To Peter it was clear evidence of the power of the word. Few persons in this theater would have read *Domestic Life of the Americans* by the Englishwoman Frances Trollope with its harsh criticism of the so-called crudity of American manners, but her name had become a popular reprimand for a breach of what was deemed to be etiquette on any occasion.

If he found the farce less than compelling, the same was not true for a young soprano who struggled in some embarrassment to sing straight and sweetly amidst the clownish antics. She had a mass of high-piled red hair and prominent breasts that threatened to spill over her low-cut bodice when she breathed deeply to strike her notes. Wanting to attract her attention, Peter jumped to his feet at the end of her aria to lead the applause. He was a leader with almost no followers, and as a result was rewarded by her full attention and a grateful smile. Good; she would remember him. There was no point now in waiting through the third performance, so as soon as the curtain dropped he went around to the stage door and sent in his card, which might prove impressive to anyone who hadn't seen his damp basement office with its plain plank desk and three straight chairs. Under the legend, "Peter Schuyler Van Alen, editor and publisher, the *New York Evening Call,*" he scribbled, "I am the man in the second tier who appreciated your performance, and I would appreciate even more your company at supper." A black woman, evidently her dresser, came out with the information that her mistress, Miss Shields, would join him as soon as she changed. His vague hope was rapidly turning into reality as he lit a cigar and puffed away furiously to try to keep his growing excitement under control.

When Miss Shields did appear, the reality was, as usual, a bit short of the expectation . . . . Without her stage makeup, her features were rather plain and unformed, the face of a girl of no more than eighteen. She did, however, have a soft and somewhat exotic southern purr to her speaking voice, and she let him know right off that she was a stranger to New York and in her first part. A bit ashamed of himself for doing so, he hastily revised his plan of taking her by hack to the Astor House for oysters and champagne and decided to walk her back to the Atlantic Garden for sausage and beer. It wasn't, he told himself, a matter of what she might be worth but where she might feel more comfortable. Trusting and obviously pleased to have attracted the attention of a gentleman of the press, she put a hand in the crook of his arm, lifted her skirts with the other, and tripped lightly along by his side.

As they stepped out to the street, a fire engine, bell clanging, the men in its shafts calling for "Way! Way! Way!" careened through the crowd to the accompaniment of shrieks from the women and curses from the men scattered from its path. Did she like New York? Oh, yes, it was so exciting with something always happening night or day, like that clanging fire engine. By now the Bowery B'hoys were out in force, and one of them, gal on arm, bore down on Peter and Miss Shields. Now was the time. Peter took off his hat and bowed elaborately at the couple. The b'hoy shoved his own hat a little back on his head, revealing the soap curls that looked a bit like crushed horns, scowled and said, "Hey, watchyer do that for? Hey, I'll bet it's him. You Mr. Van Alen?"

"Well, yes . . ." Peter admitted, smiling broadly. To be recognized in the streets was a new and elevating experience. Miss Shields would really know that she was with somebody . . .

But the boy had shoved his girl behind him and, speaking to a ring of other b'hoys who had seemingly sprung out of the pavement, he said, "It's him. It's the fellow who called our gals in the paper common street girls. Lam him, b'hoys, lam him!"

As the b'hoy pulled back his fist, Peter also shoved Miss Shields away but held out his open hands. "Don't you understand? I was trying to say what fine fellows you are, you and your gals . . . I didn't mean—"

The fist caught him on the jaw. Another blow from somewhere behind stung his ear. Still another fist coming into his solar plexus doubled him over. Miss Shields let out an operatic scream, but the blows went on until he was down on the sidewalk. Boots made for standing in blood or water came at him. He could do nothing but try to curl into a ball to protect his head and face as each stomp shot pain through another part of his body. One caught him in the testicles, and then he could hear his own scream. All that came from the lips of his tormentors were short, satisfied grunts of exertion. He was vaguely aware that Miss Shields had run off, calling for help, but no help came. Even the law would not interfere with the business of the Bowery B'hoy. Only God could do that, and he did—with the blessed gift of unconsciousness . . . .

There was some mystery but mostly logic in the next step that brought Peter to Amelia. Befuddled and temporarily deranged, Peter gave the address of his old Broadway home to the men who picked up his battered body and finally brought him to some degree of consciousness with whiffs and sips of brandy from the nearest saloon. In his confused state he was both a boy badly hurt and a man aware of the danger of going to the hospital where some eager doctor might take it into his head to saw off the arm that hung useless by his side. The rescuers, understandably wanting to risk no possible reprisal on themselves from the Bowery B'hoys, bundled him into a hack and sent him off. It turned out that he had been robbed as well as beaten, and in the early hours of a Sunday morning an angry and unsympathetic hack driver pounded on the old mahogany door of the Broadway house until Amelia herself, an angelic vision in flowing nightdress, came to pay his fare and take him in. While at the time he had been beyond realizing that Amelia would be there, had been, in fact, expecting to find his mother, Peter had to concede that some level of his mind had been aware of the true situation.

Not long after their visit to Washington Amelia had sold off her Georgetown house and come to New York to reestablish her school in a place where her abolitionist principles might not prove so abhorrent to the parents of her pupils. Whatever he thought about Amelia's activities, Cornelius had seized the opportunity to offer her a lease on the Broadway building, since he wanted to move his offices closer to the factory he'd built on the North River shore. And whatever her feelings about Cornelius's attitudes, Amelia had jumped at the chance to have a place in which she'd been happy as a girl. Cornelius' alterations for business purposes made it easier to convert the upper stories into dormitories for the girls; the parlor served well for a classroom as did the study for a library, and the diningroom, built for lavish colonial entertaining, was ideal for the candlelit meals at which Amelia gave her charges pointers in the gracious living for which most of them were intended. Amelia also turned the dusty old counting room on the first floor into a sitting room for herself and the storerooms into an office and bedroom. In keeping with her generally forward look, Amelia not only installed a bath and water closet for herself but a similar facility upstairs for the girls. Since the lavish Astor House was the only other building in New York with water available above the first floor, she used this facility as a very effective selling point for her school, but some of the girls were less than enchanted when they discovered that assigning them to work the pump that conveyed the cistern water to the storage tank on the roof was Amelia's favorite form of discipline.

Before the night of his beating, Peter had visited Amelia several times to see the wonders wrought in the old house and to enjoy the generally lively conversation between them, and so only derangement could account for his delusion that it was still his home, the place he had to go to ground.

When he came in the door, filthy with blood and mud, clothes torn, arm dangling, barely able to keep his feet and unable to speak for pain, Amelia asked no questions. She led him to her own bed, still warm where her body had lain, stretched him out and began to undress him. Since he groaned with every slight movement, she scissored off most of his clothes. As they came away, she could see that his whole white body was blotched with purplish bruises, red welts, weeping cuts, and the left arm he'd used to defend his head was askew at the elbow. She needed help. She covered him and went to blow up the kitchen fire and put a pot of water on to heat, then slipped quietly as she could past the dormitories and up to the attic to wake up one of the Irish housemaids, whom she sent to fetch the doctor, pretending it was herself in need. Having no idea what circumstances had brought Peter to this state, she thought it wise to keep his presence in the house to herself.

While she waited for the doctor, Amelia began to bathe his wounds as tenderly as possible. He would moan and cry out from time to time but showed no other signs of consciousness; his eyes, when occasionally he opened them, had a glazed, uncomprehending look. She felt curiously alone with his body, free to examine it inch by inch, which she found necessary since the damage was so extensive. Bruised though it was, it was the kind of body she'd imagined he would have —lean and sinewy from little eating and much walking, bone-white and hairless except in appropriate places. There was a bad bruise on his groin which she tried to soothe with warm water and then, feeling modesty foolish under the circumstances, she also bathed his genitals and was startled to see, as she did this, his soft penis stir, begin to rise, as if it had feelings of its own, deeper than consciousness, deeper than pain. She was startled, too, to feel a response in herself. She was not totally without experience, but it had been a deliberate and quick yielding in the dark to the importunings of a safely married man, temporarily adrift in Washington, for the purpose of ridding herself of romantic illusion. Her purpose had been well served—her pain and the sweaty passion of her partner had left her without any desire. She had never, of course, seen, much less caressed, the unclothed body of a man, as she was now doing, and, as much in confusion and embarrassment over her own reaction as his, she hurried on to dab at his knees, which had been scraped to bloody pulp, and then quickly to cover him up.

When he came, the doctor splinted the arm and concluded after his examination that Peter had suffered a mild concussion that would probably take care of itself with rest. He promised to keep his patient's presence unknown to the rest of the household and, to that end, put on a convincing charade in front of the maid at the door, advising Amelia loudly to take the medicine he'd prescribed for her and to call him again whenever she felt faint.

Amelia spent the rest of the night in a chair to keep an eye on Peter, who finally fell into a whimpering sleep. When sometime after dawn he woke up, his eyes were clear, though not his comprehension . . . . "My God, where *am* I?"

"You're home—or what used to be home, Peter," Amelia said. "Tell me what happened—"

"I've got to get out of here or the paper won't come out," he said and tried to get up. One movement was enough; he'd never imagined such pain possible—*everything* hurt. He sank back with a groan, and Amelia asked again, "Peter, what *happened?*"

He told her the story as well as he could, not omitting the singer on whom he'd had designs, and Amelia said, "Well, at least some good may have come out of this . . . her virtue may still be intact."

"It's not funny, Amelia, not funny at all. Oh, God, how I hurt, I never knew a body could hurt so much. I don't know what to do about the paper, I don't know what to do about anything—"

"From what the doctor says you're not going to be doing anything about anything for quite a while. You'll just have to rest here . . . and I think it wiser that the girls not know you're here, so I'll be your nurse myself. I'll send word to your mother, of course, but she can come without arousing suspicion since she often visits me. And I'll send word to the paper—"

"I write the whole damned thing myself, you'd better tell them to suspend publication—"

"And give those Bowery B'hoys a real victory?"

"Why not? I have an odd feeling that they've actually done me a favor, though they could have been a little less thorough about it. I've been thinking about giving up the paper for a long time. You know I've been using up mother's money—that's supposed to be a secret from Cornelius—and sure as hell nobody out there has been listening to me . . . what better proof of that than the way those thugs misread me?"

"I wouldn't do anything hasty, Peter. You've had a concussion, and you're probably not thinking right—"

"Oh yes I am, Amelia. In addition to hurting, I'm so damn tired . . . I've been working six, seven days a week for two years now and . . . well, I'd just like to sleep and sleep and sleep . . ." He was already nodding again. She went out and closed the door softly behind her.

For the next few days Peter found himself drifting lazily in and out of sleep, waking up when Amelia would bustle in with food or when his mother came calling, feeling relief that he'd given up the paper and concern for his health. He didn't know what he would do when he felt better, nor did he seem to care. There was some chagrin in this ignoble end to his role as self-appointed savior of the downtrodden, but all he had to do was visualize again those boots coming for his head to reaffirm his judgment. Strangely, he felt no bitterness toward his attackers, only a deep sadness . . . . In their way they were victims as much as he, and he knew that this experience would not change his belief that the struggle had to go on to eliminate man's rottenness to man and that he would try to play some part in it. For the first time, though, he'd come face to face with the possibility that it was a struggle in which he could be a loser, a battle in which those signed up under his banner would be few and far between, a cause in which patience and sacrifice were the orders of the day, a conflict in which subtlety and compromise might well be the weapons of choice. Through all history, men of good will had been beaten and reviled, often, as in his case, by those they tried to serve. What sustained them? What made them go on? Maybe he'd find out. Meanwhile he gave in to being nursed, indulged, and Amelia, for all her sometimes bitter humor and unwomanly independence, was proving remarkably good at the job, so good, in fact, that even after the pain subsided Peter continued to lie there and let her wait on him, even unto the indignity of carting away his slops. He hadn't since early childhood so enjoyed being irresponsibly helpless in feminine hands. He decided to make the most of it, and he did.

"You're going to get weak and lose the use of your limbs," she told him one day.

"But it still hurts to move," he protested, lying more than a little.

"Then I'm going to have to massage you to keep the blood moving, whether it hurts or not," she said, and seating herself beside him on the bed, she began rubbing his good arm. It did cause just enough pain so that he could wince convincingly, but, at the same time he enjoyed the touch of her hands, which were large and capable, in proportion with her goddesslike stature. "Roll over," she ordered, and with an arm around his shoulders, she helped him. She started working on his neck and, peeling back the covers, his back. The feel of her fingers, gentle but firm in their kneading, warm even through the cloth of his nightshirt, was soothing and exciting; the small tremors of pain when she touched a sore spot tended mostly to add to the pleasant stimulation. Then a lash of cold air across his bare buttocks made him realize that the inadequate nightshirt his mother had brought from Cornelius' wardrobe left him exposed. "Oh, Peter, you're still so black and blue down here. Does it hurt?" and she tentatively touched the sensitive skin. He didn't know whether it hurt there or not, only that his cock was stiffening against the mattress. He didn't dare speak, afraid she'd stop, and afraid that she'd go on . . . However she interpreted his silence, she did go on, massaging the bruised cheeks until he shuddered more from delight than pain, and she said, "I'm sorry. I *am* hurting you, I didn't mean to," and moved quickly down his thighs, his calves. If her innocent purpose had been to get his vital juices flowing, she was succeeding very well: his balls were literally beginning to ache—

"All right, this side's finished, roll over again," she commanded.

Didn't she know anything about men? Well, naturally she didn't . . . she was the family spinster . . . he had better stop her . . . "I can't —"

"Of course, you can. It didn't hurt that much before, did it? Here, let me help you." She was stronger than he'd counted on and flipped him before he could resist. As he'd known it would, his cock stood up straight.

"Don't be embarrassed," she said. "There's precious little I don't know about you, Peter Van Alen. When you were too hurt to be embarrassed the other night I bathed every inch of you, and I must say you've obviously gained some strength since then."

Peter was grateful for the note of humor instead of spinsterly shock in her voice—grateful and surprised. "You know, if it makes any difference to you, I'm not entirely innocent," she said, as she resumed her massage, beginning with his ankles. "I just hope you enjoy the good nursing you're getting."

"Oh, I do, Amelia, I do. But you *must* stop. You don't know what you're doing to me—"

"I'm not really hurting you, am I? What am I doing to you?"

"I'd say it's rather obvious."

"Oh, that. That doesn't hurt, does it?"

"Yes, by God . . . look, please stop . . ."

He could, of course, have covered himself, but her hands were on his thighs and working upward and he was much too worked up to try. Damn his broken arm in its heavy cast, and then her massaging hands were around his stiff cock and she was asking, "Will this help make it feel better?"

"*Amelia* . . . oh, my God, Amelia . . ."

And all his juices escaped with a whoosh, sending him into a convulsion of relief.

Now, finally, she was shocked. "Oh, Peter, I'm sorry, I didn't—"

With his good arm he reached up and pulled her down to him, pressed her face next to his and covered her with kisses . . . "For God's sake, don't be *sorry,* don't be sorry, Amelia . . ."

She was returning his kisses now, and he could feel the warmth and weight of her body as she stretched out next to him on the bed. She buried her face in the pillow, her cheek hot against his, her lips teasing his ear . . . "Peter, do you think I'm awful?"

"No, of course, not, you didn't know—"

"But I did . . . I was . . . I was curious, that's the truth. Ever since the night you came here . . . I don't know what's got into me . . . or maybe I do . . . Peter? . . ."

She had stopped talking, he could feel her body shaking. She lifted her head from the pillow and looked him in the eyes. For the first time he was aware that her eyes were green when they had no blinding surface sparkle of laughter . . . "Peter, not now, but when you're better . . . well, would you make love to me? I need to know . . ."

"But I thought you said you weren't innocent—"

"It was pretty terrible," she said, "but I hope it isn't always. Is it?"

"Good lord, Amelia . . . I've always liked you, but we're not—"

"In love? Is that what you're trying to say? I didn't say anything about that—"

"We'd have to get married—" He felt foolish as he said it.

"Why? Were you going to marry Miss Shields?"

"No, damn it, but you're—"

"I'm *what* . . . ? A good woman, too decent to be a real woman . . . ?"

"You're my *cousin*—"

"All the better. What are cousins for but to help each other?"

"Amelia—"

"Peter, I do believe you are really shocked—aren't you? I wouldn't have dared throw myself at you this way if I hadn't thought you a . . . a freethinker . . ."

"Well, this . . . this takes some getting used to . . ."

"I didn't notice you shoving me away when I—"

"I should have, I'm sorry—"

"You aren't sorry at all, and you know it. Let's at least be honest with each other."

"You're right," he said. "There's an old saying that isn't fit for a lady's ear but since it suits the occasion I'll tell you—'a stiff prick has no conscience.' "

Amelia laughed. "Well, now I'm getting somewhere, or at least you aren't treating me like a lady."

"I didn't mean that."

"I wish you did."

All through this astonishing conversation, Peter was acutely aware that he was becoming erect again . . . His own previous experiences had, in truth, been brief and guilt-ridden vettings with what he assumed, *presumed,* to be rather mindless partners. Making banal conversation with them was simply a necessary part of a game in which the rules forbade honest reference to its purpose. He didn't even have any idea of whether the women he'd been with had enjoyed the experience, though he suspected they hadn't. Even when sometimes

330

preceded by a mock struggle, submission had pretty much been the extent of their participation. He had assumed it was the way of their sex, a disinterest that Cousin James defined as a God-given guarantee of virtue; the reported bawdiness of whores was a sign of, a result of, unnatural depravity. To have a woman of such beauty and breeding and intelligence as Amelia all but pleading with him to take her was nearly irresistible, but he still tried to hold back . . . "It isn't right, Amelia. You'd probably hate me for it—"

"Obviously, you don't want me."

"It isn't *that*. God, Amelia, I've always . . . well, admired you, from way back . . . I shouldn't tell you but I guess it doesn't matter now. Once when I was about thirteen I got myself in trouble with Cornelius and mother by trying to watch you undress through the keyhole. Cousin James accused me of worse than lust—incest almost . . ."

"Why, Peter Van Alen!"

"Now even you're shocked."

"Or maybe a little flattered. I always thought you had your mind only on poetry then. And what, if I may ask, did you see? Her eyes were laughing.

"Not much. You were just down to your chemise when Cornelius caught me."

She got up from beside him and turned her back to him. "Would you like to see me undress now?"

The time for resisting had passed. "Yes," he said.

She sat on the bed, still with her back to him, and removed her gaiters and stockings, then stood and fumbled with the buttons of her bodice and skirt. "Say something," she said as she stepped out of her skirt, revealing the full white curves of her long legs.

He said what he felt. "You are beautiful."

"Am I? Am I *really*? I've always hoped so, but nobody's ever known —"

"You are, you are. Go on, please . . ."

With a quick gesture of defiance, of abandon, she pulled the chemise up and over her head. Like the Greek goddess he'd always thought she resembled, she was generously endowed with flesh in perfect proportion—broad shoulders, long smooth sweep of back, round hips. When she turned to face him he saw her breasts, lovely and firm, the cup in the roll of her belly, the hair curling over the

331

mound between her legs. He tried to speak his feelings in the trite words that come as much to poets as to any other men in such circumstances . . . "My God, you *are* beautiful," he said. "Come here to me—"

"But you aren't well . . ."

"Well enough. Can't you see? Come on . . ."

And she started to, but turned suddenly shy, paused at the edge of the bed and tried awkwardly to cover herself with her hands. He heaved himself up as well as he could on his damaged arm, removed her hands with his good one and buried his face in her pubic hair, damp and smelling with the flow of her. Her hands dug into his hair, pressing him closer, and then she was over him, covering him with her warm and pliant flesh, taking him up into her. He felt consumed, as if his very life were being drawn out of him and into her, as if the moment of release were also a moment of divine death . . . This was what it meant to be transported, to possess and be possessed, to "know" one other in the biblical sense, to become one flesh.

She must have felt the same way. When she finally lay quiet by his side, she whispered, "Thank you, oh, Peter, thank you . . ."

"Amelia, you must marry me—"

She put a finger over his lips. "Shh. Don't talk about that now."

"Why not? After this I can't ever let you go. Don't you feel the same way about me?"

"I don't know, but I do know that you've ruined me—"

"*Ruined* you?"

"Not that way. It's just that I was happy without men. Now—"

"Now you need me, you know damn well you do."

"Yes, now I need you, and isn't it lucky that you aren't quite well yet? And isn't it fortunate that nobody knows you're here but your mother? We still have days and days together. Please, Peter, let's just think about them . . ."

It was an idyll, a time out of time, when they explored together the wonderful ways of knowing each other. Since bringing up the subject of marriage seemed to upset her, Peter decided to let it go—for then.

Finally, though, there came the inevitable day when she told him, "You've got to get out of here. The girls are beginning to suspect something, and it would ruin my school if it got about that I was harboring a man in my bedroom, cousin or no cousin. Oh, don't look so sad—we'll be seeing each other." . . . Since then, and for months,

332

"seeing each other" was all they'd been doing. Once they were out of hiding they couldn't risk using her room, and his own chamber in a boardinghouse was out of the question as was any hotel with its prying clerks and porters. During the summer months, a ferry ride could have brought them to a spot in the woods of Jersey or Long Island, where even if seen they wouldn't be recognized, but she was oddly resisting. "I've never been a girl for picnics, Peter, and I just know it wouldn't be the same . . . I'm afraid of that, spoiling what we've had, even more than I ache to have you." So he had to be content with their meetings in public places, like those of proper cousins or proper courters, where they walked and talked and occasionally kissed and argued, always about marriage . . .

"I've thought and thought about it, Peter, and I know that I'm not *right* for you, not for any man. You deserve a young thing who'll give you babies and darn your socks and cook your supper," she would insist. "I've never boiled an egg and don't intend to start now, and I may be too old to have children. At least, thank God, there's been no sign of any."

"I wish there were, and then you'd have to marry me," he would say. "God, Amelia, I'd go barefoot and eat weeds just to be able to love you—"

"You say that now, but for how long? Familiarity breeds contempt, you know. You've never seen me when I'm sick or angry or tired, which I am more often than I like. Peter, we've shared something wonderful, something I doubt few people ever know, and I want to keep it that way. I want you to go on *liking* me, being cousins, being friends . . ."

"How can we be *friends* after what we've known? I can hardly keep my hands off you right now—"

"And that frightens me, because I feel the same way. But I know myself too well, and I know that there would come a time when I'd resent your wanting so much of me, or even my wanting you. I *like* my work. I like opening young minds, and I want to be free to do it, and I want to be free, too, to speak my own mind about freeing the slaves, freeing women. I'd become an embarrassment to your family —and possibly to you too. Oh, don't you see?"

"No, I don't see. I don't see that anything matters to me but you —"

"Then I truly am bad for you. You're a man to whom so much else

333

ought to matter—your poetry, your work for a better society—"

"So you'd just give me up?"

"Not give you up—ever. To the day I die I'll love you in my own way for literally opening me up to something I couldn't imagine. I'm hoping that you can learn to love me that way too. Let's just say we were blessed for a while with what I believe you poets call a divine madness—"

"Let's just say we'll get married. You're talking romantic rot."

. . .

That night as he followed Amelia along the causeway toward the blaring band and the crowd roaring "Tippecanoe and Tyler Too," Peter had, in spite of his brave words, the first real feeling that all of his arguments would fail. With her broad shoulders and skillful thrusts of her folded parasol, Amelia made her way through the dense pack of people to the wagon, where she managed to get a cup of hard cider for them to share. The song had shifted to another favorite of the followers of the Whig candidate, the old Indiana Indian fighter, General Benjamin Harrison:

> Old Tip he wears a homespun coat,
> He has no ruffled shirt—wirt-wirt;
> But Mat he has the golden plate,
> And he's a little squirt—wirt-wirt.

"Isn't that dreadful?" Amelia shouted over the singing. "I wonder how your Cousin Matty feels when he hears such things."

"They say he's unruffled, if you don't mind a bad pun," Peter replied. "But I'm sure he's going to lose. Right or wrong, they've blamed him for the depression, and they don't need any other issue. I'm just glad I'm not trying to run a newspaper during this campaign."

It was, most serious-minded people agreed, the most disgraceful campaign yet in America's young history. The Whigs would not even let the old general, Harrison, speak, out of fear that he'd turn up on the wrong side of some vital and divisive issue; instead, and totally ignoring the fact that Harrison was living out his retirement on a handsome spread in his home state, they created the image of a poor man of the people—a dirt farmer dwelling in a log cabin and solacing himself with cider. "Little Van"—the kindest name they had for the

President—was depicted as living in a palace, dousing his beard with eau de cologne and soothing his palate with "sparkling wine" while the country starved. Even the good things Van Buren had done, such as signing an executive order creating a ten-hour workday in summer months, were sneered at as sleight of hand on the part of the little magician to get votes. He was, in Peter's opinion, doomed as more and more thoughtless people swallowed the Harrison myth along with their hard cider. Already Maine in its early election had gone for Harrison, and the cry was, "As Maine goes, so goes the nation." But then Cousin Matty had proved as powerless as Peter had sensed him to be. The real problem was that Harrison and that nonentity on his ticket, Tyler, would clearly be worse. Yes, Peter was glad that he didn't have to try to tell readers whether they should stick to the frying pan or jump into the fire, glad that his only activity in the hours when he couldn't see Amelia was trying to put his love for her into verse.

"I've had enough. Even their cider is sour," Amelia said. "Take me home, Peter. I have to get up and work in the morning, you know."

As they reached the edge of the crowd, an almost ghostly figure loomed in their way. Tall, stooped, white-haired and white-suited, the man called out, "Peter! Peter Van Alen!"

If possible, Peter would have avoided this confrontation. As it was, he said with some sarcasm, "Why, if it isn't Go-west Greeley, or is it Log Cabin Greeley now?"

As much as he was glad that he himself had no part in this campaign, he was grieved that a man he had once admired had gone so far in selling his soul, in Peter's opinion, to the Whig forces of Albany —Thurlow Weed and his puppet, Governor Seward. The man who had launched the *New Yorker* saying "nor shall we adventure our barque among the whirlpools and quicksands of politics" was now publishing with Weed and Seward's help a campaign sheet called *Log Cabin* that was spreading the Harrison myth. Greeley had adapted one of the *New Yorker*'s most popular features—a back page devoted to the words and music of popular songs such as "Meet Me by Moonlight Alone"—to the *Log Cabin,* but the songs he was publishing now were the ones they were hearing right here in the park. In his leading editorial, Greeley had announced that "this journal will be the advocate of the cause of the log cabin against that of the presidential palace." Seeing Greeley now reminded Peter of what Cousin

Matty had written to his mother: "If I'm defeated, it will be without a why or wherefore but only because I've been sung down and drunk down." Though still as staunch an advocate of temperance as Cousin James or Cornelius, Greeley was certainly responsible for much of the singing.

"Now, Peter, you sound bitter," Greeley said, and then, seeing Amelia, bowed to her. "Good evening, Miss Downing . . ."

"I didn't know you knew each other," Peter said.

"Oh, yes, Mrs. Greeley and I are in the same cause of promoting the health of women by eating Mr. Graham's cracker bread," Amelia said. "How is Mrs. Greeley?"

"Well as might be expected, though I must say that her diet doesn't agree with me—"

"Yes, I remember you had quite an appetite," Peter said.

"For everything but this damnable cider," Greeley said. "Peter, I'm sorry about your paper. Whether you think so now or not, we share many of the same causes."

"Such as?"

"Slavery for one. You know one reason I'm opposed to your cousin in the White House is that he and his party have been so wishy-washy on this issue, whereas Governor Seward has at least done something practical by pushing through legislation to protect fugitive slaves here in New York. You would agree with me on that, wouldn't you, Miss Downing?"

"Yes, I . . ."

"By the way, I hear you have a Negro girl in your school," Greeley said. "I think that's capital."

"Yes, I'm very excited. Now that Oberlin College out in Ohio is accepting both women and Negroes, there may be a real future for her," Amelia said.

Not much given to small talk, Greeley turned to Peter. "I'm glad I ran into you because I'm planning to start a new newspaper, and I'd like you to join me—"

"One like this sheet you're running now?"

"Please, bear with me," Greeley said. "This will die with the campaign. No, I'm going to be truly independent, though Thurlow Weed doesn't know it yet. I'm going to call it the *Tribune* because I plan to make it a real forum for the people. In addition to fighting the extension of slavery I'm going to take to task the unfair employers

336

who work our people for too many hours for too little wages. That sounds like what you were trying to do, doesn't it, Peter? And I'm going to do more than talk. I'm already organizing a union of printers to stand up for their rights against unscrupulous publishers. I have a good many plans—"

"What about the magazine?"

"I guess I'm a newspaper man at heart," Greeley said. "I want to make things happen. It didn't seem enough to be publishing love songs or even the first story by the now celebrated Boz—Charles Dickens. Will you join me, Peter? I promise you won't regret it, even though we won't see eye to eye on everything."

"Certainly not on temperance, Uncle Horace. I'm on my way now to the Astor House for something to wash out the bad taste of your friends' cider," Peter said.

"But you haven't answered my question. Promise that at least you'll think about it. I'm going to get going early next year."

"All right, I will. Goodnight. I have to take this working lady home."

They were silent for a while as they walked up a gaslit and nearly deserted Broadway. Then Amelia reached out and took his hand. "I think you should do it, Peter. I know you're writing poetry, but I think it would be good for you to get back into action. Mr. Greeley's as bad as his wife when it comes to fads, and I think this *Log Cabin* is a kind of fad, an overreaction to having been out of politics for so long. But even you've said he's basically a sound man—"

"You're just trying to get my mind off you, aren't you?"

They had reached her door. She turned to him and took both of his hands.

"Look at me, Peter." Her eyes almost on a level with his were as lake-green as when she'd asked him to make love to her. "This really can't go on . . . if we're going to be friends you must get this marriage idea out of your head, and we must never again try to . . . well, repeat what we've had. Otherwise I'll have to stop seeing you, and I *don't* want to do that . . ." She kissed him lightly and disappeared behind the heavy old door that had opened and closed on so many important moments of his life.

He did walk on up the street to the Astor House, where he stood at the bar and proceeded to get maudlin drunk. He ignored the crude bonhomie of the men drinking around him. Not one of them, he was sure in his sanctimony, could appreciate such sorrow as his, for not one of them could ever have tasted Amelia's sweet love. The Bible said that Adam was banished from Eden when the fruit opened his eyes to the knowledge of good and evil, but Peter's drunken poetic mind played with a train of thought that had begun earlier in the evening. Couldn't the fable really mean that Eve had introduced Adam to a passion that would be forever consuming, forever unfulfilled? Wasn't covering their nakedness a symbolic way of saying what Amelia kept saying in her own way: that a true openness, a true blending of flesh between man and woman was incompatible with the harsh realities of life? If it ever did happen, as he was certain it had in the deep memory of man who'd created the fable and again in a sheltering house on Broadway in New York City, it could not last, because God had thrown man out of Eden. He could even remember the words: "He drove out the man; and at the east of the garden of Eden he placed the cherubim, and a flaming sword which turned every way, to guard the way to the tree of life."

Without realizing what he was doing, Peter had been speaking these words aloud. The man next to him at the bar turned to him and said, "Hey, fellow, you must have a real snootful. This is a bar. It ain't a ruddy church."

Peter pulled himself erect and delivered an alcoholic homily: "My dear sir, the church is where you find it."

"Say, you'd better take yourself home, fellow."

"I will," said Peter, trying to recoup. "I think I will—if I can ruddy find it . . ."

Chapter **XVI**

The Politician, The Poet and The Pilot

There had been a time when he could take a walk up Broadway from the Battery as far as the canal and know who lived behind almost every door without even looking at the nameplates. He'd encounter a dozen or more familiar faces in such a stroll, and the men would tip their hats and the women would curtsy, and they'd call him senator. But now in this year of our Lord eighteen hundred and forty-seven, there was hardly a private dwelling of consequence in lower Broadway, the last of them, including the old Van Alen house, having been wiped out in the fire of '45. If he met in a month of constitutionals one person who knew him, or whom he knew, it would be a miracle comparable to finding a needle in a haystack. About the only place in the whole city where he could count on having his name or fame recognized was the new Century Club, and there it was only the doorman, who in gratitude for small gratuities always made a point of saying loudly enough for anyone within earshot to hear, "Afternoon, Senator Schuyler!" So these days after his walk he spent much of his lonely time at the club, dozing off his after-luncheon brandy and wondering what to do with another empty evening.

Ever since that ungrateful whippersnapper Cornelius had replaced him as company counsel with young Smith, he'd had nothing to do with his days. Cornelius had tried in his fashion to be nice about it. "You know you're over seventy now, Uncle Peter, and you deserve a rest," he'd said and then put a sting in it by adding, "Things are moving awfully fast in business these days since the depression's over, and we need a young man to keep up with it." What they needed in Peter Schuyler's opinion was a lawyer without any principles, and John Charles Smith, Jr., certainly filled that bill. He was the spitting image of his late father and his older brother George, not only in looks but habits; he spent half his time over at the Union Race Course on Long Island and the rest at the Astor House bar. Peter wondered that a hard-working Puritan like Cornelius could put up with any of those Smiths, but then Cornelius had always baffled him.

Sally was forever making excuses for Cornelius, not that he could blame her. She did really owe her son most everything she had, and he had no doubt that however she tried to hide it, Sally had a guilty conscience over the matter of her other son's conception. Still, it rankled him to have her say when Cornelius came out with one of his priggish pronouncements, "He's just like our father, isn't he, Peter?" As far as Peter could see, Cornelius wasn't at all like Jacobus, who at least was willing to suffer, as well as make all of them suffer, for his convictions. Cornelius had a capacity to trim his convictions to catch a favoring wind, and Sally was probably closer to the truth when she'd shrug off her son's involvement in something like this unholy alliance between Commodore Vanderbilt and Dan Drew by saying, "He takes after his grandfather old Cornelius, who'd never let anybody beat him on the river." Of course, women weren't exactly rational creatures, and Sally, for all her worth, was no exception, though she did at times have an uncanny instinct about people, and her paradoxical comments about Cornelius made a good deal of sense . . . he *was* a strange combination of both of his grandfathers. While Peter had often thought that Cornelius had inherited the worst traits of old Jacobus and old Cornelius, he was also aware of being out of step with popular opinion, particularly here in New York. In a place and at a time when the measure of a man's stature was material possessions, Cornelius Van Alen, despite his measly five feet, six inches, stood among the tallest: he was worth at least half a million, perhaps more, and it was said that even old Astor, living in misery on milk-toast up there in his place at Hell Gate, had called his falling out with the Van Alens one of his few regrets, since staying invested with them might have turned out to be far more profitable than acquiring that land which had lost a quarter or more of its value as a result of the renters' revolt.

Old men were prone to regrets, as Peter knew only too well, but he was glad that his were not, as Astor's seemed to be, mean reflections on every dollar that might have escaped him. Much of the Scripture his father had once thundered at them stuck in Peter's mind, and when he thought of Astor he was always reminded of that part of the Sermon on the Mount where Jesus said, "For where your treasure is, there will your heart be also." Peter hadn't seen old Astor in ten years, but that literary fellow Cogswell who'd feathered a fine nest for himself by becoming Astor's companion at Hell Gate was a member of the Century, and, worshipful fool that he was, he would bore everyone in sight—often only Peter on those long afternoons —with stories that were supposed to show how keen his employer remained at eighty-three. To Peter these tales were simply and purely sad, for they revealed that the farsighted "landlord of New York"— a man worth at least $20 million, more perhaps than any other man had amassed in history—remained as hungry in spirit as in his old stomach that could no longer tolerate solid food. Those unfortunate enough to be invited to dinner at Hell Gate were obliged to endure watching their host slobber over the gruel that a servant fed him as if he were a baby, and to observe his once large frame, now so wasted and weak that Coggswell and the coachman, William, had to exercise him by bouncing him up and down in a blanket.

"But he's still sharp as a tack," Coggswell would say. "Nothing escapes his attention. The other day while we were bouncing him one of his rent collectors came in, and Mr. Astor asked him, 'Did you get the rent from Mrs. O'Hara yet?' He must have thousands of properties, so imagine his remembering the name of one tenant! Well, the agent said, 'No, sir,' and, though it's hard for Mr. Astor to talk now, he almost sounded his old self when he said, 'Vy not? She *must* bay.' 'She's had reverses, sir, and we must give her time . . .' Mr. Astor made us put him down and prop him up while he shook a finger at the man and said, 'I tell you she can bay it, and she *vill* bay it. You just don't know the right vay to vork vith her. By damn, I'll fire you if you don't get that rent.' We have to humor him sometimes lest he be carried away by stroke, so Mr. Bill gave the agent the money out of his own pocket and told him to tell his father it came from Mrs. O'Hara. Well, you should have seen Mr. Astor smile. 'Ach, I told you!' he said. 'You can always get money if you use the right vay.' Yes, sir, sharp as a tack he is.''

In a way, Peter had to thank the Lord that nobody would ever call him sharp as a tack these days. He knew that people were either irritated or amused by his tendency to nod his way through dull meetings, dreary sermons and deafening concerts, but for him the virtue in growing old, if virtue there was, lay in the realization that much of what excited and agitated men in the present would be forgotten in the future. The trick, of course, was to latch on to things that really mattered and let the rest go. The irony was that, by the time you learned the trick, it was generally too late to play the game. But you could get a certain satisfaction out of watching through educated eyes the way other people went on playing it. It was a little like being the fellow he'd sat beside at the Italian opera the other night who was following it with an English translation: when he'd groan or break out laughing, everybody else would look around at him as if he were queer, but he was the only person in the house who knew what was going on.

One of the things going on right now that most people didn't understand was this war with Mexico. You'd think any fool could see the game President Polk had been playing, and yet there were men right here in this club who insisted, as Polk did, that the mighty United States could not tolerate having "American blood shed on American soil" and editors like that O'Neill fellow who justified any amount of bloodshed on the grounds that it was America's "manifest destiny" to expand to the Pacific. The truth was that Polk had sent General Taylor's troops clear down to the Rio Grande, which, as that young Congressman Lincoln from Illinois pointed out, was invading Mexican soil and then had screamed like a stuck pig when a few of them got shot by angry Mexicans in the process. Anyone with an ounce of brains could see that Polk was really after California and was just looking for some excuse to force the Mexicans to give it up. Well, with General Winfield Scott marching right up to the "halls of Montezuma" like one of those old Spanish conquistadors, it was beginning to look like Polk would have his way, and then, of course, there would be more hell to pay about whether or not slavery would be allowed in the new territories. Peter thought that James Russell Lowell had the whole thing about right with his jingle: "They just want this Californy / So's to lug new slave states in / To abuse ye, an' to scorn ye / An' to plunder ye like sin." Yet, except for some young fellows like that Lincoln and that Henry Thoreau who got himself arrested up in Massachusetts for refusing to pay his taxes in protest against the war, there wasn't even a Whig politician of any note who had the courage to question Polk's jingoism. Peter certainly wasn't one to cast stones at them, however, since he'd got his own political start by going along with Mr. Madison's war back in '12 when the Federalists who opposed it were virtually wiped out forever. Once they got going, wars were like holy crusades for Americans, no matter how they came about, and people who had opposed them were deemed infidels to be burned at the stake. It was only when you grew old enough and had seen enough of them come and go that you came to understand that wars seldom had anything to do with the incidents that provoked them, and that for every problem they seemed to solve they created others, as this war would surely do. The people who opposed wars were probably as right in the eyes of God as those who favored them, and they quite clearly had more common sense. But common sense was not a commodity widely distributed among the people of the earth, as poor Matty Van Buren was also learning in his old age.

Poor Matty? Peter found it amusing and rather comforting that he could think in that way about the man who had occupied the throne to which he had once aspired and who just might sit upon it again. He was, he realized, indulging in the kind of comfortable arrogance that had been both his birthright as a Schuyler and a somewhat unexpected compensation for having grown old and forgone the ambitions that make men craven. Yes, poor Matty. He had climbed so high and fallen so far. Quite incredibly, if you viewed man in terms of the myths he created about himself rather than, as Peter had come to do, in terms of the reality of his methods, Matty's fall coincided with what almost everybody would concede was a favorable change in his character. Despite, or perhaps because of, the silks and silver and champagne and china with which he surrounded himself in the palace, the former beer boy from Kinderhook had behaved like a real statesman as president. Almost nobody, least of all Peter, would have expected the little magician, the Red Fox, the political spoilsman, to ride out a depression that was blamed on him without a whimper of protest over the Jackson policies he'd inherited, without committing a foolish or expedient act, without once losing his almost naive faith in the ability of the American people to save themselves. Now that everybody was making more money than ever before and the country's financial capital had shifted from Philadelphia to New York, even men here in the Century had a good word for Matty, and some of them conceded that that monetary devil Andrew Jackson might have ascended to heaven after all when he died in '45. The clincher was when Jackson's archenemy, the angel of the financiers, Nick Biddle, was caught stealing from his own Bank of the United States. Peter could still remember Philip Hone, of all people, coming back from a trip to Philadelphia and ranting, "The Bank of the United States is in a terrible smell. It would appear to have been an immense sack, in which everyone put in his hand and took as much as he wanted, from Mr. Biddle to the lowest employee. As the contents of the sack were dwindling away so fast, and those who had charge of it knew that it would soon be empty, perhaps it was as well, they thought, to feather their own nests. The notes of the bank are being discounted at twelve percent with a terrible effect on the merchants who hold them. Why, I've got one for $100 right here in my pocket, worth only $88. Is it to be wondered that the people of this country rail against banks?" Whatever else was said of Matty, even in that low mudslinging campaign of '40, nobody ever accused him of dishonesty with a dollar, which was more than could be said of Webster or Benton or Cass or any other of a number of so-called statesmen.

Poor Matty. It's said that power corrupts, but in his case it seemed to have purified. The man who once wouldn't be tricked into saying where the sun rose began spouting principles like a regular Clay or Calhoun. Peter was surprised, shocked really, when Matty joined his probable Whig opponent Henry Clay before the conventions of '44 in issuing a warning against a too speedy annexation of Texas. Not only that but he put it in writing, arguing in his letter that such a course would lead to war with Mexico. Though a majority of the delegates were said to have favored Matty, the "manifest destiny" boys put across a two-thirds vote rule and managed thereby to enter their dark horse Polk into a race in which he beat Clay. So now we had a war Matty had warned against, and a brand new Matty. The man who was once scorned by all the antislavery people as a "Northern man with Southern principles" was being talked about as the

344

candidate for a Free Soil Party that his son, "Prince John," was putting together out of the old locofoco Democrats and the abolitionist Whigs for next year's campaign. They called themselves "barn burners"—they were willing to burn down the Democratic barn to get the rats out. Peter guessed that they would burn the barn, that tottering old party structure that had thrown a roof over men of varied views from north and south, east and west, and that the rats would come out wearing wigs. Pretty good. He'd have to share that pun with somebody. Maybe young Peter could get it printed . . .

Peter still didn't think that it was right for the government of the United States to take away a man's private property and he still hadn't seen any evidence that Negroes were any more competent . . . or less . . . than women to exercise the privileges of free men, but he agreed with Matty and the barn burners that letting slavery spread west to the Pacific would ruin the country. Among other things, it would make it harder for free men to go west and get jobs, as that fellow Peter worked for, Horace Greeley, kept advising, and all these immigrants would be bottled up right here between the rivers in New York. It was getting out of hand already, what with that potato famine in Ireland. Somebody told Peter that more than 75,000 immigrants had come into New York in the last year alone, and he could well believe it because he sometimes whiled away an afternoon over at City Hall watching them come through the naturalization lines. In addition to the half-starved Irish, there were those Italians who looked like they'd climbed out of the depths of Naples, and, even as he watched the farce of naturalizing all these people who couldn't, after all, make a go of it in their own countries, Peter was concerned that they'd march right out the other door of City Hall to the almshouse for free board or, if they were smarter, to the Tammany Wigwam to sell their votes. One reason that he didn't regret leaving politics was that he couldn't have faced himself in a mirror if he thought that his seat in the Senate came from the votes Tammany bought, and he couldn't understand how a man from a respectable merchant family like that James J. Roosevelt let himself be used by the Irish Indians. Peter had even gone so far as to vote for James Harper when he ran on the Native American party ticket for mayor, but the stupid fellow had misused his office to try to pass blue laws and put uniforms on the police and had, of course, been thrown out. Peter would have to say for the Tammany sachems that they had more sense than to try to legislate against human nature—no law was going to stop a thirsty man in need of a drink or dress a proud man in what he thought of as "livery." The interesting thing about Matty was that he remained a hero to Tammany despite breaking out in a rash of principles, as was certainly evident in the way they cheered him when he came down from the country to help President Tyler bless the flow of Croton water.

Thinking about the Croton water, Peter had to laugh at what his old friend Attorney Strong's son George had said when he predicted that it would be worse than Manhattan water because the aqueduct through which it ran had been used as a necessary by all the Hibernian vagabonds who worked on it. But young Strong was probably as wrong about Croton water as he'd been when he said that Harper's election was "the worst blow to befall the Hibernian race since the Battle of the Boyne." One thing for sure: the water was creating a new trade for at least some of the immigrants who claimed to be plumbers, though they'd never before seen a bathtub or a water closet, and Peter had heard that there might be as many as five thousand water closets in New York now. But *poor* Matty. Peter was sure that Matty was in for another fall when the Irish learned that his principles were bringing him antislavery support, for if anyone hated Negroes more than a plantation overseer it was a New York Irishman. Matty was sixty-five or so, and Peter wondered why age hadn't robbed Matty of ambition, as it seemed to have him, and left Matty content with playing squire up there on the estate he called Lindenwald.

In Peter's mind the fact that a tavernkeeper's son had bought, remodeled and was dwelling in the old Van Ness mansion near Kinderhook was more improbable than the fact that he'd once occupied the White House and was, in a sense, a sorry sign of how far the times were, as Shakespeare had put it, "out of joint." That renters' war a year or so ago when tenants had run around dressed up as "Injins" and threatened their landlords had just about done in the patroons, including his own brother Jacobus, who'd either been frightened or angered into a fatal stroke and had left things in such a mess that his widow had had to sell off all that remained of the Schuyler property. Though Governor Seward had sent troops to stop the Injins, the law had finished what they had started in the constitutional convention of '46, and now no Hudson River landlord could count on his feudal rights—his "four fat hens" a year, his tithe of wheat and labor, and worse, his quarter money due if the tenant sold out his lease. Likely all the old properties would fall into the hands of people like Van Buren or those Roosevelts who made their money right here in the city in sugar and banking and hardware and were pretending to be patroons. He could remember meeting one of the older Jameses, as colorless a merchant as he'd ever seen, at Sally's house, and now he'd heard that the fellow's son, Isaac, had given up medicine and was just idling up there in a place near Poughkeepsie he called Rosedale. Well, the fellow had married right when he'd got hold of one of the Aspinwall girls, who now that her family was connected with the Howlands was heir to one of the biggest shipping fortunes in the city. Although it rankled him that he had no more part in it, Peter did agree that Cornelius was smart to get Van Alen & Son back into shipping with Vanderbilt since, aside from real estate, that was where the money could be found. It was one of those jokes with the bite of truth that people called the "N.L. and G." stamped on the merchandise handled by N.L. and G. Griswold—"no loss and great gain." Well, perhaps Cornelius or even Sally might be moved to buy their way back onto the river again, but if so he'd probably never live to see it. Another of his old man's regrets was that he'd ever sold them his land to finance a political career without future—and lose a son. He didn't yet know whether he was grateful to Sally or angry at her for finally telling him that the young man was living out Chicago way under the name of Francis Livingston and apparently doing very well. He'd been too proud to risk rejection by trying to contact his son and had been convinced again of that old saying that it was better to leave well enough alone. Still, if he hadn't sold the land, he'd probably be living up there with his son and perhaps a passle of grandchildren instead of dozing here in this club or wandering around alone in a marble house that was blacker than the face of an actor in Christy's Minstrels what with everybody burning coal and steam engines that had taken over from the horses on the Harlem Railway puffing smoke that lay like a black blanket over the whole lower city when the weather was unfavorable. There were times when he'd lie there at night and listen to his neighbors' horses cough and stomp in their stalls and think about how wonderful it would be to be able to get out and ride along the river and through the forests as he'd done nearly every day of his boyhood. He'd given up even trying to keep an animal since you had to get clear north of the Croton Reservoir at Fifth Avenue and Forty-Second Street to find open country, and it was too harrowing for an old man to try to keep a beast under control in the shambles of all the omnibuses and carriages and wagons and dodging pedestrians you had to thread your way through to get there. The city was no longer a good place for an old man with country tastes, and yet there was nowhere else for him to go.

It might be different if he cared enough for reading like Sally and that impossible niece of hers, Amelia Downing, and wasn't bored to death at all the receptions they put on for the so-called literati or if he liked the theater as young Peter did or if he were gullible enough to enjoy being fooled by the "wonders" that Barnum was always trotting out at his American museum. He did have to admit to being amused and fascinated by one of these—that little General Tom Thumb—but it was probably owing to an old man's vanity. When Peter had finally gone over to see the midget, a little fellow who came about to his kneecaps ran up to him and bowed and squeaked, "I'm proud to meet you, *Senator* Schuyler. You honor me with your presence." No doubt Barnum was back there in the wings coaching his star, because Peter had heard later that acknowledging any claim to fame on anybody's part was a feature of the act. Having been nearly taken in a dozen years before when Barnum produced at Niblo's that old Negro woman who was supposed to have been Washington's slave, Peter wouldn't have gone to see Tom Thumb at all if it hadn't been for a letter that Amelia Downing got from one of her brothers in London about how the tiny Yankee midget had almost literally twisted the British lion's tail, and Peter had to admire any American for doing that in these days when it was the fashion for Englishmen like that writing fellow Dickens to reward American hospitality with sneering comments about American manners.

"You should have been here, Amelia," Henry Downing had written. "You would have split your sides with laughter. I was invited along to General Tom Thumb's audience with Queen Victoria by reason of helping Barnum arrange some of his showings here in England where he's said to have taken in an incredible 150,000 pounds, of which I saw not so much as a pence, but the show at Buckingham Palace was reward enough. The queen, you know, is a dumpy, stuffy little person, but people are terrified of her. Not so Barnum, who has the looks and manners of one of those Yankee

peddlers who could sell wooden nutmegs off his wagon—or his protege who also comes from Connecticut. Though he's only a bit over
three feet tall, Tom Thumb's a perfectly proportioned little man.
He's really Charles Stratton, born of normal parents in Bridgeport,
but I'm sure you know all that. Anyway, the audience took place in
the royal picture gallery where the queen, dressed all in black, stood
with Prince Albert beside her and a dozen or so leading members of
the nobility behind them. Barnum was dressed in knee breeches at
my suggestion, but the little general wore a black velvet cutaway with
fawn pantaloons. When he marched down that gallery and up to the
queen he looked like a wax doll in motion and when, after bowing
to her majesty, he said, 'Good evening, ladies and gentlemen!' they
were startled into laughter by his being able to talk so clearly and
sensibly. He asked to see the Prince of Wales to measure himself
against him but was told that the prince was in bed. 'Well,' said
General Thumb, 'I'd rather have a little miss anyway,' bringing on
more laughter. Queen Victoria was so intrigued that she began asking Barnum questions about his protege, and Barnum just spoke
right up to her, which caused the queen's lord-in-waiting, through
whom replies to royal questions are supposed to be made, to go into
a fit and me to be proud of the American character which acknowl-
edges no royalty here on earth. God help me, I forget it from time
to time from living here for so long.

"Well, small as he is, General Tom Thumb is as proud and irreverent as any other American. After he'd done some of his dances and
imitations—the one of Napoleon particularly pleasing Her Majesty—
the sign came from the still-fretting lord-in-waiting that the audience
was over. Barnum started backing down the long hall with his face
always to the queen as he'd been instructed to do, but the midget with
his short legs couldn't keep up and so would turn and run a few steps,
then back a few steps, then run again. The royal audience broke up
with laughter, but the royal poodle took offense and started barking
and growling at the general. At this point, Tom Thumb decided that
his valuable small hide was more important than any foreign protocol
and with his stick began attacking the poodle. There followed a
hilarious fight in which the general sent the poodle scurrying for
safety behind his mistress's skirts and brought the house down. When
the general finally reached safety in the anteroom, the ruffled lord-in-
waiting followed with Queen Victoria's personal apologies for her

dog's manners, a rare and wonderful concession to the feelings of her American cousins."

Peter often wondered where Barnum turned up the things he displayed in his museum, most of which were preposterous hoaxes like that petrified mermaid, but he did have to hand it to the man for livening up New York. By the time Barnum took it over, the old Scudder's museum was as dead as its exhibits. But Barnum draped the building with colorful posters of the attractions within and kept a band playing from morning until night on the balcony to attract passersby on Broadway or in the City Hall Park. As with some of his hoaxes, Barnum evidently relied upon the American sense of humor when it came to music: the band's playing was so bad that it was a kind of wonder in itself. This was a result of Barnum's Yankee penury, as Peter gathered from the story of one young man who applied for a position in the band and was told by Barnum to go ahead and play without benefit of an audition. When at the end of the first week the man asked for his pay, Barnum said, "Pay? Why, the honor of playing in Phineas T. Barnum's band is pay enough for a young fellow like you." Barnum had such a knack for getting his name in the papers that even the atrociousness of his amateur band got turned around into a kind of virtue in a poem Peter had read the other day:

> I love the city, and the city's smoke
> The smell of gas; the dust of coal and coke;
> The sound of bells; the tramp of hurrying feet;
> The sight of pigs and Paphians in the street;
> The jostling crowd; the never-ceasing noise
> Of rattling coaches, and vociferous boys;
> The cry of "Fire!" and the exciting scene
> Of heroes running with their mad "mercheen";
> Nay, now I think that I could even stand
> The direful din of Barnum's brazen band,
> So much I long to see the town again!

While he'd have to agree with the poet about the band, Peter imagined that only a young man who'd never known better days and ways could feel that way about the rest of the city. He didn't usually agree with the Reverend James Schuyler who was so often quoted in Greeley's *Tribune* because of his prohibitionist views, but James had got off a pretty good one when he called New York "the anteroom of hell." Of course, James and he had very different ideas of what constituted hell. In that interview James was all worked up about the police raid on the Odeon Theater the previous Sunday. Bad enough, James thundered, that the theater was open at all on the Lord's day in violation of the law, but when the police arrived they discovered on the stage "three well-formed ladies attired in short skirts" performing in a religious mockery entitled *Jacob in the House of Laban.* The minds of the audience were so inflamed by the lewd scenes on stage, according to James, that they turned on their own guardians and pelted them with everything that came to hand, thus proving the infectiousness of sin. The shamelessness of the performers knew no bounds: when the police finally worked their way backstage into the dressing rooms, a number of scantily clad women pulled their nether garments up to hide their faces and shocked the good officers by exposing their private parts. Peter thought that this scene must have surpassed anything ever put on stage for comedy, and of course accounts of the raid, augmented by the Reverend Schuyler's diatribe, resulted in the Odeon's being packed every night thereafter. No, the hell New York was becoming in Peter's mind was not a place in which a man might enjoy the sight of female flesh but a place in which it was no longer possible for a man to be known, a place in which every physical landmark by which a man oriented himself was periodically wiped out by fire or sacrificed to progress, a place in which a man's ears were deafened by noise and his eyes clouded by smoke, a place in which men were driven by starvation to prey on their fellow creatures like beasts in a jungle.

If anyone from the papers had cared to interview ex-Senator Peter Schuyler as he dozed in his chair at the Century, he would have received a prophecy of doom strikingly like that from the lips of the senator's nephew, the Reverend James Schuyler. "Not only is New York going to hell but the whole country with it," the senator might have said. But after that, there would be a distinct difference between the senator's views and those of the parson. Whereas the Reverend Schuyler had ended up his polemic about lewdness in the theater with a call for the people to return to God, Senator Schuyler would have closed his interview with a little laugh. "Yes, I guess that's where we're all going," he would have said, "but the journey ought to be interesting, and I for one ought to find a lot of good friends down there."

Among the five hundred thousand or so souls who could be found in New York in that year of eighteen forty-seven, there was one who had already stepped out of the anteroom into the shadowy recesses of hell itself, but he was beyond the saving reach of the Reverend James Schuyler. Looking out over the upturned faces of his fashionable congregation of a Sunday, the Reverend Schuyler would never see the pale, handsome features of Edgar Allan Poe, never look into those startling eyes with pupils often shrunk to a pinpoint by laudanum or blurred to a watery sadness by alcohol. Poe was not one for seeking God in church; the angels upon whom he counted for salvation were right here on earth in the faces and forms of the women who found him irresistible. If James Schuyler had known that his twenty-year-old daughter Martha was one of these angels, he would have been horrified, because he regarded the weird stories and strange poems from Poe's hand that were appearing in the newspapers and magazines as the work of the devil, compared with which the pantheism of Bryant and unitarianism of Emerson appeared almost divinely inspired.

But there was a great deal that James Schuyler didn't know about Martha, who as the third of a series of increasingly lovely girls, sired by a Schuyler out of a Roosevelt, could often hide from the vigilant pastoral eye behind the skirts of her sisters. All of the girls were of course raised in the fear—or, as Martha said, boredom—of the Lord by being in attendance every time the doors of the uptown Presbyterian Church were thrown open, which became somewhat less of an ordeal for them when they were old enough to realize that they were the focus of more young masculine eyes than their father in the pulpit. At home they were subjected to morning and evening prayers in the parlor, and Martha could never see a rose in bloom without being reminded of the floral covering on the chair at which she stared while kneeling uncomfortably through these sessions. When she was small, the familiar, musical sound of her father's voice in prayer combined with the hypnotic effect of the rose pattern in front of her eyes often put her to sleep, a minor sin for which her mother would rap her sharply on the head. But there were compensations for this sometimes painful piety, among them being their father's undeniably prominent position in the city which brought them into contact with the very best and wealthiest people and, of course, their sons. Because of his profession, it didn't matter that their father's family had been "land poor," as he always said, or that they had lost even the land when their grandfather Jacobus died; in any case, their mother's Roosevelt relatives were wealthy enough that they were always getting beautiful hand-me-down clothes that could be made over so that nobody would ever recognize them and family heirlooms of jewelry or fine china or silver for their hope chests as presents on important occasions. More practical than their father, their mother kept copies of *Godey's Lady's Book* and Mrs. Farrar's *The Young Lady's Friend* under the Bible and would read them social scripture after the prayer meeting was over and their father had left. Martha always stayed awake through *that.* She was happy that Mrs. Farrar approved of eating your peas with your knife which she did anyway, distressed that the social arbiter thought it improper for young ladies to blow their noses at table since hers had a way of tickling when she was bored and absolutely devastated by the author's comments on jiggling, an art she'd practiced for hours in front of her mirror after she'd seen the older girls doing it at her first ball.

"Some girls have a trick of *jiggling* their bodies (I am obliged to coin a word to describe it); they shake all over, as if they were hung on spiral wires like the geese in a Dutch toy; than which, nothing can be more ungraceful, or unmeaning," Mrs. Farrar had written. "It robs a lady of all dignity, and makes her appear trifling and insignificant. Some do it only on entering a room, others do it every time they are introduced to anybody, and whenever they begin to talk to anyone. It must have originated in embarrassment, and a desire to do something, without knowing exactly what; and being adapted by some popular belle, it became, at one time, a fashion in New York and spread thence to other cities."

Although Martha stopped jiggling after hearing that, she didn't stop attending the Bachelor Balls that made up the city's social season. She was what she guessed everybody would call a belle, and in that way as in others, she was luckier than her sisters who'd had dreadful rows with their father over whether dancing was harmful to a girl's morals. By the time Martha came along, he'd given up the fight, only insisting that she be properly chaperoned and escorted, which wasn't difficult with all those Roosevelt boys. Her mother's cousin, Cornelius Van Schaack Roosevelt—"C. V. S.," as everybody called him—had four lively sons, and she'd often played with them in their big house at Broadway and Fourteenth Street. Since they had no sisters they were fascinated with her as she, having no brothers, was fascinated with them. She didn't know whether she liked Theodore best because, although he was a little young for her, he was full of mischief, or Robert because he had gumption enough to shuck the family glass business and start a newspaper to reform the world. Whatever, to appear at a ball on the arm of one of the Roosevelt boys was enough to attract attention, since C. V. S. had been listed in Mr. Beach's book as one of the half dozen or so millionaires in all of New York. Sometimes Robert seemed almost ashamed of his father's money, claiming that it had all come from cheating the poor by using the inheritance from their grandfather to buy land from people wiped out in the depression of '37, but Martha would jolly him out of it by quoting about the only part of her father's preaching in which she really believed—that wealth, like beauty, was a sure sign of God's favor.

If she were, as she felt, blessed by God with beauty and the right connections, Martha Roosevelt Schuyler considered such rewards just return for spending so much time on her knees and saw no reason not to enjoy them. She was, therefore, a sunny girl, full of confidence and optimism and the good health that usually accompanies these attitudes. She was, indeed, a belle. Though she'd inherited her mother's pale gold hair, Martha was petite with finely chiseled features, dark brows and dark eyes, and she was said to take after her great-grandfather Jacobus and her Aunt Sally and Cousin Cornelius Van Alen and, when she was naughty as a little girl, her father would insist that it was the French blood coming out in her since he considered the French a wicked race. Far from being upset by her father's teasing, if that's what it was, Martha found it fascinating to be different from all the stolid Dutch in her lineage. Her mother, for instance, looked like a bolster tied in the middle and Cousin C. V. S. was so short and fat and solid that someone once described him as "a Hindu idol, roughly carved in porphyry." His sons, she thought, should thank the Lord that he'd married a Barnhill and watered the blood. While Martha wasn't sure she liked looking like Cousin Cornelius, who always sat behind them in church and frowned through the service, she was intrigued by her resemblance to his mother, about whom there were hints of a dark mystery. She'd sometimes be sent from the room when Aunt Sally's name came up in conversation, and Aunt Sally was never, never seen in church or in their house.

Fortunately from Martha's point of view, her father regarded it as a Christian duty for her to spend a lot of time at Lafayette Place as a companion for little Sophie Van Alen, who had no brothers or sisters. While the girl herself had seemed too dumb and drab and young to be of interest to Martha, going to see her had been turned into an alluring risk by all those mysteries surrounding the Van Alen household. When Cousin Cornelius had first invited her to visit Sophie, her mother had said, "I'm not sure we ought to risk it, James. Nobody seems to know what disease Augusta is suffering from—it could be consumption, or worse; you know, Commodore Vanderbilt has had to have her mother locked away in McDonald's Asylum over on Long Island. Besides, I don't think your Aunt Sally and her friends would be the best of influences on a young girl." And her father had replied, "All you say may be true, my dear, but Cornelius is one of the finest Christian gentlemen I know, and we are obliged to do anything we can to help relieve his sad situation. I'm sure, if we pray over it, our Martha will be protected from harm and with her sunny disposition she should do them all a lot of good."

Again fortunately, Martha was not at all protected by prayer from what she was certain her father would look upon as harm. It wasn't infection of the body to which she was exposed since she seldom saw Sophie's wraith of a mother, who kept to her bed; it was contagion of the mind from Aunt Sally, who seemed to like her right away. "You've got all the charm your father used to have as a young man," she said, "but, without, thank goodness, his piety. I think we can do a lot with you." The "we" was not only Aunt Sally but her fascinating friends who would drop by of an afternoon for tea and sometimes a spot of very old Madeira. Almost as much as the conversation, a conspiratorial secrecy spiced these affairs for Martha. "When you see Cousin Cornelius, I don't think you should tell him Miss Fuller was here," Aunt Sally had advised her after the first such occasion. "Your Cousin Cornelius is a very fine man, as I'm sure your father has told you, but it upsets him to think that Sophie is exposed to such outspoken women. We've found that what father doesn't know, doesn't hurt him, haven't we, Sophie?" And Martha had begun to feel less sorry for Sophie, who had looked almost attractive when she grinned

355

and said, "Oh, yes, grandmother. Do you think I could grow up to write for the papers like Miss Fuller?" and her grandmother had said, "I don't see why not. As she was saying, a woman can do anything these days. I envy you young girls."

Martha had never heard a woman talk as Margaret Fuller did. She'd come down to New York to work for Mr. Greeley's *Tribune* from a place in Massachusetts called Brook Farm, where young men and women from the best of families lived and worked together in what they called an ideal community. The women actually wore bloomers the way that Mrs. Amelia Bloomer advised in her magazine *Lily* and let their hair flow long and naturally. The women did all the cooking and cleaning while the men tended the farm, and in the evenings they would have discussions together in which even the men agreed that women ought to be equal partners in marriage. "I'm writing a book now," Miss Fuller said, "and in it I'm going to say that it is the fault of marriage and of the present relations between the sexes that woman belongs to man instead of forming a whole with him. Woman, if self-centered, would never be absorbed by a relation; it would be only an experience to her as it is to a man. It is a vulgar error that to woman love is her whole existence."

Aunt Sally had clapped her hands and said, "Oh, how I wish some woman had had the courage to say things like that when I was young. I would have known I wasn't alone."

It was easy enough for Martha to understand why her Cousin Cornelius, an elder in the church where her father was always preaching that woman, a creature out of Adam, must be submissive to man, would be upset by Miss Fuller. And she didn't even have to be warned about discussing the visits of Miss Amelia Downing, the one who always asked for Madeira, since she'd heard her father rant about Miss Downing all her life. When once Martha had wanted to go to Miss Downing's school, her father had said, "Never! I can't understand how any self-respecting parent would subject his daughter to the influence of such a woman. I think it unnatural that one so comely remains unmarried and downright sinful that she fills young female minds with the idea that, contrary to the word of God, they are equal to men." When in '45, her school was burned out, he had been almost gleeful: "It's the punishment of the Lord for her trying to tear this country apart by talking about freeing the sons of Ham."

Her father's attitude about slavery was a puzzle to Martha that became more complicated with her visits to Lafayette Place, where old Flossie, the only approach to a slave she'd ever known, was kept like a secret up under the eaves. "Look at Flossie," her father would say, "she was just as happy being a slave as she is now, and I can't see that her being free has made any difference." Martha had to admit that there was some truth to the remark. Flossie never went anywhere or did anything but spent her time waiting hand and foot on the sick Augusta or spoiling little Sophie with special delicacies she concocted when the cook was out of the kitchen. Moreover, Flossie tended to confirm her father by telling tales about life on the manor, about being with her own pappy and mammy and taking care of Martha's father when he was a baby that sounded as if it had been the best time of her life. Once Flossie said somewhat bitterly that these idyllic times came to an end because of "Mis' Sally's troubles when she disobeyed de Lawd," but no matter how she pried Martha couldn't get any more detail about the matter out of the old woman, and so the slip of the tongue, if that's what it was, simply added to the mystery surrounding Aunt Sally. Aunt Sally herself seemed a little embarrassed about Flossie. "I never wanted her, you know," she told Martha. "She was more or less thrust upon me, given to me by your great-great-grandmother, and I must say that I was relieved when the state made it impossible for me to keep her on as a slave since it had never rested well on my conscience. I don't think she's ever quite approved of me, but she dotes on your cousin Cornelius. She thinks of herself as more his mother than I am and credits herself with saving him for the Lord, as she does your own father, though James couldn't have been a year old when she left him. Well, I'm sure she'll get a reward in heaven for the way she looks after Augusta. For that I'm glad she never took advantage of her freedom to leave us, as my son Peter wanted her to do." About all that Martha could conclude from knowing Flossie was that her father might have a point: freeing the slaves didn't seem, as Miss Downing claimed, to be *just* a matter of passing a law.

If the fire had been divine punishment for her abolitionist activities, as the Reverend Schuyler claimed, Amelia Downing evidently didn't get the message. She had, in fact, given up her teaching and was always getting her name in the papers, like one of Mr. Barnum's oddities, for speaking out about freeing Negroes and women wherever and whenever she could be heard. Not only that, but it was a scandal of New York that she lived alone in a suite at the Astor House, instead of with one of her relatives, and that she was often visited there by men like Cousin Peter Van Alen whom Martha was dying to meet after she'd heard more about him from Aunt Sally and the others.

Amelia Downing was almost as formidable in person as in reputation. She was large in every way and handsome rather than beautiful. Like Aunt Sally, she dressed in the height of feminine fashion, corseting herself into tight bodices, wrestling with hoopskirts, fussing with ostrich feathers. "I'd love to get into some of those bloomers," she said, "but people think me queer enough as it is. Anyway I find that what I say startles them more when it comes from somebody looking like a lady." She was outspokenly but not unkindly critical of Martha's aspirations as a belle. "God, can you imagine being raised on the Bible and *Godey's Lady's Book!*" she hooted. "The poor girl hasn't had a chance. I wish I could have got my hands on her in school, but it may not be too late. We should sneak her into some of our literary evenings, Sally. It might open her eyes before she gives herself to some dull hardware merchant because he can waltz without stepping on her feet. I'm sure Poe, at least, would appreciate the scenery. Do you read anything, my dear?"

Martha, who was not without spirit, said, "Oh, yes. The Mr. Poe you mention appears often in *Godey's Lady's Book.*"

Amelia Downing sneered. "That trash. It's not the best of his work, or his mind, that you see there. But the poor man has to try to make a living. Yes, we'll have to take you along. I think he might be quite enchanted with you."

"I agree, and I wonder if it would be wise," Sally cautioned.

"Why not? Sally, I'm surprised at you. You aren't jealous, are you?" Amelia said. "Oh, I know you're half in love with Poe yourself, as I am, and Margaret Fuller, and . . . well, most of the women I know. But he doesn't belong to any of us."

"What about Fanny Osgood?"

"Fanny either. As far as I can see, women aren't quite real for Poe. We're figments of his imagination, his dreams. Except perhaps for Virginia—and she isn't quite real herself, like that wraith you've got upstairs here. Maybe Poe wouldn't be so damned melancholy if he could see that a girl can be both beautiful and healthy."

"I'm not so concerned about Poe as I am about Martha here. She could lose *her* head, as both of us know, and James would never forgive us if—"

358

"Heavens, Sally, you are getting cautious in your old age. Martha's old enough to take care of herself, and—"

"But I know something about the wrath of a pious Schuyler, and if I know James, he wouldn't approve of introducing his daughter to Poe—or any of the rest. Am I right, Martha?"

Martha nodded. More than Aunt Sally guessed, her father disapproved of what he'd heard about the New York literary scene; it was, in his eyes, almost as destructive of morals as the theater. Worse than what they wrote was their habit of gathering together in some salon, men and women alike, often without benefit of husband or wife, and indulging in radical talk about slavery, women's suffrage, love, and, for all he knew, some outlandish new religion like that of the Millerites with their wild talk of the end of the world or the Mormons with their lustful bigamy. Some of the women like that Miss Fuller and Miss Lynch and Mrs. Oakes were bold enough to have writings published under their own names. They were called the "starry sisterhood," but the Reverend James Schuyler could use a better name for them if there weren't ladies present. "They're the sort of people that Amelia Downing and Peter Van Alen consort with, and you girls know what an embarrassment they've been to Cousin Cornelius and the rest of the family," her father would say. It was more than implied that no daughter of the manse would ever be involved in such goings on, and, indeed, until Amelia brought the matter up, Martha, happy enough in belledom, had never aspired to join the "starry sisterhood." But with her eyes gradually opening through the conversations of Aunt Sally and her friends to the possibility of becoming something other than a wife, Martha wanted to test her wings in a society made, of course, more intriguing by her father's forbiddance.

"But . . . but I'd *love* to go, Aunt Sally," she said. "Why does father have to know? I could come over here to spend the night and—"

"That's the girl!" Amelia said. "What about it, Sally?"

"You two are certainly putting me on a spot," Sally said. "I'm supposed to be the older generation, you know, the guardian of morals. How would it look if I connived with a young girl to deceive her father?"

"Oh, come on, Sally, don't go holy on us," Amelia said. "You're already doing it when you expose her to me and Margaret and the others. Let's give this girl a chance to open her eyes."

"Well, all right. I have to admit that it could be interesting . . . ."

So on a cold, late fall night in '46, Martha Schuyler went with her Aunt Sally and Amelia Downing to her first literary evening at the home of Miss Anna Lynch, the poetess, in Waverly Place. A mild sense of sinning made her more nervous than she'd been at her first ball. She would have been happier with a robust Roosevelt boy to escort her, but then she had been promised the probability that her cousin, Peter Van Alen, would be there and would, if he were, look out for her. She might have felt more secure if it weren't true, as Amelia had suspected, that she read very little. Neither of her parents stressed wide reading as among the accomplishments essential for young ladies, her father judging from his knowledge of women so addicted, such as Aunt Sally and Amelia, that it tended to make them restless at the very least and rebellious at worst. Music had, however, been approved, and Martha, spending much of the idle time that would otherwise be devoted to reading at the keyboard of the family piano, had developed a real passion for it. So at least she had read one of the more famous poems by her hostess, Miss Lynch, *Farewell to Ole Bull,* since, music being without the power to corrupt, she had been allowed to attend the popular concerts by Mr. Bull, the Swedish violinist, and was attracted to the title.

If the Waverly Place house were a den of iniquity, it was certainly deceptive. A scrubbed little Irish maid of twelve or so met them at the door and led the way upstairs where they entered a gathering place that consisted of two parlors thrown open to each other to create a room the length of the whole house. Coal fires burned at either end; gilt-edged chairs and sofas lined the walls which were hung with portraits and two large and misty scenes of the Hudson River highlands by Thomas Cole. The only touch more daring than the furnishings in any other wealthy New York household Martha had seen was a plaster reproduction of Hiram Powers' statue, "The Greek Slave," which had caused such a fuss in the papers when it was shown at the National Academy for being the first exposure of female nudity in the city. The women were dressed as if for a ball, and the men wore black frockcoats except for one tall, stooped figure in a rumpled, slightly soiled white coat that was both out of place and out of season. Miss Lynch, standing with her mother by the black mantel of one of the fireplaces to receive her guests, was especially elegant in a tulle overskirt figured in lace and silver thread over pale blue silk. She was nearly as tall as Amelia but poetically thin, with large dark eyes and dark hair falling in water curls from a part in the middle. Martha had the wit to mention how much she liked the poem about Ole Bull, and Miss Lynch said, "Oh, it was just a trifle—at least that's what Mr. Poe thought of it. Isn't it dreadful the way he patronizes us? But I have to go along with Mrs. Smith and accept him for what he is—a genius. Look at him—he's over there now in the other room probably telling Margaret Fuller how shallow the criticism she writes for the *Tribune* is and making her like it."

When Martha turned she managed to pick out among the crowd the familiar figure of Miss Fuller sitting on a couch beside a man with a high pale forehead and full gray whiskers. They were staring in apparent fascination at a figure standing above them, as was another small and pretty woman who was sitting childlike on the floor at their feet. The man they were listening to was short, but he had an erect, almost military, bearing and was emphasizing his words with the practiced gestures of an actor. While he was dressed like the other men in a dark frock coat, his soft collar and loosely knotted cravat implied a careless scorn for the dictates of fashion. This must be the famous Mr. Poe! Just then a masculine voice sounded in Martha's ear. "So you're the Martha I've been hearing so much about? Has mother given you the cast of characters here yet? I see you've already picked out the darling of the ladies, my friend, Edgar Poe. And, in case you can't guess, I'm Peter."

Martha looked up into a pair of smiling, sea-gray eyes. Tall and thin, with a thick mane of wavy black hair, Peter Van Alen was, in Martha's instant opinion, even handsomer than Mr. Poe. From all she'd heard of him, she half expected he'd be wearing horns and a tail and breathing fire instead of flashing a sweet, dimpled smile like his mother's. He was unhappily quite old—over thirty-five—and, from what everybody said, a confirmed bachelor, though there was muted talk in her family about some Jewish girl and another scandalous affair when he'd been beaten up in the company of an actress. All she knew of him from hearing her parents talk was that he was a journalist who lived above his station in one of the suites in the new Delmonico's on lower Broadway that had to cost at least $60 a month; he was, in her father's description, "one of those ungrateful leeches, like that Amelia Downing, who suck up the blood Cornelius creates in the form of dividends and then spit it out as if it were poison." But

361

it was obvious from the way she spoke of him that Aunt Sally had a very different view of her second son; her only complaint about him seemed to be that he hadn't stuck to the writing of poetry that, she was sure, would have made him as famous now as Mr. Bryant or Mr. Poe or that Mr. Longfellow up in Massachusetts.

"Now let's see," he was saying. "Sitting on the couch there in front of Poe is Margaret Fuller—"

"Oh, I know her."

"That's right, you would—from mother's teas. Beside her is Mr. Bryant, the editor and poet. That matron pretending to be a little girl is the notorious Mrs. Osgood. And that fellow over there, the one in the white suit, is my boss at the *Tribune,* Mr. Greeley. Now, who would you like to meet? Poe, of course . . ."

Before she could protest that she'd be happy just to stand here and watch, Peter took her firmly by the elbow and started toward Poe. But there was a sudden silence in the room. The little clusters of chatting people broke up and receded toward the walls. Poe stepped out into the center of the opening between the parlors which was bordered with rich velvet drapery almost like the proscenium of a theater. "Oh, oh, he's going to recite," Peter whispered in her ear. "Probably *The Raven* again. Do you know it?"

"I . . . I'm afraid I'm not much of a reader."

Peter chuckled. "Well, at least you're honest. But listen, you'll like it."

When he raised and projected it, Poe's voice, though light, was as beautifully controlled as his gestures, and each word was pronounced distinctly with a modulation proper to its sense and feeling. *"The Raven,"* he announced, and began . . .

> Once upon a midnight dreary, while I pondered, weak and weary,
> Over many a quaint and curious volume of forgotten lore—
> While I nodded nearly napping, suddenly there came a tapping . . .

On and on the words flowed, and to Martha's ears they were like music, needing no meaning to convey a sense of melancholy beauty. Like a sad little melody threading through a sonata was the word of the raven, "Nevermore," and then the piece ended in a haunting minor cadence.

Transported, Martha found the polite applause that followed the

362

reading as shocking as if it had greeted one of her father's prayers in church. Before she could recover, Peter had propelled her right in front of Mr. Poe. His eyes were the most amazing she'd ever seen. Light gray and large, made larger by the tiny black dots of the pupils, they still seemed to be staring at that raven. Then suddenly they were looking at her, through her, into her soul. "Mr. Poe, it was . . . it was beautiful," she got out in some embarrassment. "I don't know much about poetry, but I do know music and it sounded just like music . . ."

Poe smiled broadly, took her hand and whirled her around as in a dance figure and called out to the whole company, "Look at this girl! I don't know who she is, but she is a *real* critic! She supports all I've been trying to say—that poetry should *be* music."

Martha blushed, and Poe took both of her hands and looked directly into her eyes and began speaking to her softly as if there were no other people in the room. "You are beautiful when you blush, Miss . . . Miss Martha, is it? Beautiful . . . tell me, do you dream?"

Somewhat startled at the quick shift, Martha said, "Yes . . . I suppose everybody does—"

"And of what do you dream? The soul lives in dreams, you know."

"I . . . I usually don't remember them. But I do remember one when I saw this angel, all shining and beckoning to me, and there was music all around. But it was around Christmas, and . . ."

Ah, I knew it," Poe said. "I knew it by your eyes that you are in touch with that other world, as I am, the shadow world of dreams, whose hidden music swells through space. It was your own soul you were seeing, I'm sure—all shining and blond like you . . . ."

Nobody had ever spoken this way to her (or perhaps to anyone else). Her father was always talking about souls, of course, but never in this way. Pinpointed by Poe's eyes and mesmerized by his voice, she felt dizzy . . . much like in the whirl of a waltz. Now she knew why so many women loved him, the way they loved a graceful dancer for the time that they were in his arms. Still, she was a little relieved when Peter Van Alen plucked at her sleeve and insisted that she come away to meet other people. Mr. Poe accepted the interruption graciously, bowing and saying, "You must come visit me at Fordham, visit me and meet my Virginia, my Lenore. She is too ill now to venture out —and in great need of angels."

When the time came to go, Peter went down and handed them into their carriage. In what Martha took to be a nice, if somewhat awkward, compliment, he said, "It seems to be my fate to find cousins fascinating," but he was looking beyond her at Amelia, who laughed. "This one's *very* distant, Peter, *and* young, so she's fairer game." Martha wanted to ask what that was all about, but, as soon as they were settled in the carriage, Amelia got onto another subject. "Fell right in love with Poe, didn't you, Martha? I could see it by your face. Well, join the crowd. It will do you a world of good if it just inspires you to read his work." . . .

It did. She read everything of Poe's that she could find, and of course she liked the poetry best because it was so like music, was music. The one about the bells absolutely rang in her head . . .

> Keeping time, time, time,
> In a sort of Runic rhyme,
> To the tintinnabulation that so musically wells
> From the bells, bells, bells, bells
> Bells, bells, bells,
> From the jingling and the tinkling of the bells . . . .

One day when she dropped in at Lafayette Place not long after the literary evening at Miss Lynch's, Martha found her Aunt Sally quite disturbed. "I've just had a visit from Mrs. Clemm—Mr. Poe's mother-in-law, you know," she told Martha. "I'm afraid that things are much worse out there at Fordham than we've supposed. Though she's a proud woman, Mrs. Clemm asked me for a little money to get a letter out of the post office, as she said, but I suspect it was for food. Ever since the *Broadway Journal* stopped publication Mr. Poe's had no regular income, and of course he had little from that. Mrs. Clemm is afraid that her Virginia may be dying—"

"Oh, is that what Mr. Poe meant when he said she was in need of an angel?"

"Probably . . . I've half a mind to go out and see for myself what's going on," Sally said.

"Oh, let's do go. *Now.* Both of us. Mr. Poe invited me," Martha said. "There's a train to Fordham, isn't there?"

There was a train that afternoon, and they managed to find a hack at the station to take them to the little cottage where the Poes lived. Though it was as spotless as the one Sally had visited so long ago on Carmine Street, it was smaller and more sparsely furnished, and there was no healthy aroma of cooking. There was, in fact, an odor-less chill in both the atmosphere and Poe's reception. He seemed embarrassed that Mrs. Clemm had gone to Sally and miffed that they had come to look on his shame. "I'd offer to take your wraps," he said, "but you'd best keep them on. We must conserve fuel. Coal is too dear and wood too scarce." He waved toward the little fireplace in the parlor where a few sticks were burning, then rubbed his hands together as if the warming gesture had become habitual. Sounds of coughing came from a door open to the parlor. "It's Virginia," Poe said. "Well, come . . . come see her, see the worst. Maybe she *will* think you're an angel, Miss Schuyler—an angel come to take her out of her misery. Come."

Uneasily, they followed Poe through the open door into a tiny room. There on a straw pallet on the floor, struggling for breath, lay Virginia. Her face flushed and eyes fired with fever, her hair loose and flowing, she was still strangely beautiful—and still shockingly young to be so wasted. Her only covering was an old military coat. Poe bent to snug it closer around her, saying as he did so, "Good material—sixteen years old—all I ever got out of my studies at West Point." Within the folds of the coat, next to Virginia's bosom, they could see a large tortoiseshell cat looking out at them with unblinking eyes. When Virginia wasn't coughing, they could hear the cat purring as if generating what heat it could for the sake of its mistress. Poe knelt and gently rubbed his wife's cold hands and feet. "Some grand ladies have come to see you, Virginia. You remember Mrs. Van Alen?" The girl's eyes turned up to them, and when she tried to speak, she started to cough again. Poe dabbed at her lips with a handkerchief that was soon spotted. He waved it at them like a flag and said, "This is what I live with day and night. Is it any wonder I dream of suffering souls? Go now, for God's sake, go."

Martha who had never before seen real poverty or illness could hardly wait to get into the crisp, clean December air. She thought that she might be sick in her stomach . . . as well as in her heart. Poe's eyes, those eyes that had so riveted hers at the party, were red and misted. Poe's tongue was thick and his breath smelled of alcohol. The shock of it all was almost too much to absorb. Having seen Virginia, she could hardly blame him for seeking some sort of solace, some oblivion, but it was all so terribly sad, like a scene from one of Mr. Dickens' books. How could a mind go on singing the way his did under such circumstances . . . ? Their hack was still waiting, and when Aunt Sally joined her in it she said, "Aunt Sally, what can we *do?*"

"I was hoping you'd feel that way, Martha. Well, to begin with we can certainly get some blankets to that poor girl, and I can spare some money for Mrs. Clemm to buy food and fuel. And perhaps we ought to get Peter out here. He might be able to do something about getting Mr. Poe more work . . ."

And so Martha became an angel more practical than the one in Poe's mind. Though they were able to make Virginia more comfortable, they could not save her, and early in this year of '47 she slipped away, leaving Poe to lament her passing in the only way he knew how . . .

> Come! let the burial rite be read—the funeral song be sung!—
> An anthem for the queenliest dead that ever died so young—
> A dirge for her the doubly dead in that she died so young.

During the months that Martha, often in company with Peter or Aunt Sally, visited the Poes, she became aware of rather frightening and perplexing changes in her outlook on life. She still went to the Bachelor Balls, but she found the young men who danced with her insipid compared not only to Poe but to her distant cousin, Peter Van Alen. She began reading works that Peter recommended and was finding new depths in the music she played, preferring now the full harmonics of Beethoven in something like his Sonata Appassionata to the bright trills of Mozart. Life, she was discovering, demanded the minor key for its fullest expression. When after Virginia died Mr. Poe wanted to go on seeing her, she agreed, deceiving in the process her Aunt Sally and Peter as well as her father. Only Amelia Downing knew about her activities . . . it was in her rooms at the Astor House that the secret meetings took place.

"Without you, I'm sure the poor fellow would come apart altogether," was Amelia's excuse for participating. "He's not only lost his Lenore, but all those silly married women, like that Mrs. Osgood, who thought it safe to flirt with him while *he* was married have fluttered back to their perches like a bunch of chickens when the fox gets into the coop. I can certainly understand how you've been losing your heart to him, Martha, but, for God's sake, don't lose your head. Just be nice to him for a while until he gets over this. For the long run, he's a weak man who's bound to bring grief to any woman, and you don't need that. If you get too involved, I'll never forgive myself for starting this thing, but right now I'm happy about it . . . you're surely much more of a woman than the pretty belle I first met."

Despite that advice, Martha wanted to be in love with Mr. Poe, wanted to find in the man himself what she heard in his words, and she almost managed it. When they met, he was gentle and gentlemanly, asking only for her presence. "Just being in the same room with you, I absorb your health, your strength. I'm uplifted by your beauty. I only wish that I had something to offer you in return," he'd say. She tried to reassure him that he'd given her more than he could ever know by opening her mind to the beauty of the word, but he was not consoled. Soon he began missing meetings. Once she heard that he'd been up in Massachusetts knocking at the door of a woman with whom he'd corresponded and later found unconscious in a hotel room from an overdose of laudanum; another time Peter Van Alen had discovered him dead drunk on the steps leading up to Mr. Greeley's office, fortunately before the editor could see him. He was pitifully apologetic about these lapses, going literally on his knees to her and asking forgiveness and then saying, "they'd never happen if only I could have you always by my side. But I can't ask you to share the life you've seen, and I know that your family would never help us." Martha would talk bravely of getting employment, perhaps taking in music students and he would shake his head. "No, I couldn't live that way . . . we must wait until I get my magazine started. It's to be called the *Stylus* and have the best of American literature in it and will, I'm sure, make money. I'm giving a lecture at the Society Library this month to raise funds for it . . ."

By staying over at Lafayette Place again and persuading Peter, despite his reluctance to visit his brother's house, to escort her, Martha arranged to attend the lecture. It was a raw, blustery February night, and less than sixty people struggled out to huddle together in the cold hall. A simple counting of the house made it obvious that the lecture was a financial disaster, but she was sure that Poe would at least make an artistic triumph of it with the melody of his verse. Instead, he ruffled a sheaf of papers on the lectern in front of him and said, "Tonight, ladies and gentlemen, I shall discuss my ideas on the cosmogony of the universe . . ." Though he recited the words with the same theatrics he would have used with poetry, they meant nothing to her, nothing at all

... "An inspection of the universality of gravitation—i.e., of the fact that each particle tends, not to any one common point, but to every other particle—suggests perfect totality or ..."

Peter whispered in her ear, "My God, the man's gone mad!" It was exactly her own thought, and Martha felt so embarrassed for him, so fearful for him that she could no longer stay another second. Her heart was already beating oddly. When she got up to go, Poe glanced up, shrugged and went on with his reading.

In the vestibule she broke down, leaned against the wall and cried. Peter, following, found her there and offered her a handkerchief. "I'm really sorry, Martha. I didn't know he meant so much to you. I just thought you were playing Lady Bountiful like a proper New York belle when we went up there and—"

"Oh, please don't talk about it."

"But we *must.* Poe isn't the only poet who's lost his heart to you."

Shock after shock. All she could think of to say was, "But you're my cousin, Peter."

And he said, "Yes, and isn't it wonderful that the Dutch believe in marrying cousins?" ...

That same night, lying awake and listening to the February winds howl outside their bedroom windows, the Reverend James Schuyler said to his wife, "You know, I think Martha's spending far too much time over there at Lafayette Place."

"It was your idea," she reminded him.

He let out the despairing sigh of a man confronted with irrefutable feminine illogic and said, "Well, I guess we'll just have to pray that she comes to no harm," and then began, "Dear Lord . . ."

It wasn't often that Peter Van Alen was "summoned into the presence," as a call to see the editor in his office was known around the *Tribune* shop and he was a bit apprehensive. Not that Horace Greeley was inaccessible—far from it; almost any citizen of New York could climb the single flight of iron stairs leading to Greeley's office overlooking City Hall Park and just walk in. Like the rest of the *Tribune*'s new building at Nassau and Spruce streets, the editor's office was wholly functional. There was a tall stool at a reading desk, two cane-bottomed chairs that were uncomfortable enough to encourage short visits, a huge desk littered with papers anchored by a paste pot and box of sand behind which Greeley sat in a swivel chair on a small island of rug in a sea of bare pine. Above the editor's head a huge pair of scissors swung on a pulley and weight arrangement so that he could haul them down to clip any item that caught his interest. Beside this contraption hung a cord on a bell to summon a copy boy who, in turn, summoned Peter.

It was near noon on a day in late May and Greeley had just come into an office he wouldn't leave until near midnight or whenever the paper was put to bed. When he took off his hat, a shower of memos he'd stored overnight in its crown drifted to the floor. One of them read, "Send Van Alen to cover the race." By the time Peter arrived, Greeley was already "pushing the quill," as he called the act of writing. With his left hand anchoring a sheet of paper, his right hand covered it with ink as fast as he could move the pen. He didn't stop or look up. Some visitors regarded this as a gross discourtesy, as had Peter's cousin, the Reverend James Schuyler. Because of Greeley's reputation for giving away money and because of their shared interest in prohibition, Cousin James had come to ask for help in a project to save the souls in Five Points from the demon rum. He had talked away for half an hour to a writing Greeley who finally had glanced up and said, "What do you really want? Make it brief." The Reverend Schuyler had replied, "I want help to save thousands of our fellow New Yorkers from going to hell." At that, Greeley had snapped, "Not a cent. Not a damned cent! Not half enough of them go there now." When Cousin James indignantly repeated this to Peter, he had trouble controlling his laughter. It was typical of a Greeley who, when he was tired or out of sorts, could be, as one staff member described him, "ferocious as a baited bear." It wasn't, however, typical of a Greeley who would risk his own reputation and that of his paper on behalf of almost any worthy-sounding cause. The reforms he favored were as serious as curbing the extension of slavery and promoting the unions of workingmen and as silly as advocating his wife's Graham bread cult and Mrs. Bloomer's pants. He'd been nearly laughed out of town when he treated the first women's suffrage meeting up in Worcester, Massachusetts, seriously; the other papers cartooned his ungainly figure in skirts and cried, "The Reign of the Petticoat!" So Peter had been surprised at the treatment accorded Cousin James— surprised and secretly pleased . . .

Now as he stood before Greeley's desk, the editor said without missing a stroke of his pen, "I guess I gave one of your relatives shabby treatment the other day. That gruel Mrs. Greeley served me for breakfast didn't sit well or something. Probably too late to make amends except that I got a request from another of your relatives yesterday . . . ."

"Oh?" Peter said, wondering who it could be. Amelia, no doubt, since she doted on Greeley for his stand on women. He was in for another surprise.

"Your brother Cornelius," Greeley said. "Wants the *Tribune* to cover the great race the commodore's rigged up between his modestly named vessel the *Cornelius Vanderbilt* and Captain Law's *Oregon*. Seems it will prove Van Alen boilers superior to all others, or something like that. Ordinarily I think steamboat racing's a sin because it's killed too many people, but I think there may be more than meets the eye in this race, so I want you to cover it."

"Why me? Isn't it a conflict of interest? I still own stock in Van Alen & Son, you know—"

"I have faith that such a circumstance won't alter your judgment, Peter. It will just give you more access to the story than others. I hear for some reason that the commodore wants your mother with him in the pilothouse. Please give her my regards—she's a woman I much admire."

Greeley sanded the sheet he'd been writing on and reached for the copy boy's bell cord; Peter understood that he had been dismissed. Back at his own desk, Peter groused to everyone within hearing: covering a steamboat race was an assignment for a cub reporter and not the paper's literary editor. Henry Raymond, whose view of the boss was being soured by the editor's devotion to what he called "Greeley-isms," agreed: "Sometimes I think the man's mad. I'm going to get out of here and start my own paper as soon as I can scrape together some money, and I think you should too. But then you tried that once, didn't you?" Charles Dana, who had the sweet disposition one might expect in a former inmate of that ideal community, the Brook Farm, took another tack: "Uncle Horace never does anything without good reason. I think he wants more than the story of a boat race, Peter, and he knows you're the man to give it to him."

As he thought about it, Peter decided that his only recourse would be to dignify the assignment by giving Greeley much more than the story of a boat race; whether he'd print it or not would be up to him. Peter knew as much, if not more, of what was behind the race as his editor suspected. Largely through Amelia who persisted in harassing Cornelius by attending the stockholders' meetings of Van Alen & Son, Peter was kept abreast of the business. It remained one of the wonders and mysteries of life for Peter that he and Amelia were still such good friends after what they'd known and experienced with each other, and it was one of the reasons he could go along with Greeley's faith in the inscrutable wisdom of women. Having, as they both agreed, nothing to hide from each other and having, as she'd finally made him realize, nothing to gain from each other, they were extraordinarily free to talk together about anything and everything. He knew that it was considered somewhat of a scandal that he was so often in her rooms at the Astor House or she in his at Delmonico's, but as Amelia was always pointing out, this flaunting of convention made their relationship an important statement to the world about how men and women should be free to associate with each other as friends as well as lovers. She was always making statements of one kind or another, and gradually Peter acknowledged that she'd been right in insisting that she wasn't the woman to share his life. The trouble was that he hadn't been able to find a woman enough like her—with enough independence to be interesting—yet different enough—with, to be honest, enough respect for the superiority with which a man was supposedly endowed—*until* he met Martha Schuyler. One of the things he liked best about Amelia was that she'd recognized the possibilities immediately. "A charming girl, really, though how she's managed it with a father like hers I don't know. Must take after her Aunt Sally," Amelia had said. "But let me give you a bit of advice . . . let her get Poe out of her system. He's doing a lot of work for you in touching her heart and wakening her mind. Every woman has a Poe she ought to get out of her system before she settles down to something more reasonable. I suppose you were mine. Well, keep after that girl, Peter—and don't let Cousin James stand in your way."

Among the things that Amelia had told him when they weren't talking about more interesting affairs of the heart was that Commodore Vanderbilt with his boats on Long Island Sound coining money had decided to go back into competition on the Hudson River. The situation on the river was changing so that the commodore thought that there were lots of dollars to be made by the kind of competitive daring he'd shown in the early days of steam. The novelty of just being able to get to Albany more or less on schedule by way of a steamboat had long since worn off, and people were tiring of the Spartan accommodations, the noise and filth of the old clunkers that the Hudson River Association kept in service until they blew up or sank. Travellers with long memories talked longingly of the old days of the great sloops when a vessel like Cornelius Van Alen's *Lady Lydia* with its elegant appointments, good food and wine, made the voyage a delight instead of a drill. Much to Commodore Vanderbilt's chagrin, the first man to sense this change in mood was his shrewd competitor, Daniel Drew, who built for his People's Line to Albany a three hundred-foot steamer with berths for five hundred passengers which he called the *Isaac Newton,* but which the press dubbed "the floating palace." At one of the Van Alen & Son meetings the commodore, seeking assistance in the form of both funds and a new and improved engine, said, "By damn, there *must* be money in it. That bastard Drew ain't wasted a cent all his life 'cepting trying to buy his way into heaven by putting up that seminary."

"What about the agreement you signed when the Hudson River Association bought you out, commodore?" Cornelius asked.

"Dead as a doornail—time's run out on it."

"Drew's a pretty strong competitor," Cornelius said.

"Oh, I ain't worried about Drew," the commodore said. "Ain't we gettin' along fine together splittin' up the Stonington run on the Sound? 'Sides, I got my brother Jake skippering one of his boats and my son Billy clerkin' down in his bank. Drew can't put anything over on me I don't know about. But if anybody else tries to get into it, there will be hell to pay."

By the time that the *Cornelius Vanderbilt,* more than matching Drew's boat in size and magnificence, was put into commission, another Hudson River captain, George Law, who was tired of watching other men's wakes, launched the *Oregon.* Law's advertisements in New York claimed that the *Oregon* was the fastest ship on the river. The commodore fumed, "Only one way to settle it—race the bastard." Law accepted Vanderbilt's challenge, and a course was laid out from the city to a buoy off Croton Point and return—a distance of seventy-five miles—and a date decided, June 1, 1847. Nobody doubted that Vanderbilt, whose name was already legendary for great feats in the waters around New York and whose fortune, listed by Mr. Beach at $1.5 million established him as a winner in that trickier race for the dollar, would win. Still, it would be well worth watching, and a chance for the city's more daring gamblers to make a fortune on the odds against the *Oregon* if the impossible should happen. Informal races between steamers had long been one of the regular thrills and hazards of river travel: safety valves were tied down, pressure gauges ignored, and some eager skippers would even refuse to put lines out when they dipped into smaller ports en route, letting long-skirted women and doddering old men jump for it as they made a pass close to the wharf. But this would be the first match in which racing was the sole object of putting to sea. For those who found betting on the outcome too tame in view of Vanderbilt's reputation, bookmakers were also giving odds on which of the boats would explode first.

By the day of the race, excitement was high enough in the city that Peter Van Alen found himself the object of envy by his fellow editorial workers on the *Tribune* as he set out for the wharf. It was somewhat humbling to reflect that his account of the race would be read more avidly by more people than his lyric critique of *Omoo, a Narrative of Adventures in the South Seas,* by a promising young New York writer named Herman Melville. Whoever this Melville was, he hadn't made his way into the salons of the literati, and Peter made a mental note to look him up. Together with the book Melville had published last year—*Typee: A Peep at Polynesian Life, or Four Months' Residence in a Valley of the Marquesas—Omoo* sparked Peter's appetite for adventure like nothing since those days when he wanted to be fighting in Greece with Lord Byron. He wondered why he'd allowed himself to be trapped in this city that grew dirtier, noisier, more crowded by the month instead of shipping out to the South Seas like Melville or around the Horn to California like that fellow Dana who'd written so well about it in *Two Years Before the Mast.* But over thirty-five, it was quixotic even to allow himself to dream of such adventures. He'd thought briefly about getting a commission to join the armies in Mexico, but it was in his view a war without cause, and he let himself believe that principle rather than age and distaste for danger kept him home. The time to have gone was back in '37 when Cousin Francis Livingston had invited him to Chicago. He knew by the exchanges that Livingston's paper was one of the most influential in the West, and he would have been its editor instead of an ink-stained wretch that Greeley could order around as he pleased.

Except for the lovely Martha, Peter could have felt sorry for himself this day. Participating in this event on the river reminded him too forcibly of that other, earlier time during the Erie Canal celebrations when he'd been virtually out of his skin with an excitement that came not so much from events without but stirrings within, from those dreams of the glory he'd see in what he was sure would be his charmed life. What had happened to that Peter Schuyler Van Alen who'd thought he could, should, be everything, do everything, know everything? Had he had the stuffings truly knocked out of him on that dark night on the Bowery or had his spirit been drained with his sperm in that time out of time in a Broadway bedroom? Or—and this he could not bring himself to face—had there never been such stuffing, such spirit? Other people still had faith in him, particularly his mother, who thought that he should go back to writing poetry, and Amelia, who thought that he should embark on a great novel about America's greatest city, New York, and now hopefully Martha, who didn't seem to care what he did but called him the nicest person she knew. Knowing himself, he often wondered why they felt this way. One gift of the last twenty or so years, a gift he hadn't wanted to accept, was an unnerving realism. As for poetry, he was intelligent enough to be aware that he had not the mad imagination of a Poe nor the abandon to enhance his visions with drugs at the probable cost of his life, and while he could perhaps be a Bryant, who labored as drudgingly as a clerk at his desk at the *Post* and with his flowing beard and mane looked as stately as a man aspiring to be a statue, he had no taste for verse born out of logic rather than that passion in which his own Dutch nature seemed deficient. Writing a novel did remain a possibility, but he doubted that he would ever find the energy for it unless he withdrew from the hectic world of journalism, which at least kept him too busy to indulge often in this kind of morose thinking. With an income from his stock that made pleasant living possible and a time-consuming job, he was, in fact, mostly comfortable, and comfort was not, he felt, the soil in which greatness grew. Was he doomed, as so many other sons of the New York rich seemed to be, to fritter away his life in essentially frivolous pursuits? He hoped not; he profoundly hoped not. The sorriest fact of his situation was that he had lately found himself envying from time to time his brother Cornelius for the avarice that drove him and the religion that sustained him. There was no evidence from any quarter that Cornelius had to endure, as he did, nights of doubt or days of despair. Cornelius had always known who he was and where he was going:

heaven was his destination, and dollars stood as milestones on his upward path. At halfway through the biblical span of life, Peter was uncertain both of the road he was traveling and where it led. When he'd complained about this feeling once to his mother, she'd said, "I'm a good deal older than you, and I feel the same way." When he'd discussed it with Amelia, she'd said, "Well, at least you have your eyes open . . . most people who think they know where they're going are like horses with blinders, and you wouldn't want to travel that way, would you?" Perhaps there would come a time and place for a call on the only gifts he was conscious of possessing—that realism that came from honesty and those open eyes that came from curiosity —but it was not yet, and it was not here, and it was galling to discover that when he went aboard the *Cornelius Vanderbilt* the most important thing about Peter Schuyler Van Alen was that he was his mother's son . . . .

Commodore Vanderbilt at fifty-three still had the strength and vigor he'd banked in his body in those early years of personally tending sails and oars on his periagur, and he studied Peter boldly with his bright blue Dutch eyes much as he'd probably appraise one of the trotters he was always buying to improve his stables. "Humm, Sally's other younker, eh?" he said. "Well, any son of my favorite lady's welcome, though I don't hold much with writing. Only book I ever read's *Pilgrim's Progress,* and I ain't planning to read more. Must say, though, you're a sight more of a man than that squirt of a son-in-law I got."

"Will my brother be aboard, sir?" Peter asked—the probability of encountering Cornelius had been one of the reasons Peter hadn't liked his assignment.

"Him?" Hell, no. He'd never take a day away from that damned desk of his. But your mother's coming and that little younker of his, Sophie. Wouldn't sail without your mother. Did she ever tell you how she helped me break the goddamned monopoly?"

"Yes, sir, I was always proud of her for that."

"Damned well ought to be. Got a lot of Dutch in her, that woman. Come, let me show you around this craft."

Peter had already admired the lines of the *Cornelius Vanderbilt.* Long and narrow of beam, she had a hull that would slice through the water like a knife. Amidships she had paddle wheels two decks high on either side and above and between them the swinging metal rocker arm that would drive them. Just forward of the wheels were the twin stacks and boilers of the engine. Her length was such that the double decks of windowed cabins and salons seemed trim and low, offering a minimum of resistance to the wind that would flow over them when the vessel was under way. The commodore, who'd met Peter at the gangplank, first led the way aft on the lower deck through a seemingly endless passageway on to which opened the doors of snug sleeping rooms. Rather astonishingly, sweating crewmen were dragging the mattresses and bedding from the rooms and piling them on the wharf. When they saw the commodore, whose brass-buttoned uniform was as close to that of a navy officer as regulations would allow, they dropped their burdens and saluted. "None of that, damn you," he told them. "Get busy and lighten this ship." At the stern they climbed a stairway to an awninged deck from which more crewmen were flinging every chair and bench that wasn't bolted down to hands below them on shore. "Every ounce counts," the commodore said over his shoulder as he proceeded through swinging glass doors into the main salon, where their footsteps on planking stripped of its carpeting echoed in an empty shell of a chamber from which all the overstuffed furniture had been removed. "Ain't much of a floating palace now, is it?" The commodore chuckled. "Takes a lean horse to run a good race." But Peter could easily imagine how the salon with its large windows on either side and its mirrored columns running down the middle would normally be an elegant perch from which to watch the high, wooded cliffs above the Hudson flow by. Forward of the salon was a bar where a black man was packing away bottles to cart ashore. "Hurry it up," the commodore said. "No need for spirits this trip, though my guests will be disappointed. From what I hear Law doesn't have the guts to run a dry ship, and he'll catch hell from me for it." Next came the machinery, about which Peter knew so little that he could only look in awe on the maze of wheels, gears, pistons, boilers all freshly painted, polished and oiled, but he felt a surprising twinge of pride when he noted a Van Alen & Son stamp on one piece of metal. Husky, bare-chested men, as sooted as actors in black face, were already shoveling coal into the fireboxes. "Keep that steam up and forget about the gauges, boys," the commodore said. A winding stair led them on up to the pilothouse. A curious five-sided affair perched above all decks, it offered a commanding view to either side and out over the needle-nosed forward deck, where passengers who wanted wind in their faces could promenade; angled half-windows on either side of the stairwell allowed the pilot to see astern.

Peter's mother and his niece Sophie were already in the pilothouse by the time they reached it. The Commodore gave Sally an affectionate hug and picked the little girl up and chucked her under the chin, saying, "Not much of a younker to look at, but smart as her grandmother, ain't she?"

Peter who'd never before seen Sophie thought that her grandfather was cruelly correct about her looks. He'd heard that the child was outrageously spoiled by Flossie and part of that spoiling had to be too much food, for she was far too fat; her only redeeming feature was blazing blue eyes like her grandfather's. "Now you stop that, Corneel," Sally said. "Wait till the child gets her growth. How's *your* Sophie by the way? I hear you're bringing her home from the asylum."

"Wouldn't if it were up to me," Vanderbilt grumped. "Can't stand her around the house, but the younkers are always after me. They say I'm cruel to leave her there."

"I agree with them . . . oh, this'll be good news for Augusta. She's been so worried—"

"Ought to worry about herself 'stead of her mother, if you ask me," the commodore said. "At least Sophie was able to have a passle of younkers even if half of them aren't worth a damn—"

"Corneel!"

"Now you know me, Sally. You can say a lot of bad things about me, but I ain't one to mince words about anything. Billy's beginning to show some promise, and so's little George, but if I could take my name back from that Cornelius I would. Ain't enough that he falls down in fits but he's been falling down drunk too. Good Christ, I don't know what I'd do if I couldn't get out of that house and tend to business. But no more talk about the family. We've got a race to run . . . . Ready to go, captain? Everybody else aboard?" the commodore asked a quiet, bearded man who except for a nautical cap was wearing civilian clothes in suitably humble contrast to his splendidly uniformed employer.

"Aye, aye, sir," the captain said, and stuck his head out the open pilothouse window and called out, "Cast off all lines," then picked up a speaking tube to the engine room and ordered, "Full ahead, slow." As the paddles began to turn and churn the water, he said quietly to the seaman at the wheel, "Left rudder."

The *Cornelius Vanderbilt* slid away from the wharf and headed out to the middle of the river, where the *Oregon* was already maneuvering along a starting line that had been set up between two ferry boats that were dangerously topheavy with passengers who'd paid to get a close look at the racers. The commodore invited Peter down to meet his other guests but said, "Sally, you and the younker best stay here. Some men think women aboard on a thing like this bad luck, though I know different." There were a dozen or so men looking lost in the empty reaches of the main salon. Some were aldermen whose names Peter recognized; one was a congressman, another the pastor of the Dutch Reformed Church from which the commodore stayed away—"Need God on our side today," he said in a winking aside to Peter. The commodore apologized for the sparse accommodations and lack of refreshment but assured his guests that there would be plenty of excitement. "Stay off the foredeck," he advised, "or you'll lose those expensive top hats to the wind we make."

At the starting line, the two vessels saluted each other with a dip of the ensign and then parted to make wide circles that would bring them across the line just as the gun sounded. The commodore stood with a watch in one hand and the speaking tube in the other. As they straightened out and headed toward the line, he shouted down the tube, "This is the commodore. Get up that steam, goddamnit, get up that *steam.*"

The double stacks of both boats were laying down long black streamers. White froth spouted from their wheels and sprayed from their bows as they charged across the line. They were running bow to bow and stern to stern and so close that it was possible to make out the faces of Captain Law and his crew in the *Oregon* pilothouse and to recognize some of the distinguished guests crowding the windows of the salon. There were far more of them, and most were holding glasses which they raised in taunting salute to the guests aboard the *Cornelius Vanderbilt,* whose dry state had evidently been made known to them. "Law thinks it's a goddamned party, but he'll soon learn," the commodore said, and shouted down the tube, "More steam, damn you, more steam . . ."

Peter left the pilothouse and wandered around the vessel in search of color for his story. Despite her size, the *Cornelius Vanderbilt* was

378

shivering with strain; her great rocker arm clanked and clattered; the water washing through her wheel housings and under her counters hissed like escaping steam. In the engine room, the black gang cursed and groaned as they shoveled, and the engineer, a phlegmatic man, betrayed a nervousness he tried to deny by sending a stream of tobacco juice sizzling against the pipes every time he glanced at the gauges that were bouncing against the upper limits of pressure. In the salon and on the afterdeck the guests were in a grumbling mood. "Wouldn't have come if I'd known the commodore took this so seriously—man could die of thirst on this ship," said one. "Know something about engines, and I see he's got the safety valves tied down—think we're in need of prayer, reverend," said another. But, as the racing vessels passed one of the old Hudson River steamers and left her stumbling in their heavy wakes, a kind of awe silenced the passengers. "This is incredible," said one of them who'd had some experience at sea. "I calculate we're making close to eighteen knots. If we live through it, we can say we've gone faster on water than any men in history."

When Peter got back to the pilothouse he saw that the seaman had stepped aside and the diminutive figure of his mother was handling the big wheel. For all her sixty-seven years, Sally looked like a girl . . . her cheeks were rouged with the flush of excitement, her eyes were dancing. "She feels like something alive," she was saying. "Just a touch and she'll turn. It isn't like the old *Bellona,* is it, Corneel?"

"Not by a damned sight, but we ain't gained an inch on Law," he said and turned to the tube. "More steam down there, you bastards!"

Incredibly, in little more than an hour, they had the turning point in sight. The commodore took over the wheel, saying, "It ain't that I don't trust you, Sally, but I want it said that Corneel Vanderbilt won this race, and here's where we'll get him."

As they neared the buoy, the *Oregon* suddenly began dropping behind. "What's the matter with the bastard—bust a boiler?" Vanderbilt said, and his captain replied, "No, sir, I think he's just slowing for the turn, and we should too."

"Like hell!" the commodore said, "This is where we take the chicken-livered bastard. You watch me and you'll learn a thing or two, captain."

The *Oregon* had the inside position on the turning buoy, but they were now just far enough ahead that the commodore spun the wheel and brought the *Cornelius Vanderbilt* across the frothing bow of its rival with only inches to spare. Little Sophie covered her eyes, and Peter could hear the captain whoosh as the breath he'd been holding came out in a rush. But the commodore was chuckling. "Learned that on the track where you've got to get the rail to win. Now we go!"

The buoy was abeam, and the commodore threw the wheel hard over. The huge boat heeled so sharply into the turn that its off-side paddle wheel came clear of the water and ran free, shaking every timber in the hull. For the first time, Peter's pulse began racing; something would surely break. But his mother, while absently patting a terrified Sophie on the head, was jumping up and down and saying, "Go, Corneel, go . . ." The vessel righted herself and raced on, but her forward motion had been so great that she was sliding sideways in the turn. Astern, the slower *Oregon* came around tight to the buoy and began pouring on steam again. By the time the Cornelius Vanderbilt was back on course, they were looking squarely at the *Oregon's* saucy stern.

"Damn," the commodore shouted. "It's sunk me. What the hell's the matter with this tub that she don't turn? You oughta known that, captain. You're fired . . ."

Peter never admired his mother more than he did in that moment. "It's not his fault, Corneel," she said. "He tried to warn you and you wouldn't listen."

Her words brought the fuming commodore back to his senses. "You're right, Sally, it's my own damned fault." Then he turned to Peter and said, "Don't you put a word of this in your goddamned paper. Nothing all them old birds sitting around their stuffy clubs in the city would like to know better than that Commodore Vanderbilt lost his own race. That is, if we don't catch the bastard."

They didn't catch the bastard. For the next tense hour and a half, the *Cornelius Vanderbilt* plowed through a black fog of smoke rolling from the *Oregon's* stacks. There in the pilothouse, they almost had to eat it. Nobody could think of anything helpful to say except for an occasional curse of sheer frustration from the commodore. When the finish line was in sight and it was clearly impossible for them to overtake the *Oregon*, Sally Van Alen put a tentative hand on the commodore's arm. "I'm sorry, Corneel," she said. "I guess I didn't bring you luck this time. Maybe I've outlived my luck."

The commodore, who'd been chewing all this while on an unlighted cigar, took out a match, struck it, puffed the cigar into life and blew a cloud of smoke into the air. He seemed curiously at ease for a man who hated to lose. "Ain't your fault, Sally," he said, "and don't you worry about it. I been thinkin'. If that bastard won the race, he's just lost himself a boat. Captain, tomorrow we cut our rates in half, and if that don't work in a few weeks we cut 'em in half again. If necessary we'll *pay* people to ride the *Cornelius Vanderbilt* to Albany until that son-of-a-bitch Law knows he's out of business. You can put that in your paper, son. For a while anyway, the real winners of this race will be the people of New York."

It wasn't a bad line, and all the way back to the office Peter pondered using it. Actually, though, the long-range significance of the race was that it had taken only three hours and fifteen minutes for the boats to cover seventy-five miles, an amazing rate of speed that, if it could be attained and sustained by larger boats on the ocean, would make possible a crossing to Liverpool in five or six days. In the end, Peter decided to turn his piece into a paean to progress instead of a carping comment on the commodore's ruthless commercial tactics as he'd half had in mind. Greeley, who tried to look on the good side of things, would like that, and so would his mother. For the first time he thought that he understood why his genteel, poetry-loving mother seemed actually to like a foul-mouthed old sailor like Vanderbilt; she'd exhibited in that pilothouse a reckless streak of sheer delight in physical adventure that matched the commodore's own. What a man she might have made, Peter thought, and then rethought and starting laughing aloud at himself: wouldn't Amelia want to strangle him with her bare hands if he ever expressed such a thought? Somehow he'd got himself mixed up with the most baffling women, women who neither thought nor behaved like other people's mothers and sweethearts. He didn't know whether to consider himself blessed or damned by this; perhaps only time would tell . . . Meanwhile, he ought to be working out a lead on that story. It could go something like this . . .

"Although the smart New Yorkers who thought that they had their money riding on a sure bet might not agree, the whole world won in yesterday's great race between the *Oregon* and the *Cornelius Vanderbilt*. The speed generated by these two floating palaces will ultimately shrink the globe on which we live and bring all mankind into closer touch . . . ."

Yes, old Greeley would like that sort of thing . . .

Chapter *XVII*

The Nuptials and the Nightingale

Sally Schuyler Van Alen didn't know when it was that she began to think of herself as a survivor. Quite possibly it had something to do with reaching in this year of 1850 the biblical definition of man's alloted time on earth, "three score years and ten." Except for a little stiffness in the joints on cold mornings and a little more trouble with her alimentary canal than she could remember from times past, she didn't feel old, and yet so many friends and family members had gone before her that her own condition of survival did become a matter for reflection. Many had been the times when she'd thought surviving a curse, God's judgment on her sins, but, oddly, the longer she carried on, the more she valued the simple fact of waking up alive every morning. If and when she did have to go, though, she'd like it to be in sleep, as it had happened a year or so ago with her brother Peter. One afternoon he'd stayed slumped in his chair at the Century longer than usual, and when a worried porter tried to wake him, it was discovered that he'd fallen into eternal sleep.

She wondered whether Peter had been blessed with any interesting insights about life or visions about death in those last slumbering minutes. They'd said that he had died with a small smile on his face, and she liked that. Quite probably he'd been rolling over in his mind one of those wry jokes that he seemed to treasure increasingly toward the end. Perhaps it was the one he was always telling about the election of '48 when poor Cousin Matty didn't get a single electoral vote. "Shows you what new principles can do to an old politician," Peter had said. "When the once loved 'northern man with southern principles' came out against the extension of slavery, he got only nine votes south of the Potomac—all in Virginia. Van Buren's Free Soil Party screamed that the count was a fraud, and one of the Virginia election judges agreed, 'Yes, fraud! And we're still looking for that son-of-a-bitch who voted nine times.' " Poor Matty up there in Lindenwald tending his famous onion patch and trying to rewrite history in an autobiography. Poor Peter, dead with only the smallest notice in the papers that he'd once been a senator. It took a great effort of her will to see them once again as they'd been in those days of the hopeful little band at Richmond Hill. They'd had such high hopes, and now she wasn't sure whether, in the light of all that had happened, Peter's quiet, tolerant pessimism or Matty's gallant and crusading last stand was the way a life ought to be brought to an end. She guessed that the difference was that a lot of people laughed with Peter, and a lot of people laughed at Matty; what they shared was that nobody in recent years had taken either of them seriously.

Whether life itself ought to be taken too seriously was becoming a large question in Sally's mind. She'd had her worst troubles with the serious-minded like her father, like her son Cornelius, like her nephew James. Both Cornelius and James had raised almost as much of a fuss as her own father when Martha had eloped with Peter, and she had very nearly had to leave Lafayette Place for good for her part in it. Both Martha and Peter had wanted her to make her home with them, and she had thought long and hard about it but had decided that, regardless of what he'd said, Cornelius needed her more. Augusta, poor thing, was incapable of running a house or being a mother to Sophie, who was getting into those years when a girl most needed a mother, and now that the California gold rush was so stimulating the shipping business, Cornelius was almost frantic with work. The decision hadn't been easy even so, since her dutiful efforts to understand and love Cornelius were less and less successful with each passing year. The man was hard—and getting harder. She'd read somewhere that a diamond was made from carbon under great pressure, and she'd begun to think of Cornelius as a kind of diamond which nothing could scratch. That old joke they'd made in Wall Street after the Barker affair—"diamond cut diamond"—was no longer funny to her, and yet it bore on her conscience that it had been she, after all, who had allowed the pressures to accumulate on Cornelius. Well, better a diamond than crushed rock, old Cornelius might have said, and perhaps that was right. Nevertheless, she preferred the image of strength Aaron had once applied to her—the willowy bamboo.

There was something, she thought, of that bamboo in Peter, as well there ought to be. She knew that his sensitive nature had often been bent nearly to the ground by the buffeting of very strong winds of passion and disappointment, but somehow it had always sprung up again—and gone on growing. She had expected some form of greatness from her son born of fire, and she still did. Although he was nearing forty and was settled down with a wife and son who, thank the good Lord, put in an appearance more than a year after the elopement, Peter still seemed open to new thoughts, new adventures. If it hadn't been for the boy, he'd probably have jumped on the first ship headed for California gold. What he had done was almost as daring: he'd let himself be nominated on the reform ticket for alderman, and, even though the Tammany bullies had attacked his workers at the polls and stolen a number of ballot boxes, he'd won because of the strong support from Mr. Greeley at the *Tribune.* Peter had, of course, made light of his motives. "It's just a thank you to Uncle Peter," he'd told her with a laugh. Everybody had been surprised, and Cornelius had been outraged, when Peter turned out to be sole heir under his uncle's will, but then it had been dated clear back in the twenties when Peter was still in college. Sally knew that her brother had been disappointed in Peter, but it was characteristic of the attitude he'd fallen into in his later years that he hadn't bothered to demonstrate it by changing his will. There wasn't much left, of course—a few thousand in stocks and the old marble house which Peter promptly turned over at a good profit to a man who wanted to build a warehouse on the site. Peter was sentimental enough to salvage some of the marble to make a magnificent foyer in the new brownstone he built on Twenty-Second Street as a showplace for Martha's entertaining, and she had no doubt that there was some real sentiment, too, in his decision to go into politics. But Peter was motivated by more than sentiment, and it made her nervous to think of what it might lead to within the family.

"Mother, I think you'd better warn Cornelius and the commodore that I'm out to see that the taxpayers of the city aren't cheated on contracts and land sales and street railway franchises the way they've been," Peter had told her. "Thanks to Uncle Peter and your good sense in making me hang onto the Van Alen stock, I'm not bribable like most of those fellows. I'm going to be watching them all like a hawk, and of course they're going to be watching me too. If I let any favoritism to the Van Alen interests pass unnoticed, they'll have me by the scruff of the neck. I happen to know already that that dandy cousin of mine, John Charles Smith, Jr., was the man buying off enough councilmen and aldermen to get the city practically to give away those waterfront leases to Cornelius. With the buildup of shipping to California he's making a fortune on dockage alone, but then you probably know that. Well, I can't do much about past history, but tell him to watch out in future."

She didn't know anything about the waterfront leases, or much else about the business these days. By issuing stock in the form of bonuses to officers as planned, Cornelius had managed to put enough into the hands of himself and George Smith, as treasurer, and his brother John Charles, as counsel and secretary, to give them easy voting control of the company short of a virtually unanimous stockholders' revolt. Amelia Downing, the company's chief heckler, had seen this coming and had quietly started buying up stock on the open market, but she could still vote only two thousand shares against ten for Cornelius and five each for the Smiths. She'd tried to persuade Sally and Peter to follow her example, but Sally had been reluctant to take her money out of sound real estate and Peter had never had a dollar to spare. The result was that Sally had been voted off the board of directors in favor of John Charles Smith, Jr., with Cornelius making the same apologies that he'd made to Uncle Peter: "You're getting on to seventy, mother, and you have a right to take things easy. Besides, business is moving so fast these days that . . . well, it takes a younger mind to cope with it."

John Charles Smith, Jr. Bad enough that Cornelius had employed for so many years his older brother, George, who, in Sally's opinion, had no more morals than a shark. But then George was a salesman whose love of fast horses, fine wines and fattening foods brought him into contact with an element in the New York business world that Cornelius couldn't, or wouldn't, know. Morals were not essential equipment for a salesman—indeed, they might be an encumbrance—and for the most part Cornelius used George somewhat as he would a tool in his factory. Since she'd had so little use for George's parents, she hadn't been surprised at the way he turned out. There were times when she still thought that her husband George just might have become a decent human being without the influence of his brother-in-law, and she would probably carry to her grave the scars from the snubs her sister-in-law, Charlotte Van Alen Smith, had inflicted before her relationship with old Cornelius provided her with a shield. Well, both the elder Smiths were dead now, and she supposed that God was having a difficult time accommodating their restless, social-climbing souls. How they produced a son like John Charles, Jr., was something of a mystery. It was easy to see that, like George's, his good looks and bad habits came directly from his father, but he possessed a quality notably lacking in his parents—brains. He'd been at the top of his class in Columbia and had a reputation as one of the smartest lawyers in New York. Before his death, her brother Peter had commented bitterly and, as she thought, out of some jealousy at being replaced, "Oh, he's smart all right—smart as only a man of no principles can be. He doesn't give a fig for truth in a case before the courts, only for winning." Well, maybe John Charles, Jr.—or Charlie, as his cronies called him—would just be another of Cornelius' sharp tools, but Sally wasn't so sure. You can cut yourself with a tool too sharp if you don't handle it just right.

Like George before him, Charlie had sought out Cornelius, had almost literally begged him for a job when it became apparent that their profligate father had left nothing behind, and the only money in the family was the small Van Alen holding in their mother's name. Naturally, the Smith brothers felt that they were on a path to greater riches by improving the fortunes of Van Alen & Son, as inheritors of their mother's stock, than by working for wages elsewhere, and Cornelius was shrewd enough to see the potential value of such motivation that he couldn't find in others. Just before her death, which resulted, fittingly and horribly, from choking on a piece of underdone beef at a fashionable dinner party, Charlotte Van Alen Smith revealed that her son Charlie's brains must have come from a more distant ancestor, possibly old Cornelius Van Alen . . . "It's just humiliating to see *my* sons work like slaves for that little clerk, Cornelius Van Alen."

The funeral for Charlotte Van Alen Smith, who had kept up her pew rent at Trinity, was itself a social occasion, drawing a number of the most prominent families in the city. Sally and Cornelius had felt it incumbent upon them to attend, and she had found the rector's fulsome thanks to God "for the Christian witness of this noble woman" even more difficult to take than the Reverend James Schuyler's unsubtle evasion, all those years ago, of anything that could be construed as favorable comment on the characters of George and Aaron. It was hard to tell what effect their mother's passing had on the Smith brothers, but, as in that other funeral where Charlotte herself had been the only noisy mourner, their sister was the sole member of the congregation with the bad manners to sniffle aloud. Although she hardly knew her, Sally did feel sorry for this woman, who, having inherited an overabundance of the equine features of her mother and Lady Lydia, was living out her life in shy spinsterhood. Lucy Smith's only sustaining interest had been in acting as a kind of social secretary to her mother, and the sorrow errupting in her sniffles was no doubt the result of a sudden confrontation with the fact of the lonely, idle years that now stretched ahead of her. Why she had the impulse to get involved in such things was still somewhat of a mystery to Sally, but she decided there at the funeral that she might be able to do something for Lucy by introducing her to Martha, who now had need of that superficial but special talent for putting the right people together that seemed to run down through the Wentworth blood. Yes, she'd do it, even though Peter might not like it. There were times when she and Amelia Downing and Martha just had to go ahead regardless of Peter, who remained sweetly naive about the machinations of women.

For example, Peter still thought after two years that the elopement had been his idea, which, of course, was exactly what she'd wanted. When Martha first came to her with the confession that she'd fallen out of love with Poe and in love with Peter, Sally had been secretly pleased but openly discouraging. "Peter is quite a bit older than you, dear," she'd said, "and then there's your father to consider. What would he think?"

"Oh, I don't think Peter's that old—at least he doesn't seem that way to me," Martha said. "But you're right about father. I can't even imagine talking to him about it. You know what he thinks about Peter and his literary friends, and . . . well, even about you . . ."

"You wouldn't want to marry without your father's consent?" Sally asked, testing slightly.

"You did, didn't you?"

"Yes, and it has not made my life easy. I wouldn't wish it on anyone."

"Would you do it again?"

"I don't know, I just don't know. But I . . . well, I had no choice . . ."

"That's just it. Neither do I, Aunt Sally. I love Peter, I know it. And . . . and he loves me, I'm sure of it. Has he ever mentioned it to you?"

"Not yet . . ."

"He will. I know he will. But what do we *do,* Aunt Sally?"

At that moment she hadn't a good answer for the girl. She'd found that, in the end, life consisted more in dealing with what actually happened to you than in doing what you decided to do, but that sort of wisdom of the aged was quite fortunately lost on youth. So her stalling answer at the time had been, "Well, let's think about it . . ."

She, at least, had done a great deal of thinking. What sense could be made out of the fact that, of some five hundred thousand souls in the city of New York, approximately half male and half female, her son and grandniece had picked each other out and thereby created problems for themselves that went far beyond the normal problems of a man and woman relating to each other? Was it once again evidence of her growing belief that life was unpredictable, uncontrollable, or was it a simple and understandable cause and effect proposition? She and Amelia had begun easing Martha out of the parsonage because they had thought, or sensed, that she had talents that would otherwise go to waste and had, in the process, introduced her to Peter. In all honesty, she had never anticipated anything more than a cousinly relationship growing out of this introduction, but, again in honesty, she had to admit that she was glad that it had. Quite selfishly, she could anticipate that a wife and possibly children would more effectively anchor Peter near her in New York than anything else and, also quite selfishly, she could anticipate that Martha would be a daughter-in-law in whom she could take real pleasure. If these two married each other, she might have a refuge from Lafayette

388

Place, from the invalid daughter-in-law, from the driven son, from the often despairing granddaughter, from the doddering old slave. Sally felt entitled to see at least one house of happiness built in her time, and she thought that Martha and Peter were as likely architects of such a project as any she'd met. So her first impulse was to go to her nephew James and reason with him. But the same instinct that had guided her in the past held her back: people like James who thought they'd seen the blazing light of truth were blinded to the small light of reason. If James even suspected his daughter's interest in Peter, he would find ways of imprisoning her and perhaps ultimately poisoning her mind. And so by the time Peter did talk to her, she had decided that James must be left out of it; as old Cornelius had so often said, and demonstrated, a *fait accompli* was the best way of doing business with unreasonable people.

Peter was blunt when finally he brought it up. "Mother, what would you think if I married Martha?"

She was purposely evasive. "Isn't she rather young for you, Peter? She's a pretty girl, I'll admit, but she's had nothing in her head but being belle of the ball and—"

"Oh, that was more than a year ago, mother. She's changed. Maybe I have to thank Edgar for that, but she's serious now. You know, she's introduced me to a whole new world of music and—"

"That may be, Peter, but she's still the Reverend James Schuyler's daughter, and he'd never consent—"

"Why not? Oh, I know we've had our differences—Cousin James and I. But I *am* Cornelius' brother and . . . and your son . . . and—"

"Yes, you are my son, and that's probably the problem. But you know as well as I do that James doesn't approve of your way of life or the way you think, and I'm sure he'd rather have his daughter end up a spinster than marry you."

"Well, I'm going to have that girl; we love each other. I gave a girl up once because of her father but not again. And don't remind me of what you went through, mother. Times have changed. This *is* the middle of the nineteenth century."

"But I'm afraid that people don't change with the times."

"*Some* people do. Martha has. You've seen it with your own eyes, haven't you? She's told me that she doesn't care what her father thinks."

"Then she *is* most unusual," Sally said, but Peter missed the wry note.

"Yes, she is unusual, isn't she, mother? You do like her, don't you?"

"Yes, I like her . . ."

"Well, then, it's settled. I'm going right to James and ask for her hand."

"And what if he says no?"

"He really *can't* say no—not if he cares a whit for his daughter's happiness."

"From his point of view, that would be precisely *why* he would say no. He wants to have his daughter join him in heaven. Take my advice, Peter, and think this over very carefully. *Please.* Unless you go about it in exactly the right way, James will see to it that you never see Martha again."

"He's already making it difficult. About the only places that I can see her for a few minutes are in church or up at Lafayette Place, neither of them favorites of mine. Apparently he's suspicious of something. Martha says he's grumbling now about how much time she spends over at Lafayette Place, says Sophie ought to be old enough to find friends of her own. Mother, I'm afraid time is running out on us."

This was news to Sally, and she decided to stop playing games. "Well, I hope you're not thinking of doing anything rash, anything you might regret, like eloping . . ."

Peter's face lit up. "Why not?" he asked. "Why not? Martha's twenty-one and—mother, just tell me when she's going to be over at your place next, and I'll line up a preacher and get a ring and—"

"Now, Peter, I can be no part of such a scheme, and you know it. Cornelius would be furious to think that we used his house to violate his friendship with James, and rightly so."

"Well, there's nothing to keep Martha from taking a walk—and not coming back."

"Oh, yes there is. There's me. An old lady with any good sense isn't supposed to let a pretty young girl go out alone. Anyway, I've told you that I don't think you should do anything rash. I think you and Martha ought to have a good talk about what you really should do."

"But where? How? I've told you that Cousin James is keeping her on a very short leash."

"Well, Martha's coming over next Wednesday to go shopping with Sophie and me. We'll be looking at gloves down at A.T. Stewart's around noon—they have a sale on. I don't suppose that I can do much about your bumping into each other in a public place . . ."

To cover her own tracks, Sally had somewhat overreacted to the strange disappearance of Miss Martha Roosevelt Schuyler from the glove counter of Stewart's Department Store in the middle of an ordinary Wednesday. She summoned Mr. Stewart himself, who in turn summoned police. A search was made of the store, including all of the ladies' dressing rooms, and then of its environs on Broadway. The hubbub, of course, attracted reporters, and a story was certain to appear in the morning press. She'd tried to be vague in her descriptions of the young woman, but Sophie, still in the dark and frantic with fear for her favorite cousin, was explicit, down to the color of the buttons on Martha's dress. Sally could only hope that Peter had planned well, because Martha would be a marked woman as soon as the story broke. Her most difficult task in giving them as much time as possible was keeping the truth from poor Sophie, who sobbed all the way home in the carriage. One thing Sally had not anticipated, however, was that the police and reporters had gone at once to the parsonage with the result that when they reached Lafayette Place they found the Reverend James Schuyler pacing the parlor.

The look on his face, the anguish in his voice . . . "Oh my God, my little Martha, how could you have let her out of your sight, Aunt Sally? How? Oh, my God . . ."

He was not swearing but praying, and Sally felt genuinely sorry for him. She was trying to think just what to say when Sophie explained, "It isn't grandma's fault, Cousin James. Martha said she was going off to try on a dress, and . . . and . . ."

"I don't know what to do. I just don't know what to do," James said. "This is prayer meeting night and I've sent out word to as many of the congregation as I can to join me in prayers for her. I want you to come, you and Cornelius. I've sent word to him too . . ."

Cornelius had evidently received the word and just at that moment arrived, breathless from running up the stairs. He went right to James, took his hand. "James, I've been praying for you all the way over here."

"Thank you, Cornelius. It's all we can do."

Cornelius turned to his mother and Sophie. "What happened? How could you . . . ?"

It was time for some version of the truth. "Now listen to me, Cornelius, and you, too, James. This has been hard enough on me without the two of you accusing me of losing her, as if she were a baby or something. She's a grown woman—and a capable one at that. I've been thinking this over, and I don't see how harm could have come to her—the kind you seem to imagine—without her fighting or screaming and rousing the whole store. Hasn't it occurred to you, as it's occurred to me while I've been thinking, that she might just have run away of her own volition?"

James seemed baffled. "Run away? From what? Not her home, not her mother and me. We love her, she knows that."

"I'm sure that's so, James. You may even love her too much. I've heard that you aren't receptive to her beaux . . . ."

"Beaux? What beaux? She has none that I know of."

"James, how could you possibly be so blind? She's been the belle of the New York balls this past year or so. She must have hundreds of beaux, but I'm afraid your attitude just hasn't earned her confidence."

"If you're right, it's worse than—"

"James! You can't mean that. At least I can say this for the way you've brought up your daughter: she knows only the right people. I'm sure any man she chooses would be acceptable. If I were you I'd look into some of the young men she's been associating with . . ."

"By George, you may be right, Aunt Sally. I'll start with those harum-scarum Roosevelt boys—"

"I'll go with you," Cornelius volunteered.

As they were leaving, Sally said, "If I were you, James, I'd call off that prayer meeting tonight. It might look ridiculous if my hunch does turn out to be right."

When they'd gone, Sophie, her alarm turned to fascination, asked, "Grandmother, do you really think that Martha ran away with a *man?*"

"It's more likely than that she came to harm. We'll just have to wait and see."

"Oh, how romantic! I think I'd like to do that."

"Now, Sophie, get such nonsense out of your head. It would kill your father."

There she went, spouting the received truth to her granddaughter even as she stood guilty of plotting to "kill" Martha's father, of having long ago "killed" her own. She was constantly guilty of mouthing moral cliches, because she did think that people who lived by the rules had an easier time of it, and she could only wish for those she loved an easier time than her own. Only when there was no choice, only when something in your nature demanded that you take a chance, as it had with her, as she was sure it did with Martha and Peter, was it worth breaking the rules. There was much to be said for the excitement that only rule-breakers could know, but then there was often hell to pay. Where were Martha and Peter now? She'd made a mistake by raising such a fuss so soon, but at least she'd bought them some time by setting up a wild goose chase for James and Cornelius. It would take them most of the night, if not longer, to check out all of the young men whom Martha might know, and the process, bearing an element of hope, would relieve the anxiety of James and his wife. Knowing Peter, she was sure that he would find a way to reassure them, at least about Martha's safety, as soon as he saw the papers. She herself would have a sleepless night, for she had no idea what might happen when the truth was out. What a mettlesome old woman she was getting to be! Was she messing around in other lives because her own was so nearly gone? Why didn't she listen to her own cliches?

By midday on Thursday the New York papers had had a full run of sensation. The front pages of the early editions were dominated by the story of the mysterious disappearance of the beautiful parson's daughter who automatically became "the belle of New York" in every headline. The lack of any clues at all only whetted the imaginations of the writers who were free to speculate darkly on such fates as kidnapping, rape, forced prostitution, suicide. Strangely, elopement was never suggested; interviews with friends and family elicited the information that Martha Roosevelt Schuyler was a pious and dutiful daughter of the parsonage with no known beaux. A packed prayer meeting had been held in the uptown Presbyterian Church after all; the absent minister was pictured as a distraught father frantically searching the city's dark streets for his lost child. The supplications to God from hundreds of voices added a touch of majesty to the tale, lifting it out of the ordinary run of police stories. Martha became a symbol of all good, done in by a wicked and lawless city, and editorial writers used the event to scream for every remedial measure they favored from hiring more police to electing honest councilmen to instituting prohibition to sending niggers back to the south to limiting immigration. Whether on Wall Street or the Bowery, the talk was of nothing else; even in Five Points where mysterious death or disappearance was a daily occurrence, the idea that it might happen to one so pure, so elevated above life's miseries, was gripping to the imagination.

Reading all this, Sally was truly sick. It didn't help that when Cornelius came in, exhausted, discouraged and curtly silent after a long night of fruitlessly searching and praying with James, she couldn't find strength within herself to confess the truth. She realized that she'd have to do it—and soon—but she reasoned that it would be better after he'd rested. And then came the first edition of the evening *Tribune*. In many ways, the news it broke was even more sensational, coming as it did on the heels of the morning's horrible speculations. It was played as the classic happy ending, the princess rescued from the tower, the star-crossed lovers joined, all rolled into one. Peter had written one of the stories himself, but Sally liked to think that he had had nothing to do with the headlines: MYSTERY SOLVED—NOT MISSING BUT MARRIED; THE BELLE OF NEW YORK IS HAPPY BRIDE. What Peter had written, she was sure, would be talked about in New York for a long time to come. He had tried to save her own skin, but she doubted that it would work. She read the story over several times before she decided that the best thing to do was to go right up to Cornelius' bedroom and wake him and let him read it, too, come what may.

"The mysterious disappearance of Miss Martha Roosevelt Schuyler was," Peter had written, "a flight into love. This day, the lady who *is*, in the opinion of your correspondent, the first belle of New York became his lovely bride.

"The marriage was performed in the Afro-Methodist Church by its pastor, the Reverend Ebenezer Brown, and is, therefore, sanctified in the eyes of the Lord. It was witnessed by Miss Amelia Downing and Mrs. Ebenezer Brown and is, therefore, legal in the eyes of society.

"Both Mrs. Van Alen and this correspondent wish to extend their apologies to the press, to the police, to our families, to anyone who feels deceived by the fact that we did not make our intentions known. We can only plead the urgency of our affections for each other and remind the reader that St. Paul advised that 'it is better to marry than to burn.'

394

"Mrs. Van Alen and your correspondent will be 'at home' at Delmonico's for those who wish to extend their congratulations. Congratulations to your correspondent are certainly in order since the furor aroused by his bride's supposed disappearance shows the esteem in which she and her family are held by the citizens of New York. I can assure you that, however high this esteem, it is no match for your correspondent's own."

It was a most curious story, but it was, of course, filled out with sidebars revealing the whole circumstances surrounding it and an editorial by Mr. Greeley who maliciously chided his counterparts in the morning press for their jumping the gun before the facts were all in and for their low and alarmist view of the human condition. The new Mrs. Van Alen was, in Greeley's view, an example of the healthy, modern young woman who knew her own mind and had the courage to act upon her convictions; she would be a welcome member of the *Tribune* family. The rival evening papers were less respectful, one headlining the event as CLANDESTINE AFFAIR CONSUMMATED TO CONSTERNATION OF ALL, but most, largely owing to the fact that the "culprit" was one of their own, took a reasonably charitable view of the affair, as in another piece headlined ALL'S FAIR IN LOVE AND WAR. What couldn't be denied by Sally Van Alen, trudging up the stairs to awaken Cornelius with the news, was that the marriage of her second son had become the talk of the town at a time when even the most celebrated nuptials were decorously announced in a paragraph or two and would, therefore, be an embarrassment to them all. Well, life had a way of getting you by the throat. As if the elopement weren't enough, that touch of being married in a Negro church was a true nose-thumbing to society, and she wondered whether it had been Peter's idea or Amelia's. Whichever, it would make matters worse.

Possibly because she'd been raised to accept slaves as a natural order of life, Sally could not get as exercised about the institution as these young people, like Amelia and Peter. She could recognize slavery as a theoretical evil that should not be extended and would, therefore, have supported Cousin Matty in the elections if she'd had the vote. But there was an emotional, irrational element involved on both sides of the actual practice of slavery that young people like Amelia and Peter didn't recognize or appreciate. She'd found Peter's frustration at not being able to get Flossie to take advantage of her

395

freedom rather sadly amusing. In truth, she herself would have preferred to have Flossie go, because she'd found hired help easier to manage and more efficient—a fact that she thought would finally dawn upon Southerners and bring an end to the institution. But, for good or ill, all of them, and especially Cornelius, were "family" for Flossie who would no sooner leave them than leave her own children, if she'd had any, and, in return, Sally could no more "fire" Flossie than she could fire family. They were thus bound together by invisible chains of emotion stronger than those monstrosities that abolitionist cartoonists draped on runaway slaves, and she could imagine that much the same situation existed on southern plantations. Secure in this relationship, Flossie, more meddlesome maiden aunt than servant, was freer than any mere employee to try with either favors or frowns to manipulate their lives. Though she'd never come out and said as much, Flossie had made it clear over the years that she didn't approve of Sally, whose "sin" had resulted in her being snatched away from her own family and from her "firs' chil'," the baby James, but Flossie's adoring devotion to Cornelius in a difficult time had more than made up for her attitude of disapproval as far as Sally was concerned. Having Flossie around was for Sally like having one of those familiar small aches that remind you that your body is mortal and would be missed if it went away. In any case, out of her experience with Flossie and her parents on the manor, Sally had a feeling that the slavery issue was too complex to benefit from gestures such as Peter had just made. Even if true, this public acknowledgment that the black people were as good as whites would arouse the rabid on both sides of the question, among them James and Cornelius. It was one of those inexplicable ironies that both of them, so beloved by Flossie for turning out to be such Christian gentlemen, had accepted her slavish devotion as proof positive that "good niggers" enjoyed servitude, as God had intended. Yes, Peter had quite definitely thumbed his nose at them, adding insult to injury.

So Sally was understandably anxious as she shook Cornelius out of a too-short sleep and handed him the papers. He grunted and fumbled on the night stand for the half glasses he'd recently taken to wearing, a discouraging reminder to Sally that her son—her *son*—was nearing fifty. She watched his face while he read. Those dark brows of his came together to form a straight line, his thin lips worked, his jaw muscles tightened. He threw the papers aside in disgust and looked up at her over the glasses. "Mother, what did you have to do with this?" he asked.

"Why . . . why, nothing. You can see that Peter even writes that he deceived his family—"

"Mother, I don't believe you. I hate to accuse my own mother of lying, but I do. Martha wouldn't even have known Peter if you and Amelia hadn't taken her to one of those literary meetings you're always attending—"

"How . . . how did you know that?"

"Thank God Flossie isn't a liar. I know a lot more than you think I know about all those freethinking ladies you've had here to tea who have obviously corrupted James' daughter."

Oh, Lord, she really should have got rid of Flossie. What more had Flossie told Cornelius? Her heart began to thud. "They're my friends. I have every right to entertain my friends."

"In my house?"

"It's half mine—"

"I'll buy you out."

"Cornelius!"

He was speaking in that calm monotone that Sally knew expressed more rage than a shout. "Now, mother, I'm going to try to keep my temper and speak reasonably," he said. "It's long past time that we had a talk. I've tolerated what I've known was going on here out of gratitude for what you've done for me and out of respect for a pledge I made to God that I would take care of you when I saw the way my father treated you. And I'll admit to being selfish, too. With Augusta sick all the time, and a child to raise, having you here has been the easy way out for me. But it has gone too far. I now fear for my own daughter's morals. You're putting nonsense into her head the way you did with Amelia and Peter and—"

"So you want me to go?"

"I don't *want* you to go. I just wish you could . . . could change."

"I'm a little old to change, Cornelius, and if I did, it probably wouldn't be in a direction you'd approve of. Now that we're having this honest talk, I want you to know that it hasn't been easy for me all these years to tolerate your . . . your priggishness. I've done it because I've felt responsible for your having had the kind of father you had, for having had the kind of life you've had, and because I've been grateful for the load you've borne . . . . No, it hasn't been easy for me—torn between two sons . . . . But you wouldn't really have had a home if I couldn't have endured it . . . and . . . and now . . ."

She hadn't meant to resort to tears, a feminine weapon she'd always considered unfair in dealing with her sons. She'd expected anger from him but not rejection. This on top of the tension and emotion of the last day were more than she could contain. Although she didn't exactly break down, she could feel the damp of tears running down her cheeks and couldn't trust her voice to go on. But Cornelius who'd dreaded to see her cry on the few occasions when she hadn't been able to help herself seemed this time unmoved. He kept staring at her over those ridiculous glasses without a flash of feeling in his dark eyes.

"Well you might weep, mother," he said. "This is truly a sad day. Can you imagine what this is going to do to James? His daughter's disobedience spread all over the front pages. The girl he raised in the fear of the Lord married to a noted freethinker and . . . and libertine. And in a *nigger* church . . . I don't see how James will be able to rise and face his congregation. I can only thank the good Lord that I've gone to the trouble to inform most of my friends that I have nothing to do with that brother of mine. Yes, well you might weep, mother. If I didn't know you better, I might be able to understand this as some foolish female sentimentality, but you've never been that kind of woman. Why *did* you do it? *Why?*"

At least his voice was rising, and he was losing his awful calm while curiously hers was returning. "Your assumption that I did anything is unfair, Cornelius," she said. "*I* could not prevent Martha and Peter from falling in love with each other, *I* could not keep your brother from coming into a public place—and I swear to you that I didn't see him there. As you know, I did everything to try to find Martha after she disappeared. But if you want my honest opinion, I don't think that this is a sad day at all. I'm delighted with this marriage, and I think James should be, too."

"Mother, you've always been blind about Peter—"

"No, it's you who are blind about Peter—you and James. Peter is a good man, a kind man, a sensitive man, an intelligent man, and the day will come when you'll be proud to call him brother and James to call him son."

Cornelius snorted, "I'll never live to see that day! Nor James ei-

398

ther, I'm sure. What sort of a *kind* man would embarrass all his relatives by getting married in a nigger church and boast about it in the papers? No, mother, for once you can't excuse him—"

"Well, perhaps there was no other place—"

"Nonsense, and you know it. Why didn't Peter go like a man to James and ask for her hand?"

"He wanted to, but . . ."

"Ah, so you did know about it?"

"I wasn't sure . . ."

"But you could have warned James. Mother, why *didn't* you?"

"Because in matters involving the heart, James is an unreasonable man. And you are, too. I think it may be high time that I leave. I've always thought that you needed me, but I guess I've been wrong. I'm sure your God will take care of your sick wife and lonely child and tell you when you've taken the wrong track in business. I'll go—I know when I'm no longer wanted." She started to leave, then turned back and added, "By the way, I know something about real estate, Cornelius, and I'll be wanting a very good price for my share of this house . . ."

It had taken a long while for this storm to blow over. She had left Lafayette Place on that same day and had gone down to live with Amelia Downing in the Astor House. Cornelius' first feeler toward reconciliation had been unfair and rather cowardly in her view; he had let Sophie come down to plead with her. The girl had been so devastated by her grandmother's going that Sally had almost caved in, but fortunately she had held out until Cornelius came himself, literally hat in hand, to fumble out a form of apology. It was an act so difficult for his nature that it almost amounted to a touching declaration of love. What he'd actually said would have been funny if it hadn't been so sad in all its connotations: "Mother, I just can't work for thinking about what might happen to you. I've been taking care of you for so long that . . . well, this just isn't *right.*"

So she'd come back, against everyone else's advice. After all, Cornelius *had* been right in suspecting her part in an affair which from his point of view had brought disgrace and disaster upon his friend and pastor, and playing the injured innocent beyond reason didn't become her . . . .

As to whether Cornelius was also right about the damage the elopement had done to the Reverend James Schuyler and his family she wasn't so sure. James had certainly seen the affair in as black a light as Cornelius. He had, however, been able to force himself to climb into the pulpit on the next Sunday where he had delivered the shortest sermon of his career; "I, who cannot control my own daughter, feel no longer competent to lead this flock. I therefore tender my resignation as your pastor." His congregation would not, of course, accept it. They reassured him that it was the sort of thing that could happen in the best of families; some ladies even went so far as to suggest that it was all rather nice and romantic. While he had been sufficiently consoled to stay at his post, James had proved a true chip off the old Schuyler block in his letter to Martha: "You have broken your mother's heart, and shamed me before the world. Under the circumstances, you would only add to our embarrassment by appearing in what was once your church or making any effort to return to what was once your home. As for your husband, if I ever set eyes on him, I will cane him on the spot. I would urge you to pray for God's forgiveness, but I am too weak and human to offer mine." In the two years since, however, the splash that Martha and Peter had been making in the society and politics of the city had, according to Sally's information, been mending Mrs. Schuyler's heart and easing James' embarrassment. The Reverend Schuyler's real embarrassment had, in fact, become the necessity of inventing lies to hide the family rift when people kept congratulating him on his stunning daughter and prominent son-in-law and new grandson.

This was far from being an accidental development, as Sally well knew. As soon as she'd received her father's note, Martha had come to see Sally at the Astor House. With her spirits still high from all the excitement of her daring deed, Martha had been more angered than aggrieved. "Can you imagine—disowning me for getting married, and to one of the city's most famous journalists? How old-fashioned!"

"What did you expect, my dear? I warned you."

"Oh, I know, Aunt Sally. But I guess I did think that, once it happened, he, or at least my mother, would accept it. Peter put that thing in about St. Paul to show them that we were trying to do the right thing."

"I rather thought that it sounded as if his tongue were in his cheek, and perhaps your parents did too," Sally said. "Couldn't you at least have found another minister?"

"Amelia found him for us, and we really didn't have time to make other arrangements, but he was a dear—and so sweet and solemn. I really do feel married in the eyes of the Lord, and I can tell you I'm not ashamed of it. Oh, I do love Peter so much—"

"That's nice to hear, Martha. At least you have each other."

"Oh, we do, we do! Aunt Sally, I'm not going to let daddy make me unhappy. Do you know that I've already received notes and some visits from my friends, even some of the young men who claim they're crushed that Peter got me first? Everyone thinks it's so exciting and romantic, and they're dying to have us to dinner to hear all about it. We'll be in all the best houses in New York, and when *that* gets back to my parents, they'll change their attitude—"

"Are you so sure, Martha? Your father has a lot of his grandfather in him."

"Yes, I'm sure. If there's one thing daddy, and particularly mother, admire as much as piety it's social success, and I'm going to be such a success that they'll come to me. You watch . . ."

Well, Sally had been watching, *was* watching, and it was one of the things that made waking up each morning still an adventure. She no longer saw James, who had chosen to express his anger for whatever part she might have had in the affair by staying away from Lafayette Place, but she could get an occasional glimpse of his thinking from Cornelius. For instance, when the boy had been born, Martha had sent a loud and clear message by naming him James Schuyler Van Alen, and the Reverend James Schuyler had nearly relented. "He wants to baptize his grandson because he's afraid they'll have him baptized by that nigger," Cornelius had reported, "but I argued him out of it. I told him that, if our pastor condones elopement, no parents of girls in our congregation, including myself, could rest easy. Anyway, I doubt, knowing Peter, that they'll even bother with baptism." At that point, Sally had thought it prudent not to tell Cornelius that, indeed, the child had been baptized by "that nigger." Aside from sending Lucy Smith over to help Martha with her social arrangements, Sally was trying not to meddle with, and possibly muddle up, a campaign that was promising success; already Martha was meeting her mother and sisters clandestinely at their Roosevelt cousins', and the day James would come around couldn't be far off.

This was important to Sally, because, in her heart, she hoped that she would live to see a miracle: a reconciliation of her sons. If Cousin

James could be brought to accept Peter as a son, wouldn't Cornelius accept him as a brother? So far, though, Cornelius exhibited only scorn for any signs of weakness on James' part, and he viewed Peter's political and social success as alarming evidence of decadence in certain elements of New York society. "Bad enough that people like you and those young socialites condone his private morals," Cornelius would grump, "but only an idiot could vote for a man with Peter's public views. Why, did you know that John Charles Smith found out that it was Peter who persuaded Greeley to run those despatches from London by that socialist Karl Marx in the *Tribune?* From what I know, Marx nearly started a revolution in Europe with his *Communist Manifesto* before they threw him out, and I tell you that Peter's notions about freeing the niggers will bring on worse than a revolution here. The South will secede, as they've a right to, and New York will go bankrupt—and us along with it. It's the worst cross I have to bear to see the good money I earn by the sweat of my brow going out to support Peter's politics and that silly wife's social aspirations. I'd rather he'd taken after father and been a drunk. If you weren't his mother, you'd see it my way too, because at least you've always shown good sense when it came to business." . . . Trying to answer such a diatribe always provoked Cornelius to more invective, and so Sally would keep her silence. But hearing Cornelius talk made her realize that, for the sake of her hope, it was good that she was a survivor: the miracle would still be a long time in coming.

One of the things that Alderman Peter Schuyler Van Alen liked most to do on a pleasant day like this one in September, 1850, was to walk from his home on Twenty-Second Street up to the Croton Reservoir at Forty-Second Street and Fifth Avenue, where he would pace the ramparts and look south over what he secretly thought of as *his* city. There weren't many of the half a million or so people living and working under the roofs that spread like a patchwork quilt of tar and slate and shingle from river to river who would be able to recall, as he did, when most of the landscape under his eye had been open fields where he'd come with his friends to sled ride in winter and shoot rabbits in summer. Grand as it had seemed to him then, the city he'd known as a child was little more than a village compared to what he saw spread out around him now, and new patches to this crazy quilt obliterating all nature were being added every year. Vanishing along with the ground's greenery was the sky's clarity. Except when there was a washing wind from the northwest, the view was hazed with smoke pouring from the stacks of factories, trailing from steamers crisscrossing the rivers, chuffing from engines plying Fourth Avenue. A continuous, clamorous sound broke around and over the ramparts of the reservoir like the pounding of surf. As a man nearing forty, Peter might well have indulged in sentimental regret over the passing of an opener, cleaner, quieter way of life as he paced, but he didn't: the sheer energy assaulting his eyes and ears excited him, and he would feel a kind of exultation in being an important part of this city that was the gulping mouth of a growing and greedy nation, which, with California's coming into the union, now stretched from sea to sea.

Peter was shy of trying to communicate this feeling to anybody but his friend Walt Whitman, who, when he was over from Brooklyn, often accompanied him on these rambles around the reservoir. Peter had come to know and respect Walt when Whitman had lost his job as editor of the Brooklyn *Eagle* for being too enthusiastic in supporting Cousin Matty Van Buren and the Free Soilers in '48. Until then, Whitman had aroused more amusement than admiration in New York newspaper circles for his verbal slugging matches with rival Brooklyn editors. Peter had counted Whitman the loser in one contest with the *Advertiser:* a paragraph in the *Eagle* speculated that, if Goethe was right in claiming brainless persons the happiest, life at the *Advertiser* must be heaven on earth; an ad in the next day's *Advertiser* read, "TO BE LET—The upper story of the editor of the *Eagle.* No foreigner need apply." When, however, Peter finally met Whitman he found that upper story fully tenanted with the most astonishing poetic visions. The loss of an editorial chair was no great sacrifice to Whitman, a footloose bachelor who could as easily earn a living with his square and competent carpenter's hands as with his words. At the moment, though, Whitman was turning out literary and musical criticism for the *National Era* while secretly composing on his kitchen table in Brooklyn what he boasted to Peter would be the first great American poetry. A big, bearded man, perpetually tanned from striding along Long Island beaches, dressed in workingmen's style with open shirt and pants tucked into boots, Whitman was a perfect walking companion. He more than shared Peter's enthusiasm for the surge of what he called "Manhatta" and kept urging the new alderman to greater efforts in building a city that would fulfill his vision of what it could be.

Once when they were walking the reservoir together Whitman shouted out a poem on which he was working:

City of orgies, walks and joys,
City whom that I have liv'd and sung in your midst
  will one day make you illustrious,
Not the pageants of you, not your shifting tableaus, your spectacles,
  repay me,
Not the interminable rows of your houses, nor the ships at the wharves,
Nor the processions in the streets, nor the bright windows with goods in
  them,
Nor to converse with learn'd persons, or bear my share in the soiree or
  feast;
Not those, but as I pass O Manhattan, your frequent and swift flash of
  eyes, offering me love,
Offering response to my own—these repay me,
Lovers, continual lovers, only repay me.

From this poem and snatches of others that Whitman quoted from time to time, Peter was aware that his friend was struggling to create something very new. Schooled as he'd been in precise meter and rhyme, he wasn't sure how much he liked it, but he did feel a chaotic power in it like the power in the city below him. As he walked alone this day, thinking of Whitman, he found himself admitting gratitude to the man for unknowingly finishing a job that Poe had begun— convincing Peter that he himself was no poet. Whitman's free-swing- ing gusto was as beyond his emotional reach as had been Poe's mystical, mysterious melodies that rang like the chimes of an opium den. The fresh, strong wind of Whitman's poetry also made it easier for Peter to reconcile himself to Poe's sad death, which for almost a year now had haunted both him and Martha with thoughts that they might somehow have prevented it. Giving up on New York, Poe had evidently headed back for Richmond, which had been his only real home, however unhappy. But in Baltimore he'd gone on a binge, been held captive by the political gangs who were rounding up drunks to vote in the local elections, fallen ill and died, alone and in delirium, in a hospital ward. Poe could no more have come to terms with Whitman's poetry than with the steamships he hated for driving the grace of sail from the sea. So perhaps in God's wisdom, if God cared for such things, it was time for Poe to go. He'd have to share this thought with Martha, who might also find some ease in it.

On the other hand, maybe he shouldn't, since Whitman was not one of Martha's favorite people. Because Whitman and Martha were both interested in music, they often met at an opera or concert. At these events, Peter just liked to sit back and let the music wash over him like the warm water of a bath. But he noticed that Whitman, out of professional necessity as a critic, and Martha, as a musician herself, would sit on the edge of their seats, alert for every flatted high C by the tenor or fumbled trill by the soprano. If they would get together for a chat between acts, Martha and Whitman would like as not argue hotly over what he planned to write about the performance, and it was this frequent difference in their opinions that made Peter a little nervous about the dinnerparty they were hosting this night in their marble-foyered brownstone. Martha herself was so highly strung by what she called "the most important event in my whole life"—a somewhat wounding statement in view of such other events as their elopement and the birth of their son—that he'd taken this walk to get away from her fussing. He didn't feel guilty about it since she had Lucy Smith to help her. He'd at first thought it odd of his mother and had been frankly irritated with her for bringing Lucy into their lives, but he'd finally come to appreciate the calm professionalism that this maiden lady, gifted with experience and devoid of those hopes for personal conquest that bred butterflies in so many women's stomachs on social occasions, brought into the house. It was Lucy, in fact, who had proposed long in advance of the lady's arrival that a dinner for a select group in honor of Jenny Lind might prove an advantage to the new alderman and his wife.

Nobody, least of all Lucy herself whose acquaintance with the arts was as limited as her knowledge of literature, could have foreseen what a social coup it had now proved to be. Lucy's hunch had been based solely on the fact that the singer was being imported by Mr. Barnum, whose uncanny knack for having his every doing reported in the papers would undoubtedly result in some favorable mention of the kindness showed by Alderman and Mrs. Van Alen in welcoming a foreign visitor to New York. In her capacity as self-appointed social secretary to Martha, Lucy had gone about her business well. To assure the singer's attendance, she'd made up a guest list that would guarantee a dinner fattened with politicians, salted with critics and sweetened with social figures, a list that Mr. Barnum, himself invited, would find irresistible. She'd also picked a night—this night —far enough away from Miss Lind's debut to assure maximum publicity if the singer were a success. A capable woman, Lucy, but who could have detected the glow of prophecy in her homely, horsey face?

The events of the last few days had been so incredible that Peter's mind still reeled when he thought of them. Because of their dinner invitation, Barnum had included him and Martha in the group to greet the singer on her arrival on Sunday, September 1. As a newspaperman, Peter of course knew Barnum; there wasn't a city room in New York in which his massive figure was not a familiar sight. Though only two years older than Peter, Barnum was prematurely bald, and his round cheeks, bushy eyebrows, prominent nose and smiling mouth gave him the look of what one inspired reporter called "a Yankee Santa Claus." Despite the sour notes from his band and the phony marvels he'd frequently foisted on the public, it was hard not to like Barnum, who relied upon his fellow Americans to laugh at themselves, just as he did. It was also hard not to admire his ability again and again to create, even among cynical members of the press, the illusion of coming up with the ultimate wonder. In the matter of importing Jenny Lind, Barnum had waved a wand more magical than he'd ever held before. Reams and reams of copy about the poor but pure little Swedish girl whose God-given voice, as sweet as that of the nightingale, had charmed all the crowned heads of Europe flowed from Barnum's office directly into print on the front pages of every newspaper across the country. By the time she departed Liverpool on the *Atlantic,* with a personal note of best wishes from Queen Victoria in her reticule and an entourage comprising a British knight, Sir Julius Benedict, as her conductor, an Italian singer for duets, Giovanni Belletti, a secretary, a friend, a valet, a Barnum agent, anticipation in America was rising like the summer temperatures. From what Peter had heard through friends in the press, the Barnum ballyhoo was a matter of sheer necessity: he'd guaranteed this woman, sight unseen and song unheard, the enormous sum of $1,000 a concert, or something like $100,000 for the tour.

That Barnum's blast of publicity had been heard in every corner of the city was evident when Peter and Martha tried to make their way to the pier where the *Atlantic* was docking. They had to abandon their hack almost half a mile from the site and enlist the aid of a policeman who recognized the alderman to get through the dense crowds. "Our captain says must be thirty thousand here," the policeman reported between shouts of "Here you, otta the way! Make way for the alderman!" Peter rather enjoyed this performance, his first experience with the fact that even petty power had its perquisites. They'd barely reached Barnum's side before the ship, hooting a salute to the crowds, got its lines out and began lowering the gangplank. "I can't wait to get a look at her," Barnum said. "Couldn't sleep a wink all last night."

"You mean you've never seen her?" Martha asked in astonishment.

"No, nor heard her either."

Almost before the plank was secured, Barnum bounded up, followed by Peter and Martha and a few other dignitaries. They found Miss Lind in her cabin, surrounded by trunks into which a maid was frantically stuffing last items. It was, Peter thought, difficult at first glance to tell the difference between mistress and maid, so plain was the little nightingale. Though her face remained unlined at thirty, it was the face of a peasant woman, broad of cheek and nose and bare of makeup; only a kind of merry intelligence in her blue eyes suggested anything unusual about her. There was nothing peasantlike about her body, though, with its tiny waist and singer's voluptuous bosom. If Barnum shared Peter's feelings, he didn't show them; he bestowed upon his new prize his most radiant Santa Claus smile and introduced her around with the deference due a queen. "She'd better sing like an angel," Martha whispered to Peter, who had trouble not laughing.

However humble her appearance, Miss Lind entered America in a manner grander than any royalty. As she made her way on Barnum's arm down the gangplank which had been covered with crimson carpet, the crowd erupted in whistles and cheers; hats sailed into the air and handkerchiefs fluttered like an immense flock of white birds. An open carriage waited at the foot of the plank, and, with the way cleared by what looked like the entire city police force, she and Barnum rode in state, bowing and waving, under two great arches of greenery and flowers topped with signs, one crying "Welcome to America!" and the other, "Welcome Jenny Lind!" Their destination was the Irving House on Broadway, where another noisy congregation of five thousand or more blocked the street and sidewalk and had to be pushed aside again by police before she could get into the hotel. By the time Peter and Martha reached the vicinity of the Irving House, they gave up even trying to get to the door. Peter sent his wife home but, curious and rather aroused by the excitement, stayed on himself to prowl the fringes of a crowd that was growing larger by the moment.

Chants of "Jenny, Jenny, Jenny!" and "Sing for us, Jenny!" and "Let's hear the nightingale!" grew into choruses. When finally the singer emerged on the balcony of her suite, waving a white handkerchief, the chorus became a roar. An almost ethereal figure in the light of the gaslamps lining the street below, Jenny could be imagined as more angel than peasant girl by those who hadn't seen her close, Peter realized. She withdrew without song, but the crowd continued to grow and persist. By midnight a column of three hundred firemen, holding blazing torches that made their red shirts glow, parted the sea of humanity flooding Broadway to make way for a two-hundred-piece band from the New York Musical Fund Society. Ringed by the firemen, the band stood under Jenny's window and serenaded her with patriotic melodies until at last she emerged again with Barnum and stood for an hour in full view. Peter tried to imagine what could be going through her head, what it would be like to receive such accolades from a people who had never seen her or heard her sing. What if, when she finally did open her mouth, her voice was as plain as her face? To Peter, the prospects of pleasing in the face of such expectations seemed terrifying. So far, though, the show had really been Barnum's, and the big man was acknowledging this fact by waving his arms wide and taking more bows than his star.

For the sake of the peace of the city, Peter hoped that Barnum knew what he was doing this time. Barnum had once been quoted as explaining his success with the cynical comment that a sucker is born every minute, an attitude which, if true, might be harmless enough in the running of a museum but could bring disaster under circumstances such as this. The potential for mayhem if these crowds were disappointed was awesome, for New Yorkers were passionate about players, as last year's riots at the Astor Place Opera House had so sadly demonstrated. To Peter particularly, it had seemed incongruous that the Bowery B'hoys could have been worked up into a fighting fever over two actors playing, of all things, *Macbeth,* but it had nevertheless happened. The American actor Edwin Forrest was playing the role at the Broadway Theater when on May 7, 1849, the English actor Charles Macready was scheduled to open in *Macbeth* at the Opera House. Blaming his unfavorable reception in London the year before on Macready, Forrest and his supporters handed out free tickets to Bowery B'hoys in search of fun with the result that Macready's appearance on stage was greeted with a barrage of rotten eggs, vegetables and, ultimately, flying chairs. The actor and the respectable members of the audience hastily vacated the theater, and it was virtually torn apart. When Macready announced that he would abandon the play and return to England, a committee of distinguished citizens headed by Washington Irving persuaded him not to bow to mob rule. And so, while on May 10, Macready managed to get through a halting performance by shouting over the hisses of an audience kept in control by a regiment of police, the Bowery B'hoys turned the streets outside into a nightmare of violence, which ended only when a troop of three hundred militia, coming to the aid of the police, fired several volleys, killing more than twenty people.

Riots were too common in a volatile population such as that of New York to leave much doubt in Peter's mind that such a tragedy could happen again. During the ten days before Miss Lind's debut at Castle Garden, Peter watched with fascination and some trepidation as Barnum's drumbeat of publicity rose to a deafening crescendo that stirred the pulse of a whole population. Whether each beat was planned or the result of the serendipity that somehow attends the fortunate was hard to tell. For instance, Miss Lind's outward placidity proved to be deceptive when at her first rehearsal she refused to sing before an invited audience of dignitaries, including Peter; all were therefore expelled but a few music critics, who in gratitude for such preference used all the superlatives at their command to describe her voice. Then Barnum decided to hold an auction in Castle Garden for the sale of first-night tickets. A hatter named John Genin who kept store next door to Barnum's American Museum had been advised by the impresario to pay whatever it took—as it turned out, $225—for the first ticket; the average ran between $6 and $7, guaranteeing an amazing gross of $17,864 for one performance. In the face of such proceeds, Barnum changed the contract, offering Miss Lind half of every dollar over his costs of $5,500; in the face of such generosity, Miss Lind offered to distribute her share to charity, beginning with $3,000 to the firemen and $2,000 to the musicians who had so splendidly welcomed her. By opening night, New Yorkers were thus prepared to see an authentic angel, whether she could sing or not.

When Peter and Martha arrived at the Battery, their hack joined a procession of carriages clattering over the wooden bridge to Castle Garden. The bridge had been turned into a tunnel of light by a canvas awning, and the circular Garden was itself a striking quartet of different colored lights, each hue designating a section corresponding with the color of the arriving patrons' tickets. It was, Peter thought, a marvel of organization, and the effect was to awe the audience into behaving as if in church. Over the stage stood a white and gold arch decorated with flags of Sweden and the United States and from the balcony hung a banner saying, "Welcome, Sweet Warbler!" The only commotion came from rowdies without the wherewithal for tickets who circled the Garden in boats, tooting and yelling. At precisely eight o'clock, Sir Julius lifted his baton, and the orchestra launched into Weber's "Oberon" overture through which the audience of five thousand stirred restlessly, awaiting the nightingale. A touch more suspense was added by what seemed an interminable solo by Belletti before, at last, Miss Lind, dressed all in angelic white, came through the orchestra. The audience rose, waving handkerchiefs and shouting welcome; Jenny just stood there for long minutes until they quieted down. "I think I'd die if I were in her shoes," Martha whispered to Peter, who agreed, "Me, too. Lord, I hope she's good . . ."

She was. From her opening rendition of the "Casta Diva" from Bellini's *Norma* through a simple little Swedish "Herdsman's Song," her voice swooped and soared like a bird set free. What was more amazing to Peter was that, in singing, her face took on a radiance that could only be described as beautiful. He agreed with Martha's verdict: "She really is an angel," and so did the critics. His old friend at the *Tribune* trumpeted: "Jenny Lind's first concert is over, and all doubts are at an end. She is the greatest singer we have ever heard, and her success is all that was anticipated from her genius and fame." By next day, what the papers called Lindomania had set in. Genin's hats were selling for twice as much and twice as fast as the day before, and a man clear out in Iowa, where the story had been picked up by local papers, auctioned an old Genin hat from the post office steps for $14. Pipes, pianos, shawls, gloves, whiskeys, playing cards appeared with the name Jenny Lind, and a shipbuilder launching one of the new clippers being built for the California gold trade christened her *Nightingale.* Crowds continued to block Broadway around Irving House so badly that the nightingale had to be removed secretly to another gilded cage, and when her carriage would appear in the streets enthusiastic young men would try to pull the horses out of the traces and pull her themselves . . .

Such was the personage who would be dining this night at Peter's house, and he guessed that Martha's anxiety was understandable. He kept his own under control by reminding himself that Miss Lind was, after all, just an entertainer, one of Barnum's passing marvels, while the Van Alens were just about the closest thing to nobility that New York could boast. He did wish, however, that Whitman, despite their friendship, hadn't been invited; the man was unpredictable both as to dress and opinion, and his review of Miss Lind's concert had not yet appeared.

Walking back down Fifth Avenue, where new homes with facades of stone and marble, brass and wrought iron, were blossoming each building season as regularly as summer flowers, Peter tried to make sense in his own mind of Lindomania. Though she was good, she was, as he'd seen close up, a very human being who probably wouldn't turn a head were she walking beside him right now. The adulation accorded this plain girl from Sweden, he thought, might reflect a people's need to find, or create, a shining hero or heroine at a time when so many idols were falling. However many bullets he had faced, the lion of the Mexican war, President Zachary Taylor, turned out to have a digestive system unequal to a Fourth of July feast in Washington's hot weather and had died, leaving the White House to Millard Fillmore, a relatively obscure lawyer from the village of Buffalo whose nomination on the Whig ticket as vice-president had only been meant to counterweight Taylor's southern associations. At approximately the same time, Daniel Webster, who'd towered above the New England landscape like a great and indestructible pine tree, turned out to have roots of clay—ha! a pun Peter would have to remember to pass on to Greeley. In the Senate, Webster had gone along with Henry Clay's complicated compromise to admit California as a free state and abolish the slave trade in the District of Columbia in return for no mention of slavery in the organization of the New Mexico and Utah territories and a stringent fugitive slave law under federal auspices. Webster's reward was to be named secretary of state by another compromiser, Fillmore. With a peace supposedly assured by

411

compromise and a prosperity assured by California gold, the people of New York, and perhaps elsewhere in the nation, felt free to pursue their personal goals. Anything was possible for anyone—even a plain, ill-bred girl, as Jenny Lind so blazingly demonstrated—with the gumption to get it. So Jenny was the kind of star that a people uncertain of its collective destiny was seeking, and while she was among them they'd follow wherever she went.

Peter hadn't expected his thought to be so literally translated into action, but by the time he reached home, all of Twenty-Second Street was packed with Jenny followers, waiting for a glimpse of their star when she arrived for dinner. It was the other side of the golden coin of publicity that they'd so carelessly tossed into the air, and yet, shoving his way through the people, Peter was rather pleased to hear mutterings of "That's the alderman himself!" and to have one or two actually seize his hand and call him by name. He found Martha in their bedroom, peering through a crack in the drapes she'd drawn against the curious eyes outside. She was fresh from her bath, wrapped in a loose negligee, her golden hair, still undressed, flowing to her waist. He was inconveniently seized with a surge of physical desire. He went to her, caressed the silk shawl of her hair and put an arm around her still small waist.

She shook him off with a nervous, instinctive gesture. "Please, Peter . . . oh, look out there! Look at all the people! Everyone in New York will know Jenny's been here. I think even daddy will be proud when he hears . . ."

Desire dissolved into acute irritation, and he stomped out. "I'll go get dressed."

Would she never give up on that pompous prude? This business of trying to woo her father back was a subject so touchy that he never dared discuss it with her lest he say things too hurtful to be forgotten. Personally, he could do without seeing Cousin James for the rest of his life. He had glimpsed the man a few times in the streets, and he was sure that James had seen him too. Instead of carrying out his threat to cane him, James had suddenly become interested in the nearest shop window or had found it necessary to cross the street. Peter would have welcomed a violent confrontation in which he was determined to turn the other cheek; it would demonstrate to the world, and Martha in particular, that Christianity lay in practice not preaching. Since he'd never considered James a coward, he had to

412

assume that the man had thought better of his rash threat. Now that Martha was seeing her mother and sisters, he had to assume also that one day they'd have to make some sort of peace with James, and he didn't look forward to it. He was still busy trying to pluck out the ugly weeds of piety, sprung from the seeds that James, as a father, had sown so deeply in Martha's soul, and he didn't want him around trying to plant more.

From the night of their elopement down to this very night, for instance, Peter had not been able to persuade Martha that the making of love could, and should, mean more to a woman than a kind of chaste surrender. It wasn't that she didn't love him, and, except for inconvenient moments like this, she was quite willing to surrender. After what he'd once known, it was truly like trying to subsist on crumbs falling from a richly laden table. She was achingly beautiful, at least what she'd let him see of her . . . their couplings took place under cover and in the dark. He was beginning to believe that, ironically, the very beauty of her body that inspired him to lust was part of the problem. In addition to having been raised to think of her body as a pure and holy temple to God, she'd found it, in her flirtatious role as belle of the ball, a chalice whose glitter was more alluring to aspiring knights when it remained untarnished by touch. Even passive surrender was difficult for her on that first night, and the accompanying pain must have served as proof of all she'd heard of God's displeasure with impurity. She'd also had a painful time bearing James, but then she had found comfort in the biblical assertion that pain was divinely ordained in childbirth. James. *He* hadn't wanted that name, but giving in had seemed the least he could do for her after watching her agony in delivery. Now the child was part of the problem too. Whenever he'd try to talk about these things to her, Martha would say, "I have been a good wife, haven't I? I've given you a son. What more do you want?" And when he'd try to explain, "It isn't what I want for me, but for you, for us together," she'd counter, "But I have all any woman could want. I have you—and you're going to be famous one day. And I have James—and he's going to be even more famous . . ."

Soaking now in his bath, Peter felt his anger gradually wash away with the dust from his walk. He had Martha, too, and in an imperfect world that was a great deal. For all of her quirks, she was good company, and he knew that her beauty, however unpossessible it

413

might be, made him the envy of other men. She still was quite young, and patience on his part and experience of the world on hers might work some unforeseen miracle. He supposed that he couldn't blame her for wanting her father's approval; indeed, getting it might well give her even more confidence in the kind of woman she was becoming, which in itself was a matter for interesting speculation. Peter had thought that Martha's willingness to elope with him had also been a sign of her willingness to sever past ties and join him in that world of literati and journalists and theater people where he found himself most comfortable. Though she'd done so to an extent, her daring and romantic gesture had drawn the younger, more adventuresome members of her old set to her like moths to a bright lamp and had aroused again her old ambition to be *the* belle. Proud of her, he'd gone along with her social aspirations, even to the extent of building this house where they could royally entertain, and his reward had been the new respectability that had led to his election. Martha's ambition for him and for herself, as satellite, were greater than his own, and, if indeed he rose to a position of real significance, he'd have her to thank for it. But he wondered where, if anywhere, she'd be content to stop. A large part of this business with her father, he was sure, had to do with Martha's serene conviction that she—and he, as *her* satellite in this case—was born to be the best, and her father's disapproval was an intolerable challenge to that conviction. Often Peter still didn't know where he was going, but since the day he'd joined his life to Martha's he'd had the feeling that he was on his way somewhere. It was Martha, too, who had suggested the direction, saying that it would be only decent gratitude to use the surprising support from Uncle Peter's will for a career in politics, and gruff old Greeley, who, eyes fixed on the paper he was covering with chicken tracks of ink, had confirmed it as the right one: "Yes, get out of here, Peter. Get out and do some real good in the world. I'd do it myself if I had any other talent—or, better yet, a rich relative with the decency to die. God bless you . . . !"

Dinner, with Miss Lind on his right and his mother on his left, began well. Martha, at the foot of the table and flanked by Barnum and Whitman, was stunning in a new sequined gown that made glittering, globed jewels of her perfect breasts. The sound of the crowds still jamming the street, muted to a murmer by the heavy scarlet drapes of the dining room, gave the air of a royal feast to the gathering. Peter noted that Whitman had worn a tie and kept his pantaloons over his boots in honor of the guest and forgot any apprehensions he'd had about his friend. Within minutes of talking to her, he thought that he understood why Miss Lind was able to face with such apparent ease the challenge of the wild adulation she provoked. She *was* a simple peasant at heart, so supremely confident of a talent that had been with her since birth that the possibility of failure never crossed her mind. Moved by a new admiration for her, Peter rose to propose a toast. Everyone lifted a glass with him, but Barnum. Martha, noticing it, said, "Why, Mr. Barnum, how can you not drink to the little lady who's brought you such fortune?"

"Madam, as Jenny well knows, I would do anything for her, even kiss her feet—anything but touch a drop of wine. I am a teetotaler, and proud of it. Since I've taken to drinking nothing but pure water, I am a better man, and I can recommend it to all of you."

As they sat down, Peter's mother said, "Cornelius would have loved that speech."

Peter, a little miffed at what he considered a kind of discourtesy to his hospitality, said, "Yes, I can well imagine. By the way, has Cornelius heard Miss Lind sing yet?"

Too polite to tell the truth—that Cornelius thought Lindomania a sign of insanity on the part of most of his fellow citizens—Sally said, "I'm afraid not. You know he is *so* busy. Would you believe it, he's even talking of having a clipper built?"

"What—the steam king of New York going into sail?"

"Well, he was very impressed when the *Sea Witch* made San Francisco in only ninety-seven days out of New York. You know, it's been taking the average ship 159 days, and with all that gold to be brought to market it's tempting. I don't know whether he'll do it yet. He says he has to balance speed against the fact that the clippers can't carry as much in their narrow hulls and need quite a crew to handle all those sails . . . By the way, Miss Lind, I hear they've named a new clipper after you."

Jenny clapped her hands. "Oh, yes. I was taken to see her. She is beautiful . . ."

Letting his attention drift away as he tended to do when his mother started talking about Cornelius' business, Peter caught Barnum's voice at the other end of the table . . . "Well, what about you, Mr. Whitman? We haven't seen your review yet."

Peter could not hear Whitman's reply, but Barnum's voice rose, confident, persisting . . . "You have it with you? Well, then, read it. I'm sure you agree with all of your colleagues. Silence, everybody. Mr. Whitman is going to read us his criticism . . ."

The table fell quiet as Whitman rose, fumbled in his coat pocket and brought out a sheaf of papers. He seemed uncharacteristically apologetic, uncertain. "Well," he began, "since Mr. Barnum has put me on the spot and since you'll all be reading it tomorrow anyway, I might as well . . . uh, I should say that from what I've seen of her here tonight I think that Miss Lind is a good, honest Swedish girl who can take good, honest criticism . . ."

Oh, my God, here it comes . . . what I'd feared, Peter thought as Whitman began reading. "The Swedish Swan, with all her blandishments never touched my heart in the least. I wondered at so much vocal dexterity; and indeed they were all very pretty, those leaps and double somersets. But even in the grandest religious airs, genuine masterpieces as they are of the German composers, executed by this strangely over-praised woman in perfect scientific style, let the critics say what they like, it was a failure; for there was a vacuum in the head of the performance . . ."

While he read on, Martha suddenly jumped up, knocking over a wine glass in the process, and all but shrieked, "Walt—how could you . . . ?" and ran from the room.

Excusing himself, Peter followed her. He found her sprawled on the bed, crying. When he tried to stroke her hair she said, "Don't touch me. That . . . that uncouth friend of yours ruined everything, everything . . . insulting our guest right at our table—"

"But Barnum insisted . . . I heard him . . ."

"Walt didn't have to do it, and you know it. He was just showing off. Oh, I'm *so* embarrassed!"

"I never did think that we should have invited Walt. It was Lucy who—"

"Don't blame *her*. She doesn't know a thing about your newspaper people. *You* should have warned her. Or done something instead of just sitting there and listening. I'd so wanted this evening to be perfect and now . . ."

He did dare touch her again . . . "It's not that bad, honey. Nothing's perfect, nobody's perfect. I'm sure Walt's right that Miss Lind can take . . . a little criticism. Now dry your eyes, we have guests."

"I can't. I just can't face them."

"All right," he said, "I'll tell them you are taken ill. Have a good cry, it may be the best medicine."

Going back down the stairs, Peter wondered whether he might not one day be grateful to Walt. It was time that Martha learned that life could not be made perfect, and Walt's lone voice had done something to cure him of incipient Lindomania. All the guests had the good taste to try to ignore the incident, but the party broke up early. On her way out, Sally Van Arlen asked her son, "Is Martha going to be all right?" When he nodded she said, "It *was* dreadful of that Whitman man, and I can understand how she feels. You know, Peter, I'm beginning to be glad that you haven't become a poet. They have such colossal egos. Goodnight—and send for me if Martha's really ill."

When his mother had gone, Peter went around checking on the gas jets, winding the clocks, letting the cat out, looking in on his sweetly slumbering son—anything to delay facing Martha's anger, or sorrow, or both . . . Finally he tiptoed into the bedroom and, thinking her asleep, slipped under the covers beside her as deftly as he could.

She wasn't asleep. Her wideawake voice came at once. "Peter?"

"Yes . . . ?"

"Promise me that you'll stop associating with people like Whitman? They'll ruin everything I'm trying to do for you. Besides, the man doesn't know a damned thing about music."

It was the first time Peter had ever heard his wife swear, and it shocked him into laughter.

"Why are you laughing? I don't think it's a bit funny."

"You swore," he said. "Didn't you hear yourself? You know, Martha, my love, I think there might be hope for you yet. We'll worry about Walt tomorrow. I think you were just overwrought from all the preparations. Do you know what mother said tonight? She said she was glad I'm not a poet, and so am I. I'd rather be your husband."

There was a silence before her voice came again. "Peter?"

"Yes . . . ?"

"I love you and . . . and I'm sorry for being a silly goose."

He reached out to touch her, and, though under the covers and in the dark, she came to him . . .

417

Later he lay wondering whether, under the other roofs quilting this stirring city, there could be other lovers as rewarded as he was this night. He hoped so. And he thought again of Walt and of those lines shouted into the wind from the ramparts of the reservoir . . .

> . . . but as I pass O Manhattan, your frequent swift flash of eyes
>   offering me love,
> Offering response to my own—these repay me,
> Lovers, continual lovers, only repay me . . . .

. . . and he knew that they were true. They could keep him away from poets but never, he hoped, from the truth of poetry. Whatever he did in his city, for his city, should be done out of feelings he'd shared this night with his wife . . . He thought about giving such a speech to the beefy board of aldermen on which he sat, and he went to sleep quietly laughing to himself.

Chapter **XVIII**

The Man Called Charlie

John Charles Smith, Jr., kept his law offices in Wall Street where, by strolling up to the exchange, he could take the pulse of the economy at virtually any hour; he kept his home on Gramercy Park where, by taking a turn around the square in the latest and largest of crinolines, his wife and daughters could remind the best people of New York of the family's fine style; he kept his horses on Long Island where, by running in every event at the Union Race Course, they could increase his odds on gaining a fortune; and he kept his mistress in a small house in New Jersey where, by visiting the new Van Alen Engine Works nearby, he could also avail himself frequently and secretly of her services. There were many men around the Astor House bar, where John Charles Smith, Jr., regularly took his lunch, who were consumed with envy of this tall, handsome man with his long waxed mustache, twinkling eyes and jingling pockets. There in the bar, they all called him Charlie and almost fought to stand next to him, because Charlie was always good for a tip on the races or the market or the whereabouts of an amiable lady grown bored with her husband, and he was forever standing drinks. So liberal was Charlie with his information and his cash that few men thought a thing about it when he would approach them for some small favor in return. Good, old Charlie wasn't the sort who ever stood in need of the kind of help that might be embarrassing, like a loan; mostly all he wanted was a little inside gossip on how the vote in the Board of Alderman might go on a certain contract, or whether Mayor Wood had been seen with so-and-so, or what members of the legislature were having trouble making ends meet. Actually, few of the men who traded confidences for drinks with Charlie Smith were really aware that a transaction had taken place. Everybody knew that good, old Charlie couldn't care less about politics; his interests were easy women, fast horses, long cigars and strong brandy. He was one of the lucky ones—a grandson of old Cornelius Van Alen with some kind of a cushy retainer from his cousin, the present Cornelius Van Alen.

But on a fall day in 1857, Charlie Smith counted himself lucky to find a place at the bar that was not only conveniently near the oysters but beside a man whose absence from New York had been making the kind of work he did do rather difficult. Charlie clapped the man on the back and said, "Well, hello, Tweed. Welcome back—and congratulations!"

Turning away from the bar, William Marcy Tweed seized Charlie's hand and said, "Mr. Smith—I mean, Charlie! Well, well, good to see you. You're a smart man, Charlie. Most people wouldn't consider trading a seat in Congress for a seat on the Board of Supervisors a matter for congratulation."

Charlie winked and said, "Most people don't know what I know, Bill—how much you love Manhattan. Well, you couldn't sentence me to Washington, either. This is where the real race is being run—"

"Speaking of races, how are your horses running, Charlie?"

"Can't be beat. I've got a new one with Morgan blood in him—named him Buchanan, after our new president. You should put your money on him next Sunday."

"Not racing a nag named Fremont, is he?" Tweed asked, and they both laughed. "Say, Charlie, what are the odds that this Republican Party will last? You're good at odds."

"I never bet on politics. You know that, Bill. In fact, you can ask anyone around here—I'm not even *interested* in politics."

"Like a horse isn't interested in hay," Tweed said. "Seen anything of Don Fernando lately?"

"Who can miss him?" Charlie said. "If he isn't leading his police

420

in pitched battles with the governor's, he's out there on the steps of City Hall haranguing all the unemployed and promising them free flour, jobs in Central Park—the moon. He'll have the city bankrupt in a year."

"He's an ass," Tweed said.

"I'll drink to that," said Charlie. "Here, barkeep, another drink for Mr. Tweed on my account."

Charlie Smith's comments about Mayor Fernando Wood were, like his life-style, somewhat deceptive. Actually, Charlie had considerable sympathy for the mayor's position that the state had no right messing about in city business, first by establishing a metropolitan police force in rivalry with the municipal police and then by Governor King's appointment of Dan Conover as street commissioner. This summer Wood had gone rather further in defending his position than Charlie thought reasonable. He'd had his municipal police physically eject Conover from his office and then, when Conover filed suit and tried to serve papers on Wood in City Hall with the aid of the metropolitan police, Wood's men, abetted by that gang of soap locks from the Sixth Ward, the Roach Guard, stood them off with bricks and gunfire. The Seventh Regiment had finally moved in to take care of that one, and while it appeared that Wood would win the battle of the courts, it also appeared that he'd lost the war: the state was in the city to stay. Too bad. Charlie guessed that he and the mayor had the same reasons for opposing state intervention, and it had nothing to do with constitutionality: having to go all the way to Albany and deal with those hicks would just complicate their business.

But that was as far as Charlie's sympathy went; otherwise, he could agree entirely that Wood was an ass. A spectacularly handsome man, handsomer even than Charlie himself, and gifted as much as Charlie with gab, Wood had climbed from a waterfront saloon where he once shortchanged stevedores into the ranks of the half millionaires. He'd been convicted of defrauding a partner along the way, but nobody seemed to remember or, if they did, they took the "there but for the grace of God go I" view. He was entertained in some of the best of houses, including that of Alderman and Mrs. Peter Schuyler Van Alen—a matter of surprise, considering Van Alen's Republican sentiments, but Charlie's sister Lucy explained it by saying that the mayor was invited for his "amusement value." In any case, all this had gone to Wood's head. He considered himself bigger than the Tammany which had spawned him, and he was tearing the place apart—literally, since his Roach Gang and others of his saloon constituency would often resort to fists and flying furniture to settle arguments in the Wigwam. This made it difficult for Charlie—a Tammany man himself for practical reasons—to know with whom to spend his time and drinking money these days. But the worst part of Don Fernando's new grandeur was that he was pricing himself out of Charlie's market. Charlie had it direct from the mouth of Charles Devlin, for whom he'd stood countless drinks, that Devlin had paid Wood $50,000 in cash for his appointment as street commissioner in addition to some promises as to the sharing of profits on contracts, a circumstance that could explain the mayor's willingness to see blood shed in protection of that office. Charlie didn't feel sorry for Devlin, who'd already let half a million in contracts at seventy-five percent above going prices and would certainly recoup his investment regardless of Conover's victory, but the magnitude of the mayor's demands had until now been very disturbing.

Charlie's pleasure in seeing Tweed again was roughly in proportion to his displeasure over the rising prices at City Hall. As a member of the state appointed Board of Supervisors for New York County, Tweed would have the kind of power that Charlie most relished. It not only put him in contact with Albany, but his board, controlling the polling places which had been at the mercy of Wood's goons, would have a lot to do with who was elected to what. The chances of getting a lower priced class of public servants in office seemed good, because Tweed was no Don Fernando. For all his having served in Congress, he was still in Charlie's eyes a tradesman. He could close his eyes and still see young Tweed standing there in the foyer of his new house on Gramercy Park, bowing and scraping and smiling to please as he delivered those gilt chairs he'd made down in his shop on Pearl Street. That wasn't all that long ago—Tweed couldn't be much more than thirty yet—but like all the young roustabouts, Tweed had got himself into the volunteer firefighters—the Americus Company, as Charlie remembered—and on into Tammany Hall. It hadn't been difficult when Tweed became an alderman to take care of him; back in '53 it had cost only $3,000 for his vote on the Third Avenue street railway franchise to go to one of Charlie's clients. Tweed's price would be up a little now, and Charlie had to remember to treat him with the convivial familiarity he'd bestow on an equal, but he always had a pleasant feeling that Tweed remembered those chairs too, and looked upon him with that useful awe in which tradesmen held gentlemen. With Tweed around, he might be able to do business again, and he was in great need of doing business.

Until a month or so ago he'd been on top of the world—his horses winning and his stocks rising. Then came the failure of Ohio Life and Trust Co., then Attwood & Co., and on and on. The market had gone into its worst slide in twenty years, and he'd been caught short. He wasn't yet in as bad straits as the members of that rabble Don Fernando was trying to placate with his promises of bread and city jobs, but it might get to that. So far he'd held on only by pledging his good Van Alen stock, a fact he didn't dare have known. He'd gone to a moneylender and was fairly certain that his transaction wouldn't get back to Cornelius, but he remained uneasy. What he needed now was a deal that was no gamble, a source of money unaffected by hard times. If the city of New York could afford to hand out picks and shovels and let a lot of Irish laborers dig up the new park, it could also afford to keep one smart patrician lawyer alive. The difference was that, instead of bankrupting the city, Charlie would enrich it with his deal, providing service to its people and income to their public servants. There were a lot of self-appointed moralists like that stupid cousin of his, Peter Van Alen, who considered Charlie's kind of business venal, but thank God there were still enough hardheads around who could appreciate in monetary terms the fact that he was rendering a service. One of them was undoubtedly Bill Tweed.

"Been out on Broadway much since you've been back, Bill?" Charlie asked.

"Yeah. Liveliest old street in the world . . ."

"Too lively, if you ask me. I was damned near killed by one of those omnibuses careening down on me while I was walking over here from the office. What we need is a street railway."

"Why talk to me about it, Charlie? It's your fancy friends who killed it. We had it all set with old Jacob Sharp—remember?—and if that cousin of yours, Van Alen, hadn't been on the Board of Aldermen it would have been built by now."

Charlie did, of course, remember. It had caused quite a stench in the courts. Nobody knew how much Sharp had paid for the franchise, but it must have been a good deal; the aldermen had seen fit to grant

423

it to him with no strings over a competing offer by Tom Davies to pay the city $100,000 a year plus a license fee of $1,000 a car for ten years. There was heavy opposition, not only from omnibus drivers and their employers but from a wealthy segment of society who either still maintained homes wedged in between the shops and hotels and theaters or who were afflicted with a nostalgia for old Broadway, as Alderman Van Alen was said to be, and who feared that the tracks would ruin the street. The mayor vetoed the bill granting the franchise, but so hefty had Sharp's sweetening been that the Board of Aldermen repassed it over the veto and in defiance of a court injunction obtained by the opposition. For this blatant illegality one alderman went to jail and most of the rest were fined. Testifying against his colleagues, the lone dissenter, Van Alen, revealed that it had been moral indignation over bribery and not nostalgia that had put him in opposition. He'd earned the nickname "Unbuyable Pete" and almost automatic reelection in his ward.

"I have other friends," Charlie ventured.

"Oh yeah? Well, there's still that Van Alen to contend with," Tweed said. "One bad apple can spoil a whole barrel."

"It has occurred to me," said Charlie, "that it's mighty strange how an announced Republican was returned in that ward when Buchanan swept the whole city. I would think that the Board of Supervisors might want to look into that."

"Not a bad idea, Charlie, but I thought that he was your cousin."

"He is. He is. But every family has a black sheep, you know, Bill."

"Well, in that case . . . How interested are your friends?"

"I don't know, but I could find out."

"Do that, and look me up, Charlie. Well, here's to you!"

Tweed tossed off his drink and left. Charlie ordered a brandy over which he could meditate. There was no question about the message Tweed left behind: if Charlie could come up with the money, Tweed would come up with the franchise. What a plum! The potential profit from a Broadway franchise had increased ever since Davies had made his astounding offer. Now the rich residents of Murray Hill were mounting what was looking like a successful effort to have steam engines on the New York and Harlem banned below Forty-Second Street, so a street railway linking the new station, wherever it would be, with all the city's major theaters and hotels would be more valuable than a California gold mine. No sane person would risk his neck riding the omnibuses or those cold, swaying sleighs in winter if he could use the cars. The only problem facing Charlie now was to find one of the "friends" to whom he'd glibly alluded.

Cornelius Van Alen was a possibility—but not a good one. He'd certainly see the value of having the franchise; Charlie could almost picture the way Cornelius' black eyes, looking up over those half glasses, would shine with the reflection of the dollars his accountant's mind would be casting up if he heard of it. There wouldn't be any problem, either, with the negotiations. Despite his Sunday-go-to-meeting piety, Cornelius had been most understanding back when they were getting the wharf rights. Cornelius was one of those hard-headed ones who made doing Charlie's kind of business a pleasure. "Give the devil his due," was all he'd said. But Cornelius was cautious, had been ever since he nearly got wiped out by the great fire. It was a good thing on the whole since, while other stocks were falling like rocks, Van Alen & Son was still trading at five hundred and paying fifty. As Charlie's brother George put it, "Selling anything with the Van Alen name is as easy as peddling gold bricks." So Cornelius would hem and haw and wait until he was sure that they'd got rid of that brother of his before he put up a dime.

That brother was, in Charlie's view, a royal pain in the ass, the kind of fellow who was out to ruin this city and the whole damned country with his talk of forming unions, freeing niggers and giving women the vote. How a maverick like that came out of such a sound family was a real mystery. Charlie often thought that it had something to do with Aunt Sally, who was a little odd herself and who, from hints his mother used to pass along, hadn't been any better in her time than an interesting woman ought to be. She was still a pretty good-looker for an old lady, and he could only remember vaguely how beautiful she'd been. He often wished that their families hadn't been so far apart back in those days so that he might have learned more about that odd Van Alen household. It was a funny thing that Peter didn't even look like a Van Alen, though he might be a throwback to somebody on Aunt Sally's side. On the other hand, his mother used to say with that little simpering smile of hers that Peter had eyes like that Captain Roberts who was always hanging around Aunt Sally. Of course his mother wouldn't go so far as to make any accusations; her bread and butter depended on the Van Alens, as his did now. Still, it was food for interesting thought for Charlie, who had a bastard son

425

of his own named Charlie Brown growing up in that house over in Jersey.

Well, having a good deal to hide himself, Charlie wasn't one to pry into such matters—at least until it became a matter of survival. It rather pained him that Aunt Sally so obviously didn't like him, but, blessed with a rather cynical turn of mind, he shrugged it off on the grounds that "it takes one to know one." What perplexed him was how Cornelius put up with her, but then people had to put up with their mothers, as he certainly ought to know. But if Cornelius didn't watch out Aunt Sally would turn that Sophie into another willful woman; now that she was losing her fat, the girl was almost pretty, and they said she had brains as well. Charlie wouldn't know, because he discreetly stayed away from Lafayette Place. He wasn't eager to tangle with Aunt Sally, and the sight of that sickly Augusta used to depress him. Now that Augusta was dead, things might be different, but he doubted it. For all he admired Cornelius as a businessman, Charlie could hardly abide him outside the office. You couldn't get a drink or smoke a cigar in his house, and all he wanted to talk about was that damned Presbyterian church where he spent every hour he wasn't at his desk. No, Lafayette Place was no place for Charlie.

The damnable thing was that, for all he detested Peter's do-gooder politics, Charlie felt pained that he was never invited to Twenty-Second Street. That wife of his, Martha, was a real knockout, and there was no question that her parties, now that they'd got away from that scruffy literary set, were the best in New York. He knew all about them, of course, from his sister Lucy. He'd been a bit miffed that Lucy was willing to spend so much time in what he thought of as the enemy camp until he realized that it was keeping her busy, if not happy, and providing a source of information that might one day be useful. So far, though, he'd heard nothing valuable except that Peter was obviously spending every nickel that came into him from his Van Alen stock and those few other stocks his uncle had left him. He didn't know exactly what these were but they'd probably gone down with everyone else's which could mean that Peter would be soon hurting and that *was* a useful thing to know about a politician. From the way Lucy talked, Peter couldn't, or wouldn't, deny his extravagant wife anything, which was so often the case with these fellows who married beautiful, younger women; a sensible man like himself got that sort of thing on the side from someone who was grateful just to eat and have a roof over her head.

If Charlie didn't know all too well himself the price of silks and laces and beef and champagne, not to mention horses and nurse-maids and servants—why, a good cook was getting as much as $10 a month and keep these days—he'd have to wonder how Peter was getting rid of the $50,000 or so that Cornelius was paying out to him every year. He knew that supporting his brother's political and social posing galled Cornelius almost more than anything else. When Cornelius heard that they were calling his brother "Unbuyable Pete," he snorted, "By whom? He doesn't mind letting *me* buy him. I don't know where he thinks money comes from, but it comes from getting your hands dirty, literally and figuratively. I think if it weren't for mother's meddling I'd have had him out of my affairs long ago. I can forgive her since she is a mother, but not him. Sometimes I'm glad I never had a son; he might turn out like Peter or my brothers-in-law, and I don't think I could tolerate that."

His mind, straying wide from the point on which he should have been concentrating had suddenly served Charlie well. In remembering Cornelius' little speech about Peter, he was reminded of the "friend" he most needed at the moment. Cornelius' brothers-in-law were the sons of the commodore, and the commodore was one man in New York who could be counted on to have cash in times like these. Not only that, but one of his sons, Billy, was messing around with a little railroad on Staten Island. Charlie's knowledge about that was tinged with bitterness. Young Vanderbilt had brought up the road's stock from less than nothing when it went bankrupt in the first days of the crash to $175 a share, but, because he'd heard Cornelius talk so often about how worthless the commodore thought his sons were, Charlie had not only failed to buy in himself but had lost a few good drinking friends by tipping them off against it. The more Charlie thought about approaching the commodore, the more certain he was that he was on to a winner. He couldn't exactly call the commodore a friend; in fact, he'd never met the man. The commodore had long since become too busy, or too high and mighty, to serve on the Van Alen & Son board, but his affairs were still intertwined with those of his son-in-law. The commodore had been one of Van Alen & Son's best customers ever since, back in '50, a Van Alen engine drove his yacht *North Star* all the way to Russia at twelve knots when the old pirate went visiting the crowned heads of Europe; now he was ordering Van Alen engines and locomotives hand over fist to supply his riverboat and railline across the Isthmus of Nicaragua to link up the Vanderbilt Atlantic and Pacific steamers on the California run. Although Charlie had come along too late to get to know the commodore, his brother George, the Van Alen supersalesman, had swung all those deals. Even though it had meant dropping a few thousand from time to time to the commodore at the whist table, it had been well worth it for George. He'd sold both Cornelius and the commodore on the proposition of having Van Alen take back an interest in the Vanderbilt shipping in return for supplying machinery, and that interest was pulling in so much money that George could thumb his nose at Cornelius whenever he wanted to and get away with it. Charlie could only hope that the commodore was satisfied with the arrangement, but it probably wouldn't matter since the commodore had more money than he could count and Cornelius was, after all, his son-in-law and, for some strange reason, Aunt Sally was his friend. So Charlie had no doubt at all that he would be welcomed by the commodore as his brother's brother—as a Van Alen.

Whether Charlie's business would be as welcome as his person was another question. A street railway on Broadway might seem small peanuts to a man who was said to be financing a whole army under that filibuster Walker to take control of Nicaragua in his interests. If so, Charlie could always fall back on Billy, suggest that the commodore might want to give it to Billy for a toy as, according to Cornelius, he'd done with the railroad. They said that the commodore had been so surprised at Billy's success that for once he had almost boasted about one of his children. "Beats me, that feller does," he'd told Aunt Sally. "I didn't think he was worth a hoot in hell—a soft pup if I ever saw one." Billy could very well be the key. Once he got the commodore interested, there would be no trouble with the part of the business that Charlie would conduct. The commodore was noted for not being squeamish about either taking bribes, as in that business with the U.S. mail contract to Liverpool, or giving them out. Nor was he stingy: he was willing to pay for whatever he wanted, lose money for years if necessary to win out in the end. Charlie rather thought that he'd like the commodore and rather hoped that the feeling would be mutual . . . .

No use wasting time. Charlie tossed off his brandy, went out into Broadway and hailed a hack. Since it was still early afternoon, the commodore would probably be in his office on Fourth Street. The driver recognized the address and asked, "You gonna see the commodore?"

Ordinarily, Charlie didn't like to discuss his affairs with hackeys, but his euphoria about the venture in hand caused him to be generous. "Why, yes," he said.

"Well, then," said the driver, "you tell that old son-of-a-bitch from me that he should stop fooling around with that bastard Walker down there in Nicaragee. He's got American boys with him, Walker does, and pretty soon they'll be screaming that American boys is gettin' killed and drag us into war like they did in Mexico."

"Would that be so bad?" Charlie asked. "We need a route to California—"

The driver let go a spurt of tobacco juice that splattered on the rump of his horse and sent him into a trot. "Bad? You don't know how bad, mister! That Walker, he's for slavery, wants to make it slave territory. If that happens all these crazy abolitionists up in New England'll get sore and want to do away with the compromise, and then, you'll see, we'll have war right here at home—and all over them niggers—"

"I think you paint too black a picture, if you don't mind a pun," Charlie said, and chuckled.

"What's so damned funny about war, mister? You and your kind don't fight 'em; it's me and my kids . . . . well, here y'are, and don't forget to tell the old bastard for me . . ."

Charlie, usually lavish with such menials, didn't tip the man. In the glow of approaching a perfect deal, he resented being reminded by an ignorant hack driver that his personal fortunes were of little concern compared to a possible national calamity. From his point of view, that Senator Douglas from Illinois had settled things properly with his Kansas-Nebraska bill giving people the right to decide about slavery themselves in the new territories. So what if those rowdies and drifters who couldn't make a decent living in the East were shooting each other up in Kansas? Let the best of them win out, and a few less of them wouldn't hurt the country. Anyway, the Supreme Court had pretty well answered the slave question early that year in the Dred Scott decision . . . a slave was still a slave wherever he was under the Stars and Stripes. A lot of people were screaming that it did away with the Missouri Compromise that had kept slavery south of that 36° 30′ line, but any lawyer or businessman with his head screwed on right ought to agree with the Court that it was unconstitutional for Congress to make any law depriving an American anywhere of his private property. If people would just settle down and stop sticking their noses into other people's business, everything would be all right. Charlie personally blamed a lot of the unrest on that sentimental trash Mrs. Stowe dished up in her *Uncle Tom's Cabin,* which was bad enough as a book but worse now that it had been turned into the longest running show on Broadway, where ignorant people who couldn't read a line would go and get themselves all steamed up about little Eva. It was the white people—people like that Mrs. Stowe and Horace Greeley and his own cousins, Peter and Amelia Downing —not the niggers who were at the bottom of all this. He wondered who had put Scott up to that suit, but he would bet it had been some white do-gooder. Why, he'd read in *Harper's Weekly* a while back that Scott himself was going around laughing about "de fuss dey make dar in Washington 'bout de old nigger." And who in tarnation here in the city of New York could give a good goddamn whether they had niggers down there in Nicaragua as long as the trains ran and the ships kept moving? If it weren't for sensible people like the commodore, like Charlie himself, it wouldn't be possible for a man to own a horse and a hack and make himself a dollar or two a day here in the city. Grass would be growing in the streets . . .

Since Charlie had seen the commodore's tough features in one of the daguerreotypes on display in Brady's window on Broadway he was prepared for the man, but he wasn't prepared for the office. It reminded Charlie of his grandfather's old counting room on Broadway, where he'd been taken occasionally as a boy, or that ugly box up in one corner of the old factory over on the Hudson, now turned into a warehouse since they'd built the new factory over in Jersey, where Cornelius insisted on conducting business. It must be something in the Dutch character that made men who could afford the best spend their days in such dreary surroundings. Charlie thanked the Lord that the Dutch in him was so well watered down. Even though he spent little time in it, his office on Wall Street had an Oriental rug, soft leather chairs, a Chippendale desk said to have been used by George Washington himself when he was in New York as president

430

and on the wall, one of the best copies of Stuart's Washington he'd ever seen. Like most of the rest of his style of life, Charlie's office furnishings were calculated to serve an end greater than comfort: they let clients who visited him know that they were in the hands of a man of means whose fees would be accordingly high. A person who didn't know better might think that the commodore sitting stiffly behind a bare oak desk in this carpetless, pictureless, dingy office and chewing on a dead cigar was an overaged clerk waiting for a summons from his boss. There was another table in the room at which a young boy sat picking his nose and a young man, presumably the commodore's clerk, hunched over scratching away with a pen. Just as Charlie entered, the commodore took the cigar out of his mouth and said to his clerk, "Write it so the bastard understands, Wardell. Tell him I want money instead of soft soap. And don't make it flowery neither . . ."

The Commodore didn't bother to rise when Charlie approached his desk with outstretched hand, saying, "I'm Charlie Smith, George's brother, commodore—you know, Cornelius Van Alen's cousin."

The commodore stuck the cigar back in his mouth and studied Charlie with eyes like blue diamonds that seemed to scratch right through to the quick. When he'd evidently seen what he wanted to see, he said, "All right . . . what's your name—Charlie? What's your business? I ain't got much time. I'm busy as hell."

There wasn't a sign of busyness on the Commodore's desk—not a scrap of paper, not a pen. Charlie had thought of working in gradually, chatting about horses which the commodore loved, or whist, perhaps. But he could sense that it would be better to come right out with it. "Commodore, I have a proposition to make . . ."

"Get to the point, I ain't got all day."

"Would you be interested in the street railway franchise on Broadway?"

"Huh! Who the hell wouldn't? But Sharp got his ass singed when he tried for it, and I ain't about to go through that."

Half the sale already made, Charlie thought jubilantly; the commodore already knows what it's worth. Now for the other half. "Things have changed, commodore. I was just talking to a good friend of mine, Bill Tweed—you know, the congressman. Gave up his seat in Washington to come back to town as a member of the Board of

Supervisors. He's very civic-minded, you know, and he thinks that a street railway would improve Broadway, and—"

"How much does he want?"

It was breathtaking—the whole sale made in a few seconds. But careful, Charlie, don't hem and haw, get enough. "I think fifty thousand might do it, commodore," he said, trying to sound as casual as if he were speaking of fifty cents.

The commodore bit right through his cigar, spit out the end on the floor and said, "That's a hell of a lot of money—what's your name, Charlie? You don't think I keep money like that in my hat, do you?"

Oh, oh—too much? Charlie looked at the commodore, who was rummaging around in his drawer for a new cigar. Though he couldn't see the man's expression, instinct told him not to back down. "If you remember, commodore, Davies offered the *city* a hundred thousand a year. This would be a one-time thing with no strings, but we've got to move fast. Once Tweed gets an idea, well . . . Couldn't you just write me a check?"

The commodore, lighting his cigar, studied Charlie through a veil of smoke which Charlie would realize later must have hid a twinkle in those blue eyes. "Easy as that, eh? I think we're fresh out of checks. We don't have any checks, do we, Wardell?"

"No, sir," his clerk said.

How in the world did the man do business, Charlie wondered. He'd heard that the commodore was a little odd, but never in the way of business. Like a man with a fish nibbling at his hook, Charlie gave a desperate jerk. "I just happen to have a blank check here, commodore. I could make it out and you could sign it."

"Well, now, that's obliging. Wardell, a pen for the gentleman."

More and more incredible. Within minutes, Charlie was back out on the street with fifty thousand dollars in his pocket—and still time to get to the bank. It was faster to walk than to hire a hack, faster yet to run. Charlie was panting when he slipped the check across to the teller. The incredible was compounded. The man studied it for a while, frowned and then left his cage to go and show it to an officer. Returning, he said, "I'm sorry, sir, we can't honor this."

Charlie exploded. "My God, man, don't you see that signature?"

"Yes, sir, but we can't honor it."

"*Why?*"

"I'm not at liberty to explain, sir. Good day."

432

Charlie was stunned. He wandered out into the street in such a daze that he was nearly run over by a hack. Was this a joke? Or were things worse than he thought? Were the banks failing too? He'd have to get right back to the commodore with the news. There was a kind of comfort in the smell of total disaster: at least his own failure would go unnoticed. He ran again and was panting even harder when he stood before the commodore and stammered out the terrible news.

The commodore leaned back in his chair, took a puff on his cigar, and, still incredibly, cracked a thin smile. "You hear that, Wardell? The man couldn't get any money. Well, well. Maybe we should try one of my kind of checks. Give me one, Wardell."

While Charlie, still catching his breath, stared, Wardell tore off half a sheet of paper and brought it to the commodore with a pen. Vanderbilt scratched for a second and then handed it to Charlie. Under the name of a bank, it read, "Pay the bearer fifty thousand dollars. C. Vanderbilt."

Charlie was both confused and furious. He simply didn't know what to say. But the commodore answered all the questions in his mind. "Guess you have to wait till tommora," he said. "You was in too much of a hurry to get money outta me, Charlie, and I thought I'd show ya it ain't that easy. Now listen here . . . I want results, and I want an accounting of every penny. I don't want more'n twenty percent sticking to *your* pockets. Wardell here and that nose-pickin' boy is witness to this transaction. Understand, Charlie?"

Well, let him have his joke; Charlie had the money now for sure. It stood to reason that a man named Vanderbilt wouldn't have to waste good money buying fancy checks. So Charlie had ten thousand clear at the end and fifty thousand to play with and perhaps outride the panic if he doled it out carefully enough. "Yes, sir, I'll get started right away," he said. "But you do understand, commodore, that these delicate matters may take some time. We might have to wait another year until we can get that Peter Van Alen off the Board of Aldermen."

"Don't understand what the hell's eatin' that feller," Vanderbilt said. "Got a sound mother and a sound brother. Only reason I'm trusting you, Charlie, is I know you work for Cornelius, and he don't keep men who don't know their business. But you play fair with me, and I might find more use for you. Now get out. I'm busy."

"Yes, sir," Charlie said, and started to leave.

Before he reached the door, the commodore called after him,

"Charlie, if you're as bad as your brother with a hand of whist, I'd welcome you up to Washington Place some night to play with me."

Charlie turned and gave the commodore his smoothest smile. "I'm worse, commodore, much worse," he lied. "Just name the night . . ."

Out on the street, Charlie started to laugh his head off, unmindful that people stared at him. That was a hell of a good joke the commodore had played on him, and Charlie, who was always joking himself, ought to appreciate it. Yes, he and the commodore would get along fine. He was so much better than his brother at cards that he could lose for a year and still make the other man think he'd won. With that check in his pocket, the present was secure and the future bright with promise. Let the market crash; he'd buy in at the bottom. A couple of thousand ought to keep Tweed in line until he could get some action going and by then the market should be up again. If it wasn't, the whole city, the whole country, would be shot to hell, and even though he was fifty-six Charlie could disappear out in California and pan gold like the rest of the old codgers who'd fallen on bad luck. But bad luck had never been in the cards for John Charles Smith, Jr., as today's events had proved, and there would yet come a day when that pious little clerk, Cornelius Van Alen, would be beholden to him.

Charlie pulled out his watch. Going on to four. As the commodore had said, the banks would be closed, but there was still time to get over to Jersey and "inspect the factory" and get back again for the late supper that his sensible wife, Janet, always kept waiting for him. With all that money tucked safely away in his pocket, Charlie felt free to duck into a store and pick up a gold bauble for Mary and a toy soldier for little Charlie. They were always so grateful for anything he gave them that it might have brought tears to his eyes if he were a sentimental man. But Charlie was not a sentimental man; he was a sensible man. Unlike that stupid cousin Peter who was bankrupting himself for what he considered a good piece of ass, Charlie was getting it the way the kings and lords of the earth in societies that recognized privilege got it, from a woman who would lick his boots for a kind word. And why not? His mother had always told him that he was named for two kings—John and Charles. He had no doubt that Mary would lick his cock, too, if he asked her, as some of the whores were said to do, but he was afraid to go that far. It sounded like a sin, like sodomy, and Charlie, who'd taken over his mother's pew rent in Trinity, wasn't willing to gamble on actually sinning; he hadn't too many years to go before he might want a fitting mansion in heaven. Armed with his gifts, King Charles hailed a hack and headed for the ferry. His usual "factory inspection" would be enough to calm his nerves after such an exciting day.

This was the kind of day that made life still worth the while for Amelia Downing. She didn't even mind cinching herself into a corset and draping herself with silk over hoops that, considering the irreducible core of her body, made her an impediment to traffic in the streets. She'd laughed heartily at the story in *Harper's Weekly* about a lady in Boston who was brought to court by a policeman on the grounds that the width of her skirts drove men off the sidewalks and endangered their lives. The court had had the good sense to exonerate the lady; from Amelia's point of view, it could only be men who wanted women to be crippled with crinolines and hobbled with hoops. They'd managed to laugh Mrs. Bloomer off the stage, but Amelia was certain that the day would eventually come when women would sensibly wear pants that would let them run and jump as fast as the men who chased them—and have the vote too. Last year's meeting here in New York of the Women's Rights Convention had opened a lot of eyes when Lucy Stone had recited the litany of the increasing number of females working in factories and going to colleges like Oberlin and Wheaton and Mount Holyoke, and next year they'd really shock them by bringing on that young fireball, Susan Anthony. Amelia didn't agree with Miss Anthony's prohibitionist sentiments except that she might be as wise as a serpent in concluding that the right to get drunk was as exclusively a male privilege as the right to vote; if women could force men off the booze, they'd have them where they wanted them. But Amelia still liked her brandy and was convinced that there would be no freedom for women until the slaves were free, and so she devoted what time and money she could spare to the cause of abolition. In the interests of not confusing one cause with another, she thought it smart to look as feminine as possible, especially since she'd been described by a male chauvinist reporter, who would be shocked to know how she'd once behaved in bed, as "a clipper with all stun-s'ils set and drawing."

One of the great things about this day was that she had, at last, persuaded Peter to join her and Sally at a stockholders' meeting of

Van Alen & Son. Martha was coming along just for the fun of it. Amelia could just imagine how, when he saw them all, Cornelius' black brows would come together in a line of frowning concern, how the Smith brothers would joke and fawn, how the Reverend James Schuyler, who'd replaced the commodore on the board, would pray with special fervor for God's blessing upon the meeting. She had a few sharp questions to ask, and she hoped that Peter did too, except that she doubted that their interests in the company were quite the same. The only way to account for Peter's agreeing to go along was that he must be worried about money to support Martha in her extravagances, which would probably be greater when this new child on its way arrived.

If she let herself go, Amelia could be jealous of Martha; Peter had turned out to be a husband that even she might have been able to live with. But in honesty she had to admit that Martha was doing for him what she'd predicted—settling him down and giving him children, *still* giving him children. She'd have thought that James and that darling little girl they'd christened Sally would have been enough, but Martha probably knew what she was doing. Martha usually did know what she was doing. It seemed nearly incredible that Martha and Peter and their children could be found nearly every Sunday in a front pew of the uptown Presbyterian Church, listening to the aging but still mellow voice of the Reverend James Schuyler. The only greater miracle would be if the brothers Van Alen exchanged more than mute, embarrassed nods of recognition on these occasions, but Amelia wouldn't put it past Martha to pass that miracle too. It would be fascinating to see what happened today.

Because the day was bright and warm for fall, Martha and Peter were picking her up with the new phaeton and team he'd bought on the excuse that he wanted to take his pregnant wife for airings in the park. What he wanted to do, of course, was exhibit her; one advantage of these hoops was that a woman's condition never showed, and Martha was never a more blooming rose than when she was with child. Amelia sometimes wondered whether those children were conceived in the kind of passion she and Peter had known. It would forever have to remain a matter of speculation since it would be unthinkable to discuss it with Peter, and Martha fortunately knew nothing of that sweet and curious interlude in both of their lives. Peter's pride in Martha was at least enough assurance that neither she nor Sally had been wrong in bringing them together. Theirs did seem to be what the world would call a happy marriage, and Martha's astonishing ambition was making of Peter a figure to be reckoned with in the city, and perhaps, now that he was one of the winners in the new Republican Party, in the country.

Getting into the phaeton and arranging her hoops so that they wouldn't tangle with Martha's was no mean feat. At least it was easier than lifting and sliding them sidewise through the door of a closed carriage; she'd heard that some clever women had rigged a string arrangement from the waist that would let them hoist the hoops like blinds, and she ought to try that. Peter had to sit up with the coachman, a not uncommon sight in this day and age when even one silk-clouded lady could preempt the whole interior of a small carriage. As soon as they were settled she found that Martha, as she supposed most of the rest of New York would be, was full of Mrs. Cunningham's acquittal in the Burdell case . . .

"What bothers me," Martha said, "is that now we don't *know* who did it. Suppose it was one of those awful garroters after all? He could have been surprised in the act and had to resort to a knife."

"Well, I'm glad she got off," Amelia said. "Every time a woman gets pregnant it's assumed that she's trying to trap some man, as if she got into it on her own. I just hope those ghouls aren't still standing around watching her house. But I suppose it does take their minds off their empty stomachs."

The attention being given the Burdell case was one of those things that made Amelia Downing despair for the intelligence of the human race. For most of the early months of this year of 1857, it had preempted both the press and private conversation, overshadowing even news of that dreadful Dred Scott decision and reports from bloody Kansas where men were at last showing their courage to die for other men's freedom. Like those queer birds the ostriches that Dr. Livingston said he saw in Africa which stuck their tiny heads in the sand and left their great bodies exposed in time of danger, the people of New York preferred to concentrate on a sordid murder than to think about the fate of thousands of black human beings. The case did, Amelia had to admit, have overtones of just about every sin in the book. It broke in February when Dr. Burdell, an obscure dentist, was found dead of stab wounds in the rooms he rented from Mrs. Cunningham at 31 Bond Street. In the early hearings it had been charged that Dr. Burdell was having an affair with Mrs. Cunningham from which she had become pregnant, and when she introduced testimony to a secret marriage with the dentist the previous October, countertestimony was offered to the effect that another boarder with whom she was also intimate, a Mr. Eckel, had stood in for the doctor at the ceremony as part of a plot, culminating in murder, to inherit the doctor's property in the name of the infant. All very spicy, indeed. Rooms where the various hearings and trials were conducted during the spring and summer had been crowded to overflowing with onlookers, and people had been standing in the streets around the clock to stare at 31 Bond Street. What perhaps so excited the public, even before the details of sexual misbehavior came out, was evidence that the killer, or killers, had first tried to do Dr. Burdell in by garroting, a crime so common in the streets that people were afraid to go out after dark. This was what was bothering Martha . . .

"I can't help it," she said. "I worry about Peter every time he has to go to one of those night meetings."

"Isn't he carrying a gun like most sensible men do these days?"

"Yes, but those garroters are so sneaky. They could get behind him and choke him before he could do anything."

"Now, Martha, Peter's a big man, and he knows New York like the back of his hand. I'm sure that he stays to safe streets like Broadway. I think it's just your condition upsetting you. You wouldn't want a poor woman convicted on circumstantial evidence just for your comfort, would you? As I say, I'm glad she got off, and I think it's high time everybody started to think about more serious matters. I don't think this garroting has anything to do with original sin, as your father was quoted as saying. I think it's a matter of economic conditions. The first thing these shortsighted businessmen start doing when the market's off a little is to turn workers out into the streets. No wonder they steal—"

Peter leaned back from his perch beside the driver and interrupted, "What are you ladies so busy chatting about?"

"About how distinguished you look, now that your curls are turning gray," Amelia teased.

"Distinguished?" Peter said. "Why, the other day Martha and I were taking a turn around Gramercy Park, and a woman who didn't know me complimented her on her handsome *father*!"

"Cheer up, Peter," Amelia said. "An aspect of dignified age is an

438

asset to a politician . . . . Well, it looks like we're here."

"What a dreadful place!" Martha said.

"Yes, isn't it? Cornelius believes in holding meetings in the warehouse to make stockholders as uncomfortable as possible and to remind us of his frugality," Amelia explained.

The phaeton had drawn up before a square building of smoke-blackened brick just off the Hudson River wharf where ships paying sufficient tribute to the Van Alen leaseholders loaded and unloaded. Just now there were two steamers flying the British flag from their gaffs and evidently making ready for departure since clouds of black smoke rising from their stacks and rolling eastward on a breeze off the water dimmed the sun and forced the ladies to mask themselves with handkerchiefs until they could get inside the warehouse door. There, in a small, cleared space surrounded by shadowy hulks of boxes, bales, casks, a makeshift platform of planks had been set up facing a few decrepit chairs on which such stockholders as cared to attend the annual meeting of Van Alen & Son could sit. Years of accumulated grime on the few high windows ringing the hall screened out whatever light or heat the fall sunshine might have offered, and it was chilly and gloomy despite two gas jets hissing and flaring from columns on either side of the platform. The directors were evidently having their own meeting elsewhere, for the chairs set out for them on the platform were empty. There were perhaps half a dozen men on the chairs in the audience, more than Amelia remembered from previous meetings, no doubt because of the market uncertainties, and one woman—Aunt Sally. Amelia experienced her usual slight twinge of envy at noting how petite and trim Sally remained, though she was nearing eighty, while her own body, going through the climacteric, grew heavier by the day. Perhaps she ought to try this hydrotherapy, though the idea of wallowing about in sitz baths and drinking nothing but water wasn't very appealing. Still, the Strongs had spent this whole last summer at the Brattleboro Water Cure House, and she had to admit that Ellie Strong looked the better for it—several pounds lighter and much rosier in her cheeks.

Surprised at seeing Peter and Martha, Sally said in a worried way, "I hope you haven't come to cause any fuss, Peter. Cornelius has been so worried about conditions that I've been worried about *him* . . ."

"It has nothing to do with Cornelius. At least, I hope not," Peter said.

Just then the directors filed in, looking, Amelia thought, with their black business uniforms, topped for the most part by solemn, gray-fringed faces, like pallbearers at a first-class funeral. If Cornelius was surprised at seeing his brother, he displayed it only as Amelia had anticipated with a frown; Cousin James nodded stiffly in his daughter's direction; George and Charlie Smith, the only ones who looked as if doing business could also be a pleasure, smiled and waved. Cousin James was the first to rise and come forward.

"For the past several years," he said, "it has been the custom to open the meetings of the stockholders of Van Alen & Son with a prayer to Almighty God that he might continue to permit this firm to prosper and to guide our deliberations. Let us bow our heads . . ."

It was a ritual, overlong prayer during which Amelia let her mind wander to the phenomenon of how such a pompous person could produce a child like the woman by her side. Physically, it was understandable enough since James, graced with the Schuyler capacity for aging well, was still strikingly handsome at sixty-two; indeed, it had been acknowledged for years that much of the feminine half of his congregation attended mostly for the pleasure of looking at him. The extent to which James might have reciprocated this almost palpable feminine ardor had been a matter for interested conjecture and gossip, but Amelia doubted that there was any truth to the rumors that cropped up from time to time: his sins were unfortunately not of the flesh. What beguiled Amelia was how a girl, raised under the lash of a tongue like James', could develop the kind of spirit that Martha had shown. True, she'd devoted an inordinate amount of time and effort to win what Amelia understood to be James' still somewhat grudging blessing on her marriage, but she hadn't done it by knuckling under. Martha had, instead, demonstrated spectacularly to her father that, far from striking her dead for disobedience, God seemed to be showering her with blessings, not least among them the accepting admiration of the city's most prominent citizens.

Ever since the Jenny Lind affair which, at least in public, had been a social triumph, being invited to dine at Martha's table was considered in itself an acknowledgment of prominence, and few declined. Amelia didn't know quite what had happened at that dinner, and she thought that Martha and especially Peter might have regrets that they no longer saw anything of Whitman since his *Leaves of Grass* had made such a splash and had proved that he was, after all, a prophetic poet and not a tramp newspaperman. Still, Martha probably knew what she was doing in this, as in other matters; Whitman continued to dress crudely and do odd things like ride atop an omnibus all day, exchanging rough talk with the driver, and there were stories about his sexual preferences that would damage any politician known to be his friend. Martha nevertheless kept Peter's image as a cultural light burnished by having to the house those old national monuments, William Cullen Bryant and Washington Irving, and seeing to it that she and Peter appeared regularly in a box at the opera and the philharmonic. She also kept Peter's name in the papers by such timely affairs as a dinner in honor of Cyrus Field and old Professor Morse just before Field set off to lay an Atlantic cable to carry Morse's telegraph to Europe; though the cable had recently broken beyond repair this season, Martha's purposes had long been served. She had the courage, too, to offer a few shocks and surprises to her guests to prove that Alderman Van Alen's house was open, whatever his politics, to all sorts of citizens. Bishop Hughes, a gold cross glittering against his black vest, was known to have toasted his hostess's health in the fine French champagne the Van Alens always served; Mayor Fernando Wood, his well-tended curls barely concealing horns in the opinion of most of those present, had been seen leading off the after-dinner waltzing with Martha in his arms; Rabbi Golden, whose plump wife was scandalously whispered to be his host's first love, had been heard blessing the Van Alen house and its offerings of food and wine in Hebrew; and, most startling of all to an assemblage of Roosevelts, Schermerhorns, Livingstons, Waltons, Belmonts and the like, Sojourner Truth, that brave black woman who would stand up in front of packed halls and speak out for the freedom of both women and Negroes, had once been seated at table on Alderman Van Alen's right.

Amelia had to hand it to Martha, who was accomplishing as much or more with feminine guile as she, Amelia, had done by raising her often too strident voice, and she was not above handing it to herself, too, for realizing that a Martha was what Peter had needed. With the Roman Catholic bishop, who was in the process of erecting a marble and granite cathedral to his alien faith on upper Fifth Avenue, blessing his house by his presence, Peter couldn't be faulted by all those "nigger-hating Irishmen" for also having entertained a black woman, for example. What Martha had perceived was that the belle of the ball can do no wrong, and she had gone on being the belle of the ball. Martha used her feminine charm the way a cat used its purr to lull certain men into thinking that they were loved for themselves instead of their value as providers, but she kept her claws sharp enough to draw blood when the occasion called for it. As long as Martha remained, as she seemed to, mostly on the side of the angels, Amelia didn't feel it becoming or intelligent of her to fault Martha's methods. It was galling, to be sure, that men, who ran everything, had to be seduced or traduced by anyone in skirts who had an idea to put across, but Aunt Sally had tried to apprise her of this fact of life, and she had been too headstrong to listen. Of course, much as she loved her, she'd always thought of Aunt Sally, who'd actually *seen* George Washington, as somewhat old hat. Watching Martha now, she wondered. Not much more proof of her power was needed than to see Cousin James bend his stiff neck, however slightly, in his daughter's direction. The man—thank God—was finally winding up: " . . . in the name of the Father, the Son, and the Holy Ghost, Amen."

Cornelius was next to get onto his feet. He stood and scowled at the smattering of people before him, and Amelia thought how peculiar it was that a white-haired man could manage to look so much like the determined little boy she'd first known when her parents almost literally dumped her at the Van Alen house on Broadway. She'd tried to joke with him without success then, and she still couldn't; he was as devoid of the joyous juices of life as a sun-dried prune. She'd had to believe Aunt Sally's conclusion that Augusta's ailing condition had been a kind of blessing to Cornelius, since his wife had been able to put so few demands upon him. He could have shown more gratitude for this blessing than by working until noon on the day of Augusta's funeral, but then, gratitude, except to his mother, had never been Cornelius' long suit. He certainly didn't seem grateful to any of them now for their trouble to come over and shiver here in this gloomy warehouse.

"On behalf of the directors of Van Alen & Son, Incorporated," he was saying, "I . . . uh . . . welcome you all here. I trust that the . . . uh . . . unusual number of stockholders present does not reflect any . . . uh . . . loss of faith in the management of this company in

442

view of present economic conditions. You will all be . . . uh . . . delighted, I'm sure, to hear the report that I've asked our secretary, Mr. John Charles Smith, Jr., to read to you. You will all agree, I'm also sure, that, thriving as it is in a time of troubles, this enterprise is, indeed, blessed by God, as acknowledged in Dr. Schuyler's moving prayer . . ."

Doctor Schuyler? Amelia had almost forgotten that Princeton College, his alma mater, had recently granted Cousin James an honorary Doctor of Divinity, an action that had made Peter, also an alumnus, squirm. Peter should be smart enough to understand that the good Dr. Schuyler, who as pastor stood close to so many wealthy men at the coming time of death, could be influential in suggesting where their earthly treasures might be deposited, but then Peter, dear soul, was often still afflicted with the stigmatism of idealism. He actually thought, as he'd once ungallantly complained to Amelia, that Martha gave all those parties that threatened to bankrupt him for her own personal pleasure. It was, after all, good that Amelia hadn't tried to live with a man. If they were decent, like Peter, they went around with their heads in the clouds, and she'd have a hard time concealing her contempt; if they were the other kind, like Cousin Charlie Smith, who was now coming forward to speak, they couldn't be trusted out of your sight, and she'd have a hard time concealing her feelings about them.

Cousin Charlie, holding papers in his hand, fumbled on the glasses that were a giveaway of his real age and then, peering over them, indulged in a small smile at the clever words that were apparently on his mind before he said, "Ladies and gentlemen, our president has noted an increase in your numbers over years past, but he failed to take note of the fact that among you sits a representative of one of the most powerful boards in our city, Alderman Peter Schuyler Van Alen. We, as directors, are honored by your presence, Mr. Van Alen, and I am hoping that, after you hear our report, you will be able to inform the city fathers that at least one of the vast number of enterprises in this great city is holding its own against the falling financial tide which threatens to leave this whole metropolis high and dry. And I am certain that, as an important stockholder, you will be personally pleased to know that, in a meeting just prior to this gathering, your directors voted to pay again next year a dividend of ten percent as a sign of their faith, despite the present panic, in the future of both

443

Van Alen & Son and of this great city and country. Now, with your permission, let me read the report . . . "

Charlie ran as rapidly as possible through confusing columns of figures: accounts receivable—numbers of engines and locomotives on order, dockage and warehousing fees due, shares of shipping ventures in prospect, and on and on; accounts payable—supplies requisitioned, rents, salaries, interest, and on and on. Nobody could possibly keep up with it all, least of all Amelia, but she could grasp the final prediction of a profit that, notwithstanding the times, would equal or exceed the proposed dividend. There was a scattering of applause from the little group of men in the audience, and one rose to say, "I for one would like to thank and congratulate the officers and directors of this company on the stockholders' behalf. I suggest that they be unanimously reelected and that their report be unanimously accepted. I must say that when the news of this report gets back to Wall Street, we shall benefit from the strange sight of a stock going up instead of down."

Cornelius, on his feet again, said, "Thank you . . . Mr . . . . uh, Griggs, isn't it? You know, my grandfather, the first Cornelius Van Alen, who founded this firm, used to say that he got his start on the river by being able to sail against the tide when other men had to anchor, and we would still seem to be carrying on in his tradition. I take it you have made a motion, Mr. Griggs. Are we ready for a vote on the motion?"

Amelia jumped to her feet. "I'd like to raise a question first, Mr. Van Alen."

Possibly because of the good news in the report, Cornelius came close to humor. "Ah, yes, Miss Downing. This wouldn't be a regular meeting—would it?—without a question from Miss Downing. What is it this time, Miss Downing?"

"Mr. Van Alen, can you tell me why the company has been laying off men with years of service who were making two dollars a day to hire mere novices at seventy-five cents a day?"

"If Miss Downing had been a teacher of mathematics instead of languages, she would not have to ask such a question. It is plain that with labor a glut on the market there is no sense in paying now the wages demanded of us when labor was scarce. If you had listened carefully to Mr. Smith's figures, Miss Downing, you would realize that our present savings in labor is offsetting the losses we must necessarily take in those few investments we have that are suffering in the falling market. Indeed, it is the reason we can offer you all such favorable dividends."

"But don't you lose in efficiency, in quality?"

"Hungry men learn rapidly . . ."

Amelia would not be put off. "Then let me ask Dr. Schuyler if it doesn't say somewhere in the Bible that a laborer is worth his hire?"

Cousin James came to stand beside Cornelius. "I think perhaps it does, Miss Downing," he said, "but couldn't that as well mean worth what he can get? I know of no biblical injunction that we must impoverish the stockholders and risk the very life of the company by paying more than circumstances require—"

"Didn't Christ himself say to take all and give it to the poor?" Amelia asked, annoyed that she felt perspiration beginning to run even in this clammy warehouse and that she heard her voice rising into the shrill register of exasperation. "As a stockholder of the company, I object to treating loyal workmen like so many interchangeable pieces of metal. I—"

Cousin James had been shaking his head and whispering to Cornelius, who interrupted. "Miss Downing, may I repeat what I've said at virtually every previous meeting? This company stands ready to purchase at ten percent above current market value the shares of any stockholder who is not happy with the management. So in this case I suggest—"

"Save your breath, Cornelius," Amelia said, dropping formality in frustration. "I guess I might as well save mine too. I just hope Mr. Secretary Smith puts my objections into the record for future reference."

As Amelia sat down, Sally whispered, "Are you sure they're doing that, Amelia?"

"You didn't hear them deny it, did you? Yes, I'm sure. The wife of one of the men came to me, caught me outside my hotel. The poor thing has eight children, and I felt obliged to give her money out of my own pocket."

Sally shook her head, whether in grief or anger or despair was difficult to tell. But Peter was now on his feet, asking for the floor, and curiosity let Amelia forget her own defeat. "Mr. Van Alen," Peter was saying, "it has come to my attention in my official capacity as an alderman of this city that Mr. John Charles Smith, Jr., secretary and

445

counsel to Van Alen & Son, is seeking a street railway franchise on Broadway. As a stockholder of this company, I should like to know whether Mr. Smith is acting on the company's behalf. If so, I should like to point out that the operation of a street railway seems entirely outside the interests and competency of this concern."

Peter had caught them off guard, like a man who throws a punch before an angry word has been spoken. Cornelius' frowning eyebrows lifted and he turned toward Charlie, who came up to him and engaged in rapid, whispered conversation, punctuated by much handwaving. Cornelius then turned back to the audience and said, "I can state categorically that Mr. Smith is engaged in no negotiations for any street railway on behalf of Van Alen & Son. I would agree that such an enterprise is not at this time in the interests of this company. Mr. Smith is, however, an attorney with other clients and whether he is representing one of them in this matter should not, and won't, be discussed at this meeting."

"Thank you, Mr. Van Alen," Peter said. "As a stockholder, I am satisfied. But my purpose in coming here today was to let you and the other directors and stockholders know that, in my capacity as an alderman, I oppose the granting of a street railway franchise on Broadway or anywhere else except to the highest bidder in open bidding. I wanted to make certain that my opposition would not prove embarrassing to this company."

When the meeting was over, Sally walked out with her son. "What was that all about, Peter?" she asked.

"Just about what you heard, mother. I didn't think that Cornelius knew that Charlie Smith is trying to bribe aldermen and councilmen, but I had to be sure. It's going to be an awful mess when and if I get the evidence I need, and we could all be hurt if the company's involved. I think you ought to talk to Cornelius about getting rid of that fellow; he's sure to get him into trouble."

As the phaeton pulled out of the gloom and into the blessed autumn sunshine, Amelia said, "Well, Peter, neither of us got anywhere, but at least you seemed to make them sit up. I hate to say it, but I wonder if you were getting the truth."

"At least half the truth. Whatever else you can say about Cornelius, he's not an outright liar. I'm sure he didn't know what Charlie's up to until now. And I've already discovered that Charlie's acting as agent for the commodore, which, the way things are, means that

Cornelius is inevitably involved. What he'd do if Charlie is forthcoming with him I don't know. Unfortunately, brother Cornelius hasn't proved too scrupulous in the past when there's a dollar to be made. Still, one can hope . . . Well, let's forget about business. It's a nice day. How about a ride in the park?"

"Oh, good," Martha said. "I thought you said those stockholders' meetings were amusing, Amelia. I found it a bore—all those figures, and everybody so solemn and formal. Daddy looked more serious than he does in church."

"Maybe he thinks this is a more serious business," Peter said.

"Now, Peter, I thought we had a truce on that," Martha said.

"Sorry, my dear, but I do agree with you—it wasn't very amusing."

"Both of you are really too nice to get pleasure out of watching a bunch of hypocrites strut and squirm. When it comes to that, there isn't a nice bone in my fat body."

"Honestly, Amelia, I don't know why you don't take Cousin Cornelius up on his offer and sell out if you feel that way," Martha said. "There are other places where you could invest—"

"Not and get as much return. Besides, I think they're all about the same. Cornelius, for heaven's sake, has the reputation of being one of the most honest businessmen in the city, and I guess he is when it comes to meeting his obligations," Amelia said. "Actually, I'm buying more stock because I think I'm more effective when I'm working from within. That's why I suffer with these damned hoops to pretend I'm a lady. You, of all people, ought to understand that, Martha."

"Yes, I guess I do, I just wanted to hear you say it. What I think, then, is that, if you and Peter don't like the way things are going with the company, you ought to get together and *do* something about it. I'd bet Aunt Sally would join you and . . . and my father too. He couldn't *afford* to have anything going on that would hurt his reputation. I think you could start by getting Cornelius to fire that Charlie Smith. I like his sister, but I don't like him."

"I've tried to explain to you, sweetheart," Peter said, "that we still wouldn't have the votes. That's really why I've stayed away. All that could result from my getting into it would be more arguments with my brother that would add to mother's distress."

"But there are other stockholders, aren't there? You could talk to them," Martha argued. "Say, I have an idea—get some of their names

447

for Lucy and me . . . good dinners work wonders, you know."

"Dear," Peter said, "I haven't yet paid for the last two parties—"

"Don't worry about that," Amelia said. "For that, *I'll* pay the bill. I can't think of any better use for the money Cornelius earns for me than to undermine his iron rule. Martha, you really are a love."

Amelia had known it would be a good day, and it was getting better all the time. They'd reached the park, and Peter asked the coachman to get down and wait for him. The paths in the park were where gentlemen took over their own rigs and displayed their skill with whip and reins. They were still so new that they could be perilously slick or hopelessly mired in the rains of spring or summer, but there'd already been a hard frost, and the going was reasonably good this day. As Peter pulled in among the carriages of all descriptions circling and weaving through the park, another phaeton came so close alongside that the hubs touched. It was a friendly challenge to a race, and the young man in the driver's seat smiled and tipped his hat to the ladies before he touched his horses into a trot with a flick of his whip.

"It's Cousin Ted Roosevelt," Martha said. "They say he drives so fast that the grooms fall off at the corners. You're not going to let *him* get ahead of you, are you, Peter?"

Peter turned and frowned. "Now you know, dear, I can't afford to take chances with you in your condition. We just came up here for the air—"

"Oh, Peter, life is full of chances. It wouldn't be any fun otherwise, would it? Look at the chance I took on you. Go on . . ."

"That's the spirit," Amelia agreed.

"Well . . ." Peter's tone was doubtful, but it was obvious that it galled him to have young Roosevelt, not only a cousin but a neighbor, show him up. "You two hold on, then," he said, and let his own whip crack across the rumps of his team.

Round and round they flew, sometimes ahead of, sometimes behind their rival. Above them the yellow and orange tapestry of fall leaves wheeled like the chips in a kaleidoscope. Amelia and Martha laughed and shrieked like girls, and Peter cursed like an omnibus driver. Amelia couldn't remember when she'd had such a marvelous time. More than once her heart skipped beats, particularly when at the end Peter pulled ahead and cut off Roosevelt with a sharp turn that sent the phaeton into a screeching careen on two wheels. Crush-

448

ing her hoops, Amelia grabbed for Martha who'd been jumping up and down, shouting, "Win, Peter, win!" and just kept her from flying out.

Martha seemed not to care about her narrow escape. When they came to a stop, she stood up, put her arms around her husband and kissed him. "You *did* it, Peter!"

"Are you all right?"

"Perfectly. Oh, I'm so proud of you, Peter. By nightfall everybody in town will know what a sportsman Alderman Van Alen is. You know those Roosevelts—they can't keep from talking even if it hurts them."

"You devil," Peter said.

Amelia turned away. She couldn't help feeling a little stab in the heart from the words and looks Martha and Peter were exchanging. There always came a time like this for her in the presence of happy couples. But her life had been her own choice, more than it was for most, and she wasn't going to let this grow into a cloud that would shadow a nearly perfect day. She turned back, clapped her hands for attention and said, "All right, you two, I want you to come back with me to the hotel and drink a toast in champagne—champagne is good for babies, isn't it?"

"I'm not sure, but I'm willing to try," Martha said. "What will we toast?"

"The winner of course. May good men always win!"

"What about their wives?" Martha teased.

"Oh, they've already won," Amelia said without much thought, and the look that Peter gave her over Martha's shoulder let her know that he had not forgotten, would never forget. Yes, some days did make life especially worth living.

Chapter XIX

The House Divided

"Mr. President, it will not make a very pretty story for my grandchildren that I spent this most crucial time of the war battling my own brother in New York," Peter Schuyler Van Alen protested.

The president, his long face sadder, more full of anxiety, than Peter had ever seen it before, had no jokes or parables at the tip of his tongue as he so often did when trying to explain the workings of his almost unfathomable mind to subordinates. "I know, Peter," he said, "but unfortunately this is a war of brothers—some of Mrs. Lincoln's brothers wear the gray, you know. I appreciate what you and your colleagues on the Sanitary Commission have been doing for the troops, but I cannot think of an assignment more important, with the possible exception of capturing Lee, than the one I am now asking you to undertake. Wouldn't you agree, Stanton?"

The secretary of war, wheezing with asthma, peered owlishly at Peter through his thick glasses. "I most certainly do, Mr. President. I can only hope that you have selected the right agent. It seems to me that somebody outside the family would better serve us."

It was, as Peter had heard, not unusual for Stanton, who before entering the cabinet had gone around calling Lincoln the "original gorilla," to challenge the president's judgment. In this case, he possibly had a right to do so since the project was primarily his; indeed, the meeting itself was taking place not in the White House but in the telegraph room of the War Office nearby, where in this late spring of 1863 the president was spending much of his time awaiting the latest reports on the whereabouts of the enemy army that General Lee was leading into Pennsylvania; if Lee succeeded in reaching Harrisburg and cutting the rail lines, the consequences were unthinkable. Peter rather agreed with Stanton, but it was apparent that the secretary would no more prevail on this than on other occasions when the president's mind was resolved.

"Mr. Stanton, I'm sure you've heard the old saying of setting a spy to catch a spy," Lincoln said. "In any case, Peter here has my fullest confidence. Now that Greeley's flaying my hide for moving so slowly, Peter may be the only man I could trust in that strange place called New York. But for the brave boys from there who have given their lives, I often think it would have been better if Fernando Wood had had his way and made of it a separate country. Will you undertake this mission, Peter?"

"I've often said, sir, that I would follow you to hell, and I think that may be where you're sending me," Peter replied.

A slight flicker of light came into the president's sunken eyes, and his lips lifted in the hint of a smile as he said, "Well, I might agree with that. I am sure you're in for some very warm work. My best wishes for your success."

The president took Peter's hand in both of his huge, hard ones. Stanton just stroked his beard nervously and said, "Remember, you will report to me, Mr. Van Alen . . ."

Out in the hot Washington sunshine, Peter walked and walked. Before he could do anything else, he had to get control of himself. Since it was unseemly for a man of fifty, healthy and unmaimed by war, comfortable in his circumstances, moderately famous for his humanitarian activities, to feel like crying, he tried to persuade himself that the blur in his vision came from sweat in his eyes or the shimmer of sun bouncing off the pavement in front of him. Of all the disappointments he had suffered in his life, this seemed now to him the worst. He had been waiting for two years for a summons from the president, and when it had come, he had expected at last to be offered an office in which he could make up for all of the shortcomings of an

451

uncertain career. To be asked, instead, to go back home and try to take over Van Alen & Son, the one job he'd shunned for a lifetime, was being offered the bitterest kind of pill to swallow. It stuck in his throat, and it made his eyes water.

The President's hint that his mission was equivalent to that of a spy's provided some sense of urgency and intrigue but not enough. However courageous they were, however valuable their work, spies necessarily went unloved and unsung as Cooper had suggested in his novel so long ago. Peter had had his share of that kind of unrewarding service in those long years as a New York alderman. The hope that he and Martha had shared in those times was that by carefully walking a tightrope to stay in office as a maverick—first a reformer and then a Republican—in a Tammany-run town he would be seen as exceptional, as a winner and logical contender for City Hall, for the governor's mansion in Albany, for . . . there was *no* limit to their dream, especially Martha's. But then the rope had let go under his feet, mysteriously severed when the Board of Supervisors had impounded the ballot boxes in his ward for a recount in '59 and had claimed that his victory had, after all, been a defeat. Unthanked, unheralded, "Unbuyable Pete" had been cast out into that utter darkness reserved for politicians who have the wrong friends. And then . . . a new light had come in the form of an unexpected letter.

Chicago, Illinois
November 10, 1859

Dear Cousin Peter:

I guess it has been twenty years since I have written to you, but I have been so busy that it seems only yesterday. I still wish that you had come out here then, because my paper is going great guns, and, with the railroads coming through, this fair city is growing so fast that I expect it to eclipse New York. My own fortunes have thrived, and I have lately entered the business of building stockyards and a slaughterhouse to handle the cattle being driven in from the western ranches. People here say that Chicago will become butcher to the whole world, and I want to be in on the ground floor of that. So I could still find something for you to do if you ever want to change your mind and take the advice of your old boss Greeley to go west.

But right now I am glad that you are still in New York, because I am hoping that you can do a favor for me, and for our country. I was very interested to read that you had gone into politics. I guess it proves that you are my father's son more than I ever was, and for what it's worth I think you deserve whatever you got from his estate. It would be nice to see a Peter Schuyler Van Alen in the Senate or the cabinet, and if you go along with me and play your cards right, I don't see why this couldn't come about. If you read any of the exchanges, you probably know that I and my paper have been strong backers of the Republican Party in which you have made a considerable name as one of its few successful candidates in that Democratic city of yours . . . (obviously, the news of the recount hadn't yet reached Illinois) . . . and now I think that we have found right here in our own state a man who can be elected to the highest office in the land in '60. His name is Abraham Lincoln, and you may have heard of him through his debates with Senator Douglas last year. Though he lost the election in the legislature to Douglas, he won the popular vote.

The problem now is to get a name for Mr. Lincoln in the East, and the favor I am asking of you is for you and some of your Republican friends to arrange for a speaking engagement in New York where he can be seen and his voice heard. I have to warn you that there are those who say that Mr. Lincoln is the ugliest man ever born of woman, and he speaks in a high, backwoodsman's twang. But from listening to most of his debates, I can assure you that you forget all that when he speaks. In any case, Mr. Lincoln is in the tradition of Old Hickory and Log Cabin Harrison, and we are calling him the "Rail Splitter" to emphasize his humble beginnings. I know that he will be opposed by your Mr. Seward who expects and probably deserves the nomination which is one reason I am appealing to you instead of Weed and the others in Albany who have so long identified themselves with Seward. I think that Mr. Lincoln may be as strongly opposed to slavery as Mr. Seward, but he hasn't yet been tarred with that brush and should, therefore, be able to get the moderate vote.

Let me know as soon as you can whether you can arrange for a speaking engagement for Mr. Lincoln, who is free to come at your convenience. I would suggest a fee of at least $200 to cover his expenses since he is virtually without funds of his own and since it would be better that he earn his way than to appear with the support of some faction here. I am sure that, if Mr. Lincoln is as successful as I predict that he will be, he will be eternally grateful to you and will find a means of showing that gratitude.

Your long lost cousin,
Francis Livingston

While he had only the vaguest idea of who Lincoln was and what he stood for, Peter jumped at the opportunity. Since, as his cousin had shrewdly surmised, Peter was himself unrelated to the Whigs-turned-Republicans under Senator Seward's leadership, he decided to keep the event out of the ordinary line of politics and to seek a high level of civic sponsorship. This was the time to cash in on all the wine and food Martha had been dispensing over the years, and he found it comparatively easy to persuade some of the men who had sat at his table to join him in inviting Lincoln to speak in New York. As chairman for the event, Peter chose his old employer, William Cullen Bryant. The old poet and *Post* editor, with his flowing white mane and beard, had become as visible as—and not unlike—a public statue; hardly a notable in New York was either laid to rest or tendered an honorary public dinner without a eulogy or tribute from Bryant. While Bryant was solidly Republican, he was less blatantly so than, say, Horace Greeley, whose editorials on the subject of slavery over the last five years had been sounding more and more like a trumpet call to war. To add to the dignity of the occasion, Peter engaged the hall at Cooper Union for February 27, 1860.

Over the weeks of waiting, Cousin Francis dropped teasing notes about how his candidate Lincoln was toiling through tomes on constitutional law and history in the state library to prepare his speech. Lincoln was taking it very seriously as his debut on a national stage, and Cousin Francis was orchestrating his paper to make public announcement of its Lincoln-for-President campaign just before the New York appearance. Greeley was cooperative, informing New Yorkers in the *Tribune* that they were about to hear "a man of the people, a champion of free labor." But God was not; on the night of the event a huge snowstorm blanketed New York, snarling traffic and discouraging the faint-hearted. Only about 1,500 people, among them Peter's loyal wife and mother, made it to the hall—just enough, at twenty-five cents a head, to get $367 from those who actually paid and cover expenses. They were, however, Peter noted as he looked around, among the city's most distinguished citizens, and his fears that he had been trapped into a situation that would make him a laughingstock grew.

If Peter had felt misgivings at first sight of Jenny Lind, they were nothing compared to his reaction to Abraham Lincoln. Delayed himself by the snowstorm, Peter had missed Lincoln at the station but had finally caught up with him in the Astor House, where he was invited up to Lincoln's room. When Lincoln himself opened the door to Peter's knock, the shock was extreme. Cousin Francis' warning about the man's looks had not been enough, especially since his tall boney frame was clad only in a flapping shirt, open at neck and cuffs, and baggy woolen underdrawers. His head seemed outsized, even on that rangy frame, and his features looked as if they'd been whittled out of hard white wood with a blunt ax. His voice was incongruously soft and high, but the hand that shook Peter's was possessed of nearly crushing strength. He was a rail-splitter, all right, but was he an orator? Peter simply couldn't imagine anything coming out of that crudely carved mouth that would satisfy the sophisticated audience they were likely to draw.

"Mr. Van Alen? Much obliged for your bringing me here. Come in, come in, and help me get decked out," Lincoln said. "Didn't expect to speak at Cooper Union, thought I was going to be at Mr. Beecher's church over in Brooklyn. So I guess it's a good thing mother insisted I get new duds—best in Springfield."

Lincoln was pulling a suit of black broadcloth out of an old valise laid open on the bed, and Peter said, "I'm sorry about the snow, Mr. Lincoln. I would have met you at the train if—"

"I've learned there's no use in apologizing for God," Lincoln said. "Anyway, a man who's chased Injuns ought to be able to find his way around a city as well laid out as New York. Mighty pretty stores on your Broadway. I'll have to remember to get mother a bonnet before I go back. She favors pretty clothes, you know. Now how's this?"

Lincoln was snapping into place the suspenders pulling up the pants of his new suit. Days of being crushed in the valise had left them as nearly crumpled as the underdrawers they covered. Peter offered to send for a valet. "No need and no time," Lincoln said, and Peter saw a little sparkle in the eyes looking out from the dark caverns made by his brows. "If they were perfect, the audience might take me for one of the New York swells like Mr. Seward instead of a man of the people like Mr. Greeley so kindly described me. If you'll just permit me to have a few minutes to change my text to acknowledge what Mr. Cooper has done for culture instead of what Mr. Beecher has done for God, I'll be ready to go with you." . . .

Whatever shock he may also have had at the sight of Lincoln, Bryant, like Barnum, was equal to the occasion. Reminding his audience that the speaker would have defeated the mighty Douglas, were it not for the legislative apportionment in Illinois, he said, "I have only, my friends, to pronounce the name of Abraham Lincoln of Illinois, I have only to pronounce his name to secure your profoundest attention." Since the audience was comprised of men of manners, they applauded politely as Lincoln stepped forward. Again, like Jenny Lind, this bag of bones in a rumpled suit seemed transformed in public appearance: Lincoln displayed a curious and benign dignity as he stood there, hands clutching lapels, rocking back and forth slightly, smiling even more slightly, and waiting patiently for silence. When it came, though, he destroyed the illusion by turning to Bryant and uttering in his high-pitched voice his first mispronounced word —"Mr. *Cheer*man . . ."

It was a while before Peter, looking around nervously at the half circle of listening faces to sense their reaction, could himself begin to understand the words that Lincoln read from his manuscript in a soft, conversational tone. When he did, he realized that Lincoln was delivering a meticulously researched, highly reasoned argument that the Founding Fathers had never proscribed the government's right to limit slavery in its territories, nor, in fact, included in the Constitution the words "slave" or "slavery," intending to exclude from that fundamental document "the idea that there could be property in man." As he listened, Peter lost all consciousness of how the man looked or sounded, and was aware that the hall had grown so attentively silent that the soft hiss of the gas jets could be heard in every pause of the speaker's voice. While Lincoln, speaking directly to Southerners, proposed that they be let alone to solve slavery in their own way, he grew increasingly adamant and eloquent in opposition to its spread. Like a great symphony in the minor mode that modulates into a closing, major cadence, his speech, rumbling with the potential perils of divisiveness, ended with, "Let us have faith that right makes might; and in that faith let us to the end dare to do our duty as we understand it."

456

As Lincoln quietly folded his papers, the audience rose to applaud, and many of them rushed forward to shake his hand. Noah Brooks, a reporter friend of Peter's from the *Tribune*, hurrying out to write his story, paused long enough to tell Peter, "He's the greatest man since St. Paul. Nobody since Jenny Lind has ever made such a first impression on a New York audience. You've sure got a winner." Peter felt so, too, felt it in his guts, and he tried to get this feeling across to Lincoln as they crunched through the snow toward the cars with Martha and his mother in tow. While Peter raved on, Sally, with a woman's eye for the human detail, noticed that Lincoln was limping and asked in a pause, "Are you lame, Mr. Lincoln?"

Lincoln chuckled. "Oh, no, ma'am, mother thought I ought to have new boots for this affair as well as a new suit, and after all that time standing they're troubling my big feet."

Just as they were about to board the car to see him back to his hotel, Lincoln asked, "Do you folks live down my way?"

When they admitted that they didn't, he insisted on finding his way alone. As the car pulled away, Sally said, "I like your Mr. Lincoln, Peter—he's so human. But I can't help thinking that what the country needs now is somebody like General Washington. I can never forget how large and majestic he was."

"You were a lot smaller then, mother," Peter said.

Sally laughed, "Perhaps you're right."

"I thought Mr. Lincoln was marvelous," Martha said. "I think we should have gone with him, Peter. He looked so sad and lonely riding away from us."

Peter had been thinking the same thing. There was a quality about Lincoln that made him feel that something far more complicated and noble than political ambition was making this man force himself into tight-fitting shoes and ill-fitting clothes to stand up before strangers and ask for their votes. Lincoln really did think that it was possible, by reason, to persuade men to govern themselves wisely, and so from that moment did Peter too. Going on through New England, Lincoln got an even firmer grip on Peter's heart by commenting on the strike of the shoe workers who claimed that they couldn't live on $250 a year. "Thank God that we have a system of labor where there *can* be a strike. I like the system which lets a man quit when he wants to, and wish it might prevail everywhere."

From then until the election, former Alderman Peter Schuyler Van

457

Alen spoke himself hoarse on behalf of Lincoln at every meeting to which he could wangle an invitation. Though his nickname changed from "Unbuyable Pete" to "Nigger-Loving Pete," he didn't care; Lincoln would prevail, and he along with him. Prospects were especially promising since Don Fernando Wood and his followers had split off from Tammany to form their own Mozart Hall, but Peter had underestimated the powerful political instinct for survival. In the end, the state's Democrats got together to form a fusion ticket, supporting any of Lincoln's three rivals—Douglas or Bell or Breckenridge—and with the unwatchful eye of a Board of Supervisors with the likes of Tweed on it perpetrated election frauds beyond any in the city's history—sixty-three fictitious names were voted in the Third Ward, five hundred in the Twelfth Ward, nine hundred thirty-five in the Seventeenth Ward. The sachems of Tammany, mindful of their followers dislike and fear of "niggers," railed against John Brown, considered a martyr in other parts of the country since Virginia had executed him for his raid on Harper's Ferry, as an instigator of "riot, treason and murder." Lincoln's spectacular showing at Cooper Union had mostly gone over the heads of the saloon contingent, and although he won the nation against his divided rivals, he got only a third of the city's total vote. Mayor Wood, triumphant again, publicly proposed that the city get ahead of the game and declare itself a free country so that it could continue its lucrative trade with the southern states should they go through with their threats to secede upon Lincoln's election. There was no job in the city for "Nigger-Loving Pete," but he had high hopes, in the light of Cousin Francis' letters, for one in Washington.

By the time President-elect Lincoln came through New York on the way to his inauguration, southern states were already seceding and setting up their own government, United States facilities in the South were being seized, and a solution short of war seemed impossible. The city's reception was as cool as the February weather; the crowds who watched the presidential procession of thirty carriages move through the streets were sullen and silent. Acknowledging their evident sentiments as well as the mayor's well-known treasonous statement, Lincoln at City Hall was humble in thanking Mayor Wood for being received at all "by a people who do not by a majority agree with me." At the opera, Lincoln committed another sartorial gaffe by wearing black gloves instead of white, and antagonistic papers like

458

the *Herald* and Wood's own *Daily News* made much of the quip by a Southerner in the audience who, seeing Lincoln's black-gloved hands resting on the rim of his box, remarked, "I think we ought to send some flowers over the way to the Undertaker of the Union." Even Mrs. Lincoln was the recipient of sneers: Mrs. August Belmont demanded of the papers a public retraction of their report that *she* had been among the guests at Mrs. Lincoln's reception in the Astor House. Seeing all this, living through all this, Peter, and especially Martha, were dismayed. As a result of being counted among Lincoln's supporters, Martha, once the belle of New York, felt like a pariah in her own city; they might as well go to Washington, if they could.

As the first president of a new party, the Republican Party, Lincoln was expected to turn the rascals out and replace them with the faithful in unprecedented numbers. From the moment he arrived in Washington, the lobbies and corridors of the Willard Hotel, where he was staying until the White House was vacated, were a seething mass of office-seekers and their sponsors. Men who couldn't get through to him would try to waylay his carriage, and one of them drew a rebuke from the usually patient Lincoln: "I don't do business in the streets." Peter, too proud to be part of this mob, tried to emulate the Lincoln patience by waiting quietly in New York for a call. Though on his visit to New York Lincoln had warmly remembered that snowy night the year before even to the point of saying, "At least my boots are broken in by now; whether I am remains to be seen," no call came. When Martha chafed, Peter kept reminding her, and himself, that it took time for a new president to see what had to be done and by whom. Seward's appointment as secretary of state was understandable as a way of placating his disappointed rival for the nomination and keeping the old Whig element of the party in line; other appointments had similar logic. The name of a New York alderman who couldn't get himself reelected would be far down the list of essential political payoffs. So Peter waited, and waited . . .

The firing on Fort Sumter did more for the Lincoln cause in New York than years of fiery editorials by Greeley or months of speeches by former Alderman Van Alen. The president's call for troops on April 15, 1861, was answered immediately by such standing units as the Seventh Regiment which had so long been the last resort to keep order in the streets; new units were hastily formed—the thousands of Irish coming up with the 69th, the Irish Zouaves, the Irish Volunteers, the St. Patrick Brigade; the Italians forming the Garibaldi Guards; the Germans supplying the Steuben Volunteers. On April 20, a crowd of fifty thousand milled around Union Square, shouting enthusiastic responses to patriotic and bellicose speeches. Unexpected voices were raised, Archbishop Hughes saying that "the Stars and Stripes has been my flag and shall be to the end." Foot-dragging businessmen who had more to lose, they thought, than anybody else —$169 million in southern money was due in New York City—nevertheless gathered and pledged funds to equip the troops. Their attitude was reflected by their spokesman, the *Herald,* which a few days before Sumter had called for "the overthrow of the demoralizing, disorganizing, and destructive sectional party, of which 'Honest Abe' is the pliant instrument" and now shouted: "The business community demand that the war shall be *short;* and the more vigorously it is prosecuted the more speedily will it be closed. Businessmen can stand a temporary reverse. They can easily make arrangements for six months or a year. But they cannot endure a long, uncertain and tedious contest." The city's all-out response caused publisher William H. Appleton to predict, "We shall crush out this rebellion as an elephant would trample on a mouse."

War fever was as infectious as the old plagues of yellow fever and cholera had been, and Peter Schuyler Van Alen, of course, caught the disease. He at first sought out friends and political acquaintances in the rapidly forming city legions but soon discovered that a man of fifty with no military experience and three small children at home was unwanted. Cocky, twenty-four-year-old Colonel Elmer Ellsworth, who'd raised a regiment of red-trousered Zoouaves in ten days from the ranks of the New York firefighters, told Peter not unkindly, "Go on home, dad, and mind the store while we're gone." He finally humbled himself to wire Lincoln directly, offering his services anywhere in any capacity and received a somewhat enigmatic reply: "Offer much appreciated. Am certain a man of your capacities will find own way to serve." Before long, an opportunity did present itself. Letters from Amelia Downing, who had at once enlisted with Dorothea Dix as a nurse to soldiers in the field, made very personal the deplorable conditions with regard to food, shelter, sanitation and medical services in the camps of a hastily raised army, and Peter, along with a number of other prominent New Yorkers too old for

460

military service, joined the Sanitary Commission. It was rewarding service in that it did get him out into the field on inspection trips, but it was an on-again, off-again thing. He couldn't bring Martha and his family to Washington, and he remained frustrated at not being in a position to have some direct influence on a war that, as Lee's surprise invasion of the North was demonstrating, could still be lost . . .

And now, however important Lincoln tried to make it seem, this peculiar assignment he had been given would take him completely out of the fighting. The nature of the mission was rather vague and ominous. At best, it would be distasteful; at worst, it would be disastrous to the already precarious relationships within his family. It had come to the ears of Secretary of War Stanton that certain men on Capitol Hill were about to expose the involvement of Van Alen & Son in an unsavory, if not downright treasonous, gouging of the government for supplying shipping to transport General Banks' forces to New Orleans in '62. Though procurement had been assigned to Commodore Vanderbilt, as the nation's leading shipper, he had, according to Stanton's information, delegated it to a Van Alen representative. Since his own appointment had been brought about by revelations of graft and collusion between the War Department under Secretary Cameron and business interests selling the government defective rifles, lame horses and thin blankets for outrageous prices, Stanton couldn't afford a scandal. But, more important in the view of both the secretary and the president, was the need to keep in operation Van Alen & Son, a major supplier of engines and locomotives upon which vital military transportation depended. If the ugly rumors were proved true in a congressional investigation, the Secretary might be forced for political reasons to cancel contracts and suspend the company—unless, of course, it could be clearly shown to be in control of a person or persons who could not be held liable for past misdemeanors. It was Lincoln's idea that Peter, as a stockholder and family member, could not only ascertain the truth of the allegations but if they were true work quietly to transform the company management before hearings started on the Hill.

That was all Peter knew as he plodded the streets of Washington in a sweaty funk. He'd been out of New York so much in the last couple of years that he'd lost touch entirely with the company. Amelia was no longer around to insert her heckling presence into stockholders' meetings and report back, and his mother, though remarkably spry for eighty-three, seemed little involved with the business beyond mentioning from time to time that Cornelius was in danger of killing himself with overwork. In view of the scenes of agony he'd witnessed at field hospitals, it had struck Peter as almost indecent that the dividends from Van Alen & Son not only kept coming regularly but increased sharply each year of the war, but Martha, in need of the money to run a household and raise three children, had soothed his conscience by arguing, quite truly and logically, that the money was making possible his own patriotic volunteer service. With that issue settled in his own mind, he'd told himself to be content to let well enough alone—to stay away not only from the company but, as much as possible, from New York itself.

Once it had become evident that the clumsy elephant could not stamp on the elusive mouse, the war fever quickly subsided in New York. Although Mayor Wood had been replaced by a Republican, Opdyke, there were times when it seemed that his call for New York to become a separate country was being heeded. Impatient, uninterested, suffering loss, many New York businessmen thought that they could do as well or better trading with an independent Confederacy. Voices critical not only of the administration but of the war itself were so strident that the government suspended from the mail four New York newspapers, among them the *Daily News,* and an exasperated Horace Greeley coined the word "copperheads" for men he considered traitorous to the Union cause. More than most cities of the North, New York had long and fruitful commercial relations with the South that had spilled over into the most intimate personal relations. Southern wives with brothers fighting for the Confederacy were, as in the case of the White House itself, captive in many New York homes. One of these, the former Martha Bullock, lived just two blocks away from Peter on Twentieth Street with his own Martha's cousin Theodore Roosevelt, and, with their youngest Aaron almost of an age with little Theodore, they were often in and out of each other's houses. Seeing Martha Roosevelt's genuine suffering made it hard for even Peter to maintain a bellicose spirit. And the Emancipation Proclamation, hailed wildly in many parts of the North, was greeted in New York's workingmen's saloons with growls . . . "Ain't no nigger coming up here to get my job." Even old Flossie was said to have grumbled that those "no 'count southern niggers" would ruin things for her people in New York. On Wall Street men talked more of what Commodore Vanderbilt's sudden interest in railroads was doing to the New York and Harlem stock than of despatches from the front. Although Julia Ward Howe's new *Battle Hymn of the Republic* was dutifully being sung at public meetings, it was very difficult to retain, in New York, the feeling that the country was engaged in a great crusade for freedom, as Peter had come to believe it was. Little surprise then that he was reluctant to go back.

But in time of war a good soldier obeys his commanding officer. Peter wasn't altogether surprised to find that his blind walk had brought him to the door of his boardinghouse. He bounded up the steps, hurriedly packed his things and headed for the station. A troop train, pulling into the capital, passed Peter's train pulling out. He was sitting in the smoking car, surrounded by other civilians, mostly drummers in a jovial mood. They were passing around a whiskey bottle, and one of them, seeing the troops, said, "Look at them, I don't know where they all come from, but I'll bet Lincoln's going to have to start drafting men to fight this damned war." Another agreed, "Yeah—I don't like the idea of Lee getting up to Harrisburg and cutting the rails. I've got to get that iron out of Pittsburgh, or I'm a dead duck." One man, offering the bottle to Peter, asked, "What line are you in, mister?"

Peter shoved the bottle away, got up and ran for the platform, having to fight down the gorge of disgust and anger.

Most people would consider it a terrible thing to use one's sister as a spy. Not Charlie Smith. He'd never had much use for Lucy anyway. Maybe because she was so ugly that she hadn't had any fun herself, she'd been jealous of his good looks and easy ways and had tattled on him all the time. Well, let her do some tattling now that could be of real use. He didn't have to stretch the truth all that much to give her a scare which was the equivalent of twisting her arm the way he used to do when they were kids. All that Lucy had to live on for the rest of her life was the income from her share of the Van Alen stock she'd inherited from their mother. So it wasn't hard to convince her, since she knew his spenthrift habits and fuzzy philosophy so well, that Peter Van Alen had no business messing around with the company. After that, Lucy kept Charlie apprised of every guest invited to the Van Alen home on Twenty-Second Street, and, although seldom a guest herself, she took to hanging about to see that "everything went well for the party," and would eavesdrop from the pantry.

It was Lucy who had unwittingly aroused Charlie's suspicions in the first place. He'd bumped into her on Broadway one day coming out of a stationers with a box of invitations under her arm. She'd been excited by the fact that, with Peter Van Alen back from Washington, they'd asked her to help plan a dinner party "just like in the old days." The whole thing had at once smelled bad to Charlie. Why would Van Alen, the great humanitarian, give up his work just when, from what Charlie heard, the biggest battle of the war was about to take place out there in Pennsylvania? And why, in what these Unionists were calling their darkest hour, would the Van Alens start having parties again? As an echo of the first gun fired on Sumter, Martha Van Alen had announced loudly—so loudly that it managed to make an item in the *Tribune*—that she would not entertain for the duration, that, in fact, her large dining room at Twenty-Second Street would be converted into a place where her social friends could come any afternoon and help wrap bandages for her husband's commission. At the time he'd had to hand it to that woman: no politician could ask for a better wife; he'd been surprised that the Republicans hadn't put Peter up then and there for mayor instead of Opdyke, but then even Republicans were probably leery of unbuyable servants. Since Martha was too smart by half to go back on her word without reason, something had to be in the wind. And the clue to that something became plain as day when Charlie wormed out of Lucy a guest list that included Mr. and Mrs. Horace Griggs and Mr. and Mrs. Francis Schermerhorn.

So they were up to their old tricks? A while back when Peter had got a whiff of the Broadway franchise deal, he and Martha and that Amelia Downing had started wooing stockholders to get him, Charlie, thrown out of the company. Nobody had come out and said as much, but their strategy had been quite evident to a man as sensitive as Charlie. Of course it hadn't come to anything then. People holding stocks going up in a market going down don't listen to complaints against management, as Peter and his crowd ought to have known if they had any heads for business at all. Besides, that little storm of '57 blew itself out so quickly that Charlie, with the aid of some of the commodore's fifty thousand, was not only able to hold onto his Van Alen stock but his others as well, riding them back up to where he was floating higher than ever before in his life. Unless something untoward happened, he would die a millionaire which, for a man in his sixties, was a consoling thought, whether he could take it with him or not: the handsome bequest he had in mind for his old alma mater, Columbia, would enshrine John Charles Smith, Jr., for the ages.

Well, he deserved it. Whatever else you might say of him, Charlie Smith delivered, as the commodore had come to appreciate. It had taken longer and had been more complicated than he'd expected, but he and Tweed had used that money well, and the commodore's men were even now laying tracks from the Harlem's terminal all the way down Fourth Avenue and Broadway to the Battery. It was in the nature of his work that Charlie could never take any credit for what he'd done, but the commodore had shown his appreciation by throwing that shipping deal to Van Alen & Son and then tipping them to buy into the Harlem along with him in the fall of '62 when it was down to $9 a share. Only a few men who knew the inside of things as well as Charlie could understand what happened after that, but Cornelius Van Alen had grasped it very well when Charlie had had to come clean with him in order to take advantage of the commodore's plan for the ships. In his own clerical way, Cornelius could be a farsighted man: with the federal government backing a transcontinental railroad, Cornelius was following the commodore out of ships and into railroads, and he owed it all to Charlie. He'd said as much the last time Charlie had gone up to visit him at Lafayette Place. Charlie had actually been touched when Cornelius, lying there in bed and looking pale and old, had reached up and taken his hand and said, "I don't know where we'd be without you, John Charles."

Charlie didn't either, but it had taken almost as much patience as they said this Lincoln had to bring it about. First, they'd had to clean up the city boards by engineering a few elections like the one that had sent Peter Van Alen packing. Even then, they'd had to wait until war got people's minds onto something bigger than whether a track was running down their street. But when they did start to move, the action was more exciting than any horserace he'd ever been in. The stakes were tremendous: the commodore figured the franchise to be worth ten million for itself and a good deal more as an adjunct to the New York and Harlem which, through neglect of its facilities and the inconvenience of its station, was falling on bad times. With encouraging messages from Tweed, they started quietly picking up the Harlem stock, and then another horse entered the race. Since it was a question whether the city or the legislature had a right to grant the Broadway franchise, the commodore's old rival, Captain Law, still burning from having to pay Vanderbilt blackmail to keep the U.S. mail franchise on his Liverpool line, started placing a few shrewd investments in Albany. Charlie, who had put the commodore's money on the city's Common Council, really began to sweat when he heard that, but, by this April of '63 his horse had pulled ahead in the turn when the Common Council voted an ordinance first. Within a few days, the commodore's men were tearing up Broadway, the commodore got himself elected president of the Harlem, and the railroad's stock went up to $100. Charlie had just started to breathe easy and count his money when still another horse, the trickiest of them all, came pounding up behind them. Old Dan Drew, probably on the advice of that spidery character Jay Gould who worked for him, got to some councilmen to whom the commodore had shown gratitude in the form of gifts of stock and suggested that, if they rescinded their ordinance in the light of possible state action, they could sell short and buy in at $50 or $60 for delivery. On top of that a hungry judge was found to issue an injunction stopping the work on Broadway. Harlem stock dropped overnight to $72, and sweat was no adequate description for what Charlie's body was doing to him when he showed up for his weekly whist game with the commodore—a man who was known for not liking to lose in high stake races.

Amazingly, the commodore said nothing about the business as they sat down to the table. It had nothing to do with the company since the other players were Wardell and Billy, who knew as much as anybody ever knew about the commodore's affairs. The commodore was serious about whist, and for an hour or so, they sat there, puffing on cigars and concentrating so hard on the cards that the ticking of the mantel clock got on Charlie's taut nerves. Finally, he couldn't contain himself. "I'm sorry, commodore, I really thought I had those fellows fixed—"

"Don't worry about it, Charlie," the commodore said, pouncing on Charlie's lead with a trump and a satisfied grunt. "Those bastards are gonna be *really* fixed now. I hope you didn't sell short, too, did you?"

"Oh, no, I'd never do that," Charlie said, wondering why he hadn't thought of it . . . he must be slipping.

"Well, then, guess who's gonna own them shares they'll have to deliver? When they get through tryin' to save their shirts by settlin' up with me, there won't be any trouble with franchises. That sneaky old son-of-a-bitch Drew must have eyes in the back of his head. He's already been to see me, whinin' and dribblin' tobacco juice, and talkin' about how we wuz both poor boys together, and if I corner all that stock I'll ruin him. I told him I'd let him off the hook just once more for bein' nice to Billy here, but that's the end of it. Now pay attention to your cards, Charlie, or you'll owe me more'n you make when the stock goes up again. By the way, you'd better get your rear end over to the exchange when it opens tomorra and get what you can before it's too late . . ."

Thanks to the ships, Charlie was able to get a good deal of stock in the name of Van Alen & Co., and with the New York and Harlem at $179 and still climbing, Cornelius *should* hold his hand. Good as it had been to them, that ship business still worried Charlie, and he thought that it might be the rat he was smelling in Peter Van Alen's sudden return from Washington. He'd heard that some investigators from the Congress were sniffing around, and, if enough people talked too much, they could get the wrong impression. People on the outside just didn't understand business. In Charlie's mind, it was a lot like machinery; it would squeak and bind and come to a halt without oil, and the oil of business was money. With a war on, you had to keep pouring out the oil to make the wheels turn. He'd done that, and as far as he was concerned he was just as much of a patriot as that drunken store clerk Grant who'd used the war to get back into uniform and make a name for himself killing people. The commodore understood this, and so did Cornelius. Why, what Charlie had done had saved the Van Alen good name just as much as paying off their debts after the fire.

"Charlie, you been doin' me a good turn in this franchise business, and I got a chance to do one in return for you and that son-in-law of mine, Van Alen," was the way that the commodore had opened the negotiations. "Now maybe because of that ship I loaned them, the War Department's come to me with a very secret and urgent mission. They need lots of ships to send General Banks and his troops down around to New Orleans, and they need 'em quick. I'd go for 'em myself, 'ceptin' there's lots of fellers in the shippin' business who've been starin' at the Vanderbilt wake too long and don't exactly love me. But Van Alen's got just about the best name there is in business,

467

so your shippers'd trust him. What he ain't got is a good name in public. He and that preacher of his went around yapping too much about how niggers ought to be slaves, and from what I hear around they're callin' him a copperhead. Now, I don't pay attention to those sorts of things, but people get touchy in war. So if he got them ships for the Union in a hurry, he'd be a patriot. You understand, Charlie?"

"Yes, sir. Will there be any trouble about money?"

"Oh, no. The government'll print it if it ain't got it. You pay top dollar, Charlie, and if some of them shippers are smart enough to appreciate the business you're givin' them—if you know what I mean —you might split it with me. I already loaned 'em a ship and bought a sight of bonds and now they're puttin' that five percent income tax on me. A man could go broke that way if he don't figure out how to get it back, couldn't he, Charlie?"

"Yes, sir . . ."

Charlie and Cornelius were also hit by that income tax, just another of the unconstitutional things that that dictator Lincoln was shoving down everyone's throats. You'd think it would be enough that they were working their tails off around the clock to get out all the locomotives that that crazy little white-haired Scotchman from Pittsburgh, Andy Carnegie, claimed he needed to keep the railroads running. The least they could do would be to let a man keep the money he was earning from honest work. Everybody forgot that they'd lost half their business and were holding debts from the South that would never be paid. That ass Fernando Wood had probably been right when he suggested making New York into a separate country, because the way things were going this one wouldn't be worth saving. What did freedom mean if it didn't mean having the government keep its hands off a man's money? But the commodore knew how to handle it: a smart man would just take it back.

In those early days of 1862, Charlie knew that he wouldn't have any trouble selling the commodore's proposition to Cornelius. Van Alen & Son was badly in need of cash. The war hadn't ended in the few months that most businessmen had been prepared to tolerate, and the squeeze was on. At the same time that he had to write off all those bad debts from the South, Cornelius had to go out and borrow to tool up for all the war orders pouring in, and it would be months, if not years, before he could pay it off from sales. To a pious and cautious accountant like Cornelius, running in the red was like living in sin;

it almost physically hurt him. At the same time Cornelius too was aware of the talk around town that he was a copperhead. It infuriated him since he saw himself as a man of principles higher and more everlasting than those of the emotional, shallowminded people who gave in to the hysteria of war. While, in his opinion, justification for slavery of the black race could be found in Scripture, no such justification could be claimed for a particular political arrangement called the United States of America. Union was, therefore, a purely political cause, disguised in a false mask of morality by the abolitionists. Though, as an elder, it grieved him to see the church split, he had understood very well the sentiments of his southern Presbyterian brethren when they broke off and set up their own general assembly. Some of the most devout men he knew were Southerners, and God was as likely on their side as that of the North. This war wasn't a struggle between right and wrong; it was God's judgment on the people of both sides for their sins. To be called a copperhead for holding a clearer view of what was happening than most men was galling, but he was conscious that the brand, however misapplied, could hurt him if the war went on so long that the warmongers got control of everything. Already, they were suspending habeas corpus, taxing incomes; when might they start seizing a man's property, his company? If Lincoln could emancipate the slaves as he was threatening to do, no property would be safe, at least in the hands of men perceived to be enemies of the cause.

Although Cornelius wasn't the kind to spell all this out, Charlie had a pretty good idea of what went on in his boss's mind from interpreting the terse comments he heard from time to time. So he presented the plan as a God-given opportunity to keep the company on its feet until the profits from production rolled in and at the same time to earn a reputation for efficient patriotism. Like a hungry fish, Cornelius swallowed the whole hook. "Praise the Lord; it sounds like an answer to my prayers," he said. "You say it's perfectly legal to take commissions on this service?"

"That's my understanding from the commodore," Charlie said. "Of course, we'll have to split commissions with him. It's only fair . . ."

"Yes, I can see that," Cornelius said. "Well, go ahead, John Charles. I'm afraid I won't have time to help you with it, but you can use my name." . . .

Within weeks Van Alen & Son came to be known around town and as far as the War Department in Washington as a kind of patriotic miraclemaker. At a time when shipping was tight, a fleet for General Banks' expedition was conjured up almost overnight. It was, of course, no miracle. Charlie Smith simply got the wheels spinning fast by pouring on more of that business oil, money, than anybody before him. Charlie Smith was no haggler. When the owners of the *Eastern Queen* seemed reluctant because they'd only got $500 a day to charter her to the government for the Burnside expedition, Charlie proposed $900 a day; cheaper vessels like the *Shetucket* and the *Charles Osgood* that had been chartered out to government service for $150 a day were taken over by Charlie for $250 a day. Under the circumstances, none of the shipowners found Charlie's suggested five percent commission unreasonable, and the idea of paying it out in cash to avoid a lot of government bookkeeping made good sense. Not being a seaman himself, Charlie had to take the owner's word for it that ships like the old *Niagra* from Lake Ontario were sound enough to make it out around Cape Hatteras and down to Florida. Charlie began to consider himself some kind of hero for just getting the ships at all, and it wasn't until the soldiers who were transported in them started writing back to their mothers and the newspapers that a gnaw of worry began to eat at his stomach.

Of course, none of the complaints had anything to do with him. It was the army's fault that they put nine hundred men aboard a ship that was only supposed to carry three hundred people. It was the owners' fault that there weren't navigators or charts on some of the vessels. And how was Charlie supposed to have known that the *Niagra* was rotten? One soldier wrote that they had ripped up her planks when they were out at sea and found her timbers so soft that they wouldn't hold a nail; only prayer, he claimed, held the thing together until they could get back on dry land. When Charlie mentioned these reports to the commodore, the old boy growled, "What the hell do them farm boys they got in the army know about ships? We got the ships for 'em, and they all got there, didn't they? Don't trouble your head about it." But naturally the possibility that a lot of pockets had been richly weighted by government money at the expense of the comfort and safety of "our boys in blue" aroused the interest of those fellows in Congress who had nothing better to do than to throw a wrench into the machinery of business just when it ran smoothest.

Some of them started asking the commodore questions, and it was unsettling to Charlie's digestion to discover that the commodore was referring them to Van Alen & Son, who had, as he explained it, "done the whole damned job for me."

Considering everything, it was probably an act of Providence that Cornelius had been stricken about that time. The doctor thought that exhaustion from overwork had affected his heart, and it certainly looked that way to Charlie. About the only thing that could save him, according to the doctor, was complete rest; he not only ordered Cornelius to bed but ordered everybody else to keep him from reading the papers or worrying about the business. Cornelius was sick enough that for the first time in fifty years he just lay back and let that old slave Flossie wait on him hand and foot. She was older even than Aunt Sally, and Charlie thought from the way she moaned and creaked like a ship in a gale that she was in worse shape than Cornelius, but Aunt Sally insisted that the chance to feel useful by nursing her "baby" was the best thing that ever happened to old Flossie. As for the papers, Cornelius had never had much time for them anyway, letting his mother read them for him, and so it was easy for her just to tell him the news she thought he ought to know. Keeping Cornelius from worrying about the business was Charlie's problem. The only way to do it was for Charlie to show up every day and tell him how well things were going. Mostly it was the truth, and Charlie considered it an act of Christian charity, rather than a sin of omission, not to bother Cornelius with the thought that the sweet shipping deal might be turning sour.

And then Peter Van Alen showed up from Washington, and it was only a matter of weeks before Charlie's worst suspicions were confirmed. This time Lucy didn't have to hide behind the pantry door at one of those strange parties on Twenty-Second Street to get the information Charlie wanted. She'd been asked to include herself among the odd assortment of people she'd been instructed to invite. The ostensible purpose of the occasion was a welcome-home party for Amelia Downing, who was on leave from nursing at the front—also odd in view of the need for nurses at that bloody battle going on around Gettysburg—and Lucy had been rather perplexed that most of the guests, like the Griggs and the Schermerhorns who were invited back and Martha's father, the Reverend Doctor James Schuyler, could hardly be described as friends of Amelia's. In fact, the only

471

one who would fit in that category at all was Aunt Sally Van Alen, who hadn't been able to come because she was having one of her "bad days." At first the party had been one of those strained affairs of almost strangers making small talk which Peter tried to ease by having the serving girls keep the wine glasses filled. But when the dessert had been cleared away, Martha did not rise to lead the ladies into the parlor while the men had their brandy and cigars. Instead, she nodded at Peter who himself rose, lifted his glass and said, "To the Union cause!"

When everybody drank but Dr. Schuyler who never touched wine, Peter said, "I was sure that would be a popular toast in this company. You may not be aware of it, and I apologize for motives other than those of pure friendship, but the dinners which all of you have attended seperately in the last few weeks and which my wife, Martha, has so graciously arranged contrary to her public vow, have had a most patriotic intent. Before asking you all here tonight, we had to be certain of your Unionist sentiments which, I'm glad to say, were quite evident in your conversation on those other occasions. But your patriotism is not the sole nor most important reason for your inclusion in this gathering which may have perplexed a number of you in view of the fact that you scarcely know my cousin—of whom, by the way, I am exceeding proud—Nurse Amelia Downing. What we all share in common is that we are stockholders of Van Alen & Son, Incorporated, and, as such, have been given a vital mission to perform on behalf of the Union by no less than President Lincoln himself . . ."

With that introduction, Peter went on to describe very openly and as best he could the problem as it was seen by Secretary Stanton and the president and then said, "Together with a few proxies I have in my pocket, those of us in this room should have more than enough voting power—it takes only a simple majority—to overthrow the board of directors, saving yourself, Dr. Schuyler, if you're with us, and institute a new management. I am also counting on the votes of my mother, who as most of you know is eighty-three and subject to sudden indispositions and therefore couldn't join us tonight.

"Even though we've seen little of each other and have had serious differences over the years, I do not find it an easy task to ask you all to join me in what amounts to wresting a company to which he has devoted his life out of the hands of my own brother. Were it not for

472

what I understand to be the very precarious state of his health, I might have confronted him directly. As it is, I see it almost as the hand of God—and I hope you won't consider me blasphemous, Dr. Schuyler—that, by electing a new board of directors at this time, Cornelius Van Alen can be honorably retired for reasons of health. Another among us, Miss Lucy Smith, will suffer the same remorse as I since, from all the information I've been able to gather, her brother, John Charles Smith, Jr., is chiefly responsible for the situation in which we find ourselves and will, of course, have to be removed from the board of directors and from his offices as secretary and counsel to satisfy the congressional investigators as to our patriotic intentions. I can only say to you, Lucy, what the president said to me: this is a war that pits brother against brother, sister against sister, father against son—and we cannot be exempt. Your other brother George seems not to be involved, but I think that, like Cornelius, he should be honorably retired because of age. I certainly, and I'm sure the rest of us, will understand if you don't feel that you can go along with us, Lucy. With my mother's vote on our side, your holdings are not enough to affect the outcome.

"I realize that I am asking you as stockholders to commit the cardinal sin of ousting a management that has been very good to us all—in monetary terms, at least. It could be argued that they are guilty of nothing more than employing common business practices uncommonly well. In this particular case, the greedy owners who supplied shoddy ships, improperly manned, at prices they knew to be outrageous are as culpable as Van Alen & Son. So, too, is Commodore Vanderbilt, who, as I understand, shared in the commissions. But I'm sure that my good father-in-law would agree with me that another's sin is no excuse for our own. In any case and being practical about it, we have to consider seriously Secretary Stanton's warning that Van Alen & Son, whether fairly or not, could be made the scapegoat for the whole affair unless we act. Now I invite your comments."

The way Lucy told it to Charlie, everybody just sat there for a long time, stunned into silence. She could actually hear her own heart thumping; while it had been nice of Peter to let her off the hook, it was so obvious that he trusted her completely that she felt terrible, like a spy or something right in the tent of the enemy general. Then Dr. Schuyler got up to speak—"he's so handsome with all that white hair and has such a warm voice—" But what did the old bastard *say*, Charlie wanted to know.

Well, as nearly as she could remember it, Dr. Schuyler said, "Ladies and gentlemen, as a director of Van Alen & Son, I am profoundly disturbed by what I have heard here tonight, because I can assure you that I know nothing of this affair. I am also profoundly moved that my daughter and son-in-law would include me in this gathering in faith that I would join them in their efforts to right this wrong. Some of you, even yet, may be surprised to find me in this house and at this table, and I can only say that the Lord in his infinite wisdom and mercy opened my eyes and my heart a number of years ago to the fine qualities that these, my children, are displaying here tonight. I know perhaps more than any of you what a sacrifice it represents for Mr. Van Alen here, and for his wife, to leave the national stage at Washington, where it was anticipated that his good friend, the president, would make use of him in high office, to straighten out the affairs of a business in which he has had no personal interest. And I know, more than any of you can know, the feelings he was trying to express with regard to his brother, for, as all of you do know, Cornelius Van Alen has been closer than a brother to me. As my leading elder he has been my right hand in the building of my church; as friends we have shared the same opinions and concerns; as cousins we share the Schuyler blood. I have known Cornelius Van Alen since he was a boy, and I know that he has never been guilty of a sinful deed, or harbored a sinful thought. His integrity as a prominent Christian businessman of this city is legendary, and I would go further than his brother to assert that the involvement of Van Alen & Son in the procurement of vessels in a time of national emergency was, on the face of it, a deed of patriotism and perfectly in accord with practices accepted by the finest men in the business community of our city. I hold Cornelius Van Alen blameless, and, indeed, I think we all owe him a vote of gratitude for maintaining at what has proved the gravest risk to his own life the dividends upon which we all prosper . . . ."

"Jesus, I couldn't have said it better myself," Charlie said when Lucy paused in her remarkable recital. "I hope the old hypocrite had sense enough to stop right there." Lucy shook her head and went on with what she remembered of the rest of Dr. Schuyler's speech:

"Nevertheless, and with apologies to his sister, for whom I have the

474

profoundest respect, I cannot, unhappily, vouch for the purposes and methods of my fellow director, Mr. Smith. Indeed, I have expressed privately to Mr. Van Alen my gravest doubts about Mr. Smith, whose personal conduct is notorious, as a fitting representative of Van Alen & Son, but I have felt obliged to accept Mr. Van Alen's judgment as superior to mine when it comes to the conduct of a business. In view of my feelings about Mr. Smith and in view of the malicious and irresponsible manner in which members of the Congress deal with business affairs that they don't understand, I would vote to accept the procedure proposed here tonight. At the risk of possible personal financial sacrifice, I, as a minister of the Gospel, urge this action as our Christian duty, for by making public Mr. Van Alen's illness and consequent retirement we could thereby at least salvage his well-deserved reputation, as well as our own. Will you join me?''

Lucy assured her brother that *she* had not joined in the amen chorus that followed this speech, but she now suggested, "Why don't you just resign, Charlie? I'm sure you have enough to live on and—''

"The hell, you say! That pious old fraud's just throwing me to the wolves. Can't you see that? He knew all about the ship deal. Lord, I included the income from the commissions in my report to the directors, so he's either too lazy to read or lying in his teeth. That company will go right on the rocks if I'm not there, and Cornelius knows it. You'd all go down the drain, and so would I. I hope you're not stupid enough to vote with them," Charlie said.

"Well, if the president himself—''

"The president? That goddamned hick country lawyer? He knows nothing of business. He never met a payroll in his life. All he wants to do is get everybody and everything under his thumb, and he knows a weak sister like that Peter Van Alen when he sees one. You stick with me, Lucy, and we'll all be rich when Lincoln goes back to splitting rails where he belongs. I'm going to see Cornelius right now—''

"Don't tell about me," Lucy pleaded. "I don't want them to know.''

"Why should I do that? I may need you again. But I swear, if you vote against me, I'll kill you, and myself as well.''

"Charlie, you wouldn't do that—''

"Try me," he said in the same tone and with the same little laugh he'd used to pronounce the same words when they were kids and he'd threaten to throw himself out the window if she told about whatever she'd found him doing.

It still worked. He left her in tears and confident of her vote. Now for Aunt Sally. This was one bit of bad news that he'd have to deliver to Cornelius, whether it killed him or not. He doubted that it would since Cornelius' anger when he heard what his brother was up to should start enough adrenalin flowing to keep the weakest heart pumping. Once he heard about it, Cornelius would probably be able to straighten his mother out; over the years Charlie had observed with some interest that Aunt Sally usually voted with Cornelius in matters of business, and there was no good reason why she shouldn't do so now. Still, she had been going down to Peter's house and rolling bandages with Martha on her good days and talking about how even her cousin Matty Van Buren had voted for Lincoln before he died and about how everybody ought to sacrifice to preserve the Union. If she was that full of it, she just might be taken in, like the others, by whatever Peter told her. You never could rely on these old people to use their heads. Well, he could only try in hopes that whatever mysterious hold Cornelius had on his mother was still strong. The important thing was that, from what Lucy had spilled, Aunt Sally's vote was crucial.

It was late in the evening by the standards of the sickroom and the habits of the elderly when Charlie Smith burst into Lafayette Place, shoved his way by the protesting maid who answered the door and ran up the stairs. Sophie Van Alen, hearing the pound of his feet, came out of the parlor and tried to stop him at her father's door. "He's sleeping, Cousin Charlie. You can't wake him. The doctor said —"

"I don't give a damn what the doctor said. This is urgent."

"Is it bad news? He's not supposed to have bad news. Please . . ."

Charlie looked at the girl and suddenly felt a little sorry for her. She hadn't turned out to be really pretty after all, and at something like twenty-six she could be considered an old maid. She had no life of her own, as far as he could tell, and Aunt Sally used her like a cane. But if something happened to Cornelius, she might be his inheritor . . . he ought to try to be nice to her.

"No, don't worry, Sophie. It's not necessarily bad news, it's just something your father has to know about. How's your grandmother?"

"Not well. She's in bed too. She's had one of her spells."

476

"You poor girl. You must feel like Miss Dix herself taking care of all of these people. Has your Uncle Peter been to see his mother?"

"Oh, yes. Just today. I shouldn't have let him in, but it usually makes her feel better to see him. I guess he stayed too long and tired her out, because she seemed so sad tonight, said she didn't care whether she wakes up or not . . . ."

"You poor thing," Charlie said again. "Your Uncle Peter never did have much sense in my opinion. Well, I won't make the same mistake with your father. I'll be only a minute."

Stepping through the door and shutting it firmly behind him so that Sophie couldn't hear, if she lingered, he thought—too late, goddamn it, too late. There was an oil lamp burning on a table beside the bed, and its flickering light and acrid smell reminded Charlie of the sickrooms of his youth. In a corner by the head of the bed, old Flossie sat like a crumpled black shadow on a rocker. She seemed to be sound asleep, and Charlie thought of waking her and sending her out. Then he thought better of it. She probably wouldn't understand what she heard if she woke up, and he might have need of her if the news proved overwhelming to Cornelius. Charlie had no taste for dealing with death.

Charlie'd have to say this for Cornelius: sick as he was, he came alert at once when Charlie started to spill out the story as straight and fast as he could, omitting for the sake of brevity and dramatic effect the part about retiring Cornelius with honor. Cornelius hitched himself up against the back of the bed, and even in the dim light Charlie could see a choleric red rise and spread across his pale face as the adrenalin went to work. "How could he dare, how could he *dare* to do this?" Cornelius fairly shouted, and the sound of his voice, strangling to a snarl, awoke Flossie.

She heaved herself up and came to the bedside, thrusting her humped body between them and saying to Charlie, "What you doin' to Mr. Cornelius this time o' night? You like to kill him . . ."

Cornelius shoved her away. "Let him be, Flossie. He's come to discuss important business."

"Ain't no business as important as you gettin' well," Flossie grumbled.

"This is," Cornelius said. "My brother's trying to take the company away from me. I might as well not get well if he succeeds. You say mother holds the deciding votes, John Charles?"

"Yes, and I gather from Sophie that Peter got to her just today . . ."

Cornelius went into his familiar frown of concentration. "I can't think what we can do if he convinced her," he said. "Mother and I hardly have talked these past years, ever since the elopement, and I don't really know what she thinks except that she's always been soft on Peter. My God, why was I cursed with a brother like that?"

It was a prayer, and it was answered at once . . . "Mr. Cornelius, he ain't your brother . . . your real brother," Flossie said.

Both men had forgotten her presence, and it was seconds before they could react. Charlie, trained to catch slips from the mouths of witnesses, was the first to find his voice. "What was that? What did you say, Flossie?"

"I said Mr. Peter he no real brother. He from that Captain Roberts . . ."

Cornelius seemed to be trying to say something, but no sound came from his bobbling mouth. The color drained from his face, as if a spigot had been opened flushing away his blood. If my news didn't kill him, what this woman's saying will, Charlie thought, but he also suddenly knew that she was right . . . she'd just come up with that last, missing piece to the puzzle about the whole Van Alen family that he'd been trying to put together in his mind for years. But he had to be *sure*.

"Flossie, look what you've done to Mr. Cornelius! You'd better be telling the truth—"

"It's true as God gave me eyes. I seen them carryin' on, but didn't say nothin' to hurt Mr. Cornelius about his mamma, but if she gonna do this . . ."

Charlie could have hugged the old woman, but it wasn't seemly under the circumstances. "You'd swear to that in court?" he asked, and she answered, "Yessuh, if it help Mr. Cornelius. I just knowed it would come to this when he weak and like to die . . ."

"I don't think he'll die now, Flossie . . . . Cornelius, can you hear me?" Charlie said. "Do you realize what this means? I think we've got your mother in a situation where she'll never vote against you . . . Cornelius?"

Cornelius did appear to be pulling himself together again. His lips had hardened into a pencil line, his jaw muscles tensed, his dark brow indented in the middle like an angry arrow aimed at his nose, but his black eyes stared straight past them. When he spoke, it was to himself, "I know what it means . . . my mother a whore . . . my *own mother* a whore . . ."

"Now listen, Cornelius, it isn't all that bad," Charlie said soothingly. "A lot of us have had . . . well . . . adventures. You've always been a praying man, Cornelius, and maybe this is just God's way of answering your prayers and delivering your enemies into your hand. You don't have to hurt your mother, and nobody but the three of us need ever know about this. It's just that, once you make it clear that you know, she'll be reasonable. I'm sure after all these years she won't want the world, and especially Peter, to know about it, so—"

"My mother a whore, oh, Lord God . . ."

"*Cornelius,*" Charlie said, sterner now, "we've got to act fast. You've got to get yourself out of that bed and go talk to her—tonight —"

"I never want to see her again, *never* . . . all these years . . . deceived by my own mother . . ."

Wrought up and excited by this unexpected delivery, Charlie lost his temper with Cornelius. "Cornelius, you *are* a little prig," he said. "This is just a matter of reasonable people making a reasonable deal that would be good for all of them. All right, *I'll* talk to her . . . . Flossie, do something about Mr. Cornelius, he looks like he's going to pass out. Give him some brandy, whether he likes it or not. I'm sure the Lord will forgive him this time. Here, I've got a flask in my pocket." When he handed it to the old woman, he whispered, "Bless you. If he'd lost that company, he really would be dead—all of us would."

Fortunately, Sophie had not hung around in the hall, and Charlie was able to tiptoe past the parlor where she sat reading and steal up the stairs to what he knew to be Aunt Sally's bedroom. A gas jet burned in the hall, and the door was ajar, evidently so that she could be heard if she called out in the night. Charlie stepped in without knocking. He could feel the hair rise on the back of his neck in surprise and a kind of fright when he realized that she was not asleep; her wide-open eyes, so like those of Cornelius, glittered dully in the shaft of light from the door. They widened with fright of her own at seeing his black shape, and he was worried that she'd scream or faint or something. "Aunt Sally, Aunt Sally," he said in a whisper he hoped

479

was loud enough for her old ears. "It's just me—Charlie Smith
. . . don't wake the maids."

She seemed even more alarmed, too startled to bother to whisper,
but her aging voice had little carrying power. "What's happened?
What are *you* doing here? Has something happened to Cornelius?"

He went over and sat on her bed. Her small, old body shrank away
from him and huddled against the headboard. He tried to reassure
her. "No, it's not that. Cornelius is all right, I've just been with him."

"Then what is it? What are you doing here in my bedroom in the
dead of night? Get out—"

"Are you wide-awake, Aunt Sally?"

"Yes, old ladies never sleep. But I'm not well. Didn't Sophie tell
you?"

"Yes, I'm sorry about that, but I have business that won't keep, and
you probably know what it is if Peter was here today."

"There isn't any business that I know of that won't wait until
morning."

"Oh, yes, there is. Peter asked you to vote your stock with him and
retire Cornelius and get rid of me, didn't he?"

"Well, I think it's a good idea—Cornelius will kill himself with
work. And as for you—"

"Let's leave me aside. Cornelius does *not* think this is a good idea.
Even the news of it damned near killed him, and if you want to ruin
the company—"

"I gave my promise to Peter, and that's an end to it. Now get out
of here, I'm not well . . ."

"You'll feel a lot worse if you force me to tell you what I know
. . ."

Charlie thought he saw the flash of a new kind of fear in the old
lady's eyes, but she was game. "Are you trying to threaten me with
something, Charlie Smith—you, of all people? Get out of here and
leave me alone. Sophie. Where's Sophie? *Sophie*!"

She could have strength in her voice when she needed it, and she
picked up a cane lying beside her bed and began pounding the floor.
There was no time left to talk around it.

"Now listen, and listen well, Aunt Sally," he said. "I've just been
with Cornelius, and we agree that no bastard is going to take over this
company. I've advised him as his counsel that we can go into court
and contest Peter's ownership of stock obtained under the fraudulent

480

assertion that he was a legitimate heir to the first Cornelius Van Alen . . ."

It was an improvisation—a brilliant one, he thought, though he wasn't at all sure of his legal grounds. But it was cut short when the cane Aunt Sally was wielding cracked across his face. In pain and fury, he lunged—to hit her? choke her? But the cane was raised again, and the old lady was hissing like a cornered snake. He jumped away. He could feel blood with the hand he put to his cheek. He could hear the rustle of Sophie's skirts in the hall, and her worried call, "Coming, grandma . . ."

"Proud, aren't you, Aunt Sally?" he said. "Think you're better than the rest of us because you got away with it? Well, you didn't. We've got a witness—that old nigger you should have got rid of long ago. Just because it's easier for us, though, not a word of this will come out if you vote your stock the right way. Think about it . . ."

He met Sophie in the hall. "What's happened? What's wrong with grandma?"

"Nothing," he said blandly. "I just thought I'd look in to see how she was, and I guess I startled her."

Charlie took the steps down and out two at a time. He could have flown. He was sure now that the company would remain safely in the right hands. He just hoped that that old bitch hadn't left a scar on his face. Still, it would be a very small price to pay, and he could have some fun with it: he'd tell all those fellows around the Astor House bar who thought that he was over the hill that it was an honorable wound from a boudoir battle. Well, in a way it was . . . wasn't he fighting for his honor . . . his life . . . ?

When, on that hot morning of July 13, 1863, Sally Schuyler Van Alen, cane in hand and with little more than the clothes on her back, walked out of Lafayette Place and hailed a hack, she wasn't sure what she would do. Whatever, though, it would likely be painful beyond anything she'd yet experienced, but life had at last caught up with her, as it had a way of doing. She would have to decide whether to go along with Charlie Smith or compromise the secret of Peter's fatherhood that she'd kept so long. She'd tried once to escape the total consequences of her actions and it hadn't worked. However short of ultimate wisdom her long years might have been, they'd at least convinced her that life could not be manipulated. It could only be lived. She would, in the end, do what she had to do . . .

In one of those ironic tricks that life seemed forever to be playing on people, the events of the night before had, in fact, made Sally all but forget that she was supposed to be so terribly sick. Whether it stirred up some magic chemical like adrenalin or aroused some more mystical force like the spirit, Charlie Smith's midnight visit had, literally, put her back on her feet. She'd gotten out of bed, and with the aid of her cane paced back and forth for the longest of the many long nights she could remember while she worked up the courage to confront her son, Cornelius. She could imagine what was going on in his mind—a fearful storm of hurt and wrath. Unfortunately, she was also only too aware that forgiveness was something that Cornelius had left out of the Christian creed that had stiffened his backbone all these years.

In some ways it was a relief to have the secret so long cradled in the depths of her surface at last. She even regretted striking Charlie Smith who, slimy as he was, was after all only an agent of Providence, like the snake in the Garden of Eden. And she could hardly bring herself to blame Flossie. She had to guess—and she was certain she was right in so guessing—that the old black woman had finally delivered herself of her suspicions out of genuine concern for Cornelius . . . she couldn't really have known what she was doing. In any case, she had no intention of trying to deny the fact to Cornelius or even of throwing herself on whatever mercy he might possess. She would, at the least, depart with dignity.

By dawn she began to dress as carefully as she'd always done when she was going out, particularly to Peter's. Instead of the old lady's black, which even she'd taken to wearing in deference to custom, she picked out a sky-blue dress starred with white lace patches. It was a little out of style with only the suggestion of hoops in the bustle and padding around the waist, but it would have to do. Her hair was the only thing she could not cope with since arthritis had stiffened her arms, and she waited impatiently now, galled by the irreversible frailties that were rendering her dependent on others, until Sophie arrived with her breakfast tray. The girl was shocked. "Grandmother, what are you doing up—and dressed like that? You ought to be in bed—"

"Not today. I have things to do. Here, help me with my hair."

"Grandmother, are you sure—?"

"Yes, I'm sure. Now, come help me . . ."

While the girl dutifully got busy with comb and brush and pins, Sally offered an explanation of sorts. She hadn't the heart to tell Sophie the truth—why she was going, why she wouldn't be back. She'd even decided not to take a bag to deceive her granddaughter. She'd have to leave the explanations to Cornelius, if he chose to make them. It was his right—and duty—as a father, and, besides, he needed Sophie; Flossie and the maids couldn't really take care of him alone. Sally had the feeling, the hope at least, that forgiveness *was* part of Sophie's creed. She'd have to risk it so she said only, "I got to thinking, Sophie, that it's been a long time since I've seen Martha and the children. I'm going over there today and I don't want them to think of their grandmother as a dowdy old frump—"

"Nobody could think that of you, grandmother. Do you want me to go with you?"

"No, you stay here with your father. I wouldn't feel right in going if I didn't know you were here."

"Well, *he* hardly does. He doesn't speak two words to me."

"That's always been his way when he was sick, ever since he was a little boy . . ." and suddenly, with that poignant memory of Cornelius as her son, she found it difficult to control her voice.

"Should I tell father you're gone?"

"No, I'll look in on him. I gather from what Charlie said, he didn't have a good night."

"That was awful of Cousin Charlie—bursting in on you like that—"

"Charlie Smith has never been known for his sensitivity."

"I think he's dreadful, I wish father would get rid of him."

"Well, if anything ever happens to your father, you should inherit the controlling interest in the company, and the first thing you perhaps ought to do is get rid of Cousin Charlie—"

"*Grandmother,* that almost sounds like a deathbed speech—"

"I didn't mean it that way, dear. Charlie's just on my mind after last night . . . Well, you've done absolute wonders with what's more a wornout mop than a decent head of hair. I'll be going now."

"You haven't had breakfast . . ."

"I'm not hungry. Why don't you sit here and eat it, Sophie, and save the girls from making another?"

It was a fortunate improvisation . . . she didn't want Sophie within earshot when she went in to see Cornelius. There would be unpleasant, angry words, she was sure.

But as it turned out, it wouldn't have mattered. When she went into his room Cornelius pulled the covers over his head. Flossie, stirring in her chair at his bedside, said apologetically, "He not feeling well this morning, Miss Sally."

"Obviously," Sally said. "Why don't you go down and get him some breakfast, Flossie?"

After the black woman had creaked her way out, Sally addressed the lump in the bed. "I've something to say to you, Cornelius."

For what seemed a long while there was no response. Then finally came a strangled mumble, "Go away, I never want to see you again —"

"You won't have to, Cornelius. I'm going now—to Peter's. But I do hope you'll think it over carefully before you and Charlie carry out your plan. Not for my sake. I'm too old to be hurt. Not really for Peter's sake, either . . . I believe he may be a big enough man to survive this. I really wonder, though, if you are, Cornelius. And you might also think of what it might do to your daughter, as well as Peter's children. All these years I've kept my silence for the sake of *my* children—you as much as Peter. I know how much precious respectability has meant to you . . ."

It was hard to tell whether she was reaching him. The shape in the bed was as still as a covered corpse. She thought possibly she detected something like the sound of muffled crying, but she suspected, unhappily, that he was immune to any comforting from her . . . *oh, God, and oh, God,* must she *always* be the family sinner, rejected in the end by a son as she'd been rejected in the beginning by a father? Well, so be it . . .

"I'm going now, Cornelius . . . I don't know whether you'll be at the next stockholders' meeting, but I'll be there . . . and"—she realized she'd known it was the only thing she could do but hadn't wanted to admit it to herself—"I'm going to vote with Peter, but *not* because of all that nonsense in Washington. I've been in business here long enough to know that you, at least, did not do anything you thought wrong. I'm voting with Peter because I agree that you ought to be honorably retired, as he's promised—to save your life . . . Well, I'll say good-by now . . . I know what you're thinking about me, Cornelius, and I suppose I can't really blame you. There's surely no law that says children must love their parents no matter what, though there does seem to be a law that parents must love their children . . . well, I'll be going now . . ."

Still no response. A kind of anger rose up to fuel her pride. She turned and walked out without another word. When she got into the hack and gave Peter's Twenty-Second Street address, the driver looked around and said, "Best go the long way, ma'am, over and up Fifth. Not by way of making more fare, mind you, but—"

"I'm in a terrible hurry," she said, almost adding that she didn't want to lose her nerve. She was going to tell Peter everything right away before there was any chance of backing out and accepting Charlie Smith's deal. *Oh, God, and oh, God,* what would he say, or do? She wondered whether she shouldn't have dressed in black after all, as befitted a woman who had lost her sons.

The driver touched his hat in compliance but went on talking as they rattled off: "Your funeral, as they say. There's a mob comin' up the Bowery and Third . . . they say they've already set fire to the draft office up at Third and Forty-Third . . . must be more'n that from the looks of the smoke up there . . . Can't say as I blame 'em, with bringin' niggers up to break the longshoremen's strike and takin' good workers into the army . . . worst thing they ever done was freein' all them niggers . . . man won't be able to make a living here soon . . ."

Within minutes, she knew that the driver had been right about the mobs. On Third Avenue their hack had to inch and fight its way through a river of people flowing north toward a pillar of smoke that stood above the scene of action. For the most part they looked to be honest workingmen, some accompanied by their women and children, but the flashily dressed Bowery B'hoys and their gals were out in force too. Fortunately, the mood was jubilant and carefree. The weather was hot and damp, and most of the men seemed to be using the demonstration as an excuse to take a holiday. They were ducking in and out of bars, passing bottles, breaking into song. Someone had the nerve to strike up "Dixie," the most popular song in the minstrel shows just before the war, and everyone joined in. Crudely lettered banners bounced above the sea of hats and bonnets, making plain the sentiments under them—"To Hell with the Draft and the War" . . . "No $300 Arrangements with Us" . . . "Tell Old Abe to Come to New York!" . . . "We'll hang old Greeley to a sour apple tree and send him straight to hell!"

Deep in her own thoughts, Sally ignored the commotion other than to fret over the loss of time. Somebody or other was always rioting

485

in New York, and she'd long since given up caring too much what it was about. Nothing in her experience was so quickly passing as the passion of "the people" . . . like a lover's quarrel it usually erupted at the wrong time and for the wrong reason. She was so fearful about the outcome of her mission that she thought it might be the providence of God if the crowd overturned and burned the hack, sparing her another kind of fire.

God. She closed her eyes and thought about praying for some kind of guidance as to how to deliver the news to Peter. It was no use. Her prayers had never been answered, and she rather respected God for that. She still hadn't been able to bring herself to believe, as Cornelius did, as her nephew James proclaimed, that there was a God who concerned himself with the affairs of each and every one of the millions of human beings on earth. It was a vanity and weakness for a person to plead with God for favors she hadn't earned by her own actions, and a sin to seek divine preference over others. Though it would have been nice in her age and growing infirmity to think that she had access to some special power for the asking, she knew very well that she did not. One of the few secrets she'd learned by growing so old was that age itself was neither a virtue nor a reward; it was simply another, and often painful, state of being in which the uncertainties of life were greater than ever . . . .

When she arrived in front of Peter's house he came rushing out to help her from the hack. "Mother, what on earth are you doing out on a day like this? I thought you were sick, and, besides, it's dangerous—"

"What *is* happening?" she asked.

"You don't know? They're rioting over the draft. They started pulling out the first names yesterday. I predicted this in a letter to Stanton, but I guess the President didn't see it in time. It's done me a world of good, though. I think he wants me in his cabinet . . ."

Inside the heavy, brass-jeweled door of Peter's home, Sally found herself in the midst of a joyful excitement that contrasted almost painfully with her own feelings and the disorder in the streets. They were still at breakfast, but the children jumped up and crowded around her shouting, "We're going to Washington! We're going to Washington!"

She was a little too bewildered by this sudden turn to respond except with grandmotherly clucks. Martha rescued her, sat her down and poured a cup of coffee. Peter pushed two letters at her. "Here, you've got to read these, mother, to know what we're talking about. Take them in order—mine first."

One of the small blessings of age was that her sight had suddenly improved, and she now ran her eyes hastily down a copy Peter had made of his letter to Stanton.

New York, July 5, 1863

Dear Mr. Secretary,

First let me offer what I am sure will be regarded as a favorable report on the special mission to which I have been assigned. I have managed to secure the agreement of enough stockholders of Van Alen & Son to call a meeting for July 20 at which it can be confidently expected that a new management satisfactory to the most prejudiced member of Congress will be installed. While it is likely that I may be elected president to succeed my brother, Cornelius Van Alen, who will be retired for reasons of health and *not* malfeasance, I wish to assure you that I will be available and eager for a new assignment in Washington. I have ascertained that the manager of our works in New Jersey, a graduate of the Rensselaer Polytechnic Institute, is fully competent to manage the company in my absence, and of course my brother should be available for consultation.

But, while this matter is well in hand, I feel obliged to warn you —and, through you, the president—that the new draft law may provoke ugly reaction here in New York. I think it must be remembered that fully four hundred thousand of our citizens are foreign-born, many of them men and women who fled their native lands expressly to escape military conscription in causes not of their own choosing. Perhaps contrary to what you in Washington may believe—and what I personally believe—the Emancipation Proclamation has been perceived here among our foreign-born laborers not as an assurance that we fight for freedom but as a certain threat to their livelihood when, and if, free Negroes are available for the labor force. The unfortunate use of Negroes to break the longshoreman's strike is, to them, most convincing proof that their fears are well grounded. In addition, the provision of the draft act permitting the wealthy to avoid service by purchasing substitutes is being given a radical interpretation by certain editors and publishers, who are inciting the people to a class war that would be more devastating than the sec-

487

tional conflict in which we are now engaged.

Unfortunately, our Democratic opponents understand these sentiments all too well and are ruthless in employing them to their own ends. Their papers here in New York, for instance, made much of ex-President Pierce's Fourth of July oration in Concord, N.H., in which he charged that "even here, in time of war the mere arbitrary will of the President takes the place of the Constitution," and of remarks on the same date by our own Governor Seymour to the effect that the national government is bringing us to the verge of destruction by "seizing our persons, infringing on our rights, insulting our homes with men deprived of the right of trial by jury, men torn from their homes by midnight intruders." The *Daily News* reacted to the draft law by saying, "The people are notified that one out of about two and a half of our citizens are to be brought off into Messrs. Lincoln & Company's charnel house. God forbid."

In the light of such comment from men they believe to be their leaders, is it any wonder that the people here in New York are confused, if not resentful? Indeed, tempers, aided and abetted by the summer heat, are running extremely high here in New York just at a time when, because of General Meade's call for reinforcements at Gettysburg, we are virtually without means of enforcing law and order beyond the city's force of some 1,500 policemen. I would, therefore, urge that you delay initiating the draft, at least in the city of New York, and that you, meanwhile, consider the possibility of eliminating the paid exemption before you do enforce it.

Please extend my regards to Mr. Lincoln and my best wishes for his health and safety and do, I pray, consider most seriously my plea to be granted responsibilities commensurate with my party loyalty and great desire to be of more effective service to the cause of union.

Your respectful servant,
Peter Schuyler Van Alen

The next letter was on heavy, embossed paper, in a strong hand:

The White House
July 10, 1863

Dear Peter Van Alen,

By the exercise of the full powers of my high office, I finally persuaded Mr. Stanton to let me see your report which he had felt would deflect my purposes with regard to the draft. I do wish that I had seen it sooner, but I am afraid that the train is now running down the track too fast to be flagged down. With the likelihood that Lee will make good his escape from Gettysburg, I cannot now unduly worry about what might transpire in New York. I am reminded of an experience in my youth when I was a circuit-riding lawyer. It was during the spring rains and all one day my fellow lawyers and I had the devil's own time fording the swollen streams in our path, and one of our number said, "If we're having such trouble with these little streams, how are we ever going to cross Fox River?" We were so worried that we decided to put up for the night at a tavern where we luckily fell in with the Methodist Presiding Elder of the circuit who rode it in all seasons and ought to know how to cross the Fox River. But when we gathered around him with our anxious questions, he told us, "Oh, yes, I know all about the Fox River. I have crossed it often, and I understand it well. But I have one fixed rule with regard to the Fox River: *I never cross it till I reach it!*"

In any event, I was delighted to note that your own mission will so soon reach a successful conclusion after which I do hope that you will come to see me in Washington. While I can make no definite promises at the moment, I have observed that the tempers of some of my cabinet members, notably Mr. Stanton, are being adversely affected by the strain of their duties, and the time may be coming when new energy will be required.

Sincerely yours,
Abraham Lincoln

When she'd finished reading, she looked up at the smiling faces and said, "Well . . . well . . . it's what you've been wanting, isn't it—both of you, all of you?"

"Yes," Peter said. "The President's letter just arrived this morning. I was going to bring it over for you to see today—but, well, it's better you're here to celebrate with all of us."

It was obviously not the right moment to blurt out her devastating story even when, after Martha had shooed the children away and gone herself to the kitchen to tell the maid to clear the table, Peter asked, "How's Cornelius?"

"Not well."

"But you do think he could act as a consultant, don't you? I mean

489

if it's put to him right. You're so good at handling Cornelius, mother, that I'm counting on you—"

"We'll see," she said, as she had said so often so many years before to a young Peter hell-bent on having his way.

"Fine. Then you'll stay the day? The children have been wanting to see you, but I was afraid to take them up and bother Cornelius."

"Yes, I'll stay, but I think I need a little rest right now. I didn't have such a good night."

What she wanted was a little time to think alone. Martha led her up to the spare front bedroom, helped her to take off the blue dress. "It's so pretty, Aunt Sally," she said. "I'm glad you don't let yourself get old . . ."

If she only knew, if she only knew, Sally thought when she was left alone. She'd never, never felt older than she did at this moment. Peter's good news had only made the burden she was bearing heavier. In addition to the undoubted private shock her revelation would create, the public scandal that Cornelius and Charlie threatened would be multiplied many times over if Peter were in the cabinet. And that would be another kind of heartbreak to confront . . . Still, she had to do it—and soon. The time for deception was over. Better that Peter hear it from her than Charles Smith, who couldn't really be trusted to keep his word no matter what he said . . . But there had to be a reason why she wouldn't go home to Lafayette Place, ever again. Well, she'd just close her eyes a minute and then get up and go to Peter. Though the windows stood open, the air was heavy with heat, and the summery sound of a high whining mosquito made her drowsy. She slipped slowly into sleep, half hoping she'd never awaken . . . .

It was probably the sound of firing that brought her back to consciousness. Whatever it was, she found Martha standing by her bed, saying, "Don't worry, Aunt Sally, you'll be perfectly safe here."

Safe from what?

"There's just a little rioting over on the avenues to the east," Martha was explaining. "Some people broke into the state arsenal on Second Avenue at Twenty-First and took guns. They're drunk and firing them in the air. But Peter and some of our neighbors from Gramercy Park are patrolling to keep them away from here. He says it will be all over by nightfall when everybody gets tired and sobers up."

But it wasn't over by nightfall, nor by dawn of the next day, nor by midday. She needed no excuse for staying in Peter's house, but it was still no time to break her news to him . . . The burning of the whole block around the draft offices on Third Avenue had been but a spark to the dry tinder of a resentful, fearful people. Blood had been shed on both sides at that fiery scene when a detachment of police and a company of marines from the Brooklyn Navy Yard, the only troops within miles of the city, tried to disperse the crowds. Infuriated rather than intimidated by the killing, the mob had moved east to tear apart and put to the torch another draft office at Broadway and Twenty-Ninth Street and twelve adjacent buildings. Roving bands of armed rioters fanned out from river to river and north to Harlem. Encampments were set up in Central Park; liquor stores everywhere were looted to fuel the forces and burned when resistance was met; windows of other establishments were smashed and goods appropriated; wherever and whenever police tried to head off the mob, barricades were flung up in the streets and pitched battles were fought.

As the second day wore away it was clear that a mindless, murderous mob was tearing apart the largest city in the land. A paralyzing panic disrupted everything. Horses were shot; streetcars stopped running; stocks fell; officials wrung their hands. The Board of Aldermen, having no quorum at their meeting, simply adjourned and sought safety in their own homes; a slightly more courageous Governor Seymour, who happened to be in the city on other business, stood on the steps of City Hall and tried to appease the angry crowds, Democratic voters all, by telling them that the draft, which he himself opposed, would probably be thrown out by the courts. What few militia the governor could summon were as outnumbered and ineffective as the police. With the draft offices destroyed, the roaming bands turned on the black people they so hated and feared. The Colored Orphanage at Forty-Second Street and Lexington Avenue was set afire, and its escaping inmates chased through the streets. A black man was hung from a tree on Clarkson Street and his body turned into a torch. Frightened Negroes headed for the water; they crowded ferries, stole boats, swam—anything to get away. One trying to escape in his wife's clothing was caught, stripped, beaten to death in the street. A ferryhouse where fleeing blacks huddled was burned. Police did fight back as well as they could, killing and being killed.

The rumored toll kept rising—a hundred dead, two hundred dead. Hospitals were jammed with wounded. As night came on, columns of fire stood on every horizon. Homes were now being burned. Mayor Opdyke's. Postmaster Wakeman's. Torches in hand, the roving mob began looking for the houses of known "nigger lovers."

Until they heard this, the mood at the Van Alen house on Twenty-Second Street had been more one of annoyance at the disruption of routine than real concern. When there was a rumor that the mobs planned to cut the Croton Water mains, the children were sent scampering to fill every tub and pan they could find, and nobody could risk a wash in case they'd have to drink the water. No ladies showed up for the afternoon bandage rolling sessions that had become Martha's wartime substitute for the social life on which she thrived. But the Reverend Doctor James Schuyler and his wife and maids did show up, uninvited, when it was heard that the gangs, some said Catholic, had fired a Methodist Church, and there had to be a great reshuffling of children and beds to accommodate them. It didn't help to have the preacher express something close to satisfaction: "I've always said this sinning city would go to hell, and it appears that we've arrived." But nobody imagined that they, quiet people on a quiet street, were in real danger. And then came the ugly rumor of a vendetta against abolitionists and with it fear. Peter had been such a visible figure during the Lincoln campaign that the press on both sides had called him "Nigger Loving Pete"—the *Tribune* in praise and the *Herald* in scorn. Peter's sentiments were so well known that they might as well have had a sign on the house, in the opinion of Dr. Schuyler who argued that they all move back to the Presbyterian manse and take a chance on being Protestants. But Peter would have none of it: "Mother isn't well enough to walk, and I doubt if we could find transportation. Anyway, we've got a good vigilante committee in this neighborhood, and it's safer here than moving through the streets. You can be a help, Cousin James. I've got an old hunting gun up in the attic. You can use it to guard the house while I'm on patrol . . ."

And so, as the second day of rioting darkened into night, the people on Twenty-Second Street began living in the tension of a household besieged. The children were more excited than fearful, running continually from floor to floor and window to window looking for the "bad men" until they wore out and flopped into bed under the watchful eye of their grandmother Schuyler. Martha, too tense for sleep or even rest, came to sit with Sally, who seldom slept even on good nights. James nervously paced the marbled foyer, his footsteps and sometimes audible prayers echoing eerily up the stairwell. Martha couldn't keep her mind on anything. She tried knitting and dropped stitches, tried reading and couldn't focus, tried talking and always came back to the same thing . . . "Oh, I'm so frightened, Aunt Sally. I wish I could be out there with Peter *doing* something." Tired and troubled, Sally agreed. "Yes, waiting is the hell of women. We'll be all right, though, I'm sure."

Another of her stroking cliches to delude the young into thinking that things somehow always turn out well. She had no fear for herself; if they did come, she could probably count on her old heart quietly quitting from excitement and thereby solving all her problems. But the others who had so much to live for had a right to fear. A war between brothers on distant battlefields was hard enough to comprehend, but a city of people gone mad was truly terrifying. Gotham, Washington Irving had called it, but he'd thought it a joke, and he was gone now, too soon to know otherwise. She remembered how Aaron Burr had called America itself an experiment that might not last, and she, having witnessed its birth in innocent awe, paid little attention to what she considered his cynicism. Could he be looking down now from that slice of moon he'd probably wangled and see these telltale fires? Did those who pass on ever know what finally happened, or was life always a story without ending? Quite suddenly she didn't want to die, not now, not in the midst of this dreadful uncertainty. If she had to leave the story unfinished, she wanted to have a better guess as to how it would come out.

Along about the middle of the night, God himself seemed intent on turning the city into an inferno. Huge clouds rolled in from the west, their heavy underbellies pink with reflected flame; flashes of lightning silhouetted the darkened buildings across the street; claps of thunder obliterated the puny sounds of riot. James came bounding up the stairs and stuck his head in the door. His look, his voice were triumphant. "Hear it! Hear it!" he said. "It's going to rain. It's God's answer to my prayer! There's nothing like rain to cool off a riot. We'll be safe now, I'm sure."

Sally wasn't so sure. "Well, you keep that gun loaded, James. I hope you can shoot as well as you pray."

James, jubilant, was full of good humor. "Oh, ye of little faith," he said. "I swear, Aunt Sally, I'm going to convert you—before it's too late."

"Well, this isn't the time for theological discussion. You'd better get back down there, James."

"Aunt Sally's right, father," Martha agreed.

When he'd gone, more to make conversation than anything else, Martha asked, "Don't you believe in prayer, Aunt Sally?"

"Odd, I've been thinking about that a good deal lately," Sally said. "I suspect not—at least not in the way your father does."

"I do. Or at least I want to. I need to. It's so often the only thing you can do—like now. I've been praying for Peter, for us all . . ."

"Well, you go right on praying, dear," Sally said. "I *do* believe in trying everything, and I must admit that this is a dramatic demonstration. If it doesn't cool off the rioters, at least it will cool us. It's been so hot . . ."

The rains were coming—not in soft drops but in a solid, sudsy wash as if a giant tub had been emptied over the city. Martha got up to close the windows—and just then it happened . . . through the pound of the storm the loud whinny of a wet, impatient horse, the sound of knocking and a voice shouting, "Open up, open up—"

"Oh, my God," Martha said, pulling back from the window.

From below came James' voice—no rounded pulpit tone but a frightened uncertain quaver. "Go away . . . I'm armed . . . I'll . . . I'll shoot . . ."

The voice outside responded. "Open up for the love of Mary, it's the police and we've got an injured person here—"

"Oh, my God—Peter!" Martha screamed, and ran for the stairs.

This was the time when her old heart ought to stop. Instead, it just pained—a gripping angina that made Sally clutch at her chest. Within minutes they were coming up—two policemen bearing something wrapped in a blanket, Martha beside them. "We'll have to put her in here with you, Aunt Sally. We don't have another bed," she was saying.

Her? When they dropped the body on the bed beside Sally, she had difficulty recognizing at first that it was Sophie. Her hair and eyebrows were singed away, the red welt of a burn covered half her face and neck. Bits of her clothes, showing above the fold of the blanket, were charred. One of the policemen, a young Irishman, was explaining, "Pulled her right out of the fire, we did. Tried to stop her but she rushed in. Just like a torch, she was, until we rolled her in this blanket. Can't get near a doctor or hospital this night, so she told us to bring her here. Gave her a little morphine, but that's all we could do—"

Sally interrupted, "*What* fire? Where?"

"Down on Lafayette Place, ma'am. Said it was the Van Alen house . . ."

"Was there . . . was there anybody else?"

"Wouldn't rightly know, ma'am. Couldn't get through the flames. Girl kept saying something about her father, but the place is a goner now. Nobody could have lived through that. Well, I'm sorry, ma'am, but we're needed . . ."

First things first. No time now for her own pain. They sent James out of the room and went to work on Sophie, peeling away the scorched clothing, buttering the burns, giving her sips of brandy and water. She was moaning, incoherent, but at last she began gasping out words, reliving in delirium her experience. It seemed to be rolling backward in her mind, but, listening, they could grasp much of what had happened . . . "He's in there, my father . . . he's in there . . . Let me go . . . he's . . . oh, my God, let me go . . . go away . . . no, no, it's *not* your 'Nigger Loving Pete' . . . no . . . *Cornelius*, my father . . . he's ill, go away, *please* . . . no, no, noooooo . . ."

Oh, my God, and my God. Peter, who had heard the news from the police while he was on patrol, came rushing in, and Martha blurted it out. "They thought it was *our* house, Peter. Oh, Peter . . ."

"Lord . . . I've got to get over there, who else was there, mother —Flossie? the maids . . . ?"

Sally nodded. "I'll go with you, Peter. Help me get dressed, Martha."

"Mother, *no*," Peter said. "It's a battlefield out there, and we'd never get a hack this time of day—"

Day? For the first time she realized that the windows were gray with a sodden dawn. The rain had stopped, however, and she was determined. She had to go, she had to know. She started to cane her way to the door. "I'll go myself, go this way, walk if I have to. I *must* go."

Peter understood there was no use in arguing with her. "All right. I'll wait downstairs, but hurry. Someone might be alive . . ."

In the end, he carried her, half running. This time they did go the long way through back streets to avoid the avenues where riot, un-quenched by water, still flared. They didn't speak. Light as she was, Peter needed all his breath to bear her. She was busy trying to understand the curious deadness in her mind, in her heart. The numbness of shock, probably. She'd gone through it enough times before to recognize the symptoms. In shock you went on doing what had to be done, hoping what shouldn't be hoped, but it was the reason why people could endure. At the site, Peter put her down on the curb and both of them, still silent, stood there staring. The front door hung ajar like a drunkard's jaw, and the foul breath of smoke poured out at them. The marble columns were black, and the broken windows were like the empty sockets of the blind. The policemen were undoubtedly right: nobody, especially a sick man, could have survived such a gutting. Still . . . "I'm going in," Peter said, "the rain has cooled it enough . . ."

And he was gone. She leaned on her cane, feeling nothing. Within minutes, he was back, handkerchief to nose, eyes teared. "They're there . . . Cornelius . . . Flossie . . . the maids . . . I found Cornelius up in the attic, in Flossie's room, he must have gone to rescue her . . ."

She barely nodded.

"They . . . they were intact," Peter said in a monotone that betrayed his own numbness. "Died of smoke . . . at least they can have proper funerals . . ."

"Yes, yes, I'm sure James will do well with that—"

"Mother, we must go . . . I'll send for them," Peter said, taking her by the arm and leading her away from the pyre.

They did find a hack on Fifth Avenue, and when they were inside it Peter started to break. "Mother . . . they thought he was me . . . I'll never be able to—"

"You *must*," she said, "it isn't your fault."

"Isn't it? . . . isn't it? . . . then, why . . . *why?*"

"We don't often know why, Peter . . . it was a dreadful thing . . . a mistake . . ."

And hearing her Peter seemed to gather resolve. Eyes still wet, his voice was surprisingly firm. "Well, dammit, I'm going to try to *do* something about it. I'm going to take over and run that precious damned company of his so he'll know he had a brother after all—"

"Peter, you're still in shock, there's no reason now for you to change your plans to go to Washington where you could do more good—"

"Oh, yes, there is—every reason. This horror has got to be made to have *meaning* . . . Anyway, I can't leave this awful mess to you . . . or Martha . . . or Sophie . . . or even James. The president will survive without me, I'm sure . . . It's going to take a Van Alen to straighten this out, and I'm the only Van Alen around . . . Odd, isn't it, but I've always had the feeling that something like this would happen—well, not like this, but something—because I never really had it in me to sell out what I am, my heritage . . . I guess, in the end, what we possess possesses us . . . oh, I almost forgot—on the way down from the attic I looked into your room and I'm afraid everything you left behind is ruined . . . but I did find this lying on the floor, I remember how you used to hold it all the time when I was little so I picked it up . . ."

Fumbling in his pocket, Peter brought out a small jade dragon, unscorched by fire, and put it in his mother's hand. It was miraculously cool against her palm, cool as it had been after another fire when she'd stumbled through the smoking ruins with hope in her heart. Because she'd had courage to go through that fire, she had this son. She reached over, put her hand on his and squeezed it. She didn't trust herself to speak.

Apparently Peter felt the same way. They rode silently, hand in hand. They found the street in front of Peter's house full of soldiers wearing the uniform of the Seventh Regiment, New York's own. They were mere boys, weary from a long forced march from Pennsylvania, perplexed, a little frightened. One of them who had been kneeling and snapping off shots in the general direction of the avenue just as they drove up said, "Lord, mister, get that old lady in the house. It's dangerous out here . . . worse than fighting the rebs, at least you can tell *them* by their uniforms. Hell, one of them fellows over there might be my brother, he ain't *about* to be drafted, and I know he's a hell of a shot . . ."

Brother against brother, all over the city, all over the country. In the most terrible way, the miracle she'd hoped for had come to pass . . . her own sons had become brothers again, though it was tragically late. Would it be too late for all the rest, for all these? Surely there must be a better way to make brothers of men. She was surprised to find herself thinking like this in the midst of such an overwhelming

personal tragedy. But, as she'd learned, and learned again, few tragedies were totally overwhelming and fewer still were personal. They
were the common lot of mankind, and mankind was meant to survive—

Peter was lifting her now out of the carriage and carrying her into
the house, shielding her body with his against any stray shots. As he
started to carry her up the stairs she said, "Peter, put me *down.*"

"No, mother, after what we've been through you must be exhausted . . . God, I know I am—"

"I need to get to the kitchen, make some coffee for those boys out
there. The poor things look so tired, and it wouldn't do at all to let
them go to sleep. Our lives depend on them."

For long minutes Peter just stared at her. The etched lines that
days of worry, weariness and finally shock had carved into his face
lifted in something like a smile. He shook his head. "Mother, you're
an amazing woman."

He had never spoken more heartfelt words.

Postlude

Sally Schuyler Van Alen, survivor. As soon as the streets of New York were cleared, they filled with thousands upon thousands of people scurrying about their business as if nothing at all had happened. Backs to the past, faces to the future.

Prominent among them was Sally Van Alen, for there was much to be done. First the funeral for Cornelius, the largest in the history of the uptown Presbyterian Church, to be sat through still dry-eyed. Then the stockholders' meeting of Van Alen & Son, where Peter Schuyler Van Alen, the new president, presented two surprises. He insisted upon the election of Sally Schuyler Van Alen to the board, despite her age, and indicated that he would, indeed, have succeeded in politics by securing the quiet resignation of John Charles Smith, Jr., on the promise of giving him more work than he could handle as a "special counsel." Peter also showed a, to some, surprising promise that he would be an astute businessman when he explained: "Mother, I don't want you on the board just to make you feel better. I want your advice . . . I'll *need* it. As for Charlie, we simply can't afford to be out of touch with Commodore Vanderbilt. He's going to run the railroads, and the railroads are going to shape this country's future."

Through all this, Sally's mind continued to roll over the events of her long, long life, in search of what she could consider wisdom. It did not come, but did it really matter?

She was, God help her, a survivor, and if one was a survivor, life had a trick of getting in death's way.